DEATH STRUGGLE

Tough Sergeant Steiner commanded ten men, a German rear guard trapped fifty miles behind the Russian line. Their path to survival led straight through the entire enemy army. All the murderous hazards of war blocked their march—hunger, exhaustion, terror, treachery, death. Finally Steiner and his men were no longer fighting for Führer or Fatherland, but for their naked, desperate lives.

THE CROSS OF IRON

A SAM PECKINPAH FILM

"CROSS OF IRON"

starring

JAMES COBURN
MAXIMILIAN SCHELL
JAMES MASON

DAVID WARNER
SENTA BERGER
in the part of EVA

MUSIC COMPOSED AND CONDUCTED
BY
ERNEST GOLD

EXECUTIVE PRODUCER
ARLENE SELLERS

SCREENPLAY BY
JULIUS J. EPSTEIN AND WALTER KELLEY & JAMES HAMILTON

PRODUCED BY
ALEX WINITSKY AND WOLF C. HARTWIG

DIRECTED BY
SAM PECKINPAH

A WINITSKY - SELLERS/RAPID FILM PRODUCTION

TECHNICAL SERVICES AND FACILITIES BY JADRAN FILM, ZAGREB

TECHNICOLOR®   AN AVCO EMBASSY RELEASE FROM (I)(T)(C) ENTERTAINMENT

THE CROSS OF IRON

WILLI HEINRICH

Translated from the German by
Richard and Clara Winston

BANTAM BOOKS · TORONTO · NEW YORK · LONDON

THE CROSS OF IRON

*A Bantam Book / published by arrangement with
The Bobbs-Merrill Company, Inc.*

PRINTING HISTORY

Bobbs-Merrill edition published April 1956
2nd printing .... April 1956
3rd printing .... September 1956

Bantam edition / May 1957

2nd printing ...... June 1957	*7th printing ... January 1961*
3rd printing .... July 1957	*8th printing ... January 1967*
4th printing .... October 1957	*9th printing .... March 1967*
5th printing .... March 1959	*10th printing ..... April 1968*
6th printing .... January 1960	*11th printing ...... June 1972*
12th printing......June 1977	

13th printing

CONTENTS

**BOOK
ONE**

I

WHILE the Russian artillery was savagely blasting away, the sun went down behind the enormous woods. It had been the same yesterday and the day before yesterday, and it would be the same tomorrow and forever. The men sat around the bunker. Schnurrbart pried at the tar in the bowl of his pipe. Corporal Steiner felt for a cigarette in his pocket. The shrilling of the field telephone cut the silence. Steiner attended to it. He listened at length, then slammed the receiver down with a curse. Startled, the other men looked up, their peaked, unshaven faces all anxiety.

"What did he say?" Kruger called from the table.

Steiner did not answer. His haggard face was glum; when he set his lips the deep creases at the corners of his mouth brought out the hardness of that face.

The silence persisted. The two candles burning on the table cast huge shadows of the men on the wooden walls. Outside, a German machine gun hammered out a short burst. Kruger cleared his throat and repeated his question: "What did he say?"

"He said the whole war was senseless."

The others stared at him. "Lieutenant Meyer said that?"

Steiner nodded. "Why not? After all, a company commander is entitled to a private opinion about the war, too."

"Why, yes . . ." Dorn, whom they called the Professor, rubbed his slender hand over his bristly chin. "But I think . . ."

"Don't think so much," Steiner said.

"Ah, let him think." Schnurrbart put his feet on the table and grinned. "You can't order him not to think. Once he has that Russian bullet in his brain he'll stop of his own accord."

The men chuckled, their shadows jerking on the walls.

"The regiment is pulling out," Steiner remarked indifferently.

Kruger was the first to react. "Why don't you say so right off?" he cried, springing to his feet. With one swift movement he pulled the blanket off his cot and began to bundle it up. One after another the men of the platoon followed his example. The lethargy in the bunker gave way to the furious bustle that comes before sudden departures.

Steiner had remained in his seat, his cigarette drooping from

3

the corner of his mouth. He turned his head and looked at Schnurrbart, who was still sitting, pipe in mouth and feet on table, making no move to join in the packing. Steiner grinned. Schnurrbart was the only man who saw through him. Actually Schnurrbart's name was Karl Reisenauer; the heavy black stubble on his face, a vigorous growth that withstood the strongest razor blades, had earned him the nickname of "Mustache"—Schnurrbart.

Steiner studied the men. They were deeply absorbed in their work. Zoll and red-haired little Maag bumped into each other but for once forgot to curse in their eagerness to get ready. Hollerbach quietly helped Kern fold up his shelter-half, which the latter in his customary clumsy manner had packed into a messy lump. Kneeling on the floor, Dorn was neatly rolling up his blanket while the three youngsters, Dietz, Pasternack and Anselm, were already hoisting their packs.

"Idiots!" Steiner muttered.

"Why?" Schnurrbart grinned. "If I didn't know you so well, I'd be packing, too."

"They're idiots all the same," Steiner replied moodily.

The men, their gear packed, became aware that Schnurrbart and Steiner had not moved. Dorn looked at each of them in turn, an uncomprehending expression on a thin face to which glasses gave an air of insignificance.

"Dorn's thinking again," Schnurrbart said.

Now the other men became attentive. They stared uneasily at Steiner. An uncanny silence fell. From somewhere came the blasts of another heavy battery and the staccato chattering of a machine gun.

At last Kruger stirred. He approached Steiner slowly. "What sort of a game is this?" he asked through his teeth.

Steiner regarded him with amusement. "It's your own game," he said. "I didn't tell you to pack your stuff."

"You said the companies were pulling out," Dorn said reproachfully.

"No, I didn't," Steiner said.

"You sure did," Kruger shouted. "We have ears!"

"Pig's ears," Steiner said. "I said the *other* companies were pulling out."

"Of all the crap!" Kruger said heatedly. Suddenly he wrenched the pack from his back, smashing it to the ground and strode off to the bunks along the wall of the dugout. With a crash he let himself drop on the lowest and stretched out, clasping his hands under his head. Steiner grinned and turned to the others.

"Battalion is pulling out in twenty minutes. We—that is, our platoon—are to stay here as a rear guard."

All the color drained out of the men's faces. Unsteadily Kern dropped into a chair, mumbling, "What a mess."

Dietz clasped his hand to his throat. "Those idiots are crazy," he said in a trembling voice.

"Idiots are always crazy," Steiner stated. He rose, took a map from his pocket and spread it out on the table. The men crowded around him. His finger traced the route which led west. Not far beyond Krimskaya lay the Crimea and the northern reaches of the Black Sea.

"Here is the situation," he explained. "Tonight the division is moving into new positions east of Krimskaya. Tomorrow night it will move on into permanent positions west of the city. Every battalion has left one platoon behind as a rear guard. The plan was for us to stay here until five o'clock tomorrow morning. Now they've found out that the Russians have smelled a rat and have at some point advanced beyond the evacuated positions. . . ."

"You mean they'll get to Krimskaya ahead of us?" Kruger asked.

Steiner shrugged. "Very likely. But orders are orders."

"You don't mean to stay here until tomorrow morning, do you?" Dorn asked in a shocked voice.

"Not till morning, no. But for two hours we have to hold this position. Maybe three." Steiner grinned. "Otherwise we might get to Krimskaya before the battalion."

The faces of the men turned pale. Maag forced a hoarse laugh. "That wouldn't do, would it?" he said. His white face twitched under the mane of red hair.

Zoll brought his fist down on the table with a crash. "It is sheer idiocy," he said violently. "I'm for clearing out now, right this minute! This is so unreasonable. . . ."

He fell silent under Steiner's cool, steady gaze and tugged nervously at the flashy yellow silk scarf he wore around his neck.

"What you are for interests nobody," Steiner said coldly. "If I wanted your advice I'd ask for it. And you ought to know by now that an enlisted man talking about reason is like a Jew shouting 'Heil Hitler.' "

Kruger slapped his thigh in appreciation and the others grinned vindictively. None of them liked Zoll. He was the eternal trouble-maker in the platoon.

Steiner watched him clench his fists in helpless rage. The scene disgusted him. He straightened up, buckled his belt and spoke to Schnurrbart.

"You better hit your bunks till we're ready. Who knows when we'll next have a chance to get some sleep? Put a sentry out—take Maag, Dietz and then the Professor. By then it will be time to go."

They watched gravely as he picked up his cap, slung the tommy gun over his shoulder and moved toward the door.

Schnurrbart involuntarily took a step forward. "Where are you going?" he asked tightly.

"Recon," Steiner said. The door slammed shut behind him.

There were eleven men in the platoon. Too few by far to keep watch on the tricky wooded terrain. By morning the Russians would be on to the enemy's weakness. Anselm could not bring himself to think of what would happen then. A regular suicide assignment, he told himself.

One of the men sat down beside him. He looked up and recognized Kern. "What do you say about this?" he asked.

Kern shrugged. "What's there to say? A stinking deal if there ever was one. The bastards won't be satisfied till we've all croaked."

Anselm regarded him with disgust. Kern's vulgar manner jarred on him. From the first he had disliked the man. He drew in his lip in contempt, and his voice sounded hostile as he said, "If that's all you have to say, you can keep it to yourself."

Kern gave him a mean glance. "If you don't like what I say don't ask me," he growled. His thumb darted under his collar at the back of his neck. He had huge, hairy hands.

Anselm studied his flat, ugly nose, his low forehead and mane of shaggy hair. I'm glad I don't look like him, he thought. He ran his hand over his own boyish face.

He did not know much about Kern, who had joined them only two weeks ago, transferred from a bakers' unit. No one knew the reasons for the transfer. No one cared particularly. Perhaps it was a punishment. All they actually knew about him was that he had owned an inn back home; he brought this up on every possible occasion. When he talked about the bottles of wine he had stowed away in a corner of his cellar, the men listened raptly. He implied that the inn brought in a tidy income, and Anselm felt resentment whenever he thought about this. Moodily he watched as Kern rolled a cigarette with unpracticed fingers; half the tobacco dropped to the floor. The man's clumsiness filled Anselm with fresh contempt.

The others were sitting around the table. Kruger took a pack of cards out of his pocket, saying, "There's no sense trying to get any sleep now." He rubbed his nose and frowned. He looked angry, but then he usually did. Anselm, watching him, remembered that he was an East Prussian from Königsberg. Rumor had it that his father had been a Russian, for he spoke the language. Kruger himself maintained a stony silence on the subject.

Dorn, the Professor, was sitting beside him. He was easy to get along with. Anselm liked his quiet way of talking. He had often wondered why Dorn had not become an officer. Kruger said the Professor did not want to. That didn't make sense, as far as Anselm was concerned.

The last man at the table was the soldier Dietz, a Sudeten German and the youngest of the group. Steiner's name for him was Baby; Kruger said he was a dreamer. Anselm looked them over as though their individualities might somehow cheer him up. The thought of having to leave this bunker depressed him. He sighed heavily and said, "Too bad."

"What's too bad?" Kruger asked.

"That we have to leave this place."

"I should think you'd have got used to moving by now."

"I'll never get used to it," Anselm said vehemently. "We worked a whole week fixing this place up—the devil take the army."

"Amen," Kruger said, slamming a trump down on the table so hard that the candle went out.

"Watch what you're doing, you idiot!" Kern snapped.

"Idiot yourself," Kruger retorted.

For a few seconds the two stared at each other like fighting cocks, until Kern threw his cards down on the table. "I'm sick of the whole thing," he growled .

Kruger grinned. "You're scared stiff."

Kern folded his arms across his chest, obviously wondering whether to let this pass. He contented himself with a mocking smile. "If you think I'm scared, you don't know me, that's all."

"No reason why I should," Kruger baited him. "You've only been with us for two weeks."

Kern flushed. "You've got nothing to boast about," he said angrily. "Two weeks at the front is as good as two years. Once you've learned the ropes, all you need is luck."

Kruger appealed to the others. "Did you guys hear that?"

"We're not deaf," Anselm said. "That man can't tell a Russian from a *landser* and thinks he's on old vet."

Dietz looked toward the door. "I wonder where Steiner went."

Schnurrbart yawned with great deliberation. Then he turned to Kruger. "You might take a look around for him," he said. "The rest of the company must have left long ago."

"Why me?"

"You're the most reliable man here."

Kruger stood up and reached out for his tommy gun. He seemed to detect something in Schnurrbart's face that he did not like. He quickly dropped back into his chair again. "I'm not a nursemaid," he said sullenly. "Steiner can look after himself."

"I'm sure of it," Schnurrbart said, getting up in turn. "If he had to depend on you, I'd be sorry for him." Before Kruger could reply, he had left the bunker.

In front of the door he paused. The position ran through a dense forest, but it was too dark to see even the nearest trees. Schnurrbart groped his way to the trench. He found Maag, who wanted to know when his relief was coming. "In ten minutes," Schnurrbart said. "Was Steiner here?"

"Sure, he went over there."

Schnurrbart peered at the dim white blur which was all he could see of the man's face. "Over where?"

"To the Russians, of course," Maag answered. "To see what's doing."

"Alone?"

"Naturally—he always does. What about it?"

"That idiot!" Schnurrbart exclaimed. He ought to have looked for Steiner earlier.

The forest smelled cold, spicy with old leaves, sodden with snow recently melted into the spongy ground. The trees were full of noises. Tiny insects fell from above and rustled through the layers of dead vegetation on the forest floor. Schnurrbart stared into the darkness. "Did he say how long he'd stay out there?" he asked.

"How could he? That depends on the Russians."

Schnurrbart nodded. If only I knew what to do, he thought.

For a while they remained silent. The dampness of the forest began to penetrate their clothes and pierced them like a frost. Finally Schnurrbart took a few steps down the trench. His uneasiness had continued to mount. He returned to Maag. "Go back to the others and tell them to get ready," he said. "We'll wait another ten minutes. If Steiner isn't back by then, we'll look for him."

While Schnurrbart settled down behind the heavy machine gun, Maag climbed out of the trench and sped off. Schnurrbart looked thoughtfully over the rim of the trench, his mind still on Steiner. Probably he was a fool to be concerned. He grinned to himself as he pictured Steiner sitting somewhere in an abandoned Russian bunker reading the book he always carried with him. Just the sort of thing Steiner would do. Ever since Schnurrbart had known him he had carried a volume of Schiller's poems in his pocket, and he would start leafing through it in the craziest situations. He must have read the thing a hundred times over. Odd, because otherwise reading didn't seem much in his line.

Schnurrbart remembered how highhanded Steiner had been toward him at the beginning, until one day their casual and almost hostile relationship had changed to friendship. The change had come about a year and a half ago. The battalion had held positions south of Kramatorsk, on an endless plain of Russian snow. . . .

For days the snow had been coming down, a wild blizzard. They were sitting in their bunkers warming themselves by the small drum stove. It was late evening. The other men were already asleep on their cots. Steiner was reading, Schnurrbart toasting some slices of bread on the red-hot top of the stove. Suddenly Steiner laid his book aside and asked, "You play chess?"

"So-so," Schnurrbart replied. He watched Steiner take a traveling chess set out of his pack and arrange the pieces on the board. They started. After the first few moves Schnurrbart realized that Steiner was several classes above him. The game was over in half an hour. He had no better luck in the second game. When by an oversight he lost his queen, he angrily swept the pieces from the board.

Steiner expressionlessly rolled a cigarette. "Tough losing her."

They sat in silence. The storm drove powdery snow through the cracks in the door. Schnurrbart took out his pipe and began filling it. After lighting it he looked up at Steiner and said, "I'm not inquisitive, but . . ." He hesitated, considering how best to put his question. Finally he gave himself a mental push and went on, "But I'd be interested to know whether you have a girl."

Steiner's features hardened, and Schnurrbart hastened to apologize. "I don't mean to step on your toes," he said hastily, already regretting having brought up the subject. Steiner had indicated on former occasions that this was something he did not want to talk about. But after all, they had been together for more than three years now. What harm was there in asking? Annoyed, Schnurrbart knocked out his pipe against the leg of the table and crammed it into his pocket. If he doesn't want to talk, that's all there is to it, he thought, yawning ostentatiously. "Think I'll sleep," he murmured. "I'm dead tired."

But this time Steiner relented. "Wait." He glanced quickly over at the sleeping men; then he laid his arms on the table and leaned forward. "I had a girl, but she's dead," he said.

In the silence that followed, the roaring wind shouldered the door as though it would knock it down. So that's it, Schnurrbart thought, trying to keep his expression blankly polite. He leaned back in the chair, crossed his legs and met Steiner's eyes squarely. "I can imagine how it must feel," he said carefully.

They fell silent again. Somewhere near by a heavy shell burst. The bunker rocked, and one of the men groaned in his sleep and mumbled something. Schnurrbart looked at the door. A thin ribbon of snow grew on the floor just below the threshold. "This will go on forever," Schnurrbart murmured. Steiner said nothing, and at last Schnurrbart turned to face him again, "What was her name?"

"Anne."

Schnurrbart nodded. "Nice name," he said noncommitally. "What happened to her?"

"She died in an accident." Steiner gestured toward the door. "It was weather just like this. The two of us used to do a lot of mountain climbing. Just below the peak the storm caught us by surprise. She slipped and . . ." He fell silent, staring into the flickering candle flame. Again there was a long pause.

Schnurrbart hunched his shoulders uncomfortably as he spoke. "Terrible. When did it happen?"

"In thirty-eight. Shortly before the war started."

"Five years ago. Seems like a long time to me."

"Seems long to you, does it," Steiner said tightly. He shook his head slowly. "It was yesterday, I tell you. Yesterday and today and tomorrow and always." A strand of dark hair fell across his forehead; he brushed it aside with an impatient movement of his hand. "You see," he said, "you see, it was all my fault, mine alone. I let go of her—these hands you see here let go of her. If you had been through it, you would never forget it, no more than I can."

His face suddenly seemed corroded, as though acid had flowed across his skin. If only I had not started it, Schnurrbart thought. In great mortification he reached for his pipe again and began filling it once more. The wood in the stove crackled and popped. He began to feel the silence like a physical pain. He propped his elbows on the table, cleared his throat several times and said at last, "I know what you mean; it is one hell of a note. But you can't go on feeling the same way forever."

Slowly Steiner lifted his hands from his face and stared at his friend. "Forever?" He moved his head as if listening for something. Then he gave a strained laugh. "No, it will not go on forever. It will stop when I meet her again," he said.

"Meet her?" Schnurrbart asked blankly.

"Sure. You may think I'm off my head, but I tell you I will meet her again. If I'm still around, she must be too. Somewhere, when this war is over, she will cross my path."

"That's going pretty far," Schnurrbart said.

Steiner shook his head. "Everyone goes as far as he can."

For a while there was silence between them, until Schnurrbart asked, "Suppose you don't meet her?"

Steiner slowly turned his face toward him. "What's that?"

"I mean, what will you do if you don't meet her?"

Steiner waved that away with a light motion of his hand. "If I live through this war," he said quietly, "I will meet her. And if I don't come out of it . . ." He stood up, stepped up quickly to the tiny window by the door and peered out.

Schnurrbart drew the pipe from his mouth and sat looking meditatively at the toes of his boots. When he glanced up he saw that Steiner was watching him with an expression of mockery. "What are you thinking about?" he asked.

Schnurrbart sensed that he was seeking a quarrel. "This and that," he said, shrugging placatingly.

"Why don't you give it up?" Steiner said with scorn. "You can't understand it anyway."

"Why not?"

"You can't," Steiner repeated with sudden anger. "None of you can understand it; you're a bunch of primitives."

"Look here . . ." Schnurrbart began, but Steiner cut him off.

"A bunch of primitives; you cannot imagine what a woman can mean. For all of you a woman is nothing but a lay, and it doesn't matter who she is as long as she puts out."

His voice had risen, and some of the men on the cots woke up. They stared sleepily over at the two, and one of them grumbled, "Be quiet, damn it. Let a man get some sleep!"

With a thrust of his hands Steiner forced himself from the wall and took four big strides over to the man's side. "You shut up!" he snarled. "Shut up, you damned idiot! Sleeping and eating and . . ." He fell silent abruptly. Disgusted, he gazed for a moment at the cowed faces of the men and whirled around.

As he went to the door, Schnurrbart gripped his arm firmly. "If you want to believe in that kind of thing, go ahead," he said quietly. "But you aren't fair to the fellows there."

Steiner stared into his eyes. Then suddenly he leaned forward and asked, "What about you? Aren't I unfair to you too?" He turned and left the bunker.

Every time he remembered that incident, Schnurrbart had felt a mingling of uneasiness and satisfaction. He was surer than ever that a wrong word at the time was all that was needed to make any future relationship with Steiner unendurable. As it was, they had become quite close. Not so close as he had hoped, for even afterward Steiner never quite dropped his reserve. There was no one at all in the platoon who could boast of sharing his undivided confidence. Every so often, in small matters, he would make it clear that he wanted to remain aloof and that he felt obligation toward none of them. He kept his thoughts to himself even at such times as this, when he was undertaking a dangerous reconnaissance which might well turn out badly.

The thought brought Schnurrbart to the present. Sighing, he peered over the top of the trench. Darkness hung among the trees like powdered soot.

A figure appeared out of the darkness and wandered toward him. He recognized Hollerbach. "What are you up to out here?" Hollerbach asked.

Schnurrbart shrugged. "Nothing. Heard anything from Steiner?"

"No, the devil only knows where he is."

"It's sickening," Schnurrbart grumbled. "Always this hide-and-seek business. He might have taken one of us with him."

Hollerbach shrugged. "You know how he is." Although Schnurrbart was quite tall, Hollerbach towered over him. He wore no cap, and his pale blond, almost white hair gleamed like a helmet in the night. He, with Kruger, was one of the few "old men" in the platoon. A steady, easygoing fellow, he was noteworthy for receiving a letter from his girl in almost every mail.

For the past week, however, no mail had reached Battalion, and Schnurrbart recalled the rumors of a huge encirclement in which the entire Caucasus army was trapped. Although he took little stock in these tales, he was aware of the possibility that a good many unpleasant surprises might be in store for them all. If only Steiner were here, he thought. Aloud he said, "He's stubborn as a mule."

"Since he came back from furlough he's been in a hell of

a mood," Hollerbach said. "Wish I knew what happened back there."

"So do I." Schnurrbart had given the matter much thought these past several months.

"At any rate—" Hollerbach lingered on the subject—"he must have started some fireworks to get himself broken from sergeant to private and four months in a punishment battalion besides."

Schnurrbart scratched his belly thoughtfully. He didn't particularly want to go into this matter. The platoon had heard one thing and another, but the reasons for Steiner's demotion remained obscure. "There's less to it than you think," he replied in a standoffish tone. "All a man has to do is shoot his mouth off once and they get him for it."

"That's true." While the conversation lapsed, Schnurrbart reckoned out the time on his fingers. It was just half a year ago that Steiner had rejoined the company. He had been wounded at Izyum and hospitalized back home. There something must have happened that he refused to talk about. At any rate he had been transferred to Disciplinary Battalion 500. After doing his spell in that outfit, he had been promoted to corporal, and six months ago had turned up in the company again—a bit more closemouthed and grim than he had been before. Schnurrbart recalled how he had responded to all questions with an indifferent shrug, until at last they gave up asking him. In any case, the hectic pace of recent weeks had kept them concentrating on the present. The retreat from Tuapse to this position could no longer be termed "an elastic defense." It really looked like the beginning of the end.

Thinking of that, and of Steiner, Schnurrbart sighed. "I guess we'll have to look for him," he said impatiently.

"I've been thinking about that. Where can you look for him in this darkness? For all we know, there are still a bunch of Russians over there."

Schnurrbart was inclined to agree. He hitched up his cartridge belt, settled back and said, "Why don't you go back to where it's warm? I'll stay here and keep my ears open, just in case. If anything comes up, you know where I am."

Hollerbach nodded and started wearily back toward the bunker.

By now most of the men had dozed off. Dorn alone continued to sit at the table. Since he had to relieve Dietz soon, there was little point to lying down now. Besides, he had been bothered for days by painful cramps, probably from the skimpy rations, which did not let him sleep.

He glanced about at the furnishings of the bunker and sighed. For two weeks they had worked like dogs, had brought stuff from the nearest villages, had dug, carpentered, made window frames, fixed straw mattresses—done everything possible to make the bunker comfortable, and now all that work was for nothing. Dorn lowered his head, thinking how hard men cling to a place, doing things to it that make for a little pleasantness. Of course it was only a hole in the ground. But for all of them, leading the soldier's nomad life, it was much more. In this land of boundless expanses and unnerving strangeness, this land with which none of their memories were linked, the bunker was a semblance of home. And as with home, they attached all kinds of emotions to it.

Now again they were pulling up stakes, forging out into the unknown, with all the apprehension such moves carried with them. Steiner's report had not sounded encouraging. Who could say where they would spend tomorrow night?

He sighed and looked at his watch. Time for him to take over. Heavily he stood up, clapped the steel helmet on his head, took his rifle and went out. As he raised his face, he felt rain falling. Cautiously he climbed the slippery steps. His glasses misted over. He removed them and tried to accommodate his eyes to the darkness. A few steps away from the door he came upon Dietz, who was leaning against a tree.

"You here already?" Dietz asked.

"It's time," Dorn replied.

Dietz took a step closer to him. His teeth chattered lightly as he said, "Dirty weather." He eased the rifle from his shoulder and shook himself. "Nice time we're going to have tonight," he said. "A regular funeral march. Just imagine it—twenty miles in this kind of weather through a swampy forest."

"It will be ghastly," Dorn agreed.

"If only the rain would stop," Dietz said, peering through the dark at Dorn's face. They both fell silent and stared gloomily into the night.

The rain drizzled down steadily; the trees let fall big drops which slapped into the dry leaves on the ground. Dorn draped his shelter-half over the steel helmet and leaned against a tree. "Well, be careful," Dietz said. He gave Dorn a helpful pat on the shoulder and disappeared into the bunker.

Minutes passed. The darkness seemed to grow thicker. From somewhere sounded the wailing cry of an owl. A gust of wind shook the trees, producing a pattering like hailstones on the roof of a tent. Dorn pushed the steel helmet back from his forehead and strained to see into the blackness of the woods.

His glasses stayed in his pocket; in weather like this they were useless.

What could be keeping Steiner so long? he wondered. His stomach cramps were getting worse. He pressed his fist into his belly and held his breath. For a few seconds the pain let up. But when he removed his fist, it returned with redoubled intensity. He bent over, and when that brought no relief squatted on his heels. It was more bearable that way. He propped his chin in his hand and became aware of his unshaven face. His skin was damp and sticky. Filth, he thought in disgust; everything is filthy, body, underclothes, everything. After a while he propped both arms on his thighs and let his head droop; his rifle he held clamped between his legs. Again and again he heard strange noises, but he was too apathetic to pay attention to them. The fear that had been with him for so long that it had become a living part of himself was gradually smothered by dull indifference.

His head drooped lower and lower. His lips were parted and he could feel the spittle trickling from his mouth. In his present state it gave him a spiteful, silly satisfaction to let himself go completely. This is what I am really like, he thought—this is me. If Maria could see me now. The thought of his wife revived him momentarily. He raised his head and closed his mouth. Maria, he thought, Maria, Betty, Jürgen. Jürgen would be going to school this year. He shook his head at the swift passage of time. Then he tried to picture his wife taking Jürgen to school every morning. He smiled happily, and the smile lingered when his thoughts had already taken a graver turn. There was Betty, Two years younger than Jürgen, a quiet, serious child like her mother. Always rather sickly, and not like other girls the same age. The doctor had said Betty ought to be sent to a rest home in the country for a few months. If only there were no war. Certainly it couldn't go on much longer, but how would it end?

He was still thinking about this when a hand gripped his shoulder brutally and pulled him to his feet. Paralyzed by fright, he stared into the face of Steiner. "Existential philosophy, Professor," Steiner said coldly, "presupposes existence. You won't exist much longer if you go to sleep at your post. Pick up your gun."

Released from his grip, Dorn stooped for the rifle on the ground. When he had straightened up he saw that Steiner was listening to the sounds from the woods.

He turned to Dorn. "You can do sentry duty sitting, for all I care, but don't fall asleep." Then he climbed down into the bunker. A few minutes later he was back, carrying blankets

and shelter-halves. He spread the blanket out on the ground,
hung the canvas over his shoulders and sat down at the foot
of a tree. "Sit beside me," he ordered Dorn. "By night you
see better from lower down."

Dorn obeyed in silence. He had recovered from his slump
and now felt guilty. Ought he to mention his cramps to
Steiner? he wondered. But oddly enough he no longer felt
any pain. For a few minutes they sat without talking. Then
Dorn asked, "Did you go to the highway?"

"Yes."

"And . . . how does it look?"

"Lovely," Steiner said with a humorless laugh.

Anxiously Dorn peered into his face. "What does that
mean? Did you see any Russians?"

"*Und wie!* Infantry, trucks, tanks—the whole damn Russian
army."

Dorn stared at him. "On the highway?"

"Not in the air, I assure you."

Dorn took a deep breath. "My God," he murmured. He
could feel his legs growing leaden; the wet uniform seemed to
weigh him down like a suit of armor.

Steiner drew his knees up closer to his body and thrust
his tommy gun between them. "We'll just have to wait until
the traffic slacks off. It ought to be quieter by tomorrow
morning."

"But that's hopeless," Dorn said, hoarse with agitation.
"Can't we avoid the highway altogether?"

"That would mean covering twice the distance. We haven't
the time. If the Russians reach Krimskaya before us, we're
sunk."

Steiner's very matter-of-factness made Dorn feel panic.
He rubbed his wet face with the back of his hand and stammered, "Then what are we going to do?"

Steiner snorted angrily. "You heard what I said. We're
crossing the highway."

"And suppose the Russians see us?"

"Then we'll say good morning and invite them to play
patty-cake."

Dorn closed his eyes before the wave of fear that swept
him. He saw Russian columns marching toward him, a thousand tommy guns pointed at him.

There was a short silence. Abruptly Steiner laughed. "You're
a philosopher, aren't you?" he asked.

Dorn looked up in astonishment. "Of course. Why do you
ask?"

"It surprises me that you don't take a calmer view of our situation."

"What has that to do with philosophy?"

Steiner laughed again. He stared into the darkness and the rain for a time. Then he replied, "Well, you are always looking for the relationships between things. But it strikes me that your so-called deeper knowledge doesn't help you any. As soon as you're up against any unusual situation, your philosophy goes to pot."

"What makes you say that?"

Steiner gestured impatiently. "If there are relationships everywhere," he said, "every situation is justified, including ours. You see . . ." he considered. "For my part, I don't believe in relationships—at most in coincidence. I also believe in encounters. But every encounter seems to me an episode in human life unconnected with other encounters. Each one is meaningful or meaningless in itself, according to how it works out in our personal life. And so no meaningless experience becomes meaningful just because you can construct a relationship between it and something else. Maybe I'm not putting it clearly. I'm not a professor. But it riles me when I see you people trying to make a meaningful incident out of all kinds of rot, looking for grand solutions, using a lot of big words, and in the end landing right back in your own muck. The way you do, Professor. Am I right?"

Dorn hesitated. Although the conversation appealed to him, he did not think they would get far. But he decided to make a stab at clarity. "Have you ever heard anything about nihilism?"

"In first grade in grammar school," Steiner said haughtily.

"The nihilist denies the meaning of existence and order. All I am denying is the meaning of meaninglessness."

"Of apparent meaninglessness."

Steiner waved his barely visible hand toward the darkness in front of them. "Is what we've got here apparent?"

"That isn't the point at issue," Dorn replied calmly. "Try to see things a little less specifically. We are placed in a mysterious and incomprehensible world. If we did not have other human beings to teach us and lead us step by step into the riddles of our environment, we might get used to their appearance but we would never fully understand them."

Steiner had been listening with knitted brows. "Keep going," he said, pulling the canvas tighter around his shoulders.

"We need the people of our environment in order . . . to give meaning and content to our lives. It is just the same with the encounters and events of our existence. All together they make up the mosaic of our life. They become meaningless only when we take them out of the picture one by one and examine them in isolation. Philosophy affirms relationships. It has to reject the idea of meaninglessness."

"All right," Steiner said. "But what has philosophy to say about war? Does it see anything in the meaninglessness of war also?"

Dorn looked up at the dense roof of foliage, through which the rain still dripped evenly. "There is not only a mosaic of our personal existence," he said, "but a mosaic composed of the history of a nation. Even the apparent meaninglessness of war can become meaningful within the whole context of a nation's life. Not that plenty of questions don't remain. We could talk about this for hours. Do you take an interest in these matters?"

"No more than I need to for living." Steiner fended him off. It appeared that the conversation was taking a course different from what he had expected, and he seemed to be losing interest. "In any case, it seems to me that philosophy, too, finds new questions in every answer."

"Not in every one," Dorn replied.

Neither spoke for a moment. Then Steiner looked directly at Dorn again. "I want to ask you a question."

His tone took Dorn aback. "Go ahead."

Steiner shook the water off his canvas. After he had drawn it over his shoulders again, he propped his chin in his hands and said, "Suppose we take the following case. Let's say we lost something especially valuable to us. Something we love more than anything else. If I decide that this loss is meaningless, I can make myself feel better by thinking that one day I will find again what I have lost, and then the losing of it will be cancelled out. Is that so?"

"That depends on the object," Dorn replied.

Steiner sternly shook his head. "The object doesn't matter," he answered with annoyance. "It's enough if it's valuable. But to go on. If on the other hand I decide that the losing of it was meaningful, had some function, that is, in my life, then I couldn't very well count on the possibility of finding it again. There was a good reason why it was lost and it would have to stay lost. Now which is right? Or to put it another way, which is better?"

"Again that depends on the object."

"Nonsense, it's a question of principle."

"It's an individual question. In order to answer it I must know the nature of the object."

Steiner's face darkened. He stood up quickly, stooping for his blanket. "Then we might as well drop the whole thing."

Dorn thought in disappointment that he had almost had him then. Steiner was even warier than he had assumed. Sooner or later he would get to the bottom of Steiner's cynicism. After all, the boy was only twenty-five.

"I'll wake the others," Steiner said. "We can continue our talk some time. You still owe me an explanation."

"What about?"

"You know what I mean," Steiner said. He rolled the blanket into a bundle. "I started off by saying that your philosophy ought to hold up even in unusual situations."

"So you did," Dorn replied.

Steiner looked at him. "I'm glad you haven't forgotten. One of these days you'll have to tell me why it doesn't work that way with you."

"I can answer that right now."

"At the moment I don't care to hear," Steiner said. "I've had enough philosophy for the day." He turned toward the bunker. Dorn followed him.

By the time Hollerbach had gone to fetch Schnurrbart, the men inside the bunker were sitting at the table, Steiner among them. Even without looking at him, Schnurrbart sensed his mocking expression. He went over to a cot and sat down.

"I hear you have been worried on my account," Steiner said. The sarcasm in his voice sent the blood rushing to Schnurrbart's forehead. The bastard, he thought, trembling with rage, the lousy bastard! He felt painfully humiliated. The hell with him in the future. He began fumbling with his pipe. Steiner watched him, his gray eyes glistening with amusement. Then he turned to the table, smoothed down the map and motioned the men to crowd around him.

"How far is it to Krimskaya?" Maag inquired anxiously, craning his neck to get a look.

"About twenty miles. If we used the highway it would be nearly forty-five."

"Then we certainly won't be using the highway," Kruger said.

Steiner stared at the map. "The stuff between is regular wilderness. At least that's how it looks to me from the map. And a stream running through. The whole region is marshy. The big question is whether we can get through."

"Then let's take the highway," Kruger said.

"Sure." Kern nodded. "It's a lot better walking on the

road. We can do forty-five miles by tomorrow night easy. The battalion must have marched along the road too."

"In the first place," Steiner explained, "the battalion didn't march; it went by truck. In the second place, I doubt that we'll be able to stay on the highway without interference."

Kern looked blankly at the map. "Why?" he asked.

For a moment Steiner sat still, looking into their anxious faces. Then he rose. "The Russians are on the highway. That means we have to go through the woods. Before we reach them we have that highway to cross." He slung his tommy gun over his shoulder and went to the door, opening it. "Come on! Stay close together and keep your traps shut."

One after the other the men squeezed past him. Steiner was last to leave the bunker. He kicked the stove so that it fell over, spilling its glowing embers on the floor. He went out, closing the door behind him. The men were waiting a few yards away. He took the lead and the platoon set off into the woods. They spoke scarcely a word as they marched. After some twenty minutes the forest began thinning out, and in another five minutes they reached the edge of it. As they stepped out upon the open plowland, a cold wind lashed the rain into their faces. By the time they had gone a few yards great lumps of muddy soil clung to their boots. They panted under the burden of their machine guns and boxes of ammunition, and with every step cursed under their breaths. Kruger kept close behind Hollerbach. He was carrying the heavy MG over his right shoulder like a shovel. Once he slipped and fell into a furrow. Tiredly he scrambled up and wiped the mud from his hands. This stinking war, he thought bitterly, and bumped into Hollerbach.

"That's what you get for falling asleep on your feet," Hollerback whispered, shifting his rifle to his other shoulder.

Kruger jabbed his fist into Hollerbach's back. "Shut up. What I'd like to know is how much farther we still have to go. This damned field is never going to end."

Suddenly Hollerbach stopped.

Kruger pushed forward toward the group in front. "What the devil's the matter now?"

The men did not answer. Out of the darkness before them rose the low drone of big motors, the creaking of heavily laden trucks. Occasional shouts, wind-blown and stirring, reached their ears.

"Russians," Hollerbach whispered.

"A whole army," Kern stammered. With quivering fingers he unthinkingly reached for his cigarettes and thrust one between his lips. As he struck a match, Steiner suddenly appeared

in front of him. There was a sharp slapping sound, followed
by a rain of sparks from the crushed cigarette. Kern uttered
a whimpering noise and pressed both hands against his
mouth.

The whole incident had taken place so swiftly that the
others only began to realize what it was about when Steiner
took a step backward and raised his tommy gun. "You god-
forsaken idiot!" His voice sounded thick with rage. The men
stared at him in alarm, while Kern still stood among them,
his hands at his face. "You ought to be shot!" Steiner whispered harshly. He whirled around and ran forward again.
Silently they followed him.

For another hundred yards they continued in the same
direction. The terrain began to slope upward. The noises
ahead became increasingly distinct. They could already hear the
crisp tread of nailed boots. But it was still so dark that they
could not see ten paces ahead. They must have been about
fifty yards from the highway when Steiner ordered a halt.
He called to Hollerbach and Schnurrbart to join him. "You
come with me. The rest will wait here." They bent low and
disappeared into the darkness.

The men squatted on the wet ground, listening to the noises
from the highway. They were all wide awake now. Kruger
looked at his watch. It was already four. The rain had let up.
Only an occasional drop fell now. I wish the hell it would
pour, Kruger thought. He said to Dietz beside him, "We'll
never get across there."

Dietz shrugged. He looked at Kern, who had buried his face
in his hands and was sitting in a posture of resentment. "He
shouldn't have hit him," Dietz whispered.

Kruger spat. "Ah, *Scheisse!*"

"What do you mean, *Scheisse?*" Dietz protested. "He
shouldn't have done it." He began to stammer indignantly.
"Where'd we be if every corporal could slap us in the face?"

Kruger rubbed his sleeve over his wet face. "What are
you raising such a fuss for?" he grumbled. "Forget it, for
God's sake. There are more important things to think about
at the moment."

Intimidated, Dietz fell silent. He sat regarding his dirty
hands unhappily. It just wasn't right, he thought. A reprimand
—all right; punishment exercises—those were all right, too.
But smashing a lighted cigarette into a man's face—that was
going too far, way too far. The more he thought about it,
the more indignant he became. Steiner had always been decent
to him personally, but that, too, might change some day. It
was a matter of principle. What had just happened to Kern

might easily happen to any of them tomorrow. Although, of course, he himself would hardly be caught making a mistake like that. After all, he was a soldier, a front-liner. At this point in his train of thought, Dietz saw the thing clearly.

"If a thing's wrong on the lowest level, it's wrong all through," he said. "That way it's a serious matter. Do you think . . ." He hesitated. "Don't you think that if they started pasting one another in the face at the Führer's headquarters, we wouldn't be feeling the effects of it quick enough? I tell you, we've got to have order. Order and discipline from the bottom to the top, but also from the bottom to the top." He spoke these last words with the utmost conviction.

Kruger grinned. "It's the same thing."

"What is?"

"Well, you said we've got to have order from the bottom to the top, but also from the bottom to the top. It's the same thing."

It took a moment for Dietz to grasp this. "That was just a slip of the tongue," he said angrily. "You know what I meant: from the bottom to the top and from the top to the bottom. In the Führer's headquarters . . ."

"Don't strain your guts," Kruger said, "In the Führer's headquarters they gargle with champagne. We'll be gargling piss by the time we're through." He wiped his hand over his mouth. "Sure we'd feel the effects if they started pasting one another." The thought amused him and he chuckled. "Maybe they will, at that; but not until all of us right here are in the bucket. You know what is important at the moment?" He brought his face close to Dietz's. "It's important that we have to get out of here. And you know why? I'll tell you." He poked his finger into Dietz's chest; indignantly Dietz moved back. "We have to get out so that we'll be on time to get into the next mess. Out of one mess into the next. That's been going on for three years, and it'll go on until we get into one mess good and deep and don't come out of it." He came to an end of words, having worked himself into a rage.

Dietz gazed at him dumfounded. Then he turned to Dorn, who had been listening to the conversation with amusement. "What do you say to that, Professor?"

Dorn forced a grave expression. "It is difficult," he said. "I shall have to consult my books."

The men grinned and turned their attention back to the highway. It was slowly beginning to grow light. The terrain was now fairly visible. In front of them the field sloped steeply up to an embankment and beyond rose the black silhouettes of mountains against the graying sky.

"Where the devil is the highway?" Zoll whispered.

Kruger shrugged. "It must be in a dip. Once we get our carcasses over it, we're in the clear."

They lifted their heads. The sounds on the highway had stopped. "Here comes somebody," Dietz whispered hoarsely.

A figure emerged out of the dim foreground, ran toward them with great leaps. "Hollerbach," Zoll whispered. At this moment Hollerbach stopped and waved his fist in the air.

"Let's go," Kruger said.

They snatched their guns and ran up the slope. Hollerbach waited a moment for them. Panting, they followed him. When they reached the crown of the hill they saw the highway beneath them in the gray dawn light, deserted. They slipped down the steep decline and raced across the trampled, rutted width of the road toward the edge of the woods which rose like a dark wall against the further mountains. Schnurrbart and Steiner were waiting there. Seconds later they were trampling through the dense undergrowth several hundred yards within the woods. They stopped to catch their breath in gasps. It had by now grown so light that they could see the wild gleam of triumph in Steiner's eyes.

Kruger raised his hand. Back toward the road they could again hear the rumble of vehicles. But now that they had made the crossing, it sounded like music to them. The fearful nervous tension of the past few hours dropped away. They grinned, slapped one another exuberantly on the back. "We're all right!" one said boastfully.

"Precision work," commented Hollerbach.

Schnurrbart studied the landscape. "What mountains are those?" he asked.

"Just hills," Steiner explained. "We have to cross them. The marsh begins on the other side." He picked up his gear. "We're ready."

Kern hung back; now and again he would rub the burned spot on his face and give Steiner a dirty look. "Don't take it so hard," Dietz said to him. Kern did not condescend to answer.

For a while their way led over springy, moss-covered forest floor. Then the slope grew steeper, and they began toiling uphill, gasping for breath. The climb seemed everlasting. Tight-lipped with determination, they gained ground slowly; every yard uphill represented a scramble. They kept their eyes fixed in the direction of the invisible peak of the hill which must lie somewhere up above the trees. Their good humor ebbed away and they started to swear.

"They ought to stop for a moment up front there," Dietz

panted. He stood still and wiped the sweat from his forehead.

Kruger, who was behind him, also stopped. "What's the matter, Child? Fuel running low?"

"They ought to make a break," Dietz repeated tearfully.

Kruger regarded him with a frown. "If you start giving out now, how is it going to be later on?" He shifted the machine gun to his left shoulder. "Let me have your boxes."

Dietz sighed gratefully and loosened his belt. "I have a stitch in the side," he said apologetically.

"You'll get over that in a little while," Kruger lied reassuringly. "Come on or we'll be holding this position alone."

The others had gone a considerable distance ahead. But after several more of the men protested, Steiner allowed a rest. It was full daylight by now. The woods filled with the noisy voices of birds. The men sprawled on the ground and looked up the steep slope. "Damned tough going," Zoll said. "We ought to be on top soon."

"We will be," Steiner replied. "You all could have done those few yards more."

Maag yawned. He stretched out on his side and asked, "Where's the fire? We'll get where we're going soon enough."

"It depends on where you're going," Steiner snapped.

Maag refused to be intimidated. "Same place you're going."

"In that case you have no time to lose."

"We'll make those eighteen miles by tonight easy," Maag declared confidently. He was happy just to sit and had made up his mind not to stand up for another ten minutes at least.

Steiner regarded him contemptuously. "If it's only eighteen miles. And, if the battalion doesn't succeed in holding the position where we're to meet them tomorrow, we'll have another fifteen to go."

Schnurrbart rolled over on his belly and explained, "To the west of Krimskaya." He turned to Steiner. "Do you know what positions they're supposed to take there?"

"Yes."

"Well then, everything's under control," Kruger said contentedly.

Steiner glanced irritably at him. None of them seemed to realize what they were facing. Perhaps it was better that way. What worried him most was the stream marked on the map as cutting at an angle across the forest. There was no reason to assume a bridge in this uninhabited area. If necessary, they'd have to fell trees. Without the proper tools that would be exhausting and time-consuming work. The sooner they reached the river the better. "Let's go," he ordered loudly.

They stared up at him in dismay. "Already?" Zoll said. "You can wait a few minutes more."

Steiner walked over to where Zoll sat. "Listen to me," he said, his voice quivering with rage, "you're beginning to get on my nerves. Maybe you better not call attention to yourself for a while."

He turned, and they saw him taking long strides up the slope. Hastily they stood up, brushed the wet leaves from their uniforms and followed. In ten minutes they had reached the brow of the hill. The ceiling of leaves was less dense up here. With surprise they saw that the sky was cloudless. The treetops glistened in the rosy light of the rising sun, which was itself still out of sight beyond the woods. Steiner turned to the right and kept to the ridge, which ran north and south. He had quickened his pace; the men trailed behind, strung out at longer and longer intervals.

Zoll lingered behind to wait for Kern, who trotted up to him with a sour expression. Last in line, they walked along silently, side by side. They were bowed over by the weight of the heavy boxes of ammunition. Sweat drew gray streaks across their filthy faces. There were burn spots around the innkeeper's mouth; Zoll saw his tongue lick out occasionally to moisten the reddened skin. Each time Kern did this, his face twisted in a grimace of pain and resentment.

"I wouldn't have stood for that," Zoll said.

Kern cursed. "You're the one to talk!"

Gradually, however, his rage was losing force and conviction. It had been idiotic of him to light that cigarette. It was the act of a green recruit. This thought had been gnawing away at him more than the blow in the face. And this toilsome climb was beginning to wear the edge off his anger. They had really been lucky. A Russian might really have seen the flare of light from his match. He shuddered. What a break, he thought, what a break! His relief made him feel almost lighthearted. If it were not for the burns around his mouth, he would be able to put the episode out of his mind. Again he ran his tongue over his lips. "Haven't you any salve?" he asked Zoll.

"Think I'm a beauty shop?" Zoll replied sulkily.

Kern grinned. "Not that!" he said. He liked Zoll no more than the others did. Zoll's appearance was as unpleasant as his behavior. There was something shifty about his face, and his eyes seemed to goggle behind his horn-rimmed glasses.

They walked in silence for a while. "I wonder where the devil he's taking us," Zoll said after a while.

Kern tried to see beyond the man in front of them. But the line was now stretched out over a good distance. Steiner was out of sight.

"There's something up ahead there," Kern said.

"Where?"

"There, above the trees."

Zoll stretched his neck forward. "What the hell is it?" he asked.

"Must be the plyon of a power line."

They quickened their steps. Before them, the girders of a huge tower rose out of the trees, and a few yards farther on they came to a cleared lane through the woods. The men were gathered around Steiner, all looking in one direction. Zoll and Kern, when they came up to them, opened their eyes wide with astonishment. Below them was one long downhill drop of land. At regular intervals the steel pylons rose above the lane. To the west, as far as the eye could reach, all the way to the purple-tinged mountains on the horizon, spread a tremendous forest. The bright, even green of the trees flowed on wholly unbroken; nowhere was there a sign of a clearing, of human habitation. The scene took their breath away. "Like a sea. A green sea," Kern murmured reverently.

They all felt stirred and solemn. "Anybody got a camera?" Kruger asked.

Suddenly Anselm cried out, "There's a city over there. See, just to the left of that mountain with the sharp peak."

"Yes, yes," Kruger said enthusiastically. "Do you see it?" he asked of Steiner.

"Sure," Steiner answered quietly. "That's Krimskaya. Where we're headed for."

With mixed feelings they eyed the fine cluster of towers and roofs set at the foot of the distant hills as clear, as still, as incisive as a pen sketch. Kruger seemed utterly lost in the sight. After a while he sighed. "If only we were there already," he said.

"We'll make it," Dietz said, looking at Steiner with trust.

Steiner nodded briefly. "Sure, by evening we'll be there with the others."

"The others," Kruger murmured. He had a queer feeling in his chest. "Funny. I mean," he went on in answer to their questioning looks, "it's a funny feeling to know that the rest of the battalion is somewhere out there."

"Yes," Schnurrbart agreed. Absentmindedly he took his pipe out of his pocket and began packing it. When Steiner sat down and folded his arms over his knees, Schnurrbart looked at him in surprise. "What's up? Aren't we going on?"

"We can spare a few more minutes," Steiner said. His impatience had suddenly vanished. He wished they could stay right here until the war was over. Nobody would look for them in this isolated region. He bit his lip. There's no getting away from it, he thought bitterly, and only then realized how familiar this pattern of emotions was to him. Whenever, after hours of climbing, he came to the top of a mountain and saw the land lying at his feet, his feelings were always similar. Always in the past the knowledge that he would have to return to ordinary life had spoiled the pleasure of the mountain solitudes. The tension which had driven him to climb steadily to the summit would snap; nothing would remain but the dull perception that the trivial burdens of existence were inescapable. Wearily he lighted a cigarette and looked at the men, who had all sat down on the ground to smoke.

Schnurrbart's eyes were fixed upon the oceanic forest below, whose western half was bathed in the rays of an as yet invisible sun. The mist above the trees shivered and dispelled itself even as he watched. The purple of the distant hills was slowly lightening to blue; the contours of the hills merged imperceptibly with the horizon. In another moment I shall start bawling, he thought. The mood he was in alarmed him. This mood was poison—it entered the blood and then there was no escaping it. It only made everything harder, the whole damned war, everything. Trying to distract himself, he concentrated on the rifle which lay at his feet. Finally he cleared his throat noisily. "Weird, isn't it?" he said to Kruger.

The East Prussian picked at his nose. "If I sit here much longer," he said hoarsely, "I won't ever be able to get up again, believe me." He glanced at Dietz, who was sitting openmouthed, staring up at the sky. "What's the matter with you?" he asked. "Seeing angels?"

Dietz raised his hand. "Shhh . . ." he said, closing his eyes.

"He's cracked at last," Kruger declared.

Dietz shook his head violently. "Be still," he whispered. "Don't you hear them?"

Kruger gave him a suspicious look. "Hear what? The angels?"

"Don't be silly, you can't help hearing them. The bells." He turned to the other men. "Do you hear them? . . . There! Now—it's perfectly clear."

They all stared at him. "What do you hear?" Kern asked.

"Bells," Schnurrbart said. "The Child hears bells, bells in the middle of the wilderness."

"Be quiet a minute, will you?" Kruger straightened up and cupped his hands behind his ears. After a while he shrugged. "I don't hear a thing. He's just trying to scare us."

"I don't hear anything either," Kern said.

They were all irked and glowered at Dietz. "You're just hearing things," Zoll growled.

Dietz lifted his shoulders helplessly. "I swear I heard them," he said uncertainly. "I couldn't be that mistaken."

"It's easy to fool yourself," Kruger said, feeling sorry for the little fellow. Dorn was standing behind him. "Isn't that true, Professor?"

Dorn took his time answering. He adjusted his glasses and regarded Dietz, who was looking anxiously up at him. His face was serious as he said, "Hallucinations."

"What is *that*?" Kruger asked aghast.

"When your senses deceive you," Dorn said briefly.

Kruger shook his head. "Never heard of it. Strange business."

Dietz addressed Steiner. "Didn't you hear them?"

Steiner, eyes half closed, took a drag on his cigarette. "The bells?" he asked. "Sure."

"There!" Dietz fairly puffed with relief, while the others stared indignantly at Steiner.

"Typical," Kruger whispered to Schnurrbart.

Schnurrbart did not answer. He had noticed long ago that Steiner had a weakness for little Dietz, who always seemed a bit lost among the others. Not that Steiner showed favoritism toward him in matters like standing guard or carrying gear. His feelings came out in the almost paternal tone he sometimes adopted toward the Sudeten German. It had happened before that he took the side of Dietz in quarrels among the men; Schnurrbart recalled incidents he had observed with just the smallest touch of jealousy. Once more Steiner's incomprehensible attitude angered him more than he would admit to himself. Naturally there had been no bells. Bells in the middle of a forest in Russia! It was ridiculous. Crossly he drew on his pipe, wondering whether to bring up the subject again.

But Dietz spoke first. He felt a little guilty. Maybe he had been hearing things. If Steiner hadn't backed him up about the bells, he would have been willing to grant that it was a mistake. Perhaps Steiner had been mistaken too. "Did you really hear them?" he asked shyly.

Steiner frowned. "Of course. I said so clearly enough, didn't I?"

"Yes, sure," Dietz murmured, intimidated. Kruger was staring tight-lipped into space. The others, too, all seemed ill-humored; a wall of hostile faces seemed to surround him with silent menace. He felt that he must placate them but could not decide how to do it, especially since he did not want to offend Steiner. Finally a diplomatic solution occurred to him. He smiled at Kruger timidly. "Still and all, it's odd!"

"There's nothing odd about it," Steiner said sharply. "What's odd about bells ringing on Sunday morning?"

They stared at him in surprise. Abruptly Kruger slapped his powerful thigh. "Why, sure!" he exclaimed. "Today's Sunday. I never even thought of it."

"There you have it," Schnurrbart said with relief. "Why shouldn't bells be ringing on Sunday?"

Their mood changed instantly. They nodded at one another significantly. "Sunday!" Maag sighed. "Back home, at this hour, I'd still be sound asleep."

"And then getting up for coffee and cake," Pasternack said nostalgically.

Kruger cursed. "Cut it out," he protested. "What's the use of water in my mouth when there's more room for it in my bladder?"

"Pretty good." Schnurrbart chuckled. He had removed his steel helmet and was busy scratching his shaggy hair.

Pasternack was still lost in pleasant recollections. He twisted his thin, hungry face into a grimace and said, "I think a man has a right to talk about cake." He sounded rebellious.

"You can talk about shit too," Kruger declared irritably.

Pasternack shook his head. "Do you have to be so foul-mouthed all the time?"

"Foulmouthed?" Kruger stared at him in astonishment.

"Yes, foulmouthed," Pasternack repeated emphatically. Then his usual melancholy expression returned to his tired face. A strand of blond hair dangled over his pimpled forehead.

"Look who's putting on an air all of a sudden." Kruger sneered.

Dietz intervened. "Cut out the bickering for once—it's Sunday."

"You can stick your Sunday . . ." Kruger said vehemently. "What the hell does the army care about Sundays? Here!" He ran his hand over his unshaven face. "Is that what you call Sunday?" In sudden fury he tore open the top buttons of his tunic and pulled out a patch of filthy shirt. "We look like pigs!" he snapped. "This is the way they let us go around, the damned bastards."

Schnurrbart grinned. He had always liked the East Prussian's crude candor. And he's right, he thought; no clean clothes for a month. The thought aroused an itchy feeling in his skin that traveled up his back all the way to his head. The damned lice. For a moment he tried to imagine what it would feel like to be standing under a hot shower and scrubbing his back with a stiff-bristled brush. The image nearly drove him out of his mind. He sighed and with his thumb scratched his neck where the itching was worst. Kruger had meanwhile shoved his shirt back under his tunic. Steiner had watched with a stony face, while listening with half an ear to a conversation between Dorn and two of the others.

"We have about sixteen miles to go," Steiner said now. "According to the map, the woods are all marsh. Besides which, there must be a stream somewhere in the middle of it. I hope you realize what we're facing. Anyone who gives out is going to be left behind." He started down the mountain. They looked after him for a moment in consternation, then shouldered their gear and followed. They kept to the middle of the power-line clearing and took care not to slip on the smooth grass. Dorn came last. His diarrhea had improved somewhat since last night, and he was glad about that. He was still thinking about Dietz's strange hallucination. After all, bells must be ringing somewhere at this hour. But a thousand miles away at least. Perhaps the bells they heard came all the way from the ruins of Germany, carried on waves of longing to wherever the armies were fighting a desperate struggle. A lost struggle. And the worst part of it was that one knew it.

They had reached the plain meanwhile. The lane came to an end here, and when they went forward among the trees, the sky vanished as the foliage closed in overhead. A cool breeze from the dim depths of the woods blew over their hot, flushed faces and made them shiver. One after the other they vanished into the green dusk.

II

THE regiment's new positions ran west of Krimskaya through hilly terrain bare of vegetation. The dominant feature of this sector was Hill 121.4, which was crowned by a wooden tower. The First Battalion was holding the positions on the southern slope of it. From here there was a good view deep into the enemy hinterland, and the artillery observers could see as far as Krimskaya, which the last companies of the division had evacuated only a few hours ago. There was great activity everywhere. Bunkers were being dug out, machine-gun emplacements sunk deep into the ground, wood for construction brought. The staff officers were well aware of the importance of the next few hours. The terrain was so open that the enemy would not be able to advance until after dark. But then the Russians would come, and from tomorrow morning on their snipers would be at work. The men did not need the admonitions of the company commanders to realize the urgency of digging in. Although they had done without sleep the night before, they set to work with a will and kept going with hardly a pause.

The battalion commander was standing in one of the Second Company's advanced dugouts. He had been scanning a patch of woods some two hundred yards away through a stereotelescope. This he considered the weak spot of his sector. Along its northern edge ran the Krimskaya-Anapa highway, which was sure to be the target of the enemy's next attack. Those woods, about a square mile in area, offered an ideal deployment area for the preparation of an enemy offensive.

The longer the commander studied the terrain, the grimmer his expression became. Finally he straightened up angrily. The commander of the Second Company was standing directly behind him. "Incredible—an irreparable oversight," he snapped. "Those woods should have been cut down or destroyed by fire."

Lieutenant Meyer's good-natured, somewhat flushed face took on the hint of a grimace. "We came sooner than expected."

"Sooner, what does sooner mean here?" the commander replied irritably. "By God, they had ample time to establish the lines for the bridgehead. I should like to know what dilettante is responsible for this." He stooped over the telescope again.

Meyer regarded him coolly. Captain Stransky, commander of the First Battalion since last week, was an interesting specimen. That longish face with high forehead and light-blue eyes gave an impression of extreme forcefulness, an impression underlined by the thin-lipped mouth and the angular chin. The man's thick hair was white at the temples, emphasizing by contrast the healthy tan of his face. His uniform was the work of a first-class tailor and effectively showed off his broad shoulders and narrow waist. He was certainly a superior specimen of officer, but in spite of that Meyer could not stand him. He watched with disgust as Stransky moved the knobs on the telescope with long, thin fingers. On his left hand he wore a heavy seal ring with the family crest, no doubt. Meyer recalled that the regimental adjutant had told him Stransky owned big estates in East Prussia. It had not impressed him. They were all the same here, he had told himself: a handful of life trying to preserve itself like the candlelight in the bunkers; a bundle of duties in uniform, feeling and thinking like human beings but trained to act like automatons.

Stransky straightened up again. "I shall send a report to that effect to Regiment," he said. "Unfortunately, it is too late to do anything about it."

Meyer agreed. "Perhaps the Russians are already in those woods," he said. "I shouldn't want to ask anyone to try to cross them in broad daylight." He glanced uncomfortably across the flat terrain, which was wholly without cover. Its rust-brown color was scarcely distinguishable from the dark strip of asphalt highway.

"I doubt that," Stransky replied. "It was already daylight when we got here. The Russians couldn't possibly have followed at our heels."

"So we thought last night," Meyer said gloomily, "and still we were unable to hold the planned positions."

"That is something else again," Stransky said with annoyance, although he was aware that the company commander was right.

According to the original plans, the battalion was still supposed to be holding the positions east of Krimskaya. Toward midnight, after an easy ride on the trucks, they had reached the reception line. But an hour later the order had come from Division to move into the final positions.

Stransky suddenly recalled the Second Company platoon which had been left behind for a rear guard. Thoughtfully he reached for his cigarette case. "I suppose we will have to write off your second platoon," he said.

"I think not, sir. I gave the platoon leader appropriate instructions in case we might have to withdraw sooner than anticipated. And then Steiner is in command of the platoon."

"Who is Steiner?" Stransky asked with a frown.

Meyer stared at him in astonishment for a moment, then he remembered. "I forgot you were new to the battalion, sir. Corporal Steiner is a soldier, let me tell you. A few weeks after I joined the battalion at Tuapse, the Russians rolled up the battalion on our left and suddenly appeared in front of my combat H.Q. If it hadn't been for Steiner turning up with his platoon at the last minute, we would all have been done for. He's a reconnaissance specialist, incidentally. One of your predecessors, our present regimental commander, thinks the world of him."

"So," Stransky said without interest.

"Yes," Meyer said. "He was still company commander when the regiment was stationed in Pribram. They got into a bad spot—that was at the beginning of the Russian campaign—and Steiner saved his life."

Stransky took a drag on his cigarette and glanced across at the woods again. These stories about a corporal somehow irked him. The man sounded like a typical Wild West hero, he thought, one of these young fellows who were quick on the trigger and had a run of luck. He knew the type—primitive and arrogant. "Sounds like a universal genius," he said with sarcasm.

"I wouldn't know about that," Meyer said. "At any rate, he's a fine soldier."

"I tend to be cautious in my estimate of men," Stransky replied coolly. "There are human as well as soldierly traits that determine the value. It surprises me, incidentally, that this—ah, what did you say his name was?"

"You mean Steiner?"

"Yes. Well, as I was saying, it surprises me to hear that this man Steiner, in spite of his remarkable talents and services, is only a corporal."

Meyer had no answer. The argument was sound. To judge by all he had heard of Steiner, the man must have been in the army at least five years. There must be some story on that. He would find out some day.

Stransky's voice cut into his thoughts. The commander had folded his arms over his chest, and a mocking smile was playing about the corners of his mouth as he asked, "Well?"

Meyer glanced away from his face. Pompous ass, he thought. He said, "I have not yet had occasion to look into the matter. Steiner was hospitalized for some time, as I understand it, and returned to the company about six months ago, shortly after I joined the battalion."

"Has he been in command of the platoon since then?" Stransky asked.

"No. In that case I would have promoted him to sergeant long ago. Up to two weeks ago he was the group leader. I assigned the platoon to him after Sergeant Graf was wounded."

Stransky dropped his cigarette butt and stepped on it. "If your Steiner succeeds in bringing the platoon back here, I'll promote him to senior sergeant."

"Then he has his promotion," Meyer declared.

"You certainly are sure of yourself," Stransky jeered.

They looked at each other, their mutual dislike plainly written in their faces. Why am I letting him get under my skin? Meyer thought. He sits so high in his saddle he will never stoop low enough to see the grass his horse is eating. A corporal hardly exists for him and, as a matter of fact, neither does a lieutenant. The thought angered him, and his voice sounded sharper than he intended: "I know Steiner well enough to vouch for him."

Stransky raised his eyebrows. Anger did not come quickly; it rose slowly into his throat and thickened his voice. "I did not ask your opinion, Herr Meyer," he said tightly. "Moreover, I am accustomed to a somewhat different tone from my subordinates."

Meyer saw the white patches under the captain's cheekbones. For a moment he regretted his impudence. With a mixture of anxiety and curiosity he waited to see what would happen next. But Stransky seemed to have regained his self-control. The spots in his face began to color, and in a moment they had disappeared. Without a word he turned toward the trench, and Meyer followed him. When they came to a machine-gun emplacement, Stransky stopped. The trench had been widened out into a square room at this point and covered over with a few planks. The man behind the gun turned his head and looked uncertainly at them. Meyer gave him a friendly nod. "Anything new, Ott?"

The man snapped to attention. "Second MG, nothing to report," he said tensely.

Stransky studied him attentively. In addition to the Iron Cross, the man wore a silver infantry assault medal. "What is your civilian vocation?" he asked.

The man's face flushed. He opened his mouth and glanced helplessly at Meyer. "He lives in Birgsau in the Bavarian Alps," Meyer said. "Until he was drafted he was the community cattleherd."

"I see," Stransky said. He dropped his official tone. "I imagine that was a very monotonous occupation, wasn't it?"

Ott grinned in great embarrassment and swallowed several times. "No," he said at last. His eyes were fixed on Meyer, who gave him an encouraging wink.

"Then it was not so dull?" Stransky asked.

"No." Ott shook his head violently.

Stransky smiled fleetingly. "Take these men away from their mountains, and they behave like fish out of water," he said to Meyer. "Still and all—" he looked at the man's medals—"they can still bite, it would seem."

They went on. Stransky had resumed his reserve and answered the men's salutes with brief nods. They ran into Lieutenant Gausser, the commander of the First Company. His youthful face was pale and sleep-starved. Because of the heat he had taken off his tunic. His green shirt was sopping, and Stransky regarded him with disapproval. "What a way to go about, Herr Gausser," he said sternly.

The lieutenant shrugged indifferently. "I have been working on my bunker, sir," he said. "This is what they call a prepared position in these parts—they haven't even provided a company combat post." He turned to Meyer. "How are conditions over your way?"

"Not quite so bad as here. There was at least a bunker for the combat post."

"Happy man." Gausser sighed. "It really is a shame. They certainly had enough time to prepare a decent position. As things are now we would have a hard time repelling an attack."

Stransky studied his well-manicured fingernails. "Good positions, Herr Gausser," he said reprovingly, "do help in keeping losses at a minimum. But you must not overlook the fact that a successful repulse of enemy assaults depends primarily on the morale of the troops. And the attitude of the officers is of the utmost importance."

Gausser exchanged glances with Meyer. To the commander he said coolly, "Perhaps you will permit me to remark that the morale of troops presupposes some sort of physical substance which, in our experience, reacts with extreme sensitivity to superior enemy fire-power."

"What do you mean by that?" Stransky asked haughtily.

Once more Gausser exchanged glances with Meyer. The little lines of irony at the corners of his mouth vanished as he said, in dead earnest now, "If none of the fighting men survive the enemy barrage, all your morale will do is add a nice touch to the communiqué."

Stransky threw a look at Meyer. Seeing the open spite in Meyer's face, he stiffened and said icily, "The probability that at least one of the four machine guns in your company will survive even the most intensive barrage is far greater than you think. But perhaps you lack the experience to judge this matter." He paused. "You will have opportunity to prove your morale with this one remaining MG."

Gausser, who had meanwhile slipped into his tunic, replied calmly, "If my physical substance survives the barrage, my morale will meet your standards, too."

"You have effrontery, if nothing else," Stransky snapped.

Meyer hastily covered his mouth with his hand to conceal the irrepressible urge to laugh.

Gausser finished buttoning his tunic before he turned politely to the commander: "Effrontery can be a good point for a soldier. It keeps him from overestimating his enemy."

Neatly parried, Meyer thought.

Stransky's frown darkened and his voice sounded even colder. "Effrontery can also lead to an irresponsible under-estimation of the enemy. To call it a good point involves a degree of naïve optimism which ill suits a company commander."

The conversation had reached a critical point, and Gausser seemed to sense this. There was no point in forcing the issue. Equably he said, "That calls for some thinking. To be frank, I've been awake all night and I've kept going on the bunkers this morning. I'm too tired to concentrate."

Stransky eyed him for a moment. Then he turned to Meyer. "I do not need you any longer. Return to your company." He dismissed both officers with a nod and strode rapidly away.

The two men watched him until Meyer cleared his throat. "I must say I've taken quite a liking to you in the past few minutes," he said.

"That's a hell of a thing to tell a man," Gausser replied, unbuttoning his tunic again. "With my effrontery, I thought you'd liked me all along." He ran his thumb between his collar and back. "Damned heat." He sighed. "And here it is only ten o'clock."

"Take your coat off again," Meyer recommended.

"So I will. I don't see how my sweating can promote the morale of the troops."

Meyer's mind went back to his second platoon. Although he had vouched for its coming through, he had no illusion about the situation of Steiner and his men. He had spent over an hour studying the map early this morning, and the picture he had formed of the terrain was scarcely reassuring That damnable forest, he thought; I should have taken the platoon along with me. In all that confusion nobody would have noticed.

He turned abruptly to Gausser. "I must make a phone call. Will you come with me?"

"Glad to." As they made their way to Second Company's combat post, Meyer spoke of his fears for his platoon. "I'm going to call Kiesel," he said. "The Second and Third also left platoons behind. Perhaps Regiment has had some report from them."

The field telephone stood on a low table in the center of the bunker. Gausser sat down on a corner of the table and let his feet dangle while Meyer made his call. The conversation was brief. When Meyer hung up he was frowning blackly. "I can't believe it. The other battalions took their platoons right with them."

"What?" Gausser stared at him. "How could they have?"

"The order came from Division. As soon as Third Battalion left, the Russians pushed up with strong forces. Well, you know Major Vogel. He said to hell with Division's order and took his platoon along. Same thing happened in Second Battalion, or must have happened. Kiesel wouldn't commit himself over the telephone. Apparently he's worried about complications."

"The hell! What complications? That's two platoons saved from certain destruction. Does Division think two dozen men would have held up the Russians?"

Meyer smiled feebly. "Kiesel will find a way to make it right with the general—if he ever finds out about it."

"And what does Lieutenant Colonel Brandt have to say about it?" Gausser wanted to know.

"I don't know. I assume . . ." He stood up abruptly.

"What's the matter?" Gausser asked uneasily.

Meyer clapped his hand to his forehead. "Why didn't I think of that sooner?" he said slowly. It had occurred to him that the regimental commander could not know who was leading the platoon that had been left behind. He would be highly interested, Meyer thought. Quickly he picked up the telephone. Hand over the mouthpiece, he said to Gausser, "If Stransky knew I was telephoning Kiesel over his head, he'd have me shot at dawn."

"That has already occurred to me," Gausser said. "Aren't you afraid he'll find out?"

"Who'd tell him? Besides, I'm on excellent terms with Kiesel." At that moment the regimental adjutant's crisp voice answered. With a wink at Gausser, Meyer clamped the telephone under his chin. "Meyer again. I forgot to report something which I am sure will interest the lieutenant colonel. The platoon I had to leave behind is commanded by Corporal Steiner."

For a few seconds there was silence on the other end of the wire. Gausser brought his ear close to the telephone, holding his breath.

"Steiner?" the voice questioned.

"Yes, Steiner."

Again a brief pause. Then, "I shall inform Lieutenant Colonel Brandt."

As Meyer hung up, the two men looked at each other. "I take it Brandt thinks a good deal of Steiner," Gausser said.

"Rightly so," said Meyer. He drew on his cigarette and blew smoke at the ceiling.

"What kind of man is he?" Gausser asked.

Meyer frowned. "A problem," he said. "First-rate soldier, often impossible as a subordinate. He doesn't seem to know the meaning of respect. But, you know, in cases like this one looks the other way."

"Why hasn't he been promoted?"

Meyer scratched his chin uncomfortably. It's like a conspiracy, he thought. He wished he had some plausible explanation to give Gausser, even though he knew the lieutenant was asking only out of idle curiosity.

Stransky had reached Battalion Combat H.Q. The bunkers were set in the midst of a small orchard where gnarled trees offered excellent cover against air reconnaissance. At the door of his dugout Stransky paused and studied the terrain carefully. The chain of hills running from west to east dipped into a tapering, trough-shaped hollow here. At its lowest point, some distance from the orchard, the hollow merged into a steep gorge. Sunlight blazed upon the naked soil, which stood out reddish-brown against the cloudless sky. A mousetrap, Stransky thought, and tried to calculate the possibilities for escape if the Russians should suddenly penetrate into the trough. We would have to retreat through the gorge, he told himself. According to the map, the gorge ran due west for about a mile to the village of Kanskoye, where the battalion's transport was parked.

The noise of someone clearing his throat behind him startled Stransky. He turned. A soldier stood some yards away. Stransky nodded amicably. "Well, Dudek, what is it?"

The man came to attention. "Your bunker is ready, sir."

"Good. Where is everybody? The place looks deserted."

Dudek glanced over toward the trees, beneath which half a dozen other bunkers were concealed. "The signalmen are all out laying lines, I think, and the couriers also. They are finding out the location of their companies."

"And Lieutenant Triebig?"

"He must be in his bunker."

"Tell him that a sentry is to be posted here at once."

"Yes, sir, sentry posted." Dudek clicked his heels again. Stransky went into his bunker. Inside, everything was extremely neat and clean. Along the wall stood a narrow army cot already made up with blankets. Stransky glanced into the mirror and nervously rearranged some of the toilet articles on a shelf. Then he took off his belt, laid his cap beside the telephone and dropped down on the bed. He found himself unable to stop thinking about his conversations with the two company commanders. The blood rushed to his face at the recollection. He closed his eyes, brooding angrily over Gausser's impudence. Steiner—a man he would have to know more about. What had Meyer said—that Brandt thought the world of him? Probably that had gone to the corporal's head.

The shrill ringing of the telephone startled him. He reached for the receiver. Nervously he recognized the regimental commander's incisive voice: "I hear you left a platoon behind?"

"Of course. I received a clear order to do so."

"The other battalion commanders also received this order. Are you aware of that?"

"So Captain Kiesel informed me," he said.

"Indeed." There was another pause. Stransky pressed the receiver to his ear and heard the rushing of his own blood, excessively loud. Then the commander's voice spoke again: "Are you also aware that the other commanders took it upon themselves to disregard the order?"

"No," Stransky murmured. "I cannot understand such conduct, sir. I, at any rate, have strictly obeyed the orders I received."

"So you have, so you have, Captain Stransky. I suppose you have not yet had enough front-line experience to use your own initiative whenever the situation demands some adjustments. Unfortunately, there was no time to send revised instructions. Vogel and Körner used their judgment in taking their platoons back with them. I have commended the good sense of these officers in my report to Division."

Stransky bit his lip. All this is only because of Steiner, the man who saved his life once, he thought bitterly. He must know that Steiner is in command of the platoon. I wonder who . . .

"Are you still there, Captain Stransky?"

"Certainly, sir. You must understand that I—I mean, that this situation is most unpleasant for me. If I had only guessed! But we had not the slightest difficulty in evacuating our positions. I therefore saw no reason for taking the platoon along. I——"

"Very well, Captain Stransky," the commander cut him off. "You certainly cannot be blamed for obeying an order. It is simply unfortunate. . . . How strong is the platoon?"

"I am sorry, I have not yet inquired," Stransky replied uncomfortably. "Ten or fifteen men, I believe. I can check immediately with Lieutenant Meyer."

"You might have done so earlier. I want to be kept informed on how this matter turns out."

The hum in the receiver faded. Stransky slowly replaced the telephone on the hook. He stood up, cursing softly. From the little window beside the door he stared wrathfully out upon the sunlit landscape. Why in the world did he have to suffer all this? After all, he himself had asked to be transferred here from France. He must have been mad, stark raving mad. He turned back to the table, took a map out of the briefcase hanging over the chair and spread it out. His eyes traveled over the vast area of forest stretching eastward from Krimskaya to the positions the battalion had occupied yesterday. The green surface was crossed in many places by fine blue lines. Undoubtedly a marsh. The observation cheered him somewhat. The commander's protégé would have a tough time getting through there. First the woods, then the city and finally the Russian front lines. Slowly he straightened up. The trouble men could make for you without your even knowing them! Meditatively he folded up the map. First of all, he had to establish himself solidly; the next task was to teach his subordinates their place. Once he had achieved a strong position in the battalion, not even Brandt would be able to undercut him. In France he had succeeded in doing that within the first week. Here conditions were somewhat more complicated. But he would manage. Although there were certain limits to the jurisdiction of a battalion commander, his opportunities for operating in depth were greater than those of a general. The smaller the pebble in the shoe, the more it could hurt. The comparison amused him.

There was a knock on the door. Stransky turned his head impatiently. 'What is it?"

The door opened, and Stransky recognized his adjutant. "I just heard that you were back, sir. Am I intruding?"

"What do you want?" Stransky asked in an unfriendly tone.

Lieutenant Triebig smiled gently. "Major Vogel telephoned about twenty minutes ago. He asks that you drop in on him some evening soon."

"Thank you. Anything else?"

"No, sir. Do you have any orders?"

Stransky regarded the lieutenant with distaste. What kind of bird was this? His voice was a little too smooth, he had slanting, dark eyes, and his wavy hair was combed back far too carefully for Stransky's taste.

"Yes, something has just occurred to me," he said in the same unfriendly tone. "Inform the company commanders that they are to report tomorrow morning for a conference. Here, at nine o'clock."

"Yes, sir. Any other orders, sir?"

"No, you may go."

Triebig saluted. When the door closed behind him, Stransky dropped back on his cot. Major Vogel. Why the sudden burst of friendship? he wondered. Last week, when they had met for the first time at regimental H.Q., the elderly major had treated him with condescension. But he was commander of the Third Battalion, and one never knew when it would prove useful to be on good terms with one's neighbors. Nevertheless, Stransky felt no great urge to accept the invitation. Their conversation last week had been very brief, but Stransky had taken away an impression that the major was highly opinionated and tactlessly outspoken.

Stransky became aware of how heavy his eyelids felt. Last night's lack of sleep was catching up with him. He stretched out full length and turned on his side. Nothing but vexations, he thought.

After his interview with Stransky, Lieutenant Triebig returned to his bunker and put through a number of telephone calls to the company commanders. Then he sat down at the table and languidly leafed through some old picture magazines. The air in the bunker was stale, and the fierce outside heat could be felt even here in this underground hole. He came to a stop at a picture of a scantily-dressed girl lying on her stomach and kicking her feet into the air. Under the low-cut blouse her pointed breasts showed clearly. Triebig studied the picture for some time. Finally he tore the page out, crumpled it into a ball and tossed it into a corner. He glanced at his watch. It was after twelve. Time to eat, he thought. He went over to the tin basin and washed his hands. Then he reached out for the loaf of bread standing on the table and cut off a few thin slices. With meticulous care, he spread the tiny portion of butter over each of the slices. From his canteen he poured cold coffee into a tin cup. Nostalgically, he recalled the aromatic coffee that had been served hot by the field kitchens in France.

His meal completed, he remained sitting at the table. There

was a knock at the door. His orderly opened it and stood hesitantly at the threshold. "Is there anything you wish, sir?"

"Not at the moment," Triebig replied. Thoughtfully he regarded the shy face. Then he beckoned the man into the bunker. "You can keep me company for a while," he said. "I really hardly know you. Sit down somewhere."

The man looked uncertainly around the bunker. Triebig was sitting on the one and only chair. "Sit down on the bed," Triebig suggested. "Are you always so timid?"

The orderly risked a shaky smile as he obeyed. "No," he murmured under his breath. He perched on the extreme edge of the narrow army cot.

Triebig studied him with interest. Keppler had been sent to the battalion from a replacement unit only a few weeks ago. Triebig had taken him for an orderly because his own orderly had just been wounded. Keppler was also a courier for First Company. No older than nineteen, Triebig guessed. His soft, unformed features bore a helpless expression which was further accentuated by the way he kept his mouth slightly open.

"Where do you come from?" Triebig opened the conversation.

Keppler clasped his hands over his knees. "Frankfurt, sir."

"Is that so? I know Frankfurt quite well," Triebig commented. "I used to run over that way frequently in my car."

With satisfaction he noted the look of respect that came into Keppler's face. "You have a car of your own, sir?"

Triebig nodded casually. "Had one for years. Though it's been taken over by the army now, like everybody else's. But we must all do our share for victory." Raising his eyebrows, he put on a lofty expression. No need for the boy to know that the car had belonged to his firm. It was always wise to impress these fellows right at the start. Made everything easier. He puffed reflectively on his cigarette for a moment, then leaned forward. "Do you live with your parents?"

Keppler shook his head sadly. "No, they're dead. My father's been dead for ten years, and my mother died seven years ago."

"Oh!" Triebig pretended sympathy. In a kindly tone he said, "That must have been very hard for you. Where did you live?"

"In an orphanage, sir. Later I went to work for a baker. I learned the trade there and lived in the baker's house."

"Didn't you have any relatives?" Triebig asked. "I mean, anybody who could take you in?"

"No, sir. You see, we used to live in Munich. Then we moved to Frankfurt, and my parents died there."

"Well, well," Triebig said. I couldn't have made a better choice, he thought happily. He felt excitement spreading from his thighs throughout his body. He moistened his lips, while his eyes rested upon the boy's narrow waist. Keppler's face slowly reddened as if he guessed the lieutenant's thoughts.

"You've had a tough time," Triebig declared. He sat down on the bed beside Keppler. "But time heals all wounds. If you get along with me, you'll have a good life here. You may go now. Come back this evening and arrange my gear."

Keppler jumped enthusiastically to his feet. "Yes, sir! When shall I come, sir?"

Triebig considered. It was clear that he would have little trouble with the boy. A naïve young fellow, just the type to while away the boredom of long, dull spells with little to do.

"Don't come too early," he replied. "Around ten. We'll have a chance to talk."

Keppler's face flushed with pleasure. He clicked his heels sharply. "Yes, sir," he began briskly, "I . . ." Abruptly he paused and lowered his eyes.

"Well?" Triebig smiled. He stood up and chucked the boy under the chin. "What did you want to say?"

His jovial tone restored Keppler's confidence. He raised his head. "I want to make good on this job, sir."

"That's the spirit," Triebig said patronizingly. He lightly touched Keppler's cheek. "Do your best and I'm sure I shall be satisfied with you."

I hit it just right, he thought, as he watched the boy go out. He felt perspiration starting all over his body. "Damnable heat," he murmured, dropping onto the cot. For a while he stared blankly at the ceiling. What the hell, he told himself. Who knows whether we'll be alive tomorrow? You had to grab your chances. But all the same he would have to be careful. For a moment he tried to imagine what would happen if Stransky found out, or one of the other officers. You could not trust anybody. His thoughts drifted back to Keppler. Closing his eyes, he allowed his imagination free rein.

The bunkers of the regimental combat H.Q. were situated on the western slope of a chain of hills that ran from southeast to northwest, shielding the headquarters from the enemy. In the commander's bunker Lieutenant Colonel Brandt and Captain Kiesel sat at the table opposite each other. The commander's gaunt face was angry. "I have to attend to every damned triviality," Brandt complained violently. "Ought to have every corporal in the regiment reporting directly to me every day."

Kiesel shrugged equably. "That would be a good deal of trouble," he remarked. "Besides, you can hardly blame Stransky. He's a conscientious officer and was obeying orders strictly."

"Don't tell me that again," Brandt replied irritably. "To me the word conscientous stinks of pedantry. I need officers able to act on their own initiative when the situation demands. Look at Vogel—by God, I wish I had more like him."

Kiesel shook his head in mild disagreement. "Not everyone can be expected to take on the burden of independent decisions when there is a chance to shift responsibility to superiors. Anyhow, if I know Steiner, he will find some way out. I count on his turning up tonight."

"It's not only Steiner," Brandt said with sharp reproof. "It's a whole platoon."

Kiesel smiled fleetingly. "Of course, I was thinking of the platoon too. But without Steiner the others would never get through."

"Hm, do you think so?" Brandt regarded Kiesel with suspicion. Brandt was tall and thin, with sparse hair covering an elongated knobby head. Under a high forehead his eyes seemed to express a permanent bitterness. When he compressed his narrow lips, the tautening skin of his face deepened the hollows beneath his cheekbones.

He gave an impatient shake of his head. "I know what you are thinking. You can't put anything over on me, Kiesel, remember that. But you are right to think so. People can think what they like of me, and have done so. But nobody can say I don't know the meaning of gratitude."

"Certainly not," Kiesel quietly agreed. He had bccn adjutant of this regiment for eight months now and had served under three commanders. With neither of the others had he reached so good an understanding as he now had with Brandt. I must look this fellow Steiner over some day, he decided. So far he knew a great deal about him from reports, but had never met the man. A few months ago Brandt had spoken to him about a black mark on Steiner's record and had asked him to investigate. He had done so, but with inconclusive results. There was no question about the charge, but there was something not quite right about the evidence, and unexplained contradiction somewhere. Brandt had had the same impression. They had let the matter ride.

Kiesel stood up and began pacing back and forth in the bunker. For a while Brandt ignored it. Then he turned on him. "For heaven's sake, stop the marathon. You bother me more than the Russians. Tell me your private opinion of Stransky."

Kiesel stopped by a chair, pulled it between his legs and sat down backward on it. "My private opinion?" he drawled. "To tell the truth, I have not yet taken the trouble to form an opinion. Herr Stransky seems to think very well of himself. But that may be because he comes from a fine old family. Or maybe he is just too rich to be human."

Brandt dismissed these remarks with a gesture. "Quit beating around the bush. You're a good judge of people. What do you think of him?"

"I have so far met Stransky only once," Kiesel answered noncommitally. He lighted a cigarette, holding the burning match in his fingers until it went out. "The few words I've exchanged with him were instructive in one sense. On the other hand, they were hardly enough to justify an objective opinion. My personal impression is that Herr Stransky considers himself an unusual personality who is above criticism. If I understood him rightly, he believes he has a great mission to perform, namely to achieve a spiritual domination of the battalion."

"A what?" Brandt asked in utter incomprehension.

Kiesel smiled. "It does sound odd, but I have an inkling of what he wants. To put the matter more clearly: Herr Stransky wants his orders obeyed not because of his rank, but because of the sheer impression his personality makes upon the men."

"If that's so, his chances are pretty poor. I've had my own experiences with the obstinacy of the First Battalion." He considered the matter in silence for a few moments. Then he laughed harshly. "You've dreamed all this up, Kiesel. I've been wearing this uniform a long time, and I've never come across anything like that."

Kiesel nodded. "I grant it is unusual for a commander to want to rule his men's emotions as well as their actions."

"And how, may I ask, does Stransky intend to achieve this—ah—spiritual domination?"

"I didn't sound him out on this. But I gather he intends to use his company commanders as his tools since, in his own words, the influence of a commanding officer diminishes in intensity the lower you go in the ranks. He considers personal contact with the enlisted men a dangerous experiment."

"Beautiful!" Brandt was highly amused. "You know, Kiesel," he said, after a moment, "I'm somewhat impressed by this man Stransky, even if he is a visionary."

"Not all visionaries are as unpopular as Stransky."

"Do you think so?" Brandt suddenly wore a look of studied indifference.

For a second there was silence between them. Then Kiesel sighed. "Oh, well." He regarded the tip of his cigarette and resolved to say no more on this dangerous topic.

Brandt drummed his fingers nervously on the table. "At any rate, in the First Stransky will find few officers or men who will go along with his little game. Less than ever now. To tell the truth, the morale of the men is troubling me. No drive in them any longer, no ambition. They're like a set of chess pieces; they'll let themselves be moved around, but they won't move of their own accord."

"Chess pieces?" Kiesel frowned reflectively. "Haven't they always been that?"

"Not at all." Brandt shook his head vehemently. "I tell you, up to a year ago we had the best troops a commander could wish for. The men knew just what they were doing and why they were doing it. They were capable of winning a battle even when it was being run by an amateur up on top. But today! I never feel easy unless I'm right up there in the trenches myself. It's impossible to have any confidence in them."

"The feeling is mutual," Kiesel remarked.

"What's that?" Brandt gave him a look of astonishment that quickly became reproach. "What do you mean by that?"

"What I said," Kiesel replied easily. "The men no longer have any confidence."

"Confidence in whom?"

"In us, of course. We misunderstand their psychology if we think that they put the blame primarily on the top leadership. If I hop into a cab which gets in an accident because the brakes fail, I blame the driver, not the company he works for. I'll say that he should have refused to drive a cab with defective brakes."

"Just what are they blaming the leadership for?"

Kiesel crossed his legs. "The morale of troops wears out after a time. The division has been on active duty for twenty-one months without a break. The men are fed up. You know yourself how often they've been promised they'd be taken out of line."

"Is that our fault?"

"I'm no general," Kiesel replied evasively. "But the way things are now, the men see in every new commander an aspirant for the *Ritterkreuz* who wants to earn his medal with their blood. Once he gets that Cross pinned on his chest, a new commander comes along. Within these twenty-one months they have changed their commanders, from general to company leader, as often as a man changes his shirt in peacetime."

"Yes, yes, I know." Brandt's fingers drummed impatiently on the table. "We burn up replacements as fast as they arrive. On the other hand, the top brass know the situation better than we do and what they say goes."

"I don't agree. I think they make some big mistakes and that this is one of their biggest."

Brandt smiled. "You might earn a living as advocate of the enlisted man's interests. Unfortunately there doesn't happen to be any such post in the Tables of Organization." He slumped back in his chair. "I agree with you that our men absolutely must have a change of climate. I'm beginning to feel the same way myself. This damned country! The men have been lured into these steppes and endless forests. At first it was all new and exciting for our *landsers,* but the excitement didn't last long. These frightful spaces, monotonous, repetitious—you can't help feeling that one of these days they'll swallow you up. You end up with a complex about it. We're getting that now. But here we are and here we have to stay. The *landsers* must be made to realize how hard it is to relieve them. Where would we get the transportation? You know how much it takes to move a division from France to Russia and vice versa. Then again, you talk of twenty-one months of uninterrupted duty. Let's be honest, Kiesel—how many of the original personnel are left?" He laughed mirthlessly. "In my former battalion I could count the survivors on my fingers. The regiment today consists ninety per cent of replacements who have served no more than a few months in Russia. The general is right when he insists that relief of the division would not be justified for the sake of the few old hands. Don't you see that?"

"No."

"Why not, for God's sake?"

Kiesel crushed out the remainder of his cigarette. Brandt's words had impressed him, less by their logic than by their psychological penetration. He would not have expected such insight from the commander. It threw a new light on the man. He gazed at all the small window near the door. Tiny particles of dust danced in the band of sunlight that fell through the single pane.

"It isn't easy to explain," he began hesitantly. "You have

to put yourself in the *landser's* place. If it weren't for the presence of a superior officer, I might express myself even more clearly. But I don't intend to discuss politics."

"If you did, I would ask you not to. Go on."

"If you wish." Kiesel puffed misshapen smoke rings at the ceiling. "It is just the few men who were here from the start that I am concerned about. They have been steady as steel all along, and they are the ones who have been keeping the replacements in line. To them we owe . . ." He stopped abruptly as he caught the faint smile on the commander's face.

"Go on," Brandt urged. "What you say interests me enormously. I'd like to hear it to the end."

"It isn't worth saying."

The commander studied him coolly for a moment. "It is always worth saying when I am your audience, remember that. But I can guess what you were going to say. You take the same view of the replacements that I do. They're no longer any good; they're infected by a spirit of tired resignation. They have experienced nothing but retreats here at the front, and have every reason to believe the myth of Russian invincibility. I started at the bottom, remember, and anything you can say about the old hands interests me now just as much as it did then."

"All right, let's talk about the old hands. To them the recent setbacks have been nothing more than the shifting fortunes of war. During the years we were on the offensive they saw the retreating back of the enemy too often to be frightened by his face now. The replacements, on the other hand, think every Russian is an infallible fighting machine."

Brandt interrupted him. "Enough," he said wearily. "With the situation as it is, we can't blame them."

He passed his hand across his forehead as though to brush away an unpleasant picture. "Perhaps it is best not to talk about all this. It seems to me such conversation only make things harder for us." He sighed and stood up. "You can accompany me this afternoon. I intend to see for myself how the positions look."

"I'll be here," Kiesel said. As he went out, he saw Brandt sit down at the table again and rest his head on his hands. The issue of the war had already been decided, Kiesel thought. They both knew it; there was no sense pretending any longer.

Late that evening the men were still working on the positions. Meyer had left his bunker a few minutes before;

he was nervous and wanted to inspect the trenches and fox-holes. He noted that the work was progressing well, and turned back toward his headquarters. Lost in thought, he trudged slowly along the head-high trench. Steiner would certainly be coming in tonight. Once the Russians built up a solid main line of resistance, there would hardly be any chance for the platoon to get through. Even as it was, the platoon would have to detour around the city, and that would take time. Meyer looked at his watch. It was shortly before ten. He stopped walking and stood for a moment, indecisive. Then, since he felt not the slightest inclination to sleep, he swung himself up out of the trench and sat down a few yards up the slope. There was a stillness all about, broken only by the clank of shovels as the men dug deeper here and there. The star-studded sky arched high above the hills, casting soft light over the terrain. For a long while Meyer stared into the night. Longing thoughts of home filled his mind. He lay back, clasped his hands behind his neck and closed his eyes. If only it were over soon. Since November the hopelessness of it all had been obvious. At that time Tuapse had been almost within their grasp, the Turkish frontier only a few days' march away, and no one had doubted that the war would soon be won. And now? The collapse of the front at Stalingrad and the resultant danger of encirclement for the divisions fighting in the Caucasian forests had reversed the picture. It was true that their division and a few others had escaped envelopment by withdrawing from the Caucasus into the present bridge-head. But what had been gained? At their back was the sea, in front of them were the superior forces of a fanatical enemy who had seized and was holding the initiative. Here were a few undermanned German divisions clinging desperately to the Circassian hills and the Kuban swamps, exhausted from end-less fighting, without hope, with nothing but endurance. Meyer sighed. He craned his neck to see beyond the positions. The moon was rising, and it was growing lighter. The highway, a pale band, ran eastward along the edge of the forest, and Meyer suddenly became aware of how intensely he hated this country, with its murderous distances and its miserable roads.

A noise in the trench roused him. There was a murmur of voices near by. He sat up, listening, alert to danger. But it was only a sentry being relieved. He lay back again and watched with half-shut eyes as the head of a man appeared over the rim of the trench. As Meyer watched him, he felt his bitter-ness slowly dissolving. Perhaps I am seeing things too blackly, he told himself; perhaps we will still make it. The sentry in front of him stood motionless. He was probably watching that patch of woods where—possibly at this very moment—the advance scouts of a Russian assault division would be groping their way forward.

Somewhere beyond the hill a flare rose against the sky, flooding the terrain with light for a few seconds. The man in the trench turned his head to the right. Meyer got up and went to his bunker. He opened the door, lighted a candle and sat down at the table. Later he pillowed his head on his arms. He waited for the platoon to arrive until the first dawnlight trickled into the bunker.

"Gentlemen," Stransky began, his voice cool and business-like, "I believe there is no need of my going into the general tactical picture. The daily army communiqué should be keeping you up to date on that."

Meyer gave a slight cough and received a stern look from the commander. Merkel clasped his hands patiently over his knees. Gausser and Schwerdtfeger stared at the floor with ill-concealed expressions of boredom.

"The map, please," Stransky said. Triebig hurried to the table, took a map out of a portfolio and pinned it to the wall. Stransky went up to it. "Very well," he said and paused until Triebig had returned.

Then he continued. "A few words are, however, in order concerning our own particular situation. Parts of the army, withdrawing through Rostov, have been fitted into the new Main Line of Resistance in the north, which runs—" his finger pointed to a spot on the map—"east of Taganrog northward in the direction of Voronezh. The front seems to have become stabilized again. The Supreme Command regards the maintenance of the Kuban bridgehead as indispensable since, as you will recognize, its tactical importance for future offensives will be of the greatest importance." Stransky paused briefly.

Halluzinationen! Meyer thought bitterly. Where were they to get the matériel and the men for future offensives? The other officers were also looking skeptical.

Apparently Stransky sensed their doubts, for his voice grew louder. "A new offensive starting from the bridgehead and moving north will shake the entire Russian southern front. Striking as it would against the rear of the Russian army, it might well decide the outcome of the war."

"God help us all!" Merkel whispered. Schwerdtfeger nodded derisively; Gausser passed his hand over his face as if to wipe away a grin.

"It may be assumed," Stransky went on, "that the enemy is aware of this danger and will spare no efforts to eliminate

the threat to his rear. Our division's sector runs from here
northwestward as far as the inlets near Temryuk. As you
see, the bridgehead resembles a bow with the Black Sea
forming the bowstring. To the south, touching our right wing,
are two rifle divisions; to the north an infantry division. I am
afraid that a Russian attack would be directed primarily
against our sector since, as you see, the marshes to the north
form a natural obstacle. Moreover, do not overlook the importance of the highway which leads through our sector.
Given the limited extent of the bridgehead, every square yard
of ground yielded would represent a serious loss. Our present
line, the Siegfried Position, must be held in all circumstances."
Stransky turned away from the map. Emphatically he continued, "See to it that the positions are sound. Put maximum
pressure on your men to get the work done. Every shovelful
of dirt, every dugout and foxhole, offsets the danger of a
break-through. Do not forget that we have only water at our
backs."

He fell silent, letting his eyes rove over the faces of the
officers. They were serious and attentive now.

Meyer cleared his throat and asked, "Where is the ferry
landing?"

Stransky turned to the map again. "We have two landing
places. The first is near Tamanskaya, the second west of the
salt marsh. Up to the present six ferries have been employed.
They require about an hour for crossing the strait. So far,
mines and low-flying planes have sunk two of our ferries.
Moreover, it is to be expected that the Russians will be sending
in submarines to stop the ferries."

"Nice prospect!" Merkel exclaimed. "What are we going
to do about that?"

"The proper measures will be taken when the time comes,"
Stransky said stiffly.

Gausser, who had been listening with obvious uneasiness,
spoke up. "What reserves have been provided?"

Stransky went over to the map again. "An assault regiment
stationed west of Kanskoye is at the disposal of the division.
Furthermore, in order to assure swift and smooth communications, the construction of two asphalt roads is planned. Engi-
neering companies have already started work. Incidently, I
must not forget to mention that the construction of a large air-
field north of Novorossiysk was decided on today. Have you
any other questions?"

The officers crowded around the map. They began vehemently discussing the chances for the bridgehead.

Meyer turned to Stransky, who had stepped somewhat to

one side. "If the Russians should succeed in making a break-through beyond Taganrog and occupying the Perekop penin-sula . . ."

Meyer did not continue. The company commanders ex-changed significant looks, while Stransky frowned darkly.

He pointed to the map again. "As you can see, Herr Meyer, Taganrog is some two hundred miles east of Perekop. The de-velopment you suggest would take a good deal of time, which would enable the Supreme Command to make the necessary preparations."

"As at Stalingrad," Merkel put in.

Stransky whirled to face the speaker. "I believe, Lieutenant Merkel, that superior authorities are more competent than you to form a proper estimate of Stalingrad. A company commander's horizon is too limited for a view of the larger problems of the struggle. In any case, in the event of such a thing, the situation would be just the same for you whether you were in the Crimea or here in the Kuban bridgehead." He took a step away from the group. "I shall expect your reports by telephone on the progress of construction work at 1700 hours. That will be all." He made a gesture of dismissal.

The officers saluted stiffly and were shown to the door by Triebig. Outside the bunker they separated. Meyer, accom-panied by Gausser, slowly climbed up the slope. They did not speak until they reached headquarters. Then Gausser asked, "What do you think of all that?"

"No comment needed," Meyer said.

Gausser grinned. They stood for a moment on the top of the steps leading down into the bunker. The sun burned fiercely. "I don't like this quiet," Gausser said. He glanced toward the woods.

"Neither do I," Meyer agreed. "The Russians ought to have got here long ago. And the hill makes a beautiful target for them."

"It sure does."

Their eyes met. "Let's hope for the best," Meyer said.

Gausser nodded. "We can use a little hope." He hesitated. Then he held out his hand to Meyer. "I'll be off. So long." A few steps away he called back, "Steiner will certainly be along soon."

Meyer smiled gratefully. When Gausser disappeared around the next bend in the trench, he sighed heavily. Where could the platoon be at this moment?

III

THE platoon had been toiling for more than four hours through the pathless woods. The thorny undergrowth ripped the men's uniforms and scratched their hands and faces. They moved through a sultry hothouse atmosphere which made them sweat from every pore, while the repulsive odor rising from the marshy ground sickened them. To make matters worse, a cloud of almost invisible stinging mites had descended on them. There was no defense against these. In places the ground was so mucky that they had to take big detours, losing precious time.

Kruger marched behind Schnurrbart. His face streamed sweat; his eyes burned as though pepper had been thrown into them. The submachine gun felt like a ton on his right shoulder. Following the example of the others, he had long ago thrown away his gas mask and steel helmet. When he stopped for a moment, as he did frequently, he could feel his legs quivering and threatening to collapse. His throat felt like a dry sponge which would not let the air pass through and which sucked every drop of fluid out of his body.

The other men were no better off. Dietz was suffering the worst. He kept his mouth wide open, and he reeled forward from one step to the next. The heavy boxes of ammunition hung from his arms like lead weights, dragging his feeble body down. Steiner had carried the boxes for him for a while. But Dietz was already so done in that this temporary relief did not help. He stared dully at the ground as he trudged on. His mind had almost ceased to function; he moved on in a stupor of exhaustion. Worst of all was the thirst. There was a steady roaring in his ears as though a clear mountain stream were pouring down over near-by rocks. But whenever he raised his inflamed eyes expectantly, he saw nothing but the endless tangle of underbrush and the labyrinth of trees.

He forced himself to go on for a while; then his knees suddenly gave way and moaning he fell forward. Dorn, who was close behind him, stopped in alarm. Then he tried to shout to make the others aware of what had happened. But his voice sounded like the hoarse cawing of a crow; he had to call several times before the men up front paused. When Steiner came running back, the men dropped where they were and did not stir again.

"What's the trouble?" Steiner asked.

Dorn shrugged helplessly. "He's collapsed."

Steiner cursed. He stooped and shook Dietz vigorously by the shoulders. "Get up," he said. "Let's have no nonsense. We *must* keep going."

Dietz did not stir. Steiner glanced quickly around at the men. They all lay gasping, and he realized that it would be some time before he could get them to their feet again. His face darkened. He took his canteen from his belt and poured some of the lukewarm water over Dietz's temples and forehead. With his other hand he unbuttoned Dietz's tunic. But it was some minutes before Dietz opened his eyes in bewilderment.

"Well now," Steiner said, pleased. "You mustn't give out on us, Baby. We still have a long way to go."

"I'm finished." Dietz struggled to sit up.

Steiner bit his lip. This was all they needed. They had not yet covered even half the distance, and already they were breaking down.

"You'll have to call a rest," Schnurrbart said.

"It's two o'clock," Steiner said tersely.

Schnurrbart shrugged. "I know, but what can't be done can't be done!"

Reluctantly Steiner had to concede: "All right." He noticed Zoll, who was lying on his stomach off to one side, his head pillowed in his arms. "Where are your ammunition boxes?" The other became attentive. When Zoll still did not stir, Steiner dug the toe of his boot into his side. "Didn't you hear me?"

"Leave me alone," Zoll grunted.

"He had them ten minutes ago," Kruger said. "The swine must have dumped them."

Steiner shifted his tommy gun to his left hand. "Then he'll go back for them." When Zoll still did not move, Steiner gripped him by his cartridge belt and pulled him to his feet.

Face twisted with fury, Zoll whirled, snatched up his rifle and raised the barrel threateningly. "Keep your dirty paws off me," he whispered hoarsely. "If you touch me again, I'm going to . . ."

Steiner looked into the man's rabid face with a sort of curiosity. "You're too much of a coward," he declared quietly. "Watch!" He dropped his tommy gun and gestured Schnurrbart and Kruger back. They watched worriedly as Steiner stepped so close to Zoll that the barrel of the rifle touched his stomach. "They'll hang you if you shoot," Steiner said. Quietly he reached out, grasped the rifle by the barrel and took it from Zoll's hands. It was done so matter-of-factly that no one was surprised.

A sigh arose from the men; their tense bodies sagged like a taut rope that has been slashed in two.

"The bastard," Kruger muttered. Zoll stood motionless, his face reflecting fear and rage and shame.

Steiner picked up his tommy gun. In the same matter-of-fact way he said, "We're going on in fifteen minutes. Get those boxes."

Zoll hesitated for just a second. Then he went off into the brush.

Kruger swore. "Next chance I have I'll let the bastard have it."

"I'll take care of him," Steiner said. He went over to Dietz. "How are you feeling?"

"Coming along," Dietz said valiantly, forcing a weary smile. Steiner gave him an encouraging nod.

The others had stretched out again, and Anselm asked, "How far do we still have to go?"

Steiner shrugged. "More than half the way."

"We won't make that today," Pasternack said.

Maag disagreed violently. "The hell we won't; listen, we've got to."

"Not through these lousy woods," Hollerbach said gravely.

Kruger cursed again. "I wish we knew where we are," he raged. "God damn this frigging forest; we should have tried the road. The devil take these pests!" He slapped at a gnat that had settled on his forehead. "They're driving me crazy."

"Crazier." Schnurrbart filled his pipe.

Kern, watching him, said, "Smoke it up. Maybe it'll drive the bugs away."

Steiner came over to them. "How you doing, Professor?" he asked Dorn.

His amiable tone made Dorn look up in astonishment. He smiled. "I'll manage if it doesn't get any worse."

Steiner stuck a cigarette between his lips. Thumb on the match head, he said, "It will sure as hell get worse."

He showed no signs of tiredness. Tough as nails, Dorn thought. He asked, "Why don't you sit down?"

"Because when the time for getting up comes around, you're more tired than you were," Steiner replied.

Schnurrbart nodded emphatically. "That's true."

"Then why have you sat down?" Dorn asked.

Schnurrbart puffed fiercely at his pipe and blew smoke into

the center of a huge swarm of insects. "I can answer that," he said grimly. "I sat down because I'm so tired now that I couldn't be any tireder."

Dorn smiled. "That coming from you!" He knew that Schnurrbart was if anything tougher than Steiner, and recalled the forty-mile marches they had put in daily on their way to the Caucasus. Evenings the men had often been so exhausted that they were unable to eat, although those rations were the first which had been distributed all day. Not so Schnurrbart and Steiner. As soon as they reached their quarters for the night, the two had scouted through all the houses and barns, requisitioning everything they could lay hands on. Long after the others were asleep, they would be sitting up in the kitchen, the smell of roasted chicken wafting through the peasant hut.

The memory reminded Dorn of how hungry he was now. He swallowed and pressed his hands against his stomach. If only I had a slice of bread, he thought. But like the others, he had finished off his last chunk of bread early that morning. A fragrant slice of fresh bread such as he used to have for breakfast every morning at home. He closed his eyes, a voluptuous shiver running down his spine as he pictured the bakery on his corner, the windows heaped with piled-up loaves. Maddening.

He looked up when Schnurrbart spoke to him. "We're going on, Professor." He forced his eyes to stay open. The other men were already on their feet. Zoll stood to one side, his face inflamed and sweaty, but a box of ammunition in either hand. As Dorn stood up, he felt how shaky he was. Schnurrbart asked, "Were you asleep, Professor?" Dorn shook his head.

"Ready?" Steiner called out.

Schnurrbart pulled his belt higher and grinned. "Ready and willing."

"You take the rear," Steiner said to him. "See that nobody drops any more ballast. Let's go!"

They followed him wordlessly. The ground where they had rested had been firm, but it soon turned to swamp again. Water welled up under their footsteps and seeped into their boots. Fortunately the underbrush was less dense and thinned out even more as they went on.

Maag shook his head. "I think we're heading straight into a lake."

"So do I," Anselm said. "What's that up ahead there? A swamp or something?"

Maag stretched his neck forward. "It is," he said, distressed. "What's the sense of going on?"

They were already sinking in up to their ankles when Steiner came to a stop. About thirty yards ahead of them an enormous expanse of reeds cut a swath across the woods. Brown water shimmered among the thick stems. Beyond the reeds the woods were thinner; they could catch glimpses of blue sky.

One by one the men reached Steiner, who was staring at the reeds with a set expression.

"We can't cross that," Kruger said.

Schnurrbart nodded. "Not a chance. What do we do now?"

Steiner unstrapped his pack, dropped it on the ground and looked about. Finally he went to a tree with low-hanging branches. He swung up to the first crotch and climbed from limb to limb until he was lost among the leaves.

The men looked expectantly at him as he came down again. "How does it look?"

Steiner dropped from the last branch of the tree. In a few words he described what he had seen: a hundred-foot stretch of reeds, open water, more reeds and forest beyond. "It's three hundred feet across at least. Worse than I thought it would be."

"There must be some way to get over," Kruger said.

For reply Steiner dug in his pocket, took out the map and spread it out on the ground. The men looked over his shoulders. He showed them the delicate blue line cutting across the woods.

"*Scheisse,*" Maag said. "Are you sure this is the creek?"

"No doubt about it."

Dietz swallowed hard. "Couldn't it be a lake?"

"No, it's the creek."

"Then we're sold," Kruger declared.

Steiner folded up the map, reached out for his tommy gun, and started back in the direction from which they had come. They followed him about three hundred yards back into the woods, until they reached a comparatively dry spot. Here Steiner stopped. The men dropped to the ground and lay brooding dully.

Schnurrbart went up to Steiner. "Are we staying the night here?"

Steiner nodded. He looked like a man who had made a wearisome climb up a mountain only to recognize just below the peak that the last hundred feet were unscalable. He leaned against a tree and closed his eyes. Schnurrbart sensed his discouragement. He felt that it was up to him to restore Steiner's confidence. If the other men guessed how Steiner felt, they would lost heart completely. There was just one thing they could do. They would have to follow the creek toward the north until they reached the road, cross the bridge there, and then turn southwest again and go back through the woods toward Krimskaya. He tried to calculate the number of miles they would have to cover. Since they had been marching steadily southwest, it would be a good thirty straight north to the highway. Then across the bridge and another forty or so southwest again to Krimskaya. Seventy miles at least.

To walk seventy miles without rations through this swampy forest was a sheer impossibility. Steiner was right to be discouraged; they were doomed. Best make an end of it before they just collapsed somewhere and perished of hunger and exhaustion. He glanced at the tommy gun which he had placed between his legs. A hell of a death. And Erika? What would she do without him? He suddenly recalled the last time they had been together. That was more than a year ago now. This filthy war. Furloughs came rarely enough anyhow, and when his turn did come, there was sure to be a general ban on furloughs. Twelve months, he thought; my God, twelve months!

He heard Steiner clearing his throat. Their eyes met. "That damned creek," Schnurrbart said.

Steiner nodded. "The map doesn't do it justice, does it? Listen, you," he said to the others. "We're going to spend the night here. Tomorrow morning we'll start before dawn."

"Straight into the creek?" Kruger asked querulously.

"Shut up!" Steiner snapped. "We'll march to the road."

"How far is that?" Maag asked.

"About thirty miles."

"Thirty miles!" Kruger laughed crazily. "Before I march thirty miles I need something to eat."

"You mean to march those thirty miles tomorrow?" Anselm inquired.

Steiner shrugged impatiently. "If we don't make it tomorrow, we'll make it the day after."

Dorn wagged his head soberly. "Even fifteen miles a day is too much without food."

Their carpings infuriated Steiner. Harshness returned to his voice. "When you're marching for your life, fifteen miles on an empty stomach is a picnic hike. I'll tell you something." He glared down the row of dispirited faces. "We'll reach the road by day after tomorrow at the latest. If you've got to have something to eat, try tree bark. Boiled soft in water, it's supposed to be edible. You've got your mess kits, you've got wood, you've got water and matches—damn it all, don't take on about this like a bunch of children."

They looked shamefaced, but Kruger growled, "If we can

drink the muck. Didn't you see what it looks like? Like a hundred cows have been shitting in it."

"Then boil it and skim it. You won't mind the filth—you've got a pig's stomach, anyway."

The men grinned; gradually they became infected by Steiner's confidence.

Schnurrbart stared at him, wondering at the sudden change of mood. But now that Steiner was himself again, they'd make it, damn it all. He grinned cheerfully. "Sure," he said, "we'll eat tree bark like the ancient Teutons."

"The ancient Teutons ate bear steak by the ton," Anselm said, rubbing his belly.

"Sure," Kern added, "and drank mead by the barrel."

"If you still had your iron rations, it wouldn't be half bad," Steiner said. "Any of you have them left?"

There was a shamefaced silence. Steiner reached into his pack and took out a small bag. "We'll make a soup," he said. "Put the meat and the bread right in it. Two men fetch water. If you can't get to the creek, dig a hole in the ground. But don't anybody try drinking the muck before it's boiled. The rest can gather wood."

For a few minutes the men bustled about. It was already growing dark beneath the trees. Steiner appointed sentries, and the fire was lighted only after these had reached their assigned places. The wood was wet and smoked heavily, but it drove away the swarms of insects. Kern and Anselm had gone to the creek for water, each carrying half a dozen mess kits. They went as far as the soft ground permitted, then dug a square hole which immediately filled with water. The water was black and stinking. Kern made a face. "Ugh, when I think of what I could be drinking back home," he said. He stared mournfully into the gathering gloom among the trees.

Anselm suddenly felt that Kern was not such a bad person after all; all the quarrels they had had now seemed foolish and needless. He watched Kern filling the mess kits and felt a great gladness that he was not alone in the woods here. All along the edge of the creek innumerable frogs had begun a concert which was rapidly rising to an unbearable fortissimo.

Kern raised his head. "Listen to that!" he said grimly. He finished filling the mess kits and straightened up groaning. "Shall we go?" he asked.

Anselm nodded. Holding the vessels carefully in order not to spill the water, they started back.

In the last few minutes night had descended fully. A feeble glimmer of light directed them toward the camp. The men

were sitting around the fire. A flat hole had been dug, and
the burning branches rested on the bottom. Kern and Anselm
dropped down with the others. Steiner sat with his back against
a tree. Beside him lay Schnurrbart, Kruger and Maag. Dietz
was chatting with Hollerbach. Dorn, off to one side, had his
arms clasped over his knees and was staring vacantly into the
fire. Zoll and Pasternack were doing sentry duty. The confidence Steiner had injected into them all a few moments ago
had already ebbed away. The uncertainty over what faced
them was as depressing as the tiredness in their bodies.

"You know what I wish I had?" Kern remarked to Anselm.
"I wish I had a barrel of vodka." He squirmed restlessly. "Boy,
how I would drink!"

"No more than you can hold," Steiner said; he was listening
with closed eyes.

Kern was wary of getting involved in a conversation with
Steiner. But he felt misunderstood, and so he said more than
he wanted to. "You don't know how much I can hold. After
ten bottles I puke it up; then I'm ready for the next ten and
the next."

The others pricked up their ears. The boasting irritated
them. Kruger said, "This guy has a big head before he
touches a drop. I'd like to see him after one bottle. I'll bet
he's done most of his drinking from a bottle with a rubber
nipple."

The others laughed. Kern spat on the ground. "Don't you
wish you had half what I've drunk in my life? Why, I can
handle vodka even better than I can women, and that's saying
a lot."

"Really?" Kruger leaned forward. "And how many women
can you handle at one time, may I ask?"

"Don't you wish you knew!" Kern grinned significantly.
Now that the conversation had taken its usual turn, several
of the men yawned.

Maag, however, spurred him on. "Come on, let's have it."

Kern pretended reticence. The presence of Dorn inhibited
him.

"Why, you can see by his nose that he's still a little virgin,"
Schnurrbart drawled. "He just talks it up. The man's so bad
off he lives from hand to prick."

"The hell I do," Kern snapped, enraged. "With all the tail
I've been having, where'd I find time for that?"

Maag looked enviously at him, recalling his one and only
experience. He'd had a few drinks for courage, then gone to
a whorehouse. He'd paid his money and the blond girl had
taken him to a small red-carpeted room. But something

funny had happened to him there; when she pulled him down on her, all his excitement had evaporated and nothing she could do helped. He had lain with his head on her breast, tears streaming down his face. Finally she had sent him home, keeping the money. Ever since, he had been scared stiff it would happen again; he kept worrying the memory. If the same thing ever happend to him with Monika, she'd quickly find somebody else. Maybe she had already done so. The idea made him sweat. He tried to distract himself, and looked at Kern, who was just relating his latest adventure with a twenty-five-year-old war widow. The men listened with mingled fascination and skepticism. Dorn had turned away indifferently. After a while he stood up, walked away a few steps and sat down by a tree. Schnurrbart had begun distributing the soup among the mess kits, measuring conscientiously and handing each man his portion as it was doled out. He looked around and asked, "Where is Steiner?"

Kruger shrugged. "I dunno. The Professor isn't here either."

Maag jerked a thumb over his shoulder in the direction of the trees. "They must be somewhere back there." Hollerbach stood up and walked in the direction Maag had indicated.

"We're not good enough for them," Kern growled sulkily. He had placed the mess kit on his knee. He sniffed several times at the dark concoction and began carefully spooning it out. The soup was hot. He burned his mouth and cursed. "Tastes like prussic acid," he observed.

Kruger grinned. "Spill the muck off the top first," he said.

"What muck?" Kern asked, examining the mess kit suspiciously.

Kruger shook his head. "Can't he tell muck when he sees it? I wonder what kind of stuff he serves his guests back home."

His professional pride impugned, Kern threw his head back and snarled, "Shut your trap."

For a second Kruger looked at him in surprise. Then his face hardened. "You want to make something of this?" he said calmly.

Kern stared into cold, icy eyes and suddenly felt frightened. He mumbled something indistinct and looked down at his mess kit again. This time he discovered the layer of filth floating on the surface. Disgusted, he dumped half the soup on the ground. "Looks like snot," he mumbled.

"You should have skimmed it," Maag advised. He was eating rapidly.

But Kern had lost his appetite. Disgruntled, he placed the mess tin on the ground.

Hollerbach returned to the fire. "What's up?" Kern asked him uneasily. The others lowered their mess tins.

Hollerbach shrugged. "I don't know. Steiner's gone off somewhere. Pasternack says Steiner walked off by himself without saying a word."

"Where to?" Kruger asked, perplexed.

Hollerbach sat down. "God only knows."

There was a monent's silence. The wet wood crackled in the fire and sent a rain of sparks spurting from the hole. "Where's the Professor?" asked Schnurrbart.

"He's asleep. Though he doesn't seem to be really asleep, Pasternack says."

"Sick?" Schnurrbart asked with concern.

There was a pause. Schnurrbart scratched his neck, wondering. Probably another of Steiner's crazy notions, he thought. Poking around now in the darkness, as usual.

"What'll we do?" Kern asked. He looked around helplessly at the men's gloomy faces. The thought that Steiner might not return terrified him. His glance fell upon Anselm's pale face; Anselm was staring over the fire at the trees beyond. They're all scared, Kern thought. When Steiner isn't here they're all scared. The realization intensified his own fear. "Should we go looking for him?" he asked Schnurrbart.

Schnurrbart tossed a branch into the fire, sending up a shower of sparks. "Where would you look for him?" he answered roughly. "He'll be back. Anyway, you can relieve Pasternack," he ordered Kern. "And you—" he turned to Anselm—"can relieve Zoll."

"Why me?" Anselm asked rebelliously. Kruger suddenly leaned over, picked up a dry stick of wood and tossed it across the fire. Anselm avoided it only by throwing himself backward. The stick clattered against a tree, and Anselm jumped to his feet with a cry of rage.

Kruger rose slowly. Something in his expression warned Anselm. His aggression died within him; Kruger was twice as strong as he. He contented himself with a glare of hatred and said to Kern, "Acting like big shots already." Kern stood up without a word.

The men watched them walk off side by side into the encompassing darkness. Dietz turned reproachfully to Kruger, who was sitting down with a grin of complacency on his face. "Why do you make trouble all the time?" he said gravely.

"Yes," Hollerbach chimed in. "Dietz is right—all this wrangling is disgusting. I should think we had other things to worry about."

"Oh, shut up." Kruger was on edge and ready to fight, even with Hollerbach.

Schnurrbart interfered. He put his hand on Kruger's shoulder. "Cut it out now. As soon as Steiner is gone for ten minutes we go to pieces. Let's get some sleep; there's a tough day ahead of us."

Kern and Anselm stood some twenty yards away from the camp. "You don't know how fed up I am with all this crap," Anselm muttered bitterly. "I'd like to walk right out on them. But you wait—I'll get that big mouth one of these days."

Kern laughed spitefully. "In the first place Kruger's too tough for you, and in the second place where would you go? To the Russians?"

"I'd like them a damn sight better than these damned hypocrites," Anselm replied.

Kern leaned against a tree and sighed. At regular intervals his stomach made protesting noises. I should have eaten that soup anyway, he thought. He was irked with himself now for not having overcome his disgust, and he began to feel sorry for himself. He took out his handkerchief and blew his nose loudly and lengthily. Anselm snapped at him, "Don't make such a racket—we're on guard, you know."

Clumsily Kern thrust the handkerchief back into his pocket. "On guard against what?" he grumbled. "Against the mosquitoes maybe?" His eyes probed the dark woods. "Who's suppose to relieve us, anyway?"

"I'll wake Kruger," Anselm offered maliciously.

Kern grinned. "Won't he be pleased? Is he going to make corporal soon? I mean, what you said about big shots?"

"Sure, he and Schnurrbart—their turn comes up at the next promotions. Listen, when they get to be noncoms we can pull in our tails. They're all alike. Rank goes right to their heads; that's the way it is from bottom to top. It stinks. The whole damned army stinks."

Anselm fell silent and shifted his carbine to the other shoulder. He felt very strongly about the whole matter, but found it hard to think of the right words to express his feelings. For a while he listened to the fading concert of the frogs. It was a sad music. You just aren't treated like a human being, he thought. That was it—"they" didn't think you were human. You were just cannon fodder for them to order around, and you couldn't do anything about it. Not a thing. His despondency deepened.

Meanwhile, Kern gazed moodily through the trees. A light

breeze had sprung up. It shook the branches, and Kern hunched his shoulders anxiously. He envied the other men who were lying by the fire, sleeping. When you were asleep you didn't know you were afraid, he thought. You could close your eyes and draw the blanket up over your head as he used to do at home during thunderstorms. His teeth suddenly chattered so loudly that Anselm exclaimed, "What's the matter with you?"

Kern hurriedly clasped his chin. "Nothing, nothing at all. I'm just cold from standing around." He wagged his head from side to side. "It's weird you know, when you start to think about it. Here we are in the middle of the woods, right in the middle of the Russian army."

His fear provoked a giggle from Anselm. With an immense feeling of superiority he recalled that Kern had come to the front only two weeks ago. "It's not so bad," he declared superciliously. "I've been through this kind of thing for ten months now—why, it'll be a year soon. We've been in spots ten times worse than this," he boasted. When Kern remained silent and depressed, Anselm slapped him on the back. "By day after tomorrow we'll be in the clear," he said reassuringly.

His confident tone did nothing to convince Kern. The innkeeper continued to peer fearfully into the unrelieved darkness. "One way or another we're sold out anyway, I tell you."

His plaintive tone increased Anselm's sense of superiority. "Now look here," he said patronizingly, "you and I haven't got along so well until now, but I tell you, if we want to we can be pretty good friends. We'll come out of this all right." His voice took on a confidential note. "Let me tell you: the friendships you make at the front last a lifetime. I'll come to see you some time after the war, with my girl, I mean. We can spend our vacation at your place." He grew enthusiastic at the idea. "We'll take a room at your place. A double room. Boy, it's a shame I didn't know you before the war. A fellow gets too old for going to the park. And no chance for anything at home; you know, the old lady keeps her eyes open. The old man, too. They watch a guy like a hawk. . . ."

He went on talking zestfully, and Kern listened patiently to his fantasies. An hour later when they went to wake Kruger, Steiner was not yet back.

Dietz and Hollerbach were the last to stand sentry. During the night Schnurrbart had given orders that if Steiner were not back by four o'clock all the men should be awakened. It was twenty minutes to four when Steiner appeared among the trees. Hollerbach spotted him first. He lowered his rifle and stared, angry and relieved, into Steiner's exhausted face. "Where did you go to?" he asked reproachfully.

Steiner ignored the question. He nodded to Dietz and walked past the sentries. His incisive voice roused the men. They scrambled up, rubbing their faces sleepily. When they realized it was Steiner, they thronged around him, hurling questions. Quietly he lighted a cigarette.

Schnurrbart studied his face; in spite of the darkness he could make out Steiner's expression, and his fear vanished instantly. The questioning gradually subsided as Steiner continued to say nothing, until at last there was silence. Schnurrbart cleared his throat. "Are we going?" he asked.

Steiner nodded. Schnurrbart knew him too well to ask anything more. Without a word he began to assemble his pack. Kruger followed his example, while the rest stood around indecisively. "Hurry up," Steiner said.

They looked at him blankly until Schnurrbart, already buckling the straps on his pack, called out, "Get ready."

Hesitantly the men began to move, angrily rolling up their blankets, tramping about heavy-footed.

They gathered in a group, shivering in the morning chill. Gray light trickled through the dense foliage above them, giving their faces a hollow, ghostly appearance. "Now for a cup of warm coffee," Anselm said, his teeth chattering.

"I'd like a warm belly better," Zoll remarked.

Maag turned toward him inquisitively. "A woman's?"

"Think I'm a fairy?" Zoll growled.

Kruger chuckled. "Everything in its proper time and place," he said. "When we get back to the company, they'll send you to a whorehouse for a two-week rest cure."

"Rest cure in a whorehouse!" Anselm laughed. "Just as likely as you going skiing on the North Sea."

Can't he ever keep his mouth shut? Kruger thought, and said, "You got anything against it? If I decide to go skiing on the North Sea, it's none of your damned business."

"Kiss your ass," Anselm retorted.

The East Prussian took a step closer to him. "What did you say?"

Steiner took two big strides and came between them. "Stop that," he said sharply. "If you have any extra energy, you'll have plenty of chances to use it up today." He paused. "Where's the Professor?"

The men looked around, bewildered. They had not noticed that Dorn was missing. "He didn't seem to be feeling well last night," Hollerbach said. "I'll go see."

"Where is he?" Steiner asked.

Hollerbach nodded toward the trees. The Professor was still lying where Hollerbach had last seen him. He had drawn the blanket over his head and seemed to be asleep. "Get up!" Hollerbach shook him vigorously by the shoulder.

The blanket was thrown back and Dorn's sleepy face emerged. "What's up?" he asked.

"We're going on," Hollerbach said. "Feeling better?"

Dorn sat up, brushing his hair back from his forehead. "I think my cramps are gone. . . . I didn't sleep most of the night," he said apologetically.

The others had drawn near. Before anyone else could ask Dorn how he felt, Steiner spoke. "There's a dirt road about five miles from here. The road leads to a bridge. By the bridge are three houses, and there are Russians in the houses. That's all."

The men stared at him, too surprised to speak. Schnurrbart recovered first, for he had been expecting some sort of surprise. Swallowing hard, he asked, "How many Russians?"

Steiner tapped the barrel of his tommy gun impatiently against the tip of his boot. "Since we've got to cross that bridge, it doesn't matter how many there are."

"What do you mean?" Kruger asked. "If there's a regiment posted there, it would be crazy to start anything with them."

"It would be crazier to imagine that a regiment of Russians have been quartered in three houses—actually, they're little more than log huts. They must be either a guard for the bridge or a column passing through. At any rate, their maps are better than ours or the road would be marked on my map. Let's go. And hang on to your ammunition boxes. We're going to need them."

It had grown considerably lighter during the past few minutes. Slender shafts of light came through the leaves of the trees like jets of so many invisible fountains. Above the tree-tops birds broke into a wild morning concert.

Pasternack, walking last in line, thought of the fairy tales his father used to tell. Most of them were set in forests which, as he had imagined them, were much like this one. After his father's death in the mine, the family had had a hard time of it. He was the oldest of seven, three boys and four girls. His mother was away all day, working as a cleaning woman. She was a quiet woman who seldom smiled and who bore her misfortune as if it were a distinction. On Sundays she washed the children with special care, dressed them in the best of their patched clothes and took them to the cathedral. There she often cried. Once, when he had asked her why she cried in church, she had said, "Other people leave an offering in the box; I have nothing to leave but tears." And she had begun to cry again.

The memory saddened him. He forgot where he was, no longer felt the painful tug of the ammunition boxes, the scraping of his belt against his hip, the pressure of the rifle slung over his shoulder. Staring at the ground, he put one foot ahead of the other as he had already done for thousands of miles, and he moved along between the melancholy memories of the past and the gloomy prospects of the future without being fully aware of his grief.

At the head of the line, a few yards behind Steiner, Schnurrbart and Kruger spoke in low voices, occasionally glancing suspiciously in all directions, although there was little to see. The brush became thicker as they advanced.

"*Scheisse!*" Kruger spat on the forest floor and peered up at the leaves and the sky beyond. "Think it will rain today?"

Schnurrbart shrugged. "I doubt it. It'll probably be the same as yesterday."

"*Scheisse*, anyhow! It doesn't matter one way or the other."

Kruger's stubborn pessimism made Schnurrbart smile. "Old grumbler," he said. He hitched up his belt and glanced at Kruger's unshaven face. "You look like a hog," he said affectionately.

Kruger ran his hand over his chin and grinned. "You should talk! With the steel wool hanging out of your holes." He raised his voice. "Slow down there—think I'm an express train?"

Steiner waited for them. "Don't yell around here," he snapped. "You might scare the Russians away."

Kruger swore under his breath. They walked on together.

"How far is it now?" Schnurrbart asked, wiping the sweat from his face.

Steiner glanced at his watch. "About thirty minutes."

"To the road?"

"Yes."

"And then?"

"Then we cross the bridge."

Dully they marched on. Steiner held to a slower pace and stopped occasionally to listen. The men spoke little. The silence of the woods seemed to radiate menace; they felt the danger like a pain that transformed their senses into super-sensitive instruments.

Anselm walked behind Schnurrbart. Although it was still cool here beneath the trees, his shirt stuck wetly to his back. His thoughts hovered on the edge of a dark chasm; every moment he expected to hear the sudden crackle of a Russian tommy gun. Once he glanced back at Dorn's pale face. The awareness that Dorn was frightened too only intensified his own fear. This damned forest, he thought, this damned forest! The noise Steiner made as he broke a path through a clump of bushes sounded like an infernal din. If the Russians don't hear that, they're deaf, he thought. For a while he tried to imagine what it would feel like to be wounded. Only not in the belly, he thought, anything but that. He pictured himself lying on the ground, writhing, while the others ran away. *"Jesus, Maria und Josef,"* he whispered. Perhaps he should have prayed before going to sleep last night.

Once upon a time he had prayed often. His parents were deeply religious and went to church every Sunday in spite of the Party's opposition. His parents had insisted on his attending mass and taking communion as they did. He'd been a good boy until he was seventeen, until he met Gertrud. She was three years older than he, a tall girl with long legs. It wasn't that he had wanted to. It had just come over him all at once. He could still remember her gestures, the way she had pulled her skirt up over her knees, saying she wanted to get a tan. And then she had just reached out and pulled him toward her so suddenly that it took his breath away. And then . . . he swallowed hard as he remembered.

The first time he had confessed, of course. Then confession had become harder and harder, and finally he no longer bothered. After a while he gave up praying, too. For the first time in years this struck him as a sin. Gertrud had not been the only girl. There were Hildegard and Gisela and Christa . . . though it hadn't worked out with Christa. She came from a good family, with a religious background. When he had tried, she had simply run away. . . .

Despite his present, repentant state of mind he grew angry even now as he thought of it and for a moment he even forgot his fear. The silly goose! he thought indignantly. Why had she followed him into the woods at all? Had she thought he wanted to catch glowworms with her? "After the wedding," she had said. When could they have married? After the war, perhaps, in the mass grave? Oh, all that nonsense! If two people wanted to, they should go ahead, church or no church. In fact, it was all "their" fault. If "they" had not been so stubborn, he would have continued praying and going to confession and every thing would have been all right. Oh well, he thought, when I am home again I shall go back to confession and just leave out the part about the women. Perhaps he would start praying again, too. All one had to do was to survive this mess. The thought relieved him. Until now he had not missed anything he could not catch up on afterward. And why should something happen to him, of all the many men? He had been in Russia for a long while, and he had survived worse situations.

There was a halt at the head of the line. Steiner had stopped. The forest floor here was covered with tall fern. Steiner looked at his watch. Kruger asked, "What's up?"

"We're at the road," Steiner said. Seeing the bewilderment on their faces, he jerked his thumb toward a fringe of brush ahead. "It's just back of that. Sit down; you'll want to know how we're going to do this thing."

"Hope nobody can hear us here." Schnurrbart sat down beside Steiner. The others sprawled in a semicircle around the two.

"It's another hundred yards over to the road," Steiner said. "If you talk as low as I am now, nobody can hear." He sounded mellow.

"All right, let's have it," Schnurrbart said.

"It's fairly easy," Steiner began, puffing at his cigarette. "The main thing is to make certain none of the Russians gets away. The houses are on this side of the bridge. If we can take the other side at once, we'll have them between us. Half of us will wait on the edge of the woods. No prisoners are to be taken. Clear?"

"Hmm . . ," Schnurrbart nodded speculatively. "Might work. With a little luck we ought to make it."

"Good," Steiner said. Now that the critical moment was upon them, his impatience had vanished. If there were no complications, they would have the bridge in their hands within twenty minutes.

He remembered something. "How's your stomach, Professor?"

His voice sounded almost friendly, and Dorn looked at him in astonishment. He knew less and less what to make of him.

Steiner reached into his pack, took out a flat bottle and handed it across Schnurrbart's legs to Dorn. "Have a drink—it's vodka."

Mechanically Dorn drank; only after he had taken a big gulp of the fiery stuff did he realize the generosity of Steiner's gesture. He coughed and made a face. "Strong medicine."

Steiner grinned as the bottle was handed back to him. "But it helps. If you'd mentioned the matter yesterday, you could have spared yourself a sleepless night." He returned the bottle to his pack.

Kruger had been watching jealously. Suddenly he thrust both hands under his belt and put on a pitiable expression of pain. "Oh," he moaned, "my stomach's gone to hell too." The men laughed softly.

Steiner did not even grin. "Go take a shit," he said brutally.

Anselm giggled spitefully. "He's got his britches full already," he said.

Kruger twisted toward him swiftly. "I'll shut your big mouth for you, my boy."

"You'll need another hundred men for that," Anselm said. He was surprised at his own bravado, but he knew that Steiner would not permit a fight.

And Steiner intervened. "Wait till we're out of here. I don't give a damn what you do to each other once we're back with the battalion."

Kruger grinned at Anselm. "All right," he said.

Now Steiner rose. "Let's go. Don't forget that anyone who is wounded is going to lie where he falls. We can't drag anyone along with us." He chose the words deliberately, and he could see that they took effect. The men looked stunned.

When they reached the road a few minutes later, Steiner stopped and waited until the last man had come up. Schnurrbart shook his head. The road was about six feet wide and ran straight east and west. At this point it was lined on both sides by high bushes. "Why couldn't we have found it yesterday?"

Dietz uttered a low cry. "Look," he said. "Tracks."

Schnurrbart stooped. "Wheel tracks, and still fresh. How many are there?"

The wheels of the vehicles had sunk deep into the soft ground. Exposed tree roots had been scoured clean by sharp rims and there were innumerable impressions of unshod horses' hoofs in the mossy ground.

Schnurrbart straightened up. "Three wagons, horse-drawn. There are some footprints too, but it's hard to make out how many. In any case, it can't have been too large a force."

"Enough to give us a hero's death," Kern growled.

Schnurrbart grinned. Kruger enterprisingly tapped the butt of the machine gun against the ground. There was a metallic click as Steiner took out the magazine of his tommy gun. They watched him check the magazine and then replace it. Silently they inspected their own weapons. Kruger put a cartridge belt into the machine gun; Zoll helped him and then slung several belts of ammunition around his neck where they would be handy.

They began to move cautiously toward the invisible bridge. The bushes on either side of the road grew denser. The ground steamed; birds twittered in the trees, and the sun cast diagonal beams of light through the leaves.

Zoll had removed his glasses. As he walked, he tried to avoid stepping on any of the withered twigs strewn all over the ground. He kept telling himself that he was not afraid, but he could not overcome a queasiness in his stomach. It hampered his walking. From his clothes a repulsive stench rose to his nostrils. As he moved along, eyes fixed on his feet, he noticed the small patches of sunlight on the ground; they changed shape, expanded and contracted each time the leaves stirred overhead. Sometimes a shaft of light would dart like a silver arrow across the road. He recalled a game he had played with other boys years ago. On a hike through the woods they had arranged a race in which none of the runners was allowed to step on the spots of sunlight. Strange that he should be thinking of this game right now. If I don't step on a spot of sunlight before we halt again, I'll come through all right, he thought. He became so obsessed with this idea that for a while he forgot the impending attack on the bridge. He found a pretext for standing still until the last man had passed him. Then he followed, his attention concentrated on the ground. In the next five minutes he crossed the road a dozen times, now taking mincing little steps, now jumping or skipping to avoid a band of sunlight. The ammunition boxes weighed him down. He began to sweat but did not notice. He was so absorbed in his game that he became oblivious to everything else.

Steiner, happening to glance back, noticed Zoll's strange process. He left Schnurrbart in the lead and stood still. Zoll was on the point of jumping over a broad strip of light when their eyes met. His intended jump became a halting step that carried him right into the middle of the sunlit band. Zoll's glance shifted rapidly from Steiner's immobile face to his foot, which still stood in the same spot. Finished, he thought. He felt paralyzed with terror.

A few seconds passed while both men stood motionless. Finally Steiner asked, "What's the idea?" His cool voice brought Zoll to his senses. He raised his head slowly and stared into those unfriendly eyes. Steiner repeated his question: "What's the idea?"

For the space of a few heartbeats Zoll fought the temptation to drop his ammunition boxes and fall on Steiner with flailing fists. But Steiner had the tommy gun crooked in his arm; only a motion and the barrel would be pointing at him. Slowly, with bowed head, Zoll walked by him, gradually increasing his pace.

A moment later Steiner trotted past and took the lead again. Zoll still quivered with rage and disappointment. The brute, he thought, the rotten brute! He could hardly restrain his tears. While he automatically trudged ahead, he tried to adjust to the idea that he would be killed in the attack on the bridge. It gave him a certain amount of pleasure to imagine himself the center of a dramatic event. Marching along behind Dorn in a haze of muddled thoughts, he ransacked his mind for the memorable happenings of his twenty-five years. He felt like a man who is compelled by financial reverses to part with precious belongings, and who examines each article in turn with love and pain.

Suddeny Dorn stopped. "What's the matter?" Zoll asked, startled out of his somber meditations.

Then he saw the men clumped together on the right side of the road, watching Steiner cautiously negotiate what seemed to be a bend in the road. Steiner vanished for a moment, then reappeared and beckoned to them.

"How does it look?" Kruger asked.

"We're there," Steiner whispered. "It's about a hundred yards to the bridge—and it's guarded." The men exchanged anxious glances. "We'll stick to the plan. Kruger sets up the MG on the edge of the woods. Dorn, Dietz, Zoll and—" he hesitated for a moment, studying their faces—"and Pasternack stay with Kruger and see that no one gets out of the windows. The doors are on the other side. The rest will come with me. Don't fire until I start. Keep your heads behind the trees. If I see that we can't silence them all, I'll send up a flare. That's the sign for everyone to dash across the bridge as fast as he can run. If worst comes to worst, we'll set fire to the houses over their heads. Let's go."

He crossed the road into the bushes. They moved forward very slowly, crawling most of the way. The underbrush soon thinned out, but it still offered some cover.

When they topped a small rise in the ground, they saw the buildings in front of them: three one-story houses made of massive logs, all on the right side of the road. Above the slate roofs rose two chimneys from which dark smoke mounted into the cloudless sky. The creek flowed parallel to the row of houses; here, too, its banks were overgrown with shoulder-high reeds which swayed gently in the wind. The bridge was close by the first house, a primitive but wide wooden bridge with rails on both sides. In the center, leaning against the narrow slats of the railing, stood the guard—an elderly man with a yellow, wrinkled face. His cap was pushed back on his head and he was staring dully at the dirty surface of the water. His tommy gun was slung diagonally across his back.

For a while the men lay motionless. Then Schnurrbart crawled over to Steiner and whispered, "Funny business. I don't like this silence." He glanced at the three wagons which stood near the long side of the middle house, their contents concealed under dark-broken canvas. "Funny business," he repeated suspiciously.

Steiner glanced irritably at him. "What's funny about it? The rest of them are still sleeping. We'll wake them up soon enough."

"I don't know," Schnurrbart murmured. "There's something in the air." He paused a moment. "The house on the right seems empty; the chimney isn't smoking and the shutters are closed."

Where were the horses? Steiner wondered. The horses could not be inside the buildings or behind them. If they had been stabled elsewhere, there must be a guard with them. He had not thought of that. If the man guarding the horses succeeded in escaping, there would be the devil to pay. As long as their presence behind the Russian lines was unknown, it was not half bad. Once the Russians found out, there'd be hundreds of men beating the bushes for them. But how could he track down the horses? Searching at random through the woods would be dangerous and time-consuming. . . . They would just have to take the risk.

He looked again at the Russian guard, who had not changed his position. Then he turned his head slightly and whispered, "Get ready!" A suppressed moan arose from the men. They stared fixedly at the bridge.

A few yards behind Steiner lay Dorn, his chin propped on his left forearm and his eyes narrowed to slits. For the past few minutes he had been afflicted with a torpor that smothered all feeling. He saw Steiner lifting the tommy gun, and he threw a rapid glance at Dietz, who lay beside him. The boy suddenly began to tremble violently. His teeth chattered audibly. Dorn felt tempted to close his eyes, press his face into the damp moss and just lie still, ignoring whatever happened. Instead he touched Dietz's arm reassuringly. As if through a curtain, he saw Steiner sighting at the man on the bridge. He tried to think of his wife. But each time he had almost summoned up her face, the outlines of it grew vague, like smoke rings dissolving in a sudden draft. He gave up trying. Then he suddenly recalled what Professor Stahl had said to him in parting:

"You have been an excellent teacher; I hope you will be just as good a soldier. But you must go into it without illusions."

Dorn smiled bitterly. With a curious sense of remoteness he saw the barrel of Steiner's tommy gun jerk a little higher. The whipping round of shots reached his ear without arousing in him the usual sense of horror. The man on the bridge started to move as though he stood on a whirling disk. Then his hands gripped the wooden railing for support. His legs sagged as though the sinews had been slashed, and he slid, knees first, underneath the railing and into the dirty water, which reached up to the stringers of the bridge. At the same moment the machine gun began to chatter.

Steiner leaped to his feet and raced with giant strides toward the bridge. Schnurrbart and the others ran close behind. When they reached the bridge, they threw themselves on the ground and immediately began firing at the doors of the huts, until Steiner changed his magazine and cried out, "Stop!"

There was a sudden stillness. Kruger, too, had stopped firing. The men looked around questioningly. Several minutes passed. Nothing stirred inside the houses.

Steiner muttered, "What do you make of that?" Schnurrbart shook his head in bewilderment.

Cursing under his breath, Steiner straightened up somewhat and stared blackly at the silent houses. "I thought there was something fishy from the start," Schnurrbart declared. Suspiciously he regarded the silent woods across the bridge. Then he turned to Steiner again. "What are we going to do?"

Steiner did not answer for a moment. If a single shot had been fired from the houses, his next steps would have followed automatically. But this uncanny silence put him in a cold sweat. He glanced down at his hands and saw that they were shaking. All of a sudden he detested himself. "We have to break in," he said. "If there's so much as a mouse inside there. we've got to make it squeak."

The others were still lying on the ground, white-faced. "Get up!" he roared at them. They rose cautiously to their feet. Steiner gripped Anselm's arm. "You go over there to Kruger. Tell him to post a guard at once about a hundred yards back along the road. Then hurry back here, cross the bridge and stand guard on the other side another hundred yards back in the woods. If a single Russian comes along, kill him; if there are more, run for it and report to me. Got it?"

Anselm nodded and began to run. Steiner motioned to Maag. "You and Kern run past the houses now. Duck your heads; we'll fire to cover you. Go as far as the last house and see whether there are any doors or windows on the north sides. If there are, see to it that nobody comes out. Get going!"

"On this side?" Kern asked.

"Of course. On the other side, I wouldn't be able to see what's happening. Hurry." He turned to Schnurrbart. "Fire high—I'll take the first house, you the second and Hollerbach the third. Get ready!"

Kern and Maag started toward the houses. They moved leadenly. Steiner shouted, "Speed!" They began to run. When the three behind them started firing above their heads at the windows, they dropped to the ground.

Steiner cursed. "Those idiots!" he raged, and shouted, "Get up. That's us, idiots! We're covering you." He waved his hand reassuringly toward Kern, who was glancing back anxiously.

Schnurrbart and Hollerbach suppressed a giggle. Hollerbach said, "Those tin soldiers." They watched as Maag, too, raised his head and looked back. Seeing Steiner point the tommy gun menacingly at him, he stood up quickly and ran again. Kern stayed on the ground a few seconds more; then he rose and stumbled behind Maag.

"Do we fire?" Schnurrbart asked.

Steiner shook his head impatiently. "Those idiots will think it's the Russians again. Anyway, they're in the clear now." The two had already reached the last of the buildings. As they disappeared around the corner, Steiner wiped the sweat from his forehead. Although they had had no trouble up to now, he was filled with forebodings. Schnurrbart was right: there was something fishy here. The Russians couldn't be giving up without a fight. Minutes passed. He stared again at the houses standing green-shuttered, quiet and peaceful in the morning sunlight. At that moment a volley of shots rang out from the north side of the house where Kern and Maag must be.

When they reached the end of the third house, Kern and Maag had looked around them quickly. The building had no doors or windows on this side. Kern sighed with relief. He leaned his back against the stout logs and said, "Nothing here. What'll we do now?"

Maag suspiciously eyed the woods, which began about fifty feet away. "I don't know," he said hesitantly. "We'd better wait here. It Steiner wants us to do something, he'll tell us." He crouched down on the ground, fished a pack of cigarettes from his pocket and handed it to Kern.

They said nothing until both cigarettes were lighted. Then Kern pushed his cap back on his head. He sighed. "I wonder what happens next?"

"We'll find out soon enough," Maag said gloomily. His freckled face twisted into a grimace. "I tell you, this thing stinks like limburger."

He again eyed the edge of the woods. How many times he had gone into the edge of dense woods just like these, on Sundays, with his girl, of course. He could see her now. She had a red dress she wore often. He recalled how he would tremble when they sat down anywhere, she with her long tanned legs folded beneath her. He would lie on his stomach and talk to distract his attention from her legs, while Monika regarded him with a faint smile. Still, she said she liked his self-control. Once she had given him a long kiss and remarked that he was the first boy she knew who didn't lose his head right away. He had swallowed the compliment like a soldier receiving an undeserved medal. What would Monika have said, he wondered, if she knew the real reason for his restraint? He had to do something about that. When the war was over, he'd go to a doctor, to a specialist in mental things. He didn't want to lose Monika. Though it would be a long time before they'd be in a position to get married. Maybe he would own his own garage some day. If it weren't for this damned war, he'd be on his way now. He sighed again. The time a man lost, all on account of those bastards, those stinkers with their damned war.

Thinking of all these things, he stared into space. When Kern suddenly gripped his arm, he looked up angrily. "What's the matter, what the devil do you want?" The outburst faded.

Kern's face was chalky white. The innkeeper was staring in terror at the woods. "Do you see him?" he stammered.

His fear was contagious; Maag became frightened too. "What?" he whispered, peering at the trees.

"Russians," Kern whispered.

Maag threw himself forward on his stomach and raised his rifle.

"Where, where the devil do you see them?"

Kern could not say another word. He pointed silently at a spot on the edge of the woods where the underbrush was particularly dense.

Maag stared intently. He could feel his heart beating in short, hard thrusts, and tried to master his excitement. Once or twice he thought he detected movement among the branches, but each time he fixed his eyes on a particular spot, he became unsure. Finally he said, "You're imagining things."

Kern shook his head violently. "I saw it, I tell you—a head with a cap, a Russian cap."

"Where, damn it?"

"Right in front of us. Over there by the crooked tree, where the branches are hanging low."

"Near the reeds?"

"No, farther to the right, over—— There he is again! Do you see him?" Kern's voice broke with excitement.

Maag raised himself a little and immediately dropped back flat on the ground. Kern was not mistaken. Above the bushes, close to the trunk of a twisted alder, he could distinctly make out the face of a man. It was impossible to tell whether or not the man had sighted them, but Maag had the feeling that the Russian was looking straight into his eyes. For a few seconds he lay paralyzed, torn between the desire to jump up and run and the feeling that this would mean disaster for the whole platoon. Kern's fear intensified his own uncertainty.

He slowly raised his rifle. He was acting against his will. Seen through the gunsight, the Russian's face looked like a white spot in the greenness of the wood. Maag lowered the barrel slightly. His finger tightened on the trigger. He fired. The shot screamed in the unnatural silence. He shot again and was conscious that Kern had raised his rifle and was firing. Wildly, heedlessly, they both emptied their magazines, opened their ammunition pouches, reloaded with trembling fingers, and again fired madly. The Russian's face had long since disappeared.

Before they could load again, Steiner came rushing around the corner, threw himself on the ground beside them and raised his tommy gun. "What happened?" he shouted.

Maag lowered his rifle and stammered, "R-R-Russians."

"Where?"

"Over there."

"How many?"

"I saw one."

"And?"

"I don't know." Maag was uncertain. "He's gone now."

Steiner turned to Kern, who had meanwhile reloaded and was raising his rifle again. "What are you shooting away at?"

"Russians," Kern responded eagerly. Dimly inside him his fear still resounded like an echo. Now that Steiner was here, he felt more confident. Grinning, he said, "We gave it to him."

"Did you?" Steiner said. He stood up slowly and looked scornfully down at the innkeeper.

But Kern did not notice. He had suddenly become aware of how courageously he had fired into the woods. The others couldn't have done any better. The thought filled him with pride. After all, this war business wasn't half bad. Keep on your toes, and you were all right. You just had to show the Russians you weren't afraid of them. His fear gave way to almost hysterical high spirits. He looked up at Steiner, who was now regarding him with absolute furor.

"You're the dumbest bastard I ever came across. Get up."

Bewildered, Kern stood up and looked at Maag, who was fussing with his rifle and glancing embarrassedly at the edge of the woods.

"Come along," Steiner ordered. He moved carefully toward the trees. They followed him at a considerable distance.

After some searching, Steiner found the Russian. He lay in the undergrowth, both hands pressed against his waist; Steiner paused a few steps away and studied him thoughtfully. As Kern and Maag saw the Russian, they stopped in alarm.

Maag regained poise first. "We got him," he said with satisfaction. "I thought so. I aimed carefully."

Kern glowered at Maag and was about to say something, but Steiner did not give him the chance.

He stepped closer to the Russian, who watched each of his movements in fear. This one, too, was an elderly man. The last reserves, Steiner thought. He looked around for the Russian's gun and found it lying half-concealed among the branches of a bush. Then he turned to Maag. "You did enough shooting to kill a regiment. But it's good you got the man. Go and bring Kruger back here. The others are to stay at their posts."

Maag hurried off, while Kern stared uncomfortably down at the Russian. He suddenly felt sorry for the old man, who lay helplessly, his face contracting with pain now and then. His eyes were still fixed on Steiner, who was indifferently studying the Russian tommy gun.

I wonder what he's going to do with him? Kern thought. Lousy business sending old men like this up to the front. Maag must have hit him; I was just firing into the air. The thought relieved him. It was rotten to feel you'd killed someone, especially when it was a sorry-looking old bird like this. He turned his head and saw Maag and Kruger approaching.

"What's up?" Kruger asked.

Steiner indicated the Russian. "Ask him where he was."

Kruger had to repeat his question twice before the wounded man moved his lips. The Russian's voice was so faint and shaky that Kruger had to stoop down to him. When the man stopped talking, Kruger turned to Steiner. "He says he was watching the horses."

Steiner nodded, pleased. "So I thought. That was the weak

point in this deal. He must have heard the firing. Ask him if there are any more men with the horses."

To Steiner's relief, the Russian shook his head.

Steiner thrust a thumb into his belt. "How many men are there in the houses?"

This time the Russian did not reply. When Kruger translated the question, he closed his eyes and turned his head aside. Steiner frowned. He was acutely conscious of how much time was passing, and he decided to act quickly. In an icy voice he said, "If he doesn't open his mouth, we'll hang him to a tree. Tell him that."

Kruger spoke in an urgent, imploring voice to the old man. Finally he shrugged hopelessly. "He won't say."

Steiner took one long step up to the wounded man and held the muzzle of the tommy gun against his head. "He has to," he said sternly. "Ask him again."

Kruger glanced at the other men's faces. The whole business sickened him, but he felt that there was no other way. He began expostulating with the Russian, illustrating his words with unmistakable gestures. The Russian slowly opened his eyes. Steiner was regarding him expressionlessly. A brief smile passed over the wrinkled, parchmentlike face, and he said a few words.

"What is he saying?" Steiner asked.

Kruger jerked his shoulders irritably. "He says he is an old man."

"We can see that," Steiner said calmly. "Nothing more?"

"No."

"Did you tell him we'll shoot him?"

Kruger nodded.

For a few heartbeats Steiner felt admiration for the old man. His mouth grew dry. His finger was resting on the trigger guard of the tommy gun, but he hesitated. He closed his eyes and pulled the trigger with the sensation of a person who is tearing a scrap of skin from a bruise, skin that hangs only by a thread. The shot sounded low, as though he had thrust the barrel of the gun into the ground. The Russian's body heaved up. The whites of his eyes bulged out, his feet beat a tattoo on the ground, and abruptly he lay still.

Steiner glanced at the white faces of the men and turned around without a word. As they approached the house, he said to Kruger, "Go back to your gun. Don't let anyone out of the windows, remember. We're going to see these places from the inside."

As they moved around the corner, they pressed close to the wall. At the bridge, Hollerbach and Schnurrbart were waiting for them, peering anxiously. When Steiner raised his hand and beckoned, they rushed up, bent low, past the houses. "What was it?" Schnurrbart asked.

Steiner explained.

"And now?"

"Now we're going in." Steiner addressed Hollerbach: "You stay out here. With your tommy gun you can command all the doors and windows from the side. Make sure nobody gets away." He gave Hollerbach the Russian tommy gun he had picked up. "Take this one—it's better than ours." The others were pressed close against the wall of the house and seemed content to stay right there. "Don't fire unless you see something, and don't run unless I give the order."

Kern rubbed his cheek excitedly. "And if you—" he corrected himself quickly—"I mean, if something should happen to you?"

Steiner stared him down. "In that case Schnurrbart will carry on. But don't worry, I won't give you the pleasure." As Kern started to protest, Steiner cut him off with a wave of his hand.

"Aren't we too few for the job?" Maag asked hollowly.

"No. In the houses we'd only get in each other's way. A few hand grenades will do it." As he spoke he drew a stick grenade from his belt.

Most of the glass in the windows had been smashed by their earlier firing. Crouching under the first window, Steiner pulled the pin on the grenade, then he rose quickly and threw it into the house. He heard the grenade thud to the floor; he leaped to safety. There was a low, booming noise as though a heavy object had been dropped in a large, empty room. The men's tense poses relaxed. They watched Steiner run to the window, hesitate for a moment and then slowly bring his face level with the empty window frame. For a few seconds he stared into the house; then he straightened. "Empty," he said quietly.

Cautiously the others approached and peered through the splintered frame. Although the interior was in semidarkness because of the closed shutters on the other windows, they could see at once that the big, rectangular room was vacant. It was utterly bare and the floor was covered with a thick layer of dust.

"I thought so," Schnurrbart said. "The chimney wasn't smoking."

"But it was smoking in the other two," Maag said.

Steiner turned to Hollerbach. "Listen, you can come with me around the next corner. The range is shorter there. There are only two houses left to worry about; that makes it easier."

He went forward slowly. Suddenly he stopped. His tense

expression was replaced by a look of incredulity. The men
froze in their tracks. Steiner stood with head cocked, listening. Then he beckoned to the others. They were only a few
steps away when he raised his finger to his lips. From the
house came low moans and sobs that were unmistakably the
voices of women. Their faces were blank with astonishment.

Schnurrbart opened his mouth, pinched his own arm and
began rolling his head back and forth.

"I've gone insane," Maag stammered.

Kern doubled over with silent laughter. He turned to Maag
and gasped, "Women!"

Maag took a deep breath, his fear vanished. He ran his
tongue over his lips, half expectantly, half fearfully. "Maybe
it's a bordel," he whispered.

Kern grinned. Why not? he thought. Maybe the Russians
have set up mobile bordels. In his enthusiasm he tugged at his
pants and shifted his weight from one foot to the other.

Hollerbach shook his head in vexation. "You're both mad.
Is that the first thing you think of?"

"Maybe it's a maternity hospital," suggested Schnurrbart,
the first to realize the absurdity of the situation. "Boys, we've
stormed a maternity hospital!"

"We'll get a maternity medal," Kern cackled. He slapped
Maag wildly on the back.

Steiner threw him an angry look. "Cut the noise," he said
sharply. "We don't know anything for sure yet." He glared
at all of them. "You're acting like a bunch of morons. Wait
and see where we stand first."

In contrast to the others, Steiner was thoroughly annoyed.
The action he had been conducting in deadly earnest had
turned out ridiculously. He felt that he had been made to
look a fool. He approached the door, his face was set and
mean. He took one leap to the top step and shook the latch.
The sounds inside stopped.

"It might be a trap," Schnurrbart whispered, raising his
tommy gun.

Steiner continued to joggle the latch. "Locked," he said.
"Two hand grenades."

Schnurrbart took two stick grenades from his belt, unscrewed the locking cap and passed them to Steiner, who with
practiced fingers took out the firing rings.

"Watch it," Kern said anxiously, retreating a step.

Steiner put a short loop of string through the rings and
fastened them to the latch. Then he gestured with his head
toward the corner of the house. The men hastily took themselves off in that direction. When the last man had vanished,

Steiner gave a powerful tug, pulling the two wooden sticks down. Then he let go.

The grenades dangling under the doorknob began to hiss like a teakettle filled with boiling water. The men began to count: "Twenty-two, twenty-three, twenty-four . . ."

Steiner came rushing around the corner; the explosion followed immediately. The thunderous noise echoed and re-echoed from the woods, and was still ringing in their ears as they followed Steiner back to the steps, which were now littered with splinters of wood. The shattered door hung askew from one of the upper hinges. Schnurrbart kicked it in. Tensely they peered into the room. It seemed to be a kind of entrance hall, at the back of which was heaped a miscellany of things. As their eyes became accustomed to the dim light, they saw two doors, one on either side of the hall. Steiner raised his gun. Slowly he stepped across the threshold. The men followed closely. The floorboards creaked under their nailed boots. From outside, where the reeds rose high in the warm sunlight, a bird's cry sounded strangely loud and penetrating in the dusk of the room.

Suddenly there was another noise. Steiner halted. At first it seemed to be coming from the back of the hall. It sounded like the hollow moan in a stove on a dark, rainy night, when the wind howls over roofs and chimney tops. The moaning swelled in volume, then faded into soft sighs. Again it seemed to be coming from above, trickling through the walls and filling the entire room. There was something horrible about it.

Steiner's eyes narrowed to tiny slits. Vainly he tried to escape the hypnotic effect of the eerie moans. His mind persistently sent orders racing through his body, but he was curiously outside of himself, aware of his own ego in all its helplessness. He seemed to stand off from himself, just a few yards away, and observe his own weakness with the eyes of an outsider who had no way to interfere. Sweat ran down his face and dripped from his chin. He could feel himself oscillating wildly, painfully, between rage and shame. From some misty distance he heard Kern's voice stammering incomprehensible words. Then there was a thudding crash which abruptly brought the moaning and whimpering to a stop. Steiner reacted like a turbine revolving at high speed that is suddenly relieved of its load. He caught a glimpse of Kern's rifle lying on the floor—that must have been the thud—and saw Kern spring to the door and rush out into the broad daylight. Schnurrbart and Maag were staring agape after him.

The episode struck Steiner as so funny that he lost all con-

trol of himself. He suddenly began to laugh in a frightful manner. He doubled over, his body jerking in unnatural, ugly
movements. Each time he raised his head, gasping for air, and
saw the horrified faces of Schnurrbart and Maag, new great
squalls of the abnormal laughter burst from him. Schnurrbart
could feel his nerves going to pieces.

Hollerbach's alarmed face appeared at the door; he stared
in bewilderment at the scene, gradually lowering his tommy
gun, which he had been holding ready to fire. "Have you gone
off your heads?" he bellowed. "What's the matter, for God's
sake?"

His roaring voice brought Steiner to his senses. He slung
the gun over his shoulder and rubbed his face with his hands,
then walked swiftly to the door on the left and opened it. It
gave on a narrow room, half of which was filled with a huge
stove built of clay. From an iron rod above the flickering fire
hung a soot-blackened kettle; the water was boiling over and
fell hissing and steaming into the flames. There was a long
table, on which cooking utensils stood, along the opposite wall.
A few chairs and a bench completed the furniture. Steiner
glanced over the room, turned around and bumped into
Schnurrbart, who was staring past him at the Russian pots and
pans. The others also tried to see into the room. But Steiner
pushed them back into the hall and approached the opposite
door. Just before he reached it he turned to Hollerbach.
"Where is Kern?" he asked.

Hollerbach grinned. "I don't know. He raced past me toward the bridge."

"Did he!" Steiner regarded him unpleasantly. His voice became a shade sharper. "And where are you?"

Puzzled, Hollerbach gaped at him. At first he thought it was
a joke. But there was nothing but anger in Steiner's expression. Uncertainly, he answered, "Right here—where do you
think?"

"Right," Steiner said fiercely. "And where are you supposed
to be?"

Hollerbach started. He suddenly realized that he was supposed to be guarding the windows outside. He rushed out the
doorway.

Schnurrbart moved closer to Steiner. "What's the matter
with you, anyway?"

"What do you mean?"

Schnurrbart hesitated. It was obvious that Steiner was behaving like a madman. The question was whether he should
be told. Perhaps it would be better not to at the moment.

Schnurrbart shrugged. "I only mean . . ." he began tentatively. Again he stopped. "Anyway, this business is beginning to get on my nerves. Did you see those pots?"

"I'm not blind," Steiner answered curtly.

Maag had been witnessing the scene uneasily. He would have liked to follow Kern's example, but the favorable moment was gone. With a worried look at the closed door, he said, "I wish I knew what that queer howling was."

Steiner said nothing. He was gnawed by the feeling that he had behaved like a woman. Twist and turn the thing whatever way you liked, the fact remained that his nerves had simply given out. It was the first time anything of the sort had ever happened to him. He looked indecisively at the door, behind which the owners of those cooking utensils must be, and he knew that he was afraid. A few hours ago that would have shocked him. Now he merely wondered why. Strangely his recent conversations with Dorn came to mind.

But before he could put it all together, Schnurrbart took the initiative. He had been watching Steiner silently. But when minute after minute passed with Steiner standing utterly motionless, his patience gave out. He brushed Steiner aside, planted himself in front of the door, raised his tommy gun and fired the entire contents of the magazine at chest height through the planks. At the first shot Steiner started. Now he watched almost indifferently as Schnurrbart pressed down the latch and shook it. The door was locked. Quickly Schnurrbart reloaded, took a step back and fired at the lock. With the first few shots the door sprang open. Steiner slowly raised his gun, while Maag crouched against the wall. Schnurrbart slowly let the barrel of his gun sink. He said a few words. Steiner slapped his left ear. The hammering of the tommy gun in the narrow hall had left a droning in his head so that he could not hear. Schnurrbart had to repeat loudly, "Come over here," before he understood. They stepped up behind him. "Take a look at that," Schnurrbart said.

Steiner gulped. The entire long wall of the room was taken up by a heap of straw covered with blankets. In the corner opposite the door stood an old wardrobe chest. Crowded together in the rear half of the room, faces half-defiant, half-terrified, were a dozen women in Russian uniforms. They carried no weapons. They stared fixedly at the men. When Steiner slowly entered the room, they moved closer together and their faces paled. At their feet, bedded down on the straw, lay a younger woman, the clothing stripped away from the upper part of her body; a blood-soaked bandage covered her right breast. Her eyes were closed, and as Steiner stepped forward she began to moan again. It was the weird sound that had unnerved the men when they were outside in the hall.

Steiner stopped in the middle of the room and looked down at the woman speechlessly. So that was it, he thought; that had made him lose his nerve —a whining woman, a . . . Rage sent his thoughts scattering in all directions; he burned with shame.

Schnurrbart, sensing his feelings, laid a hand on his arm. "Keep your head, Rolf," he said. "It can happen to anybody. We're all on edge. Better let it be something like this than anything else. Now what do we do with them?"

Steiner stared absently at him. Then he looked back at the women. Hoarsely he said, "What do you do with armed guerrillas, male or female?"

"These are not guerrillas," Schnurrbart replied quietly. "They're regular uniformed troops. Besides—" he grinned— "they have no arms."

Steiner had recovered. "If they belong to regular troops, we'll treat them as we must treat all prisoners in our situation."

"You mean, shoot them?" Schnurrbart gasped.

"Do you see any other way? If one of them escapes and gets to the Russian lines before us, we're done for."

Maag had recovered from his astonishment. "Steiner is right. The women must be killed."

They stood in the middle of the room not knowing what to do. Schnurrbart irritably gnawed his lips. The idea of shooting women shocked him, and he tried to think of a better solution. Finally he suggested, "We can tie them up. I mean, we could tie them and lock them in here."

Steiner threw him a contemptuous look. "You've read too many cowboy and Indian stories. This is Russia, not the Wild West." His voice took on a hysterical note. "What are you going to tie them with? Their panties? Or their bras? And where are you going to lock them in? This place here has more holes than all the women put together. You keep out of this, hear me? I'm going to . . ." He was silent abruptly. His glance had fallen on the woman lying on the straw. She had opened her eyes. Perhaps his loud words had roused her to consciousness. Her winsome oval face bore an expression of such wild horror that Steiner's rage evaporated.

Quickly he raised his eyes and looked at the other women. They all looked about the same to him, with Slavic cheekbones and smooth black hair combed straight back. A few of them had more delicate features, which gave their faces a certain attractiveness. They wore the usual Russian uniform.

Their full blouses, reaching down over their hips, were gathered at the waist by broad belts. They were big-breasted, stocky women, and the blouses made them look more so. Their breeches were tucked into the high leather boots Russian officers wore.

Schnurrbart said, "We better do something. The others will be going crazy out there."

Steiner nodded. He hung the tommy gun from his shoulder. "They'll go crazier when they see the women," he said. "Send Kruger in to me. Add a man each to the guards on the road. Take the rest into the next house and bring everybody who's in there over here. Watch your step; there must be another man among them."

"Why do you say that?"

"Obvious. The two men we killed must have been the drivers of the wagons, and there were three wagons."

"Don't you want to go along?" Schnurrbart asked.

Steiner shook his head. As Schnurrbart went to the door, Steiner beckoned to Maag. "You stay here," he ordered. "We'll see what's the matter with the woman."

As he bent over the wounded woman, she tried to roll back against the wall. Steiner held her firmly. "Take it easy," he said quietly. "What do you think I want to do?"

Carefully he lifted the bandage. The wound was a big one and looked bad. From nipple to waist there was a dark-brown rent almost an inch wide. When Steiner removed the bandage, it began bleeding heavily. Thoughtfully he looked down at her. Then he ordered Maag to bring hot water. The other women had not changed their posture. They were still huddled together against the wall, fearfully watching his movements. As he stared down at the woman's bleeding breast, he became aware of the absurdity of his behavior. He looked at her face; she had closed her eyes again. Above her right eyebrow was a small scar. His gaze moved down along the fine nose to the full mouth and lingered finally on the uninjured half of her breast. It quivered from the beating of her heart, and for seconds he felt tempted to close both hands around the soft flesh. With each heartbeat the blood ran down along her narrow hips. An ugly stain on the woolen blanket was steadily spreading.

When she opened her eyes again, he asked, "Are you in pain?" When she nodded, he knew she understood. "The pain will be all over soon," he said. Her face fell. She moved her lips without uttering a sound.

Maag returned and placed a bowl of hot water on the floor. "That ought to do."

Steiner nodded. While he was busy cleaning the wound, Maag stood so that he could look on, but from a sense of shame he made sure the others could not see his face. Because the wound ran to the waist, Steiner unbuttoned the woman's trousers and pushed them down a little.

Maag suddenly began shaking. His voice sounded husky. "Want help with this?" Without waiting for an answer, he put his hands on the woman's waist, loosening the clothes and as if without intention reaching his fingers far down under the trousers.

"Stop that," Steiner said sharply.

For a second Maag could not decide how Steiner meant this. But he removed his fingers. His excitement was so intense that he could feel it with an almost voluptuous pain in every part of his body. Feverishly he wondered how he could persuade Steiner to leave the room for a few minutes. He could think of no pretext. But he made up his mind to seize the first opportunity that offered. Before we kill the women, I'll lay one of them, he thought. This was the chance of a lifetime. There was no risk of making himself ridiculous here, and if it went off all right he would be rid forever of that damnable fear that he was impotent. How could he work it? It was now or never.

Steiner had meanwhile finished cleaning the wound. He took a first-aid kit from his pocket and began to lay a medicated compress on the wound. As he finished, he heard hasty footsteps outside, and Kruger, Schnurrbart and Hollerbach came noisily into the room. Steiner glanced once more at the wounded woman. Her head had fallen to one side and her eyes were closed. It looked as though she had lost consciousness again, and he thought that was best.

He turned to the men and asked, "How is everything?"

"Fine." Schnurrbart grinned. "Thirteen dames and the billygoat too. They're right outside."

Steiner nodded. "Did you have any trouble?"

"Not at all. They were sitting on the floor, scared to death."

"You should have let us know what's going on," Kruger said, his eyes studying the women. His face was twitching and he pulled at his nose. "We felt like we were sitting on hot coals."

"With your thick hide I imagine you didn't even singe your ass." Steiner suddenly remembered something. "Where's Kern?"

The men exchanged meaningful glances. "Hasn't turned up yet," Kruger said after a momentary pause. "We saw him running across the bridge like the devil was after him. Made us think they'd cooked your goose in here. What's the matter with her?" With his chin he indicated the wounded woman.

Steiner shrugged indifferently. "She was hit. Must have been a ricochet."

"Serves her right," Kruger commented. "What business have women putting on uniforms? We ought to paddle their asses so they can't sit for a month."

"They won't be sitting up much longer," Steiner said.

Kruger frowned. "Schnurrbart said something about that. You can count me out."

"I don't need you," Steiner replied coolly.

"Are you going to kill them yourself?"

Steiner did not answer. This was the question he had been turning over in his mind for the past few minutes. The longer he thought about it, the more uneasy he felt. Finally he pushed it away, postponing the problem until later. If there were no other way, he would do it himself. Russians were Russians, no matter what they had between their legs.

He ordered Hollerbach to search the wagons for food. When they found it, one man was to make coffee or tea; the guards on the road were to withdraw to the bridge; two men would remain in the house to guard the prisoners.

For a moment he stared at the floor, considering. Then he said, "That will be all for now. Kruger, I need you again."

As the men filed out, Steiner turned to the women again. Their initial fear was gradually diminishing. They still stood close together against the wall, but they were talking in whispers now and throwing curious glances at the men. As Steiner took a step toward them, they were all attention. In as rough a voice as he could muster he said, "Ask them where they come from, where they were going and whether there are any more of them on the way here. Tell them if they lie to us we'll throw them into the creek."

"Lots of work for nothing if they can swim," Kruger said. He beckoned to one of the women who wore an officer's insigne on her collar. Her face expressed fear and defiance. When Kruger raised his gun, she slowly came forward. He asked her a number of questions which she answered promptly and boldly.

Kruger interpreted. "They belong to the 34th Women's Mortar Battalion and are on the way from Maikop to Krimskaya. They are . . ."

"What about Krimskaya?" Steiner interrupted.

Kruger again addressed the Russian woman. She listened attentively. Then she exchanged a few words with the other prisoners. When she turned to Kruger again, she spoke slowly, dramatizing her words with frequent shrugs.

"Krimskaya is supposed to have been taken by the Russians last night," Kruger translated. "But she isn't sure. Her group had to wait in Maikop for new mortars yesterday, while the battalion went down the road to Krimskaya yesterday morning."

"How did they come to be here?" Steiner asked.

"A civilian told them about the short cut through the woods. They arrived here last night and were intending to go on to Krimskaya."

Steiner thought that over. The Russian woman's story might well be true, although you had to be cautious. If Krimskaya had already been occupied by the Russians, that was a hard blow. In addition to all their other troubles they would now have to detour around the city. Although he had reckoned with that possibility, he felt his earlier discouragement returning.

He heard a low cough from the doorway. Schnurrbart stood there, weary and grim. When their eyes met, Schnurrbart said, "So it's that."

"What's what?" Steiner asked.

"Krimskaya."

Steiner growled impatiently, "One more reason for making sure the women don't get to the city before us. Where is the other batch of women?"

"Outside. I was waiting until you were through. Should I bring them in now?"

Steiner nodded. "Yes, don't forget the sentries. Are the other fellows back?"

"All here," Schnurrbart said.

Steiner turned to Maag. "You and Zoll stay here. If any one of the women starts anything, shoot her at once."

"What about the man?" Schnurrbart asked. "Should we . . . right away . . ."

"Is he young?"

"No, he's an old fellow like the others."

"You can bring him in here for the present," Steiner said. "We'll take care of them all together." Kruger was staring blackly at the wall. "Don't think I'm looking forward to it," Steiner added. "It makes me feel sicker than your stupid mugs, and that's saying a lot."

They went outside, where the prisoners, guarded by Zoll and Anselm, were lined up against the house. Steiner paused on the lowest step.

On the left end of the line stood the wagon driver, his head hunched between his shoulders. His eyes were crafty, and his ugly, pockmarked face was typically Asiatic. Squat in build, he looked quite powerful still, in spite of his age. When he saw Steiner's eyes on him, he took a step forward, raised his hand pleadingly and said, "Captain . . ." Steiner pointed the tommy gun at his chest. The man reeled back, frightened, while the women screeched and ducked low against the wall.

"Take them in," Steiner said. "Where are the sentries?"

Schnurrbart pointed to the bridge. "On the edge of the woods. I picked the place myself. They can see the road in both directions from there."

"Who have you got?"

"Dietz and Pasternack."

Steiner moved away from the steps and watched as Zoll and Anselm drove the prisoners into the house. For the first time he noticed that all the men were holding large chunks of Russian bread in their hands and hungrily chewing. The sight reminded him that he had not eaten for twenty-four hours. In the open window of the kitchen Dorn's head appeared for a second. In spite of his bad temper, Steiner could not help grinning. It would be Dorn, he thought; Schnurrbart might have picked a better man for KP duty. Kern, for instance. Suddenly he realized that Kern was still missing. He would have a word with *that* idiot. Kern must be off in the woods somewhere, the piss scared out of him. Slinging the tommy gun over his shoulder, Steiner sauntered around the house toward the wagons. On the way he remembered that he had forgotten to ask about the horses. He stopped and called to Kruger. There was no answer. Impatiently, he went back. The East Prussian was standing with the others, gesticulating and speaking with great force. They always know better, Steiner thought with rising anger.

He strode up to them and addressed himself to Kruger: "Get hold of the man and bring the horses here. Take Anselm with you. What's the idea of standing around here making speeches? By God, we've got more important things to do."

Kruger threw him a rebellious look. "We're discussing something a lot more important than the damned horses."

For a second Steiner seemed on the point of smashing his fist into Kruger's face. But he controlled himself. His voice was tense. "What's said around here is important only if it comes from me."

"Says your conceit," Kruger growled.

"I'd sooner be conceited than as dumb as you. Get moving, and have those horses here in ten minutes."

Sullenly the two went into the house to fetch the old Russian. Steiner motioned to Schnurrbart: "Come along." They went around the house and ran into Hollerbach, standing on one of the wagons.

When he heard them coming, he called, "Where the devil is everyone? Do you think I'm going to sweat my ass off on this stuff alone?"

Steiner went up to the wagon and looked in. Half-ridden under boxes of ammunition lay two heavy mortars. Curiously Steiner examined the caliber. "The damn thing's murder," Schnurrbart observed.

They watched as Hollerbach tugged at a canvas cover in the back of the wagon and brought out a tommy gun. He handed it to Steiner who examined it with interest.

"It looks brand-new," Schnurrbart commented.

"Any more of these things in there?" Steiner asked.

"Let's see." Hollerbach pulled the rest of the canvas cover aside. "Sure, half the wagon is crammed with ammunition, and then some. What'll we do with it?"

Steiner turned the tommy gun over between his hands. He seemed to be struggling to make up his mind. Finally he said, "Tell you what, we'll take these guns along. Every man take one and as much ammunition as he can carry. The rest we'll toss into the creek. The best way, I guess, would be to push the wagons up on the bridge and turn them over into the water."

"Not bad." Schnurrbart yawned. He rested his arms on the edge of the wagon rack and blinked at the sun. "But what are we going to do with our own guns?" he asked. "We don't want to be lugging them too, on top of everything else."

"Of course not. We'll toss them into the water too."

"I don't know," Hollerbach said with a worried frown. "I grant you theirs are better than ours. But what a stink there'll be about it when we get back. Meyer will throw a fit."

"He can throw two for all I care," Steiner replied. "The kind of fix we're in justifies unusual measures. Why do you want to hang on to your stinking carbines? By the time you've reloaded them the Russian tommy guns can fill you full of holes. Besides, we've only three boxes of ammunition left."

Schnurrbart nodded agreement. "As far as I'm concerned, orders are orders." He grinned. "I've been waiting for years for a chance to throw my rifle into a river."

"How do we stand on rations?" Steiner asked Hollerbach. "Found anything decent?"

Hollerbach nodded. "Several dozen loaves of bread and a

few boxes of canned stuff." He put on a solemn, secretive expression. "Guess where the stuff comes from?"

"How should I know?" Schnurrbart shrugged. "It can come from Siberia for all I care."

Hollerbach chuckled and held up a can. "Made in U.S.A."

Schnurrbart spat. *"Scheisse.* What the devil are we staying here in Russia for? Just promoting international good feeling, I suppose. What a laugh: the plutocrats sending corned beef to the Communists!"

"They get along fine when it comes to beating us." Hollerbach sighed. He sat down on the wagon shaft and let his feet dangle.

Steiner laughed harshly. "Don't let it bother you," he said. "One of these days they'll be paid back for their corned beef, and then some."

They gave the matter some thought. Finally Hollerbach shook his head and with an air of profundity said, "It's only the Jews."

Schnurrbart clapped his hands to his ears. "Cut it out; it doesn't sound any better on an empty stomach."

"That's the only time I can stand politics without puking," Steiner said. He placed the tommy gun on the wagon. "Let's stop gabbing and get to work."

"Yes, let's go." Hollerback jumped up and energetically rolled up his sleeves.

"What do we do first?" Schnurrbart asked.

"Let's take out the tommy guns and the ammunition, then the food. Everything else we can dump into the water."

They started unloading.

Dietz and Pasternack were lying on the ground near the edge of the woods, on the other side of the bridge. They talked in whispers, without relaxing their close watch. Pasternack was saying vehemently, "It's out of the question, I tell you. Once I get back home I want to take things easy."

He wants to take things easy, Dietz thought. A fat chance a man has to do that. He drew a blade of grass between his teeth and propped himself up on his elbows. "It isn't all so simple," he said. "Now look . . ." He paused reflectively, considering how to explain why it was not so simple. "You see," he continued, "back home I work as a bricklayer. I wanted to go to college, but there wasn't enough money."

"What did you want to study?"

"Medicine. I wanted to be a doctor. I've been mad about medicine as long as I can remember."

Pasternack hummed thoughtfully. "Since you couldn't afford

it, why didn't you go in for something else? Salesman or something." He glanced at Dietz's thin, frail body. "I should think
bricklaying would be too tough for you."

"It is," Dietz said gloomily. He remembered how dead tired
he had always been when he came home from work; sometimes he had thrown himself down on his bed and wept from
sheer exhaustion. "There wasn't anything else, though," he
went on. "When I finished school, my old man was un-
employed. I haunted the employment bureau, but it wasn't any
use. One time I tried for an office job, but they didn't want me.
Even though my marks in school had always been high."

Pasternack nodded sympathetically, and Dietz looked grateful. "It was tough," Dietz went on. "There just didn't seem to
be anything for me. Then one day my father heard about a
construction job and I went over and got it. It was supposed
to be just a starter, till something better came along, but once
I was in it I was stuck."

"That's the way it always is," Pasternack said. "Same thing
happened to me. When my old man had his accident, I went to
work in the mine, and there I stayed until I was drafted."

There was silence. Dietz absently watched a small beetle
crawling along the ground. When it had made off, he said,
"You know, when I remember what it was like on that job, I
don't know that I'm so crazy about getting home. When I think
of our foreman—I tell you he was a hundred times worse than
any of these birds in the army. Here you can lie down and
take a snooze once in a while, but there you didn't dare take
time out for a smoke. He once threw a brick at me—hit me
square in the small of the back. It could have killed me." His
eyes filled with tears of resentment at the memory. He swallowed hard.

"There are sons of bitches like that everywhere," Pasternack
said. "We had our share of them." He shook his head and
sighed. "The bastards."

Dietz smiled dismally. "That's why I don't give a damn.
Back home they lay it into you and here in the army they lay
it into you. I don't know which is worse." He picked up a dry
stick and broke it in two. "It's a rotten deal any way you look
at it."

Pasternack stared unhappily into space. The sun was warm
on his back. The stillness and the sharp tang of the reeds reminded him of days on the banks of the Oder. His father had
taken him swimming when he was a little shaver. Being near
water always reminded him of those days—the happiest in his
life.

He was gazing abstractedly at the bridge when he suddenly

caught sight of Kern. The innkeeper was moving slowly toward the bridge, looking warily on all sides. Dietz, who had also spied him, called out his name. Kern whirled around. Then his tense pose relaxed and he walked swiftly toward them.

"What are you doing around here?" Dietz asked in surprise.

Abashed, Kern scratched his chin. He glanced uneasily toward the houses. "I had to go," he said hoarsely. "Devil only knows what I've done to get this upset stomach."

Both the others grinned. Crouching with Kruger behind the machine gun, they had witnessed Kern's wild flight.

"Steiner's been looking all over for you," Pasternack said. "You can't just run away like that."

"Run away?" Kern pretended to be indignant. "What do you mean, run away? I told you I had to go. Oooh!" He clutched at his belly in pretended pain. "Never had the shits like this before. I can hardly stand. What's been happening, anyway? What are you doing here?"

"Sentry duty," Dietz said.

"What about the Russians?"

"Russians!" Pasternack laughed. "You mean the girls?"

Kern stared at him. "So that's what they were!"

"Sure, the houses were full of women. Part of a mortar battalion."

Kern paled. His chin drooped. Steiner will kill me, he thought; what an idiot I've been! He had run only a few hundred yards into the woods, then thrown himself down on the ground with overwhelming relief. But when minute after minute passed and he did not hear the expected din of battle, he had become nervous. Torn between fear and his sense of duty, he had finally dragged himself to his feet and gone part way back. Then he had heard noises in the underbrush and his terror had returned with redoubled force; he had hidden behind a tree until he discovered that the sounds were being made by some animal. Steiner would not believe his reason for running away, any more than Pasternack and Dietz did. The somewhat malicious expressions of the two men increased his dread.

Pasternack yawned. "Go on over there and tell them to send us something to eat. I'm hollow."

Kern hesitated.

"They won't shoot you," Dietz said reassuringly.

"You know how Steiner is," Kern said sulkily, his hand touching the burned spot on his face .

Dietz laughed angrily. "He won't try that again."

Kern stood indecisive for a few moments more. Then he squared his shoulders. "Well, see you later," he said.

As he crossed the bridge, he saw the others. They were pushing one of the wagons and were so absorbed in their labors that they did not notice him. Schnurrbart was holding the shaft and steering while Hollerbach and Steiner, their backs braced against the wagon, walked backward, pushing it step by step toward the bridge.

Schnurrbart looked up. Kern quickly put his finger to his lips in a beseeching gesture, and strode rapidly toward them. When he reached the wagon, he braced his shoulder against one of the crosspieces and began to shove with the others. In a moment they reached the bridge. Since they had to lift the wagon up a step about eight inches high, they paused.

Steiner cursed under his breath and wiped the sweat from his brow. Suddenly he saw Kern. Hollerback, catching sight of him also, exclaimed, "Holy thunder!" They stared at one another in silence.

"Where have you been?" Steiner asked quietly.

Kern cringed and did not answer. When Steiner repeated the question he stammered, "In the woods—I had to—I had cramps—that soup must have upset my bowels."

"I see," Steiner said.

Kern ducked his head as though a shell were whining over him. Schnurrbart saw him begin to tremble. As always he wondered at the uncanny effect of Steiner's personality. Although Kern was half a head taller than Steiner and was certainly not inclined to be timorous, he was cringing like a schoolboy expecting a deserved whipping. Standing with drooping shoulders and white face, he looked the personification of fear, and Schnurrbart suddenly felt disgust so violent that he could taste it as a bitterness in his mouth. He had to put an end to this disgusting scene.

To Steiner he said, "Let him alone. We were all scared stiff when we stood outside that door. Don't forget Kern has been at the front just a few days. That sort of things can happen to anyone." He hesitated, then lifted his jaw aggressively. "You went to pieces too," he added sharply.

Steiner slowly turned toward him. Schnurrbart looked into his eyes and was frightened. But there was no outburst. Without a word Steiner took his tommy gun from the wagon, thrust two clips of ammunition under the strap of his pack, and started across the bridge. As they watched, he disappeared among the trees. The men stared at one another in alarm.

"Now we've done it," Kern murmured.

Hollerback turned on Schnurrbart. "Man, you shouldn't have said that!" he said angrily. "You know how he is."

Schnurrbart was still staring in horror at the spot where Steiner had vanished .He felt like a man who has accidentally set his own house afire and is standing before the smoking ruins. He stood numbed until Hollerbach shook him violently by the shoulder and shouted, "Go after him and bring him back."

"It's no use," Schnurrbart muttered. Suddenly he turned on Kern. "It's all your fault, you idiot!" he burst out.

Kern looked guiltily into their outraged faces and did not answer.

"Here comes Kruger," Hollerbach said. They looked toward the houses, where Kruger, Anselm and the male Russian prisoner had appeared. Each of them was leading a pair of small, rugged-looking ponies.

Kruger waved to them, laughing. "We've got them," he called out cheerfully. "Now we can play cavalry." Seeing their grim faces, he turned to Anselm. "Tie up the ponies and put the prisoner into the house." Then he strode swiftly toward the men. "What's the matter— has something happened?" he asked.

"Und wie," Hollerbach said glumly. "Steiner's left."

"What do you mean, left?" Kruger demanded, his heart suddenly pounding.

"Let him tell you," Hollerbach replied, nodding toward Schnurrbart, who was staring blackly at the water.

Kruger whirled around. "What the devil is the matter? Come on, talk."

"Damn it all," Schnurrbart growled, "a man can't weigh every word on a precision balance." He told Kruger what had happened.

Kruger turned on Kern. "You goddamned bastard!" he shouted. "Just wait till we . . ."

"Cut it out," Hollerbach interrupted furiously. "You'll do better to figure out what we're going to do."

There was an uneasy silence. Finally Schnurrbart said, shrugging, "There's only one thing we can do: carry out Steiner's plans. First we'll dump the wagons into the water; then each of us will take a Russian tommy gun and we'll clear out. Maybe he'll be waiting up ahead for us."

"You don't believe that yourself," Kruger growled. Again fury overpowered him. "If only you'd kept your dumb mouth shut!"

Schnurrbart was on the point of retorting angrily. But he felt that Kruger was right, and on top of his awareness of having got the platoon into this predicament came the additional sense that all the responsibility for the safety of the group now rested on him. Without another word he turned toward the wagon and began tossing boxes of ammunition into the water. For a while the others watched him. Then Kruger cursed and unbuckled his belt. "Don't stand there and gape," he burst out furiously, jumping up on the wagon. "We're going to hell anyhow." He stooped and picked up a heavy box. The others fell to and worked like madmen.

After crossing the bridge Steiner ran into the two sentries. When he heard his name called, his thoughts returned with difficulty to the present sunny April morning. He stood still and stared at Dietz, sauntering slowly toward him. "Anything new?" Dietz asked. He gave Steiner a friendly, boyish smile. "Can't you send us something to eat over here? We're starved."

Steiner hesitated. Now that his initial temper was gone, he felt uncertain of himself. Uncomfortably he looked into the smiling face before him. "You'll get something to eat soon," he answered roughly. "Schnurrbart will either send some stuff over here or have you relieved."

"Why Schnurrbart?" asked Pasternack, joining them. "Aren't you going back across?"

When Steiner did not reply, the two men began to look worried. Dietz began nervously fingering the strap on his rifle. "Has something happened?" he asked.

Steiner shook his head. He felt that it was impossible to tell the two of them that he was leaving the platoon. "I want to take a look around," he said. "Keep your eyes open."

They still looked doubtful. "Did you see Kern?" Pasternack asked.

Steiner nodded. There was a few seconds' silence. Then Dietz inquired uneasily, "Did you hit him again?"

Steiner grinned. "No, why should I?"

"That's good." Dietz sighed with relief. "I've been thinking about him. You know, Kern isn't a bad guy at all; he just isn't used to the front yet."

"I agree." Steiner nodded. "Only I'm afraid he never will get used to it. He looks to me the kind of guy who feels like a man only when he's on top of a woman." Seeing Dietz flush, he laughed and clapped him on the back. "You're still a regular baby, after all," he said.

"Do you think we'll get out of this with whole skins?" Pasternack asked.

"I hope so."

"But the Russians are in Krimskaya now."

Steiner looked down at the toes of his boots. The conversation made him uncomfortable; he was anxious to end it as quickly as possible. "We'll just have to detour around the city. We've been through worse messes."

"Sure," Dietz said with eager agreement. "You'll get us out of this. Nothing to it."

There was such vast trustfulness in his voice that Steiner looked at him baffled. Then he turned sharply, made his way through the trees to the road and walked rapidly off into the woods.

Dietz watched with admiration. Then he turned to Pasternack. "He'll do it, I tell you; he'll get us out of here somehow."

"Sure," Pasternack said emphatically. They went back to their places.

The farther Steiner walked away from the bridge, the less firm his pace became. Dietz's last words kept ringing in his ears. They were like elastic bands wound around his body and tied somewhere way back at the bridge. With every step forward their pull tautened; his legs began to feel as if he were up to his waist in a rushing stream and trying to advance against the current. Finally he came to a stop and looked back. It was utterly quiet. The road wound and twisted through the woods, flanked by dense undergrowth on both sides. Through the foliage overhead the sunlight speckled the floor of the forest. Steiner swallowed repeatedly. There was a hollowness in him that seemed to be spreading through his whole body, so that even his physical sensations were unreal. Wearily he sat down at the foot of a tree, tucking the tommy gun under his legs. He should have taken Dietz and Pasternack with him, he thought. But then he shook his head. You couldn't compromise with your conscience. For a while his thoughts dwelt on Dietz. He had sometimes tried to analyze his feelings about the little fellow, but had never really got anywhere. Dietz was a plucky little jack-in-the-box with a faithful heart and eyes of a good dog. With the best will in the world you could not see much more in him. And yet Steiner felt he would miss Dietz more than he would miss Schnurrbart and all the others. Strange. Maybe that was it; maybe the little fellow uncovered a hidden streak of queerness in himself. The idea troubled him. He closed his eyes and thought it over. But as soon as he started to visualize the thing, he grinned scornfully. No, that was out of the question. He knew himself too well not to mistake his own feelings about such filth. Crazy even to think of it.

He reached into his pocket for a cigarette and began smoking. While he sat staring with narrowed eyes at the dirt road, he reconsidered his relationship with Dietz. He recalled the many times he had favored Dietz in ways the others would not notice. Had they really never noticed? Anything was possible. Now and then Schnurrbart had made a few remarks. But those might have been sheer chance. In any case, who cared what Schnurrbart said?

In a sudden flash of rage Steiner snapped the half-smoked cigarette into the bushes. The conversation on the bridge, momentarily forgotten, came back to him. From anyone else he could have taken that, but not from Schnurrbart. In the course of his talk with Pasternack and Dietz he had come to feel a certain detachment toward his own injured pride, but that didn't mean he was going to pardon Schnurrbart. If Schnurrbart had taken him aside to make the same point, he would not have taken offense. But the public humiliation could not be borne. The more he thought about it, the more determined he felt to leave the platoon to its fate.

He continued to sit for a few moment, brooding bleakly. Finally with an impatient jerk he looked at his watch. It was half past nine; there was no more time to lose. The rest of the platoon would be coming any moment. As he stood up he thought about Dietz once more and felt annoyed with himself for not having found any explanation. You're an idiot, he told himself; the way you carry on, you might be an aging spinster who feels the last stirrings of maternal feelings and goes to bed with a doll between her withered breasts. The idea amused him; for a few seconds he doubled over like a caterpillar and shook with soundless laughter. Then he jumped to his feet. As he stooped for his gun, he caught a glimpse of a large moving shadow.

All the men with the exception of Zoll were sitting in the kitchen. To gain time Schnurrbart had recalled the sentries from the bridge so that they could eat with the others before setting out. The wagons were at the bottom of the stream and the men were now armed with Russian tommy guns. They were sipping the hot tea Dorn had brewed and eating directly out of the American tin cans. The Russian bread was moist and heavy, but they devoured it hungrily. Schnurrbart alone was scarcely eating. Until he had spoken with Dietz and Pasternack he had gone on hoping Steiner would return. But now there could be no doubt. Steiner had left the platoon. It was up to him to decide the next steps to be taken.

For a while Schnurrbart regarded Kruger's gloomy face.

Then he suddenly remembered the man guarding the prisoners. He turned to Maag and said, "Hurry up; you have to relieve Zoll so that he can eat. We're leaving right away."

Maag nodded as he gobbled a huge hunk of corned beef. Schnurrbart watched with disgust. He looked toward Kruger again, and their eyes met. Something in his face troubled Schnurrbart. He felt that they were both thinking about the same thing. What was to be done with the prisoners? Now that Steiner had gone the responsibility no longer lay in one man's hands. He knew quite well that he could not carry out the execution against Kruger's opposition. Thoughtfully his eyes drifted over the faces of the men. Dorn, Dietz, Pasternack and Hollerbach would also undoubtedly raise a fuss. What Kern's and Anselm's attitude would be he could not decide. Zoll and Maag, he felt fairly sure, were the only ones who would mow the women down without a qualm. In any case it would hardly strengthen his position as leader of the platoon if he insisted on shooting the women. Left to himself, he would not have thought of it for a moment.

"What's on your mind?" Kruger asked.

Schnurrbart hesitated a moment. He glanced quickly at the door before he spoke. "What are we going to do with the women?"

The men stopped chewing and stared at him. Although they knew this matter still hung fire, they were nevertheless shocked. They avoided one another's eyes.

Dorn was the first to speak again. He laid his fork on the table, removed his glasses and studied the lenses as he asked, "What do you propose?"

Schnurrbart did not reply.

Dorn turned to the others. "I don't see that our situation will be either better or worse if we shoot them. But in any case I am unalterably opposed."

His resolute tone aroused in Schnurrbart a spirit of contradiction. "So," he said irritably, "you're unalterably opposed. May I ask why the devil you're so opposed?"

Dorn regarded him coolly. "You certainly may ask. I am opposed because we are soldiers and not murderers. Anyway, I think we are facing a far more urgent problem. Does any of you know where the battalion is posted at present?"

No one answered. Schnurrbart shrugged. "It's marked on the map," he said crossly.

"Right." Dorn smiled briefly. With unwonted sharpness he asked, "And who has the map?"

Schnurrbart felt a sudden pang run through his body. Turning his head, he caught Kruger's look of alarm as Hollerbach

sprang to his feet exclaiming, "Steiner! The map's with him."
The men stared at one another in consternation.

Dorn alone remained calm; it surprised him how calm he
was. He was as composed as a person who has long ago understood that feeling is only a passing intoxication of the soul
which must not be taken seriously lest it introduce needless
disruption into life. To Pasternack who sat in a slump at his
side, he said, "Didn't Steiner say anything about the map
when he talked to you and Dietz?"

Pasternack shook his head silently.

"Then we haven't got a chance," Dorn commented tran-
quilly.

Kruger's repressed fury erupted suddenly. He brought his
fist down on the table with a crash and roared, "Well, then,
goddam it to hell! The devil with the map! What do I need
a map for? I'll show you my map. Here it is!"

He stooped quickly, picked up his Russian tommy gun and
slammed it down on the table with all his strength. Several
mess kits were knocked over, spilling hot tea in all directions.

The men jumped back out of the way, and Kern, his trousers
soaked, called out angrily, "You damned half Russian!"

Kruger whirled around, stared at him for a second, then
threw himself on Kern with an inarticulate cry. His body hit
Kern's so hard that Kern was hurled backward across the
table.

The men jumped aside, cursing. "Stop it!" Schnurrbart
roared. His words were drowned out in the tumult.

Kern slid across the table and fell to the floor. He rose in a
flash and met Kruger with furious blows. They were evenly
matched. Their arms moved like windmills; they seemed to be
pulling each punch from out of the air. Most of the others
formed a ring around the fighters and cheered them on. Dietz
backed trembling against the wall. Each time a fist landed
with a dull thud, he closed his eyes and noiselessly moved his
lips. When Kruger charged Kern and the two began rolling
in a tangle on the floor, he found his voice again. He turned
to Schnurrbart, who was standing by watching the fight with a
set expression, and yelled, "They've got to stop, tell them to
stop!"

Schnurrbart nodded.

He glanced quickly at Hollerbach. They cautiously approached the grappling men from both sides. Kern had just
heaved himself up off the ground, rolled over on top of
Kruger and was closing his hairy hands around his neck. Hollerbach and Schnurrbart desperately tried to separate them,
but they could not get a good hold.

Schnurrbart attempted to seize one of the thrashing legs, and caught Kern's visious kick in the groin. He reeled back and crumpled heavily to the ground. As he sat up, face twisted with pain, a tommy gun stuttered and a storm of metal lashed above their heads.

After Schnurrbart called Maag to help unload the wagons, Zoll was left alone with the prisoners. All the while the men were at work outside, Zoll stood with his back against the door, alertly watching the women. Since there were now nearly thirty persons in the relatively small room, it was closely packed. In order to simplify the problem of guarding them, Schnurrbart had ordered the prisoners to sit in rows one behind the other, legs apart and hands on the shoulders of the one in front. They had made themselves somewhat more comfortable by using one another as supports for their backs. In the farther corner, her head upon one of the women's laps, lay the wounded woman. She was still unconscious. Although the prisoners did not yet know what was going to be done with them, their initial fear seemed to have abated somewhat. They talked in whispers, and Zoll was bothered by the feeling that they were making fun of him. He could think of no other explanation for their occasional bursts of giggling. Several times he had tried to intimidate them by cursing viciously, but after looking up in curiosity and astonishment they had resumed their whispering. Finally he had given up playing the strong man.

Toward the front, close to him, sat the solitary male prisoner. In contrast to the others his expression was worried, and Zoll observed him talking steadily to the woman beside him. What the devil was all the chatter about? Zoll wished he could pound him over the head with his tommy gun. But they would be killing the man very soon now. This thought made him feel generous. Let the fellow shoot off his mouth while he still had the chance.

For a while he listened to the flow of the unfamiliar language, feeling irritated with himself for not having learned Russian. He recalled all the tutoring his parents had forced on him when he came home with poor marks in English and French. What did all the cramming get you? Half of what you learned you never used, and the other half you forgot.

He watched the woman the Russian was talking to. He had noticed her before. Couldn't be more than twenty, he would guess. Her thin face was rather pretty, and every time she looked up at him with her gray eyes he became restless. She had what it took, he thought. Too bad he was not alone with her. His eyes glided searchingly over her figure, which looked promising in spite of the shapeless uniform. Her blouse was stretched tight over high breasts, and Zoll tried to imagine how it would be if he were to unbutton that blouse. A lousy situation, he thought; here they had all the girls they could wish for and weren't getting anything out of them.

To distract himself, he glanced out the window. The men were still slaving away at the wagons. He saw them dumping ammunition boxes and mortars into the water. They pushed the empty wagon onto the bridge, rammed it into the railing several times until the wood splintered and the heavy wagon pitched over the side of the bridge. The water splashed high all around it. He grinned with satisfaction. That was one cart the Ivans wouldn't be using any more. He watched with interest as the men turned to the next wagon. Pleased, he saw Maag wiping the sweat from his brow. Good that Schnurrbart hadn't sent for him. He could do without an extra detail right now. He felt, to his own surprise, a touch of gratitude toward Schnurrbart. Until now he had automatically thought of superiors as stinkers. He might as well try to get along with Schnurrbart from now on—wouldn't do any harm. If Steiner had really gone off, Schnurrbart would be platoon leader. What a break that would be! He had felt enormously relieved a few minutes ago when Schnurrbart came into the room and told them about Steiner. He had hated Steiner from the first day he met the fellow. Maybe because Steiner was the only man he feared.

He suddenly recalled with a surge of rage and shame their run-in of that morning. The game he had played with the patches of sunlight had been ridiculously childish. But all the friction with Steiner had been to blame for that. One's nerves were shot, that was all. That damned bastard had done the rest.

He had been so deep in thought that he had paid no attention to the prisoners. Now he suddenly heard a groan behind him. Whirling around, he scrutinized them suspiciously. They were sitting as still as before. Only in the farther corner, where the wounded woman lay moaning softly, a few of them had turned their heads.

"Quiet!" Zoll yelled.

From somewhere in the room there was a brief burst of giggles.

Zoll bit his lip. Damned bitches, he thought. I ought to . . . His hand tightened on his gun. Angrily he looked over the rows of faces.

Suddenly he gaped. The woman sitting in front of him—

the woman the man had been talking to so urgently—was moving ever so slightly. Head bowed, she was fingering her blouse. The two top buttons were already open, revealing the base of her breasts. Zoll gulped and looked at the man, who sat with eyes closed, apparently dozing. The other women had stopped whispering. Most of them seemed to be asleep, or were sitting with heads drooping, staring at the floor. It was so quiet in the room now that he could distinctly hear Schnurrbart outside issuing orders. Zoll felt a peculiar sensation in the pit of his stomach. He glanced at his gun, making sure the safety was off.

When he looked up again, his eyes met the Russian woman's. She was gazing steadily at him, and had opened another button on her blouse. As he watched her in fascination, she closed one eye in a slow wink and smiled at him. Zoll held his breath. The thought crossed his mind that there might be some danger for him concealed behind this behavior, only to be immediately routed by the heady rush of vanity. He ran his tongue over his dry lips and tried to look at the woman impassively. Her thin, rather dirty fingers were busy opening the last button.

Zoll threw a glance out of the window. The men were just shoving the last of the wagons over the edge of the bridge. They stared at the water for a few seconds and then turned toward the house. He heard the heavy tread of their nailed boots mounting the stairs and thumping across the hallway. Then the door was wrenched open and Schnurrbart thrust his head in. "Everything all right?" he asked.

Zoll nodded. Out of the corner of his eye he observed that the Russian woman was holding her blouse closed and staring vacantly at the floor.

"I'll relieve you in a few minutes," Schnurrbart said. "As soon as Maag has eaten he'll take over so you can eat." His eyes roved over the rows of prisoners. "They asleep?"

"Seem to be," Zoll answered curtly. He was furious at the interruption, and he wished only that Schnurrbart would leave as quickly as possible.

But Schnurrbart still delayed. Something about the women's attitude aroused his suspicions. Queer that they should be sleeping, he thought, coming all the way into the room.

"What do you want?" Zoll asked impatiently. "Everything is all right."

"I said the women were to sit and not lie back," Schnurrbart answered.

Zoll was aware of the swift fading of all his good resolutions. If Schnurrbart was going to be a louse like Steiner, he would have to set him back on his heels in good time. "I don't know what you want," he said angrily. "Let them stay the way they are. If any of them lets out a peep, I'll let her have it."

Their loud voices had roused the women. They sat up again, throwing anxious looks at the two men.

"There you are!" Zoll burst out in a rage. "When they're lying down they've got less of a chance to make trouble." He turned around and bellowed, "Lie down!"

The Russian women looked blank.

Zoll strode over to one of them, raised his boot and kicked against her shoulder, throwing her backward. "Lie down, I said!" he shouted again.

This time the others understood. Zoll watched with satisfaction as their bodies sagged to the floor. "Don't you think I can watch them better this way?" he said to Schnurrbart.

Schnurrbart hesitated uneasily. Finally he shrugged. "You can't see their faces this way."

Zoll grinned. "What do I need to see their faces for? I prefer their arses."

"You're an old hog," Schnurrbart growled as he went out.

Zoll kicked the door shut behind him and quickly turned toward the Russian woman. She had opened her eyes and was looking at him. Now she spread her legs apart, turning her feet outward, and nodded encouragingly to him. When he did not stir, she spread her blouse open, reached under the gray cloth of her undershirt and pressed her breast upward. Breathlessly, head crooked forward, Zoll watched the white flesh appear over the edge of the shirt. He dug his teeth into his lower lip, and his whole body tautened. But he stood still as if nailed to the spot. His eyes hung painfully, greedily on the brownish circles of her nipples which rose up tense and hard. When the Russian woman beckoned him with her finger, he could feel that he was losing control of himself.

His eyes swept over the heads of the other prisoners, paused upon the face of the man. Although he was lying with closed eyes, just like the women, Zoll's suspicions revived. But it was crazy to worry, he told himself. The old goat would not dare try anything. As his gaze turned back to the exposed breast, he feverishly went over the possibilities. Nothing much could happen if he went ahead. Though it would be dreadful if another of the men came in. He would have to hurry. But here?

He shook himself. To provide an erotic spectacle for thirty women did not appeal to him. Besides he did not quite trust the sleepy and apparently indifferent man. The fellow might only be waiting for him to lie down on top of the woman. The thought sobered him a little. You couldn't trust any of this damned pack of Russians. Undecided, he looked over the rest of the prisoners once more. There was nothing about their attitudes that seemed suspicious.

Then he suddenly recalled that the woman who was baring herself had been the very one with whom the man had talked so excitedly. He glowered at her. As though she were guessing his thoughts, she smiled again, and began to push herself along the floor toward him. She moved in such a provocative manner that all Zoll's compunctions disappeared. Where could he take her? Finally he thought he had found the solution. He beckoned with a movement of his head. "Come," he said softly, *"idi syuda."*

She hesitated and glanced at the man for the briefest moment. The man seemed to notice nothing of the byplay between the two. Was he pretending?

Again Zoll hesitated for a second. But by now he was in such a state of obsessive lust that he would have killed the man instantly rather than be deterred. *"Idi syuda,"* he repeated hoarsely.

The coquettish smile on the woman's face vanished. When she looked up at him again, he saw fear in her eyes.

He grinned. "So now you've decided to be coy," he said. "That doesn't go with me, understand, not with me." He took one long stride up to her, stooped, grasped her shoulder tightly and pulled her to her feet. "Not with me," he growled.

Again he threw a glance at the man, who was still lying with closed eyes. But his face now seemed unnaturally pale. Abruptly Zoll opened the door and pulled the resisting woman by the wrist out into the hall. Madly he looked around. From the room behind the door opposite he heard the muted voices of the men. For a few seconds he listened, eyes narrowed, still tightly gripping the woman's wrist. If they catch me I'm sunk, he thought.

He turned toward the woman and saw that she was trying with her free hand to button her blouse. He grinned. "Let that be," he said, his hand darting to her breast. The touch increased his excitement. He raised his tommy gun and wordlessly gestured with it toward the outer door. The woman stared at him, her mouth twitching. "Come," he said, shoving her toward the door.

On the steps she tried to escape. But he had expected this and tightened his brutal grip on her arm. "Come," he panted, dragging her to the next house. He pushed her up the steps and into the hall. The house was just like the others, a kitchen on one side, living quarters on the other. Both doors were open. He shoved the woman into the room to the right of the hallway. On the floor lay the prisoners' blankets and equipment.

As he laid his tommy gun down in a corner, the woman suddenly broke loose and ran toward the door. In two bounds he was at her side. He threw his arm around her waist, dragged her back into the room, hurled her to the ground, and fell on her, panting with exertion and excitement. She tried to defend herself; her small, clenched hands battered against his face, and she began to scream. Had he not been so wild with the desire to possess her, he might have wondered about her contradictory behavior. But he did not think. When he had stripped her naked, he dragged one of the blankets over her face and smothered her screams. She lay like an animal under him, moaning.

Vladimir Ignatiev heard the screams as he ran toward the bridge, and his heart contracted. Poor Ninotchka, he thought, tears streaming down his face, poor little Ninotchka! From the window he had watched the German push her into the empty house, and then he had made his break for freedom. Any moment he had expected to hear the crackle of the Germans' guns, their shouts, but there had not been a sound. Now he raced across the bridge, and the forest reached out green hands toward him; the forest cried, "Run faster, Vladimir Ignatiev." He was in the shelter of the tall trees. He panted, stumbled over roots, fought with flailing arms and legs through the dense undergrowth until he came out on the road again. For a few seconds he paused, panting for breath; then he ran on. As he rounded a bend in the road, he stopped, as horror-stricken as though hell had opened before him. His heart pounded against his ribs and his gasping breath seemed to have become boiling water that seared the inside of his chest.

A dozen paces away from him sat a German, the one he had spoken to in front of the house. The German was sitting with his back against a tree, apparently lost in thought. Vladimir Ignatiev dared not move. He stood with arms dangling, his thoughts tumbling over one another like bowling pins when the wooden balls struck them square in the center. The forest had lost its friendly aspect; the trees stared threateningly down at him. "Holy Saint Basil!" Vladimir Ignatiev whispered. Under his heavy wadded jacket he began to sweat; perspiration poured down over his forehead, burned in his eyes. The German did not move. But if he turned his head just a little, it would all be for nothing—all of it, including the screams of Ninotchka who had sacrificed herself to make his flight possible. It must not, it must not be in vain. Vladimir's parchmentlike face tightened. He clenched his fists. He must kill the man, must seize his gun and make off for Krimskaya. Now, at once. As he got set to spring, he saw the German stand up abruptly, pause and then stoop for his gun. At that moment he threw himself like a falling tree on the German's back and pulled him to the ground.

Although the attack was a complete surprise, Steiner reacted instantly. Even as he fell he managed to half turn his body, and he recognized the Russian. As the man's hands were clamped around his throat, Steiner doubled up, reached over his shoulders and pressed his fingers into the man's eyes. The Russian let out of piercing scream; his grip relaxed. Like a weasel Steiner rolled over on his side, continued to roll across the road, and jumped up. He saw the man taking a tremendous leap into the bushes, rushed toward the spot where he knew the tommy gun must be, stumbled over a tree root and fell flat on his face. Although he recovered almost at once, he had lost precious seconds. As soon as he laid hands on the gun, he raised it and fired blindly into the undergrowth until the magazine was empty. But when he raised his head and listened into the sudden silence, he could hear the retreating sounds of breaking branches. In a moment these were swallowed up in the depths of the woods, and the silence closed over him like deep water.

For a second Steiner stood motionless, listening still. He was so clearly aware of the hopelessness of pursuit that he did not even attempt it. To hunt down one man in these impenetrable woods would take a whole company. As he brushed out his clothing, he smiled grimly. Leading a platoon, he thought, took more stuff than Schnurrbart had in that little brain of his. Served the bigmouthed bastard right; let him get out of this mess now.

He bent over to pick up his pack, which he had lost in the fight, and a piece of paper fell out of his coat pocket. He froze. The map, he thought—the map's with me. Slowly he reached out for the paper. Without the map Schnurrbart couldn't possibly find his way to the battalion. Furious, he stared blankly into the green woods, cursing his own taciturnity; he should long ago have told the men where the new positions were located. At the very least he might have informed them that a detour around Krimskaya was possible only from the north; on the south of the city they would run into swamps. The longer he considered it, the more apparent it was that taking the map with him was not in the game. Schnurrbart had to have as good a chance to make it as he would have had. Yet if he returned now to bring the men the map, they would not so easily let him go off again. Most of all he feared the way they would look at him. And what would Kruger say, or Hollerbach or Dietz? What would he read in Dorn's eyes? Yet there was no help for it; they had to have the map. What he did next would depend on the situation he found when he returned to the platoon.

His next movements were swift and considered. He put a new clip in his gun, picked up his gear and set out at a steady trot back down the path. When he reached the bridge, he stopped and looked around. Seeing no sentry, he shook his head and looked toward the houses. They seemed deserted and uncannily quiet. His uneasiness mounted. Inconceivable that they had not yet discovered the Russian's escape! As soon as he had crossed the bridge, he saw the horses. They were standing with lowered heads, tied to the last house. Steiner breathed easier. The men would not have set out without the horses; therefore, they must still be inside. He felt somewhat reassured, although the silence was still baffling. Cautiously he approached the house where the prionsers ought to be.

As he passed the first building, he heard a suppressed moan. Quickly he turned and peered suspiciously at the windows. The sound was not repeated. On tiptoe he stole up the steps, entered the hall and paused, listening. Now he heard the moaning again; it was a little softer but unmistakable. Rather out of curiosity than concern, he approached the door, pushed it open slightly and thrust his head into the room. The sight that met his eyes took his breath away. But he made no sound. When he came out a moment later his face was flushed. So that's it, he thought grimly; that's why it's so quiet here! He ran to the next building, rushed up the steps, noiselessly opened the kitchen door and stood still, astounded. Then he raised his gun and fired.

The men, instinctively flattened out on the floor, gaped at Steiner, in the doorway with his gun smoking. Kern and Kruger were lying in a tangle half under the table. But Kern's terrible grip had loosened, and as Kruger staggered to his feet, his eyes glassy, the innkeeper's heavy body rolled to the side to lie like a log of wood. Still bewildered, the men looked from the motionless Kern to the tottering figure of Kruger, who reeled toward the door and straightened up, breathing heavily, in front of Steiner. For a few seconds they stared at each other without a word.

Abruptly Kruger began to grin. He plucked at his nose, glanced over his shoulder at Kern and whispered, "Out for the count."

Steiner blinked. His initial surprise at the scene had given way to a terrible suspicion. He turned to Schnurrbart, who was still staring incredulously at him, and demanded, "Who is guarding the prisoners?"

It took a moment for Schnurrbart to remember. "Zoll," he said at last, breathing hard.

"I see. Zoll." Steiner nodded. All at once he came to life. He sprang across the hall, wrenched open the door and looked into the room. The women were standing pressed up against the walls, their faces white. With narrowed eyes Steiner looked them over. Then he turned to the men, who had gathered in the hallway behind him. The expression on his face appalled them.

"For Christ's sake, what is it?" Schnurrbart stammered.

"You'll find out soon enough," Steiner replied fiercely. "You idiots can't be left alone for five minutes. Get yourselves ready. Don't any of you leave the house." Before they could ask him any more questions, he pelted down the hallway.

As he went out Dorn, his voice quivering with agitation, turned to Schnurrbart. "Where in the world is Zoll?" he asked.

Schnurrbart bit his lip and did not answer.

When Steiner kicked open the door, Zoll was just pulling up his trousers. The Russian woman lay on the floor, naked and whimpering. At the sound of the opening door, Zoll whirled around. He stared incredulously at Steiner in the doorway. For a few seconds they merely looked at each other. Then Steiner came slowly into the room, and slowly approached Zoll, until he was right in front of him. The whimpering of the Russian woman stopped. With satisfaction Steiner observed the sheer terror in Zoll's eyes. He wondered what would be the consequences if he shot Zoll on the spot. Did the commander of a platoon cut off in the heart of enemy country have the same rights of summary court-martial as the captain of a warship at sea? He did not know the regulations on that, but he knew that he would not tolerate Zoll in the platoon any longer. After all, there was another solution. He looked around the room; his eyes lighted on the tall, single-doored wardrobe that stood beside the window, filling the entire left corner of the room. It was massively built but seemed to have no lock; the door could be closed only by a wooden catch.

"Open the door," Steiner said to Zoll. Zoll did not move. He was holding his trousers up with both hands, his face reflecting all the emotions that had been passing through him in these past few minutes. Steiner's order intensified his fear. Involuntarily he glanced toward his tommy gun. It was out of reach in the farther corner of the room.

Steiner caught his glance. His mouth twisted. "Don't try it," he said coldly. "You couldn't get there. Come on, open the wardrobe."

"What for?" Zoll asked loudly. He made an effort to speak firmly.

Steiner pointed the tommy gun at his chest. "You ask too many questions," he said calmly.

Zoll stared into his pitiless eyes. He did not doubt for a second that Steiner would fire at once if he tried to jump him. Nevertheless, he made a last attempt at opposition. "Not until you tell me why you want me to open the wardrobe."

His resistance threw Steiner into a fury. The urge to press the trigger was almost too much for him. "Go on," he said hoarsely, "go on, hurry up."

Zoll shrank away from that naked rage. He turned quickly, went to the wardrobe and opened the door a little.

"More," Steiner ordered.

Zoll pulled the door wide open. The wardrobe was empty inside. Steiner nodded with satisfaction. Turning his head for a moment, he saw that the Russian woman's gaze was fixed upon him. Deep within those gray eyes of hers blazed a flame that sent a shiver down his spine. If she had a gun now, she would kill us both in a moment, he thought.

"Get into the wardrobe," he said to Zoll.

Zoll took a quick step to the side, his eyes widening with fear.

This was taking too much time, Steiner thought. He stepped up to Zoll and whacked him across the face with the heavy barrel of the submachine gun.

Zoll let out a wild shriek. He let go of his trousers and pressed both hands against his nose, which streamed blood.

Ignoring his cries, Steiner shoved him into the wardrobe. "The show is over," he said coldly. "The applause has died down and the audience is heading for the exits. Do you know what happens then?"

He saw Zoll's body tensing and quickly raised the gun. "You don't understand. The show is over, I said. And when the show is over the curtain falls . . . like this." As he spoke he had been closing the door inch by inch. Now he suddenly slammed it shut, pushed the wooden catch down, and took a step back. "If you make a sound," he called out loudly, "I'll fire through the wood."

From the side he tugged at the wardrobe until he had moved it somewhat away from the wall. He enlarged the space until he could squeeze between the wall and the rear of the wardrobe. Then he braced his back against the wall, and with a mighty shove pushed the wardrobe over. The heavy piece of furniture crashed to the floor, sending up a cloud of dust, behind which appeared the Russian woman's white face. For a few seconds there was silence. Then Zoll began to shout. When he began kicking his nailed boots against the wood inside, Steiner hammered the butt of the tommy gun against the rear wall of the wardrobe. The shouting stopped.

"Stop the racket," Steiner said loudly. "Nothing can happen to you as long as you're inside there. I'm going to leave the lady here."

He turned on the woman, grasped her wrist and pulled her over to the wardrobe, where she crouched to the ground, trying to cover herself with her hands. Her eyes were still afire, and Steiner felt a tremor at the thought of the fate awaiting Zoll. For a moment he fought with himself. Then his face set. He picked up Zoll's tommy gun and turned toward the door.

As he went out, he stepped on a piece of clothing. It was the Russian woman's uniform. He halted. The thought came to him so suddenly that it took a while before he fully took it in. He stooped, picked up the uniform and regarded it. Then he went on out of the room, a triumphant smile on his face.

The men were ready to march. They stood about the kitchen looking at Kern, who lay moaning on the floor with his eyes shut. Schnurrbart was bending over him. He had unbuttoned Kern's jacket, pulled up his shirt and with both hands was massaging the innkeeper's swarthy abdomen. The others stood around discussing the jujitsu trick Kruger had used. Kern seemed to be slowly recovering. His moaning stopped. Suddenly he opened his eyes and tried to sit up.

"Good morning," Schnurrbart said, grinning with relief.

Kern stared blankly at him. Then he saw Kruger and his memory returned. He twisted his face in a grimace of pain and cursed. "What the devil happened?" he said, his astonished eyes coming to rest on Schnurrbart, who was still rubbing his stomach. He could not figure it out. He had been on top of Kruger and had had a beautiful grip on his throat. And there his memory ended. Seeing the grinning faces of the others, he flung Schnurrbart's hands off him and sprang to his feet.

At this moment Steiner returned. He went over to the table and spread out the Russian uniform. Then he turned to Kruger. "You back to normal again?" he asked quietly.

Kruger straightened his cartridge belt, brushed the hair back from his perspiring face. "More or less," he said.

"Let's hope it's more. Come along." They went across the hall to the prisoners. The buzz of conversation stopped and the women looked up expectantly at them. "Tell them to undress," Steiner ordered.

Kruger gaped at him, thinking he had heard wrong. When Steiner impatiently repeated his order, he shrugged and spoke to the women. Their faces paled and they shifted about uneasily, but made no move to obey. Steiner lifted the submachine gun and fired half the magazine into the floor. The women screamed in terror and threw their arms up in the air. "If they don't undress voluntarily we'll strip them one by one," Steiner said loudly, over the reverberations of the shots. "Tell them it's their uniforms I want . . . nobody could take away their virginity any more."

Kruger did not see what Steiner wanted with the uniforms, but the business was beginning to amuse him. His voice rang out incisively as he translated Steiner's remark.

This time the women complied at once. In their panic they pulled the blouses over their heads without bothering to unbutton them. When the other men, startled by the shots, came rushing into the room, they stopped in utter astonishment. The women had already removed their high boots and were now taking off their trousers. Their scanty and rather ragged underclothing scarcely concealed their breasts. Some of them were wearing woolen panties; most wore men's long underwear. Half naked, they huddled together in front of the men, glaring at them bitterly.

Maag ran his tongue over his lips. "Boy, oh boy," he murmured. The sight made his skin tingle. He glanced at the other men and saw that they were in similar condition. They were all standing leaning forward slightly, identical expressions of outright lechery on their faces.

Dorn lingered in the background, outraged. Although he understood the ugly scene no more than the others, he was revolted by the way all of them were, as he put it to himself, welcoming this shameless exploitation. He elbowed his way to the front and went up to Steiner. "What's the idea of this filthy business?" he said angrily.

Steiner regarded him coolly. "Haven't you ever seen a woman's arse before?"

Disgusted, Dorn stared into his impassive face. Before he could reply, Kruger nudged him roughly. "Never you mind," he growled. "If their holes bother you, take off your glasses. Otherwise, go for a walk, for God's sake."

Dorn quivered with indignation. Angrily he turned his back on the scene, went to the window and stared out into the bright daylight. So much had happened in the past few minutes that demanded explanation. Why had Steiner come back? Where was the one Russian male prisoner? Where was Zoll? What was the meaning of this disgusting undressing of the women?

The women had finished by now. Their uniforms lay in a heap on the floor, and the men's eyes slid hungrily over their bodies. Steiner, seeing the men's faces, grinned. What they were thinking was obvious and understandable. But they had no more time to lose now. The Russian who had escaped would reach Krimskaya in three hours at most. Steiner addressed the men. "We are going to change uniforms. Each of you take whatever fits and change over there in the kitchen. Wrap your own uniforms in your blankets and include them in your packs. Clear?"

"You mean we're to put that stuff on?" Maag gasped.

"Have you got anything against it?"

"No, of course not, but they're women's uniforms."

"They're the same uniforms all the Russians wear," Steiner answered impatiently. "Have you noticed any difference?"

Maag looked at Schnurrbart beside him, appealing for aid. But Schnurrbart was just as puzzled.

"The idea in itself isn't bad," Kruger spoke up, looking sour. "But those uniforms are stinking filthy."

Steiner flashed him an irritated look. "Yesterday you yourself said we were going around like pigs. The women's uniforms are no dirtier than our own; so don't be so damned fastidious." He nodded at the women, who were watching the bickering with apprehension. "Ask them when they last washed. More recently than you have, I'll bet."

There was little Kruger could answer to that. He stared blackly at the floor. Finally he asked, "What's happened anyway? Has the Ivan escaped?"

"He would have been crazy if he hadn't," Steiner said bitingly. "You couldn't have made it easier for him to get away if you tried. What I've been wondering is why the women didn't run off with him."

"Nothing surprising about that," Kruger said, stung by Steiner's tone. "They were too damn scared. Incidentally, where in hell is Zoll?"

There was a sudden silence. The men looked at Steiner. "Safe enough at the moment, I imagine," he replied indifferently. "I don't think we have any reason to worry about him."

"Has he skipped out?"

"What would you have done in his place?"

Kruger also shrugged. They had all realized that one of the women was missing. Perhaps Zoll had noticed Steiner returning and had made a dash for the woods with the woman. But then how had Steiner come to have the woman's uniform? One way or another the business was queer, Kruger thought, scratching his chin.

Steiner gave them no time to think the matter over. "Take the uniforms," he ordered harshly. "We're starting in five minutes."

"In five minutes," Maag exclaimed, looking sick with disappointment. "What are we going to do with the women?"

Steiner did not reply. The men picked up the uniforms, went into the kitchen and began changing clothes. Steiner was the last to leave the room. At the door he glanced back. The women were standing motionless at the back of the room, a grotesque sight. They had put on their boots again and their legs emerged from the black, high tops like thin, ridiculously white sticks. As Steiner looked at their faces, he felt acutely uncomfortable. He stepped quickly out into the hall and closed the door behind him. Then he stripped off his own uniform.

Kruger had already tried on five uniforms. He was sweating and cursing steadily under his breath. At last he found a pair of pants that fitted. "What an idea!" he said aloud, staring in fury at the picture he presented.

Hollerbach watched him with amusement. He was fully aware of the humor of their situation. He also felt so relieved at Steiner's return that he would cheerfully have carried out far more unpleasant orders. He had found a pair of trousers that fitted him well, and as he fished a suitable blouse out of the pile of clothes he watched with growing mirth as the men in a frenzy of haste slipped into one uniform, turned around, took a few steps back and forth, and then—anxious not to look ridiculous—searched for garments that fitted them better.

Kern had just toilsomely squeezed into trousers that reached only just below his knees when he pulled them up to his waist. For a few seconds he looked down at himself aghast. His hand reached back and felt his behind for a while; then he turned to Hollerbach who was barely able to keep from laughing. "You see how it is," he said plaintively. "I'm going out of my mind, I tell you. What a damned crazy, idiotic idea. If the Russians see me, they'll die laughing."

"They sure as hell will." Hollerbach smirked. "From now on you have to take the lead. The Russians will laugh so hard they won't be able to shoot."

Kern shook his head unhappily. "What am I going to do? I can't go around like this." He looked down at his legs with troubled gravity.

Hollerbach patted him reassuringly on the back. "It isn't so bad. Try another pair."

"I've tried them all. This is the only one that fits around the waist."

"Then take the leggings and wind them around your legs. That's how I've done it. It doesn't matter how you look; the main thing is if it serves the purpose."

"As far as that goes," Maag put in, "do you think the Russians won't see we're not Russians?" He tugged angrily at his blouse. "What a laugh—they're not that dumb. They only have to look at our caps or our boots."

Hollerbach, drawing on his belt, shook his head doubtfully. "Let's wait and see. In the dark it won't be so obvious. Don't forget we have to cross the front lines while it's dark."

"In these rags!" Kern laughed wildly. "When we get to the battalion our own men will mow us down. Us looking like a pack of damned Russians!"

"Don't wear your brain out thinking about it," Hollerbach retorted. "After all, we have our own uniforms with us."

"Which makes another few pounds to carry. Look at the size of this bundle." Kern had begun wrapping his jacket and trousers in the blanket. The bundle was distinctly bulky.

"This is ridiculous," Maag said, cursing. As he buttoned his blouse he thought of the women with acute disappointment. He had missed the chance of a lifetime. Why hadn't he made better use of the time? He'd had his opportunity when he and Zoll were guarding the prisoners together. They could have taken turns going out with one of the women. But he had felt so damnably inhibited about broaching the matter to Zoll. Then Schnurrbart had come in later and he had had to go out and work on the wagons. But how could he have known that they would be moving on so soon? It was lousy bad luck, that's what it was. They never let you have anything, the bastards, he thought bitterly. I always have rotten luck and one of these days Monika is going to chase me off. Gloomily he stared down at the floor. Here you crawled in the mud and worked your ass off month after month, and when for once you had a chance at a little fun nothing came of it. Filled with self-pity, he cursed Steiner; Steiner was to blame for the whole deal. Naturally that thick-skinned studhorse wouldn't have any such difficulties. He was the kind who took a woman without complications. The thought increased his bitterness. Do they have any idea what a fellow like me has to go through? he thought. If they knew—the slave drivers, the goddamned slave drivers!

He muttered under his breath for a while until Steiner appeared in the doorway and urged them all to hurry. They regarded him in amazement. The Russian uniform had radically changed him. He looked broader, and even his face seemed different. Harder than ever, Dorn thought, studying him.

"Don't gape like idiots," Steiner said. "If you fool around here much longer, we'll have a Russian regiment on our necks."

The men shuffled through the front door. They had wound the leggings around their calves; the long blouses fell down to their thighs; on their heads they wore their usual visored caps with the edelweiss insignia. Their swollen packs tugged at the straps. Steiner and Kruger went in to the prisoners, while the others inspected one another, shaking their heads. They strode back and forth, grimacing and strutting like women trying on new dresses.

"I'm glad he came back," Schnurrbart said.

Dorn looked uneasily toward the window of the prisoners' room. "If he shoots them, I'll transfer to another platoon," he said.

"You'll have to be back with Battalion to do that," Hollerbach reminded him. He ran his thumb along under his collar. "To tell the truth, I don't like this business either. But I keep telling myself that we come first and the women second." Since the others did not say anything, Hollerbach blinked up at the sun. "Nice weather today," he went on. "It's beginning to feel a little like spring at last."

Schnurrbart shrugged wearily. "If I were back home, I wouldn't care if it were as cold as the North Pole."

Hollerbach sighed. "I'd be content if we were back with Battalion. Dirty business, Zoll. What was that bird thinking of?"

Hollerbach fell silent and looked over toward the bridge, where the reeds swayed above the surface of the water. He suddenly remembered the trip he had taken to Würzburg with Brigitte. It had been a Sunday outing. After they climbed up to the old castle they sat on a bench and looked down on the city below them. The bells of the Cathedral and the Neumünster Church rang out. The hills across the Main River seemed to be moving gently under the shadow of the vineyards, rocking up and down in the deep blue of the sky. "I wish I could come here often," Brigitte had said.

Hollerbach smiled a bitter, painful smile as he remembered that. He had had to save every pfennig for over four months in order to spend this Sunday in Würzburg with Brigitte. They had had little money at home. As a boy he had dreamed of having a great deal of money, of owning a car and seeing the world. But the world had too soon become for him a narrow funnel with its point at Mudau, and there had been no escape from it. His horizon extended no further than the edge of the woods beyond the small church, where the mountains reached to the sky and effectively blocked all yearnings. He could already see his future, sitting behind the counter of a railroad ticket office as his father had done all his life, dully regarding the faces of travelers, annoyed by their stupid questions and their rudeness, and having always to be at their service. And then watching them enter the train to ride out into the world, he always remaining behind, as effectively bound to his little booth as if he were chained there.

He rubbed his eyes and looked hastily around. But no one was paying attention to him. Schnurrbart and Dorn had joined the others. The men were loading the horses with boxes of ammunition. The horses shifted restively. They had straggly manes and small, spiteful eyes. Maag picked up a stout stick of wood and began belaboring them. They kicked out, pranced wildly. Hollerbach shook his head. Those fools don't know a thing about handling horses, he thought, and went over to take a hand. Würzburg was again two thousand miles away.

Steiner could not have explained the impulse that made him go in to see the prisoners once more. When he and Kruger entered the room, the women were sitting on the floor, their blankets wrapped around them. They stared hostilely at him, and Kruger, too, threw a suspicious glance at his face out of the corners of his eyes. The East Prussian had no intention of playing executioner. If Steiner insisted on killing the women, he would have to do it alone. Steiner, who sensed his thoughts, smiled fleetingly. Now that the male prisoner had escaped, there was, of course, no point to shooting the women. Perhaps he had never seriously intended to anyway. He really did not know.

He noticed the wounded woman. The other women had bedded her on several blankets and covered her. Her eyes were open and she was looking at him. As he approached her, the other women shrank away as though he were a carrier of the plague. He stopped in front of her. "How do you feel?" he asked.

She did not answer. He suddenly observed that she had

beautiful hazel eyes, and wondered why he had not noted this before. "When you wear a uniform in wartime," he said quietly, "you must not expect the enemy to treat you as a woman. Do you understand?" Although she again did not reply, he could see from her expression that she had grasped his meaning. Stubborn like all Russians, he thought, frowning, and went on: "The rest of your uniforms are in the kitchen; you can go and get them. I imagine help will soon be sent to you from Krimskaya."

With satisfaction he saw her pupils widen in surprise. As he started to turn away, she spoke. "Why do you say that?" Her German was flawless; her voice was low and resonant.

He looked at her in surprise. What a voice! He felt the impulse to hear her go on talking. He bent closer and said, "You know as well as I that there are two missing from this room."

With an excitement inexplicable to himself he watched her raise her head slightly. "Vladimir got away?" she said. It sounded more like a statement than a question. But Steiner nodded anyway. "If you mean the man who was here, yes— he escaped."

The woman turned her head and said something to the other women. Their faces brightened and they exchanged significant glances. Then she turned to Steiner again. "You said two."

"She is waiting next door, in the other house."

"Is she . . ." The woman hesitated and her tongue licked out to moisten her lips. "Is she all right?"

"No one ever got sick from that," Steiner said cynically. The woman's expression darkened. "That is not for you to say," she answered quietly. "A good many have got sick from that, sick here." She drew her arm from under the blanket and pointed at her chest.

Slinging the submachine gun over his shoulder, Steiner leaned forward and asked, "How is it you speak German so well?"

She hesitated for a moment. Then she said, "I teach the language to children—I am a schoolteacher." There was pride in her voice.

"I see," Steiner said. "But why should you teach the children German?"

"Why do your children learn English and French?"

"Because we have already conquered France and are going to conquer England. Do you understand that?"

She nodded quietly. Talking had exhausted her; her face was overlaid with dark shadows. She is going to die, Steiner realized, and the thought pained him. He tried to push it away. We must all die, he told himself, and asked, "Well?"

She looked up at him for a second, then closed her eyes. "You know the answer," she said wearily.

He nodded and straightened up. "The day hasn't come yet," he said. "It's still a long way to Germany."

She opened her eyes again, and there were flickering lights in them. Slowly she turned her head, and her words reached his ears as a barely audible whisper: "Not a long way . . . for us. But . . . for you."

He looked down at her dying face. Then he turned silently and went out. Kruger followed him. Outside, Steiner stood still for a moment. Beyond the bridge loomed the woods, mute and menacing. The gnarled branches had become like the lithe limbs of an octopus, scaled with green leaves and reaching dark shadows across the water to the men on the shore. Steiner shuddered. He passed his hand over his face to wipe away the image. I'm cracking up, he thought. Against the sinister curtain of the woods the dying woman's last words rang in his mind like an oracle.

There was something else that her voice rather than her words had awakened in him. His heart throbbed and memories scattered in all directions within him. There was another woodland ringing the oval green of a forgotten meadow. The tall grass danced in the wind, the bluebells swayed, the wild pink blazed among the blossoms of the foamflowers, while black and cream-colored butterflies fluttered above them. Towering over the woods rose the spired mountain, grave and powerful, a circlet of white clouds around its granite neck. And a voice was speaking, saying foolish, lovely things, a soft voice, a dark voice, and meadow and woods and mountain and clouds and sky faded at the touch of an impatient mouth. Steiner stood breathing heavily, his face creased with grief.

He came back to himself when Kruger placed a hand lightly on his shoulder. The men were standing near the horses; he saw their haggard faces above the Russian uniforms, and he saw the woods again. Slowly he descended the steps and beckoned. Then he started across the bridge. The men followed, falling immediately into their weary tread, and the green shade of the woods closed around them.

The wardrobe had been constructed of solid planks. Only on the floor side, where the door now lay, was there a crack the width of a finger; the molding on the bottom raised the wardrobe enough off the floor to admit fresh air. Zoll lay on his stomach, his head resting on his arms, his mouth close to the crack. About ten minutes had passed since Steiner had overturned the wardrobe. Zoll did not move. He had knocked his head against the door in falling and broken his glasses. After trying frenziedly to escape the terrible confinement of his wooden cage, he had given up. He still regarded his uncomfortable situation as one of Steiner's characteristic mean tricks and expected the men to arrive any moment and liberate him. He could already see their grinning faces and was framing what he would say to their jokes. Again and again he asked himself how Steiner, of all people, had happened to come into the room just at the wrong time. Perhaps Schnurrbart had only been faking and it had all been a trick of Steiner's just to catch him, Zoll. Just like that bastard! Zoll cursed himself for a fool for having been tricked this way. In helpless rage he clenched his fists.

Lying motionless again, he thought he heard scratching noises. He raised his head to listen. Perhaps it's the Russian woman, he thought. Steiner had said he would leave her there. Another of his rotten tricks to frighten him. Perhaps the men were already standing around the wardrobe waiting for him to scream for help. Well, he wouldn't give them the satisfaction. On the contrary. He began whistling loudly, and in spite of the pain where the butt of Steiner's gun had smashed across his face, he smiled at the thought of their astonished expressions.

The heat in the wardrobe gradually became unbearable. He felt as if he were in a Turkish bath, and although he was wearing only his shirt and trousers he began to sweat. He thought of Steiner again. He'll pay for this, the bastard, he said to himself; one of these days I'll send a bullet into his spine.

He gritted his teeth and stared frantically into the darkness. The heat grew worse; finally he opened the buttons of his shirt, pulled down his trousers and turned over on his back. I won't let them think they can soften me up, he thought. When they get bored waiting they'll let me out. He closed his eyes and half dozed. Images and words bubbled up out of his memory. He saw himself sitting in the new Mercedes his father had given him for his eighteenth birthday. He saw the faces of the girls who followed the car with their eyes, whose walk slowed as his car cruised by, and who were only too glad to be invited for a drive. "Where shall we drive?" he would ask, and they would always answer, "Anywhere." Zoll grinned at the memory. He knew a great many lonely spots which were the ideal destinations for such drives to "anywhere." For a while he reveled in specific memories, and his excitement returned. He relived his recent experience with the Russian prisoner and considered how he could have improved on it. It always goes too quickly, he thought discontentedly. He clasped his hands behind his neck and lay that way for more than fifteen minutes. Then he began to worry again. It seemed unlikely that Steiner would spin this thing out so long without the other men protesting. He pulled up his trousers, turned over on his stomach and pressed his ear against the side wall of the wardrobe, holding his breath until the strain was too much for him. It was so utterly silent that his uneasiness turned to fear. Suddenly the terrible thought struck him that the platoon might already have left. He forgot his pride and began to cry out. First he called softly, timidly, then louder and louder, until he was emitting long-drawn-out roars. He crooked his body and beat his heels against the bottom of the wardrobe. He dug his hands into the crack of the door and pulled until his fingers were bleeding. At last he lay still, panting for air. It was becoming more and more of a certainty that Steiner had left him behind, locked up in this wardrobe from which he could not escape without aid from outside.

He threw himself on his back and stared into the darkness. Fiery dots danced before his eyes, became glowing circles when he closed his eyelids, whirling madly and shooting sparks in all directions when he opened his eyes again. I must not lose my head, he told himself; I must stay very quiet now. He tried to think. Again he thought he heard noises outside. This time there was no question about it. Before he could determine their meaning, the wardrobe in which he lay began to move. Twice he was jolted hard against the wood, and then the daylight came so suddenly that he closed his eyes, dazzled. Stunned, he pulled himself up to a half-sitting position and blinked in speechless terror at a crowd of mocking faces that were bending over him, at flashing eyes that sent icy chills of terror racing through his body, at rows of breasts bulging out of dirty underwear, and at dozens of hands that reached into the wardrobe, gripped his hair, his clothes, his limbs, pulled him up and hurled him to the floor of the room. As he started to defend himself, his arms and legs were pinioned, his clothes were torn off and a rain of merciless blows beat down upon him.

Just above him was the face of the Russian woman he had raped. Her hair hung in tangled strands over her forehead; her eyes gleamed like green glass lighted from within. She did not strike him or curse him as the others were doing. She only stood stooped above him, staring at him in silence. And as Zoll looked into her face, as the blood ran down his forehead, bubbled out of his nose and mouth, as he jerked and writhed under the kicks and punches that struck every part of his body, as he moaned out his torment between clenched teeth and almost but not quite fainted from the pain, he saw nothing but her face above him. He saw her breasts, still bearing the marks of his teeth, her throat branded with bruises and the pitiless hot fever of her eyes.

Then a pain flashed through him that swallowed up all the other hundred pains, that tore like a red-hot iron into his body. There broke from him a scream that no longer resembled anything human, that came down like a club upon the women's heads, so that they started back and held their ears. They clapped their hands over their ears, but the scream continued. A bestial roar, it reverberated horribly between the walls, on and on, until one of the women shook off the paralysis of horror and with both feet at once jumped on the bellowing, twitching, bleeding body. Then the others sprang on him, stamping and screaming and kicking until the last twitching and the last whimpering were crushed out under their heavy boots. When they at last were done with him and had filed out of the room, a ray of sunlight fell through the window, and the feet of the battered body lay in a pool of flickering light.

IV

CAPTAIN STRANSKY had decided after all not to put off his call on Major Vogel. He set out that same evening. Third Battalion's combat headquarters was located north of Hill 121.4, in the center of a meadow that sloped off to the west. A small brook, its banks lined by dense shrubbery, flowed close by the group of bunkers. When Stransky opened the door to the commander's bunker, he saw by the candlelight that Vogel already had a visitor. Kiesel was sitting across the table from him.

Vogel stood up. "Well, I'll be damned!" he exclaimed. "What a surprise!"

Stransky smiled, trying to conceal his discomfort at the presence of Kiesel. "I hope I'm not intruding," he said.

"Nonsense." Vogel shook hands with him vigorously. "I was expecting you yesterday; glad to see you any time."

He busied himself in a corner of the bunker and then placed several bottles on the table.

Kiesel smacked his lips. "My respects, Vogel. Producing a nineteen thirty-seven Moselle here in the southernmost corner of Russia. Keep that up and you'll be besieged with visitors."

The major began a booming laugh as he uncorked one of the bottles. "Just takes a little organizing talent, gentlemen. Comes natural to an old soldier like me." He filled the glasses. "Then again, a bottle of Moselle is no more absurd in this region than we ourselves. Your health!"

They touched glasses. Stransky sipped the wine delicately. "Splendid, Major," he said. "It's a long while since these parched lips have tasted nectar like this."

The major nodded complacently and dropped a pack of cigarettes on the table. As they lighted up, Stransky looked around the bunker. The staccato flicker of the candles cast the men's shadows on the rough boarding of the walls. The major's bed, crudely knocked together out of wooden slats, was close to the door. At the head of it stood a chest, probably containing clothing. The major's tommy gun, cartridge belt and raincoat hung from nails.

Stransky puffed hard on his cigarette, which was not burning well. When it caught evenly at last, he crossed his legs and turned to the major. "Incidentally, Major Vogel, why does our presence in the bridgehead strike you as absurd?"

Vogel's massive head, capped with snowy, close-cropped hair, jerked up. He pushed his glass a little to one side. "I can tell you that, Herr Stransky," he boomed. "If we have to go on playing fire department, there's no sense in our being several hundred miles away from the heart of the fire. Which is where we are now. That's what makes our presence here absurd."

Stransky frowned. "I don't quite follow you. After all, we are here to carry out a highly important mission. It seems to me that your opinion springs from a certain prejudice. After all—" he smiled politely—"even a force that has been cut off has a function to perform. Wouldn't you say so, Herr Kiesel? Or perhaps you can tell me where our presence would be more useful. It seems to me that the tactical importance of the bridgehead is not open to question."

Before Kiesel could reply, the major's fist pounded down on the table. "Tactical importance? You must mean decorative importance." He leaned forward, propping both elbows on the table. "You must be asleep. Consider the events of this campaign up to the present day." He laughed cuttingly. "It's like the staggering of a blind man, going in one direction until he runs up against a stone wall, then turning and backtracking. Left, right, here, there. You know what it amounts to?" The major's ponderous figure seemed to swell. His eyes flashed wrathfully under his bushy brows. Stransky watched him uncomfortably. "I'll tell you what it is. Sheer waste of strength. Waste. Muddle. Criminal stupidity." Angrily he picked up his glass and took a long swig.

Stransky smiled superciliously. "That's a matter of opinion," he replied coolly. "I do not doubt that you speak from a wealth of experience. But remember, please, that warfare has changed radically since the First World War. We no longer smash forward head on until we're covered with blood—as at Verdun, for example; instead, we seek out the enemy's weak spots. That takes mobility."

"Bah!" Vogel swished his hand through the air. "Spare me that crap. The weak spots, you say? We've picked out the strong points, not the weak spots. Prestige, big names, even if whole armies are chewed up. Look here." He raised his hands and began counting off on his fingers. "First, the boil at Leningrad, then the bloody nose at Moscow, then the amputation at Stalingrad, and finally the carve up of the Caucasus. And what have we achieved? Nothing, not a damn thing! Or do you think we have?"

Stransky suppressed an acrid retort. Vogel looked so choleric that it seemed wiser to him at the moment not to carry the argument too far.

The major refilled their glasses. "What I'd like to know is what we've done wrong," he said tightly.

"We have only continued what was begun by others," Kiesel retorted. "And now, if I am not mistaken, we are on the point of introducing our successors and stepping off the stage of world history."

"You mean the peoples of the East?" the major asked.

Kiesel nodded.

Stransky smiled sourly. "I'm more surprised than impressed," he commented. "It really astonishes me to hear such words from the lips of an active officer. After all, you have seen these Russians. How can you imagine these barbarians being capable of taking over from us?"

Kiesel grinned. "More easily than you think. You must remember that the history of a nation is not written in decades but in centuries and millenia. Communism, for instance, is nothing but the trumpet blast awakening the Eastern peoples from their enchanted sleep. In a few years it will seem obvious that it was only a brief part of their evolution, though a necessary one."

The major seemed to feel that the conversation was reaching a danger point. To change the subject he asked about the Second Company's missing platoon. "You've had no word yet?"

Uncomfortably Stransky said he had not. The major shook his head gravely. "I'm afraid you'll have to write them off. There doesn't seem much hope now. How many men were there?"

"Eleven."

Vogel nodded somberly. "That few won't get far. I know how it is. I was in a situation like that myself once. During the First World War, at Soissons. Damnable business, I tell you. When we started out we were a whole company; eight men came back." He stared gloomily into space.

Stransky seized the opportunity to steer the talk away from the platoon. Turning to Kiesel, he asked, "What do they think of the situation up at Division?"

"The general situation or our own?"

"Our own, of course."

"The Russian preparations indicate a large-scale offensive. Our intelligence people in Krimskaya report the arrival of more and more new divisions."

"Then I imagine we're going to be in for something," the major remarked. "But we'll survive this *bataille* too, At any rate, they won't drive me out of my trench," he added belligerently.

Kiesel smiled. "Spoken like a man!" He had heard a great deal about the battle-scarred old fellow's courage. "As a matter of fact, we have no choice. If the Russians break through anywhere, we're done for."

Stransky nodded animatedly. "I quite agree. Just today I spoke in precisely those terms to my company leaders. We must hold the bridgehead and we will hold it. That is my firm conviction."

"Certainly we will." Kiesel's mouth twisted bitterly. "We will defend ourselves like madmen, convert the entire bridgehead into a huge mass grave, and all to the end that on X Day we can voluntarily withdraw from the heroically defended soil because the general tactical situation requires us to pull out."

"You paint too black a picture," Stransky objected. "Why are you unwilling to see the positive aspects of our situation?

We are pinning down strong enemy forces and relieving the crucial points of the front."

Kiesel said coldly, "You are talking in romantic terms, Captain Stransky. It is ridiculous to imagine that we here can ever make any important contribution toward deciding the issue of the war."

"Bravo!" the major bellowed. "Really now, Stransky, you're talking sheer rot. Every single man we lose is a useless sacrifice." He was angry now, and his eyes flashed fiercely at Stransky, who looked sulky and offended.

"Captain Stransky is entitled to his point of view." Kiesel was obviously trying to save the situation. "It seems to me——" he forced a polite smile—"it seems to me that it is good, for all our sakes, to have officers in our midst who still contrive to see some sense even in a lost position. I wish I could take a similar attitude. It would make many things easier," he added in a low voice.

The major growled and applied himself to his glass. Then he seemed to recall his duties as a host. He took a conciliatory tone. "Good Lord, Stransky, don't set your jaw like a steel trap. I was just shooting my mouth off for a change. No reason for you to get huffy." To Kiesel he added, "It's the *landser* I'm most sorry for. You know, he's the unluckiest invention of this twentieth century of ours. I think Captain Stransky will have to admit that, at least."

Stransky had meanwhile recovered his aplomb; his customary superior smile covered his face like a mask. "I don't see your conclusion," he said. "The fact remains that every soldier suffers privations in wartime. I really don't see why the German soldier is worse off than any other."

"You don't see that?" Again the major pounded the table so hard that the glasses jumped. "I'll explain the reason to you, by God! Our men no longer have any ideals. They're not fighting for world freedom or for the culture of the West. They're not fighting for the kind of government they want. They're fighting for nothing but their naked lives, for their bedeviled, unfortunate flesh. If you don't see that . . ." He was abruptly silent.

Stransky regarded him coldly. "Is that nothing?"

"It is a great deal," Kiesel said. "But it isn't everything. Otherwise, our men would have deserted long ago. Perhaps——" he turned to the major—"perhaps I may add something to your line of argument. Flesh is patient, as paper is patient. It will suffer anything that is put on it. It can be used; it can be abused. And it has suffered abuse because it has been lured with the bait of so-called ideals. It has been killed, and it has been allowed to kill, until it seems to exist only for its own sake. But behind all that there is the common soldier's fundamental decency which doesn't permit him to leave his comrades in the lurch. And there is also a last glimmering spark of hope that everything may still turn out all right in the end."

"In the present situation of our nation," Stransky said frigidly, "such talk borders on treason. I am a soldier and as such it is my duty to subordinate my own ideas to the interests of my country."

Kiesel smiled easily. "We are all doing our duty, Captain Stransky. I hope that history will some day recognize the dreadful battle which responsible German officers have had to fight with their consciences." He leaned forward with an expression of intense seriousness. "To fight for a conviction does not require heroism. Heroism begins where the meaninglessness of the sacrifice remains the last, the only message the dead can leave behind. Never forget that, Captain Stransky."

One of the candles had burned down, and the wick, sagging into the liquid wax, snuffed itself out. The major sat with clasped hands, staring into space. Suddenly he stood up. "Getting late. I must take another look around the positions, if you will excuse me."

Kiesel drained his glass and slowly rose to his feet. Stransky followed his example. The major accompanied them to the door and shook hands with Kiesel. To Stransky he said fiercely, "In this regiment there are no traitors, only human beings endowed with reason. Some use their reason and some don't. To say this may be dialectic and it may be tactless, but that is how I feel about it. Good evening, gentlemen."

When the door had closed behind them, the two officers looked at each other. Stransky, beside himself with rage, blurted, "An impossible man!"

"Do you think so?" Kiesel retorted. "My opinion of Major Vogel was formed long ago, and I have seen no reason to revise it. He is a first-rate soldier of the old school and an admirable person in addition. It is interesting to hear your opinion of him. Good evening." He bowed formally and strode off.

Stransky started up the hill looking neither to right nor left. His mind was entirely possessed by fury, making him incapable of any consecutive thoughts. The land lay dark and still at his feet, a motionless beast with a crooked back, and Stransky felt cold shivers prickling his skin. The rude comforts of his bunker seemed suddenly very good to him and he hastened down the south slope. Halfway down he stopped abruptly. Out of the stars broke a whining noise that swelled rapidly to a fearful roar. Instantly Stransky threw himself to the ground and pillowed his face on his arm. The shell exploded with a shattering boom. A fiery blast of wind swept along the ground, carrying with it the ugly odor of burned powder. Stransky lay numbed; he held his breath and waited faint with fear for the next impact. When the whining began again in the distance, he dug his fingers into the sandy soil and closed his eyes. But this time the whooshing passed high over his head and ended in a dull rumble beyond the hill. Then all was quiet. And the first shells had fallen on Hill 121.4.

For a while Stransky remained lying where he was. But when minute after minute passed without incident, he pulled himself up, blew the sand from his lips and felt his limbs. It seemed a miracle to him that he had not been hurt. Never had death been so close.

Back in his bunker he threw himself down on the cot. For a long while he lay still, staring open-eyed at the ceiling. But each time he thought again of Kiesel, a blaze of rage obliterated cool thought. He began to seek excuses for his conduct. The period in France softened me up, he thought. I'm not the man I was. Certainly those two years in Paris had left their traces on him. He had been commander of a garrison battalion and uncrowned lord of several thousand civilians. Those feasts at the colonel's villa, the French wine, the ladies of easy virtue—he closed his eyes and enjoyed his recollections for a while. Then Stransky saw the colonel's mocking look when he informed him he was asking for a transfer to the eastern front. His parting words rang in Stransky's ears as if they were being spoken at the moment. "I can't stop you," the colonel had said, "since I am convinced that without you the eastern front would collapse in a matter of days. Go ahead, in the devil's name, you heroic fathead." His other friends and acquaintances had shaken their heads in bewilderment, as if he were a man exchanging a mansion on the French Riviera for a straw-roofed kraal in the Congo.

And now after only ten days here, he wished he were back in France. Fortunately his connections were good enough to enable him to transfer back at any time. But it was too soon as yet. First, there was the little matter of filling out the empty space on the front of his tunic. Eyes closed, he tried to picture the Iron Cross on the gray uniform cloth. An oval face appeared before his eyes, a hand touched his arm lightly, and a bewitching voice whispered words that stirred his blood and confused his mind: "I love brave men, men who have more courage than it takes to pay compliments, men who have lain with death as well as with women. . . ."

There was a sudden knock on the door. "Yes!" he called in a strident voice. Lieutenant Triebig entered, pausing in the doorway with a respectful smile. "Forgive me for disturbing you at this late hour, sir. "I'm sorry, but there are a few things for you to sign."

"Let me have the junk," Stransky said crossly. As he glanced through the papers and signed his name, Triebig watched him with his soft eyes, the smile remaining fixed on his face. Stransky finished the batch, pushed the signed papers toward him and looked up quickly. This bird cannot look you straight in the eyes, he thought. Time I found out a little about him. After all, it was of some importance to know what kind of creature lived inside the skin of his adjutant.

Gesturing toward a chair, he tried to inject a cordial note into his voice. "Sit down, won't you? We really have had no chance to exchange a personal word as yet."

"Unfortunately, that's true," Triebig replied politely.

Stransky offered him a cigarette. "How long have you been here—with the battalion, I mean?"

"Four months. The battlion was at Tuapse when I joined it."

"Where had you been stationed before?"

"In the south of France—Bordeaux." Triebig's voice softened.

"Oh!" Stransky raised his head in surprise. "What unit?"

"The Three Hundred Twelfth Infantry. Guarding the coast."

"Then being transferred must have come hard, eh? Why were you transferred, anyway?"

The question caught Triebig off balance. Officially the transfer had come by his own request; unofficially there had been a small incident he preferred not to mention. At an impatient little cough from Stransky he quickly pulled himself together. "I voluntarily applied for a transfer, sir."

Noticing his embarrassment Stransky began to look at him suspiciously. "How interesting."

In the ensuing pause Triebig moved his head restlessly. With mounting apprehension he waited for Stransky to speak again, and was almost overcome with relief when the captain dropped the awkward subject and began to talk about the lovely countryside of southern France. "Believe me, I have seen a good deal of the world, but whenever I visit that region I am enchanted all over again. A beautiful country—its charm is in the very air. One can almost scent it; perhaps it's the closeness of the sea."

Triebig nodded eagerly. "Yes. That's exactly how I felt." He gazed dreamily into a corner of the bunker. It was all present with him again: the undulating blue of the water, the white-pebbled beach, the flickering brightness of the caressing air, the deep, moist green of the palms.

With a little sigh he said, "All of southern France is like one garden. We lived in real mansions right on the beach. Swimming at any hour, day or night. It was indescribable: the sea, the palms, the beaches, the people, everything . . ." Overwhelmed by his memories, he stopped.

Stransky was astonished to see him swallow with emotion. With a knowing smile he winked and said, "The women, you mean."

Triebig raised his head inquiringly. "I beg your pardon?"

"I said: the women. I mean, in referring to the people you meant, of course, the women?"

Triebig shrugged. "Not so much that. I am—that is . . ." He became confused. "I didn't have much time to think about women."

"Come now." Stransky raised his finger jokingly. "Occupation duty and no time for women—I've been in France myself!"

Triebig tried hastily to correct his slip. "Of course there were opportunities now and then," he said. "But to tell the truth, I had other worries."

He felt at once how unsatisfactory this explanation sounded and watched the commander's face uneasily.

Stransky's eyebrows rose. "Other worries? You mean to tell me you had worries in *France?*"

Suddenly Stransky became keenly alert. The story of voluntary transfer sounded fishy. Anyone who talked so enthusiastically about France was unlikely to volunteer for service in Russia. Triebig didn't look the type who would risk a hero's death for the sake of a few medals, and Stransky remembered the man's reluctance to answer when asked the reasons for his transfer. He decided to probe a little further.

"If you had worries in France, that is your affair. It is not my habit to intrude on any man's private life. It is . . ." He stopped abruptly. The relief on Triebig's face was so patent that for a second Stransky lost his thread. But he caught himself quickly and continued the conversation in an even, casual voice. "Are you married?"

Triebig shook his head. "No, sir. When would I have had a chance to marry? I was only twenty when I started at Officers Training School. That didn't leave much time for anything like that."

"I suppose not," Stransky agreed. His next question was a cautious generality: "Do you like soldiering?"

"Certainly," Triebig declared with emphasis.

Stransky nodded patronizingly. "I'm glad to hear that."

"It's like living in an altogether different world," Triebig added.

The candle had burned down. Stransky rose and lighted another. Then he sat down again. "It would interest me—" he folded his arms across his chest—"to hear your definition of the differences between this world and the world of the civilian."

Triebig smiled, abashed. "Hard to say, sir. I suppose it's something in the environment, in the atmosphere . . ." He shrugged. "I really don't know."

"You are a keen observer," Stransky remarked innocuously. "But after all, isn't it always the people who make the environment, who provide the atmosphere?"

"Certainly."

Stransky lighted another cigarette and dropped the burning match to the floor. He waited until it went out. The suspicion he had been nursing during the past few minutes began to assume a definite shape.

"It is indeed a very different world, the one we live in," he said. "A world of danger and a world of men, a world without women. You know, Triebig, we experience it in ourselves. Things that seemed simply impossible in the past, in ordinary civilian life, happen here." He laughed. "For example, in the army it becomes apparent that men are not absolutely dependent on women after all. It's an old idea of mine that we men can get along even without women. Dependency on women seems to me a regrettable flaw in the male character. I tell you, man's truly natural destiny is not to breed children, but rather to be free, to rule and fight— in other words, to lead a man's existence in which women are no more than a fancy but superfluous dessert. Or do you disagree?"

Triebig looked up at him in great confusion. For a moment Stransky wondered whether he had not gone too far. But no, he had nothing to fear from the man. The bait was good; if his suspicion proved correct, Triebig was sure to bite.

He was momentarily disappointed. Triebig remained extremely reserved. His sense of caution, sharpened by many bad experiences, had been alerted. Intertwining his fingers, he regarded his thumb thoughtfully. "I don't think I disagree, sir." He hesitated. If Stransky was seriously feeling his way to an offer, he must not put obstacles in the way. He had played this nerve-racking game of words dozens of times and thought he could trust himself to risk a step further.

He forced himself to adopt a tone as innocent and casual as possible. "This seems to me an individual matter. There are men who simply cannot live without women and others who never have been dependent on them."

"And which class do you feel you belong to?" Stransky asked.

Triebig hesitated again. "That depends," he said tentatively. "I think that if I have to I can live without women."

"I'm pleased to hear that," Stransky declared. For a moment he studied the burning tip of his cigarette. Then he looked up quickly. "In other words, you prefer the company of a man to that of a woman?"

Triebig, eyes half closed, scrutinized him. He felt himself breaking into a sweat, and he shifted uneasily about in his chair. From here on every word could turn into a booby trap. "It depends on the situation."

"Really?" Stransky smiled. Triebig did not reply. "Wearing a uniform does not relieve you of the obligation to display a certain amount of ordinary, everyday courage. But if it will help you, I shall put your thoughts into words for you." Stransky's smile broadened. "You prefer the society of men to that of women in any and all situations."

The words hung in the silence of the bunker in all their brutal nakedness. Triebig retreated into himself like a snail sealing itself up in its shell. His chin trembled and he stared with mingled fear, assent and hope at Stransky's face, which still registered nothing but friendly interest. Afraid silence might be interpreted as agreement, Triebig murmured, "I did not say that, sir."

Stransky nodded reassuringly. He felt convinced that he was on the right track and decided to risk everything on a single card. Softly, insistently, he said, "Certainly you did not say it, but I wish you would." He smiled confidentially. "Let's drop the hide and seek. By God, Triebig, you don't have to put on a front with me, of all people. What I said is true, isn't it? Say yes, man, for heaven's sake."

Triebig felt his mouth opening. He wanted to stop himself, but the word was already said.

The smile on Stransky's face went out at once. He dropped back into his chanr, staring at Triebig as though seeing him for the first time. His eyes filled with contempt. "How very, very interesting, Lieutenant," he drawled, "extremely interesting indeed. To tell the truth, I've never had dealings with one of your kind before."

Triebig stared at him appalled, his mouth partly open as though he were on the point of screaming. "I don't understand, sir . . ." he stammered.

"You understand me very well," Stransky replied savagely. "Do you take me for a fool? You said yes, didn't you?"

Triebig, lips quivering, did not answer.

Stransky sprang to his feet directly in front of him. "Speak out," he bellowed. "You said yes. Don't you dare lie to my face. You said yes, didn't you?"

At the sight of the enraged face only inches away from his own, Triebig closed his eyes in terror. When Stransky gripped his shoulders and shook him, he nodded feebly. "Yes."

At once Stransky released him, took a step back and ordered, "Stand up!"

Trembling, Triebig obeyed.

Slowly Stransky looked him up and down. His voice was under control again as he said, "I can assure you of this: if I catch you trying any of that stuff, I'll have you hanged, remember that! Now get the hell out of here and keep out of my sight for the next twenty-four hours. . . . Get out!" he suddenly shouted as Triebig stood immobile.

For a second Triebig looked at the commander's distorted face. Then he wheeled around, stumbled across the threshold and vanished. Stransky remained in the same spot for several minutes. Then he fished for a cigarette, lighted it and smiled. For the first time in a week he was completely satisfied with himself and with the world at large.

Triebig stood in front of the bunker, gazing wild-eyed at the trees. From the trenches came the occasional hammering of a machine gun. Isolated rifle shots sounded disturbingly close, and tracer bullets whished in fiery trails above the dark hills. For a long while Triebig stood unmoving, incapable of a coherent thought. He felt his whole being trampled on, humiliated, reduced to a pulp. Finally he moved off toward his bunker on unsteady legs. He stumbled down the steps, closed the door and dropped onto his cot like a stone. I must shoot myself, he thought; I must shoot myself at once. He groped for his pistol. But when he felt the cool steel against his forehead, he lowered his arm and with a sudden, violent movement hurled the gun to the floor. Then he turned over, pressed his face against the blanket and began to sob unrestrainedly.

He made up his mind to kill Stransky.

V

LATE in the afternoon the platoon came upon the Russians. They had just skirted a sizable patch of swamp when a horse led by Dietz suddenly broke loose and galloped wildly off between the trees. The men stopped and looked accusingly at Dietz, who was staring in a daze at the place where the horse had been. Since it was carrying part of their rations on its back, they felt the loss keenly.

"Idiot!" Kruger exclaimed in a fury.

Steiner came striding toward them. "Can't you keep hold of a rope?" he shouted at Dietz. "You get that beast back or I'll show you something."

Dietz stared for a second at his enraged face. Then he turned and dashed after the runaway horse. His feet were covered with blisters; for the past few hours he had only barely managed to keep going. But now he forgot his pain and exhaustion. He must make good his carelessness and bring back the horse. For a few minutes he ran on among the trees and underbrush, stumbling, falling, picking himself up, scratching his face and hands on thorns and twigs till the blood ran. He panted on but slowed to a walk. Then he gave up. He leaned against a tree and dug his clenched fists into his heaving chest. Tears streamed down his face.

It was beginning to grow dark among the trees, and the woods were formidably silent. Turning his head a little, Dietz suddenly caught sight of the Russians. They were standing about a dozen yards away from him, not moving, just staring at him. There were five men in long overcoats, with sheepskin-banded caps, their tommy guns pointing at him. Dietz gaped. But he felt no fear, nothing but a vast astonishment that gradually seeped throughout his entire body and transformed his legs into wooden posts buried deep in the earth. Then he suddenly remembered the platoon. He must tell Steiner about the Russians at once, must warn the men. How surprised they would be! They would certainly forgive him the loss of the horse. This thought so comforted him that he almost forgot the menace of the Russians. When they began to move slowly toward him, he pulled his numbed legs out of the ground and rushed blindly off. At his back he heard a shout and he hunched his head between his shoulders. How surprised the others will be, he thought, how surprised they'll be. His face was contorted, but he smiled expectantly at the thought of the impression his news would make.

The shouting behind him grew louder. It bothered him, made it hard to think, but did not seem to mean very much. Suddenly something hit him in the back and threw him forward on his face. Above his head sounded the hysterical hammering of several submachine guns at once. At first he thought someone had thrown a rock at him, and he remained lying where he was, startled. Above him the bullets hissed, slapped into the trees, hummed through the air as they ricocheted. Why are they firing like crazy? Dietz thought. He tried to get up. Then he realized that his body would no longer obey him. His arms felt dead, and there was a dull, painful pressure against his back. With great effort he managed to slip his hand underneath his pack, but he could feel nothing in particular. When he tried to turn on his side, a fiery pain shot through his chest. He let his face sink to the ground and began to whimper.

After Dietz ran off in pursuit of the horse, the men sat down on the ground, their heads bent with weariness. Steiner remained standing near the other horses. It would soon be dark, and the end of the forest was nowhere in sight. During the march he had discovered that the horses were a hindrance rather than a help; their obstinacy constantly made for delay. He would long ago have released them and chased them off if he had not been worried about the condition of the men. They had been marching almost without interruption and were completely exhausted. Under normal conditions they would have covered three times the distance they had managed to march. But the ever recurring barricades of thorny undergrowth, the miles of swampy ground, the many narrow streams had forced them to swing in countless wide detours and had eaten up their strength. Their original intention to use the road had had to be abandoned since the Russian's escape. They had followed it for only a few hundred yards beyond the brook, then had struck out by compass in a southwesterly direction straight across the woods. Since the road wound and turned, they had quickly diverged from it and were now somewhere in the heart of the pathless forest.

Cursing under his breath, Steiner glanced at his watch. Three minutes had passed since Dietz had gone after the horse, and Steiner suddenly felt an intense uneasiness. "I'll see how he's getting along," he said. As he struck out in the direction Dietz had taken, he reflected that his order had been idiotic. Once a horse started running a man could not catch up with it, anyway. He speeded his pace. Since orientation was impossible in these dense woods, he relied on instinct. He had gone no more than three hundred yards when off to the right he heard voices calling. He stopped as abruptly as if he had run head on into a tree, and raised his head to listen. The calls became a furor of shouts, but he could distinctly hear single words. Russians, he thought with a stab of alarm. He peered into the darkening woods.

When the firing began, he doubled over, leaped behind a tree and raised his tommy gun. The air was suddenly filled with a vicious hissing; ricochets slapped into the tree trunks, buzzed by his head like hummingbirds and landed with a dull patter on the soft forest floor. It might be too late if he waited to get the men. If Dietz were still alive—and the Russians wouldn't be shooting if he weren't—there was not a second to lose. He dodged from tree to tree for about fifty feet. Then he began to fire at random, holding the muzzle of the gun high. Once he thought he glimpsed a dark form among the trees. But since it might be Dietz, he held his fire. Then he realized that the invisible enemy was concentrating on him. Bullets hissed over his head. Cursing, he darted behind a tree. He was in a fix. If the Russians realized they had only a single man to deal with, they would surround him quickly.

His fears were confirmed immediately. From the right side a machine gun began hammering away, frightfully close. Disregarding all caution, he exposed himself, blazing away blindly between the trees. Then he tumbled rapidly a few yards to one side, behind the next tree. The flanking fire had stopped; perhaps he had hit someone. The rattling of the guns continued only from in front, where a strip of dense underbrush cut across the woods. He tried in vain to make out the flash from the hidden enemy guns, but it was still too light. For a while he lay motionless, watching the cone of fire high above his head. They'll strip the leaves from the trees if they keep firing like this, he thought, and rolled a few yards further away.

His excitement began to subside. He had survived worse situations, after all. Had he not been worried about the platoon, he would have felt almost serene. In another ten minutes it would be too dark for the Russians to do anything. Flattening out behind the shaggy trunk of a black birch, he looked around alertly. The random fire of the Russians continued to lash through the leaves high up. He did not answer it. What could have happened to Dietz? He hoped the boy had not been hit. After all, the sight of his Russian uniform must have caused some confusion, to say the least. Undoubtedly he was crouching somewhere among the trees, waiting for full darkness to come. Where could the others be? Even as he thought this, hell broke loose behind him.

When the din of the skirmish started, the men had leaped to their feet and looked about them in shocked surprise. Kruger stammered, "Steiner," and looked at Schnurrbart.

Schnurrbart was silent. When he took the tommy gun from his shoulder, his hands shook. "Bring the horses with you," he said to Pasternack. "Take the ammunition off them."

He began to pull boxes of ammunition from the horses and issued curt orders which the men obeyed in feverish haste. A few seconds later they rushed forward toward the increasing clatter of rifles and submachine guns. When the first bullets began whistling over their heads, they scattered and began to answer the firing.

Suddenly they came upon Steiner, who had sat up facing in their direction. Maag noticed him first and burst out shouting. The men stopped firing and Steiner came dashing toward them. As soon as they recognized him, they felt an enormous relief.

"What luck!" Kruger stammered. He slapped Steiner on the shoulder. "What'll we do?" he asked hastily. "Where's Dietz?"

"We'll have to look for him," Steiner said nervously. The firing from the other side had stopped abruptly.

"They've run off," Anselm declared. "How many were there?" he asked Steiner.

"I don't know."

For a moment they stood around irresolutely, until Schnurrbart grunted with impatience. "Think we should follow them?" he asked.

Steiner shook his head. "What for? We'll look for Dietz and then clear out of here as fast as possible. Where are the horses?"

Schnurrbart jerked his thumb back, where Pasternack had just appeared with the horses.

"Let's start," Steiner said. "He must be somewhere near by."

They scattered among the trees and began searching the ground. Since Russians might still be lurking in the vicinity, they moved with extreme caution. After a while they risked calling Dietz's name. It had grown much darker, and the search became increasingly difficult. Once or twice Steiner thought of sending up a flare, but it seemed to him too dangerous. His foreboding mounted. If Dietz were anywhere near, he should have heard them calling. Perhaps it would be better to spend the night here and continue the search next morning. Suddenly he heard his own name called. He recognized the Professor's voice and hurried toward it. As he approached he made out the rest of the men, gathered in a cluster and looking toward him.

"What is it?" he asked hoarsely.

There was a moment of silence. Then Kruger spoke up: "Here he is." A dark bundle lay on the ground.

In spite of the gloom Steiner recognized Dietz at once. He knelt down beside him, removed his pack and turned him over on his back. Kruger switched on a shielded flashlight and Steiner unbuttoned Dietz's coat. The men leaned forward as Steiner opened the little fellow's shirt. There was a low sigh of relief as they saw no sign of a wound on chest or stomach. Then their features froze, mouths open. Steiner had turned Dietz over and was staring incredulously at two holes the size of hazelnuts below the right shoulder blade. There was no trace of blood, just a pink circle around the edges of the wounds.

"Verdammt," Kruger whispered. The flashlight in his hand shook.

"Is he dead?" Anselm asked.

Steiner did not answer. He placed him arm around Dietz's waist and raised him up. Then he began quickly bandaging the wounds. Dietz's heart was still beating, though rapidly and irregularly.

"Bring the horses," he said curtly.

They tied the two horses close together, made a litter of shelter-halves and cautiously raised Dietz to the backs of the horses. Not a word was spoken all the while.

"We must get out of here," Steiner declared. He turned

to Kruger. "You and Schnurrbart follow at a distance. Make sure the Russians aren't following us."

He slung his gun over his shoulder and started back in the direction from which they had come. Pasternack and Dorn led the horses; the others walked behind to guard againt Dietz's falling off. It was pitch dark. Stars shone now and then through the leafy roof. The crack of dried branches under their boots sounded alarmingly loud. Schnurrbart and Kruger followed at a considerable distance, stopping now and then to look back. The woods appeared deserted.

"They've cleared out." Kruger sighed. "It would be Dietz; that's all we needed."

Schnurrbart nodded. "That's only the beginning," he said. "The Ivans have picked up our trail now; just wait till daylight."

"*Scheisse*," Kruger said. He suddenly thought of Zoll. "That dirty bastard," he growled. "If only I could lay hands on him."

"Who?"

"Who do you think? Zoll, of course."

Schnurrbart was silent for a moment. "He paid for it, don't worry."

"What do you mean?"

Schnurrbart shrugged and said nothing.

"The whole forest must be swarming with patrols by now," Kruger muttered. "And when we get out of the forest, what a reception they're going to give us!"

Schnurrbart sighed.

Dietz was walking last in line, leading the horse by the reins and suffering terribly from thirst. Suddenly the horse pulled loose and Steiner came raging toward him. From that menacing face Dietz fled into the woods, running behind the horse. Often it was so close he thought he could reach out and grasp it. But it was always faster than he and escaped each time. He stretched out his arms, called and sobbed. Suddenly the horse stood still. But as he approached he was horrified to see that it had turned into a Russian with five heads, glaring at him with ten fiery eyes. He began to scream and the five-headed Russian began to scream, and as he stared at those malignant faces they merged into a single huge face with gaping maw, shouting at him, and abruptly he recognized it as the foreman stooping to pick up a monstrous brick. He turned and ran as fast as he could, making off among the trees, and the screams behind him grew worse, until something hard struck him in the back and threw him to the ground, where he lay sobbing.

Then it seemed to him he was lifted up. Somewhere sweet voices sang a song of unearthly beauty. He raised his head, incredulous, and a happy smile passed over his face. Someone told him he must sing also. He opened his mouth and sang: "Oh, the mountains, Oh, the valleys." Tears streamed down his cheeks; he could no longer sing because he was sobbing so hard. But he closed his eyes and listened, deeply stirred, until the song faded away.

When he opened his eyes again, his first impression was of a gentle rocking motion that lulled him and aroused beautiful images. He saw himself at home in Eger, walking through the streets of the older part of the city, going down to the riverbank and skipping flat stones over the water. He got into a boat and rowed upstream until he tired. As he let the current carry him back, he gazed dreamily at the green woods of the Fichtelgebirge and saw himself hiking among the quiet valleys and out-of-the-way villages. The boat rocked over the still water and the sun shone warm and pleasant. But suddenly his mother's harsh, complaining voice rang out, scolded him, called him a good-for-nothing for loafing around instead of working. Now he felt sad again; bitterness wrapped him in a black mantle that grew heavier and heavier, dragging him down to the ground, burying him.

A long while later, years afterward it seemed, he opened his eyes and saw Steiner's grave face. He tried to sit up, but Steiner held him firmly. "Lie where you are, Baby; you must lie very quiet."

"Lie very quiet," Dietz whispered obediently, and sank back.

Steiner glanced at his watch. It was an hour after midnight. He turned his head and looked over toward the others. All except the sentry were wrapped in their blankets sound asleep. The horses, necks lowered, stood among the tall, grim trees that surrounded the little clearing. They had reached this place after two hours of trudging through the dark woods, and Steiner had decided to stop here for the night. After arranging the order of sentry duty, he sat down beside Dietz, pillowed his head on his arms and spent the time in anguished vigil. When Dietz began to stir, he switched on the flashlight and examined his face. He knew that expression; he had seen it hundreds of times before. There were dark hollows under the cheekbones; the skin was drawn taut and waxen over the jaw, and the eyes were sunk in deep shadows that seemed to be spreading out slowly, consuming the rest of the face. Dietz would not live through the night. And since Steiner realized this, something inside him snapped. Yet he was unable really to feel grief.

A while later, when Dietz opened his eyes again, he bent over him and asked, "Are you in pain?" His own voice grated.

Dietz stared at him wide-eyed. Then he moved his head slightly and murmured, "Thirsty." He drank from the canteen Steiner held to his mouth and sighed gratefully.

"Enough?" Steiner asked.

Dietz nodded. He was probably fully conscious and he seemed to be aware of the cold water running down his throat, filling his stomach, spreading through all the channels of his body. But when he tried to speak the events of the day just passed were tangled in an inextricable knot with the fading images of his recent delirium. He turned his head slightly. "What's the matter with me?"

Steiner did not answer at once.

Dietz's voice took on a plaintive note. "Tell me what's the matter with me. Why won't you tell me?"

Steiner swallowed. "Nothing much," he said roughly. "You were creased by a bullet, that's all." He hesitated, and then added with forced cheerfulness, "That's all, really."

"Is it bad?"

"No, just a crease, I tell you. Nothing to worry about."

"That isn't true," Dietz stated. There was such certainty in his voice that Steiner caught his breath.

"What isn't true?" he asked helplessly.

"That it's nothing much. Don't lie to me; I can feel myself that my whole chest is smashed."

"There's nothing wrong with your chest," Steiner said. "You were just nicked in the back, that's all." He felt the perspiration starting on his forehead. "Tomorrow we'll fix up a stretcher on the horses and take you to the battalion. By day after tomorrow you'll be on the hospital train and headed for home."

Dietz did not reply. As soon as Steiner mentioned the horses, he remembered what had happened. Raising his head, he whispered, "I'm sorry, I mean, about the horse, that it got away from me. I couldn't . . ."

Steiner interrupted him. "My God, don't worry about the goddamn horse. We meant to get rid of it anyhow."

"You mean that?"

"Of course I do or I wouldn't say it."

Dietz closed his eyes and thought hard. He had been running behind the horse and had not been able to catch it. Then he had stood still, and then . . . He opened his eyes wide and let out a terrible cry.

The men started up, dazed and alarmed. The scream continued to issue out of Dietz like an endless coil of sound unwinding and unwinding from his throat. The men haltingly drew near. "He'll have the Russians on our necks," Kern said anxiously.

Steiner held the flashlight close to Dietz's face. "Be quiet now—there's no need to be afraid, we're all with you." At last the screaming stopped. "If only we had a medic with us," Steiner said. "He ought to have a shot of morphine."

"He wanted to be a doctor," Pastternack said. After a pause he asked, "Do you think he'll make it?"

Steiner did not reply. At last he looked up. "You fellows better lie down again."

"Lie down yourself," Schnurrbart said. "I'll relieve you. You have to get a few hours' sleep too."

Steiner shook his head. "I'm not tired."

The men returned to their places. When Steiner noticed Schnurrbart still beside him, he frowned. "What's the matter?" he said irritably. "I told you I'm not tired."

"Don't be so pigheaded," Schnurrbart said.

Steiner opened his mouth to reply angrily, but Dietz spoke first. Neither of the other had noticed that his eyes were open. "You mustn't bicker," he said softly. "Why are you bickering again?"

Steiner turned swiftly toward him. "We aren't bickering."

"You are bickering. Make up, please, make up."

Steiner switched off the flashlight. "Please," Dietz whispered. Steiner glanced at Schnurrbart, motionless beside him. He could feel Dietz reaching out for his hands in the darkness, and soothingly ran his palm over the boy's damp forehead. "Please." The word was barely breathed.

He nodded. Then he realized that Dietz could not see the movement of his head. Leaning over him, he framed the words, "I will."

When he looked up again, he saw Schnurrbart softly walking away. Dietz lay motionless. Steiner looked down at the bright oval of his face. The woods were very still. Then a rustling began among the trees, and as it grew stronger the dying man's face underwent a strange transformation. The lines narrowed, became thinner and more delicate. The eyebrows arched high beneath a clear, white forehead; the ears were hidden in an abundance of wanton, chestnut-brown curls. Steiner held his breath and bent over him. Dark rings danced before his eyes, but he could see the face before him with great distinctness. . . .

Lips, red and softly parted, reveal small, shining teeth, and big dark eyes bent on his in utter despair. His strength is giving out. He sees the snowflakes on her face, and his bare hands ache unbearably in the frightful cold. A few minutes before, she slipped on the narrow, steep mountain trail. He threw himself forward and grasped her outstretched hands. Then he slid, slid until he managed to hook his feet on something. Now he lies pressed flat against the ground, her face directly below his. She is dangling free over the cliff, while his fingers dig into her hands. He knows she is lost, and he stares into her face. She opens her mouth and speaks, but her words do not penetrate to his mind. It is as if he were dead and seeing nothing but her eyes. . . .

"You have no heart, Anne."

"Yes, I do, Rolf. Here, I'll show you I have." She places his hand on her small breast. It is always this way. When he becomes importunate, she disarms his impatience with a "No" and a simple gesture.

He shakes his head. "You don't know how tough this is on me."

"I do know, Rolf."

"A hell of a lot of good that does, then."

"Be patient with me."

He sighs, takes her face in his hands and examines it. His eyes rest on her lips, and he says, "Your mouth."

"What about my mouth?"

"I don't know. . . ." He laughs, abashed. "You see, once a man kisses it he never gets over it."

"Don't talk that way, Rolf. It sounds so strained and . . ." Her eyes avoid his, and she looks grave. "And so sad," she adds. Suddenly she throws herself into his arms. Pressing him close to her, she exclaims, "Will you always be fond of me?"

"What would I be without you?"

When he tries to sit up, she holds him fast by the hair. "That isn't an answer. Promise me."

It is still and warm. Above the meadow the air quivers and the trees reach up toward the sun. A butterfly wings past them and vanishes in the grass. Slowly he gropes out for her hand, brings it to his mouth.

"Always," he says, "always." When she laughs happily, he draws her head to his chest and whispers, "I must tell you this: You are everything that is lovely." He gazes over her head at the woods, where the mountain lunges toward the sky, and goes on: "You are like the air above the glaciers, and you are all the things I cannot understand because I am dazzled when I look at them. You are yourself, and ever so much more."

Slowly she turns her face toward him, and he sees her tears. "Say that again," she whispers.

But he shakes his head. "That sort of thing can be said only once, as all good things can be really experienced only once."

She leans her head against his chest again and says, "You talk like my father."

He smiled. "And you still behave like a child of fourteen."

"Why do you say that?"

He places his hand on her firm, slender thighs, whose nakedness he can feel through the thin white skirt. "That's why."

For a few seconds they are silent. Then she brushes a strand of dark hair away from his forehead and says, "Let us save the best for later."

"How do you know it is good at all?" he asks quietly. "Some people say it is ugly."

She leans against him, and in a confusion of feeling he is conscious of the pressure of her breasts against his shoulder. "It must be," she says pensively. "If it weren't, it would not mean so much to you."

Her wisdom is such that he has to shake his head. "You're an incredible girl." He frowns. "Before I met you I did not know what a human being could be."

"And now you do know?"

"Yes."

"Oh, Rolf!" She presses against him. "Sometimes I'm so frightened."

He looks at her in surprise. "Frightened. You, Anne? For heaven's sake, what are you afraid of?"

For the space of a few heartbeats she looks down at the ground, hesitant. Then she lifts her shoulders. "You're right, of course; I'm a silly child. But you see, you're going away again day after tomorrow, and last night Father said there might be a war and then you'd certainly go into the army and then you and I would . . ." Suddenly she begins to sob. When he tries to kiss her to comfort her, she shakes her head violently.

He waits until she is calmer. Then he says, "Your father is foolish. Even if there were a war, it would be over in a month."

There is a note of forced confidence in his voice, and she looks up quickly. "Would you promise me something, please?" He looks at her questioningly. "If there is a war you must come to our place, in Zürich. Father can get you a job and you can stay with us until the war is over. Promise me that?"

"That's impossible, Anne," he says, gravely and firmly. She turns away, disappointed, and he places a hand on her arm. "Be sensible, sweet. A man cannot simply desert. You can escape the law and the guardians of the law, but you can't escape your own conscience. I can't, anyway," he adds, in a lowered voice.

She looks down at the ground, pouting. "But you can escape from me, can't you? You can go away from me, perhaps for years, just on account of your miserable war. I don't matter to you. That's what you mean to say, don't you?"

"You're being unreasonable," he says, troubled. "I've never known you to be like this. Look . . ." He lies down again and draws her down beside him. "You must understand. If I go away from you, I know that we will be parting only for a short time. But if I desert from home, I can never go back again. I'd have to remain an exile, an outcast. Is that what you want?"

She does not answer. His eyes rest on the gathering clouds in the sky. It is going to rain, he thinks. Anne is lying beside him, eyes shut. He sees that her shoulders are quivering, and gently takes her hand. "You must understand that," he says softly, "and you don't want me to be a fish out of water. You can't want that, Anne; you're not so selfish." When she shakes her head, he kisses her. They lie close together, looking up at the silvery cone of the mountaintop.

Suddenly Anne sits up and says, "But I have one thing to ask that you mustn't refuse."

"If it's something I can do, certainly."

"I want to climb up there again tomorrow. Up our mountain once more." Seeing his worried frown, she bends over him and looks pleadingly into his eyes. "We can take the first train tomorrow morning. We'll be here by four o'clock, and there'll be plenty of time."

"The weather is changing," he says, eying the clouds.

She shakes her head willfully. "Tomorrow will be fair."

It is hard for him to refuse. There is fresh snow on the peak and he knows how unpredictable the weather is at this time of year. Still . . . Indecisive, he sits up. The political situation has been going from bad to worse these past few weeks; war is no longer so unimaginable. Although he has said nothing to Anne about his own fears, he knows she is right. This may be their last chance to be together for a long time. And if we don't reach the peak, it doesn't matter; we can turn back, he tells himself. It is "their" mountain. That was where they had met two years ago, at the peak. As she kisses him, he nods assent. . . .

Again and again he tries to find some support for his elbows, to draw in his arms, to pull her back up. But he no longer has the strength. She is still holding her head up, her eyes fixed on his face. The wind is letting up, but the snow continues to fall in big wet flakes. His arms and hands are numb, insensible. Lying face down on the slope, his head lower than his body, has brought a rush of blood to his head; there is a dull roaring in his ears. He is aware that he is gradually losing control over his body. Her face is wet. He sees the snowflakes thawing on her skin, and wants to reach out and wipe them away; he sees her lips twitching; sees the mortal fear in her eyes; and he gasps words that are intended to comfort her and that are only the inarticulate utterance of his horror. When she suddenly closes her eyes, he realizes that the grip of his hands has loosened. . . .

The roaring in his ears continued with unremitting intensity. Steady, monotonous, it seemed to fill all the air, beating its way into his consciousness, bringing him back to reality. When he sat up, he felt the dampness on his back and lifted his face in bewilderment. It was raining. The crowns of the trees were whipping about in the wind, but he knew this only from the sound; the trees themselves were lost in darkness. For a few seconds he peered about him, uncomprehending. Then he realized that his hands were clutched around something soft that felt strangely cold and lifeless. With a surge of disgust he let go and stood up. His clothes were soaked to the skin. He shivered. What has happened? he wondered. Then he was back in the present. The forest, the platoon and . . . Dietz. He knew at once that Dietz was dead. He felt along the ground until he touched the flashlight, snapped it on. Dietz's mouth was open and the whites of his eyes gleamed under half-shut lids. He was already scarcely recognizable. With horror Steiner thought that he had been clutching Dietz's hands all this while. Quickly he stooped, tugged the woolen blanket from under the dead man, and covered his face. Then he looked toward the sleeping men.

He saw Schnurrbart walking slowly toward him. He switched off the light. He could feel nothing at all. The forest panted and groaned under the assault of the wind. "He's dead," Steiner said. The storm wrenched the words from his lips. He held his face up to the rain, listened for a moment with closed eyes and repeated, "He's dead." Gripping Schnurrbart's arm, he drew him across the clearing to the shelter of the trees. Then he slung the pack off his back, unbuckled the blanket and shelter-halves and spread them out on the ground. They sat down, drew the canvas over their shoulders and stared into the tumultuous darkness.

Later, when the storm had let up somewhat, Schnurrbart said, "There was no saving him."

Steiner nodded in the darkness. He had known that wounds like that were hopeless.

"And it's really best for him," Schnurrbart went on. "We would have had to carry him all the way, and try to get him across the Russian lines. Couldn't have been done." Steiner nodded again.

Schnurrbart laid a hand on his arm. "We mustn't let it get us down," he said beseechingly. "Don't forget what we still have before us. We've never been in anything like this before —not so bad as this."

"I know."

Schnurrbart tried worriedly to see the expression on the other man's face. The tone of Steiner's voice bothered him. "Then you have to keep your chin up," he said. "Wish I knew what's been the matter with you lately. You used to be a lot different, Rolf."

"I know," Steiner said. A gust of wind shook the leaves above them and sent huge drops of rain down on their heads. Schnurrbart felt helpless. He had never liked Steiner at those times when he seemed cynical and superior. But now he wished that Steiner were like that. He had been on his mind for the past few hours. In the past, in similar tight places, Steiner had always seemed to grow more confident as difficulties mounted. His present state was incomprehensible; not even the death of Dietz could explain it. Still, the death might be a factor. He would see.

"Sooner or later it will get us all," he said experimentally. "Doesn't matter much who comes first and who last." Steiner did not answer. Schnurrbart went on: "I always liked the boy, but damn it all . . ." He spat on the ground and stared grimly into the darkness.

Steiner moved so abruptly that Schnurrbart started. "Do you believe in God?" he asked.

Schnurrbart recovered quickly. The answer to that question had been given him in his childhood, and he had carried it with him. The subject was beyond discussion. "Do I believe in

God? Of course I do. At any rate I believe we are dependent on Someone who decides our fate."

Steiner smiled grimly. It was the answer he had expected. "You make things easy for yourself," he said. "I had the same idea once. But if there is a God, He's a sadist. That's my firm conviction."

"You're crazy." Schnurrbart was alarmed by the blasphemy. He shook his head. "You really are. Otherwise you'd see that all creation doesn't indicate sadism but . . . I suppose the word for it is love. Can you deny that?"

"I won't go into it," Steiner said contemptuously. "What about the other side? If I'm dying of thirst and someone gives me a pail of water, that's love, would you say?"

Wondering where this was leading, Schnurrbart nodded half-heartedly.

"Good." Despite the darkness Steiner had detected the movement. "So that's love. But if this Someone takes the pail of water away from me when I've only had a swallow or two, that's love too, is it?" When Schnurrbart did not reply, Steiner leaned closer to him. "You haven't an answer to that one, have you? I'll tell you the name for it. It's sadism, dirty rotten sadism, the kind of trick a real bastard would think of. That's my opinion, anyway; you can stick that on your hat."

Schnurrbart closed his eyes, confused, groping for a new right answer. For a while there was no sound but the swish of the rain. When Schnurrbart spoke again, his voice was tight. "That's what you say, brother. Speak for yourself. I'll tell you this: there are certain people who go on for so long hankering for a pail of water that's disappeared that they die of thirst, when all the while a brook is flowing past them a few feet away. Good night." He stood up abruptly and walked off.

The following morning they buried Dietz. It was still raining, and the clouds hung low in the sky. The men dug a rectangular hole and stood soaked and shivering. A cold wind blasted across the clearing. When Steiner stepped up to the hole, the others silently approached. They had rolled Dietz in a tent canvas; he lay in the deep pit, small and inoffensive. The men held their short-handled spades in their hands.

"What are we waiting for?" Kern asked irritably.

Steiner sized up their dirty, unshaven faces. "Maybe I intend to hold a funeral service," he replied hoarsely. He wiped the rain from his face with his sleeve. "It's something we don't usually bother with," he went on, "but he deserves one. If Dietz had died at home, a few score, maybe even a hundred, people would be standing around his grave, in their best dark clothes. Some would be crying because they really felt bad, and others because it was the thing to do." He wiped his face again. They stared at him spellbound. "And if they met again later on they would say, 'So young; it's always the best who go first.' And they'd look sanctimoniously down at their bellies and be glad they still had bellies—the goddamned overstuffed bastards!" he suddenly shouted.

The men flinched. Schnurrbart, beside him, noticed that Steiner's shoulders were heaving.

"A few weeks later they would have forgotten him," Steiner went on. "I hope none of you will forget him. I should be sorry for anyone who did."

He stooped and threw a handful of the black earth into the grave. Wordlessly they all set to work closing the grave.

An hour later they set out, tent canvas over their shoulders; the rain had not abated. They led two of the horses, on which they had loaded the machine gun's heavy ammunition boxes. They had driven the other horses away. Since they might run into Russians at any moment, they held their guns ready to fire and moved cautiously, keeping a sharp lookout.

Schnurrbart talked in whispers with Dorn. "That was a funny business, but typical Steiner."

Dorn nodded gravely. "The strangest funeral oration I ever heard. He's an original, no matter what else one may think of him."

"One can think a lot of different things about him."

"I know, but it's hard to judge him fairly. He must have suffered a real shock once; that's the only explanation for his oddness."

Schnurrbart turned his head suspiciously. "Did he ever tell you anything?"

"Not directly," Dorn said. "But I gathered a little from things he said."

"I see."

For a while they walked along in silence. Schnurrbart considered whether he should tell Dorn anything about Steiner and Anne but decided against it.

There was a halt at the front of the line. The men were looking at a dense line of shrubbery about a hundred yards ahead. Beyond, the woods thinned out and a steep incline rose sheer and gray.

"We're there." Steiner glanced at his watch. "We'll wait here until dark. Come along." They forced a path through the tangled bushes. On the other side of the hedge was an open field overgrown with tall grass. The chain of hills which began about a hundred yards further on was almost bare of vegetation. Halfway between them and the first hill a brook flowed across the meadow. It did not look wide enough to be a serious obstacle.

The men gazed in silence at the prospect before them. In thought they traveled back over the long trail through the forest. Fifty-five hours ago they had seen in the distance the silhouette of the hills which now lay close before them in this rainy noon. A promised land then, the hills now presented a sad and dreary sight. The men thought of Dietz. A cold wind still whipped the rain into their faces. Again and again the hilltops were enveloped in drifting tag ends of mist, and the sky was piled high with ledge-like cloud formations, gray and black.

Steiner raised his head and listened to the hollow sighing in the trees. To Schnurrbart he said, "Tether the horses. We'll let them go this evening. One sentry will be enough; he can watch the meadow and the hills. I don't think we need fear any trouble from the rear. The rest of you find a good place in the bushes and keep out of sight. . . ."

The men silently followed his instructions. A relatively dry spot in the heart of the thicket was covered with shelter-halves. Anselm posted himself as sentry on the edge of the woods. The others began to unpack canned food and bread. After eating they stretched out on the ground and smoked.

They spent the afternoon sleeping. The weather continued the same, and it grew dark very early, so that they were able to set out again by six o'clock. They left the horses behind. The meadow was extremely marshy in places, and within a few minutes their boots filled with water. The brook was small. As Steiner indifferently stepped into it—he was so wet already he could not be wetter—he still wondered which direction to take. For the tenth time he tried to recall the position of the city as he had seen it from the distance two days ago. But the outlines had been too vague then, although he did have the impression that isolated hills rose out of the mist to the south of the city.

As he was about to step out on the bank of the brook, he stopped abruptly. The others, too, froze in their tracks. About five hundred yards away, above the hills, a white flare rose vertically into the air, paused for seconds as though hanging by an invisible thread, slowly fluttered down on the meadow and faded out in the grass. Then it was as dark as before.

"The front!" Pasternack stammered.

Steiner slowly climbed out of the water and squinted toward the hills. The invisible soldier who had shot the flare must be stationed only a short distance away toward the right, approximately in the direction of Krimskaya.

The others had clustered around him in the high grass. "What shall we do?" Schnurrbart whispered.

"Keep a sharp eye out," Steiner replied. "And stay close together." He had made up his mind. He slung the tommy gun from his shoulder. "If you see anything, fire at once without challenge. Clear?"

Carefully they made their way toward the hill and began climbing the slope. The bare ground was smooth underfoot; now and again one of the men would slip and slide back several yards, then get to his feet, cursing, and wipe his hands on his trousers. At last they reached the top and stopped to catch their breath. They could not see five paces ahead of them. The wind was no longer so violent, but the rain beat steadily against their faces, soaked their uniforms and seeped, cold and clammy, down their sweaty backs. Steiner waited a few moments until they all stopped panting; then he led the way due west. Within a few steps they were going downhill again. But the dip did not continue for long. They crossed a flat hollow and began to climb once more.

Suddenly a cry rang out of the darkness: *"Unimanye!"*

The men flinched as if a shell had exploded a few yards away. The call struck them so unexpectedly that they felt it like a blow. It froze their blood. They threw themselves flat on the ground. Steiner looked back toward Kruger and hissed, "Answer him, you idiot, answer him!"

It took a moment before the East Prussian understood. He raised himself up, funneled his hands over his mouth and shouted, *"Tovarishchi . . . tovarishchi!"*

They held their breath. Not a sound came from in front of them. If the Russian had a flare gun with him now, things would happen fast. They lay close together, staring tensely into the impenetrable darkness. "I don't understand it," Steiner whispered. "What did you tell him?"

Kruger chuckled. "Told him we're his comrades. He must have believed me."

They peered about distrustfully. "A real circus," Maag commented. "I feel like I'm doing a dance on a mine field. What do we do now?"

"Keep going," Steiner decided. "But we have to be more careful. Don't make so much noise. They must have heard us; they couldn't possibly see us. Come on."

The platoon followed him like a many-limbed animal tensed to spring. For over an hour they went up and down the hills without incident. The monotonous tramp over soft ground, the steepness of the slopes that seemed to stretch on forever into the rainy night, their tops never visible until they were reached, the constant menace of the enemy who might confront them at any moment, drained the men. Their caution gave way to apathy. Not even Steiner's occasional sharp rebukes could shake them out of it.

Even Kruger and Schnurrbart were completely worn out. Kruger was limping. For the past half hour a stabbing pain in his right heel had grown steadily worse. Must be a blood blister, he thought, and wondered whether he ought to take off his boot to look. But Steiner, he knew, would not order a rest on account of a blister. Kruger cursed him fiercely under his breath. For a while he tried walking on tiptoe, but the water in his boots was then doubly unpleasant; at every step it bubbled between his toes and made smacking noises. And I would get a blister, he thought, infuriated. It seemed to him incredible that his feet, so hardened to marching, should play such a trick on him—as though he were a raw recruit. His wet socks must have bunched up at his heel, and the skin, softened by water, reacted to the chafing. The pain became unbearable. His shoulder, sore from the weight of the heavy machine gun; the painful tugging at his hips, which bore the brunt of his pack with all its troublesome but indispensable equipment; the soaked uniform on his steaming, sweating skin; the plodding over soft ground where every step was an effort; the gloom and rain and uncertainty—all these other burdens vanished before the torment of his smarting heel.

Suddenly he stopped and dropped the machine gun to the ground. Its thud reached Steiner at the front of the line. "You're crazy," Schnurrbart muttered to him in alarm. Kruger did not reply. He simply sat down on the wet ground and began untying the laces of his boot. He took off boot and sock and felt the swelling at his heel. When Steiner came over to him, he did not even look up.

"Mamma's boy got a sore foot?" Steiner's voice dripped scorn. Kruger did not reply. He stretched out his foot, held the painful heel up to the rain and groaned with relief. Steiner's frown grew fiercer by the second. He stooped, picked up the machine gun and asked, "Would you mind telling me what you think you're doing?" Stubbornly Kruger remained silent. The men had come closer and were grinning broadly.

Suddenly they fell flat on their faces as though someone had kicked them all in the back. In front of them, about at the spot they would have reached by now but for Kruger, the night exploded like a ball of fire. A crashing roar broke over them, forcing their mouths open. Steiner lay with his face on Kruger's back. Kruger had forgotten his painful heel and closed his eyes in horror. The roar continued with undiminished violence. At last Steiner raised his head cautiously; he had realized he was unhurt, and he had been schooled by three years of war. A moment later he had grasped the situation. The platoon was no more than fifty yards from the emplacement of a heavy Russian battery, which must be up ahead in one of the innumerable hollows of this terrain.

Steiner slowly got to his feet. The battery was firing without pause. The others, too, got up one after the other. Only Kruger, Kern and Pasternack remained sitting on the ground. The East Prussian was clutching his boot and sock in his right hand, and his bare foot stood out, a bright shape against the dark ground. Steiner regarded him silently. Then he laid the machine gun across Kruger's legs and said, "Put on your boot before you catch cold." The men's shoulders began to quiver; they bit their lips and shook like saplings in a wind.

Ignoring their mirth, Kruger carefully laid his footgear on the ground beside him, used both hands to draw his foot up above his left knee, and with his fingers felt his abused heel. "Anybody got a needle?"

Silently Steiner reached under his belt, fumbled for a moment and brought forth a large safety pin. "Make it snappy," he said, not harshly.

Kruger nodded. He pressed the pin into his flesh and felt the lymph spurt out over his fingers. "More water in there than in all your heads put together," he said. He carefully pressed out the blister, took a packet of bandages from a pocket and bound up the heel. "There," he said contentedly, put on his torn sock and his sopping boot and quickly stood up. As he did so the artillery fire stopped.

"A short cease fire," Schnurrbart murmured. "They'll be . . ."

"Sh!" Steiner interrupted him savagely. They raised their heads to listen. Somewhere, surprisingly near, shells were falling, and the men looked significantly at one another.

Kruger turned philosophical. "If we were over there," he said, "over there where they're landing, we'd be where we want to be."

They were still quaking inwardly from shock and surprise. But they grinned and looked almost tenderly at Kruger. At this moment each of them felt about the others as he felt about himself. No better and no worse. They were very close.

They made a wide detour around the Russian emplacement.

The apathy had altogether vanished, had given place to an abnormal alertness. They started climbing again, and this time the ascent seemed to go on forever. When Steiner suddenly stopped for no apparent reason, they raised their heads in alarm. The rain pattered evenly down on their weary faces. They saw that Steiner was staring fixedly up the hill. "What is it?" Kern whispered excitedly. Steiner pointed toward the darkness in front of them. For a few seconds they stared at the sky without understanding. Then they all saw it. For brief moments the outline of the hill stood out, clearly visible against the rainy darkness; then it seemed to fuse with the darkness again, like water that is poured into a bottle of ink. At irregular intervals the same phenomenon was repeated. Before they could grasp the meaning of it, Steiner hurried on.

A few minutes later they reached the top of the hill and stood still again, panting for breath and shivering with emotion. At their feet the terrain fell away steeply to the south. Far below them stretched out what appeared to be a broad plain. An endless chain of dimmed headlights was moving from east to west. The whole of the western horizon stood in the spectral illumination of white flares. The men fought in vain against the emotion that tightened their throats and filled their eyes with moisture. They began to swallow and rub their hands over their damp faces.

"The front," Maag whispered almost reverently.

"The front," Kern repeated, placing his hands one over the other as if he wanted to pray. They stared fascinated toward the west.

Steiner raised his arm and pointed to the row of lights. His voice thick, he said, "That's the road to Krimskaya. The battalion must be dug in to the left of it. Remember that, in case we get separated."

Schnurrbart threw him a glance. He was the first to realize the significance of the heavy traffic on the road. "Friends, something's going on down there."

"What then?" Steiner said. "Once we reach the battalion others can worry their heads about it." He crouched down on the ground. "We'll take a short rest here."

Schnurrbart looked around uneasily. "Isn't this spot kind of dangerous?"

"Not especially. At least from here we can see what's going on. Sit down. The final sprint comes next."

"How do you figure to get through?" Kruger inquired. "There are whole armies rolling along down there."

Steiner grinned. "Then a few Russians like us won't make

much difference." He looked at his watch. "It's half past nine now. We have plenty of time. There's no sense trying to cross before three o'clock— too much traffic."

The men sat down, talking in whispers.

"Not a chance we'll get through there," Kern protested. "We must try it some place else. Imagine what it's going to be like when we try to cross the Russian trenches. Why, it's plain crazy!"

"Don't get all worked up," Steiner retorted contemptuously. "We've made it this far and we'll make it the rest of the way, you can depend on that." He turned to Dorn. "Won't we, Professor?"

Dorn looked shiftily down at the ground. He thoroughly agreed with Kern and could only think with horror of what lay before them. On the other hand, he did not want to provide Steiner with food for mockery. He limited himself to a silent shrug.

Steiner watched him out of the corner of his eye. Then he laughed curtly. "You seem to think differently. As you like. To tell the truth I'm enjoying this, I'm enjoying this enormously. Damn it all, what do you want? At least this is a change from sitting around in a filthy mudhole and waiting till one of those blasted things goes off over your head and turns you into fresh hash. Am I right?"

He looked around at their abashed faces. Listening to the overtones of his own words, he felt a serene satisfaction because they had arisen out of his deepest convictions. The sense of being dependent only on his own instinct for all decisions increased his boldness, gave him a feeling of immense confidence. Suddenly, in contrast to his usual manner, he surprised them by growing garrulous. He lashed them with a long string of cynical remarks.

Finally Kruger looked up angrily. "Now you can stop it," he said. "I'd like to know what's so funny. Perhaps what happened to Dietz was a big joke too, eh?"

Steiner started as though he had touched a hot iron. Grief washed over him, along with a profound astonishment that he had not thought about Dietz for so much as a moment during the past few hours. Could the boy have meant so little to him? The question was answered by the aching pain within him, which grew in intensity from second to second, sapping all his high spirits and arousing a dull rage directed solely against Kruger. The men were aware of the sudden change, and Schnurrbart gave Kruger, sitting in front of him, a furious shove. Kruger bit his lip. The words had slipped out involuntarily and he already regretted them.

Dorn, too, was distressed; it seemed to him that a harmless, casual conversation was being needlessly dramatized. He tried to stop the avalanche: "Let's not weigh every word on a chemical balance," he said. "I think we all agree that war is horrible in all its manifestations."

With a look of disgust, Steiner stretched out on the wet ground. Conversation stopped.

Later, when they began ascending the hill again, the incident was forgotten. Steiner centered his whole attention on the difficult terrain. Although the front in the main lay due west, there was a deep salient at one point, a wedge that appeared to expand far to the east. The flares which rose at regular intervals along the line gave him a fairly accurate picture of the course of the front, and Steiner vainly tried to understand why, in defiance of all tactical rules, the German commanders had permitted this incomprehensible extension of the main line of resistance. Probably the reason lay in the character of the terrain, which he could not judge properly from his present position. They had reached the foot of the hill meanwhile and were moving toward the front. They kept close to the line of hills until these turned off at an acute angle toward the north and the terrain opened up on all sides. The ground turned mucky and walking again became difficult. The front was closer. The men could already hear the boom of mortars and occasionally the hollow chatter of machine guns.

During the past few minutes Steiner had been slowing their marching tempo. Now he moved forward toward a dark barrier that crossed the land in front of them. When they reached it they discovered that it was a shoulder-high line of shrubbery running along both sides of a narrow brook. The water was not deep, but the current was surprisingly strong.

On the opposite bank, Steiner stopped abruptly. He had bumped into an obstruction which proved to be the wire of a telephone line. It crossed the brook a few yards away and ran between the bushes toward the front. Thoughtfully he slid his fingers along the wire and stared into the night. The men thronged around him, and Anselm asked, "Shall we cut the wire?"

"You're out of your mind," Hollerbach said. "We'd only bring the Russians down on our necks."

Steiner considered. The moment he had touched the wire he had perceived how the platoon was going to cross the lines. He looked at his watch. It was shortly before midnight—too early to carry out the plan. "We'll have to wait two hours. Shortly before dawn will be the best time. Take a rest."

They slipped their packs from their backs and crouched down on the bank of the brook, as deep in the growth of shrubbery as they could get. Steiner stood by for a few seconds then he vanished softly as a cat into the darkness.

He followed the wire for nearly half a mile before he came on a Russian sentry. He fell flat, eyes fastened on the dark silhouette of the man, who stood motionless some seventy feet away. In spite of the distance he could hear the Russian whistling idly under his breath. The man's back was turned to him, so that there was no great danger of being discovered, and Steiner crawled a few feet closer. I should have brought Kruger, he thought. The front line seemed almost within reach from here. Every time a flare rose up toward the sky, the figure of the sentry stood out plainly against the dark background. With satisfaction Steiner noticed that the direction he was taking led straight to the point of the protruding salient in the German front, which fitted in neatly with his intentions.

When he had got it all straight in his mind, he crawled slowly backward, careful to make no noise at all, until he was far enough from the sentry to stand up without risk. As he approached the line of bushes he looked to his left, toward the road, and found confirmation of his earlier observations. At a particular spot the headlights of the vehicles were extinguished and it was no longer possible to see their course. He guessed that the Russians must be assembling their matériel at this point, which was probably a small village. The distance was too great for him to see anything more in the darkness, but his map would probably show. When he reached the men, he disregarded their eager silence, and studied the map by the shielded beam of his flashlight. His guess was correct. About a mile and a half south of the road was a fairly sizable village, and off to the west, approximately in line with the front, lay a wooded area, its northern edge bordered by the highway. As he examined the immediate vicinity of the wooded area he came across a number that attracted his attention: 121.4. He frowned thoughtfully. Possibly that indicated a hill, which would explain the puzzling wedge in the front line.

He looked up from the map and briefly outlined his plan to the men. Concluding, he said, "Of course, we first have to find out how many bunkers there are. If you don't mess it up, it ought to work. Only you have to act fast, and with as little noise as possible. Close the doors behind you when you shoot, and don't miss."

"But the noise . . ." Schnurrbart remonstrated.

Steiner was impatient. "There's always noise at the front. I told you to close the doors behind you. Can you think of any better plan?"

They did not answer. Now that they were facing the decisive test, their excitement began to die down. Steiner's bold plan no longer seemed fantastic, and the more they considered it the more helpful it appeared.

Kern, eying the front, remarked, "This seems to be a quiet area. No artillery—nothing."

"Why shouldn't our company come in for a quiet sector once in a while?" Kruger retorted.

Schnurrbart was cheerful. "If this is a quiet sector, you won't find our company here! Take a look at that torchlight parade over there. Do you think they're laying Easter eggs?"

"Hell, no." Maag was watching the road, where the headlights of vehicles still showed.

"Our artillery is sound asleep again," Kern said grimly. "That stuff down there would be pie for a forward observer. Don't they see what's going on here?"

"Lack of ammunition," Schnurrbart replied. "You mustn't forget that our supplies have to come in over water. We'll need what we have when the big show starts."

"When it starts!" Maag laughed cynically. "When it starts, our wires will be cut and the batteries blown up. There's something going on back there right now, and it's not a little show either." He gestured toward the south where constant flashes lighted the sky and a low rumble hung steadily in the air.

"Where would that be?" Kruger asked Steiner.

"I don't know. Maybe near Novorossiysk. Won't matter to us, anyway."

"I wouldn't say that." Schnurrbart shivered and drew his shelter-half closer around his shoulders. "If the Russians break through over that way, we're sunk. They'll reach the sea and we'll be right in the trap."

Kruger nodded. "If we lose the war then, you'll never get home again."

Schnurrbart did not answer. He thought of Erika. She would marry someone else and he would spend the rest of his life pounding stone or working in a mine. His head drooped and he stared down at the ground between his legs.

"It stinks any way you look at it," Maag said gloomily. "Whether we win the war or lose it, we'll be left holding the bag. Do you think they'll ever let us take off these rags, even if we do win the war? Don't fool yourself."

"Don't be idiotic," Kruger said angrily. "What on earth

would they do with all us *landsers* when the war is over? They'll be glad when they don't have to pay us any longer."

"They will like hell," Maag said heatedly. "To win the war we'll first have to beat half the world, and if we do beat half the world we'll have to keep it occupied afterwards. Who do you think is going to do that job? The Party, maybe? They'll have enough to do celebrating the victory."

"Let me alone with the Party," Kruger growled. "When the war is over I'll fart on their Party and their army."

Maag grinned cynically at him. "You don't believe that yourself. What are you going to do when the war is over? Raise radishes?"

"None of your goddamn business whether I raise radishes or herring. The main thing is to get out of this stinking uniform and be a free man again."

The other men had been only half listening to the conversation. The artillery fire in the south was dying down, and they saw a row of red flares mount into the air. "Now they're attacking," Anselm said excitedly. "I hope they get a bellyful." They gazed toward the south, where the sky was slowly beginning to redden as though dipped in blood. "Something's burning there," Anselm commented. "What a show! Attacking in this weather—just like the damned Ivans."

Kruger whispered to Schnurrbart, "It's getting late. What the devil is he waiting for?"

"Don't worry, you'll go to hell soon enough," Schnurrbart said indifferently.

"We'll see about that. Before they get me I'll knock off a few dozen of them, as sure as my name is Kruger. What do you think about the idea?"

"What idea?"

"The bunkers. We don't even know how many there are. And maybe the wire leads right up to the trench."

"So much the better. We'll make it all the faster."

Kruger shook himself. "Damn this rain. I'm soaked to the skin. And on top of it all this darkness."

"In a few minutes you'll be glad it's dark. I think we're starting now."

Steiner had got slowly to his feet.

"Are we going?" Maag asked.

"Yes."

The men rolled up their shelter-halves. Kruger stayed close to Steiner, who went over his plan again. "And when you know where you stand," he concluded, "shake hands with him. I'll take care of the rest."

The men stared tensely into the darkness and moved forward cautiously. Everything depended on the next few minutes. The rain sprayed their faces with fine droplets and made seeing difficult. Steiner began to be anxious. Had he mistaken the direction? He paused and peered uncertainly into the darkness. Suddenly a voice called to them. They were prepared for it and did not flinch. Steiner dug his fingers into Kruger's arm. "Go on, answer him."

Kruger took a deep breath. Then he shouted, *"Potselui menya v shopu . . . idi syuda."* Nothing moved. He stood a step forward and said sharply, *"Byeda!"*

Nervously Steiner gnawed his lips. The men, breathing hard, held their guns ready to fire. Somewhere near by a Russian machine gun chattered; the noise seemed to go on forever and plucked at their nerves.

"Damn," Maag whispered, and took two steps back. Kruger, too, looked uneasily at Steiner, who was already making up his mind to resort to force.

At this critical moment a figure emerged slowly out of the darkness. Steiner swallowed; his relief was so intense that for a second he felt as if his body were no longer subject to the law of gravity. He lowered his gun. The Russian had stopped a few paces away and regarded them with curiosity. He was a skinny little fellow; his head protruded from the long coat as though he had been stuck into a sack which was tied under the chin. He was carrying his gun loosely under his right arm, the muzzle pointed at the ground. *"Kuda?"* he asked. His voice was high-pitched and a little hoarse; it was evident from his tone that he was so far without suspicion.

Kruger reached into his pocket, took a single cigarette and held it out. *"Papirossa?"*

The Russian nodded gratefully. The others could see only a little of his face. He put the cigarette carefully into his coat pocket and said, *"Spasibo."* He was looking hard at Steiner, who began to wonder whether their caps were arousing his mistrust. But he turned to Kruger again and repeated, *"Kuda?"*

Kruger waved his hand vaguely and replied that they were going on a patrol up to the front. "Where do you belong?" he asked.

The Russian began to speak freely, with the volubility of a person who is pleased to find something to break the monotony and wants to keep his visitor in good humor. By interjecting a few adroit questions Kruger learned that the man was guarding a Russian battalion combat H.Q. located in a bunker about a hundred feet away. But when the Russian disclosed that there were four bunkers, Kruger began to feel anxious. He looked at Steiner, who was standing beside him, half listening to the noises from the front. Their glances met and Kruger winked. He exchanged a few more words with the Russian, then held out his hand, saying, *"Do-svidanya."*

That was Steiner's cue. The Russian shifted the tommy gun to his left hand and held out his right. Steiner took a rapid step to the side and raised his gun high. The Russian caught the movement. Terrified, he twisted, trying to escape the steely grip in which Kruger held his hand. He opened his mouth to shout as the heavy barrel of the tommy gun struck him crushingly in the back of the neck. There was a horrible, cracking noise. Kruger caught the lifeless body and carefully lowered it to the ground. "He's finished."

"Move back," Steiner said.

"He's finished, I tell you." Kruger stepped back.

"Better to make sure," Steiner said coldly. He picked up the Russian's gun and struck twice. Then he hurled it far away. The men approached, their faces white.

"Horrible," Dorn whispered.

"You'll see things a lot more horrible in the next few minutes," Steiner said. He turned to Kruger. "What did he say?"

"The business isn't so easy," Kruger replied hesitantly. "There are four bunkers. A battalion H.Q. . . ." He retailed hastily everything he had learned.

Steiner shrugged. "We'll have to do it anyway. Two men to each bunker. One will stay outside and stand guard." He turned to Dorn. "That's a job for you." Dorn nodded, relieved. "Let's start," Steiner said. He assigned each man a bunker. "Remember, no prisoners. And don't spare ammunition. Let's go."

They moved forward again. After a few yards they saw dark mounds of earth rising above the ground and a feeble gleam of light. The bunkers were scattered, not in a straight row as Steiner had assumed, and connected by a deep trench that led, with many windings, toward the front. The light came from the crack under a door. In spite of the darkness they could see that telephone lines from all directions led into a rectangular opening near the door of one of the bunkers. "Communications center," Kruger whispered.

Steiner scrutinized the bunkers. They were covered with freshly dug earth and seemed massively built. "I'll open fire. As soon as you hear the first shot, get in and slam the door behind you. Are your flashlights working?"

They nodded. "Good. Depending on how many Russians are inside, one of you can hold the light and the other fire. Clear?" He turned to Dorn. "You stay outside. If anybody comes along, fire at once, even if it's Stalin in person."

In pairs they began to climb down into the trench. At the edge Kruger's foot slipped on the wet earth. He tried to throw himself backward, but the weight of his gun hindered him. Anselm, close at his heels, reached out, but it was too late. Kruger crashed heavily against the door of the bunker directly opposite. It yielded and he tumbled headlong into the bunker. For a few seconds he lay dazed. When he started to get up, a glaring light fell upon his face and a sharp voice rang in his ear. Anselm, close behind, stared over Kruger at a half-dressed Russian holding a battery lantern and shouting furiously. At that moment the muted but fully audible hammering of tommy guns began. The Russian flashed his light toward the trench.

Kruger, who had recovered from his first shock, instinctively reached for the Russian's high leather boots.

An officer, he thought. With a powerful jerk he pulled the man off his feet. He saw Anselm raising his gun. "Don't shoot," he panted. "Hit him on the head, on the head!"

Anselm hesitated. There might be others in the bunker. Across the two men grappling on the floor he could see a candle burning on the table, a cot in the background and blankets scattered around the floor.

"Hit him!" Kruger groaned.

The Russian fought desperately. His lantern had rolled into the trench and illuminated the scene. At last Anselm grasped his hair and slugged him with the butt of the gun.

Kruger shook himself like a dog emerging from the water. "How's it going?" he asked quickly, reaching for the gun.

"I don't know," Anselm said excitedly. "It's so quiet." He looked down at the motionless Russian. "What shall we do with him?"

"I don't know. Maybe we can use him."

He looked around the bunker. The Russian's tunic and coat were hanging from a nail. Kruger nodded with satisfaction. "A captain. Must be the commander. We're really lucky."

"If he isn't dead already," Anselm said. "But Steiner said no prisoners."

"We can always kill him later." Kruger stooped over the Russian and took his wrist. "There's still a pulse beat." The firing had stopped. No more than two minutes had passed since he fell into the trench. He dropped the Russian's arm.

"We'll have to see what's going on. It's——" He broke off. Someone came running down the trench. They ducked, then recognized Schnurrbart and Kern.

"All right?" Schnurrbart asked, glancing at the Russian.

"How about your bunker?" Kruger returned the question.

"Four men."

"Dead?"

"Yes. They were asleep. Nothing to it."

"What about Hollerbach and Steiner?" Kruger asked nervously, mopping his damp face with his sleeve.

"I don't know," Schnurrbart replied. "We'll have to go see." Kruger turned to Anselm. "Watch the Russian."

"Is he still alive?" Kern whispered.

"Yes," Kruger said. The three of them hurried down the trench.

Steiner had picked the communications bunker for himself. Maag at his side, he pressed the door open inch by inch. The first thing he saw was the back of a man sitting on a chair, head drooping, dozing. Then he heard loud snoring and thrust his head in so that he could see the whole of the spacious bunker. There were six bunks in three tiers, each tier at right angles to the other. They filled the rear long wall and the right side wall of the bunker. On each of them lay a Russian wrapped in a brown woolen blanket, sound asleep. Most of them had their backs to the door. In front of the man sitting on the left was a box containing the switchboard. Guns hung from a wooden pole driven into the earthen wall. The room was lighted by two candles.

Steiner closed the door again and turned to Maag. "You take the beds on the right. . . ." he started to say.

A low thud in the trench interrupted him. They heard a loud voice bellowing incomprehensible phrases. "Russians," Maag gasped. For the fraction of a second Steiner hesitated. Then he kicked open the door and stepped in. The Russian at the switchboard jumped to his feet. Steiner forced himself to smile. He kept smiling until Maag had slipped into the bunker. Then he slowly closed the door behind him. Out of the corner of his eye he caught a movement in the bunks. The Russian standing before him was a tall man with a mournful face under a shaved head. As he opened his mouth, Steiner shot from the hip. He saw the pupils of the man's eyes start to widen with horror, but only start. He died before his face could express the sudden emotion. Dark astonishment remained in his eyes as, spinning from the force of the bullets, he toppled forward.

Steiner whirled. The beds had come to life. He saw jerking limbs, eyes goggling with the terror of death, heavy boots swinging through the air, blankets fluttering to the floor. A loud bellow of fear was silenced by the hammering of Steiner's gun. Maag fired also. He stood crouching slightly, his back against the door, his face contorted. Steiner and Maag braced the butts of their tommy guns against their chests, took their stand with legs wide apart and squinted over the shaking barrels. Bullets tore scraps of wood from the bunks; caught leaping bodies and dropped them to the floor like sandbags; transformed openmouthed, frightened faces into shapeless, bloody clods of flesh. Steiner acted in a fever. Objects swam before his eyes. The insane roar of the two tommy guns in the confined space almost robbed him of consciousness. From one of the upper bunks a dark shadow came flying toward him, arching in a gigantic leap. Instinctively he ducked and thrust the barrel of his gun into a face—he saw only the bloodshot eyes and gaping mouth—and fired. The heavy body drove him to the floor and knocked the wind out of him. Abruptly there was silence. From somewhere Maag called to him in alarm. Groaning, he tried to free himself from the weight on his chest. Then the Russian's body was pulled to one side, and he recognized Maag's smoke-blackened face. He managed to sit up.

"Were you hit?" Maag asked in dismay. Steiner slowly shook his head. The Russian lay close beside him. At the sight of the man's face Steiner suddenly threw up. The violent gush of vomit drove his body forward. Spasm after spasm racked him, and he felt as if he were choking in his own slops. He writhed on the floor, snorting, struggling for breath. Maag stared down at him in helpless fright.

The door was kicked open and Hollerbach, followed closely by Pasternack, rushed in. They stopped short, stunned by the sight of Steiner on the floor. Before Maag could explain, Schnurrbart and the others appeared. A few seconds later the whole platoon, except for Dorn and Anselm, who had not left their posts, were bending anxiously over Steiner. Steiner had recovered sufficiently to be aware of what was happening. He felt wretched and had to be helped up; his legs shook as he staggered to his feet. Then he spied the open door, angrily pushed aside the helping hands and cursed. "You idiots, close the door, damn it!"

Kruger grinned. "I thought so. There's still some bile in him, even though half of it is on the floor. How are you feeling, General?"

Steiner rubbed his mouth with the back of his hand and

glared. After Maag had closed the door, they looked around. "A slaughterhouse," Schnurrbart said. "This war, this god-damned stinking war!"

Steiner picked his tommy gun up from the floor and replaced the empty clip.

"Where do we go from here?" Kruger asked with some urgency. "We're apt to have visitors soon. They must have heard the racket we made."

"Well, then," Steiner said. "There's room enough for more corpses around here. What hapened in your bunkers?"

The men reported. Hollerbach and Pasternack had had the easiest time. Two sleeping officers had never had a chance to wake up.

Steiner turned to Kruger. "Is the commander in condition to be questioned?"

"When I left him he was still taking a nap," Kruger replied. "I can go see."

"You do that," Steiner said. Kruger left the bunker. Steiner reached into his pocket and produced a pack of cigarettes, which he silently passed to Schnurrbart. He took a cigarette for himself, stepped over the bodies lying on the floor and with the cigarette in his mouth leaned forward to the burning candles. As he stooped one of the dark-brown jacks on the switchboard dropped and a muted buzzing sounded. The men looked at Steiner, who had frozen in the midst of his movement. The buzzing stopped.

Schnurrbart went to Steiner's side. "What'll we do? If no-body answers they'll come to see what's the matter."

"Get Kruger," Steiner snapped, taking the cigarette from his mouth. Schnurrbart rushed out of the bunker. Steiner examined the apparatus. It was similar to the type of switchboard used in the German army. As he stared at the bright brass plugs he was struck by a thought at which he first shook his head, then involuntarily grinned. He turned toward the men and encountered anxious glances. Maag opened his mouth to say something. But at that moment the buzzing resumed, and instead of speaking he glanced impatiently at the door.

"Any of you know how to say 'wait' in Russian?" Steiner asked.

All shook their heads.

"I'll see what's keeping them," Kern exclaimed.

Just then Schnurrbart and Kruger appeared. Schnurrbart had talked to Kruger and the East Prussian went directly to the switchboard, picked up the hand set and pressed the button above the jack. He brought the mouthpiece closer to his lips and said, *"Da."* The tense expression on his face slowly disappeared. With his free hand he reached out for the crank on the telephone box, turned it vigorously several times, and said, *"Khorosho."* He replaced the receiver. The jack sprang up.

"What is it?" Steiner snapped.

Kruger grinned broadly. "What a laugh. Some bird in the signal corps decided to test the line."

Steiner sighed with relief. "He ought to be shot for that."

The door opened again and Anselm appeared, pushing the tall figure of the Russian officer into the bunker. The man was pale and distraught. He caught sight of the dead bodies and swallowed. The *landsers* could see his Adam's apple bob up and down above his shirt collar. He turned still paler, and swayed from side to side, his eyes fixed on a single point. Involuntarily the men followed the direction of his gaze. From one of the upper bunks dangled the corpse of a Russian. He hung head downward; his fingers seemed to be reaching for some invisible object on the floor. The head was a dark blob from which blood was dripping onto the wooden floorboards. There was a large pool of blood.

Schnurrbart felt the urge to say something obscene. "Like a virgin after defloration," he commented.

"What's that?" Maag asked.

"What?"

"That word you just used. Defloration, or something."

Schnurrbart tore his eyes away from the corpse on the bunk. "That's the fate worse than death that a virgin always lives through."

The men guffawed and the spell was broken. Steiner turned to the Russian again and studied him. Then he asked Kruger, "Who told you to take prisoners?"

"You can kill him any time," Kruger retorted.

Steiner shook his head. "I've changed my mind, but in the future obey my orders, understand?"

Kruger fell into sulky silence.

"Come on, we'd better get out of here," Schnurrbart said impatiently. He was suddenly filled with an acute dread, intensified by the sight of all the dead.

But Steiner waved his protest aside. "Five minutes more or less don't matter," he said. "We have a little more to do here. Did you find any maps?" he asked Kruger.

"I had other things to worry about," Kruger replied indignantly.

"Well, go and look now. Since this bird is the commander, there must be maps of the positions in his bunker."

"What have you got in mind?" Schnurrbart asked.

"In a moment." Steiner beckoned to the Russian. "Come here." The Russian raised his head; he still stood by the door. The men had given him no time to put on his tunic. His high-collared shirt was smeared with mud. Steiner regarded his set face thoughtfully. The fellow did not look the type to yield easily. They would have to soften him properly.

Kern pushed him hard, bellowing, "Didn't you hear?" The Russian glared at Kern and clenched his fists.

"Bring him over here," Steiner ordered.

Kern pulled the Russian across the bunker. "The bastard is still sulking," Kern said, frowning fiercely at the glowering prisoner. "Shall I smash his ugly mug for him?"

"Maybe later on." Steiner watched as the other men cleared the bodies out of the way, tossing them unceremoniously onto the bunks. For a few seconds he fought down a renewed impulse to vomit.

The door's opening distracted him. Kruger came in with several sheets of paper and threw them on the telephone switchboard. "That's all," he said.

Steiner unfolded the maps and studied them. Then he smiled. "Nice work. Meyer will be glad to see this stuff." With his finger he traced the lines. The map was distinctly better than his. The course of the front line was marked in red pencil, and the sectors of the different companies were neatly divided, although there were no indications of the numbers of the companies. The battalion combat H.Q. was marked by a red circle. Steiner also found the explanation for the peculiar salient in the main line of resistance at this point. Schnurrbart was peering inquisitively over his shoulder. "You see that?" Steiner said. "There's a ridge in front of us, and I'll stake my head on it our company is over there. The front runs out around here." His finger pointed to the area marked out with brown crosshatching. "Now we know just where we stand."

Finger on the map, he considered for a moment. It would obviously be best to try to get through right at the point of the salient. This route was shortest and easiest. He turned to Kruger. "Now let's see what you can do. What I have in mind depends on you, because it depends on the Russian. Look here." Kruger bent over the map. "You see the point of this angle here?" Kruger nodded. "Good. That's where I want to cross. Now I have to know which company is stationed there."

"Which Russian company?" Kruger asked.

"Of course. What's on the other side of the line doesn't interest me until we get there."

Schnurrbart took the pipe out of his mouth. "Isn't that marked on the map? Which company, I mean?"

Steiner shook his head patiently. "If it were I wouldn't have to ask the Russian."

"Well, let's see," Kruger said. He turned to the Russian, who had been listening glumly to the conversation. When Kruger held the map up in front of him and spoke to him, he set his lips and looked away.

Steiner raised his hand. "He wants to play the hero," he said. "But we can knock that idea out of his head." He stood up and looked at the Russian officer. The man's trousers lacked a belt. Steiner reached out so quickly that the Russian's defensive gesture came only after the buttons had given and the trousers slipped down to the floor. For seconds the Russian stared at the grinning men, his face contorted with fury. But when he stooped to pull up his trousers, Steiner struck him in the face so brutally that he fell backward and lay groaning on the floor.

"That was only the beginning," Steiner said fiercely. "Undress him completely."

The men stared at him in astonishment. "Hurry up about it!" he barked. Silently they obeyed. The Russian's initial resistance quickly ceased. A moment later he lay naked on the floor, panting from indignation and struggle. Steiner sat down again and regarded him coldly. "Stand him up," he ordered curtly. As though he had understood, the Russian sprang to his feet of his own accord. Without clothing he looked spare and helpless. His mouth and nose were bleeding; he rubbed the back of his hand over his face. "I never knew a man who was ready to play the hero in his birthday suit," Steiner drawled.

He took his bayonet out of his belt and threw it skillfully across the bunker so that it stuck in the wooden floor close to the Russian. "If he doesn't talk, we'll castrate him," Steiner said. He spoke urgently to the men. "Everything depends on him. If he tells us lies or refuses to talk, we're going to have a damned hard time of it. Do you understand?"

They looked at Steiner's grim face, and then at the Russian. Steiner was right: the idea of falling into the hands of the Russians now that they were so close to safety drove all mercy out of their heads. Kern rubbed his fingernails on his coat sleeve and growled, "I'll cut him up piece by piece if necessary."

"Then we understand each other," Steiner said. "Tell him, Kruger."

Kruger spoke harshly, gesturing repeatedly at the bayonet

on the floor. The Russian's face reflected in turn shame, fear, rage and resolution. Steiner, studying him closely, thought he could guess his reaction in advance. He was right. When Kruger held the map up in front of the Russian, the skin tightened over the man's cheekbones and he said in a firm voice, *"Nyet!"* a collective groan went through the room. The men moved threateningly closer.

Steiner got up and slowly approached the prisoner, taking each step with deliberation. He stooped, pulled the bayonet out of the floor and toyed with it. "So you don't want to," he said softly. Then he took a step backward and ordered, "Lay him down." They threw him to the floor. When he tried to scream, Kruger slapped his mouth. They knelt on his arms and legs and held him fast. His eyes were fixed on Steiner in mortal terror. Steiner clenched the bayonet in his right hand and slowly stooped. As he raised his arm, a babble of words burst from the Russian's lips.

Kruger listened breathlessly. Finally he turned to Steiner, grinning. "Good enough. He says it's the third company at the point. The first and second are on the left and right respectively."

The men looked at Steiner with visible relief. Steiner was still frowning fiercely at the Russian. Before anyone could stop him, he quickly lifted his boot and stepped heavily between the man's legs. The Russian let out a piercing scream and doubled up in agony. "Have you gone insane?" Kruger cursed. The others looked at Steiner with outrage in their eyes.

Steiner tossed his head impatiently. "This bird wasn't nearly softened up enough for what I intend to do with him."

"You've already got your information," Kruger protested angrily.

"Sure, but that's only a starter." They looked blank. He smiled and said, "Take him over to the switchboard."

They pulled the Russian to his feet again, dragged him across the bunker and plumped him down in the chair. Steiner leaned over the switchboard and studied the numbers over the contacts.

"What are you up to?" Schnurrbart asked.

"You'll see," Steiner said. He added to Kruger, "We're going to call up the third company."

They looked at him as if he had gone out of his mind. For a few seconds he enjoyed their consternation. Then he said, "That's right, we're going to telephone the third company. This bird—" he indicated the Russian who sat doubled over on the chair, hands between his legs—"this bird is going to tell the company commander that a reconnaissance patrol is on its way."

"A reconnaissance patrol!" Schnurrbart suddenly slapped his thigh and burst into laughter.

The others had not yet understood. Kruger excitedly plucked at his nose and wrinkled his brow, until all at once a broad smile of understanding spread over his face. "Why, that's . . . I'll be damned . . . what a cockeyed . . . what a . . ." Kruger pounded Steiner on the shoulder. "You're the craziest son of a bitch I ever met," he declared admiringly.

The others still looked baffled. "Don't you understand yet, you idiots?" Kruger boomed. "This Russian will tell his company commander that a reconnaissance patrol is going to cross the lines, so the boys have to keep quiet and not shoot. They'll give us a guard of honor, I tell you, a guard of honor!"

Steiner twisted his mouth in a thin smile. "I think we had better dispense with that," he said. "It might be too much of a good thing." The smile vanished. "You've got to realize that if the Russian says one wrong word he can bring the whole company down on our necks. Listen, Kruger, and be ready."

"Depend on that," Kruger said fiercely.

Kruger told the Russian what was expected of him. If he was sensible, he said, they would take him with them as a prisoner—and he would be a lot better off than if he lay here mutilated and slowly bleeding to death. Intimidated, the Russian nodded.

He placed the reciever in the Russian's hand. Kern stepped up behind the man and almost tenderly placed his hands around his throat. The Russian hunched his head between his shoulders and pressed the reciever to his ear. Steiner exchanged a glance with Kruger. Then he pressed one of the black buttons and turned the crank. There was a dead silence. Steiner drummed his fingers on the wooden case that housed the switchboard. In a moment they would see whether he was risking too much. All at once the plan seemed to him crazy and impossible. He wished he could stop the call, but it was already too late. The prisoner began to speak. He spoke slowly; only a very attentive listener would have detected the excitement in his voice. The men kept their eyes on his face; their fists were clenched and they held their breath.

Anselm stood with eyes closed. It can't work, it just can't, he kept thinking. He was so convinced that the telephone call would end disastrously that he still held his eyes closed when the prisoner's voice had stopped and Kruger sighed with relief and replaced the receiver on the hook. "It worked," he said. Anselm opened his eyes in astonishment and saw around him the men's white faces.

"Nobody will believe us when we get back," Pasternack whispered. "If only Dietz had lived to see this."

Steiner turned slowly toward him, his mouth twitching. Impulsively Schnurrbart laid his hand on Steiner's shoulder. "If it hadn't been for you," he said, "we never would have got out of here. Never, believe me."

"No laurels in advance," Steiner said roughly. "We aren't out yet. Besides—" he looked at Kruger—"without you there would have been no way to pull this off."

"Right," Anselm exclaimed. He stepped up to Kruger and shook his hand vigorously. "You really handled that. We were lucky to have you."

Kruger was overwhelmed. He tried to conceal his pleasure. "Oh, hell," he said, "what good would my Russian do me if Steiner didn't have the ideas?"

"Do your backslapping later on," Schnurrbart said. "It seems to me high time we got out of here."

They looked at Steiner for further orders. "We'll take the Russian with us," Steiner said. "Better put him in one of the dead men's uniforms. An officer might attract attention. He'll march between Kruger and Kern. If he attempts to escape, knock him down. Don't shoot. Kruger, tell him that if he opens his mouth on the way, he's a dead man. He can make trouble for us, but it won't do him any good."

While Kruger translated, the men stripped one of the bodies. Steiner tucked the Russian maps carefully into his coat pocket. He watched as the prisoner donned the bloodstained uniform. Before they left the bunker, they ripped out the switchboard. Each of the men took a souvenir—they tore the Russian officer's uniform on the floor to pieces. Maag, Hollerbach and Dorn joined them at once, and Steiner explained in a whisper what had happened. Then they set out along the trench leading toward the front line.

It was still raining, a thin, even drizzle. The front had quieted all along the line. But flares still rose, hung trembling against the clouded sky, fluttered noiselessly down to the ground and went out. Schnurrbart followed Kern. He had slung his tommy gun over his right shoulder, buried both hands in his trousers pockets and walked with head drooping in thought. Soon the trench became shallower and ended in a grassless plain that sloped slightly upward. "Quite a bit of construction for two nights," Maag, behind him, whispered.

Schnurrbart nodded. The Russians must have worked like moles, he thought. But undoubtedly they had mobilized the

entire civilian population of Krimskaya; were it not for the
rain the platoon probably would have run into a construction
crew by now. That would have meant more trouble. As it was
there were dangers enough to pass through before they
reached the German trenches. Suddenly something occurred to
him. He hurried past the file of men until he came up with
Steiner. "Do you think all the Ivans have been warned we're
coming?" he asked.

"Yes," Steiner said. "Look up ahead. Don't you notice anything?"

The other men had caught up with them. It was impossible
to see more than a dozen paces ahead, and the occasional
glow of flares above the trenches was swallowed up in the
darkness before it reached them. "Dark as the inside of a
black cow's ass," Kern whispered.

Steiner raised his hand impatiently. "Don't you see anything?"

"Sure—" Schnurrbart nodded—"if you mean the flares."

"I do mean them," Steiner replied with a scornful undertone. "Not the ones you see but the ones you don't see."

Schnurrbart shook his head. "That's too much for me."

"Not for me," Dorn said.

The men looked at him. "We know you're smart," Schnurrbart growled.

"You don't have to be particularly smart to see this," Dorn
replied evenly. "If you look close you'll notice that the
Russians directly in front of us are not firing any flares; all
of the flares are coming from the other side."

"Right," Steiner said approvingly. "So the Russians are
just waiting until we come through. Stay close together from
now on. In case we're spoken to, Kruger knows what to do."
He slipped the gun from his shoulder and went up to the
Russian. "One word from you, you bastard," he said threateningly, "and we'll tear you to pieces!"

"He can't understand," Kern said.

"He understood that, don't worry." Steiner started forward,
taking long resolute strides. According to the map, the distance
between the battalion command post and the positions of the
third company was about a mile. They must have covered
at least half that distance by now. The men moved in a knot.

Kern was walking so close behind the prisoner that their
bodies touched. He was acutely conscious of the responsibility
resting on him, and he wanted Steiner to be satisfied. At the
first suspicious movement on the Russian's part he was determined to kill him, even if he himself were killed in the
process. The thought filled him with pride. Suddenly he felt

a part of the platoon, as though he had been with it for ten years. It's a damn fine thing to belong to a crazy bunch like this, he said to himself. We all belong together. All for one and one for all. He no longer remembered where he had picked up the phrase, but it sent strange chills down his spine, plucked strings in him that momentarily made his eyes fill with tears. It was a great thing to have comrades. As he listened to the crunch of the gravelly earth underfoot and the stirring noises from the front, he was more and more overwhelmed by this emotion. Comradeship is everything, he thought. It didn't matter if you pitched into one another once in a while; what mattered was that you could depend on the others when you were in trouble. And, by God, you could depend on these fellows here! You really could, and he was damned glad to be in their platoon and not in some other. Later, when the war was over, he would invite them all to come to his inn. The idea enchanted him. He turned his head and glanced almost with tenderness at Dorn, stumbling along behind him. The longer he thought about it, the more enthusiastic he became. He'd keep them for two weeks; they could eat all they had room for, goddamn it, and sleep in his bedrooms, and he would hang a big sign on the door: *Closed for veterans' reunion*. Yes, by God, he would do it, and every night he would bring up the best stuff from the cellar and they'd talk about the past, how they had marched through this damned dark night and through the damned woods and how they had undressed the women and almost run head-on into the Russian artillery emplacement, and how they had all been scared stiff. He could see the whole scene: all of them sitting around the big round table in his inn, laughing, slapping one another on the back, glasses tinkling as they touched. Then he would stand up and make a speech, a fine speech in plain words, and at the end they would stand up and bow their heads and think of Dietz, of Dietz and . . . oh, well . . . He ran his sleeve over his face, wiping away the picture.

Meanwhile they had come so close to the front that they had to fall flat as each flare went up. While the Russians up ahead of them remained absolutely quiet, machine-gun and rifle fire from the other side often passed close over their heads, so that for stretches they had to crawl on all fours.

"Idiots!" Kruger whispered indignantly. He stuck close by Steiner's side.

At the moment Steiner was flattened out on the ground, peering ahead.

"You should have sent them a postcard that we're coming,"

Steiner growled. "They might be getting nervous because the Russians are so quiet."

He concentrated on the rising terrain before them. It was muddy now. Progress was difficult. But the rain had stopped. On the other side, about two hundred paces away, another flare shot up. For a few seconds all the terrain could be seen. In front of them, a stone's throw away, a dark wall rose above the ground. Steiner guessed that it must be the rampart of the Russian trench. The eastern slope of the hill was also distinctly visible. The German line must run somewhere along there. As the flare went out, he glanced briefly back at the men. They were lying flat on the ground, motionless. Wearily, as though the burden of the pack on his back had suddenly increased many times in weight, he straightened up. For a few seconds he stood indecisive. "What is it?" Kruger whispered. Steiner did not reply. His original intention of leading the platoon in a body across the no man's land, across these crucial hundred yards, now seemed insane. Frowning, he considered the situation. There seemed to be only one way to keep the platoon from being mowed down by their own machine guns.

He beckoned the men to him and explained in a whisper. "And suppose you get hit?" Kruger asked uncomfortably.

"With a little luck it ought to work," Steiner said. "But if I am, Schnurrbart must try it next. We haven't much choice. You come with me now. We must first find a place where you can cross afterward without being stopped. Then you go back and wait for the flares. If nothing happens in fifteen minutes, Schnurrbart had better start out. I . . . ." He threw himself to the ground. A chilling howl hurtled toward them, and they pressed their faces into the damp earth. Then came the frightful crash of the explosion, and a few seconds later a hail of large and small lumps of earth pattered down on their backs. They waited until the vicious hum of the splinters stopped and the silence washed over them like water. Steiner raised his head and shook off the paralysis of shock. All year long they have no ammunition, he thought fiercely, and they have to pick this moment to throw the stuff around.

The men came to life again. Schnurrbart wiped his muddy face and began to curse softly. "There'll be more," Kruger warned. "They never fire only one shell."

"They always fire just one shell," Schnurrbart answered. "Ever since I've been in this damned army they fire one shell and hit their own men with it." They listened fearfully to the darkness.

"Calm down," Steiner said. "If any more come, we can't

do anything about it." He turned to Kruger. "We have to start. Everything clear?"

"Clear as mud," Kruger said gloomily.

He passed the tommy gun to Maag, who stood beside him. The prisoner was sitting on the ground, crouching forward, motionless. "Keep a close watch on him," Kruger said to Kern. "If he makes a sound now, we're sunk."

"He won't," Kern promised, spreading his fingers significantly.

"Good luck," Schnurrbart whispered uneasily.

Steiner nodded. As he and Kruger disappeared into the darkness, the men stared anxiously after them. They cowered on the ground and waited.

Flattened out, the two crawled to the Russian trench. They were within a few yards of it when Kruger suddenly hissed softly and clutched Steiner's foot. Steiner breathed, "What?" Kruger pointed to the left. For a few seconds Steiner peered; then he saw the Russian. The man was standing in the trench, his helmet rising shapeless above the mounted earth.

"To the right," Kruger whispered. With infinite caution they crawled over the slippery ground. They moved about fifty feet parallel to the Rusian trench before Steiner abruptly turned. Panting, Kruger crawled up beside him. Their uniforms were pasted to their bodies, their faces and hands smeared with mud.

"Do you see anyone?" Steiner whispered.

"No."

Steiner hesitated. Then he rose and walked on, bending low. When he reached the trench, another flare rose from the German lines. He dropped quickly to his knee and looked up and down the trench. It was not occupied here. He waited until Kruger came up beside him, whispered, "Notice this place. This is where you must cross. Right here, understand?" He straightened his belt. "You can take my tommy gun. I won't need it any more."

"Why not?" Kruger whispered anxiously.

Steiner looked across the trench. Somewhat to the right a German machine gun was firing tracer rounds. He watched them fade out in the darkness like shooting stars. The flare was dead now; no man's land stretched before him, black and hostile.

"Because deserters don't carry weapons when they cross the lines. Go back now."

Kruger hesitated. Then he quickly reached out for Steiner's hand and pressed it hard. "If anything happens to you," he said fiercely, "I'll kill all the bastards."

"Too damn many of them," Steiner murmured. "Get going."

He watched Kruger crawl off until the dark shadow on the ground was absorbed by the surrounding gloom. Abruptly he felt terribly isolated. For a while he stood staring across the trench, jaw set. He wished he could turn back and take one of the men with him. One of the men . . . He remembered that they were waiting for the signal, and pulled himself together. Cautiously he climbed up the other side of the trench, clambered over the rampart and waited until the next flare came. When it faded, he straightened up and tensed his body. His heart suddenly began to pound like mad, and he sank back on the ground. "Stand up, you son of a bitch," he told himself, "stand up!" His legs were trembling violently; he panted, gasped for air and dug his fingers into the soft earth. For a few seconds he fought desperately against his fear, against the sheer terror that pinned him to the ground and threatened to crush his will. His face was contorted, and he stared wide-eyed at the height where the German line must be located. He groaned between clenched teeth; he tried to force his body into motion. But the night lay with a terrible weight upon his hunched back. It constricted his throat until he felt that he was choking; a sound like a death rattle emerged from his mouth, and spittle trickled from his lips onto his hands. He fought like an animal. Suddenly the whole area grew light again. This time there were two flares sent up from different spots; they rose almost vertically, drifted sideways, driven by a faint breeze, and sailed down toward the ground. At that moment he pulled himself up, braced his shoulders against the returning darkness and charged forward, mouth wide open. He saw nothing, heard nothing. His feet churned the ground; in a few seconds he had crossed the level space and was flying as if hurled out of a catapult up the slope. He had come within about twenty yards of the German line when the next flare arose. He threw his arms up and began to shout.

BOOK
TWO

VI

MEYER waded through the water in the bottom of the trench, feeling the rain patter down on his face. He stumbled over something lying in the trench, and fell. Cursing, he got up and groped for the obstacle. It proved to be a length of wood that had jammed between the walls of the trench and in spite of all his efforts would not move. Irritably he kicked at it. Then he noticed an opening in the left side of the trench, which proved to be a well-constructed machine-gun emplacement. It was even equipped with a convenient bench for sitting. As he straightened up he knocked his head against a ceiling beam. He glanced through the wide embrasure, but the darkness was as impenetrable outside as in. Nevertheless, he felt a certain sense of comfort in here; the feeling was intensified by the sound of the rain outside. Sighing, he dropped onto the bench, hunched his shoulders and listened to the monotonous, lulling patter of the rain. He closed his eyes. A long while afterward—he did not know whether minutes or hours had passed—he was startled by a noise. He heard a voice, and he thought he detected the shadow of a man moving in front of the dim rectangle of the entrance. "What's the matter?" he snapped.

There was a silence outside. Meyer was wide awake now. Automatically he reached for his pistol holster and sprang to his feet. Then he heard a voice which was unmistakably Lieutenant Gausser's saying, "What little rat is hiding in this nice burrow?"

Momentary embarrassment made Meyer duck his head. But his sense of humor came to his rescue and he started to laugh. "If you mean me, Lieutenant Gausser, I must insist upon a more respectful tone toward a fellow officer."

From outside there came an exclamation of surprise. Then Gausser's lean figure appeared. "Herr Meyer," he blurted, "how the devil did you get into this cave?"

"Through the entrance, Gausser, through the entrance, same way you did." They stood facing each other in the darkness, unable to see more than blurred outlines. Meyer explained. "I must have fallen sound asleep," he concluded. "After all, it doesn't matter much whether I spend the night here or in my bunker. But what brings you out at this hour?

I would have thought you'd gone to sleep long ago. Whom were you talking to outside there?"

"Too many questions at once," Gausser said. "I stumbled over that wood in the trench just as you probbaly did. Was just making a tour of the positions. I wasn't talking to anybody, just cursing to myself. I suppose that woke you. Shall we sit down?"

"Why not?" Meyer said. They moved close together and lighted cigarettes.

"Miserable weather," Gausser said.

Meyer nodded. "If it lasts much longer," he said, "the bunkers and trenches will collapse on us. I would never have thought the rainy season could go on for so long."

There was a pause. Now that he had recovered from his initial surprise Gausser began to consider the reason for Meyer's presence here. Undoubtedly he was waiting for his platoon, he thought. Perhaps he intended to wait until dawn. He was conscious of a warm admiration for Meyer. Meyer must think a good deal of his men to stay awake night after night on their account. For a while he wondered whether he ought to bring up the subject again. But since Meyer remained laconic, he decided not to say anything. After a while they began chatting casually, occasionally taking surreptitious glances at their watches. Although they could scarcely keep their eyes open, neither of them wanted to be the first to admit it. But they spoke less and less; their conversation faded into dull monosyllables that scarcely rose above the monotonous patter of the rain. At last it petered out entirely.

Third Company's positions ran around the eastern tip of Hill 121.4. It had stopped raining about an hour before. The front was quiet. In one of the advanced weapon pits stood the soldier Faber behind a medium machine gun. His tour had begun at three o'clock in the morning. He was a broadshouldered, quiet fellow who never talked much. But the other men in his platoon felt that when he did speak there was little to be added to what he said. He picked his words painfully, and his thoughts often struck his fellows as deep and mysterious, like the still lakes of his native province. Faber came from the Black Forest. Before the war he had been a woodcutter, and the pathways through the dense pine woods were as familiar to him as the wrinkles on his mother's face. Three years before, he had received his draft call and had donned his uniform without enthusiasm. At that time he was twenty-four. Since then he had remained in Lieutenant Gausser's Third Company and was well thought of by his superiors. A steady, reliable man. Now he stood motionless and alert in the chest-deep MG position, his eyes probing the dark landscape before him, his ears attentive to every sound. The noises, however, were always the same: the suppressed coughing of the man in the foxhole near by; the metallic clank when the lever of a machine gun was moved; the smacking suction noise of boots on the muddy bottom of the trench. He was aware of these sounds only in the fringes of consciousness. Nevertheless, his attention had become alert during the past fifteen minutes. At first he could not have said himself what had shaken him out of the sleepy indifference during the first few minutes of his watch and produced a mounting uneasiness. Then he had realized that it was the unnatural silence in the Russian positions opposite.

Now he was suspicious and tense. He used his flare gun frequently, and the men in the near-by weapon pits were also shooting off flares at shorter and shorter intervals. But strain his eyes as he would, he could detect nothing to give him reason for concern. Every time one of the flares hit the ground and went out, he closed his eyes to ease the shock of the returning darkness. As he reloaded the flare pistol, he wondered whether it might not be best to communicate with his platoon leader. He had half made up his mind to go over to the adjoining sentry and ask his opinion. Suddenly he started and his hand darted out again to send up another flare.

From the right came a warning cry. As the flare mounted he saw a man come tearing up the slope bent over, saw him stop abruptly and throw up his arms. A shout reached his ear, words in German. Faber took his hands from the MG and stared bewildered at the man, apparently a Russian, who stood some twenty yards away. Then Faber displayed a presence of mind in keen contrast to his usual slow-moving temperament. He called hastily to the men within range of his voice, and before the flare had gone out he ordered the Russian, who was shouting that he was Corporal Steiner, to approach the trench slowly, with hands raised. He was quite conscious of the risk he was taking; the whole business might be a clever Russian trap. He kept his finger on the trigger of the MG and waited until the man was close enough so that he could watch his every movement in spite of the darkness. Only then he ordered him to jump into the trench. Men were hurrying up from the neighboring weapon pits, rushing into the MG emplacement with rifles at ready. Suspiciously they stared at him as he stood before them, panting and doubled over, leaning his back against the wall of the trench for support. Faber sent up another flare. After he had made sure

there were no more unexpected visitors on the way he turned
to the men who were pouring out a torrent of words at the
new arrival.

"Quiet!" Faber thrust his broad frame into the middle of
the group. For a few seconds he studied the man silently.
Then he said quietly, "So you're Steiner." The man nodded.
Faber flashed his light on the man's face. It was smeared with
mud, unshaven and unrecognizable. "Where are the others?"
he went on.

"If you waste any more time," the man in Russian uniform
replied irritably, "you can pay them a visit in Siberia. They're
waiting for the signal—green and white flares shot up in succession. Hurry up, damn it!"

Faber hesitated. He had seen Steiner only a few times.
If this man happened to be a double who was posing as
Steiner, the prearranged signal might bring a Lorde of Rus-
sians down on the position. The other men were equally wary.
They had been in the company only a few weeks, and none
of them could recognize Corporal Steiner.

Their hesitancy was understandable but nevertheless disastrous, Steiner realized. Yet a lethargy prevented him from
doing anything. The moment after he had reached the trench
and Third Company, the furious energy which had propelled
him across the three hundred feet of no man's land and up
the slope to the German positions had subsided like a foun-
tain when the pressure is turned off. Reaction set in: he felt
like closing his eyes and falling promptly asleep.

But out there in the night his platoon was waiting. He
pulled himself together, explained the meaning of his mas-
querade to the men, tore open the pack on his back and
produced his own uniform. "Don't be asses," he said with
some return of vigor. "If Meyer or anyone else from my
company were here, they'd let you know who I am, by God.
But we can't take the time to wake up one of them. If I were
a Russian . . ."

He broke off. The men had not noticed that as he spoke
these last words Faber had turned and fussed with his flare
pistol for a few seconds. He moved fast, and before anyone
could stop him a green and right after it a white flare rose
into the sky.

"Are you mad?" one of the men exclaimed angrily. The
others stared in alarm over the rim of the trench.

Faber stood squarely behind his MG watching the flares
sink to the ground and go out. Then he turned his head.
"Go back to your posts. If there's any need for shooting,
leave the first shot to me."

"You should have waited till I went for the sergeant," one man protested.

Faber shook his head. "If what the corporal says is true, we have no time."

"And suppose it isn't true?"

Faber glanced at Steiner. Evenly he said, "Then this fellow will be the first to get a bellyful. . . ." He spoke to Steiner. "Go out there."

"Out where?" Steiner asked in amazement.

Faber waved his hand toward the rim of the trench. "You sit down over there, right in front of the MG, three paces away from the barrel. When the others come along tell them to enter the trench one by one and without their weapons."

"Suppose I don't," Steiner drawled.

"If you don't I'll fire as soon as the first man appears."

Steiner climbed out of the trench and sat down; the other men scurried back to their places. Through his clothes Steiner could feel the damp of the ground. Anger filled him as he stared into the darkness. But his irritation vanished. The man's prudence impressed him; he grinned as he reflected that this was the first time he had obeyed a *soldat's* order without protest. The boy is all right, he said to himself; I couldn't have done a better job. If only he doesn't lose his nerve at the last minute. A ribbon of MG bullets in the back would be devilishly uncomfortable. He turned his head and saw the stocky figure like a dark log behind the machine gun. "What's your name?" he asked.

"I'll tell you later. Shut up now."

Steiner raised his eyebrows. Then he shook his head and began to chuckle. "You're priceless," he whispered, "really priceless." Highly amused, he kept trying to see the man's face, visible only as a white blur.

It was the hour before dawn. The night still clung darkly to the hill, lay upon the trenches and weapon pits and filled every hollow of the land. In the east, however, the face of the night was turning sallow like the skin of a dying man, and above the still invisible horizon a gash in the sky had opened, through which trickled yellowish light. Steiner drew his feet close to his body and turned his eyes ahead again. The men ought to be showing up any second now. He suddenly felt a keen anticipation. There no longer seemed any reason to worry. The loud shouts by which he had announced himself might have made the Russians suspicious, and they might have seen him standing with arms raised in the light of the flares from the German trenches. But the absolute silence on the other side was reassuring. Several times he thought he heard distinctly the rattle of weapons. But the noises might have come from the trenches behind him; he could not be sure. Again and again he glanced at the radiant dial of his wrist watch. It seemed impossible that only four minutes had passed since the green flare rose into the sky. His uneasiness mounted.

He was about to turn and say something. But the man at the MG made a hissing sound. Steiner was amazed at the keenness of the fellow's hearing, for several seconds passed before he also heard the noises. First, there was a vague, dull thudding; then he could distinguish gasping breaths and a tinny rattle. The darkness in front of him suddenly took on life, a stirring and scurrying that abruptly ceased when a flare rose behind him, flooding the area with harsh light. Halfway up the slopes, about sixty feet from the lines, he saw his men. He recognized Schnurrbart and Kruger at once, standing side by side, peering up the hill. The voice of the machine gunner cracked out a few words. Steiner ordered his men to drop their weapons and come up to the lines one by one, at intervals.

As soon as the flare died Schnurrbart appeared. "What's the idea?" he panted. He looked angrily down at Steiner. "Why're you sitting here? What's the matter?"

Before Steiner could answer, Faber spoke up. As soon as he heard Schnurrbart's voice he had taken his hands from the machine gun. Now he climbed out of his weapon pit. "Don't take offense," he said apologetically. "We had to check on you."

Steiner rose slowly. He rubbed his stiff back. "There are easier ways to check, my boy," he said. "A telephone call to Freiburg would have done it. That's my home town."

The other men had come up one by one and thronged around Steiner. He could scarcely fend off all who wanted to shake hands with him. From foxholes on both sides of the MG position sentries hurried up, and word of the successful return of the platoon swept up and down the lines. "Now for half a bottle of schnapps," Kruger said ambitiously. The men of the platoon laughed and nudged one another.

Steiner turned to Schnurrbart. "Was everything all right?"

"Well, now," Schnurrbart said contentedly, "there was a while there when we had butterflies in our stomachs because it seemed so long, but as soon as those flares went up we started out like an express train, let me tell you. On the way . . ." He babbled on about the details of their trip across the no man's land. Steiner only half listened. He was gazing out into the distance with the sudden queer feeling that he had lost something irrecoverable. But he did not know what it was.

Faber watched him in silence for a while. Then he remarked, "I think it would be better if you went on another ten paces before looking back."

Steiner slowly turned to face him. "What's that?"

"As a boy I once got lost in the forest," Faber said. "Maybe you know what it's like. Anyway, my father found me next morning. When he brought me home, that is what he said to me."

Steiner shook his head. "Quoth the raven," he exclaimed. He hesitated for a moment. "But I have a suggestion. Would you care to come over to me—I mean join my platoon?"

"I think so."

"Good," Steiner said. "I'll talk to Meyer about it." He reached for Faber's hand and shook it strongly. Then he turned to the others. "Let's go. We'll rout out Meyer." He grinned. "I don't think he'll be mad at us for disturbing his sleep."

They groped their way forward to the main trench. The others gazed after them in admiration.

When Gausser awoke, it took him awhile to realize where he was. At his side he heard Meyer breathing deeply and evenly. He shook his head. Here they had both gone to sleep in an MG emplacement instead of seeking the comparative comfort of their beds. Along with astonishment at his own conduct he was aware of intense uneasiness as he found himself wondering what had awakened him. As a rule he slept soundly during the most intense artillery barrages; an uncomfortable position never bothered him. It must be late; he glanced at his watch and saw that it was already four o'clock. Day would break before long. For a moment he considered waking Meyer, but Meyer was sleeping so soundly that he could not bear to.

He got up, intending to look around. Suddenly he heard noises. In two rapid strides he was outside, and his eyes widened in surprise. Through the graying darkness of the trench came a long line of men, led by a man of his company. Cheerfully the man raised his hand. "Oh, there you are, sir! Corporal Steiner is back."

Incredulously, and with just a touch of alarm, Gausser stared at the men in Russian uniform. He did not quite take it in until one of the newcomers raised his hand to his cap with studied carelessness and stood appraising him rather insolently. Without a word Gausser stooped and went back into the MG emplacement, where Meyer still slept. He gripped the other man's arm roughly and pulled him to his feet. "Come on out," he shouted in his ear, "come on out, Meyer, you have visitors."

He dragged the recalcitrant, still sleeping company commander outside, where the grinning men awaited them. Meyer jerked away angrily. "Are you going out of your mind, Gausser? What on earth . . ."

The words froze on his lips as he caught sight of the Russian uniforms. Involuntarily his hand flashed to his side.

Gausser seized his arm. "Calmness does it, Lieutenant Meyer. My God, you're hard to satisfy. First, you can't wait until your platoon comes back, and now that your Steiner is here you're all ready to take a pot shot at him."

"Steiner!" Meyer rubbed his eyes and shook his head unbelievingly. Steiner, who had been watching him with amusement, felt a wave of emotion which clamped his lips shut and sent a prickly sensation up his back and through the nape of his neck into his face; the corners of his mouth twitched and he had to dig his teeth into his lower lip to keep from saying something silly. When Meyer gripped his hand and held it clenched in his for a long while, he closed his eyes for a few seconds. Gausser quietly departed.

The shrill ringing of the telephone awoke Stransky from his soundest sleep of the night. As he stumbled to his feet in the darkness, he bumped into the chair on which he had placed his clothes and knocked it over. "Blast it," he cursed, kicked out at it vindictively and cursed again because he had hurt his toes. The ringing went on. Face twisted with pain, he hobbled to the table, lifted the handset and bellowed his name. When he recognized Meyer's voice, his first impulse was to hurl the telephone to the floor. But the company commander's first few words brought him wide awake. What was he saying? That Steiner was back, had brought a prisoner, wiped out a Russian battalion command post. Why, that was . . . "Is this an actual fact?" he demanded.

The cheer went out of Meyer's voice. "I am not in the habit of playing practical jokes, sir!" he replied sharply.

Stransky sat down at the table and thought for a moment. Then he instructed Meyer to bring the prisoner and the platoon to his bunker at once. He hung up. For a while he sat lost in thought, unable to decide how to act. The return of the platoon presented him with a number of problems he would sooner not have dealt with. Chief of these was his promise to promote the corporal. Naturally, he told himself, he could simply pretend to have forgotten his conversation with Meyer on the subject. But Meyer would undoubtedly make a point of reminding him. The thought of Meyer's temerity was even more unpleasant than the promotion as such. What irked him was not only that Meyer had been right, but also that he, Stransky, would have to pay tribute to Meyer's rightness by promoting Steiner. The longer he considered this the deeper grew his antagonism for his company commander.

He lighted a candle and dressed. He would look this man Steiner over carefully. If the regimental commander thought so much of him, it would certainly not be out of order to display his generosity and jump Steiner ahead. That was it: he would make him a senior sergeant.

He had just finished buckling his belt when there was a knock at the door. Quickly he stepped to the little window and looked out. Day was breaking. Above the rim of the trench stood several men; he could see only their heads. Their faces looked gray and weary in the cold light of the morning. When he stepped outside, he found Meyer before him. Stransky bit his lip at the triumph in Meyer's face. He mounted the steps and silently inspected the men. They stood close together, their heads held high, and he sensed that this was a great moment for them. They still wore the Russian uniforms. Stransky's eyebrows rose. When he turned for explanation to Meyer, the lieutenant nodded, smiling. "I forgot to mention the uniforms, sir. You see . . ."

Stransky waved his hand impatiently. "I'll hear the explanation later. Which of these is the prisoner?"

Meyer pointed to the Russian, who stood in the background watching alertly. The men of the battalion staff had meanwhile come out of the other bunkers. Stransky turned to Triebig. "Put the prisoner in a bunker and see to it that he is well guarded," he ordered.

Meyer felt obliged to point out the Russian's rank. "He is a captain, sir."

"At the moment he is a prisoner of war," Stransky replied coldly.

He looked at the men again. "Which one is Corporal Steiner?"

Steiner took a step forward and slackly came to attention. Stransky studied him, disappointed. From all that he had heard he had formed another picture of Steiner—a vague one, resembling in no way the man who stood before him and met his gaze with insulting unconcern. He felt Meyer eying him and stiffened. "You are promoted to senior sergeant, promo-

tion to be effective at once!" he declared loudly. He watched
Steiner's face. But again he experienced a disappointment.
It was as if he had spoken to a tree. Steiner betrayed no sign
of surprise; only the manner in which he flexed his arms
slightly indicated that he had heard at all.

Stransky frowned. Then he turned abruptly to Meyer. "Come
in, you and the sergeant."

As Steiner followed the two officers down the steps to the
bunker, he suddenly felt his knees shaking from exhaustion.
In spite of the half dozen shots of schnapps he had drunk in
Meyer's bunker, he was shivering with cold.

The men of the platoon watched him go. It was a chilly,
disagreeable morning, the air filled with mist. The lift of
muddy slopes on all sides made the scene even gloomier.
Schnurrbart stretched, his teeth chattering. He turned to
Kruger. "Some reception, huh? I tell you, if Brandt were still
here . . ." He glared down at the commander's bunker.

"This one looked like a stinker to me the first time I laid
eyes on him," Kruger growled.

They stood in a huddle, cross and cold, answering in monosyllables the questions bombarded at them by the men of the
staff. Their exuberant mood had been thoroughly quelled.
Standing around in filthy, soaking wet clothes did not improve
their humor; all they could think about was their need for
sleep. After a while they accepted the invitation of the signalmen and scattered among the men's bunkers to await Steiner's
return.

Meanwhile the newly appointed sergeant sat at the regimental commander's table, reporting in short, clipped sen-
tences the events of the past few days. Meyer, who had already
heard most of the story, remained silent, but Stransky kept
interrupting with questions. Steiner at first answered these
patiently, but gradually grew more and more irritable. He had
difficulty keeping his eyes open, and Meyer, well aware of
his condition, finally thought the time had come to put an
end to the conversation—all the more so since the main
events had been covered.

When Stransky wanted to know what had happened to their
original guns, Meyer cleared his throat. "Wouldn't it be possible to discuss these matters at some later time, sir?" he suggested. "It seems to me that Sergeant Steiner is too exhausted
to go into more detail. Besides, the other men are waiting
outside; they'll catch their deaths in those wet clothes."

Stransky's eyes flashed angrily. But since there was little
objection he could raise, he nodded with a hypocritical sympathy. "You should have reminded me of this sooner," he said.

"But after all I must have some of the details in order to make my report to Regiment." He crushed out his cigarette and smiled patronizingly at Steiner. "I have been in the habit of interrogating men in the uniform you are wearing, not receiving reports from them. A new experience, really. Take your platoon back to Kanskoye. Until tonight you may catch up on some sleep. I shall expect you back when the supply column comes over, since there are several points I am still unclear about." He let his eyes travel over Steiner's filthy uniform once more. Then he smiled harshly. "See to it that you transform yourself into a German sergeant by then.... Incidentally, the uniform looks very well on you; were you an actor before the war?"

Meyer raised his head, alert to the insult in the words. Steiner showed no change of expression as he replied, "Not before the war."

Stransky folded his arms. Something in the man's intonation did not please him. "You seem to emphasize the word 'before,'" he said.

Steiner appraised him. Then he shrugged. "If I did, it was accidental."

"So?" Stransky scratched his chin in vexation. There was something wrong with the fellow's attitude; he seemed to think that he was talking to an equal. The fact that he was careful in his choice of words and overstepped the limits Stransky had mentally set for the rank of a noncom only in his tone made it all the more offensive. Stransky made up his mind to cut him down to size: "I have the feeling, Sergeant, that you somewhat overestimate your importance," he said.

A little color rose in the gray of Steiner's exhausted face. His eyes darkened, turned almost black. But there was no change in his voice. "At the moment I am free of any such illusions."

Stransky stared at him more in astonishment than indignation. In a voice just a shade colder he said, "You are in the habit of speaking your mind, I see, but I would nevertheless suggest to you not to underestimate your present company. At any rate never forget that everything you are and may become is dependent upon that present company."

"I don't think I will forget that," Steiner replied coolly. "Although I may add that a man generally is what he feels himself to be."

Stransky pushed his chair back and rose. His face looked sallow and apathetic. The candles on the table flickered tiredly in the dimness of the bunker, though the daylight was seeping

in through the window with increasing brightness. The air was
heavy and stale. Steiner felt a craving to get outside into the
open air. As he, along with Meyer, followed the commander's
example and rose, fatigue almost toppled him; he had to lean
on the table for support. Stransky picked up the maps Steiner
had brought and spoke to Meyer. "I will inform Regiment;
see to it that the prisoner is taken to Kiesel at once."

He turned again to Steiner. "For my part you can feel as
you like. But when you talk with me do not forget that you
are wearing a uniform. In the future keep that in mind."
He reached for the telephone and Steiner decided that he had
been dismissed.

As he stepped outside, Meyer laid a hand on his shoulder.
"A useful tip," he said. "Remember from now on that we
have a different battalion commander."

Steiner did not answer. They collected the men from the
bunkers and Meyer shook hands with each of them. "Get
yourselves plenty of sleep. I'll see to it that you're given a
few day's rest." He turned again to Steiner and explained the
route they must take to Kanskoye. "You'll be there in twenty
minutes. Fetscher will take care of you. I've had him informed. Well . . ." He hesitated and lowered his voice. "Don't
forget by tonight what I've just said."

The platoon watched him walk off toward the bunker where
the prisoner had been put. Schnurrbart clicked his heels and
rasped, "Pull your asses together from now on; we have a
sergeant for platoon leader." Laughing, they crowded around
Steiner and pounded him on the back.

"Boy, you're a big shot now," Anselm said flatteringly. "Do
we have to say 'sir' when we talk to you?"

"Shut up, moron," Steiner replied grimly. "I've just been
told in there—" he jerked a thumb toward the commander's
bunker—"how much of a big shot I am."

"Why, what was wrong?" Kruger asked.

Steiner gestured wearily. "Forget it. There'll be a better
time to . . ." The rest of the sentence trailed off.

"Was there something he didn't like?" Schnurrbart asked
sourly.

Steiner shrugged. He slunk the tommy gun over his shoulder.
"Let's get to the village. I'll be glad to be rid of these wet rags."

They descended into the ravine and followed the winding
brook. Although the sky was still clouded, the rains seemed
to be over. The sight of the bushes that lined the brook, their
fresh green contrasting with the barrenness of the dead clay
slopes, somewhat revived the men. Their thoughts hurried on
ahead; they could see themselves already resting in comfort-

able, dry quarters beyond the next or at most the next but one turn in the path. One of them began to sing. Hollerbach took up the song, and a few moments later the echo of their voices boomed boisterously down the gorge:

> We, we are the huntsmen of the plains,
> The starvelings of the nation.
> For three years now, in snow and rain
> We've marched on dehydrated rations.

> Forward, you huntsmen of the plains,
> Forward, to do your fighting all alone.
> For the others come in cars when the battle is all done.
> Forward, you huntsmen of the plains.

Up ahead, through a cluster of trees, the first houses appeared. A minute later they were surrounded by a crowd of admirers who slapped them on the back, shook hands and hurled so many questions that it would have taken hours to answer all. Finally the massive figure of a staff sergeant thrust through the crowd, cursed furiously for silence and stood shaking his head at the appearance of Steiner and the others. He was a powerfully built man with rugged, honest features; it was easy to imagine him pacing slowly behind a plow. Several times he started to speak but was so stunned by the sight of the Russian uniforms that he could not say a word.

Steiner grinned. He had always got on well with Fetscher. Slowly he brought his heels together, performed a caricature of standing at attention, raised his hand to his cap and said, "Beg to report, sir . . ."

The sergeant's face turned red. Suddenly he found speech again, and the rest of Steiner's report was drowned out in a series of obscene curses.

"Come up for air," Steiner said at last. "You've used up two weeks' stock of profanity. Better show us our quarters."

Fetscher continued to mutter under his breath for a moment, but then he roused himself and displayed such admirable efficiency that within a few minutes the men were being guided by members of the supply column to comfortable houses. Steiner followed Fetscher to his own house. As soon as he stepped inside he dropped the pack from his back to the floor and interrupted Fetscher who was talking a blue streak. "Hold your horses. I want to eat and sleep and first of all I want to wash. Let me alone now."

Fetscher went out. Later, when Steiner came out of the kitchen, freshly washed and shaved, his mess tin stood on the table, filled to the brim with stew. He sat down. Strangely enough, he no longer felt hungry, and his weariness seemed to have washed away in the hot water. He felt depressed and ill-humored without knowing why. All right, so they were back with the battalion. Meyer had been as happy as a child on Christmas morning, he himself had been promoted, looked and smelled like a human being again—everything seemed fine, and still . . . He propped his chin on his fists and stared out the window where fragile rays of sunlight played on the fresh green of the trees. He recalled the conversation with Stransky and snorted contemptuously. So that was the sort of guy . . . Well, he would see what came of it. Stransky was only one of the many battalion commanders he had survived; he would survive Stransky, too. A stupid, self-important ass —no need to take him seriously. What the devil were they so proud of, those arrogant bastards? Of their ancestry? It wasn't their doing. Of their money? They'd inherited it. Of their education? They'd had time to get one. He laughed and pushed the mess tin aside. Then he stood up and walked slowly to the window. Maag was just passing, a new uniform over his arm, his face reflecting contentment. Steiner watched him until he disappeared into the house across the way. Undemanding and shallow, he thought bitterly. They're all tickled to be back with the battalion. Here they felt at home, safe, sheltered. But he himself, where was he at home? Certainly not back in Freiburg, where since two years ago there had been no one waiting for him. He leaned his forehead against the cool windowpane and closed his eyes. If only there were still Anne, he thought. Anne! For the first time he felt that he had lost her forever.

At Regiment H.Q. the news of the missing platoon's return was a bombshell. Brandt sent for Kiesel at once. Kiesel had rarely known the commander to be in such high spirits. In spite of the early hour, Brandt had a bottle on the table in front of him—of genuine Black Forest kirschwasser, he emphasized. Kiesel declined a glass; he could not take alcohol on an empty stomach, he said.

"You're an ascetic," Brandt declared, filling the water glass. *"Prost!"* He drained his glass in one swig. "I told you right off," he said, "that Steiner would come through. What a boy, Kiesel, what a boy! If we had a few hundred like him the Russians would never have a peaceful moment."

"Have you heard any of the details?" Kiesel asked.

"Un wie! I made Stransky cough up the story. He didn't like it a bit; it's my feeling that we'll have to watch him for a while. You keep an eye on him, Kiesel."

"I don't quite understand," Kiesel said in surprise.

"You will soon enough. Remember that Stransky has already had some difficulty over Steiner, and remember the type Stransky is. He has a damned loose tongue on him anyway," Brandt added cheerfully.

"Stransky?" Kiesel exclaimed.

"Don't be silly. Steiner, of course. So watch sharp. And now get an earful of what that hellhound has done."

He began the story of the platoon, repeatedly bursting into laughter and pounding the table with his fist. "And do you know what I'm going to do?" he concluded.

"Promote him, of course," Kiesel guessed.

"He has already been promoted. Stransky did that right away—even jumped him a grade to senior sergeant. A lucky stroke by the way, or I would have made a point of asking him to. No, I was thinking of something else—sending Steiner to Gursuf for two weeks. What do you think?"

"He deserves it," Kiesel answered. Gursuf was a small spa on the southern coast of the Crimea where the division operated a rest camp.

Kiesel held up a letter. "If you don't mind, I have a personal favor to ask this morning. I have a letter from my brother-in-law, Lieutenant März."

"What about him?"

Kiesel hesitated, then gave a rueful laugh. "He insists on a transfer to the front, and to the eastern front of all places. Right now he's a company commander in a Leipzig garrison. You know how these young chaps are. Think they're missing something if they don't get out here. He's set his heart on it, and if I know him he'll keep at it until he's where he wants to be."

Brandt nodded. "I take it you want to keep him near you."

"Exactly. I would feel a good deal better about it. Perhaps it would be possible to ask for him through Division."

"Will do," Brandt said, making a note of the matter. "How old is he?"

"Twenty-four. He comes from Villingen in the Black Forest —the family owns a watch factory out there."

Before Brandt could inquire further there was a knock at the door and a soldier reported the arrival of Lieutenant Triebig with the prisoner. Brant nodded to Triebig as he entered the bunker. "You can return immediately," he said. "Tell Stransky I want to congratulate him on the return of his platoon, and tell him furthermore that I will expect Sergeant Steiner here at six o'clock. Have you the captured maps?"

Triebig laid the maps on the table and withdrew. On the

way back he studied the terrain carefully. From the hill behind which Regimental H.Q. was located there was an excellent view of the surrounding countryside. Beyond the ravine rose the crooked ridge of Hill 121.4. The trenches and weapon pits could be seen clearly. Every detail of this terrain must be equally visible from the enemy positions, Triebig thought, and involuntarily walked faster. He did not slow down again until he had reached the ravine; then he returned to his sauntering pace. In the past few days he had thought a great deal about his conversation with Stransky and had come to the conclusion that he could not have handled his end of it more foolishly. But his nervousness had dissipated. His resolve to kill Stransky had already dwindled down to a mere wish, of no more intensity than his desire to spend one of these spring days strolling through the streets of Cologne again. He had decided not to act too hastily in any dealing with Stransky. Perhaps something would turn up; he would keep his eyes open for opportunities.

When Steiner set out shortly after five o'clock, the Russian artillery was sending occasional nuisance bursts into the ravine. He avoided the direct road and made a wide detour around the dangerous area. As a result, it took him nearly an hour to reach Regimental H.Q., and he arrived a few minutes late. As he approached he admired the skillful arrangement of the bunkers. They had been built into a part of the slope that rose almost vertically, so that it would be virtually impossible for enemy guns to reach them. Steiner asked his way to the commander's bunker, which had no outward marking to distinguish it from the rest.

Brandt strode forward to meet him and pressed his hand vigorously. "So here you are," he said loudly, "unpunctual and unsoldierly as ever." He laughed and propelled Steiner to a chair.

Steiner looked up at his large, friendly face and shrugged regretfully. "The way was longer than I thought; I had to . . ."

"No need to apologize," Brandt interrupted, taking a seat opposite him. "If that sort of thing bothered me I would have seen that you changed your ways long ago." He laughed again and shook his head. "What you've pulled off this time beats all. I wouldn't have thought you could do it."

"We were lucky," Steiner replied.

Brandt crossed his legs. "If luck was all there was to it," he said quietly, "you wouldn't be sitting here. Now tell me all about it. Don't leave anything out." He took a pack of cigarettes from his pocket and handed them across the table.

Steiner thanked him, lighted one and began his report. When Steiner came to the encounter with the Russian women, Brandt took a few notes.

After Steiner had finished, he said, "You've done a wonderful job, Steiner. It's a long time since I've felt as pleased as I do today; we know each other well enough for me to be able to say that to you. Your report is enormously valuable; I intend to transmit it personally to the general. I hope it gives him a thing or two to think about. You know the big brass think we're in a rest camp down here; maybe they'll see what's brewing when I tell them about the matériel you saw rolling down that highway."

Steiner regarded him in silence. His relations with Brandt had been good from the start, without his having made any effort. The men had felt drawn to each other, and since the incident at Studenok the commander had displayed an understandable interest in him. After becoming commander of the regiment Brandt had suggested that he stay with him, and had offered him a quiet staff post. But Steiner had politely asked permission to remain with his men. He could still see how disappointed Brandt had looked. Asked for his reasons, Steiner had referred to his feelings of solidarity with the men. It would have been difficult to explain to the commander that he did not want to be dependent on anyone, let alone a regimental commander, no matter how good a fellow. Since then he had not seen Brandt, and he was relieved to find that the commander did not seem to hold his refusal against him. Yet he could not stifle a slight sense of uneasiness, and he waited impatiently to be dismissed.

When Brandt thrust some papers across the table and told him that beginning tomorrow he was to start a two-week furlough in the Crimea, he could not rise to the occasion. In fact, he found himself raising various objections to the furlough. However, when it became apparent that the commander was beginning to be seriously displeased, he shrugged his acquiescence. "If it's your command, sir . . . You see, the reason that I don't feel easy about it is that every man in my platoon deserves this furlough and it will make a bad impression if I——"

"As far as I can recall," Brandt interrupted him sharply, "you have never given a hang about the impression you were making anywhere and at any time. You are going on furlough tomorrow, and that's all there is to it. I have already informed your company commander." He rose quickly. "Sometimes, Steiner, you make it hard for me to forget that I am your superior."

"I often wonder why you try to forget it." Steiner also stood up and looked expectantly at the commander.

Brandt's mouth began to twitch and his voice shook. "You're the freshest bastard that's ever come my way. If you aren't gone by tomorrow, I'll have you chased away from this front at bayonet point."

He gripped Steiner by the shoulders and propelled him out the door. A little bewildered, Steiner began ascending the slope and almost failed to notice an officer coming down the path toward him. The officer looked him over carefully. Steiner recognized the regimental adjutant. "You are Steiner," the officer said. Carefully, so that the slackness of his reaction would not be overlooked, Steiner placed his feet together and nodded. A fleeting smile passed over the captain's stern features. "So I thought," he said. He continued on up the hill and vanished into the commander's bunker. Steiner looked after him with a startled expression. Then he continued on his way, whistling.

He was due at the battalion command post at eight o'clock. Since the Russian fire had stopped toward evening, he reached the headquarters without incident. He had more than half an hour before his scheduled interview with Stransky, and he dropped in on Meyer first. The lieutenant gave him a hearty greeting and congratulated him on his impending leave.

"I've already informed the captain," he said. "He doesn't seem altogether delighted, but orders are orders and not even Captain Stransky can scotch them." He produced cigarettes and schnapps. "The two weeks will do you good. I'm afraid, though, that things will be popping here by the time you return."

"Really?" Steiner asked.

Meyer nodded gravely. "I'd say that the Russian preparations indicate a big offensive in the making. Since we're right in a salient, I imagine we'll be hit hard. That damned hill," he added uncomfortably. From somewhere outside came the dull thud of exploding shells. "Do you hear that? Must be a seventeen-two. They're bringing in new guns every day over there."

"They have plenty," Steiner commented.

Meyer leaned across the table. "I did want to tell you this. Be careful with Stransky. He seems to have taken a dislike to you. He's sure to make a stink about the weapons you discarded."

Steiner waved that away. "I've already reported the matter to Colonel Brandt. He let it pass without a word."

"That's good." Meyer was visibly relieved. He glanced at

his watch. "You'd better be on your way; it's nearly eight."

Steiner finished his glass and reached for his cap. As they shook hands Meyer said, "Don't forget us while you're on leave."

"I've been in your company too long for that," Steiner said.

It was dark outside, with stars gleaming among scattered clouds and a soft breeze blowing over the hill. Steiner took a deep breath. It was starting to feel like spring. At home the last patches of snow would be melting among the pine trees. He stood still abruptly, astonished at his own thoughts and emotions. Was this homesickness? Perhaps—a homesickness for memories. Violently he started forward again and went toward the battalion headquarters by the shortest route, without bothering to use the trench.

When he entered the commander's bunker, Stransky was sitting over a map. He looked up and said, "Here you are. Sit down. You're three minutes late."

"Dark out," Steiner explained laconically, taking the offered seat.

Stransky took a cigarette case from his pocket, removed one cigarette, tapped it carefully on his thumbnail several times and finally put it between his lips. Steiner watched him impassively. There was the outside chance that Stransky would offer him a cigarette and as this was the last thing he wanted, he put on an expression of refusal.

But Stransky came promptly to the point. "I've sent for you in order to clarify certain obscurities," he said. "Principally I should like to hear again how your casualties occurred. You lost two men?"

"I've been over that," Steiner said curtly. This was a subject he preferred to steer clear of. After Schnurrbart had pointed out that even if Zoll had made off, they ought to conceal the fact out of consideration for Zoll's parents, they had all agreed on a new version of the story. Zoll was simply to be reported missing. This was the story as Steiner had given in his first report and Stransky's inquisitiveness endangered it. "That time we ran into the Russians," he went on reluctantly, "it was already dark in the woods. Dietz received two shots in the back, while Zoll simply vanished."

"Did you look for him?" Stransky asked.

Steiner shrugged impatiently. "We had no time to lose. It would have been irresponsible to risk the safety of the entire platoon for the sake of one man. I'm glad we came out of it as well as we did."

"You will have to make a written report," Stransky declared. "There ought not to be any missing men in such cases.

But let us drop that for the moment. There is another matter I cannot understand. What prompted you to exchange weapons? As you surely know, the weapons are entered in the men's paybooks and each man is responsible for the equipment entrusted to him. You know that, don't you?" He did not wait for an answer. "Furthermore, you must also be aware that the quality of our arms is far superior to that of the Russians and . . ."

When Steiner shook his head, he broke off. "I beg your pardon?" he asked, raising his eyebrows.

"On the contrary," Steiner said. "In our opinion the German tommy gun is not nearly as good as the Russian. Ask any of the men in the trenches. They'll all tell you the same thing."

"That is stupid, loose talk," Stransky retorted sharply. "The weapons as designed by our engineers and produced in German factories are superior to any others. You have every reason to be grateful for the fine equipment that the Fatherland puts into your hands at the cost of countless sacrifices."

Steiner could not quite suppress a grin. "I never asked them to put the stuff in my hands, you know."

Stransky took a deep breath. "I request you for the last time to mind your tone. I haven't asked you here for a discussion. I have told you that our equipment is far superior to that of the Russians and I do not wish . . ."

The rest of the sentence failed to reach Steiner's consciousness. He had no desire to bicker with Stransky. Let him talk, he thought. For his part he let himself drop down into the bottomless weariness which still filled his body in spite of the rest he had had. From far away Stransky's voice sounded like the troublesome buzzing of a fly. Steiner looked down at his hands and tried to move his fingers. They remained stiff and motionless, and he wondered why. Disturbed, he moved his legs, tensed his biceps and, yawning, concentrated wholly on his hands.

Then he heard the commander's voice again; it was violent now, had risen almost to a shout. Uncomprehending, Steiner lifted his head and looked at the captain. He realized that Stransky was now standing; his face was red and his eyes, ordinarily so icy, were flaming. What was this about? Steiner wondered. Active passivity, he thought; I've been able to do something without doing a thing. He was still considering this when he suddenly felt himself gripped by the arm and jerked to his feet. With more astonishment than indignation he blinked at the commander's excited face. Then he pulled free and reached for the Russian tommy gun hanging from the chair. Without another look at Stransky he turned to the door. As he stepped out into the night, the stars came rushing at him. For a second he closed his eyes. Tomorrow evening, he thought, tomorrow evening you'll be in Gursuf.

He tried to think of the mountains, of the endless swells of the sea and the white beach. He opened his eyes and looked about him. The bunkers, dark and apparently deserted mounds, lay scattered among the trees. It was beautifully still. Absorbed in thought, he followed the path down the ravine and along the brook.

It was shortly after nine o'clock when he reached Kanskoye. When he entered Fetscher's house he heard the men's voices. They stopped talking as he opened the door. The whole platoon, sitting around the big table with bottles and glasses in front of them, looked up at him. Schnurrbart pointed to an empty chair. "Have a seat."

Steiner studied them in astonishment. "Why so solemn?" he asked. He sat down and looked around expectantly.

Kruger stood up sheepishly. In a somewhat hoarse voice, he began: "Fetscher told us that you were leaving tomorrow. Fetscher's a pretty good hand at rounding up things to drink. Now I'm not much of a speaker and two weeks are a long time, but the fellows here wanted me to say something."

As he hesitated, Steiner gave him an encouraging nod. The men grinned.

Kruger scowled at them and went on: "As I was saying, two weeks are a damned long time, a hell of a long time, I tell you, and we hope you'll come back and we're still here, we hope, and as I was saying . . ." He frowned and plucked agitatedly at his nose. "The devil take this war, but if this war gets us first we hope you're with us." He became aware of the broadening grins of the men and began to stammer. "I don't mean by that that I want us, I mean that I want you to be, but that all of us, all of us sitting here together, if we're with you and . . ." He stumbled to a halt, his face flushed.

Abruptly he banged the table with his fist and turned to the men, quivering with rage. "I told you I couldn't do it, you idiots." He reached for his glass and gulped down its contents, at the same time sneaking a look at a bit of paper he held in his palm. It was done so clumsily that everyone saw it.

"If I were you I'd start from the beginning again," Schnurrbart proposed innocently.

Kruger glowered at him. "You know what you can do?"

Schnurrbart nodded soberly. "I know. You've made that suggestion time and again."

"Have I now?" Kruger leaned far across the table. "Then go ahead and do it," he bellowed. 'Why don't you do it, you lousy mongrel, you mustache cup, you . . ." The rest of his explosion was drowned out in the roaring laughter of the men. Kruger dropped into his chair and stared bitterly at his glass.

Steiner placed a hand on his shoulder and quickly stood up. The men were silent.

"There are things that one cannot talk about," he said quietly. "We know one another and don't have to say anything. The fact that this great speech didn't turn out so well—" he smiled at Kruger—"isn't the speaker's fault; it's because of the subject. There are all kinds of things that make bonds between people—love, respect, habit and so on. That sort of thing can be talked about. But the bond among us is nothing like that. Our uniform isn't a bond either; it only brought us together." He paused and looked into their earnest faces. There were four candles on the table, half burned down, and for a moment he watched with his mind empty of thought as the hot wax dripped down. Then he raised his head. "Sometimes we feel what it is. But if we wanted to talk about it, it would sound silly. Better to keep it to ourselves. If we want to show one another what our mutual feelings are, there will certainly be better occasions than this. Let us just hold on to those feelings."

They remained silent a long time after he had sat down again and filled his glass from one of the bottles. The sporadic conversation which commenced again here and there around the table had none of the usual brashness about it. Steiner said little for a while. He felt that something had gone wrong; something strange and disturbing had taken place within him which he could not relate to any of his previous experiences. And the queerness was not only inside him; there was something wrong all around him also. Pondering, he stared into space. His life ever since, since then . . . hadn't it been like slowly toiling through an almost endless tunnel? Walking on and on toward a distant glimmer of light? The thought came as a vision, and for a few seconds it seemed to him that he need only open his eyes abruptly in order to see clearly where he was. But his eyes were open. He held his glass between both hands, his breathing came hard. He struggled toward the lucidity which lay just ahead, just around the corner. Finally, disappointed, he slumped back in his seat. It's hopeless, he thought; you can be almost on the point of grasping it and then . . .

To the Professor, who sat at his right, he said, "No philosophy tonight, but there's one question I want to ask you."

"Go right ahead." Dorn adjusted his glasses and was all attention.

"It won't cost anything to ask," Steiner said. He lowered his voice, and the flippancy disappeared from his tone. "Is there anything one can do to help oneself forget?"

Dorn's thin face became grave. He looked away from Steiner and his glance lingered on the wine goblets. They were part of a precious table service; more than once in the course of the evening he had marveled that things of this sort existed in Russia. Carefully he picked up one of the thin-stemmed glasses, drank the remaining wine, and raised it to the candle-light. He turned it swiftly between his fingers. The polished crystal sparkled. Then he put it down on the table and met Steiner's eyes. "There's the answer," Dorn said. "Live and be alive, see and be seen, and a few other things—but you know that yourself."

The conversation at the table had revived. The men were growing boisterous now. Anselm filled his glass. "What did the Old Man want of you?" he asked Steiner.

"Nothing in particular. I had to finish my report."

They spoke disparagingly of Stransky for a while. "We'll fix him," Anselm boasted. "Just wait till he's been here a few weeks; we'll trim him down. Anyway, you don't have to worry about him for the next two weeks. What's the name of the place they're sending you to?"

"Gursuf," Steiner replied.

Anselm sighed enviously. "Must be some hot women there, eh?"

"Maybe—I don't care. I want to relax."

Launched now on their favorite topic, the men talked about women through the next few bottles. Later they began to sing. When the general boisterousness had reached its height, Steiner went out of the house. Slowly he strolled along the dark road, taking deep breaths of the clear night air. After a while he heard footsteps behind him. Dorn came up quickly. "Am I in the way?" he asked.

Steiner suppressed a rude reply and thrust his hands into his pockets. "Hardly. What brings you out?"

"I need a little air."

They walked side by side back toward the house. "We might sit down for a while up there," Steiner said, indicating the hill that rose up behind the house. Halfway to the top they dropped to the ground and looked silently down at the buildings. The men's loud singing reached their ears. Steiner closed his eyes.

Im Feldquartier auf hartem Stein
Streck ich die müden Glieder
Und sende in die Nacht hinein
Der Liebsten meine Lieder.

As he listened to the time-honored soldier's song, he felt a great tiredness that drained off all the bitterness and restored a profound sense of peace within him. The mild night air stirred memories, aroused nostalgia and a rare gladness. For the first time he felt pleasure at the thought of two weeks of rest. An impatience to be there took hold of him. To see the sea stretching before him—he could hardly wait. Again he gave ear to the singing. Hollerbach's tenor rose distinctly above the voices of the others:

Vielleicht werd ich bald bei dir sein,
Annemarie,
Vielleicht scharrt man schon morgen ein
Die ganze Kompanie, die ganze Kompanie.

The song ended. The two men sat together in silence. In the sky the multitudinous stars sparkled, and the houses lay bedded down among the still trees, sleeping. They slept, and everything was strangely close and vast. Steiner looked down below and the song ran through his head, the song and the men who sang it. The predatory Nazi hordes, the Huns and barbarians—his comrades.

Many minutes passed. Then a band of light appeared among the trees below. Someone had opened the door. Schnurrbart was silhouetted on the threshold; he took a few steps away from the house and looked around, apparently searching. "They're getting worried about us," Dorn said.

"I guess so." Steiner stood up and called out in reassurance. Schnurrbart went back inside. The door closed and the darkness flooded back.

Down below in the house the men started singing again. Steiner hummed the melody under his breath. Then he drew Dorn to his feet. They stopped in silence a few minutes longer, looking over the dark hills.

"By himself a man is scrap iron," Steiner said roughly. Dorn nodded. As they walked down the hill, Steiner kept his hand on Dorn's shoulder. His hand was still there as they entered the house.

VII

TOWARD noon two days later, Steiner rode the last leg to his destination in the back of a heavily laden truck. He stood at last somewhat dazed on the cobbled pavement, watching the vehicle rattling away down the road. Now that he was no longer cooled by the wind of its motion, he could feel how searing hot the sun was. The heat was doubly unpleasant because of the heavy camouflage suit he wore over his uniform. Fetscher had thought it best for him to take all his stuff with him—one never knew. Fetscher had also swapped the Russian tommy gun for a German one. "As long as you're on furlough," he had said self-importantly. "Any MP would arrest you on the spot if he saw you carrying that thing. You're going back to rear echelon, don't forget that, my boy." He was right, of course, and so Steiner had set out with his pack loaded and festooned with all the regulation equipment.

He slung the straps of his pack over his shoulders and stood for a few minutes perplexed. The street was still and deserted. Apparently the inhabitants of the little resort kept to their houses at this time of day. The houses which lined both sides of the street were set among gardens of tropical lushness. The village lay at the foot of a mountain slope, which from this point seemed almost vertical. On one hand the restless sea gleamed with the same blueness as the sky. Low pines and tall palms bordered the pebbly white beach, and out of the water gigantic rocks rose like petrified fountains above the white surf.

Steiner tore his eyes away from the peacefulness of it and set out down the street. A soldier lounging under the arch of a garden gate was dressed only in shirt and trousers. When Steiner spoke to him, he barely moved his head. But he was awake enough to point the way to the Division Rest Home. It was only a short distance away, a huge building with tall windows and marble pillars in the façade, set close to the beach in the midst of spacious grounds. The flat roof was shaded by a large grove of pines. As Steiner approached the door opened. A sergeant and a Red Cross nurse came out. Steiner sauntered toward them. He did not like the sergeant's leathery face, nor his brand-new uniform with the knifelike creases in the trousers. He was only too familiar with that type from back in the barracks.

The sergeant scrutinized Steiner from top to toe. "What do you want, soldier?" he asked.

Steiner thrust his thumb under his pack straps and stared coolly at the man. "Do you mean me, soldier?" he retorted.

The leathery forehead flushed. Steiner ignored the angry sergeant and looked at the nurse. She had a pretty, insipid doll's face with bright, watery eyes, and she looked at him indignantly.

"Who do you think you are?" the sergeant bellowed. "What are you doing here? What do you want?"

Steiner grinned. "A room with running water, central heating and a view of the ocean. Anything of that sort available, my man?"

The sergeant gaped at him while the nurse giggled foolishly. Steiner reached into his pocket and handed the sergeant his papers. The man leafed through them for a moment, and the expression on his face slowly changed. When he handed them back, there was embarrassment in his voice. "How's a fellow to tell who's inside one of those damned play suits you've got on?" He turned to the nurse. "Where can we put him? All the rooms are taken."

"Is he to stay here?" she asked in surprise.

"Yes. Sergeant Steiner—two weeks' leave." He laughed angrily. "God only knows how they figure it. We always receive our men by groups, each group to stay ten days. The whole place is filled up."

Steiner was growing impatient. "You must have a closet empty. Otherwise I'll look for private quarters."

"There's a regulation against that," the sergeant replied quickly. He thought for a moment.

"We could put him upstairs," the nurse said with sudden eagerness.

The sergeant looked at her. "You mean upstairs?"

She nodded. He hesitated. Then he turned to Steiner again. "We do have one room for special visitors, but it's on the third floor."

Steiner scrutinized his face and then the nurse's. "For special visitors?" He noticed the nurse blushing and grinned. "I'll take it. I don't suppose you have an elevator?"

The sergeant laughed. "The servants didn't have it that cozy. You see," he went on conversationally, "the house used to be the summer residence of some Russian government official. The upper rooms were for the servants. We'll get that room ready now. You can wait on the bench there. We won't be long." He pointed to a white bench under the trees. Then he beckoned to the nurse and went back inside. Steiner slung his pack from his back, unbuttoned the camouflage jacket and dropped onto the bench with a sigh. He looked out over the sea. Somewhere out there, beyond the horizon, lay Turkey, Syria, Arabia and the Indian Ocean: the great wide world, adventure and distance, the islands and dreams of youth, longing and its fulfillment. He looked at the white beading of the surf. There was an almost unnatural silence here, broken only by the rhythmic slapping of the waves. Eyes half-closed, he let the song of the sea lull him. Pleasantly weary, he felt grateful now for the warmth of the cloudless April day. Now and then a cool breeze wafted across the water; then the pines were stirred out of their immobility and their shadows danced across the gardens.

He completely forgot where he was. When he heard a voice in his ear, it took him a while to recover awareness of his surroundings. The nurse was standing at the door, her face under its white cap turned toward him. He stood up slowly, picked up his pack and walked toward her. "Had you fallen asleep?" she asked.

"No, but I was pretty close to it. The room's done already?"

"Yes. You'll like it." As they mounted the stairs side by side she talked steadily. "You're really in luck. The other noncoms are two or three to a room. This is the first time anyone has arrived so irregularly. Incidentally, your room is right next to mine."

He glanced at her face out of the corner of his eye and said, "I hope you don't snore. I'm very sensitive to noise."

They had reached the third floor. She approached one of the many doors. "This is it," she said, letting him go ahead of her.

On the threshold he paused for a moment to study the room. At the left stood the bed, its head beneath the large casement windows. In the center of the room stood a small table and two chairs. The right wall was taken up by a wide couch with several cushions.

Steiner turned and saw the nurse close behind him. "Do you like it?" she asked.

He nodded, went over to the table and laid his pack on it. Then he stepped to the window and looked out.

"You can see the sunset every evening from here," she said, still right behind him.

As he turned to face her, he found his arm brushing her breast. He wrinkled his brow. "Can the sunset be seen from your room, too?"

"Of course." She laughed. "I told you mine is right next to yours."

"That's good," he said coldly. "It would be a bother if you had to watch your sunset from here."

As he slipped off the camouflage jacket, the nurse glared at him. Her face was pink and her voice trembled. "There are lots of other rooms in this building."

"I don't doubt it," Steiner said. "I wouldn't be surprised if you knew them all. Where's the roster here?"

She was already on her way to the door, and she turned to look at him with fury. "We don't have any roster and we don't have ranks here, either; we have a house schedule and guests who are supposed to follow it. It's posted here." She angrily indicated a printed card on the wall and went out, slamming the door behind her.

Steiner grinned. He studied the schedule carefully. From one to three was a rest period. That explained the peculiar quiet in the building in which, he guessed, seventy or eighty men must be housed. Supper was served in the dining room at half past six. He looked at his watch. It was not yet half past three, and he decided to take a swim. After stowing away his belongings, he strolled slowly down to the beach. There he undressed and dived in. With vigorous strokes he swam to a rock that rose out of the waves about a hundred and fifty feet from the beach. From the top of it there was a good view in all directions. The coastline was full of indentations and the shifting surf lined the beach like a silvery girdle. The town itself stretched in a single line for about half a mile. From his perch on the rock the sharp slopes of the mountain seemed to loom directly over the houses, threatening the safety of the town.

Steiner was totally absorbed in the view when he heard a loud call. He looked down and saw a man thrashing the water energetically. He reached the rock at last and climbed up, panting and shaking himself like a wet poodle. "Well, *Kamerad*," he said, "this is the life." He beat the water out of his red bathing trunks, brushed it out of his blanched blond hair, and finally settled down on the rock close to Steiner. His body was on the puny side, but he had a good head with blue, cheerful eyes and rosy cheeks. "Boy, oh boy," he talked on gaily, "couldn't be better. The upper crust of the socialist worker's state sure knew how to appreciate the good things in life. Don't you think?"

"They would have to be idiots not to."

The blond boy nodded. "Where are you staying? I haven't seen you before."

"Just arrived an hour ago," Steiner said.

"Has a new shipment come?" the boy asked in surprise.

"No, I came alone."

"Oh. Well, where are you staying?" He made no attempt to conceal his frank curiosity.

Steiner pointed to the rest home.

"An awful place," the towheaded fellow said contemptuously. "Swell front and nothing inside it."

"What do you mean?" Steiner asked. "There are at least seventy *landsers* staying there."

"I don't mean the men. You ought to come over to our quarters. Six houses down the street. Not such an elegant building, but we've got a canteen that's the best."

"So?" This boy talked a little too much and Steiner wanted to be left alone. To get rid of him he nodded. "Maybe I'll drop in tonight."

The boy slapped him on the back. "Fine. Don't forget. By the way—" he leaned confidentially closer—"we have a bunch of women there who are really something. Especially two of them. There's one of them wears her breasts like I would wear the Iron Cross."

"Women?" Steiner queried.

"Sure. The nurses, but high-class, let me tell you. Great girls. They're in on all our parties."

"All?"

"Sure. You can go the limit with them. Only the one with IC breasts is reserved for Lieutenant Mannheim, the paymaster. Nobody else gets a chance at her." He sighed and gazed gloomily over the water. "It's always the same; if there's anyone around with a star on their shoulders, we *landsers* get left out."

His chagrin seemed so genuine that Steiner smiled. "If so, you aren't missing much," he said. "I'd sooner have a decent glass of wine or beer than a dozen of these whores."

The blond fellow protested indignantly, "They're not whores. When you see Gertrud you'll change your mind."

"Don't keep at me about it," Steiner replied irritably. "I'll take a look at your canteen tonight. If I needed women I wouldn't have to go six houses down the street." He nodded good-by, dropped into the water and swam back to the beach. As he dressed he wondered for a moment whether he had been too sharp with the boy. He recalled his conversation with the nurse. That kind were the same everywhere. He'd make it up

to the blond fellow this evening over a bottle. After all, he
should be grateful for the tip about the canteen. As he
thought of it, his mouth watered. It was a long time since
he had tasted beer. He frowned. Had the blond boy said anything about beer? He couldn't recall. He would see; a canteen
without beer was no canteen.

The swim had wonderfully refreshed him, and the act
of having rid himself of the dirt of the road seemed to bring
back the mood of bygone Saturday nights when, still a civilian,
he had washed and shaved and gone out. As he approached
the house he saw several men standing by the door and talking in loud voices. They caught sight of him, stopped talking
and studied him with curiosity. For a few seconds he was
undecided whether to join them or not. Then they apparently
recognized his rank, and their faces set. He went past them,
answering their salutes with a brief nod. When he reached
his room he lay down and promptly fell asleep.

It was dark when he awoke. He lay for a while staring up
at the ceiling with eyes half shut. He began thinking about
the nurse. Perhaps he shouldn't have told her off so roughly.
Cursing under his breath, he got up, combed his hair and
slipped into his tunic. It was high time for supper. He hurried
downstairs. The dining hall was a long, lofty room. Three
rows of tables took up nearly half of it. Most of the chairs
were already occupied and Steiner had difficulty finding a
seat in the further corner of the room. He squeezed between
chairs. The men inspected him frankly, put their heads together and whispered. When he started to sit down, someone said, "You'll be served up front; this section is for
landsers."

"Then this is where I belong," Steiner said, sitting down beside the man who had spoken. The soldier looked at him in
astonishment, then grinned and resumed eating. The faces
of the others brightened and they moved so that he had
more room. Since the place in front of him was not set, Steiner
looked around. The food was being served in big bowls. When
one of the nurses approached, Steiner asked her for a plate
and silverware.

She pointed to the other end of the table. "You'll have to
go up there. That's where sergeants and corporals are served."

"As you see, I am a sergeant," Steiner said sharply. "Bring
me a plate or I'll get one for myself."

Their interest piqued, the men all raised their heads. The
nurse set her bowl down on the table, her pretty face flushing.
"If you want to change the regulations," she said defiantly,
"tell Sergeant Müller, not me." She started away, but Steiner

caught her arm. The clatter of spoons stopped and all eyes turned inquisitively toward him. Steiner looked down the table and caught sight of the leather-faced sergeant, who sat at the other end of the table with a half dozen noncoms, staring hard at him.

Steiner raised his voice. "In the first place I don't like your tone, miss, and in the second place I don't intend to be told where I have to sit to choke down your dehydrated rations. Now bring me a plate."

Helplessly the nurse looked toward the noncom table. The sergeant strode rapidly toward them. "There are regulations here," he said angrily, "and even a senior sergeant has to obey them. You sit with us. No one gets special treament here, understand?"

Steiner took a deep breath. He released the nurse's arm. "What regulations say I must?" he asked quietly.

"There's a copy of them hanging in your room," the leathery skinned sergeant replied curtly.

"In all the rooms?"

"Of course."

"Really." Steiner tapped one of the men in front of him on the shoulder. "Bring me the regulations from your room."

The man stood up and hurried to the door. "I'm not out for special treatment," Steiner declared coolly. "This is a matter of principle and we'll settle it right now."

The sergeant's voice was thick with rage. "You'll find out soon enough what it's a matter of. Don't think you can play the leader here."

"That's a part that suits you a lot better than it does me," Steiner replied coldly. The scene disgusted him, but on the other hand he did not want to give in now. He looked over toward the door.

The man had come back. He made a wide circle around Leatherskin and handed the printed card to Steiner. "Here it is, sir."

"Thank you very much," Steiner said. He looked the regulations over again and noted with satisfaction that he had not been mistaken.

The sergeant regarded him darkly. "Well?"

Steiner smiled scornfully. "Do you think I'm an illiterate?" The smile vanished abruptly. He glanced briefly at the men, who were listening in eager suspense. "There's not a word here about noncoms having to eat separately from the men. Is there?"

"That's taken for granted," Leatherskin replied violently. "It doesn't have to be specifically mentioned."

Steiner frowned. "There's only one thing I'd take for granted: that the enlisted men here are being fooled with unwritten as well as written nonsense. I came here to rest up, not to be reminded of the barracks and the drill ground." He snatched the card from the speechless sergeant's hand and slapped it down on the table. "You can just pull in your horns. If I am not served right here tomorrow morning, I'll see that I get my rations elsewhere. Good appetite." He strode to the door through a wall of icy silence. As he passed by one of the windows outside, he saw that everyone in the dining hall was still sitting motionless and silent. His appetite was thoroughly ruined by now, so he fetched his cap from his room and left the building.

He counted the houses on the left side of the street. The sixth house lay in the midst of large grounds. The building was hidden far back among the trees. He went up a paved walk toward the brightness of its windows. On the threshold of the open door he collided with a fellow who was hurrying out, and at once recognized the towheaded boy of his afternoon acquaintance. He grabbed his arm roughly. "Well, here I am."

The boy stared at him incredulously. Steiner laughed. "What's the matter? Have you forgotten me already?"

"No," the boy stammered, confused. "I didn't know that you . . . I mean, sir . . ." He gulped, and sweat actually started out on his face at his discovery of Steiner's rank.

Steiner gave him a poke. "Don't talk crap, my boy. If we always knew the whole truth about other people, sooner or later we'd turn hermit. Where's this canteen of yours? My throat is dry as a hot stove lid."

"We can take care of that." The boy laughed, at ease again. He led Steiner inside. "I was going out to look you up," he said. "Things are getting gay downstairs." As they descended he told Steiner that the canteen was intended only for the use of occupants of the house and their guests. "If you came alone, they'd throw you out. Otherwise the mob in this town would drink us dry in two days."

At the bottom of the stairs was a long corridor leading to a door from which came a din of laughter and singing. "Sounds good," Steiner murmured and followed the boy in. It took a few seconds for their eyes to adjust to the dense cloud of cigarette smoke which enveloped the whole of the large room. Some two dozen men were sitting around small round tables, bottles and glasses in front of them, loudly singing to the harsh notes of an out-of-tune piano in the corner opposite the door. Steiner followed the boy to the bar. A soldier in rolled-up shirt sleeves was acting as bartender. He scowled at Steiner.

Towhead leaned forward, whispered a few words, and the man's face cleared. He nodded and asked, "What will you have?"

"What have you got?"

"Red wine and beer."

Steiner chose beer. When the man set two bottles on the counter, Steiner opened his eyes wide in astonishment. "Pilsener in Russia!" he exclaimed, overpowered by emotion. "This is a dream. Give me five bottles."

"The two of us will finish them off in good shape," Towhead said serenely.

"The two of us!" Steiner laughed harshly. "What do you mean, the two of us? I'm going to drink these five alone. What do you think I am, an infant? I've been waiting for this moment for six months. You don't know what it's like to go without beer for six months. I don't know what the stuff tastes like any more."

"It's three marks a bottle," the bartender said.

"I wouldn't care if it was a hundred," Steiner replied. "What good is this crap in my pocket? Here!" He brought out a roll of big bills. "Six months' pay with extra combat pay and not a chance to spend the stuff." He tossed a bill on the counter, tucked the bottles under his arm and strode over to a table, where he lined the bottles up in front of him. Towhead followed, shaking his head, and sat down beside him. Two other men at the table were so absorbed in a chess game that they scarcely noticed. Steiner picked up a bottle, regarding the label lovingly. His mouth was parched as if he had not drunk even water for days. As he opened the bottle, his hands shook.

"Here's your change," Towhead said. "You had five marks coming to you; you left it on the counter."

With the back of his hand Steiner swept the bill off the table. He disregarded the glass and set the bottle to his lips. As he drank, he closed his eyes. "My God, you can stow it away," Towhead said enthusiastically. "I've never seen anything like it. He laughed. "That stuff will knock you over, believe me. It's prewar."

Steiner wiped his mouth and grinned. "The first three bottles won't, and after that it doesn't matter." He opened the second bottle.

"Here are your five marks." Towhead held out the money which he had picked up from the floor. Steiner took it from him, cursed and tore the bill to pieces.

The boy stared at him in dismay. "What's wrong with you?" he asked.

"Another word about money tonight and I'll hit you over the head with a bottle. What the hell is it good for? To drink myself to death?"

"But you can always send it home," Towhead stammered.

"Home!" Steiner laughed raucously. The two chess players lifted their heads. He paid no attention to them, raised the second bottle to his lips and drank half of it. "Do you send your money home?"

"Of course."

"Why, may I ask?"

Towhead shrugged. "So it will be there for me later."

"Later! You mean so they can put up a tombstone for you? With your name on it, and under the name 'Died for Folk and Fatherland,' and all that crap?"

Towhead shifted uncomfortably in his chair. Steiner leaned across the table. "Don't worry; I don't get plastered on a bottle and a half. I'm still cold sober; it takes me at least five to get going. I want to tell you this: later, when you're walking barefoot over the heavenly prairies you won't need your money, and if you're shoveling coal in hell you certainly won't."

"No need to get so pessimistic," Towhead replied crossly.

"Sure. Maybe you'll be lucky enough to pound rock in Siberia or clear ruins at home and shout 'Heil Hitler.' "

"Be quiet." Towhead glanced anxiously at the men, who had turned back to their chess game but who must be hearing every word.

Steiner snorted. He was starting on the third bottle. "We're all miserable bastards," he said vehemently. "We're all sick to death of it and scared to death, all of us." He spat.

"That's a hell of a thing coming from you." Towhead threw a somewhat envious glance at the decorations on Steiner's chest.

Steiner laughed contemptuously. "You mean on account of these things? If you only knew . . ." He broke off and stared down darkly. "Why aren't you drinking? Go on, get yourself something to drink." He tossed money across the table. Towhead went to the counter and returned with two bottles.

"Now we're really getting started," Steiner said, opening the fourth bottle. More men had come into the room. The pianist was worn out and had taken a seat at a near-by table.

Among the uniforms the white of a nurse's costume gleamed, and Towhead began shifting impatiently in his chair. "Piles bothering you?" Steiner asked maliciously.

Towhead shook his head. "I'm just wondering where Gertrud is."

"Is she the IC breasts?"

"No, that's the other one."

Steiner took out his cigarettes. He passed them across the table. "I don't smoke," Towhead said.

Lighting one for himself, Steiner smiled pityingly. "You don't smoke and you hardly drink and you send your money home. What in hell do you live for?"

Towhead shrugged. "I'm satisfied. As for the money, they can use it back home."

"Your parents."

"Sure."

Steiner glowered at him. "Oh, sure, they can use it. That's what I thought two years ago. I wrote mine to take a vacation, to have a good time with the money I was sending them." He stared down at his hands and his lips quivered.

"Well?" Towhead asked. "Did they do it?"

"Oh, they went off on their vacation all right," Steiner said. His voice was hoarse.

Towhead leaned forward, intensely curious. "And then?"

Steiner puffed at his cigarette. His face was red and his forehead beaded with tiny drops of sweat. He picked up the bottle and finished it off. "And then," he said, "and then . . . ah . . ." He snapped the cigarette to the floor and opened the last bottle. "Shut up," he said roughly. "You ask too many questions. You ought to drink, not ask questions. Drink, drink."

They drank in silence. After a while Towhead went back to the bar. He walked unsteadily, touching a chair for support now and then. Milksop, Steiner thought, watching him; these children can't take it! He began mumbling to himself and rested his head on his hands. The sounds in the room reached his ear in a vague, distorted manner. Someone started to sing. The pianist was playing again. Steiner hummed the melody.

All at once he felt a gentle indifference. The canteen began to sway; the walls rose almost imperceptibly; all the harsh, sharp angles disappeared and everything became soft and round as a woman's breast. When Towhead returned with several bottles, Steiner slapped him on the back. He was in high spirits. "Them and them and more to come; today we drink, today we swill."

"Today we swill," Towhead said thickly, opening a bottle with a loud pop. "In four days," he went on, "I'll be on my way back into it again, back to Smolensk. Ever heard of the place?"

Steiner nodded. "Sure. Birthplace of Shakespeare. Everything comes from Russia, everything stays in Russia. Everything."

They guffawed and clinked bottles. The chess players dumped their pieces into the box and moved closer. Steiner thrust two bottles toward them. "That's it; why wear your brains out? The game is lost either way." He suddenly began to sing, pounding the table with his fists in time to the music.

> *Auf der Strasse nach Tuapse*
> *Marschiert ein Bataillon.*
> *Und das sind die Reste*
> *Von unserer Division.*

Silence fell at the other tables. Laughing, the pianist looked toward them. In one corner someone joined in, then a third voice followed, and when it came to the refrain almost all of them roared out:

> *Wir konnten schon Tuapse sehn*
> *Und mussten wider stiften gehn*
> *Wie einst Napoleon.*

The song faded out. The men raised their glasses, drank thirstily and started another song. As Steiner opened the seventh bottle, a voice behind him roused him.

Towhead stood up quickly, exclaiming, "Gertrud, here you are! Come over here, sit down. I'm so glad you've come." He dragged a chair over from the next table. His face was radiant; he was so excited that he seemed quite ridiculous.

Steiner placed his bottle on the table and slowly turned his head. He looked into a pale face, a face which kept its distance and knew its worth. A wealth of chestnut hair gathered in a bun at the nape of the neck emphasized the high arched forehead. The girl's large, almond-shaped eyes had a look of great self-assurance in them. There was a fineness and regularity about all her features, and the corners of her soft mouth were disturbingly sweet. Steiner stared at her and slowly lifted his hands from the bottle. He watched with narrowed eyes as she sat down opposite Towhead and greeted the other men with a friendly smile. Then she turned to Towhead. "You've drunk too much, Klaus," she said. She had a throaty voice, and Steiner felt a painful stabbing sensation around his heart. He crouched a little and pushed his chair back as though intending to get up.

At the reprimand in the nurse's tone Towhead had looked

guiltily down at the floor. He seemed absurdly embarrassed. He raised his head, shrugged in comic despair and said to Steiner, "This is Gertrud, finest girl I ever met. But when she sees a fellow sitting over a bottle, she acts like he'd thrown away his chance at Paradise."

Steiner cleared his throat. He felt out of control and bad-mannered and tried to steady himself by lighting a cigarette. But the seven bottles of Pilsener were taking effect. His face seemed to have become a stupid mask, and he rubbed his hand over his mouth. Hoarsely he muttered, "Maybe she reads the Bible too much." As soon as the words were out he was sorry he had spoken. The nurse looked at him. He saw her face as a vague whiteness through the smoke of his cigarette, and reached for the bottle again. The hell with her! he thought. What do I care what these uniformed whores think of me?

He finished the bottle and rapped it down on the table. The nurse continued to look fixedly at him, and his insecurity grew. Angrily he thrust out his lower lip. "Don't you like what I say?"

She pretended not to have heard. Turning to Towhead, she asked, "Who is this?"

"An acquaintance," Towhead replied, abashed. He looked imploringly at Steiner.

"I'm surprised," the nurse replied coolly. "Where did you pick him up?"

Steiner had had enough. Before Towhead could answer, he used both hands against the table to push himself to his feet. "You sound as if I were his new pair of pants," he said. "But if I were I'd prefer to be on the part of you where pants belong. Good night, everybody." He staggered to the bar and dropped a fifty-mark note on the counter. "Two bottles; the rest is for you."

The man behind the bar stared unbelievingly at him. "Do you mean that?"

"Sure. You can do me the favor of wiping your ass with it one of these days." Paying no attention to the man's baffled face, he picked up the bottles and weaved his way among the tables to the opposite end of the canteen. Out of the corner of his eye he saw Towhead talking earnestly with the nurse.

He stopped at the piano. For a few seconds he watched the man's fingers moving over the keys. Then he gripped his shoulder and said, "Play the Volga song. Do you know it?"

"Sure. I played it only five minutes ago."

"Did you now?" Steiner pondered that. He shook his head. "I don't remember—play it again."

The man nodded. "Often as you like."

Steiner found an empty seat at one of the rear tables. The other men at the table looked at him but didn't speak. He set his bottles down and said, "Don't you like my face? Sorry, it's the only one I have." He sat down and opened a bottle. The men grinned and drank to him. Through the racket, bits of the Volga song could be heard.

"Be quiet a minute," Steiner said. He tilted his head and felt his heart beating in short, hard thumps. Although he was completely drunk, he had not entirely lost mastery of himself. He looked across the room to where the nurse was still sitting with Towhead. For a brief moment their glances met. She quickly looked aside.

Steiner lighted another cigarette. I shouldn't have drunk so much, he told himself. But he promptly shook his head in anger. What did he care about the woman—and a nurse at that! He grinned scornfully. Had he gone so far that he thought every skirt was another Anne? He puffed hard at his cigarette, thinking. You had to have something you could cling to—something real that was meaningful because you felt it, not something you imagined just because you wanted something meaningful. His head was growing heavier and heavier. With a terrible effort he forced his eyes open, emptied the last bottle and pushed his chair back. As he stood up, the canteen began to whirl around him. He compressed his lips and took a deep breath. The other men at the table watched him, grinning. He became aware of them and stiffened. Then he steered himself toward the door, left the canteen and stumbled up the stairs.

In front of the building he stood still for a moment. The fresh night air, far from making him feel better, affected him badly. He reeled down the path in the direction of the beach, with a vague idea of cleansing himself. On the way he stumbled and fell so heavily that he cut his forehead and lay where he had fallen, half-conscious. Suddenly he heard a voice: "How could you get yourself in such a state?" He rose on his knees and began to curse. When someone gripped his shoulder, he struck out wildly with his fist. He heard a suppressed cry of pain.

"Go away," he panted. "Go away, or . . ."

He staggered to his feet and plodded on, blood running down his forehead and into his eyes. Half-blinded, he reached the sand and stripped off his clothes. As he was about to plunge into the water, someone grasped his arms and again the voice, imploring and insistent, spoke in his ear: "Are you mad, for heaven's sake? You're in no condition to . . ." He stared into the anxious face of the nurse.

It was a bright night. A full moon hung like a round yellow lamp in the sky. The waves were rolling heavily against the beach, digging into the pebbles and flattening out as though a crack in the earth were absorbing them. Steiner wiped the blood out of his eyes. "You touch me again," he said hoarsely, "and I'll throw you into the water. What do you want anyway? Anything special about me that interests you?" He looked down at her and suddenly grinned. "From what I hear, a man's no good when he's drunk, you know," he added.

He saw disgust in her eyes. But she stood her ground. "Clear out!" he said roughly.

He strode forward up to his waist in the water, drew up his legs and let the waves carry him. After a while he swam against the tide and did not return to the beach until he could feel his arms and legs growing stiff and numb. From far out he could see that she was waiting for him, like a statue against the background of the dark garden. As he emerged from the water, his teeth were chattering. Before he reached his clothes, he felt sick. He turned quickly, dropped down with his face in the water and vomited. His body heaved; he could feel all the air leaving his lungs, but he allowed himself to slide deeper and deeper into the water.

Suddenly he was gripped by the feet and pulled back. Struggling for breath, he lay on the ground and saw her horrified face above him. "What are you doing?" she stammered. "My God, what are you doing?"

He turned over on his back and looked at her. Abruptly he felt a surge of rage and shame. The repulsive taste of vomit was on his tongue, and he felt his stomach drawing together again. But he fought down the new fit of vomiting. Blood began streaming down his face afresh. Suppressing a groan, he sat up. When she tried to support him, he knocked her arm back. "Are you still here?" he growled. "If you don't go away I'll smash . . ." He broke off and stooped for his clothes.

Something else occurred to him. He glanced at the chest-high wall which surrounded the garden only twenty feet away. Heavily he went over to it, pulled himself up and dropped to the soft ground on the other side. Before the surprised nurse could follow him, he crawled a few yards forward into the darkness of the garden and flattened out on the ground. He waited quietly. If she went to the canteen to fetch help from the men, he would have to clear out in a hurry. The thought worried him. Now he could distinctly hear her footsteps as she ran along the wall. She must have reached the little gate

by now. He tensed his muscles. Although he was trembling
violently in the cool night air, he did not move. The trees almost shut out the moonlight. Nevertheless, he could see her
white uniform nearing; she was evidently looking for him. He
pillowed his head on his arms and began to moan softly. A
moment later he heard her voice in words of concern, and
then she was close beside him.

He moved so swiftly that he smothered her resistance and
her outcry before she could recover from her initial shock. He
pulled her to the ground, brutally threw himself upon her,
pulled her skirt over her head and pressed his knee between
her legs. Then he suddenly released her and stood up. He
stood watching her as she slowly sat up, rearranged her clothing and stared at him without speaking.

"Why did you follow me?" he asked in a low voice.

She did not answer. He shook his head slightly. "You are
reckless, Nurse Gertrud. In the future keep your humani-
tarian paws off drunken men. It might be misunderstood."

"You're insane." Her face was as white as her uniform, and
she was breathing heavily.

"We are all insane," he replied. "We are living in an age of
absolute madness; the few normal people are safely behind
barbed wire because they have failed to understand that it's no
longer worth being normal." He laughed and felt the wound
on his forehead. His voice grew quite cheerful as he went on:
"Our century is changing everything. What was thought bad in
the past will be thought good in the future, and what was good
once will become bad. We will no longer lie on top of but
under women, and some day we'll reach the point where the
men will bear the children and the women go out and earn
the bread." He laughed. "We're heading for a great age, sister;
madness will be totalized and the insane asylums emptied." He
took a step toward her and lowered his voice. "You're just as
insane as I am, because if you were normal you'd stay home
and darn socks and study cookbooks instead of hanging
around places where every man has two glands too many.
You get me?"

"My father is a doctor," she replied calmly.

"So much the worse. Then he ought to know what comes of
leaving his daughter to a horde of two-footed billygoats. If I
were your father, I would have pounded your backside black
and blue and locked you up in the cellar."

He turned away abruptly, climbed over the wall and found
his clothes. He was dead sober now, but his head ached as
though it were locked in a vise. Dressed, he looked over the
wall into the garden again. The nurse still stood motionless.

Her face seemed dark now, scarcely distinguishable against the background of the night. For a moment he was tempted to say a friendly word to her. Then he shrugged, turned away and strode along the beach until the massive structure of the Division Rest Home appeared among the trees. With few exceptions the windows were dark. He remembered that ten o'clock was curfew. It must be within a few minutes of ten. He hurried, found the front door open and slowly mounted the stairs. In front of his room he hesitated. Then he went softly to the next door and leaned forward, listening. He glanced up and down the hall to make sure no one was there, and slowly depressed the latch.

As he entered the dark room he heard a hasty sound and a sleepy voice asked, "Who's there?"

"Three guesses," he said, closing the door behind him. For a few seconds there was a dead silence. Then he heard a sound like that made by a blanket being thrown back. His eyes had grown accustomed to the darkness, and he saw a figure in white get out of the bed and hesitantly approach him. She seemed to recognize him, stood still and said indignantly, "Leave my room at once."

"You've got that out of the movies," he said. "But don't worry; I just wanted to ask you whether you have any aspirin. I've got a frightful headache."

She came two steps closer, her long nightgown trailing around her ankles. "You're drunk," she said with disgust.

He regarded her speculatively. "Not any more. I got rid of it all in the water. Have you any aspirin?"

She hesitated. As she turned toward the door, he gripped her shoulders and held her tightly. "Were you going to turn on the light?" he asked.

"Yes."

"You don't need any light," he said, feeling along her arms. The nightgown had slipped off her right shoulder and he knew that she had slid it off deliberately. But she defended herself and panted, "Let me go. I'll scream. I *will* scream."

"Sure, you'll scream," he said.

Her breasts were firm and soft. When she tried to kiss him, he turned his face aside and laid her on the bed.

Later, when they were lying side by side, he mused about Gertrud. Why, he wondered, had she not run to the canteen for help? There was no doubt that she was a different sort, different from this girl beside him, whose name he did not even know. In the darkness he grinned and asked, "What is your name?"

"My friends call me Inge." When he said nothing, she

pressed close to him and stroked his chest. "Don't you like the name?"

"Why, of course I do; why shouldn't I like it?"

"How many girls have you said that to?"

He laughed. "Up to this moment I've never met a girl named Inge. At least not in bed," he added.

He tried to sit up. She held him tight. "Where are you going?"

"To bed."

"But you can sleep here with me," she said, disappointed.

He shook his head. "I wouldn't be able to sleep."

She pulled the blanket up under her chin and watched him dress. When he was finished, he came over to the bed once more and said, "Good night."

"Aren't you at least going to kiss me?" Her voice was quivering with anger. He stooped and casually kissed her shoulder.

"Is that all?"

"Isn't it enough? Do you want to be paid?"

She started up as though the pillow under her back had become a hot iron. Then she threw herself face down on the bed and began to sob wildly. Steiner stood for a moment looking at her in embarrassment. Then he slowly withdrew, closing the door behind him. He paused in the corridor and closed his eyes. When the sobbing stopped, he went to his room. For a long while he stood at the window, staring out at the sea. He felt oddly wakeful and not at all tired. He slowly undressed again. His headache was almost gone, but the cut on his forehead throbbed painfully. By the light of a candle he examined the narrow, blood-encrusted slit over his right eyebrow. Irritably he shook his head. Then he threw himself down on the bed and closed his eyes. The candle burned down and went out. Outside the open window the sea breathed, gasping, rolling blindly up on the beach, and the moon hung above the water like a savage mask, grinning like a faun.

Steiner awoke early next morning. He felt as fresh and rested as if he had slept for twenty-four hours without a break. Carefully he washed the encrusted blood from his forehead, put a bit of adhesive over the wound and appeared punctually in the dining room. As he approached the enlisted men's table he saw that a place was set for him. Several of the men were already at the table; in response to his greeting they winked meaningfully.

The one who had fetched the card of regulations last night

pulled out the chair for him, saying, "Congratulations, Sergeant."

"You gave it to them," another man commented. "What did you do to your forehead? Been rubbing elbows with the big chief?"

Steiner sat down. "No, just rubbing noses with the ground." He leaned back comfortably in his chair.

"Here come their lordships," someone said. Everyone turned to look at the door, where the noncoms were entering. Leatherskin came last. They sat down without so much as a glance in Steiner's direction. Later Steiner noticed Inge serving at the noncom table. After breakfast he went to his room, straightened it up and then set out for the beach. In spite of the early-morning chill he drifted about in the water for a long time. Suddenly he caught sight of Towhead sitting on a bench, apparently watching him. Steiner pretended not to notice him; he swam back to where his clothes lay and dressed.

He suddenly felt the impulse to talk with somebody about Nurse Gertrud, and the only person to talk to was Towhead. He sauntered idly in his direction and stopped in pretended surprise when his name was called. "Well, what are you doing here so early?" He sat down on the bench.

"What happened to your head?" Towhead asked.

Steiner touched the adhesive. "Slight accident," he said casually. "Did you stay long?"

"In the canteen?"

"Yes."

They looked out over the water. After a while Towhead asked, "Did you see Gertrud later last night?"

"Why do you ask?" Steiner countered, feeling his way.

"Oh, I was just wondering. She went out after you. Said you were so drunk you had to be watched."

"Why didn't you come with her?"

Towhead laughed in vexation. "She said I was so pie-eyed myself I wouldn't be any help. I waited over an hour in the canteen, but she didn't come back."

"Well," Steiner said pensively.

Towhead regarded him suspiciously. Then he stooped, picked up a pebble and skipped it over the water. "At any rate," he went on maliciously, "she was awfully queer this morning."

"Just one of her days, I guess," Steiner said.

Towhead shook his head vigorously. "No, it's something else. I'm not usually nosy, but I'd give a lot to know what happened last night."

"You can ask her."

They sat in silence. The beach was gradually coming to life. Alone and in groups men were appearing. Most of them headed straight for the water. Others stretched out in the sun. Since it was obvious he would get no further information from Towhead, Steiner stood up. "I have things to do."

"Won't you be coming over this evening?"

Steiner shook his head. "No, thanks. I've had enough for the present."

"But you haven't even met the other girl yet," Towhead said insistently. "The one with the IC breasts. She wasn't around last night. There's a woman for you."

Steiner raised his eyebrows. "I thought the paymaster had reserved her."

"Hell, what would that mean around here? A guy like you would put that old barrel-belly in the shade."

"Too strenuous," Steiner said, grinning. Towhead's jealousy was all too obvious. He was surprised to find himself slightly pained by the thought that there might be something between Towhead and Gertrud. What the hell did he care? Nevertheless, as he walked along the beach, his early-morning good humor was gone.

In the evening after supper, Steiner decided to take a walk through the town. He strolled aimlessly down the street between the spacious lawns whose scent mingled with the tang of the water. A strange mood had taken possession of him; he stopped frequently to gaze up at the massive mountain slopes or over the sea. He had the feeling that he was walking on a narrow path that led between the heights and depths, between serenity and restiveness, to the intersection of all roads; he smiled bitterly at the thought that there should be a new road from there, one going in a different direction. There was only one road for him, and it was the road taken by all the men who stopped in this resort for a brief breathing spell—the road back to the front. For a moment he clossed his eyes. Better not to think about that, he told himself. Every such thought was like a razor-edged knife cutting another sliver off the little time remaining to him.

Slowly he walked back the way he had come. Scarcely anyone was on the street at this hour. From the windows of the houses light flowed out on the dark yards. He turned his steps toward the beach. Like a barrier of black clouds the mountains towered up against the sky. They seemed to be staring westward, breathlessly, where the crimson last light of day rent the heavens like a flaming sword. The sky was bleeding, and as far as the eye could reach the sea lay incarnadined. Steiner shuddered. He felt an acute need to talk to someone, to make contact with some human being, and he was pleased when he saw Towhead coming toward him. The boy hailed him excitedly, "There you are!" and broke into a run. "I've got her, I've got her all lined up for you!"

"Got whom?"

"Ilse," Towhead said hastily, "you know . . ."

At the mention of the name Steiner started. He gripped the boy's shoulder hard and whispered tensely, "Ilse? Who is Ilse?"

"The IC breasts," Towhead said eagerly, wrenching away. "She's right on my heels." Although the moon was overcast, it was possible to see a long way down the beach. Steiner recognized the white uniform of a nurse.

"Listen, I don't want . . ."

"Have fun."

Before Steiner could finish, Towhead ran off into the night. Slowly the nurse came up to Steiner. He pulled his cap down low over his forehead. It's crazy, he told himself, there are a million girls named Ilse. But when he heard her voice, he began to tremble. He pulled his flashlight out of his pocket and flashed it full in her face. She closed her wide, dark eyes; her mouth was smiling. "Turn out that light—" she raised her hand to her eyes—"I can't see."

Without a word he switched off the flashlight and thrust it into his pocket.

"Do you study all girls so thoroughly?" she asked. Her voice was flat and rather common.

Turning his face to one side, he murmured, "Excuse me. I always like to see who I'm dealing with."

She gave a cooing laugh. "Are you satisfied?"

He glanced quickly to the right and left. He reached out so fast that before she could make a move to defend herself, he had pulled her close to him. His face was right above hers. She was still smiling. He took off his cap, quietly stuck it into his coat pocket, and said, "Good evening, Ilse."

Her smile froze.

"I'm very well satisfied!" He laughed hoarsely, dangerously, and held her more tightly. "Nothing is lost," he said. "Nothing is lost and the past is never so dead that we may not meet it again."

She tried to pull away. Her face was twisted into an ugly grimace and she groaned under the hard pressure of his arms.

Suddenly she went limp. He let go of her and she slid slowly to the ground. He stooped over her. She lay still, with face averted, her mouth open and twitching. My God, he thought, my God. It still seemed to him that he was dreaming. But this was no dream, this was reality. He closed his eyes. Thirteen months had passed, more than a whole year since . . .

May nights in the Bohemian forest are mild and full of promise. The fragrance of cherry blossoms hangs in the air over the big park attached to the hospital. The pines stretch up the mountain slopes, an enchanted woods against the night sky. This is the end of his second week in the hospital. In another week, at the latest, he will be discharged. His leg wound has healed without complications; he has every reason to be content. If it were not for this nurse, Ilse. From the moment she first tended him his thoughts had been busy with her. Perhaps he would not have become so involved if she were not so obtrusively showing interest in him. And now she is sitting beside him frankly offering herself to him.

"What do you see in me?" he asks. "There are over a hundred beds in this hospital. You can find yourself plenty of company more grateful than I'll be."

She raises her hands in comic resignation. "Perhaps it's only the ungrateful ones who attract me."

He moves a little away from her and looks at the white foam of the cherry blossoms. "You talk like a . . ." He swallows the word and bites his lips.

"Like a what?" she asks. Her face is right above him. A strand of her long, dark hair hangs down to his mouth. "Like a what?" she repeats. When he does not reply, she places her arm around his shoulder and smiles. "How do you know how prostitutes talk? That's what you meant, isn't it?"

Against his will he feels admiration for her. "Perhaps from knowing you," he says thickly.

"From knowing me?" She speaks as though he were an obstinate child. He feels her breath against his face. "Then you haven't known much about me," she says softly. "Don't you want to know me better?"

I'm an idiot, he thinks. Her face is so close to him that all his surroundings are blotted out. Slowly he reaches forward with his teeth for the lock of hair dangling in front of her mouth. As their lips touch he pulls her violently into his arms. . . .

That was how it had begun. But it had lasted only three

days. He became aware of how long he had been stooping, looking down at her now as she lay on the sand.

He straightened up and saw that her eyes were open and fixed on his. "Get up!" he ordered harshly. His voice was so imperative that she obeyed at once. She made no resistance as he led her to a bench a few yards away. "Sit down," he said curtly. He sat down beside her. For the moment he did not know what he ought to do. The meeting had come too unexpectedly. With unsteady hands he lighted a cigarette. He stared at its glowing tip until he heard suppressed sobs at his side.

"Tears, Ilse?" he said. "Why? More to the point if you'd done your crying last time."

She turned toward him and spoke with unbending fury. "You stinking bastard."

He laughed, liking her courage. "Is that what I am?"

"Yes," she said violently. "You always were a bastard. You don't know how to treat a woman."

"When a woman forces her way into a man's bed," he said coldly, "she must expect something of the sort. Sooner or later she'll find herself lying alone in it, or be thrown out on the other side. That's the fate of all whores," he added brutally.

She cringed. He noticed it and grinned. "You didn't use to be so sensitive about words," he said. "You're slipping, Ilse."

As she made a move to spring to her feet, he gripped her arm hard. "Stay here; we're not through with each other yet." He tossed the cigarette away. "You know how that little romance started. I didn't want it. I grant you that I learned something from you. But all there was to learn I found out the first night, and I knew there wasn't any more." He laughed cynically. "A man can't forgive himself for his clumsiness with his first woman, especially when she's as experienced as you. I told you what I thought of you that third night. Two nights were enough to bring me to my senses again. And then . . ."

Suddenly his fury returned. He would never forget the expression on the face of the staff doctor, Major Dietrich, who had searched his room, assisted by several nurses and medics, and had found the watch among his things. The rest had been an ugly dream. The courtmartial, the sentence, the countless humiliations that he had undergone up to and all through the period in the penal battalion. At the recollection he clenched his fists, faint with hatred. It had not been a chain of unfortunate accidents; he knew that. It had been rigged from start to finish. He wanted to hear the confirmation from her own lips.

She shook her head. "I don't know what you're talking about." She tried to make it sound genuine, but he heard the waver in her voice and smiled malignantly.

"So you don't know," he replied softly. "Of course you don't know. But we have plenty of time now. You'll remember before this evening is over. In the next room a wrist watch was stolen from an amputee. Next morning it was found among my clothes, wasn't it? There was only one person who could have put it there, Ilse, and that was you."

In spite of the darkness he could see the unnatural wanness of her face. She tried to laugh, but produced so strange and forced a sound that she stopped abruptly. "You're crazy," she said at last. "Why should I have done a thing like that?"

"Why?" He laughed wildly. "Because on that third night I told you I was a human being, not a studhorse. That's why."

She did not answer. It was gradually growing lighter. The moon had risen above the mountains and seemed to be hesitating before taking the leap over the sea. Steiner took his paybook out of his pocket, leafed through it until he found a piece of paper. He switched on his flashlight. Ilse was watching his movements nervously. As he bent over the paper and began to write with a stubby pencil, she asked, "Are you writing me a letter?"

Her light tone sounded false. He said nothing until he was finished. Then he read through what he had written and nodded with satisfaction. "That will do," he said quietly, placing the pencil and paper on her lap. "Now sign this."

"What is it?"

"Your confession. I want it in writing."

Suddenly she jumped to her feet and tried to run. But he was prepared. He caught up with her in two strides. She kicked him and pummeled him with her fists. Her blows inspired him to harsher measures than he had intended. He dragged her down to the water, waded in knee-deep and thrust her head under. Then he pulled her up by the hair and asked, "Will you sign now?"

She coughed and struggled for breath. When he carried her back to the bench, she lay utterly defeated in his arms. He set her down, picked up the paper and pencil and flashed the light into her face. Water was dripping from her hair down her forehead and onto her hands. "That was unnecessary," he said quietly. "You might have spared us both the unpleasantness. In bed you were superior to me, but not here."

He placed the paper in her lap again with the hard surface of the paybook under it. "If you don't sign, I'll duck you again—and for good this time, believe me."

He watched as she signed her name with trembling hands. When she was finished, he carefully pocketed the paper and the paybook. Then he switched out the flashlight. "You may go now."

She did not stir. "You may go," he repeated sharply.

Unsteadily she got to her feet. She looked up at him. "You're going to report me," she said tonelessly.

He nodded.

"Jesus," she stammered. "Jesus, what am I going to do?"

He shrugged. Slowly she walked away, her wet skirt clinging to her long legs, her head bowed, shoulders twitching. He felt no pity at all. For a while he stared across the water. Then he reached into his pocket and took out the sheet of paper. In spite of the wavery handwriting the name was quite legible. Ilse Baumann. He was struck by the realization that he had never known her surname. For only a moment he hesitated. Then he tore the paper into tiny scraps and tossed them into the water. He watched them being carried out on the waves, dancing and scattering until they vanished from sight. As he set out for his quarters, he recalled a phrase he had once read: that the person who cannot forgive carries his unhappiness across his own shadow. He thought about this for a while as he lay in bed, but could not quite understand it.

Next morning as he walked toward the beach, he saw across the street a nurse coming in his direction. He recognized Gertrud immediately and crossed the street, but her steps swerved; she seemed to wish to pass him by. He blocked her way and said, "I wish I were meeting you for the first time now."

She stood still, the corners of her mouth quivering. When she spoke her voice was cool and distant. "You will have to accept things as they are. Wishes don't undo what is done."

By daylight her face seemed even better-wrought than he remembered, and he suddenly realized that she was lovely—more than that, she was beautiful. His hands felt awkward and he thrust them into his jacket pockets. "Perhaps you are right," he said quietly. "But what is done can sometimes grow or diminish in importance, as one likes."

She shook her head firmly. "I see things as they are, not as I might like to see them afterwards."

He listened to her voice with delight. "You are a person

with principles. But just between the two of us, wouldn't you rather like to see our first encounter different from what it was?"

"I was speaking generally," she replied coolly. Her face flushed slightly, like a glacier at sunrise.

"If I were a woman," he said genially, "I would never talk in generalities." He changed the subject abruptly. "As for the Pilsener in your canteen, my compliments. I'm going to drop in this evening. Will you be there?"

She shook her head. "No."

"I won't drink more than one bottle."

"I would recommend a water cure for you."

She walked swiftly past him. Somewhat taken aback, he watched her until she was out of sight among the trees. He set out for his quarters, thoughtful and a little sad.

VIII

STAFF SERGEANT FETSCHER had worries. From his office he stared grumpily out the window without the slightest awareness of the brilliance of the spring day. At irregular intervals a low, long-drawn-out rumble broke the noonday quiet, and each time he raised his head uneasily, cursed at length and relapsed into gloomy brooding. At last he got up and went out. He gave a wide berth to several ugly craters that had meanwhile appeared on the street and walked slowly toward one of the buildings. As he approached he noticed a group of men digging a hole behind the wall of a house. They raised their heads expectantly.

"You'd better quit," Fetscher said morosely. "You have to go back up front tomorrow morning."

"So soon?" Pasternack exclaimed. "I thought we had a full week back here."

"So did I," Fetscher growled. "Commander's orders. You're going to be assigned to the battalion headquarters."

Kruger climbed out of the hole and shook the dirt from his clothes. "Those sons of bitches! They promise us a week of rest and send for us after three days."

The rest of the men angrily tossed their tools aside. "What does Meyer say about it?" Schnurrbart asked.

Fetscher shrugged. "How should I know? It wouldn't matter anyhow." He turned to Dorn, who was cleaning his glasses.

"They want to see you, too, about officers' training. Triebig wants to talk to you."

Dorn opened his mouth to reply, appeared to change his mind and said nothing.

Hollerbach grinned. "Well, well," he said. "Before long you won't know us."

"Don't be silly," Dorn said curtly.

Kruger lighted a cigarette. "If we had only known," he said to Fetscher, "you would have had to dig your bunker yourself."

He turned to the others. "Actually, it doesn't matter much whether we're here or at battalion headquarters. Since Ivan's got the range it's getting uncomfortable here. I wonder what we're supposed to do there."

"Same thing," Fetscher said.

"You mean dig bunkers?" Kern asked.

"Yes."

"But they already have theirs," Anselm said.

Fetscher grimaced. "The battalion commander thinks he needs a deeper one."

"Scared, is he?" Schnurrbart sneered.

Fetscher looked disapproving. "That's his order and that's all there is to it." He walked away.

"What'll we do now?" Schnurrbart called after him.

"Whatever you like for the rest of the day. Fix up your uniforms."

Back at his desk, Fetscher sat down, sighing, and leafed unhappily through a sheaf of papers. For the tenth time that day he told himself that there must be some special significance to it when a battalion commander asked for the personal papers of a platoon leader. Two days ago Stransky had called and ordered him to send Senior Sergeant Steiner's service record book up to the battalion command post. He had sensed trouble at once, and his feeling had persisted even though the papers were returned the following day. Of course Stransky now knew that Steiner had once been broken. Fetscher had long known all about this black mark on Steiner's record and had formed his own opinion about it. But he had guarded his knowledge carefully and had made sure the incriminating papers were never seen by anyone else. Why Stransky's knowing should disturb him so acutely he could not say. He wondered whether he ought to write to Steiner about it. Then he realized that the letter would reach Gursuf too late. He could only let things take their course and be prepared for a talk with Meyer, who would certainly get wind of the matter before long. Cursing again, he tried to concentrate on the papers in front of him. But the work went miserably. Two hours later, when he left the house to find the clerk, he had with him the recommendation for Kruger's promotion to corporal.

"Say what you will," Schnurrbart remarked, "the silence in this sector isn't going to last another week; I feel it in my urine."

Four of them were sitting in their quarters, smoking. Kruger spat and remarked to Dorn, "If you're smart, you'll clear out. If Ivan starts getting nasty here, we're through. Don't be a fool. By the time the training course is over the war will be over too, and when the war is over it won't matter a damn to you whether you were an officer or a *landser*."

"I cannot reconcile that with my conscience," Dorn said.

"Conscience!" Kruger puffed contemptuously. "When you're a corpse you can shove your conscience up your ass. You're married, aren't you?" Dorn nodded silently. "Well, then, what is there to consider? Think of your wife. You have children too?" Dorn nodded again. Kruger turned to Schnurrbart, who was sucking vigorously at his pipe. "What do you say to such an idiot? Has a wife and children and refuses to leave this rattrap because he can't 'reconcile it with his conscience' to be one of Adolf's officers."

"He's crazy," Schnurrbart said quietly.

"Plumb insane." Anselm was sitting on a wooden box, a harmonica in his hands.

Dorn sat with drooping head. It was late evening. In the east the front continued to rumble; for seconds at a time the sky was bathed in red light. Schnurrbart asked a question: "What's your wife's name?"

Dorn raised his head. "Maria."

"And the children?"

"Betty and Jürgen."

Schnurrbart nodded. He removed the pipe from his mouth and spoke in an oddly hoarse voice. "If I had a Maria and a Betty and a Jürgen, I would seriously ask myself whether I had the right to determine for myself alone what was to become of me and of them. That's what I'd think about, otherwise to hell with my conscience."

Kruger looked at him with admiration. "You sound like a preacher, but you're right." He turned to Dorn again. "It shouldn't matter to me what you do. Principles are neither here nor there. But I'll tell you this: if you decide to play the hero again, I'm through with you till the next Ice Age. Remember that."

Dorn raised his head dolefully. Everything the men were saying he had considered. If it were only a matter of overcoming his distaste for an officer's career, he might long ago have given in. But there was something else. He made the effort to convey it to them: "You make the matter out as more simple than it really is. After all, we've grown used to one another and . . ."

There was a moment's silence before Kruger growled, "That's sheer sentimentality. You're unhinged, my friend." He waved his arms violently in an effort to conceal his real emotion. "I want to tell you something. One of these days every one of us sitting here will be laid out stiff as a poker. What good will we be to you then, eh?" He fixed Dorn with a fierce gaze. "Not a damn bit of good, that's what. If you clear out now, at least you won't have to watch them chop us into mincemeat. And they will, let me tell you." To reinforce his declaration he let out a fart so loud that it brought from Schnurrbart a respectful grunt. Then he stood up. "I'm going to hit the sack. Tomorrow morning the circus starts again."

Schnurrbart also stood up, yawning. "Think it over," he said to Dorn. "You won't miss us like your children are going to miss you. Good night." He followed Kruger into the house.

As Dorn was about to get up also, Anselm placed a hand on his shoulder. "Hold on a minute, please," he said. "There's something I want to ask you."

Although Dorn felt little inclination to talk, he nodded encouragingly. There was a long pause as Anselm pondered how to begin. At last he asked, "You're a Catholic, aren't you?"

"Yes," Dorn answered in surprise.

"Are you a good Catholic?"

"I hope so."

Anselm clasped his arms across his chest. "I thought you were, but I wanted to make sure. I've been meaning to talk with you for a long time. And now that you may be going away I don't want to put it off any longer."

The elaborate preface aroused Dorn's curiosity. He tried to catch an impression of Anselm's face in the darkness. "By all means tell me what's on your mind."

"It isn't easy to talk about," Anselm stammered. He pulled himself together. "You see, I'm Catholic too. Maybe you have a low opinion of me on account of the stories I've told about women and so on."

Dorn shook his head. "We all have our weaknesses."

Anselm nodded, relieved. "A fellow can talk with you," he said in a pleased tone. "Anyway, it isn't half as bad as it sounds; I mean, a fellow likes to boast a bit." He laughed abashedly. "Of course, I've got a good deal behind me in that field, but it was always just the way things turned out, and after all a fellow is only human." Dorn's continuing silence revived his uncertainty. He scratched his throat and lowered his voice. "I don't know whether you as a married man can understand that, but when a fellow gets to a certain age and has no chance to marry it's damned hard to get along without it. Or don't you think so?"

"Of course it's hard."

Anselm moved closer, and his voice took on a pleading note. "I want you to believe what I say—I've always gone to church and to confession gladly, but since the first time I had a girl there was just no sense to it. I confessed it twice. Lord, you should have heard what a pig he made me out to be, talking about irresponsibility and sinful lust of the flesh and so on. He took on like it was high treason, and pretty soon I just stopped going to confession or even to church." He fell silent and looked uneasily at Dorn, whose head was still bowed.

Dorn placed his hand on Anselm's shoulder. "You yourself must know how strong you are."

Anselm laughed contemptuously. "What good does my strength do me if I can't sleep at night and go crazy when I see a woman? I've thought about it often, believe me. It would be different if I could say today that in one year or two I would marry, and if I could begin saving up for a house. But even then it would tear me apart. My body needs it, that's all, and when I don't have it I don't feel human."

Dorn sighed. Without conviction he said, "The human body finds a way to cope with it."

"I know that." Anselm nodded. "But you must admit that afterwards it's only worse. When you get to the point where you start dreaming about it at night, you're really off your head next morning. Besides—" his tone became scornful— "what is it you dream about? Heaven? Or hell maybe? No—" he shook his head vigorously—"it's lucky you're not supposed to take your dreams to confession. It would be funny if it weren't so sad."

There was little point saying anything. Dorn thoughtfully lighted a cigarette. He wondered how many men had lost contact with the church on this same issue. He was aware of

Anselm's eyes upon him, and shrugged. "I can't help you," he said quietly. "I married fairly young and can sympathize, but I don't really know how you feel."

"But you studied philosophy," Anselm said helplessly.

Dorn smiled painfully. "Yes, I studied philosophy, but this is a problem you would do better to take to a priest. He will be able to discuss it with you far more sensibly than I can. Try our divisional chaplain one of these days. He is a man with both feet firmly on the ground. Tell him everything. He won't just condemn you; he'll give you some guidance to help you along."

"I'm filled to the gills with all of them," Anselm said in disgust.

"You ought not to say that," Dorn replied gravely. "Perhaps you ran into a priest who was particularly stern in his judgments. Not all priests are alike. If you feel the need to find your way back, it is always open to you. But in God's name you must also give up your prejudices."

"I'll think it over," Anselm said. "Are you coming in?"

"I'll stay out a while."

Anselm said good night and walked off swiftly. Dorn sighed again. He tossed his cigarette away and remained sitting under the clear April sky for a long time. Should he become an officer? The longer he thought about it, the more difficult it was to decide. He recalled his wife's last letter: that he must not worry and that all was well at home. At home . . . He clasped his hands over his knees and lifted his face to the stars. Home, he thought, and felt his eyes filling with tears. It was long past midnight before he went into the house.

They set out early next morning and reached the battalion command post in short order. Schnurrbart went into the adjutant's bunker to report the arrival of the platoon. Triebig received him in his shirt sleeves, his face lathered and his razor in one hand. He turned his head, annoyed at being disturbed so early. When he had finished shaving he went outside with Schnurrbart and gave the men their instructions. "And be snappy about it," he said. "The bunker must be ready by tomorrow night. You can ask the signals platoon for tools."

He beckoned to Dorn and went back into the bunker with him. Offering Dorn a cigarette, he came to the point at once. "We don't want you to feel pressed," he said in a friendly tone. "But a man of your abilities must know himself where his place is. At any rate I cannot imagine that you feel com-

fortable in your present situation. We need officers, men who
are above average, and I really see no reason why you hold
back. In a few days you can be on your way back home,
which would surely be a treat for you. Moreover, it's a chance
of getting out of Russia for good. I assure you, I wouldn't
hesitate for a moment if I were in your position."

Dorn hunched his shoulders in torment. Although he had
scarcely closed his eyes during the night, and had been turning the matter about in his mind the whole night through, he
had not yet been able to decide. Triebig talked a while longer
and spread out a number of papers on the table. "All you
need do is sign. Naturally, you'll be given a furlough first and
can be back home with your family for Easter."

"I don't know." Dorn stared at the papers.

Triebig rose. "I'll give you a few hours more to think it
over. Come to see me again around two and let me know."

Dorn nodded and slowly rose to his feet.

"I really don't understand you," Triebig said irritably.
"Anybody else would be overjoyed."

Dorn suppressed an unfriendly comment, saluted and left.

The men had meanwhile begun to dig a large rectangular
pit somewhat to one side of the other bunkers, in the center
of the orchard. Ten feet deep, the signals platoon leader had
said, according to the commander's orders. Kruger drove his
sharply filed spade viciously into the tangle of roots in the
ground and poured out a steady stream of curses; even
Schnurrbart finally had enough. He straightened up from his
stooped position, wiped the sweat from his forehead and said,
"Save your wind, will you? Your filthy mouth is beginning to
get on my nerves."

The others also stopped work and looked reproachfully at
Kruger. Kruger went right on. "Ten feet deep!" he snarled
furiously. "Have you ever heard the like of it? This isn't a
bunker, it's a mine, I tell you. First thing you know we'll be
putting in an elevator shaft. That bastard of a captain is scared
out of his pants."

He would have gone on railing if Dorn had not returned,
looking as if he had seen a ghost. Schnurrbart called out,
"What's the matter? Have they been raising a stink about
something?"

Dorn shook his head mutely and began to remove his tunic.

"What is it?" Anselm insisted. "Aren't you going?"

"Yes, I'm going," Dorn replied somberly.

Kruger grinned. "Well, at last you've come to your senses.
By your face a guy would think you were going to your own

funeral, but you'll get used to the idea. Once you're sitting in the train bound for home, you'll feel better."

Dorn picked up a spade without another word.

By midday they had dug a hole chest deep. "Mealtime," Schnurrbart said, throwing down his shovel.

Stiffly they clambered out of the hole, unpacked the rations they had brought with them and scattered among the trees. Dorn sat down by himself. After a while Anselm joined him and tried to strike up a conversation. But Dorn answered in monosyllables, and Anselm at last concentrated silently on his sausage. Although there were some scattered clouds in the sky, the sun burned down on them fiercely. The front was quiet, the silence broken only now and then by the thud of heavy mortar shells or the agitated chatter of a machine gun. Dorn stared down at the ground, feeling mournful, like a person who has lost something precious forever. He forced himself to think of his family again, reached into his pocket and took out his wife's latest letter. His features softened as he studied the toilsomely drawn letters at the bottom of the paper: "Dear Papa come home soon."

As he let his hand drop, he chanced to turn his head. The other men were lying flat, pressed against the ground. What is the matter? he had time to think. Then the earth exploded. The blast knocked him backward. He lay staring up at the sky, his expression unchanged; the quiet joy had lingered on his face. The shattered lenses of his glasses lay beside his head.

The black pillar of smoke began to collapse. The torn branches of trees emerged again, stripped of their leaves, and the men came to life. Faces pale with fright, they sat up. Beside the crater Anselm and the Professor lay as though asleep. Schnurrbart was the first to recover; he approached slowly. Seeing the red flesh among the remnants of the Professor's uniform, he turned away and knelt beside Anselm, who lay on his belly, his fingers dug into the ground. Schnurrbart turned him over on his back. There was no face left.

The others now stood beside the two dead men, looking down on them in silence. At the bunkers men were stirring also. Stransky appeared for a few seconds, glanced toward them and vanished into his bunker immediately.

A few minutes later Triebig came over. He asked, "Dead?" They nodded. His face was chalky. He ran his tongue over his lips. "Let them lie there until tonight," he said. "The supply column can take them back." He walked a few steps further on and looked at the shell hole. Then he turned back toward his bunker.

"That one came like a flash of lightning," Kern said.

"It always comes like lightning," Schnurrbart said tonelessly.

They looked down at Dorn. His lifeless eyes seemed to be staring through the twigs up at the fragile ribbons of cloud. "He was a good man, the Professor," Kern said tightly. "This stinking, this miserable war—just to croak like that—a man of his learning." He wiped his eyes and swallowed.

Pasternack, standing beside Kruger, suddenly turned away. He pressed his forehead against a tree trunk and stood motionless.

"What are you turning weepy for?" Kruger growled hoarsely. "You think any of you are going to make out better? You make me laugh." He walked back to the pit, picked up his spade and began digging furiously. Hollerbach followed him silently.

"What are you waiting for?" Schnurrbart said to the others.

"Are you going to let them lie like this?" Maag asked.

"I'll cover them. Let's finish up here."

Hesitantly they moved off. Schnurrbart stood beside the bodies for a while. Then he went to the Professor's pack, extracted shelter-halves and blanket and spread them over the two dead men so that only their heavy nailed boots could be seen. As he started to put Dorn's right arm under the blanket, he noticed the piece of paper in the clenched fist. With some effort he pulled it away and discovered that it was a letter. Slowly he straightened up. His eyes rested on the boots. German army boots, size 10. He suddenly recalled that these were the boots of a man who had joined the company shortly after Dorn, and had died under a hail of machine-gun bullets. Dorn, who had been equipped with uncomfortable clodhoppers, had asked Fetscher for the boots, then relatively new. The nails had since become worn down and the soles were full of holes. What a long way those boots had come since their nails first rang challengingly on the cobblestoned street of a small Czech town and the March sun was reflected in the high polish of the uppers. Schnurrbart knew all the paths they had walked. They had trodden the clean highways of Slovakia, the sandy paths in Poland, the corduroy roads of the Ukraine, the crushed flowers of the steppes, the lonely forest paths of the Caucasus. In light and dark, on hills and valleys, over land and water. And the road had always been there. Dust and searing heat had dried the leather and cracked it. The boots had slogged through rain and bottomless swamps, through cold and deep snow. With a kind of insane clarity Schnurrbart calculated: perhaps six million footsteps lay behind them. Now they had reached their final destination and were resting, unsightly, used up, worthless, with the warm sun beating down on the cracked leather. They lay waiting patiently, patient as the hide of which they were made. Schnurrbart suddenly became aware of the tears streaming down his face. Now the soldier Dorn had left his boots and his body behind.

In the evening the men of the supply column would load the flesh and the boots on a horse. Somewhere among the hills was an army burial ground where the earthly remains would be put. A simple wooden cross would be all that was left— that, and the grief of a wife and a Betty and a Jürgen.

Schnurrbart looked at the letter and then back at the boots. It occurred to him that he had forgotten something: the philosophy and its unrest. But then he told himself that Doctor of Philosophy Dorn must at last be recognizing the ultimate meaning of his existence and the relationships among all things, for death solves all questions. Perhaps he was now in possession of an understanding that had no need of knowledge because it was terrifyingly simple, like all great matters. Slowly he thrust the letter into his pocket. He noticed Pasternack still leaning against the tree. He went to him and placed a hand of his shoulder. "Come," he said softly. They joined the other men.

It was the last evening in Gursuf. They sat on a bench by the beach looking over the water. Steiner, his elbows propped on his knees, his chin in his hands, tried in vain to fight back his melancholy. The fourteen-day dream had come to an end. He would have to answer the call of the front as the others had, as had Towhead, who more than ten days ago had been absorbed by the boiling caldron of the Central Sector. The front forgot no one. Well, he had known that from the start, and the knowledge had scarcely troubled him. It would have mattered to him as little as everything else. The prospect of seeing the men of his platoon again would certainly have overlaid the sentimental, little regret at leaving this island of rest and peace—the present was always overshadowed by the demands of the next day. But something had happened that extended from the present into the future. Ten days ago such a possibility would have seemed preposterous to him. But now . . .

He looked at the sea and the choking sensation in his throat grew stronger. When he was gone from here the melody of the sea would still sound; the waves would pound on the beach, the pines rustle in the sea breeze, and the sun sink into the sea as it did every day at this time. All would remain, remain behind.

He felt a hand touching his arm. "You must not think about it, Rolf."

He smiled bitterly. "It is so close now," he said softly. "I can't help thinking about it, whether I want to or not."

She sighed and laid her head on his shoulder. "Yesterday it was still so far off," she whispered, "as far away as the stars."

He drew her close. "The stars are often closer to us than human beings; tomorrow you'll be thousands of light years away from me."

"How far is that?" she asked seriously.

"How far?" He wrinkled his brow. Then he nodded toward the water. "If you walk across the sea until you are so tired that your feet can no longer carry you, you've taken the first step."

"And how many steps are there?"

He raised his face toward the sky. "As many as there are stars."

"Then it is far," she breathed.

He nodded. After a while he placed his arm around her waist and studied her face. "You shouldn't have come into the canteen that evening."

"Would you have liked that better?"

"If you had asked me that yesterday I would have said no."

"And today?"

He smiled desperately. "Today I no longer know what to say."

"I didn't want to come."

"But you came anyway."

"Yes."

"You don't know how I waited for you, and I really did crink only one bottle."

She kissed him quickly and ran her hand over his hair. "You kept your word," she affirmed gently.

They were silent. Steiner thought about that meeting. Even now he still felt a certain surprise at how quickly she had agreed, that evening, to walk with him on the beach, although her experience should not have encouraged her to take such a risk. They had spoken little, but next night they had met again; each time there had been more between them. Each through the other discovered new things in their surroundings, things they had not noticed before, and as they drew closer to each other Steiner's front of cynicism dropped away without his even noticing. Whenever, alone in his room, he thought over their last meeting and the things she had said, he felt a quiet joy that quelled the bitterness within him and uncovered long-buried, deeply overlaid feelings.

And yet, he suddenly realized, all this had taken place and still he knew scarcely anything about her other than her name. The thought bothered him, and he said, "I know so little about you."

She smiled. "It isn't good for a man to know too much about a woman."

"I don't see that."

Her voice dropped lower. "Knowledge is often quickly forgotten."

He still did not understand. "I think you and I are talking about two different things," he said cautiously.

She shook her head firmly. "No. Why do you want to know more about me?"

"That's simple. Because I want to see you again some day."

"And why do you want to see me again?"

His face hardened. Seeing this, she quickly took his hand. "We are both sensible enough and old enough," she said, "to know that there has to be more between a man and woman than walks by moonlight and an occasional kiss."

"Why do you talk like that?" he asked quietly.

She hesitated, avoiding his eyes. Then she lifted her head. "Because," she explained firmly, "I don't want you to go on feeling until the last hour that you have something to make up to me."

Breathlessly he stared at her. "Is that feeling unjustified?" he asked at last.

"Yes." When he looked down at the ground, she added, "If it were justified, we would not have met again." Her voice became stronger. "I don't want you to misunderstand me. I know less about you than you do about me. But what I know is basis enough for what I said."

He thought he understood her now. He nodded and drew her head tenderly against his chest. "It's all right, I know what you mean. Maybe it was because things need time to develop and time was just what we haven't had."

"Maybe we have not used it properly," she replied pensively, "or perhaps this is the way it had to be."

"You sound like the Professor and Schnurrbart," he said.

"Who are they? You've never told me about them."

"I know," he said. "You'd have to actually know them; it wouldn't be any good describing them. Perhaps I would never have come to know you if it had not been for them."

"You're talking in riddles."

"There are no such things. What we call riddles are only the inadequacies of our minds."

"That is philosophy," she said gravely.

He began to laugh, stood up quickly and drew her to her feet. "Come," he said softly.

A dark shadow of evening trailed across the sky and only on the margin where the sea plunged into the blackness a strip of bright light clung, trembled for a time, and then shrank up like a dead man's face, scattering a rain of blinking lights on the water, until the shadow fell over the horizon like a black curtain, hiding everything beneath it.

Arm in arm, they walked along the beach. Steiner regarded her face from the side. Later they went out to the tip of a narrow sand bar that extended far out into the water, and sat down. He felt her body close beside his, and when he put his arm around her she let herself fall back against it. "Why must that be?" she whispered.

"What?"

"The war and all these terrible things."

"Perhaps so that we could meet each other." He sat up a little. "Do you believe in fated meetings?"

"I don't know," she answered thoughtfully, her finger following the lines of his mouth. "I don't know what I believe and I don't know what you want me to say. But it's obvious that many things had to come together so that we two could meet."

He nodded. Her words sounded echoes in him. He leaned over her so that he could feel her breath on his face. "And where will we meet again?"

She closed her eyes and whispered, "Somewhere above or below the stars. Perhaps . . ."

He closed her mouth with a long kiss. When his hand felt for her knees, she started and opened her eyes. Then she threw her arms around his neck and sighed. Her skin was smooth and firm; he began to undress her slowly, with great care and tenderness. She did not resist, and he felt her trembling under his hands in the cool night air.

A long while later they walked back the way they had come. When they reached the wide grounds around the building where they had first met, Steiner stopped and drew her close. "I still don't know all about you," he said softly.

"I'll write to you."

He nodded. "As you like. Don't forget the address."

He looked across the low wall at the building. "I'll be leaving very early and won't see you again. Perhaps we'll not meet until the war is over. Why won't you tell me where you live?"

"I'll write you all about it." She leaned her head against his chest. He could not understand her strange conduct and looked down on her, frowning. When he took hold of her chin to see her face, she turned her head aside quickly, whispering, "No, please don't." Suddenly she wound her arms around him and kissed him wildly. Then she broke loose and ran.

He watched her until she disappeared in the darkness of the lawns. He wanted to call out to her, but his voice would not obey him. Unsteadily he staggered forward a few steps, then stood still. At his back the surf roared, monotonous, heavy and mournful. For a while he stood peering among the trees. Then he turned away. Slowly he returned to the beach and walked with bowed head toward his quarters. At the gate he stopped for a moment and looked up at the mountains. They crouched black under the weight of the sky. Over their bent backs hung the moon, its face cold and expressionless. Steiner hunched his shoulders and moved his lips. His voice sounded strange to himself as he said, like a prayer, "As you like." He went up to his room.

IX

EASTER passed almost unnoticed in the monotony of their existence. Spring they were scarcely aware of. Only now and then, when they went out of the dugouts and bunkers and stood in the deep trenches, lifting their weary faces to the warm sunlight and closing their eyes, did they forget their surroundings for a few minutes—until somewhere in the vicinity a shell exploded and the dark cloud of smoke and dust rolled over their heads. Then they crouched like beasts and their faces turned hard and angry. They cursed and went back into the bunkers where they sat, longingly looking up at the narrow strip of blue sky that showed above the edge of the trench.

The expected Russian grand offensive had not yet begun. But more and more big guns were raining shells down on their positions. The hill was veiled in the dust of detonations all day long, and at night heavy bombers flew so close over the positions that the men in their bunkers hunched their heads between their shoulders. Uncertainty as to when the enemy offensive would come hardly bothered them. For months and years they had been learning the art of waiting. With the skill and indifference of long practice, they moved about their trenches and weapon pits like acrobats, for any false step, any awkward movement, could swiftly put an end to all movement. The daily artillery fire on the positions, the reconnaissance attacks of strong Russian patrols almost every night and the heavy bombardment of the rear positions cost the battalion more and more casualties. Scarcely a day passed without some dramatic incidents. The soldiers—thousands of miles from home, waiting under a cloudless sky in that decisive spring of 1943 for the Russian general offensive— learned in helpless despair that the war, in a new and terrible form, was being carried over the front lines into their homeland. The familiar faces around them grew rarer; more and more they felt that their struggle was meaningless, and they grew steadily quieter and more hopeless.

Second Company's bunkers were dug deep into the walls of the trench at intervals of seventy-five to a hundred feet. The men who were not on duty lay dozing on the hard plank beds. Steiner was with them again. He had rejoined the battalion the previous week. He had rejoined the battalion the previous week. Immediately after his arrival Fetscher had called him in for a long talk and had gravely warned him that it would be better for him to accept the regimental commander's offer and transfer immediately to the headquarters staff. Shaken though he was by the news of Dorn's death, Steiner had flatly rejected the sergeant's well-meant advice. It would take more than a dozen Stranskys to make him leave the company, he had said.

The reunion with the men of the platoon had been subdued and rather grave. Schnurrbart and Kruger were already wearing their corporals' insignia—they received his congratulations with somewhat dreary smiles. "What good does this crap do me," Kruger said bitterly, "if a month from now none of the bastards I always wanted to order around are left?" They had not yet got over the deaths of Anselm and Dorn. Steiner, too, was soon affected by their mood, which only deepened the depression he felt whenever he reflected on Gertrud's strange evasiveness. Luckily he had little time to think too much about that. He had redivided the groups and was devoting most of his energy to training the replacements brought in only a few days before. He instructed them in the possibilities and perils of positional warfare and sketched for them the probable phases of the impending battle, so that they would not lose their heads when the time came.

His thoughts were with them now as he sat at the table in his bunker, absently watching Faber conscientiously divide up his meager piece of sausage. Faber's big, earnest face, with its vigorous nose, cleft chin and thin lips, was concentrated on his task; he held the knife poised as though picking the next spot on a tree before swinging his ax. His eyes were a deep lake-blue. Faber's transfer from the Third to the Second Company had been accomplished only over Lieutenant Gausser's resistance. Gausser had been unwilling to release his reliable machine gunner, and it had taken all of Meyer's persuasiveness to move him. Later Meyer had told Steiner that next time he wanted a man he'd better go out and capture one from the Russian lines. But the transfer had finally gone through and Faber was now machine gunner in the second platoon.

Five men were lying on the cots in the bunker, snoring loudly. Of the five, Kern was the only former member of the platoon. Maag and Pasternack were assigned to Kruger's group in the next bunker; Hollerbach and Schnurrbart shared the next but one bunker with four replacements. Although the platoon now numbered over thirty rifles, the "old men" had not been particularly enthusiastic about the reinforcements because it meant that the regulars were split up. Hollerbach had been emphatic about sticking with Maag and Pasternack, but Steiner had pointed out that it would not be fair to the new men to leave them without front-line veterans. In any case, Kruger had remarked sarcastically, within another two weeks it would be possible to stow the whole battalion away in a single bunker.

The Black Forester had finished his meal. He wiped his greasy fingers on his trousers. Now he caught Steiner thoughtfully regarding the men on the cots. "Not much to them," he remarked laconically.

Steiner, startled out of his thoughts, looked up distractedly. He nodded. "I know, but what can we expect? Those fellows have picked a bad time to come out to the front. Four weeks' training and right smack into the soup. I'm afraid we're going to have trouble with them."

"So am I," Faber said. "Even a tree must learn to bow at the right time. If it doesn't, it breaks in the first storm."

Steiner grinned. "Do you always talk in terms of trees?"

"Almost always," Faber replied quietly.

Steiner took out his cigarettes and held them across the table. "Do you smoke?"

"No."

"Oh, well." Steiner shrugged and lighted a cigarette.

He had talked with Faber several times and knew that his folks owned a small farm near St. Blasien. But the woodsman was so taciturn that he had not found out very much more. Only once had Faber dropped his reserve somewhat. They had been talking about trees, the one subject he really seemed to know and care about. Thinking of this, Steiner took up the conversation again. "I've never been one to hear the grass growing. As for your trees, all I know about them is that they look pretty and are useful for lumber. I guess I can stand learning a bit more about them."

Faber's face remained expressionless. He laid his big hands on the table. "When it comes to trees, a person can always learn a little more. Back home in our valley there was a man who wanted to know how many trees there were in the forest. He wanted to know exactly, and so he counted them."

"Counted the trees?" Steiner exclaimed incredulously.

"Yes. He took a brush and a pot of white paint and went into the woods. Every tree he counted he marked with a white cross."

"He was crazy."

Faber shook his head. "He was living on a pension and was sixty-five years old when he started. For over fifteen years he walked in the woods painting his crosses on every tree."

"He should have been put in an insane asylum."

"That's what some people said," Faber continued, "but he had influential friends who saw to it that he was let alone; he had been a university professor and a famous astronomer. When people tried to persuade him to stop his senseless work he only smiled and said he had spent his whole life investigating the stars but he didn't know how many trees there were in the forest."

"The story is pointless," Steiner said. "Maybe he stared up at the sky so long he lost touch with the ground under his feet. What became of him?"

"He died a few years ago."

"Best thing he could do. How many trees did he count in those fiften years?"

"He kept that to himself. But one day he came home and said that now he knew exactly how many there were. The trees told him, he said. He passed on not long afterwards."

"Peace to his ashes," Steiner said. "I suppose we ought to feel sorry for a fellow like that. I hope to spend the last fifteen years of my life more profitably. When I get to the point where I hear the trees talking, I'll drink a bottle of nitroglycerin and jump off the Jungfrau. But seriously, do you believe any of that?"

Faber stood up slowly. "The peasants where I live have their work and they have their beliefs," he said quietly. "They know the trees have their own language and they believe what the trees tell them, because what the trees have to say is sure and steady. Our peasants are like the trees."

Steiner studied him suspiciously. "Sounds to me like you're saying something about us—I mean, about us city people."

The ghost of a smile passed over Faber's grave face. "You are the leaves on the trees."

"Are we? Well, that's something; what would a tree be without leaves!"

"A tree without leaves is still a tree," Faber said. "But a leaf without a tree is a withered nothing, and the leaf always dies before the tree." He left the bunker.

In the MG emplacement Maag and Pasternack were sitting on empty ammunition boxes, peering through the loophole at the woods. It was warm and they had taken off their tunics. At regular intervals they heard the dull explosion of heavy mortar fire. *Plop, plop, plop.* It sounded like the hammering of a woodpecker. The shells were landing somewhere on the hill in back of them.

Pasternack sighed. "I wonder how long this war is going on."

Maag twisted his freckled face into a grimace and spat. "Until final victory," he declared pompously. "One of these days we'll turn the tide, all right."

"I can't believe that any longer."

"Neither can I," Maag said. "But what the hell, who cares? The cart is stuck in the mud and that's all that matters."

Pasternack shrugged. "That's ridiculous," he said crossly.

"It isn't ridiculous," Maag retorted. "It's better for it to be stuck in the mud than to go rolling over the cliff. But that's politics and I'm sick of it." He spat again. Then, seeing Pasternack's troubled expression, he clapped him reassuringly on the shoulder. "We'll get through one way or another. I just want to live through this war; that's all I care about. As long as the cart stays in the mud, I'm sticking with it; when it starts rolling again, I'll jump off."

"A good way to break your neck."

"True enough, but I'll jump carefully, you can depend on that."

Several shells landed close in front of them. They flattened out on the floor. Acrid black smoke entered through the loophole. When the air cleared, Maag got up, groaning, and looked at the crater. "Those stinking mortars," he growled. "Another ten feet and it would have made our bones rattle." Another thought occurred to him. "Maybe those girls from the bridge are firing at us. I said right away we should have killed them."

Pasternack pounded the dust from his clothes. "What would have been the use? They have plenty of replacements. Women are women, in or out of uniform."

Before Maag could reply, Schnurrbart appeared. Maag grinned at him. "What's new, Corporal?"

Schnurrbart pulled up an ammunition box for a seat. "If you say corporal again, I'll throw you out of the trench." He filled his pipe and voluptuously puffed smoke at the ceiling. "What could possibly be new? You know already we're losing the war."

Maag dug the tip of his boot ill-humoredly into the sand. "There's no proof of that."

"Any map proves it," Schnurrbart replied.

They sat in silence for a while, looking out through the loophole. At last Maag cursed. "So what? Any army can retreat. So maybe the others will win the war, but it's nothing to boast of. Dozens against one country. Our allies don't count. Except for the Japs they're good for nothing." He was hit by sudden fury. "Today they shake hands with you, all smiles, and next day they kick you in the behind. The devil take them!"

"Who?"

They turned their heads and saw that Kruger had come up quietly and now stood, head ducked, in the entrance.

"All of them and you too," Maag growled.

Kruger threw out his chest. "You are talking to your superior officer."

"In that case come over here and kiss my ass."

Kruger's face flushed. "One of these days somebody's going to let out a howl," he threatened.

Schnurrbart raised his hand. "Cut the bickering," he said mildly. His glance fell on an earthworm wriggling across the floor. "Learn from this lowly creature," he said with mock solemnity. "It lies in slime all the time and yet it doesn't complain about it."

Maag shook his head in aversion. "Disgusting things," he said. "I wonder what they exist for."

Kruger studied the worm thoughtfully. "Nevertheless," he commented, "if you cut off its head, the rest of the body goes on living."

"Too bad that isn't the case with a certain type of corporal," Schnurrbart said.

Maag chuckled, and Kruger glared at him. Then he turned to Schnurrbart and said frostily, "You might refrain from such remarks in the presence of the men."

Schnurrbart swallowed the wrong way and coughed, and the others regarded Kruger's flushed face half in astonishment, half in amusement. Kruger stepped forward quickly, crushed the worm under his heavy boot and turned toward the entrance. "One of these days you'll find yourself thinking of me," he said.

Schnurrbart nodded. "Often as you like—in the latrine."

Kruger went out. "What's eating him?" Maag asked. "He was only joking, wasn't he?"

"Sure." Schnurrbart looked down at the crushed worm, which was still twitching. He stood up. "Everything's a joke," he declared, and also left.

Maag shrugged. "They've got trench fever," he said angrily. "They can kiss my ass."

Pasternack said nothing. He was thinking of home in Breslau, and everything suddenly seemed much harder and far more hopeless.

In the evening they sat around in their bunkers. Steiner lay on his bunk leafing without interest through his volume of Schiller's poems. He felt an uneasiness he could not explain. Faber sat at the table writing a letter. His big, hairy paws covered most of the sheet of paper; now and then he stared absently into the candlelight for a while, then carefully set down a few more words. Beside him, on the other half of the table, Kern and two of the other men were playing cards and exchanging low comments. For a while Steiner watched their faces. Then he decided to look in on the other bunkers. He stood up.

At that moment the door was opened and the broad face of the company commander appeared. As the men started to rise, he waved his hand. "Don't let me disturb you." To Steiner he said, "You can accompany me through the positions." His voice sounded so impersonal that Steiner was taken aback. Without a word he picked up his tommy gun and went out behind Meyer.

The night was warm and still. They inspected the MG and sniper positions. Meyer remained uncommunicative; he received the sentries' reports without his usual word or two of encouragement. When they reached the right wing of the company's sector, he turned about and started back. Abruptly he stopped to look over the top of the trench. "If the Russians keep pushing their trench in the direction they've been doing, they will land just about here."

Steiner nodded. He had known for two days that the Russains were working hard on an assault trench leading from the edge of the woods across the open field straight toward Second Company's positions. "When they get close enough," he answered off-handedly, "we'll pay them a visit. But they won't be finished before day after tomorrow."

"Let's hope not." Meyer took a step back, and Steiner felt his scrutiny. Meyer's odd behavior was beginning to get on his nerves. "A nasty business," Meyer said uncertainly. "I ran into Triebig this afternoon. He says you were degraded a year ago. Is that true?"

Steiner closed his eyes for a moment. He had expected this, but it had come sooner than he thought. Stransky works fast, he thought, his mouth twisting in contempt. He answered frigidly, "It's true."

Meyer nodded. "And why were you degraded?"

"I assume you already know," Steiner replied calmly.

Meyer nodded again. His face hardened. "I've heard one side of the story; now I'd like to hear the other. I hope you have something to say about it." As he spoke these last words, his voice took on a tone of command.

Steiner frowned. "I see no reason to," he declared icily. "I owe explanations to no one, including my company commander."

"Do you mean that, Steiner?"

"I damn well do, if you want to know." His voice sounded stubborn and unyielding.

They stared at each other for a few seconds. Then Meyer turned away without a word and strode off. Steiner stood motionless, grinning scornfully into the darkness. Idiot, he thought contemptuously, you damned idiot! After a while he began to whistle softly. He felt a grim amusement that extended into his fingertips and produced a whirling sensation in his head as though he had been drinking. Pilsener, he thought with a feeble spasm of laughter. Suddenly the chatter of a Russian submachine gun burst out of the night, and the bullets whistled so close over his head that he involuntarily dropped to his knees, cursing wildly. His fright lasted only for a second. Then he bounded to the next MG emplacement and squeezed in through the shaft. In the darkness he bumped into a man apparently trying to get into the trench. He recognized Maag's voice and clutched his shoulder. "Where to?" He had to shout to make himself heard.

"To fetch reinforcements," Maag stammered.

"Leaving your post for that?" Steiner bellowed angrily, pushing Maag back into the hole. As he felt for the MG in the darkness, he went on berating Maag.

He peered through the loophole. The Russian fire had

stopped. A few shells whined through the air and exploded near by. "I wish I knew . . ." Steiner interrupted himself, turned to Maag and snapped, "Where is the flare gun?"

"Here." Maag handed it to him. As Steiner fired a flare through the loophole, there was a rattling against the metal of the MG and the hideous noise of richocheting bullets buzzed around their heads as though they had stumbled into a beehive. "They must be right in front of us," Maag gasped. "In the shell holes down there."

Steiner recalled that there were a number of big craters on the slope below the MG emplacement. "Go get the other fellows," he ordered. The firing had diminished somewhat in the past few seconds, and Steiner considered what to do next. Before he could take any action he would have to inform Meyer, although that thought was distasteful. The arrival of the other men turned his thoughts in a different direction.

Schnurrbart squeezed into the emplacement first. "Good evening, everybody," he said cheerfully. "Where's the field kitchen? I'll take bullet stew, if you please."

Steiner grinned. He waited until Kruger and Hollerbach had come in. Then he briefed them on the situation. "We've got to get them out of there," he said. "They could be on top of us before we got started shooting. We'll have to . . ." He broke off.

From the entrance came Meyer's incisive voice. The lieutenant squeezed into the hole. "What's happening?"

In silence he listened to the report. When Steiner finished he stood frowning for a few seconds. Then he raised his head. "Signal for a barrage," he ordered. "I'll inform the commander." He hurried out.

Steiner picked up the flare gun again, took cartridges from Maag and followed the company commander out into the trench. He sent up the first flare and then the second. Watching them burst, shedding red and green light as they sank to earth, he hoped the artillery observers would see what they illuminated. In his mind he followed the action a few kilometers back of the lines as the men rushed to their guns to begin loading the big shells. He waited with bated breath. Minutes later, he heard hasty footsteps and Meyer reappeared just as a hollow roaring sounded above their heads. It swelled rapidly to a mighty moan and a moment later the heavy detonations came. Steiner followed the lieutenant into the MG emplacement, where the men waited impatiently.

"Commander's order," Meyer said. "The second platoon is to undertake a counterattack at once. You are to occupy the craters and take as many prisoners as possible. Sergeant

Steiner, you will command. How do you think to proceed?"

Steiner considered briefly. "We'll attack from three sides: Kruger from the west, Schnurrbart from the east and I from the south." He outlined his plan hastily. "When the firing starts we'll need artillery support—but only on the Russian positions at the edge of the woods. I guess that's all."

Meyer nodded. "Good in theory; let's hope it works out in practice."

Steiner ordered the men to get ready. Before he left the MG emplacement, he turned to Meyer again. "Who will take over our positions?"

"The first platoon. I've already given the order. One moment, Steiner." He waited until the other men were out. "I wish you all the luck in the world in this business," he said hesitantly. "But before you go I must tell you that it is often hard to understand you."

"That may be," Steiner replied. "That may be." He followed the men.

The artillery fire had ceased. The air was saturated with the smell of burned powder. As he walked down the trench, he felt his heart beating faster. In his bunker he hooked four reserve clips to his belt, exchanged a few words with Faber and urged the men to hurry. Shortly afterward the platoon was ready to go. There was an air of nervous tension about them all. The clatter of weapons persisted, and Steiner had to remind them several times to tone it down. Now and then a Russian submachine gun hammered away; the bullets whipped harmlessly over their heads.

Kruger grimaced disgustedly. "Haven't you got anything better for me to do? That's a crazy assignment—to lie out on the slope and do nothing."

"Be nice if that were all," Steiner said. "When Schnurrbart attacks and I turn up in their rear, the Russians will be able to retreat only to the east. You'll probably find all hell letting loose in your direction before it's over." He turned to Schnurrbart, who had come up behind him. "All clear?"

Schnurrbart nodded. From somewhere Meyer's muted voice could be heard.

"Let's go," Steiner said. He waited until Kruger disappeared in the darkness. Then he raised his arm. The rest of the men followed him. He led them about a hundred yards westward down the communication trench. From there they cautiously descended the slope.

When they reached the level field, he gave them final instructions. "You wait here," he said to Schnurrbart. "Attack in exactly five minutes. As soon as the first shots are fired, we'll come in. Clear?"

"All clear," Schnurrbart grunted, shaking hands with him.

"Good luck." After taking leave of Hollerbach also, Steiner led his men across no man's land in a southeasterly direction.

Schnurrbart watched them go. To the others in his group he said, "Stick close together and don't save on hand grenades. Remember, the eyes of the entire German nation are upon you."

The men chuckled low, and one of them said, *"Scheisse."*

Schnurrbart looked at him. The man had come in the last group of replacements—a pale eighteen-year-old. "Sorry, child," Schnurrbart said, "you can't now. You probably will anyway when the shooting starts."

"I don't see why we should start the thing," another spoke up. "I say we ought to wait here until the sergeant gets to the Russians."

Schnurrbart whirled around. "You shut your trap, my boy. Any more of that silly stuff and you'll be sorry."

"We weren't born yesterday," the man replied rebelliously.

"Day before yesterday, I guess." Schnurrbart looked at his watch.

"It ought to be time," Hollerbach said.

Schnurrbart put the watch back into his pocket. "One minute more." He turned his head in the direction in which Steiner had disappeared. Suddenly his eyes widened. He raised his arm.

"Someone's coming," Hollerbach breathed.

In spite of the starlit sky there was almost impenetrable darkness here at the foot of the hill, but they thought they could make out dark shadows slowly moving toward them. The men dropped to the ground, pushed the steel helmets back from their foreheads and scarcely dared to breathe. The shadows took on visible forms, and now they also heard the harsh tingle of arms. They pressed flat against the ground and settled the butts of their rifles against their shoulders.

Steiner and his men had marched toward the clump of woods. They were approaching the Russian assault trench when Steiner suddenly dropped to the ground. To one side of them, marching from the south in a northeasterly direction, appeared a long row of dim forms moving cautiously through the darkness. Steiner realized that if they continued they would pass by only a dozen paces away. He hastily began to crawl to one side, his men following. They covered a considerable distance. When the Russians were out of sight they sat up. "How many do you think there were?" Steiner whispered.

"Hard to say," Faber answered. "I'd guess a hundred."

"They're going to run smack into Schnurrbart."

Faber nodded. "What should we do?"

Steiner hesitated. They were really in a jam. On one side lay the woods, the outlines of the trees vaguely visible in the darkness, and on the other side the Russians—so large a force that they could roll right over Schnurrbart's dozen men. Schnurrbart ought to be warned. But firing prematurely would endanger the whole counterattack. Agonized by the urgent need for a decision, he clenched his teeth and felt sweat start on his forehead. Behind him he heard Kern's voice but could not make out the words. The others waited motionless, staring tensely toward the north, where fighting would surely flare up at any moment.

Steiner started forward. But at that moment an inferno broke loose back toward the German trenches. Steiner threw a harried glance toward the edge of the woods, then started back toward the spot where a few carbine shots were almost drowned out by the hammering of several dozen submachine guns. Quickly light flooded the area as five or six flares rose simultaneously. The air was suddenly filled with loud shouts and the crackle of rifle fire. They've broken in, Steiner thought in horror, they've broken into the trenches.

Abruptly he stood still. A howling roar swelled above their heads. They dropped flat, pressing their faces into their arms. When they realized it was their own artillery, they sprang to their feet and ran on. Steiner's thoughts were in a turmoil. Seeing several dark bundles on the ground, he turned and ran straight up the slope to the trench. The platoon had the advantage of surprise on their side, and a dozen well-aimed hand grenades created wild confusion among the Russians who had broken through. Faber settled behind the MG and began firing.

But the Russians adjusted to the new situation with amazing speed and stiffened their resistance. Steiner saw two of his men rolling down the slope like wooden dummies. Just as he decided to break off the unequal combat, they received unexpected aid.

Kruger had reached the assigned spot with his group. Crouching, they talked in whispers. "The plan is cockeyed." Maag tugged nervously at the strap of his submachine gun.

Pasternack disagreed. "Why? Seems good to me. It'll give

those Russians a turn when we suddenly start firing on them from the rear. They won't expect that."

Kruger was peering alertly into the darkness.

"What do you think?" Maag asked.

The East Prussian shrugged. "Wait and drink tea. Anyway, you'd better keep your traps shut and your ears open. It's going to start in a minute."

"Let it," Maag growled, trying to appear superior.

Kruger glanced impatiently at his wrist watch. "I don't want any of you shooting up the air," he said to the replacements. "When the Ivans start coming, I'll fire a flare and you can pick them off at leisure."

There was an uncomfortable silence. He looked at his watch again. His uneasiness was infectious, and several of the men stood up. He was about to snap at them when there was an outbreak of furious rifle fire. "Here it goes," Maag whispered excitedly.

Kruger sprang to his feet. The trenches were suddenly bathed in light. "They're crazy," he exclaimed in dismay. "What are they shooting flares for?"

"Giving it all away," Maag stammered.

Kruger raised his hand. But the artillery barrage had begun, and the mighty explosions drowned out the noise of rifles and tommy guns.

"Something's up over there," Maag shouted. "Those are Russian guns."

Kruger thought feverishly. If the counterattack was going wrong, as seemed to be the case, they would be needed. For a moment he was sorely tempted to stick by Steiner's order. He could stay right here and let the other fight, whatever it was, go on without him. Then he thought of Schnurrbart and suddenly knew that everything up in the trenches was hanging by a thread. His throat tight with apprehension, he shouted orders. The men obeyed reluctantly, holding their guns ready to fire. They began marching toward the shell holes. Flares still rose steadily from the trenches, throwing dancing shadows over the bare terrain, chiseling details out of the darkness with merciless clarity. They had come within thirty paces of the shell holes when rifle fire roared at them. Pasternack sank to his knees with a groan, and another man reached into the air with both hands as if trying to grasp some invisible object, whirled around his own axis and toppled heavily to the ground.

Kruger raced forward with huge strides, hurled one, two hand grenades at several heads which showed just above the ground, as though their owners were buried there up to the neck. He scarcely waited for the thunderous detonations to end; seconds later he jumped into a deep hole. He stumbled over a twitching body, fell, rolled over on his back and raised his tommy gun. He saw two Russians disappear over the edge of the crater and heard the lash of several rifle shots, then there was silence. As he staggered up he heard Maag shouting his name. His voice would not obey him, and he clambered out of the hole. The men were standing in a knot a few yards away.

"Where are the rest?" he asked hoarsely.

Maag gestured silently over his shoulder. His right arm was dangling stiffly, and Kruger asked him, "What's the matter with you?"

"My arm. I don't know." He said dully, "Pasternack got it."

"Dead?"

"Yes. Right through the chest."

Kruger began to blink as though a grain of sand had got into his eye. From the shell hole came a loud moan. Several of the men started toward the hole, but Kruger held them back. "That one won't bother us. We'd better look through the other holes."

"No need," Maag said. "All the bastards have disappeared. There couldn't have been many. What are we going to do now?"

"Look for Steiner and Schnurrbart," Kruger said firmly. "Where are the other fellows?"

"Wounded. They're lying over there. Should we take them with us?"

Kruger considered for a moment, then shook his head. "There'll be time for them later. How many are there?"

"Five," Maag answered.

"Good enough. Maybe there'll be a few more; that will make it worth while picking them up."

They stared at him outraged. One man said, "Now look here . . ."

"Shut up," Kruger ordered sharply. "None of you has any reason to shoot his mouth off. Why didn't you follow me?"

They evaded his menacing glance and did not answer. The artillery barrage had stopped, but farther to the west the noise of fighting continued; they distinctly heard the shattering explosions of the hand grenades. Loud shouting rang out from the top of the hill, where more and more flares were being fired. Kruger beckoned to the men. At the top of the hill they ran into men of the first platoon, who shouted excitedly at him.

Kruger cursed wildly. "What's going on up there?"

One man explained that the Russians had got into the trenches and that Meyer was gathering all available men for a counterthrust.

"Then let's go," Kruger declared, and started forward.

The first platoon men joined his group. About a hundred paces farther on they heard several violent explosions and at the same time loud cheers. On the run they reached the spot where the Russians had broken in. A few dark figures climbed out of the trench and ran forward. For a moment Meyer's powerful voice could be heard. Then an ear-shattering hammering began and many fleeing Russians came tearing down the slope. Kruger fired until his magazine was empty. As he reached for a new clip he caught sight of Steiner and Faber only a few yards away. For a second they stared at one another in amazement.

Kruger cursed again. "Where the hell is Schnurrbart?" he asked.

Steiner looked down the slope. Singly and in groups, pursuing Germans were coming back.

Meyer appeared among them. He saw Steiner. "What's up?" he asked tensely.

Steiner shrugged. The question seemed superfluous.

Kruger took a step forward. "We cleaned out the shell holes."

"Really?" Meyer whirled around. "And you only tell me that now?"

"Haven't had a chance to before," Kruger growled.

"How did all this happen?" he asked curtly.

Steiner reported laconically. "I was just about to withdraw when your show started. If you had attacked later we . . ." He stopped abruptly, recognizing Hollerbach. Hastily he pushed through to ask, "Where is Schnurrbart?"

"He must still be lying down there," Hollerbach replied softly.

"Down where?"

Stammering, hesitant, Hollerbach explained: "First we fired till our magazines were empty, and then the Russians came at us and we ran up the hill. But I saw nothing of Schnurrbart."

"So." Steiner glowered at him. Then he started down the slope, followed by several men, including Kruger, Hollerbach and Faber. They found Schnurrbart at last, lying on his face, and Steiner looked down at him for long seconds before he knelt and quickly examined him. "He's alive," he said hoarsely. "Let's get him to the infirmary." They lifted Schnurrbart carefully and toiled up the steep slope.

The infirmary bunkers were jammed. The medics had their hands full, and it was some time before they found a doctor to look at Schnurrbart. Among the severely wounded men lying side by side on the floor, Steiner saw many familiar faces. Near the door lay one man with his torn abdomen exposed. His face was too smeared with blood to be recognizable. Looking at him, Steiner had to clench his teeth to fight down the sickness that threatened to overpower him. It seemed incredible that a man with such gruesome wounds could still be alive. They had laid Schnurrbart on a blanket. Kruger unbuckled the chin strap of his helmet and cried out in horror, "Head wound!"

Steiner closed his eyes, paralyzed with apprehension. Then he heard Faber: "You're crazy. It just grazed him, that's all." Steiner took a deep breath. He opened his eyes.

The men had cut open Schnurrbart's trousers. Kruger said, "He's been hit in the leg, too."

"In the calf," Hollerbach said. "Shot went clean through."

Steiner now had the courage to look at Schnurrbart's face. From his temple a red streak ran down to his chin, where it vanished in the thick growth of beard. His face was pale, dirty, sunken-cheeked; all its familiar character had been erased. The sight aroused a dull pain in Steiner. He could feel a choking, burning sensation in his throat. The noises in the bunker, the suppressed moans of the wounded men, the lowered voices of the medical personnel, the soft clinking of instruments, the curt instructions of the doctors, working with rolled-up shirt sleeves, the flickering light of the candles—all of it merged into an unreal, stagy background. And close to him was the masklike, bearded face of a man who had been at his side for more than five years.

A violent dispute caught his attention. One of the medics was arguing with Kruger. "You've got to clear out," he asserted angrily. "This isn't a hospital ward." He turned to Steiner. "I'm sorry, Sergeant, but you must realize we need the room."

Steiner ordered the men outside. They left reluctantly. "I'll go as soon as you tell me what the story is," he said to the medic, gesturing at Schnurrbart.

"We'll be ready for him in a minute," the man said.

The doctor had approached. He wiped his bloodstained hands with a piece of gauze, attended to a man lying in front of Schnurrbart and then stopped before Steiner. "Wounded?" he said curtly.

Steiner shook his head. "Not me. I want to know what's wrong with this man here."

He watched with outward calm as the doctor bent over Schnurrbart and felt the bloody welt above the right temple. "Wasn't the man wearing a helmet?"

"Here it is," Steiner said. As he picked up the steel helmet his eyes widened. "Look at that," he said, pointing to a round hole on the back of the helmet.

The doctor took it from his hand and examined the spot curiously. "Was he lucky!" he said slowly. "The bullet came from behind, penetrated the metal and bounced around inside until it fell out. Incredible luck."

"Is it bad?" Steiner asked.

The doctor stooped over Schnurrbart again. "Not at all. Slight concussion of the brain. He'll come to soon."

"And the leg?"

"I don't know yet. If the bone isn't injured, he'll be on his feet in a month." He turned to the next patient.

"Well?" Hollerbach asked outside.

Steiner waved his hand. "Everything is all right. He may be back here in four weeks."

They sighed with relief. "The idiot." Kruger swore cheerfully. "I always told him to watch out for that dumb noodle of his. Did you know that Pasternack got it?"

"Dead?" Steiner asked hoarsely.

"Yes."

Steiner bit his lip. "Who else?"

"Maag," Kruger answered. "He's on his way to the rear already. Half the platoon is knocked out. Incidentally, Meyer is looking for you. We said you would be right along."

"He can wait," Steiner growled.

Captain Stransky had put some exciting experiences behind him. Originally he had intended to await the outcome of the patrol action in his bunker. But soon he was seized by uneasiness and, accompanied by Triebig, had set out for the Second Company's sector. They had reached the first foxholes when the enemy breakthrough began. Stansky had turned about promptly and raced back to his bunker. As soon as he had reached it, breathless and trembling, he had commanded his frightened adjutant to take up positions in front of the bunker with all the men attached to the staff. Then he had placed telephone calls to the combat train and to Regiment. Staff Sergeant Fetscher was ordered to bring everybody who could carry a gun to the battalion command post at once; to the worried regimental commander he gave a vivid description of the events, weaving into his report phases about resistance to the last cartridge. Shortly afterward, just as Sergeant

Fetscher arrived with a heavily armed group of communications personnel, Lieutenant Meyer telephoned him that the positions had been retaken from the enemy and the bomb craters cleared. The result was that Fetscher and his men, cursing but visibly relieved, started back and the regimental commander received a report calculated to warm his heart.

Now Stransky waited impatiently in his bunker for Meyer and Steiner. He was explaining to Triebig the proper way to meet any repetitions of such "unfortunate incidents," as he called them. "Everything depends on keeping calm and acting quickly and precisely," he said.

When Meyer and Steiner came in Stransky greeted them curtly and asked Steiner to describe the course of events in sequence. The three officers listened closely, and Stransky repeatedly gave vent to low exclamations of disapproval, which Steiner studiously ignored. When Steiner had concluded, Stransky turned to Meyer. "Bad business. The penetration of the trench could have been prevented."

"Under normal conditions certainly," Meyer said. "But in the first place the positions were weakly held, and in the second place the men did not know what to expect, since their own men were in front of them. By the time they realized the men coming up the hill were Russians, it was too late."

"All the same," Stransky retorted testily. He picked up a candle from the table and rolled it several times between his hands before he turned to Steiner. "You should have taken into consideration such a possibility," he said sternly. "A shock troop leader must count on all eventualities."

Meyer drew in his breath indignantly. But Steiner answered before he could intervene. "My assignment was to clear the bomb craters," he replied coolly. "An encounter with a hundred Russians was not expected by me or anyone else."

"You should have attacked the Russians right off," Triebig interposed. "If you had done so, they would never have got so far."

Steiner threw him a contemptuous glance. "The reasons why I did not," he said, "are so obvious that an explanation is unnecessary."

Stransky pounded his fist on the table. "I cannot agree with you," he said savagely. "In fact, it is perfectly clear that you are not able to cope with such situations." He turned to Meyer. "It would have been better after all if you had led the patrol. Apparently I overestimated your platoon leader's abilities."

Meyer exchanged a rapid glance with Steiner. In spite of the harsh words between him and Steiner earlier, his sense of justice was outraged. His anger was apparent in his voice. "I disagree, sir. As I see the situation, I would have acted precisely as Steiner did in every detail."

Stransky regarded him without change of expression. "It grieves me to hear that," he said. "If you equate your qualities as a leader with the sergeant's, that is your affair, of course, but it suggests regrettable conclusions."

Triebig spoke up. "I must agree with the captain," he said softly. "Such situations call for not only a high degree of coolness, but certain traits of character. Whether or not Sergeant Steiner possesses them you would know. Certainly there is reason to doubt that he does."

There was a silence. Steiner's face was drained of color. Meyer stood up quickly. "Perhaps you are an authority on character, Herr Triebig," he said scornfully. He turned to Stransky. "Have you any further orders for me?"

Stransky, still seated, looked up at him, a glint of mockery in his light eyes. "Not at the moment. You can inform me about your casualties tomorrow. I shall expect your written report at nine o'clock. You may go."

They had gone some distance from the bunker when Steiner stopped. "There's something I have to take care of," he said tightly.

In the darkness Meyer could scarcely see Steiner's face, but the tone of voice gave him concern. "You'll get into trouble," he warned him. "Don't do anything foolish."

Steiner shook his head. For a moment Meyer still hesitated; then he shrugged and walked away swiftly.

Steiner stole back quietly, detouring around the command post, and found a good spot among the trees, where he could not be seen. There was a sentry in front of the commander's bunker. Steiner prepared for a long wait. He thought over every detail of his plan. It was relatively simple. It would only be necessary to work up a suitable alibi. That was easy Kruger and Hollerbach would swear to high heaven that he had been with them all during the time in question.

Minute after minute passed. Then a light shone from one of the bunkers. A man came out slowly, looked around, closed the door behind him, exchanged a few words with the sentry and disappeared among the trees. Steiner stepped behind a crooked trunk. The sentry shifted his carbine to the other shoulder and began pacing back and forth. Finally he turned to the right, went over to the western edge of the orchard and again stood motionless. He was only dimly visible now. Steiner was about to step out from behind the tree when he heard a sound. A dark shadow emerged from the trees, stood poised for a while, approached with footsteps silent as a cat's and disappeared into the bunker Steiner knew belonged to Triebig. Steiner shook his head in wonder. Another ten minutes passed before Triebig appeared. He came from the commander's bunker and went straight to his, without glancing right or left. To Steiner's amazement no sound of conversation broke the silence. The glimmer of light from the small window beside the door went out. He stood suspended. What was going on here? At last curiosity won out over caution. After making sure that there was no immediate danger from the sentry, Steiner carefully approached the bunker, felt his way down the steps and paused for a moment at the door, listening, his tommy gun tucked under his arm. Nothing stirred inside. Inch by inch he pushed the door open until he could squeeze in. He stepped quickly across the threshold.

He heard hasty movements; then there was silence. Slowly he closed the door behind him, pressed his back against it and switched on his flashlight. On the low cot lay two men. It took a moment for him to recognize one of them as Triebig. His pistol in his hand, he was staring wide-eyed into the light. The man beside Triebig he knew only by sight—he was a member of the battalion staff. As Steiner stepped forward and placed the flashlight on the table, he saw the clothing strewn on the floor. The silence became agonizing. He walked around the table to the bed, the Russian submachine gun held like a club in his hands.

"Put that down," he whispered, pointing to the pistol. Triebig did not stir. The waxen pallor of his face was suddenly washed away by a rush of blood that mounted to the roots of his hair and seemed to flow even into the whites of his eyes. He uttered an inarticulate sound and tried to pull the blanket over his naked shoulders. But Steiner's hand flashed forward, caught a corner of the blanket and wrenched it off the bed. He tossed it behind him on the floor.

"Stand up!" he said to Triebig. Steiner gripped his wrist tightly, took hold of the pistol and laid it and his own gun beside the flashlight on the table. Uncertainly Triebig stood up. The other man pressed against the wall, drawing up his legs. His childish face reflected such abysmal terror that for a moment Steiner felt sorry for him.

"You should have barricaded the door," Steiner said. "Then you wouldn't have been caught, you damned swine."

"What do you want?" Triebig whispered.

"I almost forgot." Steiner smiled savagely. "Thanks for reminding me."

Triebig backed away from him to the wall and stood still, trembling. "I meant," Steiner said, "to beat you up for what you said over at Stransky's bunker. The problem would have been to keep you from shouting for help. Now I'm going to give you that beating and you won't shout."

"I will," Triebig stammered.

Steiner shook his head. "No, you won't," he declared grimly. "If you do, people will come and see what's going on here. What do you think Stransky will say?"

Triebig moved his lips without making a sound. Suddenly he propelled himself from the wall and ran to where his clothes lay. As he stooped for them, Steiner brought his nailed boot heavily down on his fingers. Triebig opened his mouth to scream. But only a low moan emerged.

"So you're keeping that in mind," Steiner said hotly. He lifted his foot and pulled Triebig up by the shoulder. "For all I care you can stick a handkerchief between your teeth. Only you'd better keep quiet. It will cost you your neck, remember."

He struck abruptly. His clenched fist hit Triebig squarely in the face. Triebig tried to defend himself, but Steiner's blows followed one another mercilessly, with all his strength behind them. He pounded the man until his fists ached. Then he picked him up and tossed him on the bed.

The other man pressed even closer against the wall.

"What's your name?" Steiner snapped.

The man did not answer.

"What's your name?" Steiner repeated sharply.

"Keppler," the man whispered.

"Are you his orderly?"

The man nodded.

"Get up, get dressed and get out. If you tell anyone about this, you'll be up for court-martial yourself. Clear?"

The man nodded silently. He stepped over Triebig and got off the bed. Steiner picked up his tommy gun. He glanced at Triebig. The fellow had passed out. It would be a while before he came to again. Without another word to Keppler, he left the bunker. Cautiously he climbed the steps and peered about.

The figure of the sentry was outlined indistinctly in the darkness. Steiner watched until he was able to make out that the man's back was turned. Hastily, crouching, he stole among the trees to the trench and started up the slope. It was the hour before dawn. Night still lay blackly over the land. Beyond the hill isolated rifle shots cracked meanly. The light was ebbing tiredly out of the stars. Reaching his bunker, Steiner paused, wondering whether he should go to see Meyer. But the company commander must be asleep by now. Indecisively he looked over the rim of the trench. He felt soiled.

Suddenly a glow passed over his face. He raised his head in

astonishment. In the east the heavens were cracking open. The horizon became a darting sea of flame, and a few seconds later a roar like a monstrous wave surged over the positions. He jumped down the steps, kicked open the door and found half a dozen horrified faces staring at him. A candle was flickering on the table. He shut the door behind him and looked at his watch.

"It's just three o'clock," Faber said quietly.

"Yes," Steiner murmured. "Just three."

X

LIEUTENANT COLONEL BRANDT was sitting on his bed, half-dressed. As he reached for his shoes, still dazed with sleep, he fiercely cursed the unreliability of the intelligence men in Krimskaya, who had predicted that the Russian offensive would begin in the middle of May. If you got to the bottom of it, he thought angrily, you'd probably find they were hand in glove with the Russians and deliberately feeding us misinformation.

He had managed to put his shoes on, but he sat for a while with drooping head. Outside there was a rumble as loud as a hundred trucks passing over a cobblestoned road. Objects in the bunker vibrated; the window glass hummed and the light of the candle dipped and flickered and threatened to go out. Suddenly the telephone buzzed. Brandt picked it up and recognized Captain Kiesel's voice. "It's starting, sir."

"It never stopped," Brandt growled. "Come over here in five minutes." He replaced the receiver and remained bent over the table for a moment. The enormous barrage had startled him out of sleep. He had been dreaming vividly that he was at the opera. But he could no longer remember what opera was being played. Perhaps the *Marriage of Figaro*, he thought, closing his eyes.

There was a knock. He quickly slipped on his tunic as Kiesel, tall and energetic, stepped in. At the same moment the telephone buzzed again. Brandt lifted the receiver. "The general," he murmured, winking at Kiesel.

The smile vanished. He listened, nodded thoughtfully. "Of course, Herr General. I shall issue the appropriate orders at once." He dropped the telephone. "Drum fire along the whole line. All available reserves have already been alerted. The general thinks this is the greatest massing of artillery the Russions have yet achieved. It really looks like the expected offensive." He turned the telephone crank and exchanged a few words with the operator. "There we have it," he said irritably. "Communications with the front are already broken.'

"We have radio," Kiesel replied.

Brandt nodded. "They're busy establishing connections now." He went to a corner of the bunker, produced a bottle of kirschwasser and filled two glasses. "You'll make an exception to your rule today," he stated. "We have a warm day before us and are going to need a tonic."

Kiesel nodded. They drank. Brandt set the glass down hard on the table and looked at his wrist watch. "Twenty after three," he noted. "The overture will last another two hours at least."

As time went on, the radioed reports coming in from the battalions were increasingly disturbing. Stransky reported loud motor noises from the edge of the wooded area. Kiesel shook his head as he read the message. "If Stransky can hear motor noises while this barrage is going on, the tanks must be right in front of his bunker," he said.

Shortly afterward telephone communication with the battalions was restored and Brandt had a chance to say a few words to the commanders. He tried to reassure them by pointing out that an assault regiment was on its way up front as reinforcement. A few moments later the wire was broken again. The signals officer informed Brandt that in attempts to restore the line more than half his men had fallen. Brandt ordered him to give up trying; radio communication would be good enough until the attack began. Slowly the sky grew brighter. The barrage had increased in violence and seemed to be drawing closer. Brandt looked at Kiesel, who was smoking a cigarette and looking calmly out of the window. "We'll take a look at the show from outside," he said to him. "Do you feel like it?"

Kiesel smiled. "Even if I didn't feel like it I wouldn't admit it. In ninety-nine out of a hundred cases our courage is nothing more than an expression of common politeness or sense of duty."

"And the remaining case?" Brandt asked.

Kiesel opened the door a crack and flipped the cigarette out. "An expression of our insanity."

It was already light enough for them to have a good view of the steep slope. The dull gray of the sky was shot through with silvery threads, and the stars were fading rapidly. Beyond the hill the artillery fire rumbled on undiminished. An inferno, Kiesel thought as they plodded up the slope. When they reached the brow of the hill, they halted together as if they had come to a wall. Toward the east, as far as the eye could reach, a volcano was raging. The horizon was a writhing dragon that lunged, stretched and twisted its giant length, spewing yellow flame over the land, puffing fiery clouds, never pausing for a moment. Between the blue-black hills there still hung pockets of darkness into which torrents of sparks showered. The knife-edged ridges stood out distinctly against the burning sky. Far to the west the moon stared down like the half-shut eye of a cyclops. Brandt gripped Kiesel by the shoulder.

They walked on a short distance to a trench which had been dug a few days earlier at the commander's order. Intended for observation it had been provided with a number of solidly built dugouts with broad lookout slits. In one of the dugouts they found Lieutenant Spannagel, the forward observer of the Second Artillery Battalion. He had a radio section with him, and was visibly delighted by the unexpected visitors. Since Spannagel also had a telphone connected to the regimental switchboard, Brandt informed the communications platoon of his whereabouts and ordered all messages and calls for him to be switched to the forward observation post. Then he questioned Spannagel about the situation. The lieutenant said that the guns were ready to fire, radio communications were intact and the supply of ammunition should be adequate to hold the Russians.

With the artillery officer's telescope Brandt studied the opposite hillside. Meanwhile Kiesel talked in low tones with Spannagel. In spite of his sanguine words, the thin-faced, likable young lieutenant seemed nervous. He kept shifting his weight restlessly from one leg to the other. "If I had only half the stuff the Russians are throwing away over here, I'd sure make things hot for them," he said.

"I thought you said you had enough ammunition," Kiesel remonstrated.

"Oh, I do, I do, but I'll need it when the attack starts. As long as the Ivans are hiding in the woods there's not much sense wasting my shells. The battalion has let me have five hundred rounds. You have no idea how fast they use up!"

"I know, I know. How many guns would you estimate they have on the other side?"

Spannagel shrugged. "Hard to say. I've been with the battalion since the start of the Russian campaign, but I've never seen anything like this. Just listen to it. You'd have to go back to the First World War to find a parallel for this kind of squandering of matériel."

"Which goes to show how seriously the Russians are taking

us," Kiesel said. "They seem to know they're facing the crack divisions of the southern front."

"Not much consolation in that. I just wonder what's left of our front lines."

Kiesel gave a worried nod. He looked at his watch. "It's been going on for two hours already. Before long their bombers will come."

"And then their tanks. They couldn't ask for better terrain."

Brandt interrupted. "The fire seems to be concentrating primarily on one-twenty-one point four. I don't think the Russians are going to attack along the road. They'll try to take the hill. If they succeed in that, our tank barrier on the highway will be worthless, and they'll pay us a visit from the rear."

"They must not take the hill," Kiesel said gravely. "If they do, we're done for."

They stepped to Brandt's side and followed his gaze out across the landscape. The sky's dull gray was taking on more and more color and the frightful glare on the horizon waned under the cold light of the new day. Slowly the light moved from the east over the hills, almost imperceptibly drawing the gentle lines of the terrain out of the dusk. The grayish-black cloud of dust hovering above the churned-up hills was becoming clearer, but a huge banner of smoke blocked all vision to the more distant east.

Kiesel suddenly raised his head to listen. At first there was only a delicate humming that set the air vibrating; then the sound swelled to a drone that seemed to fill the whole of the sky above their heads. Their faces paled. "The second phase," Brandt said coolly. "Planes."

The shrilling of the telephone startled them all. Spannagel picked up the receiver, listened and turned to Brandt. "The general, sir."

Brandt took the telephone, and his body involuntarily stiffened. "Herr General?"

"How do things look out your way, Brandt?" The voice sounded thin, remote, as though coming from a distant planet.

"Unchanged," Brandt replied. "Violent artillery fire on the trenches. I'm afraid the casualties will be high."

Outside a penetrating howl approached a crescendo. Out of the corner of his eye Brandt saw Kiesel and Spannagel pressing against the walls of the dugout. The radio section men lay flat on the floor. He pressed the receiver to his ear. "Herr General . . ."

The voice at the other end sounded concerned. "What's the matter? Brandt, what——"

The dugout began to sway. A deafening crash drowned out

every other sound. With his free hand Brandt clung to a prop and stared at the ceiling of the dugout. The buzzing in the receiver stopped. Dark smoke poured through the lookout slit. He heard Kiesel shouting. Sand trickled between cracks in the plank ceiling, and the doorless opening vanished in white smoke. Brandt coughed. He had let the receiver drop; now his legs sagged and he slid to the ground, with his back against the wall, gasping for air. In a few minutes the crash and roar of explosions gradually slackened, and the air slowly cleared. Brandt rose and stared at Kiesel, who stood near the entrance, his hand covering his eyes. Spannagel sat on the floor.

Kiesel took his hand from his eyes and blinked vigorously. His glance met Brandt's and he nodded. "The third phase," he said loudly. "The barrage is rolling over the communications zone now."

As if on command they stepped over to the lookout slit and peered out. The sound of motors hung in the air. Scattered heavy detonations indicated that the bombardment was not yet over. The officers stared at the white pall of fog spreading over the entire landscape. Kiesel recalled reaching the peak of a mountain several years ago, to find himself standing high above a solid bank of clouds.

He felt the commander's hand grip his arm. "Smoke," Brandt exclaimed, "they've fired smoke shells." He took two strides to the field telephone and turned the crank. But the line was dead.

As he started toward the door he bumped against a man who was just coming in. The man clicked his heels. "They're attacking now, sir. Radio message from the second battalion: tanks approaching; request artillery."

The radiomen were already at their apparatus, headsets over their ears, looking at Spannagel, whose nervousness had entirely disappeared. He stood beside Kiesel at the telescope. Now he straightened up. His voice sounded calm, sure, distinct. "Firing command."

"Firing command," one of the radiomen repeated in a monotone. Spannagel leaned forward over the telescope again. "Entire battalion: fire!"

The attack took place on a thirty-mile front, with the main blow directed against the positions west of Krimskaya. Little ground was gained, although the German side estimated that between twenty and thirty Russian assault divisions were employed. The spearhead was formed by several tank brigades which rolled over the smashed trenches under cover of the smoke screen. In spite of the vigorous German barrage they reached the peak of Hill 121.4. The army communiqué that day reported a grand Russian offensive against the Kuban bridgehead, with an expenditure of matériel comparable to the battles of the First World War. Local penetrations, the communiqué went on to say, had been sealed off and thrown back by counterattacks, and the offensive had been halted by the concentrated fire of the German defenders.

To the men on Hill 121.4 that morning, it scarcely seemed that there was any serious resistance to the surging tide of Russian infantry. The survivors of the artillery barrage rushed in wild flight down the battered trenches and tried to reach the battalion command post. Those who got through were assembled by Triebig for the defense of the post. Steiner's men stayed at their positions, wondering how long these posts, already as good as lost, would hold out. They had sat in dull apathy through the three-hour barrage, smoking countless cigarettes and scarcely exchanging a word.

The moment everything abruptly fell silent outside, and even the drone of airplane motors faded in the distance, Steiner had picked up his submachine gun, slid the strap of his steel helmet under his chin and climbed up into the trench, followed by Faber, Kern and the others. White swaths of smoke blotted out everything; the men had to grope their way to the next MG emplacement. Now they were standing around the loophole, staring in perplexity into the impenetrable smoke that covered the terrain. Steiner slung the tommy gun over his shoulder. "I'll look for Meyer," he said. "Set up the MG; it's going to start soon."

Faber shrugged. "I'm afraid you won't find anyone. Where do we meet if things go wrong?"

"Battalion command post," Steiner replied. "But not until you've used up all your ammunition." He lingered for a moment watching the woodsman place a belt in the machine gun. Kern crouched, his face twitching. His nerves seemed about gone. Besides Kern and Faber there were three other men in the dugout. They seemed somewhat calmer, although they had come with the latest batch of replacements. A little rough for a starter, Steiner thought, regarding them with pity. It suddenly occurred to him that Schnurrbart was no longer here. Lucky he was out of this. But Hollerbach and Kruger must . . . Concerned, he climbed quickly into the trench and looked around, listening. He could not see ten feet ahead. Isolated rifle shots sounded feebly from all directions. And the noise of motors could again be heard. He could not be sure whether the sounds came from the air or from the slope of the hill below. For a few seconds he stood still, wondering which way to go. Since Hollerbach's bunker was on the way to the battalion command post, Kruger must be somewhere to the left, near the company command post. The noise of the motors was growing louder and he realized that he had little time for reflection. He decided to look for Kruger first; that way he might be able to contact Meyer at once. Crouching, he began to hurry down the trench. Here and there the sides had collapsed, and in many spots huge craters blocked the way. The rifle pits he passed by were unmanned. His uneasiness increased. Suddenly he came across a man lying in his path. The head was separated from the body and had lodged among clumps of earth a few paces farther on. The mouth was open for a terrible scream, as if the head wanted to shout to him to turn back. Steiner closed his eyes and stepped over it. A head, he thought, just a head. He felt his whole body trembling.

The trench made a sharp turn to the left. The company command post ought to be beyond the next bend. Involuntarily he speeded his steps. Then he stopped abruptly. Before him yawned an enormous crater made by a bomb. Out of the black earth protruded splintered bits of beams and wood siding; smoke had sunk thickly into the pit, forming a pool of whiteness at the bottom. Steiner dug his fingers into the hard earth of the trench wall. His legs felt oddly numb, lifeless. The company command post, he thought. Lieutenant Meyer. For a few seconds he stood unable to move, then he detoured around the crater, stumbled into the trench on the other side and felt his way slowly forward.

The smoke was even denser here; it clung viscously to the ground. He passed another roofed emplacement and glanced in. He did so without intention, without hope. Then he stood still in astonishment. He saw a back, a broad, uncannily familiar back. His mouth opened to call, could not produce a sound. But when the back moved, he crawled into the hole and laid a hand on that familiar shoulder. The man whirled around, and Steiner found himself staring into Kruger's face. They looked at each other in silence.

Kruger turned to the loophole. "They're coming now," he said. His voice was strange, low and toneless.

"Tanks," Steiner whispered. He stepped to the other side of the heavy machine gun. The sound of the motors had risen to a horrible drone that filled the air and inexorably drew nearer. The steely clank of the treads were clearly audible. Visibility was gradually improving. The smoke screen was sliding down the hill, so that it was possible to see a few yards of the precipitous slope. Further down, however, it lay like thick soup, lazily drifting eastward toward the sun, which was just beginning to rise.

"If they have infantry with them," Steiner said, "we won't get out of here."

Kruger nodded. His set, masklike face did not change.

"Where are the others?" Steiner asked.

"I don't know. When the bombs started falling they were in the bunker."

"And where were you?"

"I was right here."

"Through the whole barrage?" Steiner exclaimed.

Kruger nodded. "We were waiting for you," he explained, speaking slowly and with effort. "Me and Hollerbach. When you didn't get here by half past two Hollerbach left and I—" he shrugged—"I didn't feel like sleeping. So I relieved the boy at the MG here, and then it started. I couldn't get out any more so I just sat, and later the bombs fell and the bunkers blew sky high and . . ." He was silent.

"It was horrible," Steiner said.

Kruger turned his head slowly. "What was horrible was that I sat here for four hours all alone. There's nothing worse than being alone. I know that now."

They listened to the roar of the motors. The sound was so near by now that they wondered why they could not see the tanks. Kruger was standing, legs spread wide apart, behind the machine gun.

Suddenly he raised his head. A roar passed overhead, swelled and dimmed as it plunged into the swaths of smoke below them. "Our barrage," Kruger commented at the top of his voice.

They watched as a black cloud surged up from below, smothering the noise of the tanks. They should have started sooner, Steiner thought. Why did they wait so long, those damned idiots? With a kind of mad satisfaction he watched as out of the turbulent caldron below a long barrel appeared and a tank with churning tracks and steel-plated sides rolled up the slope, a dozen Russian infantrymen clinging to its broad back. T34, he thought—always these damned T34's.

Apathetically he watched Kruger swing the MG around and begin to fire. The men on the tank tumbled off like so many stones, to roll down the steep slope, where they were swallowed up by the boiling smoke. The tank continued on and vanished from sight. It had not fired a shot. But behind it another appeared, and behind that one still others. Kruger pulled the MG off its pedestal and shouted, "Let's go!"

Steiner barely nodded. A terrible numbness was creeping over him; he could not stir.

"Come on," Kruger cried.

At the same time the tanks opened fire. The sharp crack of their cannon was louder than the barrage; the explosions resounded menacingly up the slope. The hammering of several dozen machine guns was suddenly interrupted by many voices screaming, "Oorraaaay!" Kruger and Steiner crouched down on the floor and stared at the entrance to the dugout. The Russians must already be in the trench. The German barrage moved back, pounded for a few seconds on the trenches and then rolled on up the hill.

They've given us up, Steiner thought. "We won't get through now," he said. His words were drowned out in the din.

"Too late," Kruger bellowed in his ear.

Steiner nodded again. Emotionlessly he looked at the white lines in Kruger's blackened face. He ought to wash, he thought, he ought to wash up right away. Aware of the absurdity of the thought, he grinned weakly. At that moment he saw a shadow in the trench, and from a sitting position fired several rounds. The shadow disappeared. Steiner imagined the Russians' next actions. Now the hand grenades would come, several explosive blocks tied together. There was nothing to do but shut his eyes and wait to be blown to smithereens. They stared from their emplacement into the trench, hardly daring a breath. Dawnlight was flooding the upper half of the trench.

Waiting in wearied resignation for the end, Steiner thought of Gertrud. Perhaps the supply column would bring a letter from her tonight. It would be returned to the sender as undeliverable, and Fetscher would note on it in red pencil, *"Gefallen für Gross-Deutschland"*—he had done so with innumerable letters before. The meeting in Gursuf would remain an episode on the margin of the war.

The waiting became unbearable. Kruger was crouching forward, peering into the trench entrance. It was quieter outside now. The racket of motors sounded further away, and the firing also seemed to proceed higher and higher up the slope. Only now and then could a German MG be heard. The artillery barrage had stopped. Kruger slowly, with terrible slowness, moved toward the entrance, paused motionless for a few seconds and finally stuck his head out into the trench.

Steiner, watching his back, saw his tense posture relax. He stepped quickly up to him, tommy gun held high. "Nothing here," Kruger whispered in bewilderment. The trench was deserted; there was no trace of the Russians.

But from the left came a new sound, like that made by several dozen boots thumping at a run along a trench. "Russians," Kruger stammered.

Steiner dropped to his knees and raised the barrel of his gun. The steps came closer; they heard panting, and men came in sight—not Russians, but men of the Third Company. They were running for all they were worth, one behind the other, most of them without weapons, with tattered uniforms and contorted, blood-smeared faces.

Kruger groaned with relief. When the last of them passed, he wanted to follow, but Steiner held him back. "Wait," he whispered sharply. "Not with the crowd." They listened.

Suddenly, alarmingly close, a motor whined, several terrified screams rang out; a tank cannon cracked and violent MG fire began. A series of shattering crashes that could only have come from hand grenades completed the unseen drama.

"They ran right into the Russians," Kruger whispered.

Steiner wet his dry lips with his tongue. The temptation to glance over the rim of the trench was enormous, but he controlled himself.

Kruger stared at the gun in his hands as though it were somehow the key to their desperate salvation. Finally he shrugged. "No sense," he murmured. "We can't go back; we've got to stay here." His perplexed helplessness made Steiner smile, but the smile flitted over his face as if it did not belong to him. Although he had no illusions, he suddenly felt that the worst was behind them. His head was clearing rapidly.

"We can't stay here," he said firmly. "The Russians will be here any minute. They must be rolling up the whole trench. What do you think those men were running from?"

Kruger plucked at his nose. "I don't know. If we stay here they'll come to us, and if we go out we'll come to them. We'll get it just like those others did."

"We've got to try," Steiner said. "Stick close behind me." He turned to the right and began walking at a low crouch along the trench. Kruger shifted the gun to his right hand. They reached the bomb crater under which the ruins of the company command post lay, climbed down into it and scrambled out the other side. It was so quiet now that they had to walk on tiptoe to keep their boots from crunching. Only above them, on the brow of the hill, some random rifle shots were still being fired.

In a dozen paces they reached Steiner's bunker and glanced

in briefly. The door was open. No one was inside. Now came the hardest part of the way; they continued forward on hands and knees. As they turned a corner they came across a man pinned to the bottom of the trench by a heavy bomb. The bomb fin protruded from his back like a ventilator, the metal red and gleaming dully in the sunlight. Went right through his back and chest and into the ground, Steiner thought. He closed his eyes and crawled over the man's guts. Kruger followed close behind him. Their faces were filthy, the sweat pouring down their foreheads and into their eyes.

But they moved steadily along over discarded equipment, pieces of uniform and human limbs scattered about the half-collapsed trench, as though the barren soil of Hill 121.4 had suddenly become a womb bearing waxen faces, clenched fists and bloody rags. They crawled over three men who had been mashed into a single heap of flesh, their mouths open in death, as if to scream curses at a sky that now arched velvety blue above the hills.

As Steiner wiped a ghastly, sticky mess from his fingers, a cry above their heads threw them flat on their faces. *"Stoi!"* They lay numbed. A Russian submachine bun hammered metal above them. At the same moment Steiner sprang to his feet, fired blindly over the trench wall and raced on. Stumbling, panting, Kruger ran behind him. Hand grenades exploded; loud shouts sounded down the trench. From somewhere to one side of them a dark face under a fur cap appeared for a few seconds. Steiner fired without taking aim. The face withdrew, and a dark object rolled toward them, hissing meanly. His eyes widening with terror at sight of the hand grenade, Steiner was about to throw himself backward. But he could already feel Kruger's panting breath right on his neck. Instead, he took an incredible leap over the grenade, dashed several yards farther on to the next turn in the trench and threw himself flat. The detonation came just as a heavy body fell on top of him. He heard Kruger's voice again, felt hands pulling him up and stared incredulously into Kruger's contorted face.

"Keep going," Kruger groaned, "keep going, keep going."

Exhausted, they stumbled ahead, heard the shouts and the firing behind them growing feebler. Abruptly they stopped. Some thirty feet away, diagonally across the trench, stood a Russian tank. "This is it," Kruger said tonelessly. The monster's turret slowly swerved around until the cannon was pointed directly at them. With an inarticulate cry, Steiner hurled himself forward, Kruger following as though they were one body.

* * *

Things were happening fast at the regimental command post. As soon as the barrage ended, Brandt had hurried to the message center, run through the reports that had arrived and talked by radio with Division. He had described the tactical situation in the blackest colors and persuaded the general to give him the support of a Stuka wing. Shortly afterward Kiesel had come into the bunker to report that the Russian assault had apparently bogged down in front of Second Battalion's positions, but that it was rolling steadily up the hill over the trenches of the First Battalion. Meanwhile, alarming radio messages from Stransky had come in. He reported that dispersed remnants of the Second and Third companies were reaching the battalion command post. There could no longer be any doubt that the main line of resistance had collapsed on Hill 121.4. Through the artillery observer's telescope Brandt had personally verified the disastrous situation. Now he stood in his bunker bent over the maps, with Kiesel and two other officers of the regimental staff at his side.

Brandt raised his head. "The break-through must have come at Gausser's part of the line," he said gloomily. "We have no time to lose. By the time the assault regiment arrives it will be too late. Look here." The officers bent closer over the map. "Vogel was almost untouched," Brandt went on. "He'll still holding his positions. If the Russians have reached the top of the hill, they'll turn up in his rear."

"How is Körner's company?" Lieutenant Mohr, the communications officer, asked.

"Körner's holding firm," Brandt replied. "He's in the least danger. His right flank is covered by Stransky, who is gathering the dispersed soldiers at his command post and will attack in ten minutes."

"With the assault regiment?" Kiesel asked.

"No. If we wait for it, Vogel will be encircled. I've already radioed orders to him and Stransky. Vogel will abandon the positions as far as the battalion command post and attack from the south up the hill, where he'll meet Stransky."

"I see." Kiesel nodded. "Then the main line of resistance will no longer run around the hill but over it. A simple rectification of the front."

Mohr spoke up. "That seems clear to me," he said. "But it looks as though advanced Russian sections—mainly tanks, I should think—will already be west of the point where Stransky and Vogel are supposed to close the gap in the main lines."

"That's true." Brandt rubbed his unshaven chin. "But those isolated Russian forces will run into the assault regiment attacking from Kanskoye. If it makes you feel any better, that regiment has ten self-propelled assault guns with it."

The gloomy faces around him brightened. Brandt tapped his knuckles on the table. "Once the assault regiment gets here, we'll take the hill back, you can depend on that. We'll attack with Stuka support and the comrades will find things a bit hot for them."

The other officers seemed partly convinced by his confidence. They consulted their watches and discussed the situation in low voices while Brandt conducted several telephone conversations. Lieutenant Stroh, regimental special-missions officer, was less optimistic than some of the others. "The attack on the hill will not be easy," he brooded. "Think of the artillery the Russians have massed over there. As soon as our men appear on the hill there'll be a barrage that will make them reel."

Kiesel glanced at Brandt, who was sitting at the table talking over the telephone. "I assure you," he replied quietly, "that the commander is aware of that. But, after all, it's the commander's duty to show optimism even against his better judgment."

"Has there been any news of the company commanders?" Mohr asked.

Kiesel nodded sadly. "Yes, some. Meyer is presumably dead. Merkel and Schwerdtfeger wounded. There's no trace at all of Gausser."

Stroh sighed. "In other words, the First Battalion is without officers."

"Except for Stransky and Triebig, yes. Körner has also lost two of his company commanders. It's pretty raw."

They looked up eagerly as the commander rose to his feet. "Good news," he said. "Division reports that the attack was beaten off almost all along the line. Small penetrations here and there, most of them already cleared up." He turned to Mohr. "Radio message to Stransky and Vogel. The counterattack is to be postponed ten minutes. The Stukas ought to arrive at any moment. I don't want our own men coming in there just when the bombs are falling. That would be all we need."

As Mohr hastened out, Brandt turned to Stroh. "Inform Spannagel and get in touch with Potzenhardt. I need every one of his guns. As soon as the Stuka attack is over, have him put covering fire on the hill until he doesn't have a round left."

"Is he still with Vogel?" Stroh asked.

"Yes, his observation dugout is near Vogel's command post.

Try to reach him through his battalion. The wire to Vogel is still out."

Stroh went tearing out. "And now," Brandt said, "a little refreshment. I feel we've earned it."

He filled the glasses and pushed one across the table to Kiesel, who had silently seated himself. They drank. Kiesel searchingly regarded the commander's exhausted features. "May I give you my frank opinion?" he asked quietly.

Brandt settled back in his chair with a groan. "I can't remember ever saying that you couldn't," he replied grumpily, "though you've never asked permission before. What is it?"

"We won't recapture that hill," Kiesel said firmly.

Brandt regarded him from half-closed eyes. He smiled unpleasantly. "Are you giving me advice, Kiesel?"

"I should like to remind you of the several hundred guns on the other side."

"Do you imagine I've forgotten them?"

Kiesel shrugged. There was a silence for a few seconds. Brandt reached for the bottle and refilled his glass. His voice rang out clear and cold. "Division has ordered me to throw the Russians back to their starting point at all costs. The general thinks it is possible."

"The general?" Kiesel asked hesitantly.

Brandt drained his glass at one swallow and leaned across the table. "I want to tell you something, Kiesel. If you as my adjutant try to impose your personal views upon me, you are at liberty to do so. All you are risking is my good feelings toward you and perhaps your position as adjutant. But if I as regimental commander want to prove a point of mine with the general, I can do so only by bleeding the whole regiment to death." His voice rose. "My regiment, Kiesel, and because my regiment consists for me not of figures but of men, and because that fact is with me every minute of every day, because I have to think not only for myself but for four thousand men, I find it just too goddamn much to have to sit and listen to your damned ideas."

Kiesel, seeing agony on the lined face, bit his lip. "Forgive me."

"Oh, shut your mouth," Brandt commanded sharply. His face looked more normal again. Noticing that Kiesel had scarcely drunk, he urged him to finish his glass.

"The thing is," Brandt went on in a somewhat lower voice, "you have to be either up at the very top or down at the very bottom, either a *landser* or commander in chief, not one of these thrice-damned middlemen like us who have no breathing space to the right or left, who neither produce nor consume, but simply receive and pass on. Ah . . ." He clenched his big hands in disgust.

Kiesel folded his arms over his chest and nodded. "The purchase price was too high," he said quietly. "Can you still remember what your uniform cost you?"

"Is that a joke?" Brandt asked sharply.

"The subject is too grave for joking. We did not buy our uniforms; we swapped them. Swapped them for our consciences, and now we'd like to take back the swap, but it is too late."

"Too late?" Brandt whispered.

"Too late," Kiesel repeated boldly. His eyes glistened. "It was already too late when we raised our hands and took the oath for Führer and Folk and for something else—we knew at the time what it was, although we did not have the guts to admit it to ourselves."

Brandt's face was chalky. "Shut up!" he barked. "For the last time I order you to shut up, Kiesel. I won't permit you to talk that way; do you hear, I won't permit it!"

He sprang abruptly to his feet and paced back and forth. Finally he came to a stop at the table again. "Even if it were true," he said, "as long as our men are bleeding and dying out there, you have not the right to talk like that, you have no right and I have no right. Here—" his hand came down heavily on the maps scattered over the table—"here is my job; here is my regiment's sector and here is where the Russians have broken through. Nothing else interests me, not today and not tomorow, not at all. If this war is lost I'll be able to stand before any mirror without spitting in my own face, and I will not permit anyone to work with me who cannot say the same for himself. Have I expressed myself clearly?"

"You have, indeed," Kiesel said. He had listened in perfect calm to the commander's outburst. Obviously this was an inappropriate moment for such a discussion; he made up his mind to return to the subject some other time. But he could not refrain from remarking that he personally would prefer not to look in any mirrors at all, since it might well be that his better judgment would be grinning scornfully over his shoulder, awakening doubts that he could easily escape by keeping his eyes shut. At that Brandt left the bunker without another word. As he did so, a swelling drone in the sky announced the arrival of the expected planes. Kiesel also went outside in time to see about a hundred of the thick-set dive bombers flying in a gigantic V and heading straight for Hill 121.4. They disappeared beyond the brow of the hill. Seconds later the air was filled with a volley of thunderous detonations; the sound waves battered their ears as they listened in breathless exultation.

The officers were all standing in front of their bunkers, their faces expressing grim satisfaction. Kiesel wondered whether he should follow the commander, who had gone up the hill to watch the counterattack from the observation post, but then he told himself that it might be advisable to leave him alone for a while. He went into his bunker. He sat at his table dozing until the telephone shrilled. It was the voice of Sergeant Hüser breathlessly informing him that, according to a radio message just received from Battalion, the counterattack had been successful. The connection with the Third Battalion had been re-established. Kiesel breathed a sigh of relief. "I shall inform the commander," he said, and added that if further messages came in they could be reached at the observation post.

He hurried out, climbed the hill, and found Brandt standing behind the telescope. The radiomen were watching through the loophole.

As Kiesel approached, Brandt said happily, "They're up there. They've made it, Kiesel: the gap is plugged. Here, see for yourself."

He drew him by the arm over to the loophole and pointed. He looked like another man, and seemed to have entirely forgotten their bitter exchange of a short while ago. Kiesel reported the radio message from First Battalion. Brandt rubbed his hands gleefully. "A pity you weren't here," he said. "In all Russia I've never seen an air attack like this one. A hundred planes." He laughed boomingly. "Wouldn't have thought we had that many left." He turned to Spannagel. "You can start now. The assault regiment ought to be along any minute." He drew Kiesel along outside the shelter. "Maybe the line has been repaired by now," he said. "I must talk to Stransky."

In silence they returned down the hill and on the way encountered Sergeant Hüser, hurrying up toward them. "The wire is fixed," he reported hastily. "Captain Stransky wishes to speak to you, sir. The assault regiment has arrived."

"Good, good." Brandt joyfully patted him on the shoulder, hurried on into his bunker and picked up the telephone. Kiesel could hear Stransky's voice, loud and seemingly excited, but he could not make out any of the words. Finally Brandt nodded several times and said, "Very well, Stransky. Start at once. We will give you ample artillery support. Follow close behind the assault regiment and occupy the positions again. How are things over your way otherwise?"

When he replaced the receiver, the smile had vanished from his face. "So it's true." He turned to Kiesel. "Stransky has no officers left. Do you know who led the counterattack on the hill?"

"Triebig," Kiesel guessed.

Brandt shook his head. "No, it was Steiner. The boy was wounded in the course of it. In the arm."

"Steiner?"

"Yes." Brandt pondered for a moment and then suddenly inquired about Kiesel's brother-in-law.

"He ought to be arriving within the next few days," Kiesel replied uncomfortably.

"We'll give him the Second Company," Brandt said. "Today I'm going to put in an urgent request for replacements. The First Company is practically wiped out and . . ." Outside violent artillery fire had begun abruptly. "It's starting," Brandt said with enforced calm. "Come along, we'll watch from up above again."

Kiesel followed him.

Steiner acted without thinking. It was as if he were being propelled forward. Kruger, too, had lost all his faculties, as though the black muzzle of the tank cannon had been a telescope showing him a ghastly pit that made the blood freeze in his veins. Nevertheless, he reacted a fraction of a second faster than the invisible gunner inside the tank. The explosion struck like a club against their ears. They were lying on the ground about ten feet away from the tank, their faces in the moist earth. Behind them the trench had vanished in a dark cloud of smoke. Even before the hail of earth stopped pelting down on his back, Steiner crawled forward on all fours. Between the crushed walls of the trench he had discerned a narrow crack, into which he squeezed himself, closing his eyes as he did so. Thirty-four tons, he thought, thirty-four tons above me. And he crawled underneath the thirty-four tons, followed so closely by Kruger that he could feel the East Prussian's hands touching his legs. Every second he expected to hear the motor roar. He imagined he felt the masses of earth starting to shift, starting to crush his body. His head, arms and shoulders bumped and pushed desperately at some soft, dark obstacle in the way. Suddenly it gave, the ground sank beneath him and he fell several yards. An instant later a heavy body fell on him and Kruger's voice made him open his eyes. Panting, trembling with exhaustion, they gaped at each other. They were lying in a deep bomb crater, and Steiner noticed that his hands were still clutching the soft obstacle that had nearly stopped him. It was the body of a man. It felt strangely spongy, and from neck to knees it was nothing but an empty, bloody sack. He let go and looked up.

The tank stood unmoving, and he saw that the right-hand track hung slack on the wheels, ripped in two. Steiner groped for his tommy gun and stood up. He noticed that Kruger no longer had his MG, but asked no questions. They clambered out of the crater, crawled into the trench and went on without turning their heads. They moved slowly. From somewhere on the hill came the sound of firing. Isolated shells whined high above their heads from left to right and right to left. But they paid no attention. They were utterly weary and totally indifferent.

They reached the fork where the branch trench led off to the battalion command post. Their way led downhill now, and the sun shone warmly in their faces, but they scarcely felt it. Their legs moved as though no longer part of them; it was as if they were dead. But the sun shone warmly and it was a lovely spring day.

The men lay behind their rifles on the edge of the orchard. Their faces were marked by the experiences of the past several hours. Hollerbach was staring vacantly at Faber, who sat beside him with eyes closed.

Kern, carrying a canteen, came up to them and tossed the canteen on the ground, muttering a curse under his breath.

"None?" Hollerbach asked.

Kern shook his head and dropped down beside them. "Nobody has any," he said glumly. "The water down there is too filthy for me. Corpses in it. I'd rather go thirsty."

"We'll have to wait till the field kitchen gets here," Hollerbach said.

Kern gave a short laugh. "By the time it comes we won't need anything. By that time the whole battalion'll be able to feed out of one mess tin." He looked up the hill. "They won't be coming now," he murmured. "They should have been here long ago." He turned to Faber. "We should have looked for them."

"It was too late," Faber said. "You know yourself it was too late. The Russians were in the trench, and we had no more ammunition."

"Not a round," Kern said.

Hollerbach sighed. "I never thought Steiner could get it," he said. "I still can't grasp it."

"Neither can I," Kern said blackly. "A guy like him should have realized what was happening."

"Death isn't something you realize," Faber said. "It comes like the night. When the twilight falls among the trees, it's there already and you can't avoid it."

"What a way to put it." Kern was strangely moved. He hunched his shoulders as if he were cold.

Four men came by carrying a wounded soldier. His legs dangled at an odd angle over the edge of the canvas. They watched as the stretcher-bearers and their burden disappeared among the trees. Kern removed his steel helmet and scratched his head. His mournful sense of loss deepened. Even now he was tremulous with the shock he had experienced when the tanks appeared. He recalled how Faber had kept firing at the oncoming Russians until a man dashed into the emplacement shouting that the Russians had broken in on the right. For all that, Faber had stuck by the gun; they had not started to retreat until the last belt of ammunition had been fired. On the way they had encountered Hollerbach and his men and had reached the battalion command post together. But neither Steiner nor Kruger had turned up. They would have to assume that the two were lying dead somewhere in the trench. The longer Kern thought about this, the more painful the dull throbbing in his chest became. Recollection of past ugly scenes between him and both the missing men did nothing to abate his grief.

Suddenly Hollerbach produced a sound halfway between a squeal and a shout. Kern looked up in time to see him jump to his feet and throw his hands in the air like a madman. Faber, too, was staring up the slope. Above them, in the chest-high communications trench, two figures appeared, trudging along with bowed heads as though nothing in the world would ever arouse their interest again.

"Steiner," Kern murmured incredulously.

The orchard was suddenly full of excited men pressing forward, calling out to the two. Almost half an hour had passed since the last straggler had arrived at the command post; no one was expecting any more survivors. As Kern and Hollerbach rushed forward to meet the two, someone carried news of the return of Sergeant Steiner to the commander's bunker. A staff courier promptly appeared with orders for Steiner to report to the commander's bunker at once.

Steiner took his time. He exchanged a few words with Faber

and the other men before following the courier down a lane
of inquisitive faces.

When he entered the commander's bunker, he found
Stransky bent over a map. Stransky's face looked aged and
expressionless. Silently he pointed to a chair. Steiner sat down.
Arms clasped behind his back, Stransky strode about the
bunker several times, finally halted in front of Steiner. "You've
come from up above?" he asked curtly.

Steiner nodded. In an effort to conceal his dislike, he looked
down at the floor.

"How do things look?" Stransky asked.

The question seemed pointless to Steiner. He shrugged
apathetically and replied, "Unchanged."

"What does that mean?" Stransky's eyes became narrow and
spiteful.

"The Russians are still holding our positions," Steiner said
quietly.

Stransky suppressed an angry retort. He went over to the
map. "We are going to undertake a counterattack," he declared. "The purpose is to restore contact with the Third
Battalion." He outlined briefly the plan of the counterattack.
"The Stukas ought to be along any minute now. I need a man
to lead the counterattack. Would you like to?"

Steiner had been expecting something of the sort. "I don't
think I would like to," he said slowly. "I don't believe I have
the qualities needed to cope with such a situation."

Abruptly Stransky stalked to the door and looked out the
little window for a few seconds.

"You are forgetting one thing," he said over his shoulder.
"You forget the fact that actually it doesn't matter at all to
me whether or not you would like to. May I suggest that you
examine your mind to see what, if anything, justifies your
attitude?"

"What makes you think that I haven't already done that?"
Steiner asked coolly.

Stransky leaned against the door. "I make that assumption
because of your total lack of discipline and . . ." He hesitated.
Then he went on: "And because young people do not take the
trouble to think when they know that, if need be, someone
else will do that thinking for them."

Steiner frowned. "I don't understand."

"I can put it more clearly," Stransky said scornfully. "You
need not be honest toward me. I am quite accustomed to having my subordinates lie to my face. But for once be honest
with yourself."

Not knowing what he was getting at, Steiner shrugged. "I try," he said, somewhat contemptuously.

"Good. Then perhaps you can answer this question: isn't your display of independence based simply on the fact that you have—I'll put the thing in terms of civilian life—that you have an influential uncle."

As Steiner started to rise angrily, Stransky raised his hand quickly. "No one likes to be reminded that his so-called individualism depends on his being backed by another man's authority. . . ."

Having delivered that insult, he remained silent.

Steiner leaped to his feet and stared balefully at him. "You wanted to talk about the counterattack," he said loudly.

"Right," Stransky said. "I'm coming to that in a moment. You see, Steiner, even if we did have something in common, there is one highly essential difference between us."

"Your rank," Steiner interjected.

Stransky smiled superciliously. "I was not referring to that," he said calmly. "If I were to proceed from that angle, I assure you that our conversation would take an entirely different course. You are very young. I don't doubt that in my position you would not hesitate to throw into the scales your authority as a superior officer. The fact that I forbear ought to give you something to think about. And there you have the difference between us."

Steiner regarded his amicable face with distrust. Then he laughed aloud. "You overlook a few facts. In the first place, those good connections you harp on didn't come about by chance and are not undeserved. In the second place, I never tried for them and have made a point of never using them. If I had, you would scarcely have had any chance to give me orders at all. As for . . ."

He broke off. Stransky had raised his hand for silence. A low drone filled the bunker. "The Stukas," Stransky said hurriedly. "We'll have to continue our conversation some other time. Look here." He bent over the maps and sketched briefly the details of the counterattack. "When you reach the hill," he went on, "wait until the assault regiment arrives and follow behind it into your old positions. All clear?"

Since the bombing began at that moment, Steiner merely nodded briefly and left the bunker. The men were standing in a cluster. Up on the hill a dark cloud of smoke was mounting to the sky.

Steiner stood for a few seconds watching the planes dive vertically and release their bombs. The sight gave him grim pleasure, and he clenched his fists. For Meyer, he thought, for

Meyer and Pasternack and Dorn and all the others lying dead up there.

A loud voice reached his ear. He saw Kruger striding toward him. "What's up?" the East Prussian asked.

"Scheisse," Steiner growled, and ordered Kruger to assemble all the noncoms. When they had gathered around him, he explained what they were to do and began dividing up tasks among the various platoons. Finally he turned to Kruger, who stood gloomily plucking at his nose. "You stay near me. You and Hollerbach and Kern and Faber."

"The bastards," Kruger cursed fiercely. "They don't give a man ten minutes' rest."

"When you've got six feet of ground over you you'll have more rest than you like," Steiner said.

The group of about a hundred men were holding their weapons, awaiting the signal from him. Raising his hand, he started up the slope. As the hum of airplane motors faded away in the west, the men spread out in a skirmishing line and followed the point group up the hill over the shell-torn terrain. Not a shot had yet been fired. Steiner walked with bowed head, wondering what they would do if a Russian tank turned up. Although most of the tanks were undoubtedly somewhere beyond Kanskoye, raising hell in that area, there might still be a few stragglers on the hill. Even one would be enough. Steiner had no illusions about that; he knew that the men, exhausted as they were and with their morale at zero, would turn back in wild flight at the first sound of motors.

As he skirted a large crater, Hollerbach came over to him. He had evidently been considering the same question. "What are you going to do if tanks come?" he asked nervously.

Steiner shrugged indifferently. "How do I know?"

The hill was steep, and they panted with the climb, but the top was slowly drawing nearer. Steiner glanced back to reassure himself that the men were following, and for a moment he felt a grim satisfaction and pride that he was leading the whole battalion. Then he grinned ironically. He had no more than half a company behind him. For a few seconds he thought of Stransky; it should have been the captain who was heading the line, not some low-down platoon leader. The conceit of the bastard! he thought with infinite contempt. The hill was flattening out and they could already see part of their old positions, which ran along the hill on the left. Nowhere was there any sign of life. It looked as if the Russians had long ago advanced behind the hill, further to the west. There was hardly any incline now, and they walked faster.

"They'll start shooting in a minute," Kruger panted.

As though set off by his words, violent sounds of skirmishing suddenly broke out far ahead of them. They stood still and looked around. The scorched earth, still covered by swaths of smoke in many places, seemed to stretch all the way to the horizon, where several white flares were now rising.

"That's the Third," Steiner said. And in answer to Kruger's uncomprehending look he explained: "The Third Battalion is attacking from the other side of the hill. We must send up flares."

He took the pistol from Faber's hand and shot up two flares in succession. Looking back, he saw far below the orchard where the command post was situated. Behind stretched the long ridge on whose other side the regimental command post must lie. The sky was quite cloudless; visibility was splendid that way.

The noise of fighting to the north increased. Most of the men had dropped into shell holes, their steel helmets protruding above the ground like huge dark mushrooms.

"What are we waiting for?" Kruger asked, looking down uncomfortably at the barren moonscape beneath their feet.

Kern was sitting with his legs dangling over the edge of a bomb crater. Faber stood beside Hollerbach, who was leaning on the machine gun.

"Why the hell should we pull the chestnuts out of the fire?" Kern growled. "What's the sense of rushing on?" He turned to Steiner. "We've reached the top; we can wait here until the men of the Third get to us."

There was something tempting about the proposal. The men exchanged glances. "If we go on," Hollerbach said, "they're going to see us from the woods, and then there'll be hell to pay."

Steiner seemed indecisive. Kern watched him closely. He had made up his mind to disappear into a shell hole at the first shot and wait until the fighting was over. He'd had more than enough for the day; a man should not push his luck too long.

"I tell you what," he volunteered when the others remained silent. "It seems to me we've carried out our orders, and now they can just kiss our behinds, the damned idiots. What the hell do they think they're doing, sending us against tanks without anti-tank guns?"

Faber, listening in silence, had been watching two of First Company's noncoms. They were sitting about a dozen paces away, taking in the whole incident. He suddenly had the uncomfortable feeling that they were amused by Steiner's indecision. He thumbed his steel helmet back on his head. "I think we'd better go on," he said quietly, indicating with a half gesture the sounds of battle. "We've got to help them—those are our orders."

Steiner frowned. "You don't have to tell me what our orders are," he said hoarsely. "Are we on top of the hill or aren't we?"

"We aren't," Faber replied firmly.

Steiner thought he detected a trace of disdain in the woodsman's blue eyes. He opened his mouth for a retort. But then he set his lips, turned his back on Faber and started forward with huge strides toward the sounds of fighting. Faber and Hollerbach followed him at once; Kruger remained standing, looking after them with annoyance.

But when he saw the other men clambering out of their holes, he turned to Kern. "Let's go."

"I'll be along," Kern grunted, not stirring.

Kruger took a step closer and glared down at him. "Handing in your resignation?"

"None of your business," Kern replied rebelliously. But he picked himself up, pounded the dust from his trousers and cursed furiously. "Trouble with you bastards is, you can't wait till you're dead."

"I'll be glad to have it over with," Kruger said.

They joined a group of men who were moving forward slowly, crouching low. Kern's rage evaporated. His face gray with fear, he kept close beside Kruger, who moved along with bowed head as though nothing mattered. They advanced several hundred yards. With growing alarm Kern noted that with every step the horizon around them moved back several kilometers. He did not dare to turn his head because he knew that they were now visible from the edge of the woods, where the Russians had their artillery emplaced. For a while he clung to the desperate hope that the Russian artillery observers would, from the distance, be unable to distinguish the German infantry from their own men. But he felt like a man walking naked in front of a crowd. Even with several dozen others around him, it was as if he were entirely alone, a solitary target for the Russians.

Suddenly he stopped. In the distance a series of dull explosions sounded; instinctively he bent his back. There was a howl over their heads, dark mushrooms of smoke burst up out of the earth, and they lay pressed against the ground with their eyes closed in terror. Steiner dived into a crater beside Hollerbach. It seemed likely that they were in for a long and systematic shelling. He recalled that Fetscher had once insisted that shells never struck twice in the same place. Nonsense. But he began listening alertly.

As suddenly as it had begun, the shelling stopped. Steiner took a while to believe it. Still skeptical, not trusting the quiet, he clambered out of the hole. Nothing happened, and he went into action. Even before the thick veil of dust and smoke could disperse, he shouted to the men at the top of his voice. Seconds later they were running after him, taking grotesque leaps over obstacles.

The encounter with the Russians was a surprise to both sides. Unexpectedly the terrain sloped off to the north; as Steiner and his men reached the top of the hill, they stood still for a few seconds, staring at the scene before them. The steep slope below them was, like all the rest of the terrain, pocked with innumerable shell holes, almost all of which were occupied by Russians. They lay side by side, firing steadily at some invisible enemy further down the slope below them. The sight of those backs turned unsuspectingly toward the top of the hill was so utterly fantastic against the vaporous background that the men were momentarily stunned.

Then, out of the corner of his eye Steiner saw that Faber was setting up the heavy MG with almost reverential care. As he crouched down behind it, the others came to life. Steiner raised his fist into the air, and a deafening roar of concentrated rifle and machine-gun fire rolled like an avalanche down the slope. Steiner had time to see the Russians whirl around to throw agonized glances up the slope, while below them a white flare rose triumphantly. While he blindly emptied his magazine he felt an intoxicating, nameless gratification that made him forget to take cover. When the painful blow twisted his body around in a quarter turn, he did not realize what had happened until the submachine gun dropped from his hands and a cry of alarm reached his ears. He staggered back, grasped his right shoulder and sank to his knees with face contorted by pain.

Kruger was at his side in a moment. Anxiously he bent over Steiner shouting something which was lost in the din of the firing. Hollerbach and Kern came immediately. They carried him back several dozen yards and laid him down with infinite care.

"Is it bad?" Kruger asked worriedly.

Steiner shook his head. He felt the need to reassure them. "Flesh wound or something," he said tightly, looking at his shoulder, where his tunic was gradually darkening. The pain was bearable, but he had a queerly numbed feeling in the whole top part if his body.

Up ahead the men of the battalion had vanished as though a sudden gust of wind had blown them down the slope. He recalled that it was his duty to lead the attack. Before he could say anything, loud shouts, then cheers came from down below.

"Got them," Kruger exclaimed. He raced ahead to the spot where Faber still lay behind his MG, and peered down the slope. "They've met the Third," he shouted. "You ought to see the Ivans with their hands up." After a while he returned. "We'll have you at a dressing station in a shot," he said to Steiner. "But first let's see what you've got."

Carefully they removed the tunic and cut open the blood-soaked shirt. "Shoulder wound." Kruger delivered his verdict. "The bullet must still be in there. Let's hope it didn't touch the bone."

They put an emergency bandage on the rapidly bleeding wound. Steiner's face was gray, but he was able to stand on his feet fairly well. While Kruger and Kern supported him on both sides, Hollerbach picked up his light assault pack, slung the Russian tommy gun over his shoulder and followed them. Since they did not want to go back by the exposed route over the hill, they cautiously descended the slope where the men were rounding up the prisoners. Within a few minutes they reached the Third Battalion's command post. Only then did they notice that Faber had trailed along.

The dressing station was in a hollow a few hundred yards further to the west. As they walked on Steiner reflected with satisfaction that the counterattack had been a complete success. They could set up the switch position now and wait quietly for the assault regiment to arrive. He felt somewhat better; aside from the dull throbbing in his shoulder, he was all right. The terrain before them began to drop, and shortly afterward they came on the dressing station bunker, hidden in the midst of dense shrubbery. Several men with minor wounds, wearing white bandages on their heads and arms, were standing or sitting around.

Steiner's shoulder was freshly bandaged. The doctor advised him to wait here until dark, since it was inadvisable to take the risk of going on to the clearing station while Russian tanks were prowling around. "I'll just give you a shot," he said, "and you can go back tonight with our supply truck. They've established the clearing station in Kanskoye for the past hour."

Steiner hesitated. "I'd rather get started right away," he said. "I can manage to walk to Kanskoye."

"You'll have to go over the hill," the doctor warned.

"I know. But I can try it over to this side, and further to the rear."

"As you like. You need only follow the brook till it turns north, and then go straight over the hill. You can't miss the way." He returned to the bunker.

Steiner turned to his men. "I'll be back soon," he assured them. "Don't put on such faces. You're really glad to be rid of me."

"Who's glad?" Kruger demanded loudly, plucking furiously at his nose.

Steiner grinned. "You more than anybody."

Kruger gasped angrily and shouted, "Me!"

"Sure."

"Easy, easy," Hollerbach said.

But Kruger was working himself into a rage. "You know what you can do for me?" he bellowed still louder.

Steiner nodded. "You'd love that, wouldn't you?" he said cheerfully.

Hissing between his teeth, Kruger turned and stalked away past the medical bunker. He disappeared in the bushes.

"You shouldn't have said that," Hollerbach reproached Steiner.

"Rot," Steiner replied; he was a little irritated with himself. "He's as thin-skinned as a girl, but in five minutes he forgets all about it." Faber stood silent and grave beside them. "If I get back to Freiburg," Steiner said to him, "I can look up your family. Shall I?"

"They'd be glad," Faber replied. "Tell them not to worry about me. And if you see Barbara, say hello to her for me."

"Who is she? Your girl?"

A faint, mischievous grin passed over Faber's face as he answered, "A birch, a sapling birch."

It was hot and still now, as if there were no war at all, no Hill 121.4. A narrow stream wound westward through green bushes, and the landscape stretched on for mile on mile. Steiner felt the sadness of parting as if it were a harmless but troublesome disease. You never get used to it, he thought. It's always the same and always new. He stretched his good arm. "Maybe I'll meet Schnurrbart somewhere. If he comes back before me, tell him to look after all you little children." He hesitated. Then, impatience and emotion in his voice, he began rapidly saying good-by and shaking hands all around.

Hollerbach offered to accompany him to Kanskoye.

"Drop us a line once in a while," Kern said. His watery eyes were sad. With surprise Steiner saw that the corners of his mouth were twitching. He turned rapidly away.

Kruger was waiting for him and Hollerbach a short distance away, glowering fiercely at Steiner.

"You can bring something for me. When you come back, I mean."

"A gravestone?" Steiner asked.

Kruger curled his upper lip, exposing his fine set of teeth. "I'll get one of those for you some day," he retorted. "No, I mean something else. You can bring me a bottle of Cologne water."

"What for?" Steiner asked suspiciously.

"Just in case we have to live in the same bunker again," Kruger replied.

Steiner nodded. "I'll do that because my nose is so sensitive!"

"You have no idea what a relief it'll be not to have to see you for a while," Kruger said malevolently.

Hollerbach grinned. Steiner said calmly, "No, you're wrong, I do have an idea. I so often feel the same way myself."

Before Kruger could speak again, Steiner started off. "Take it easy," he called loudly.

Kruger stood looking after them. They had gone quite a way before he funneled his hands over his mouth and shouted, "Come back soon."

Steiner raised his sound arm and waved.

For a long while Steiner and Hollerbach walked in silence side by side. Hollerbach glanced at him admiringly now and then. He's tough, he was thinking, to be able to walk this distance with his wound. After a while he caught himself wishing that he himself would not have to go back to fighting.

"I'd like to be going with you," he said.

"Where to?" Steiner asked.

"Home, of course."

They slowed their pace. Steiner looked off toward the hills. "Home?" he repeated softly. "Where is that?"

"What do you mean?"

"Do you know where your home is?" he asked.

"I'm not an idiot."

"That's open to discussion." Steiner grinned. Then he became serious again. "You're at home where you're happy, isn't that so?"

"Of course."

"And were you happy at home, really happy?"

Hollerbach hesitated.

Steiner nodded. "So you weren't. Being home is nothing more than crude habit and the fact that we don't have to worry about where we're going to spend the night. It's being with a few people you like, and when you lose them, you can't stand the place any more because everything around you reminds you of them. And being home means giving up voluntarily all the things you don't have at home. It's the damned commonplaceness of daily life and an infernal mirror that shows you the wrinkles coming in your face. Believe me, of all the illusions in our lives the biggest is the idea that somewhere is home for us. There isn't any place really where you can keep your balance without dancing like a tightrope walker. Do you see what I mean?"

"No," Hollerbach said.

Steiner frowned. "No wonder. Thére's a lousy clever system in it. From childhood on they put blinkers on us so we won't see to either side of us. Every time, just before you're about to see, they toss you a bone like you were a dog. You can sink your teeth into that and forget about it all for a while. The older you get and the more demanding you become, the bigger the bone. And when the time comes that you're sick of it all—school, job and so on—then they throw you the biggest bone of all. That's the one that really does the trick; it's guaranteed to wear your teeth down because it keeps you busy even in bed, so that you don't have a minute to spare to think about other things. Ah . . ." he waved his sound arm disgustedly.

"What's the matter with you?" Hollerbach asked.

"I don't know," Steiner answered tonelessly. "You always think you no longer have any illusions. But believe me, the biggest illusion of all is believing you're without illusions."

They had covered somewhat more than a mile by now, and his shoulder was beginning to ache viciously. They ought to be level with Kanskoye soon, and they would have to cross over the hill. He looked up along the road, marked by the tracks of innumerable vehicles. It ran almost due west and disappeared in the distance beyond a gentle undulation in the landscape. Probably it led to Kanskoye, swinging in a big arc around the hill. On their left, about twenty yards away, the brook turned sharply off toward the north and appeared to lose itself in an endless plain. This must be the spot the doctor had mentioned. Steiner came to a stop.

"What's the matter?" Hollerbach asked, wiping the sweat from his brow.

"We have to cross over here," Steiner said. "But let's have a cigarette first."

They dropped to the ground where they were, and Steiner swung off his tunic, which had been hanging loosely over his back. He was glad to see that the bandage was not yet soaked through with blood. As they lighted their cigarettes, Hollerbach looked down with a troubled expression.

"I'm not sure I follow you," he said, "when you talk about somebody tossing us bones. Who the devil is this 'they' of yours?"

"If I knew that, I'd know everything," Steiner replied. "But it isn't something you can prove; you just believe it or you don't. Maybe some day I'll get to the bottom of it."

He looked at the other man. Hollerbach's face was flushed and dirty. He had removed his steel helmut and his blond hair straggled over his forehead. How little I know about him, Steiner thought suddenly. We never have time for each other; we lie in the same mud for three years and hardly know more than the other's name. It's a shame.

"It's a shame," Hollerbach said.

Steiner grinned at the apparent harmony of their thoughts and asked, "What?"

"It's all a shame," Hollerbach explained. "Everything. In the old days I always wanted to get away from Mudau, my home town, and now I'm away from it and I wish I were back. Then when I think of working my ass off for the lousy railroad, I'm not so sure. Why does it have to be like that?"

"I guess it's always a mistake to do more thinking than we're supposed to," Steiner said thoughtfully. He felt his shoulder and went on: "They say man is the perfect creature when he's nothing more than a pretty poor compromise between an animal and something better than himself. A contradiction, dreaming of nectar and ambrosia and eating pig's flesh, talking about love and whoring around every chance he gets, talking about goodness and giving hell to the other fellow. A dirty deal altogether."

He suddenly felt no inclination to go on with the discussion, and frowned into the distance. Hollerbach started to answer. But at that moment a succession of violent crashes sounded behind them. The rolling echo rumbled above their heads, weird and heart-stopping. "Tanks," Hollerbach exclaimed.

Steiner nodded. They sat motionless, listening. Those first

explosions seemed only the beginning of a regular battle. The cannonade grew in intensity, and interspersed between the louder explosions came the crackle of rifle fire. "That must be the assault regiment," Steiner said. He recalled Stransky's mentioning anti-tank guns.

Now they could hear motors too. Hollerbach glanced at the underbrush that grew beside the brook. It would afford good cover. But they sat still, staring up the hill. From where they sat they could see only a little of it because the initially steep slope flattened out somewhat higher up.

By the time they saw the Russian tank tearing down the slope, it was less than two hundred feet away. Steiner uttered a warning cry and made for the underbrush as fast as his legs could carry him. Hollerbach followed at once. But he had taken only a few steps when he remembered Steiner's pack. He turned, snatched it up and then ran with desperate leaps after Steiner. He saw that Steiner had come within a few yards of the brook. He wanted to shout to him to stick to the left, where the brush was somewhat thicker. At that moment a shattering roar sounded behind him; the earth burst open and he plunged to the ground like a felled tree. He could feel nothing at all, but he was still conscious. He saw Steiner stop abruptly and stare toward him. And he shouted to him to go on, to throw himself into the brook. But although he shouted as loudly as he could, he was unable to hear his own voice, and astonishment at this fact occupied his mind so completely for the next few seconds that he forgot everything else. His attentiveness returned only when Steiner disappeared behind a cloud of smoke that suddenly appeared between them as though fallen from the sky. Then he saw Steiner lying on the ground. Strangely he seemed to be crawling like a crab, and it struck Hollerbach as astonishing that he was not moving forward so much as a yard. It looked so funny that he giggled. Then it occurred to him that there was a stillness all about. He turned his head, and his eyes froze.

Steiner, too, was quite conscious, although he felt as though every inch of his body had been pierced by splinters. Faint with pain, he tried to crawl over the ground toward the motionless Hollerbach. He was completely unaware of the senselessness of his efforts. From the moment he had seen the advancing tank heading straight toward the helpless Hollerbach, he had lost all sense of what he was doing; he writhed like a madman, eyes popping, foam dribbling from his mouth. His arms and legs flailed wildly like ripples around a point where a stone has been thrown into water,

self-consuming and ineffectual. At last he lay still like a body
already dead, only his eyes burning in a white face. The
tank had approached within ten yards of the motionless
body. Hollerbach turned his head. Steiner opened his
mouth and screamed. He screamed so that the land heaved
and a storm rose that carried the hills before it as though
they were tower-high waves of water stretching from horizon
to horizon. When he looked up he saw the space between
sky and earth beginning to fill, darkening with a horde of
withered leaves that whirled closer and closer and showered down on him like snow. He saw without seeing the
tank pass over Hollerbach's twitching body, mashing it into
the ground and leaving a bloody track on the hard soil
as it moved off toward the east. The landscape lay unchanged under the hot noonday sun. Only where the bushes
crowded up against the narrow stream a few paces beyond
Steiner's still body a few dry leaves were strewn, and beyond
the underbrush there yawned between sky and earth a fearful void.

BOOK
THREE

XI

STEINER was only dimly aware of the telegraph poles sweeping by the train window. The song of wheels on rails faded. He lifted the letter again.

Somewhere in the East

DEAR ROLF,

I am sitting on an old sand bar, tanned like a South Sea islander, dangling my feet in the water. And those feet need it, by God. Last night a Russian gunboat tried to make a landing. Kruger was on guard and drove it off with his carbine. So he says. He spent two hours diving today and found two old leather boots, both of them for the left foot. Kruger insists they belonged to the captain and first mate of the boat. We chucked them back into the water. (The boots, of course.) It's about time you were coming back. For the past three weeks we've been stationed here on the Black Sea, heroically battling against boredom. We rest all day long, and sleep all night. What a life, I tell you. It's a pity you're not with us. None of these birds can play chess, just when we'd have plenty of time for it. Have I written you that Maag is back again? He really stuffed his belly while he was back home; he's put on lots of weight. Faber looked at his calendar yesterday and discovered that it's exactly three months since you were wounded. Time flies. This is all for now. Writing a letter in this heat is tough work. Kruger and Kern are looking over my shoulder and both of them say I have a handwriting like an old goat. But my beautiful style makes up for it, don't you think? Keep well and watch out that they don't pick you up and stick you in some other unit when you start back for here. Things are supposed to be pretty hot back on the main front. All the best.

Your old friend
SCHNURRBART

Steiner let the letter sink to his lap. Three months, he thought. It seemed to him that ten times three months had passed. Thrusting the letter back into his breast pocket, he closed his eyes. He had been wounded at the beginning of May, and now the hot August sun was searing down upon the parched earth of the bridgehead. He had hoped the division would be in the Crimea by the time he returned to it. But although the front in the north was daily shifting further to the west, although the situation was growing more precarious with every passing moment, no move had been made to abandon the Kuban bridgehead. More and more people were predicting another Stalingrad.

He looked out the window again, abstractedly watching the countryside. Now the sound of the wheels on the rails was lulling. Most of the other men in the compartment were sitting with heads drooping, eyes closed, slumped into queer positions on the uncomfortable seats. In a state halfway between sleeping and waking and dreaming of the end of this interminable trip—he had been riding trains for almost ten days now—he went over the events of the past three months.

He recalled the moment when he had come to again in one of the dirty cots at the clearing station—the first stage of his journey back home to Germany. He had never learned how he got there. Perhaps some men of the Third Battalion had picked him up that evening. During the night he was operated on, and when he awoke again from deep anesthesia he was already on the way to a field hospital. Two days later he was sent in a hospital train nonstop as far as Przemysl and ended his journey in a hospital back home in Passau.

He had recovered with surprising speed. The nasty splinter wounds all over his chest, arms and legs had healed without complications. Nor did the wound in his shoulder prove troublesome.

About a month after his arrival in the hospital, the first letter from Schnurrbart had reported with disappointment that he had not got as far as Germany. Schnurrbart's wound had been good only for a trip to Odessa, and a month later he had been sent back to the division as fit for service. He wrote that the attack of the assault regiment had been stopped by Russian artillery fire, and the front line now ran definitively straight across the hill. He spoke of rumors of relief, of new replacements and a new company commander, and said that all they needed to hold the bridgehead was Steiner's presence.

Three more letters had come from him since. The rumor was confirmed and the division moved to quiet positions on the coast for a few weeks' rest. The last letter, the one Steiner had just been reading, had reached him on the day of his departure. When he reached Kerch he learned that the division had meanwhile been transferred to Novorossiysk. There could only be a few miles more to go. The big, boxlike passenger car had poor springs and Steiner was often startled out of his thoughts when the wheels thumped hard over switches, or when a shrill whistle from the locomotive shrieked through the glassless windows.

He studied the faces of his fellow travelers. All of them seemed to be veteran soldiers, probably returning from furloughs to judge by the indifference with which they occasionally opened their eyes and glanced out the window, only to slip back into a doze again. Slumped in the corner opposite Steiner sat a corporal. He, too, had his eyes closed, and with every jerk of the train his head bobbed about on a neck of unusual length, as though on a coil spring. His big-boned face looked weary and lifeless.

Suddenly he opened his eyes and their glances met. "We should be almost there," Steiner said.

The man stretched and threw a look out the window. "Another ten minutes." He yawned. "We're coming to a long tunnel now," he added. "Once we're through that, we're there."

"Have you often come this way?" Steiner asked.

"Yes. Courier."

Steiner regarded him with interest. Nice job, he thought; I'd like that. "Is the station in town?" he asked.

The man grimaced. "Station is good. You'll have an hour's walk into town. But the road is good, and if you're lucky some truck will pick you up."

"What's the place like?" Steiner asked. "This is my first time there," he explained.

The corporal shrugged. "A nice quiet position. The main thing is there's plenty of champagne. All you can drink."

"Champagne!" Steiner exclaimed in amazement.

The man nodded. "Haven't you heard about it? Tremendous champagne vaults there. The war could go on for ten years before the stuff is drunk up."

"I'd just as soon it didn't," Steiner replied dryly.

The locomotive let loose two piercing whistles. "The tunnel," the corporal said. "Here we are." He stood up and pulled his things down from the baggage rack. Steiner followed his example. The others in the compartment started up, dazed from sleep, and foraged for their baggage. A moment later they rolled into the tunnel and everything grew dark. When daylight flooded in through the windows again, the train braked swiftly and finally came to a stop with a sharp jerk. The men tumbled over one another and cursed.

"They act like they've got cattle aboard," one man said. The man at his side laughed. "What else do you think we are?"

Steiner opened the door and jumped to the platform. Because he wanted to shake off the corporal, he pressed rapidly through the crowd to the barrier. After his pass was checked, he stood for a moment and looked around. The railroad station consisted of a few small buildings. To judge by the many tracks, the place must have been a shunting yard. He glanced back at the train. The locomotive was being uncoupled, and for a moment he felt a faint stabbing sensation in the pit of his stomach. He took several deep breaths. This is the way you wanted it, he told himself. You could be back home in Freiburg now if you had not refused to take your convalescent leave.

He started off rapidly down the road, and in a few minutes had left the last of the buildings behind. The road led straight westward, and he hit a smart pace. Apparently the corporal had not exaggerated. The highway was flanked by vineyards. The ripe grapes were of a size and sweetness he had tasted only once before, in southern France. Again and again he stopped to pick some. Looking around, he saw the rest of the train's passengers following in loose formation. He walked faster. Here and there, behind the green of the grapevines, gleamed the white-painted walls of a small house. Everything about the region seemed neat and orderly; it was more like the landscape south of the Loire than anything he had seen before in Russia. The scent of the near-by sea was unmistakable and grew steadily stronger as he approached his destination. Silhouettes overcast with a yellowish shimmer gradually emerged out of the bright-blue mist of the horizon. Later he could see that they were the precipitous slopes of a mountain range. He was so absorbed that he did not hear a truck bearing down on him from behind, and stopped only when a loud voice reached his ears. The truck stopped a few feet away from him and a good-natured face under a forage cap appeared at the window. "Where to?" the man called out.

"Freiburg," Steiner said.

Without a flicker of a smile, the man opened the door. "That's where I'm headed for. Get in."

Steiner shifted his pack from his back and climbed up to the seat. "I don't usually give rides," the man explained as he shifted gears. The truck started forward. "Not that I'm hard-hearted," he went on. "But I've been careful ever since a couple of bastards snitched two boxes of sausage from me."

"Are you in the supply train?" Steiner asked.

"Yes, I'm sorry to say."

"Why are you sorry?"

The driver laughed. "You've got no idea all the responsibility and trouble we have."

"Why don't you transfer?"

"Where to?"

"To us. We just sleep in nice warm bunkers."

The man laughed again. "I'm not that crazy. It's no good wherever you are. The devil take this army."

The houses on either side of the road were becoming more numerous. Apparently they were in the outskirts of the town. Steiner leaned out the window. The road led gently uphill, and when they reached the top he saw the sea before him. The memory wrenched so hard that he pressed his hands against his heart. Two weeks ago he had imagined that it was all over and done with, that he had come to terms with it, and now he realized how he had been deceiving himself.

He tried to distract his mind by studying the view of the city. The mountainous coastline formed a deep indentation, and the city spread out around it in a semicircle. The terraced construction reminded him of Zürich. Most of the houses were painted white.

The driver's voice startled him out of his thoughts. "Last week the civilians were evacuated," the man told him. "A pity, too—you should have seen the women that lived here." Steiner scarcely listened as the man rattled on. He brought himself to attention only when they stopped. "You'll have to get out here," the driver said. "First street to the right. They're posted down near the water front, I think." He stepped on the brake. Steiner offered him a pack of cigarettes, but he waved this aside. "Hell, all the supplies pass through our hands. Good luck."

Steiner watched the truck until it turned a corner. The houses, some of them as much as four stories high, were quiet in the hot noonday sun. His nailed boots thumped loudly on the deserted street. On the way he met an MP and asked directions.

The company was quartered in a neat row of houses near the water front. Steiner soon encountered a man who clicked his heels and raised his hand to his cap. Steiner stopped and asked, "Where do you belong?"

"Second Company," the man replied.

Steiner looked him over. He had never seen him before. "What platoon?"

"The second."

It seemed odd to Steiner to be speaking with a man of his own platoon who was a stranger. Dropping his official tone he asked, "What is your platoon leader's name?"

The answer was snapped out like a pistol shot: "Corporal Schnurrbart, sir."

With difficulty Steiner repressed a grin. Schnurrbart's real name was evidently lost for good and all. He asked the man to take him to Corporal Schnurrbart.

The houses were set in the midst of small yards, ringed by walls and fences. The man led Steiner to one such green-fenced dwelling. The yard was planted with fruit trees which might have been battered by a hurricane, so ripped were their leaves. The flower beds were thick with weeds; only the gravel-strewn path looked tended. Steiner slowly opened the chest-high gate, careful not to make any loud noise. The front door of the house was closed, and he walked a few paces past it. As he turned the corner, he stopped abruptly. On a bench, facing the water which was about a hundred yards away, sat Schnurrbart, his face to the sun, his eyes closed, his pipe inevitably in his mouth. He looked as if he had been sitting there forever, and he looked as he had always looked, thin, wiry, heavily bearded. Steiner felt his heart thumping; he smiled and wiped his eyes. Quietly he went over to him, slipped the pack from his back and sat down on the bench. Dropping his arms over the back of the seat, he looked at Schnurrbart's face from the side.

Schnurrbart did not open his eyes. He took the pipe from his mouth, threw his head back a little and said, "Have you guys had a good rest?"

"Yes," Steiner said, watching his face. At first it showed no change. Then suddenly all his features began to move. He blinked, opened his eyes slowly and turned his head. They looked at each other silently, searchingly, unnaturally quiet.

Finally Schnurrbart turned his face back toward the water. "In this weather the fish bite."

Steiner nodded. There was a long pause. The garden sloped down toward the water's edge, and beyond the green pickets of the fence piers stretched out into the oily surface of the sea.

"Although," Schnurrbart commented, "when it rains they bite too."

Steiner yawned ostentatiously, holding his hand over his mouth.

"In point of fact, they bite in all weathers," Schnurrbart said stubbornly.

"Do they really?" Steiner murmured. He felt very content.

"We weren't expecting you yet," Schnurrbart said abruptly. "How was it back home?"

Steiner reached into his breast pocket and after some fumbling brought out a sheet of paper. He placed it on Schnurrbart's lap. "Read that," he said tersely.

The letter was short. "Dear Rolf," Schnurrbart read, "I am sure you will not understand my behavior, but I could not help myself. When we first met in the canteen, I was very angry with you. Then I felt pity for you, and later I loved you. I hoped that some day I would be able to free myself. You see, Rolf, I'm married and I thought I loved my husband. It was a proxy wedding, because he wanted it so much. After that last night together I decided firmly to get a divorce. But a week afterward word came that my husband had been seriously wounded. They have had to amputate his right leg. I struggled with myself, but now I know that I have no right to leave him. Please don't think too badly of me. I was not honest with you, but I loved you and couldn't bear to lose you. Forgive me. Gertrud."

Schnurrbart handed the letter back. Steiner was staring vacantly across the water. "So her name was Gertrud," Schnurrbart said after a while.

Steiner nodded.

"Where did you meet her?"

"In Gursuf."

Schnurrbart looked up in surprise. "In Gursuf, of all places! And why didn't you go home?"

"How do you know I didn't?"

"You wouldn't be here so soon if you had," Schnurrbart replied with assurance.

Steiner leaned forward, propping his arms on his thighs and letting his head droop. "What would I do at home?" he asked wearily. "After I received that letter at the hospital, I didn't feel like it."

It occurred to Schnurrbart that Steiner had never spoken of his family. But he did not dare to ask about it, and the opportunity passed. Steiner suddenly changed the subject and asked about Kruger and Kern.

"They're snoozing," Schnurrbart said. "Taking their siesta. Since we've been here I've never seen either of them really awake."

Schnurrbart went on to say that he was sharing this house with Kruger; Kern, Faber and Maag were quartered next door. Stransky was trying to introduce regular barracks discipline and drill. The new company commander, Lieutenant März, had been raised on dynamite.

When Steiner asked about the front, Schnurrbart jerked his thumb to point across the bay. "We're dug in over there, halfway to the right, near the big factory. With binoculars you can see the barbed wire. It's quiet here, except for an occasional seventeen-two around noon."

"Who held the place before?" Steiner asked.

Schnurrbart waved his hand contemptuously. "A navy unit. They had the life!" He warmed up and before long had told Steiner virtually all the news. Both of them shied away from speaking of Hollerbach.

Finally Schnurrbart lighted his pipe and stretched his legs. "It's nice sitting in the sun," he said. "Once I get back home I'll just spend several weeks in the sun and be glad that everything is so.

"What do you mean by so?" Steiner asked.

"Just so," Schnurrbart waved his hand vaguely. He drew violently on his pipe and looked across to the opposite shore of the bay. "You know what I think?" he said at last. "I think we've just forgotten to live in the present and it seems to me that the present is our life and the future is what we hope for and I'll pull my own beard out by the handful if we don't pass life right by when we do it the other way."

"Hold on," Steiner said. "I didn't quite follow that."

Schnurrbart sat pondering. "Now I don't know any more," he said irritably. "Yet I knew just what I meant. I could have written it down for you, I had it all so clear in my mind."

"I can tell you what you meant," Steiner offered. "You mean that the present is real and the future is illusory and if we take it the other way around we pass life by."

"That's it," Schnurrbart said. "That's exactly what I meant." Now that he heard his own thought repeated, he was amazed at it; for a few seconds he felt as though he had discovered a wonderful trait in himself which he had never before suspected. Steiner's eyes rested on his face with a curious expression, and his sense of having pronounced a profound philosophical truth grew stronger. "That's the way it is," he repeated emphatically.

It suddenly occurred to him that he had omitted something. "I haven't told you the queerest business yet," he said excitedly. "Happened a couple of days ago at Regiment. Kruger and I had to go see Captain Kiesel."

Steiner raised his eyebrows. "Kiesel? What did he want?"

"Damned if I know. He asked us whether we saw Stansky with us the night I was wounded. Did you see him?"

Steiner shook his head in bewilderment. "How could I have? He stayed at the command post."

"So I thought," Schnurrbart growled. "We said we hadn't seen him, and then Kiesel said he would have to wait till you got back."

"Funny." Frowning, Steiner considered the matter. But he could make nothing of it and shrugged. "I wish they'd leave me alone. They start hounding a man the minute he comes back."

Schnurrbart tapped his pipe out on the ground and stood up. "Want to come along?" he asked. "I'll wake Kruger."

"I want to be in on that," Steiner said. He picked up his pack.

They entered the house and walked down a long hallway. At the last door Schnurrbart stopped, slowly pressed down the latch and opened the door slightly. "He's in dreamland," he whispered.

Steiner looked in. Kruger was sprawled out on a bed, snoring loudly. As Schnurrbart started into the room, Steiner restrained him. Schnurrbart watched in puzzlement as he took a small bottle out of his pack and held it aloft, winking. "What's that?" Schnurrbart whispered. "Liqueur?"

Steiner shook his head. He opened the door quietly, cautiously approached the sleeping man and sprinkled his hair and uniform with the contents of the bottle. The remainder he poured into the boots standing beside the bed. With a happy smile, he tiptoed back to the door. "We can wake him now," he said.

Schnurrbart sniffed. There was a sweetish odor which grew stronger from second to second. Steiner identified it. "Perfume."

"It stinks something awful," Schnurrbart whispered. "Where did you get the stuff?"

"Liberated it," Steiner replied. Schnurrbart told him to wait a moment and went out. Kruger moved restlessly, then turned over on his other side. Schnurrbart reappeared carrying a dozen china dishes.

"What's the idea?" Steiner asked.

Schnurrbart grinned. "Wake him up. There's plenty of the stuff in the kitchen."

They entered the room. "Ready!" Steiner nodded. Schnurr-bart raised the pile of plates high, and as they crashed on the floor, he uttered so piercing a scream that even Steiner jumped.

The sleeping man started up as though an aerial mine had exploded beside his head.

Kruger stared at them, his face turning alternately red and white. He caught a glimpse of the pile of broken crockery on the floor and suddenly understood. He sprang to his feet, bumped into Steiner and let forth an inarticulate cry of rage. "Have you come back for that?" he roared. "Why the devil did you come back at all, why didn't you stay away?"

Steiner smiled into his burning face. "I was homesick," he said. "Homesick for you."

Kruger seemed on the point of swinging wildly at him. Then he snatched up his tunic, stepped into his boots and stormed from the room. They followed him. As he sulkily sat down on a garden bench, Schnurrbart and Steiner sat down to his right and left.

"He hasn't improved any," Steiner said.

"He never will," Schnurrbart said. "A hopeless case."

Kruger groaned and clenched his fist. Steiner laid his hand placatingly on his arm. "Come on, calm down, old ruffian."

His voice sounded so gentle that Schnurrbart raised his head in astonishment. He had never heard such a tone from Steiner before. It did not fail to take effect on Kruger also. He went on growling for a while, but his rage seemed to withdraw more and more into itself like a snail into its shell.

"That's better," Steiner said. They sat in silence, looking out over the water—three men in torn uniforms sitting close together on a bench, blinking peacefully up at the sun.

"Let's drink to your homecoming," Schnurrbart said after a while. He stood up. "I'll go get the others."

They returned to the house. Steiner looked around. The three big rooms were comfortably furnished. Apparently the civilian populace had not been permitted to take their furniture with them, and everything still stood as it had been. As Steiner entered the living room with Kruger, he heard hasty footsteps in the hallway. The door flew open and Kern appeared, with Maag and Faber behind him. For a few seconds they stared at him without a word.

He saw their familiar faces, their twitching lips, the pleasure in their eyes, and he was suddenly overcome by an emotion he had not felt for a long, long time. "So there you are," he said hoarsely.

"Don't start bawling," said Schnurrbart, coming in behind them with several bottles in his hands. He pushed the others into the room.

Kern was the first to shake hands with Steiner. Maag followed. As Steiner turned toward Faber, he saw an expectant look in the woodsman's eyes, and he suddenly recalled his promise to visit Faber's family. "Sorry to disappoint you," he said quietly. "I didn't go home."

Faber nodded. "I received a letter from Barbara yesterday," he said. "She wrote that you hadn't come yet. They were looking forward to meeting you."

"Looking forward?" Steiner smiled bitterly. "To meeting me?"

"I wrote them about you," Faber said.

Steiner smiled with gratitude and embarrassment.

"Didn't you have any furlough?" Maag asked.

Steiner shook his head but gave no explanation.

Schnurrbart had arranged the bottles on the table. "Sit down," he called noisily. "What do you say to that?" Proudly he pointed out the half dozen bottles of champagne, watching Steiner's face for a reaction. When Steiner remained blank, he shrugged. "Doesn't anything impress you?" he said in disappointment.

"Why should it?" Steiner said, grinning. "Every schoolboy knows Novorossiysk is full of champagne."

They sat down. Schnurrbart had brought no glasses, and they drank straight from the bottles. Kern made a face. "The stuff is too warm," he commented. "I'd sooner have a beer. You know . . ." He broke off and sniffed ostentatiously.

"What's the matter?" Maag asked.

"Something stinks of perfume," Kern declared suspiciously.

"I thought I smelled it, too," Maag said.

Seeing that all eyes were turned toward him, Kruger smiled maliciously. "That's Steiner," he said.

Kern sniffed again. "No, that isn't Steiner. It's you."

"You're crazy," Kruger growled. "Get yourself a new smeller. The old one isn't any good."

Schnurrbart intervened. "Don't bicker," he said. "We all stink." He raised his bottle. "Here's to the champagne-guzzling German army."

"Here's to the mass grave," Maag toasted. They emptied the bottles.

Kern wiped his mouth. "Open the window," he growled.

"Open it yourself," Maag retorted. But he stood up and pulled the casement windows wide open. Returning to the table, he paused behind Steiner. "It isn't him," he said loudly.

"Of course not," Kern said emphatically. "It's just like I've always said. There are men who just can't stand promotion. Soon as they get a little rank their true colors come right out. Damned fairies." He threw a significant look at Kruger.

Kruger's face slowly reddened. "I don't stink," he roared. "It's Steiner who stinks!"

The men began to giggle, and a fleeting smile passed across even Faber's grave face. They all looked at Steiner, who shook his head reprimandingly.

"I beg your pardon, Corporal Kruger," he said gravely. "But this is no way to talk about a superior."

Kruger sprang to his feet. "You can stick your goddamned rank! This isn't a question of rank, but of stench, I tell you, of naked stench."

As he paused to catch his breath, a lieutenant entered the room, erect in his bearing and firm in his movements. His lively gray-blue eyes scrutinized the men. They had jumped up and come to attention. "As you were!" the officer said tersely. He strode toward them. "Drinking parties so early in the afternoon," he stated rather than asked. His glance fell on Steiner, who was standing at ease behind the table. "Who is this?"

Steiner placed the tips of his shoes together and replied, "Senior Sergeant Steiner, back from hospital."

The lieutenant's eyes widened in surprise. "Steiner?" he repeated. Then he nodded and held out his hand across the table. "I am your company commander, Lieutenant März. Have you heard about me?"

"A few things," Steiner said.

März raised his eyebrows. Then he smiled. "So have I about you. Some good and some not so good. You will resume command of the platoon at once. Order and discipline. I don't stand for slackness. If there are any misunderstandings, tell me to my face, but don't talk about them behind my back. Clear?"

Steiner nodded, taken by surprise. The boy has the temperament of a young colt, he thought.

März turned to the other men. "Inspection in one hour. By the commander in person. I don't want anybody slipping up."

He was standing close to Kruger and suddenly raised his head. "Who's been dousing himself with perfume?"

Kruger threw a sideways glance at Steiner and grinned.

"I mean you, Corporal," März said sharply. "Are you a queer?"

Kruger did not know what to think. But since the lieutenant was looking straight at him, he raised his shoulders helplessly and stammered, "It's not me."

The company commander's eyes suddenly flared. "Really," he said, and with a rapid movement passed his hand over Kruger's hair. Then he held the hand under his nose. "Smell that!" he ordered.

Aghast, Kruger sniffed. He looked so thunderstruck that Steiner began to feel intensely guilty.

The lieutenant's voice rang out sharply. "If you want to smear perfume all over you like a woman, that's your affair, but if you lie to me it's my affair. Remember that!"

Before Kruger could recover from his dismay, the company commander was gone.

"You really do smell rather awful," Steiner said.

Kruger had come so close to him that their bodies were touching. He gripped Steiner by the lapels. "I don't know what's going to happen in this war," he choked. "But I can tell what's going to happen to you."

Steiner raised his eyebrows, courteously attentive. "What is that, my good fellow?"

"I'm not your good fellow!" Kruger roared, beside himself.

Schnurrbart stepped up to them, raised his head and inhaled the scent with sham delight. "What a lovely fragrance!" he whispered, closing his eyes.

"Like a rose," Kern said.

"Like a prickly rose," Maag added.

Kruger tore out of the room.

The battalion command post was located in a small group of houses about twenty-five hundred feet from the water front. The company commanders were gathered in Stransky's office for a short briefing. Lieutenant März sat in a comfortable basket chair, listening with boredom to Stransky's explanations. First Lieutenant Moninger, commander of the First Company, stared absently out the window at the cloudless August sky. Beside him Lieutenant Hahn, commander of the Third Company, tried to conceal a yawn behind his palm, while First Lieutenant Stallmann studied his fingernails with deep interest. If only he'd wind it up, März thought, watching Stransky with veiled eyes.

Stransky, standing back of the table, was throwing a great deal of emotion into his voice. But he seemed now to become aware of the officers' lassitude and spoke more loudly.

"We are in the unfortunate situation of having been forced over from the offensive to the defensive. The momentary calm must not be allowed to lull our alertness. I consider it more important than ever to keep the men well in hand. Tight discipline is the prime factor in keeping a battalion in battle trim and tiptop shape." He emphasized his words by pounding vigorously on the table. "I require my company commanders to root out every type of undisciplined behavior. See to it that the roster is drawn up accordingly. Now is the best time for the men to put their equipment in order. I shall personally look into this matter." He glanced at his gold wrist watch. "Inspection begins in fifteen minutes. I shall make spot checks on the condition of weapons." He turned to Triebig. "Have we anything else?"

"I don't think so, sir," Triebig replied obsequiously.

Stransky blew an invisible grain of dust from the sleeve of his tunic. "Then that will be all for today."

As the others left the room, März asked, "Where do you intend to begin, sir?"

Stransky was on the point of replying sharply when he recalled that März was the regimental adjutant's brother-in-law. He smiled. "With your company, Lieutenant März."

"Then I'll have the company fall in at once."

Stransky nodded. "Is there anything else?"

"Nothing important," März said casually. "I only wanted to inform you that Sergeant Steiner returned to the company an hour ago."

Although Stransky made an effort to conceal his feelings, his eyelids fluttered rapidly, and the evenness of his voice sounded forced as he said, "Steiner?" He looked down at the floor, then raised his head again. "Very well. Send the sergeant to me at eight this evening."

März saluted and left. As he emerged from the command post, there was a thin smile at the corners of his mouth. Stransky watched him through one of the big triple-casemented windows as he crossed the street. Suddenly a tremendous, swelling roar filled the air. He saw März leap for the nearest house. Stransky threw himself instantly to the floor. A terrible impact shook the house to its foundations. Glass shattered and fell inward; plaster broke from the ceiling and shrouded the room in white dust. Stransky lay holding his breath until the pattering rain of brick, wood and fragments of stone stopped. Then he rose slowly. His knees were quivering. Across the street one of the houses had collapsed. A huge blackish-yellow cloud of smoke was billowing out of the ruins and drifting toward the water front. Stransky realized that the house was the messengers' quarters.

He saw März rush out of the house next door and stop, horrified. Behind him several men of the signals company appeared, their faces white. Suddenly they threw themselves to the ground and once again that horrible hum filled the air. But it was higher in pitch this time and did not have the same sense of fatal abruptness. The shell exploded far back of the houses, in the midst of an open field, and another dark cloud of smoke shot up into the sky. The noise of the detonation was so painful that Stransky clapped his hands to his ears.

He watched while the men got up, and led by März, disappeared into the wrecked house. He wondered what caliber the shell had been. Perhaps one of those notorious 21-cm. Russian mortars about which he had heard so many ghastly tales. He waited for a few minutes. When no more shells came over, he sent Triebig and ordered him to cancel all roll calls at once and set the men to work digging bunkers near their quarters. "Inform the company commanders," he added, "and see to it that a strong dugout is built back of my command post. You can use the signalmen." He became aware of Triebig's distressed look. "Were there casualties?"

"Three men," Triebig replied hoarsely. "Dudek was one of them."

"Dudek?" Triebig nodded silently. Stransky bit his lip. "Really unfortunate," he said at last. "I was highly pleased with him. Couldn't have asked for a better orderly."

"I feel exactly the same," Triebig said softly. "Keppler was one of them too."

"Dead?" Stransky asked.

Triebig nodded. "All three."

There was a long pause. Stransky went over to the window, hands clasped behind his back, and watched the men of the signal platoon working to get at the bodies trapped under the ruins. "Steiner is back," he said abruptly, without turning around. He could not see the sudden pallor that spread over Triebig's face. "I've sent for him for this evening. As soon as I have his signature I want to transmit the paper to Regiment at once."

Triebig had recovered from the immediate shock, though his face remained unnaturally pale. He moistened his lips with his tongue. "I had not expected him back so soon. I hope he doesn't make trouble."

"Bah!" Stransky laughed contemptuously. "I'll soften him

up, rest assured." He looked at his watch. "Getting late. Inform the company commanders and see to it that new messengers are detailed. I'll look around for another orderly."

Triebig saluted and left the room. As he crossed the street, his face was rigid. When he reached his quarters he telephoned the companies, informed them of the new situation and ordered them to detail a messenger each to Battalion. Then he drew a chair to the window and stared absently at the white limestone slopes of the mountain. He felt as if a suppurating sore inside his chest had broken open and was poisoning his blood. Steiner's return struck him like a physical blow. All the past few months had been a torment; every time the telephone rang the sweat had started on his forehead. He had trembled before every meeting with Stransky, and the constant fear had brought his nerves nearly to the breaking point. Although it looked as if Steiner intended to keep quiet, the threat remained, and it would remain until Steiner had been silenced for good and all.

As he was considering rather hopelessly how that could be done, Triebig remembered that Steiner was to see Stransky that evening. He knew about the antagonism between the two men. Couldn't that be put to good use? There must be some way.

He laid his arms on the window sill and half closed his eyes. It will depend on how the interview turns out, he thought. Although he too was implicated in the success or failure of the interview, he felt malicious joy at the thought of the tight spot Stransky had got himself into. This business could lead to anything.

The thing had started, Triebig recalled, because Stransky, in his report on the events of the hours just before the Russian offensive, had somewhat overdone it when he described his own part. That was the night before that devil Steiner had played the hero. According to Stransky's account, it was due only to his initiative that the unexpected Russian penetration into the positions of the Second Company on Hill 121.4 had been repulsed. The report had pictured Stransky, accompanied by his adjutant, appearing at the last moment among the fleeing men, stemming their panic and leading them into the counterattack.

Stransky had candidly told his adjutant that he counted on an Iron Cross as the reward for this report. "Of course you must confirm the details if you're asked, Triebig. It's perfectly safe. You are the only witness. Meyer is dead so no one can prove it wasn't so. This is the way everybody does it, and if the nomination goes through, you'll get the IC Second Class for it."

The temptation was great, and in any case Triebig was in no position to oppose Stransky's wishes.

Next day the report had been sent on to Regiment. Brandt had at once informed Stransky that he was entitled to the IC First Class for his part in the counterattack. But he had also pointed out that in such cases two witnesses were required; he would have to have the signature of the company commander in addition to Triebig's. Since Meyer was dead, Brandt suggested he should apply to Meyer's deputy at the time. In case the latter could not be reached at the moment, he was to shelve the nomination until the witness was available. Although Steiner's name had not once been mentioned, Stransky realized immediately whom the regimental commander meant. "A ticklish affair," he had said to Triebig at the time. "But we can't back out now. There's too much at stake."

The more Triebig thought about it, the more pessimistic he became. But Stransky was right. They could not back out now—the affair had to be fought right on through Regiment. And it seemed highly likely that Steiner would refuse to give his signature. In that case Stransky would be forced to get rid of him as a person who knew too much. How—that was Stransky's affair. It shouldn't be too difficult to maneuver a hothead like Steiner into a situation where even Brandt could no longer protect him.

XII

WHEN Steiner appeared at the command post, Stransky received him with marked restraint and asked him to sit down. The sergeant did not accept this invitation. "You may sit down," Stransky repeated impatiently.

"If you order me to," Steiner said.

"Consider it an order." Steiner reluctantly drew up a chair, and Stransky moved the kerosene lamp so that he himself was sitting in darkness. He crossed his legs casually. "Do you recall our last conversation?"

Steiner nodded silently.

"As a result of your wound," Stransky went on, "we were unable to conclude it. I don't like to do things halfway and should like to follow it up." He continued in a completely colorless voice: "You are still quite young. That is why I prefer to excuse your past behavior. But I can do so only if you recognize that I am being tolerant."

"Are you referring to my switching tommy guns?"

Stransky frowned. "The matter of the submachine guns is only one phase of the subject. Please, let me assume a certain amount of mental agility on your part when I speak with you."

Steiner shrugged. "Maybe you're assuming too much. At any rate, certain things can be talked about only man to man, not superior to subordinate."

Stransky studied him speculatively. "You would naturally think that," he said with an attempt at a smile. "But even if we leave my rank aside, this still remains a conversation between a superior and an inferior. You are quite aware that in civil life too a distinction is made between people and personalities. Or haven't you ever been aware of that?"

Steiner bit his lip. So that's what you're getting at, he thought. Evidently Stransky was bent on humiliating him. He forced an ingenuous tone to his voice. "I have never thought much about such matters. But I'm sure you can explain the distinction to me."

"I can," Stransky said. He folded his arms over his chest, his long face with its silvery temples forming the very portrait of a distinguished man. "The difference is a matter of ethical and intellectual superiority and is caused, whether you like it or not, by class differences. Those who are reared in dirt will never or rarely emerge from it because they have never learned to see dirt as dirt. Isn't that self-evident?"

Steiner shook his head. "I disagree," he said. "What experience I have had has shown me that talent, sensitivity and character are not privileges of the upper classes. If I remember rightly, Kant was the son of a saddlemaker and Schubert's father was nothing but a poor schoolmaster. I'm sorry my scanty education makes it impossible for me to add a whole lot of big names to the list. At eighteen I had to drop my schoolbooks and pick up a spade in order to dig useless holes in the ground, instead of developing myself into a personality."

He had spoken swiftly, in a low voice. Now he became silent, looking past Stransky into the dark reaches of the room. There was a pause.

"We were talking about general concepts," Stransky said evasively.

"We are still talking about general concepts," Steiner said quietly. "I might add that useful plants and useless weeds grow on the same soil everywhere. Or are things different in East Prussia?"

Stransky's voice had become less urbane. "May I ask in which of the two categories you count yourself?"

It was an open challenge, precisely what Steiner had feared. He straightened in his chair. "This talk was going to be about general concepts," he said. "Before we go over into personal matters, I'd like to clarify one question."

"What is that?"

"To go back to the beginning: is this conversation taking place between two equal human beings, or between a superior and his subordinate?"

"I see no reason to throw the weight of my rank into the balance," Stransky declared haughtily.

Steiner nodded with satisfaction, feeling maliciously pleased at being able to overstep the limits of this conversation. "In that case," he said quietly, "I am free not to answer your tactless question."

There was a silence, such a dead silence that for a second Steiner felt as if he were alone in the room. He watched the change in Stransky's expression. He felt himself a man who has tossed a pebble down a slope and stands to watch it start a roaring landslide.

Yet Stransky did not stir from his seat. The fury showed only in his eyes as he whispered, "You are forgetting yourself, Steiner."

For a moment Steiner quailed before that fury. But he shook off the response to years of military discipline, and raised his head. "You are forgetting our argument," he said coldly. "If you feel insecure about standing on grounds of equality, we can easily go back to our regular relationship."

Stransky looked down at his hands. "Your impertinence can only arise from stupidity," he said softly. "If it came from courage, I might punish it, but I would also admire it." He stood up brusquely and paced about the room several times and finally came to a stop in front of Steiner. "I have encountered more than one person of your type," he went on, "and I have always crushed them like vermin. At our first meeting I told you that you overestimate your own importance. If you think you can impress me, you are very much mistaken. I consider you nothing more than an insolent lout with criminal tendencies who cannot keep his hands off his comrades' property."

Steiner stood up slowly. He looked down at his hands

and was glad to see that they were steady. "You'll regret that," he said quietly.

Stransky wiped his sleeve with his right hand. "For that remark alone," he replied, "back home I would have had dogs chase you over the countryside until your feet were bleeding straps."

"We're not back home," Steiner replied.

"You'll wish you were before long." He turned his back on Steiner, strode over to the table, picked up the telephone and called Triebig.

"Come over here," he ordered curtly. Turning around, he saw that Steiner was leaning easily against the wall. "Stand at attention." Steiner took a half step forward and let his arms dangle. "You'll learn that too," Stransky snapped.

At that moment Triebig entered. At the sight of Steiner blood rushed to his pallid face. "You called me, sir," he said to Stransky.

Stransky lighted a cigarette, placed the used match carefully in an ash tray and nodded. "How far has my bunker progressed?"

"The men have started," Triebig reported. "It's slow work; the ground is very hard."

"How deep is it now?"

"About a foot and a half."

"The bunker is to be ten feet deep. Sergeant Steiner will work on it tonight until that depth is reached."

"Tonight?" Triebig exclaimed, astonished.

"Tonight; in fact he is to begin at once. Give him the necessary tools. I shall hold you responsible for having that bunker ready by tomorrow morning."

"Yes, sir," Triebig stammered.

Steiner had listened with an impassive face.

Now Stransky turned to him. "You wait outside." He remained silent until Steiner had left the room. "I intend to play a different tune with that fellow now," he said then.

"Did he refuse?" Triebig asked in alarm.

Stransky shook his head. "I've changed my mind. We are going to call the whole thing off. You will go to see Kiesel tomorrow morning. Listen carefully."

Triebig listened attentively as Stransky explained his plan, and the worried expression slowly passed from his face.

Outside, Triebig found Steiner standing with hands in his pockets, a cigarette drooping from his lips. "Come along!" Triebig ordered. They walked around the house to the back garden.

"You'll find tools here," Triebig said, pointing to a spot along the wall of the house.

In spite of the darkness Steiner could see freshly turned earth and a dark rectangle in the ground. He went up to it and glanced in. Triebig was watching him uncertainly. "What are you staying around for?" he asked without removing the cigarette from the corner of his mouth.

"I want you to know that I have nothing to do with this business."

"That's fortunate for you," Steiner said. Since Triebig made no move to leave, Steiner took a step toward him. "I've heard that you suffered a terrible loss today," he said. "But bear up. There are plenty more of that type around."

Triebig stared at him with hatred. His voice shook as he said, "I have only one wish, and the commander shares it. We could court-martial you or get rid of you some other way. But we want to have the pleasure of seeing you croak."

Steiner smiled. "You'll have to take very good care of yourself if you want to outlive me."

"You're an idiot," Triebig said hoarsely, "a goddamn idiot and stupid fool." His voice dropped to a whisper. "Do you think anyone would believe you?"

"Brandt would," Steiner said. "But if I wanted to tell tales, I would have done so long ago."

"And if you had, it would be your word against mine, and you may be sure an officer would be believed rather than you, of all people." He laughed contemptuously. "You lost your chance, Steiner. You had me until you left the bunker and not a second longer."

"That may be," Steiner replied. "But you're too insignificant to be worth jawing about. You're so insignificant you're not worth the bullet I'm going to send through your filthy hide one of these days. Not worth it, but I'll have to do it sooner or later. Go on, get out of my sight."

Triebig clenched his fists in helpless fury. "Thank you for the warning."

"You're entirely welcome," Steiner said coldly.

Triebig stood for a second leaning forward as though he were going to topple over, or spring upon Steiner. Then he turned and stalked off. As Steiner looked around he saw to his surprise two figures emerge from the dark background of the garden and come toward him. He recognized them immediately.

"Where are you two coming from?" he asked.

"Over there," Schnurrbart replied, jerking his thumb over his shoulder.

"It was highly interesting," Kruger murmured, lighting a cigarette.

"Did you hear what we were talking about?"

"Not quite," Schnurrbart said. "But it was interesting anyway. Are you coming along?"

"Not at the moment," Steiner said. "I have to dig out the commander's bunker tonight."

The two stared at him incredulously. "Who says?" Schnurrbart asked softly.

"The commander."

"Well, what do you know!" Kruger growled. "This gets more interesting by the minute." He turned to Schnurrbart. "I'll get the fellows." Without waiting for an answer, he sped off.

"What's the idea?" Steiner asked.

Schnurrbart hunched his shoulders. "Do you think we're going to leave you here alone? Six will do it a lot faster."

"You're crazy," Steiner muttered, swallowing hard. "What were you doing here anyhow?"

Schnurrbart sat down. "Seemed as if you'd been gone a long time and we got to wondering. Kruger thought we ought to take a look around, so we started out. Just as we reached the house we saw you and Triebig going round the back. That looked funny, so we waited until Triebig left. That's all."

"That's a lot." Steiner took a deep breath. He fought against the impulse to place his hand on Schurrbart's shoulder.

"They'll be right along," Schnurrbart said, fussing with his pipe. Steiner looked at his watch. It was shortly after ten. Suddenly they heard a voice speaking loudly in the street. Schnurrbart jumped to his feet. "That's März," he said worriedly. "What's he doing here?"

Hasty footsteps sounded along the path from the street. A moment later five men appeared around the corner of the house. Steiner recognized the foremost as Lieutenant März.

"What's going on here?" März inquired sharply.

Behind him came Faber, Maag and Kern, anxious looks on their faces. Kruger answered Schnurrbart's questioning look with a shrug. "We ran into him on the way," he whispered. "When he heard what it was about, he insisted on coming with us." Steiner was answering the company commander's question. He merely repeated the commander's order.

"And why was such an order given?" März asked curtly.

"I don't know. We were having a pleasant chat."

"By chat you mean—?"

Steiner smiled. "A private conversation."

"With the commander's approval?"

Steiner rubbed his chin. His smile broadened. "I am cautious by nature."

März considered for a few seconds. Then he ordered Steiner to begin work. "You return to your quarters," he said to the others. Seeing their disgruntled expressions, he added, "If it turns out that the sergeant needs you, you'll be informed."

The men grinned significantly at one another. With encouraging nods to Steiner, they straggled off. März stayed long enough to see Steiner jump into the pit and pick up one of the spades. Then he turned away and went out along the garden path to the street.

Back at headquarters, he telephoned Kiesel at once. The conversation took some time, since Kiesel had to check with Brandt. When März laid down the receiver, he was smiling with satisfaction. He waited a little while. Then he picked up the telephone again. Stransky answered sleepily. März apologized for disturbing him at this late hour; he had received a telephone call from Regiment, he said. "I hear that Steiner is supposed to be with you now," he went on. "The lieutenant colonel wants him sent to regimental headquarters at once."

He was silent. It was so still at the other end of the line that for a moment he thought Stransky had hung up. Then Stransky spoke again, tensely and with effort: "Very well, he will leave immediately."

März heard several noises he could not interpret. Then the hum in the receiver stopped. The indifferent voice of the operator asked, "Are you through?" März did not answer, "Are you through?" the voice asked again, and, after a short pause: "I am disconnecting."

März turned to the window and looked out across the water. The mountains gleamed as though coated with frost, towering gravely into the star-sown sky. The night on the mountains wore a sparkling surface of a curved mirror. As he saw, with a strange, constricted feeling in his breast, how sky and earth held each other in close embrace, he was conscious of a mute melancholy. Never before had he been so painfully aware of the banalities that filled his days to the very brim.

Triebig was startled out of sleep by the persistent shrilling of the telephone. Cursing, he groped his way unsteadily to the table. He came wide awake as soon as he heard Stransky's voice. "Come here!" Stransky ordered him. "At once."

Triebig stammered something and dressed with feverish haste. He was so frightened that he was still trembling when, a few minutes later, he left the house. Before he entered the command post he tiptoed around the corner of the house to make sure that Steiner was still working. Then he went inside. Stransky received him in a state of agitation such as Triebig had never before seen him display. He stood behind his desk, leaning forward with hands braced on its surface, and shouted in a voice altogether out of control, "Where the devil have you been? Didn't I say to come at once?"

"I had to dress," Triebig replied, shaking.

Stransky's face flushed. "Dress!" he bellowed. "A soldier is always dressed, even when he's in bed with a woman. Come over here! Where is Steiner?"

"Working at your bunker, as you ordered," Triebig whispered, hesitantly stepping closer.

"You are to take him to Regiment at once," Stransky said. "Regiment wants to see Steiner today, now. At—" he looked at his watch—"at eleven o'clock. Do you know what that means?"

Triebig moved his lips soundlessly. He was so stunned by the news that he was unable to speak. In one sudden vision he saw disaster descending on his own head. "It must be the report."

Stransky nodded fiercely. "Certainly. Brandt must somehow have got wind of what happened tonight, and I'll lay ten to one that that damned sneak März is behind it."

"You should have expected that," Triebig said tonelessly.

Stransky threw him a scornful look. "Of course I expected it. Do you think I don't know that I'm spied on every step of the way here?" He laughed sarcastically. "Those gentlemen underestimate me. I'll show them that a captain is a captain and a sergeant still a sergeant no matter how many times he crawls behind the back of the regimental commander." He began to pace the room.

Triebig moistened his lips with his tongue. "What do you intend to do?"

"I need time," Stransky replied. "No matter what, you must speak to Brandt before Steiner sees him. Tell Brandt that I prefer to forgo the IC because it is beneath my dignity to have a merited decoration depend on the signature of a subordinate whose undisciplined conduct has bordered on open mutiny. Tomorrow I intend to send a written report to Regiment on his behavior. You will also tell the commander that it is asking too much to expect me to seek a favor of a man with a criminal record who has every reason to wish me ill because a single word from me would suffice to put him where he has long deserved to be: up against a wall."

Triebig gasped. "The lieutenant colonel will . . ."

Stransky cut him off with an angry wave of his hand. "The lieutenant colonel," he said loudly, "will not be able to ignore the justified complaint of a battalion commander. I am thoroughly sick of being treated like a stupid boy by a sergeant who thinks he's under the protection of the regimental commander. If my complaint is not accepted, I shall disregard channels and address myself directly to Division. I want you to repeat what I have said to the lieutenant colonel word for word."

"Wouldn't you prefer to give it to me in writing?" Triebig asked anxiously.

Stransky sneered. "I should think not. They're quite capable of twisting a noose for me out of anything written. It will be quite enough documentation for me to present my complaint on Steiner in writing tomorrow morning. And now repeat what you are to tell the lieutenant colonel."

He sat down at the table and while Triebig, acutely uncomfortable, repeated his words he made brief notations on a sheet of paper. When Triebig finished, he nodded his approval. "In general outline that is it. Even put a bit more strongly, it does no harm. One must not allow oneself to be intimidated; it's essential to keep on the offensive. Start at once."

Triebig left hurriedly. He went first to his quarters, then to Steiner, standing up to his chest in the pit. Steiner looked up indifferently as he was spoken to. "Come along! You're to go to Regiment."

Steiner concealed his surprise, although he could not understand what Brandt could possibly want of him at this late hour. Since Triebig strode rapidly ahead with no explanations, he asked no questions.

They passed through a good dozen black tunnels of streets and Steiner gradually lost his sense of direction. At rare intervals they encountered a bored sentry who regarded them curiously. Their way led finally out of the confusion of tenement houses into a dark street lined by trees. Steiner figured that they must have been walking for more than twenty minutes.

At that moment they were hailed sharply. "Regimental command post?" Triebig asked. Steiner saw the dim silhouette of a man who approached and asked for the password. "Kuban," Triebig returned, adding: "The commander is expecting us." By now the sentry had apparently recognized the officer's uniform; he clicked his heels. On the right a wall loomed up out of the darkness; they passed through a gate guarded by another sentry. A short flight of steps led to a front door, and they entered a long hallway. "Wait here," Triebig said.

Steiner thrust his hands into his pockets. He was quite calm now and observed with disdain the nervous timidity with which the lieutenant knocked on the door. But no one called to him to come in. Instead, Kiesel suddenly appeared on the threshold. Seeing Triebig, he raised his eyebrows in surprise. Then he caught sight of Steiner. For the fraction of a second a faint smile seemed to pass over his face. But since Steiner was not sure sure of it, he slowly took his hands from his pockets.

"Did you want to see me?" Kiesel asked Triebig.

"Captain Stransky has sent me," Triebig said. "I must speak with the commander."

Kiesel's expression became reserved. "Concerning what?" he asked in a stiff official tone.

"Concerning . . ." Triebig glanced quickly at Steiner and stopped. Then he gathered up his courage again. "I request permission to speak personally with the commander in regard to an official matter."

"One moment," Kiesel said, and went back into the room, closing the door.

He was unusually long about returning. At last he reappeared and with a silent movement of his head indicated that Triebig was to come in. Before he followed he turned to Steiner. "The commander asks you to be patient for a few minutes more."

"Gladly," Steiner said. Kiesel turned swiftly, but before the door closed, Steiner thought he saw an amused grin in his direction. Standing, Steiner looked down at his soiled boots.

I should have polished them, he thought. But there had been no chance.

The wait proved long. To break his boredom Steiner wandered along the corridor, which was lighted by two candles. At the end of the corridor was a flight of steps covered by a thick runner. He sat down on the lowest step and stretched out his legs. He was suddenly aware of his weariness and closed his eyes. The hell with it all and with all of them, Stransky, Triebig, Brandt and all the rest. He began to whistle under his breath. Again he noticed his dirty boots. The sight of them troubled him, and he wiped them off with a corner of the carpet. Then he settled back contentedly and tried to think of nothing at all. It was hard for him to keep his eyes open, and he began to blink. If I close them, he thought, I'll fall asleep.

Suddenly a loud voice startled him. He stumbled to his feet, straightened up jerkily and stared blankly about him. Kiesel was standing in front of him. "I think you fell asleep," he remarked.

"Seems like it." Steiner rubbed his eyes.

Kiesel looked at him, shaking his head. "I wish I had your conscience. Come this way."

They entered the room, and for a moment Steiner stood stock still in confusion. It was so stuffed with furniture that he did not see where the commander was until he heard his booming voice. Brandt sat behind a huge, clumsy desk piled with all sorts of useless objects; he held a lighted cigarette between his fingers. "So there you are," he said loudly. "Next time you're wounded, give me a week's notice that we're going to lose you, ha ha. How are you, Steiner?"

"I can't complain," Steiner said weakly, feeling foolish.

But Brandt stood up and shook hands heartily. Then he gestured toward a chair. "Make yourself comfortable. I've heard that you've worked a great deal today."

"A man does what he can," Steiner muttered, cursing his sleepiness. As he sat down and took a cigarette from the case Brandt extended across the desk, he realized that Triebig was not in the room. He lighted his cigarette and looked attentively at the commander.

"How was it in the hospital?" Brandt began.

"Pretty good," Steiner said laconically. Apparently Brandt was in good humor. But it seemed unlikely that the commander had sent for him so late at night merely to ask how he was. Besides, why had Triebig accompanied him, and where was Triebig now?

The commander was speaking. "Tell me about your wound, won't you? I hear that you were wounded again on your way back to Kanskoye."

"That's right," Steiner said, and began to tell the story, keeping it as short as possible.

The commander listened gravely. "Yes, that was a bad business," he sighed, when Steiner had finished. His face darkened at the memory of the several hundred men who had fallen in the unsuccessful counterattack of the assault regiment.

Steiner puffed at his cigarette. The presence of Kiesel bothered him, for he felt that the captain was watching him all the time.

They went on talking until Brandt suddenly leaned forward, elbows on the desk, and casually asked whether Steiner knew that Captain Stransky had led Second Company's counterthrust that night just before the beginning of the big Russian offensive. Steiner looked at him in surprise. He recalled that Schnurrbart and Kruger had also been questioned, and became alert.

"The counterthrust was led by Lieutenant Meyer," he stated. "Captain Stransky was nowhere in sight at any time."

He caught Brandt exchanging a glance with Kiesel, and Kiesel now asked whether he was sure of that. "Absolutely," Steiner affirmed. "In the first place, I would have seen him, and in the second place, directly after the business Lieutenant Meyer had to report to the captain what had been happening in the lines."

"How do you know that?" Kiesel asked.

"I was there when he made his report," Steiner replied.

Brand gave an exclamation. "When was that?" he asked.

Steiner looked in puzzlement at his flushed face. "Right afterwards," he declared, and began to sketch in the order of events.

When he finished, Brandt let his head droop and sat thinking. Something in his expression warned Steiner to step cautiously. But whatever the threat was, it apparently was not directed toward him, for when the commander looked up again there was a faint smile around his mouth. He turned to Kiesel. "Fetch Triebig," he ordered sharply.

Triebig was biting his lip when he came into the room with Kiesel and saw Steiner sitting at ease beside the desk. It was, he felt, alarmingly quiet in the room.

Brandt's voice, when he spoke, sounded unusually soft and low. "You gave your name, Lieutenant Triebig. Were you present when Captain Stransky led the counterthrust?"

Triebig hesitated. He seemed to be struggling to come to a

decision. Finally he hunched his shoulders. "I accompanied the commander to the hill and saw him calling several men around him. Then he sent me back to the command post."

"Why did he do that?" Brandt asked.

"He thought someone ought to be in the command post in case you called, sir."

"Then how do you know that Stransky really led the counterattack? You signed a statement to that effect as a witness, Lieutenant Triebig."

Triebig's reply came without hesitation this time: "I learned of it from wounded men who were returning."

Kiesel interrupted. "Will you permit me to ask a question, sir?" When Brandt nodded, he addressed Triebig: "Can you give me the name of one of these wounded men?"

"They weren't staff men but company men," Triebig replied evasively. "I knew them only by sight. Besides, it was pitch-dark when I spoke with them. I saw no reason to doubt their statements."

"You should have noted their names," Kiesel said.

Triebig shrugged. "In all that confusion?" he murmured. "I'd practically lost my head myself."

"You may yet," Brandt said icily. "I want you to know, Lieutenant Triebig, that I have had your statements checked. Captain Kiesel will now inform you of the results of our investigations."

Steiner had been listening to the conversation with mounting wonder. He watched as Kiesel took a sheet of paper out of his pocket and studied the contents for a moment. "Our investigations so far," Kiesel stated placidly, "have disclosed that at the moment there are forty-two men in Second Company who took part in the aforementioned counterthrust. They declare unanimously that the attack was led by Lieutenant Meyer. None of them saw Captain Stransky, and none of them heard that he was even with the company at the time the attack was launched."

"Very well," Brandt said. He turned again to Triebig, who looked as if he were standing against a wall watching an execution squad line up in front of him. "You are not going to try to tell me that all this is a matter of sheer coincidence. If it should turn out that Captain Stransky has deliberately sent in a false report, I shall take the matter up with Division. In that case, Lieutenant Triebig, you yourself would have to justify your conduct before a court of honor."

Steiner, watching Triebig, noticed the fine beads of perspiration on his forehead. But he felt no sympathy at all. Now that he had wind of what was going on, he could feel nothing but contempt. Iron Cross hyenas, he thought, and recalled that neither Schnurrbart nor Kruger wore any special decorations, although they had earned them a hundred times over.

Triebig seemed to have recovered somewhat. He attempted to lend firmness to his voice. "I acted out of my deepest convictions, sir."

"Whether you acted out of deepest conviction is not in question," Brandt replied coldly. "You can only corroborate what you yourself saw, not what was allegedly told to you. To my mind there is nothing more contemptible than snatching the laurels that properly belong to a man who fell on the field of battle. I shall abide by Sergeant Steiner's testimony. He was in the immediate vicinity of Meyer. If he stands by his statement that Captain Stransky was not with the company during the time in question, I shall be compelled to institute disciplinary proceedings against the captain."

He turned to Steiner. "Do you stand by your statement?"

There was a deep silence in the room. Steiner hesitated.

"Would it be possible for me to think that over for a few days?" he asked finally.

Brandt stared at him, perplexed. "Think it over?" he said, anger and disappointment in his voice. "What is there to think over? Did you see Stransky? Yes or no!"

At this juncture Steiner unexpectedly received aid.

Kiesel had stood up. "I think Sergeant Steiner is right," he said to Brandt, who sat glowering behind his desk. "A question as important as this one ought to be considered very carefully."

Brandt jumped to his feet. "Are you starting the same nonsense? Common sense ought to tell you that . . ." He broke off abruptly. Kiesel was furiously winking at him. He turned to Triebig and Steiner and ordered them to wait outside.

As soon as they were gone, Brandt asked sharply, "What's this nonsense all about?"

"Of course it's nonsense," Kiesel said. "Steiner knows perfectly well where Stransky was during the counterattack." He took a few strides about the room, then turned swiftly. "You have two alternatives," he said. "Either you can pursue the matter and perhaps bring Stransky up before a courtmartial. But Steiner would have to appear as a witness. That is a role he is not going to love. Perhaps that's why he wants to stall."

Brandt rubbed his chin. "We could leave him out of it," he said reluctantly, after a long pause.

Kiesel shook his head dubiously. "Stransky would wonder,"

he said. "If we don't bring up the principal witness against him, he'll think about it and probably draw false conclusions. It wouldn't be a good idea for us to leave ourselves open that way. Moreover, we can't load forty-two men of the Second Company on a truck and transport them God knows where as witnesses." Observing the gathering frown on the commander's face, he stepped closer to him and argued pleadingly: "If I were you, I would avoid doing anything that might bring Steiner into a case before a court-martial for the second time. Stransky would certainly refer to Steiner's past, and we'd be in for ticklish complications."

"That's ridiculous!" Brandt thundered, pounding on the table. "I can't let him pull a trick like this on me and get away with it!"

"Not at all," Kiesel replied. "I spoke of two alternatives. You can administer a much more thorough slap to Stransky another way."

"Well, what is it?" Brandt asked.

Kiesel dropped into a chair and crossed his legs. "I have been watching Steiner this evening, and I think I know something about men's reactions. I can well imagine that he not only wants to avoid testifying before a court-martial, but that the idea of being the principal witness against Stransky is also distasteful to him."

"Why, in Heaven's name? To judge by what März has said, he must have every reason to want revenge." Brandt laughed irritably. "That's sheer fantasy, Kiesel. Steiner must wish him in hell."

Kiesel smiled. "Of course. But it is my impression that he regards his differences with Stransky as a private matter. As for Stransky—what will you do if he sends in his recommendation that Steiner be disciplined?"

"Let me worry about that," Brandt replied. "If he dares to carry out his threat and contact Division behind my back, he'll find he's bitten off more than he can chew."

"He seems to have good connections," Kiesel reminded him.

"Connections!" Brandt waved his hand contemptuously. "If I convict him of presenting a falsified report, the best connections in the world won't do him any good. But we're digressing. You had a plan?"

"Right," Kiesel said, and began to explain. When he finished there was a prolonged silence.

"Only you could have hit on that idea," Brandt declared at last. He sat for several minutes with drawn face thinking it over. Then he raised his head and said, "Bring the two of them in."

He spoke first to Steiner. "I agree. You may think the matter over for a few days. You know what it is all about?"

"I think I do," Steiner replied.

Brandt nodded. "So that there will be no misunderstandings about it, it is this: Captain Stransky claims that he led Second Company's counterattack. For that he would receive the Iron Cross, First Class. But I want the action confirmed by two signatures, as is proper. The first was supplied by Lieutenant Triebig; the second should come from the company commander. Since Lieutenant Meyer was killed, you, who were his representative at the time, are the only possible person to give his signature. Any questions?"

Steiner shook his head. Brandt turned to Triebig. "I want you to inform Captain Stransky of this conversation. As for his promised report on the insubordinate conduct of one of his platoon leaders, you may tell him that I leave it to his imagination whether such an action might not refresh the memory of the person in question in a manner disadvantageous to Captain Stransky."

Kiesel barely repressed a grin at the delicacy of Brandt's wording. Triebig held his head bowed. But his relief was obvious. "I shall inform the captain," he murmured.

Brandt glared coldly at him. "That is an order," he informed him. "You are no longer needed here."

He waited until Triebig had left the room. Then he sat down behind his desk again. Steiner had remained standing in the middle of the room. From the back of the room, where Kiesel sat, came a repressed cough, and Brandt suddenly felt Kiesel's presence as disturbing. But since he could not very well send him away, he forced himself to take a distant tone. "Why were you ordered to dig Stransky's bunker tonight?"

Steiner compressed his lips.

"I asked you something," Brandt said loudly.

Suppressing the urge to retort sharply, Steiner murmured, "I would rather not talk about it."

"And suppose I order you to?"

Steiner raised his head. Their eyes met, and Steiner felt a dull anger mounting within him. "Do you want to hear lies?" he asked rebelliously.

Brandt placed the tips of his fingers together and leaned forward slightly. "I want to tell you something, Steiner. In the vicinity of this house there is room for several hundred bunkers, and it might occur to me to keep you busy for two or three weeks, just to keep you where you don't make any more trouble for me. Do you know that Stransky intends to recommend disciplining you?"

"If I were he I wouldn't lose a minute about it," Steiner growled.

Brandt turned to Kiesel, who had been listening attentively. "What do you say to that? I really think it would be better for me to place a guard over him and have him dig holes until he's blue in the face."

"A poor cure for obstinacy," Kiesel said, smiling. "Besides, why try to revise the decisions of Providence?" Since he did not want to say anything more in front of Steiner, he shrugged and said nothing.

Brandt peered questioningly at his face. Then he turned to Steiner, and his voice grew stern. "Listen to me. You know quite well that I have always shown a great deal of understanding for you. But I am beginning to get tired of battling with your superiors over you."

"I didn't ask you to," Steiner replied and stared at him defiantly. It was the greatest liberty he had ever permitted himself with Brandt, and as soon as he had said it he was frightened at his own foolhardiness. But he met the commander's eyes firmly and observed with an almost voluptuous excitement the way Brandt's expression changed.

He rose and leaned on the desk. His voice was hoarse with rage. "Didn't ask me to! You didn't ask me to? Have you gone clean out of your mind? Do you have any idea what you're saying?"

For a second Steiner closed his eyes. Anger surged up in him so suddenly that afterward he could not explain it. The bitterness locked up inside him for months spilled out with such violence that his whole body felt taut. "I do indeed," he hissed. "Ever since I've been wearing this damned uniform I've known that there are two kinds of human beings, and that the one kind consists of the Stranskys and Triebigs and other commissioned officers, and at bottom they are all the same, as much alike as one arse is like the other, and I'm glad I've said it to you at last."

He paused, shaking. His face was twitching like the restless surface of a lake, and there was so much contempt in his eyes that Brandt caught his breath. There was a dead silence in the room. A clock could be heard ticking. The commander was breathing heavily. His unsteady hands groped across the top of the desk. When at last he spoke his voice sounded broken. "Get out. Get out of here at once!"

Steiner abruptly came to his senses. Staring at the commander's grief-stricken face, he felt such remorse that his eyes filled with tears and all the objects in the room swam. Staggering, he moved toward the door, turned around once more and looked back helplessly. Then he went out.

As the door closed, Brandt dropped into his chair and looked down at his big hands until he heard a shuffling sound at his side. He raised his head and saw Kiesel standing stiffly, watching him with a strange expression.

"Why didn't you spare yourself that?" the adjutant said slowly.

Brandt looked blankly at him.

"You should either have ignored his first impertinence or punished the last," Kiesel went on quietly. "You were inconsistent. You can raise up a wildcat, but don't count on it for gratitude. The species is unpredictable. To tell the truth, I'm worried."

"About Steiner?"

"No, not about Steiner. I'm worried about Stransky. For the past five minutes I've been convinced I would not like to be in his shoes."

He watched as the blood flowed back under the commander's skin, washing away the dumfounded expression. Brandt nodded. "I know," he said.

"In that case it would be better for you to transfer Steiner to another battalion at once, or bring him up here to Regiment."

Brandt stared down at his hands again. When he raised his head, there was an incrutable expression on his face. "I wouldn't think of it," he said slowly. "A few minutes ago you yourself advised me not to revise the decisions of Providence. It seems to me that was for once a wise remark on your part."

"The case is somewhat different now," Kiesel retorted uncomfortably.

By now Brandt had recovered completely. He smiled mockingly. "I disagree. If you tried to mend a hole in a spider web, you'd tear the whole web, no matter how skillful your fingers were. I am going to keep my hands off matters as delicate as this."

He stood up and began to stride about the room. "Perhaps I've treated Steiner wrongly," he said reflectively. "The relationship between superior and subordinate presupposes a distinct barrier. I thought that in this case I could dispense with it."

"Why?" Kiesel interjected.

Brandt ignored the question. "It's hard to find the proper tone," he went on. "I don't want my men to lose touch with me, and at the same time I can't have them taking the liberties Steiner does."

"It's a matter of sensitivity," Kiesel said.

Brandt laughed harshly. "Don't give me any of that. If I started being sensitive I should have to apologize for every order I gave my men, saying it wasn't from me but from Division. No . . ." He shook his head passionately. "It's something else, and it's the thing I worry about most of the time." He halted in front of Kiesel, his face flushed. "I'll tell you what it is," he declared in an unnaturally loud voice. "It's the damned fear we carry around all the time, the fear of exposing any of our weakness, of losing our nimbus. That's it, Kiesel. That's why we don't dare tolerate any personal contact with the men. If we discuss our love affairs, say, with a subordinate, we've shown ourselves in our underwear and can no longer ask him to run blindly head-on into a tank cannon while we hang medals on our chests."

"Not always." Kiesel smiled. "You're right, though. In reality it is nothing but the attempt to maintain an illusion—the illusion that the officer occupies a special position. If you permit closer relations, you are letting the other fellow understand that you respect him as a human being. In doing that you bolster his self-assurance, but that means you run the risk of his feeling himself your equal. Letting down the barrier can be the equivalent of surrender." His smile broadened. "We are like actors who don't dare appear without our grease paint."

"I didn't put it quite that drastically."

"But that is what you meant," Kiesel answered.

They stood silent for a few moments, until Brandt went over to the desk and sat down with a groan. His face twisted in pain, and he clapped his hand to his hip. "This damned rheumatism. I can't seem to get rid of it any more."

"We're getting old," Kiesel said equably.

Brandt looked at him suspiciously. "Is that directed at me?"

"At your rheumatism," Kiesel said.

The conversation between them had bogged down once more. Somehow Kiesel could not understand Brandt. There were too many contradictions in his personality for which he could find no explanation. He recalled how a few months ago the commander had emphasized that his regiment did not consist of figures but of human beings. And now came this strict repudiation of any such feelings.

He smiled. "Stransky must have made the same mistake you did. He was too sure of himself when he started discussions with Steiner."

"Don't overlook the difference in our motives," Brandt growled.

"I've thought of that," Kiesel replied. "Stransky's I know. He received a setback to his morbid arrogance that he will have to chew on for a long time. Incidentally, that sort of arrogance seems to be a specifically German trait."

Brandt waved his hand impatiently. "That's sheer prejudice," he said irritably. "We're no worse than others."

"But perhaps more peculiar," Kiesel countered. "There's no denying that our country swarms with frustrated despots. For their own self-esteem they need someone's back to step on, just as a short woman needs high heels to feel self-respecting. They're frustrated, of course, only so long as they're not in uniform."

"You're an anarchist," Brandt said.

Kiesel shrugged. "I lack the courage to be an anarchist. I am just one of the many who know very well they're in the wrong pew and do nothing about it."

"It's not worth the doing."

"Not for the sake of others," Kiesel agreed, "but perhaps for our own sakes. What are you going to do with Steiner?"

Brandt looked up into his face. "You certainly are insistent," he said gruffly. "Why are you concerned?"

"For your sake," Kiesel said earnestly.

Brandt seemed on the point of replying in the same gruff tone. Suddenly he compressed his lips. There was no way, no possible way, to tell Kiesel that this boy Steiner had for him become the image of all the young men who had fought forever now, all the young men from whom life was taken whether in death on the field or in the longer, even more painful death of hopelessness and shattered faith. His son had been one of these young men; his son had died. It should be enough simply to say to Kiesel, "Steiner is a *landser*." He could say nothing. With a motion of his hand he indicated the interview was closed.

The sun had set beyond the peaceful swells of the sea. Faber sat in his quarters reading for the second or third time his letter from Barbara. At last he folded it carefully and placed it in his breast pocket. Thoughtfully he went over to the window. His gaze wandered from the mountains down to the water, trying to connect the present appearance of the city with the information Barbara had supplied. Her data must have come from their old village schoolmaster. He wrinkled his broad forehead. Could 95,000 people possibly have lived here? He tried to imagine the number and shook his head in astonishment. However, the big factories Barbara mentioned were here—he had seen them. The grain mills and cement works, the elevators and oil refineries—these stood. But on the water front there was none of the busy activity she spoke of, no sign of the many ships. What a babel of tongues there must have been along those piers! But now the port lay like a choked spring, and the city had been transformed into a stony wasteland at the foot of the mountains; it could not have seemed more silent and lifeless if it had lain at the bottom of the sea. A city without human beings. It was like a Black Forest without trees, unthinkable and unreasonable.

He opened the window and leaned far out. The sky was studded with stars. But they did not seem near, as they were at home when he saw them above the trees. Here they were inconceivably remote. He recalled how often at this time of day, when the sun sank beyond the trees and the clangor of bells rang across the mountains, he would sit down on top of a hill somewhere, fold his hands and murmur an "Ave Maria." And think of Barbara. Barbara with her quiet, grave face who wore her braid of fair hair in a crown about her head. He could hear her voice in his ears so distinctly that for a second it seemed to him she must be standing at his side, and he looked back into the dark room. Then he sighed and closed the window. Were it not for the war, he thought, we would have been married long ago.

Since it was still too early to go to sleep, he decided to take a stroll. Kern and Maag were with Kruger, playing skat. Buckling on his belt and plumping his cap over his unruly hair, he left the house. Outside he encountered Maag.

"Game over already?" Faber asked.

"No," Maag said crossly. "I just got sick of it and quit."

"Were you bickering?"

Maag shook his head. "No, not that. I'm just sick of letting Steiner get under my skin. He's at it again. Since that business last night he's been in a stinking mood."

"When did he get back?" Faber asked.

"I don't know. Schnurrbart says he went to the regiment command post during the night. Schnurrbart and Kruger waited up for him till two and then went to bed. He was back this morning. But won't say a word about it all. Are you on duty?"

"No, not today. Tomorrow morning at six."

"Lousy time for sentry duty." Maag lighted a cigarette. "I'd sooner have it at night. Then at least I can sleep in the morning."

They walked together across the street. Faber remained

taciturn. Although Maag tried several times to induce him to talk, he could not get a decent conversation going. Finally Maag stopped, saying, "I'm going back home. I have to stand sentry in an hour. Till then I can take a little nap."

"Hardly worth it," Faber said. "Your head just feels heavy when you have to get up."

Maag looked around. They had wandered a considerable distance beyond the company sector into a district strange to them. All around stood four-story houses, apparently unoccupied. "We might take a look at those dives from inside," he said enterprisingly. "Maybe we'll come across something worth taking."

"That's forbidden," Faber replied. "You know a special order of the day has been issued about plundering."

"What's plundering in a place like this? It doesn't matter much whether the stuff's smashed to bits by shellfire or whether I pocket it."

"In the one case it's plundering, in the other fate," Faber said firmly. "I won't have anything to do with it."

Maag shook his head in disgust. "What a guy you are," he said angrily. "Haven't you ever liberated anything?"

"Not unless it was absolutely necessary for me, no. Besides, it's pitch-dark in the houses."

"I have a flashlight with me."

"The MP's are constantly patrolling," he said. "If they see a light in a window, they'll investigate and you'll be in for a rough time. Take some good advice and keep clear of that kind of thing."

"The bastards." Maag cursed the MP's automatically. He knew quite well that Faber was right. After a few more resentful murmurs, he turned to go. Faber joined him and they retraced their steps.

"I'll be glad when we're back in regular positions again," Maag said. "This here gets me. Half front and half rear echelon. And the officers so bored they spend all their time thinking up ways to annoy us." He spat and added threateningly, "When things start getting hot here, they'd better keep out of my way. I might take a notion to puncture somebody's spine for him."

"That's just talk."

"What do you mean?" Maag flared up. "You don't know me very well."

"We don't know each other at all," Faber replied thoughtfully.

Their pace slowed. "What's that about we don't know each other?" Maag asked in astonishment.

Faber thrust his hands into his pockets. "Of course we don't know each other," he said quietly. "About all we do know is each other's name."

"I suppose that's true," Maag said, taken aback. After a pause he asked, "Are you married?"

Faber shook his head. "No, the war interfered."

"For me too." Maag nodded gloomily. "The damned war. If it weren't for the war I'd have . . ." He stopped abruptly.

"What?" Faber asked.

Maag laughed in embarrassment. "That's something else again. You see . . ." He hesitated until they had crossed a street. "I have a girl. You too?"

"Yes."

"What's her name?"

"Barbara."

"Nice name," Maag said. "My girl's named Monika."

They walked on in silence, Maag turning over the idea that had suddenly occurred to him. He had never spoken about his impotence to anyone, for fear of ridicule. But there was something about Faber's quiet manner that made Maag think he might be helpful The difficulty was how to begin. Several times he started to speak. Finally he stood still and grasped Faber's arm. "A fellow can talk with you, can't he?" he asked uncertainly.

Faber looked at his face, whose freckles showed through the pale skin even at night. "I think so," he said.

"That's good." Maag sighed. "I suppose you've been with your Barbara, haven't you?"

"Been with her? What do you mean?"

"You know what I mean." Maag gave an embarrassed laugh. His uncertainly was increasing and he already regretted having brought up the subject. But he made a last try. "I don't know how you say it in your district. I mean, when you go to bed with a woman."

Faber's expression hardened. "In my district you don't go to bed with a woman until you're married," he declared with emphasis.

Maag gaped at him. He realized his mistake and tried to cover up. "That's what I mean."

"That's not what you mean," Faber replied. "I told you I wasn't married."

"I forgot," Maag mumbled.

Faber studied him silently, then turned and walked on. Maag followed him, downcast. There just isn't anybody, he thought bitterly. A fellow can't talk to any of these idiots.

Head bowed, shoulders slumping, he trotted along behind Faber. He felt very small and very miserable.

Faber walked swiftly. Even after years in the army, conversations of this sort still filled him with disgust and annoyance. They can never talk decently about a woman, he thought, repelled.

They were approaching their company sector when Faber suddenly paused. From a house on the right side of the street had come a strange whining sound that cut one to the heart. It was not something you could miss or pass by.

Maag, too, had stopped. They looked across the street toward a dark shadow in front of a door. The shadow started moving slowly toward them. "A dog," Maag whispered in surprise. It was in fact a big watch dog that limped across the street toward them, its right forepaw held up in the air.

"Damned mutt." Maag raised his fist threateningly.

"Let him alone," Faber said sharply.

The dog stopped and whimpered. Faber held out his hand toward it and began coaxing it. "Come," he said again and again, "come over here."

"What do you want with the filthy beast?" Maag asked irritably.

Faber did not reply. The dog raised its head trustfully and began licking his hand. "I have to go," Maag said. "My tour begins in five minutes."

Faber looked around at him. "Nobody's keeping you."

For a moment Maag glared angrily. Then he stalked off, offended. They'll feel sorry for a dog, he thought bitterly. All the sympathy in the world for a dog!

Faber examined the dog's forepaw. As he ran his fingers carefully over the leathery skin, he came upon a thorn buried deep between the pads. The animal seemed aware that he wanted to help it, and held still. When he gripped the thorn between his fingernails and pulled it out with a jerk, the dog's body twitched and it whimpered softly. "There, it's done," Faber said soothingly, patting the moist snout that rubbed gratefully against his hand. He wondered whether he should take the dog along to his quarters. But perhaps the others would object. And he did not know where he could get food for it. Rations here in the bridgehead were not exactly generous. On the other hand, he could not leave the poor creature to its fate.

Hoping it would follow him, he walked on a few steps. But when he turned around, he saw that the dog had stood still and was watching him go. Now it hobbled across the street to its old place in front of the door, crouched down and whimpered softly. Faber went over to it and sat down on the doorstep. He drew his knees up, and the dog laid its narrow head on his lap and eagerly licked his hands. Tenderly Faber stroked the shaggy hide. The street was dark and silent. After a while man and dog sat still. It occurred to Faber that they had much in common. The only difference was that he knew he was homesick and the dog only dumbly sensed it. There was some comfort in their being here together, comfort for the man from the valleys of the Black Forest and for the forgotten dog who had been driven by homesickness back to the threshold of a deserted house. . . .

The dog kept its eyes closed. It felt the hand upon its back, and its whimpering stopped. Now and then, Faber saw, it raised its head and looked at the door. But there was no one here to let it in. Nor were there any of the familiar faces, the loved smells. Everything was strangely different, and the dog was mournful because of that. When Faber stood up, it watched his every movement with anxious attention. Its eyes seemed to be begging, and Faber felt his heart grow heavy. "I cannot help you," he said softly. "I am as forlorn as you." When he walked away at last, the dog's head dropped down on its paws, and it whimpered. Faber bit his lip and speeded his pace. A great, helpless rage was in him.

XIII

IT WAS October by now, and the order for departure came as a complete surprise. It snapped the men out of the reflective quiet of the preceding weeks. But they were accustomed to such changes and quickly adjusted to the idea. During the night they were relieved by a marine unit and marched west over the dark roads. Steiner walked at the head of the second platoon alongside Lieutenant März, who occasionally glanced back at the company behind him. They said little; each was busy with his thoughts.

Steiner was in a bad humor. That morning he had had a talk with Fetscher, who ventured the opinion that the divisions in the bridgehead had already been written off by the army. "There'll be a second Stalingrad," he had said. "The Russians are already close to Melitopol, and in a few days they'll reach Perekop. The Crimea is lost, and we along with it."

Steiner tried to shake off the gloom. Out of the corner of his eye he looked at the face of his company commander.

Steiner had spent a good deal of time with him of late. Once it had developed that März was a passionate chess player they had whiled away a good many evenings in the company command post, playing chess and afterward talking of this and that. In the course of their talks it had come out that März was related by marriage to the regimental adjutant. This information had rather disturbed Steiner, reminding him as it did of his last encounter with Kiesel and the ugly scene with Brandt. Although several weeks had passed since that night without any gesture from Brandt, and although Stransky had let him alone, he still had the gnawing sensation that the hardest contest still lay before him. As he studied the lieutenant's face he again became aware that März had never remotely referred to the incident in the regimental command post, although Kiesel must certainly have told him about it. There was some method behind this silence, Steiner thought. He looked back along the line.

"How far do we still have to go?" Schnurrbart asked. He was marching beside Kruger and Kiesel in the first row of the platoon, his pipe in his mouth.

März shrugged. "I've no idea. There's supposed to be a truck column somewhere that's going to pick us up."

"Truck column?" Kruger growled. "As soon as I hear that I feel sick to my stomach. That means all hell has let loose somewhere."

März tramped out his cigarette butt. "That may be. But not in the bridgehead, for sure. At present our whole sector is quiet."

"Ivan's had enough," Schnurrbart muttered, spitting sideways.

In the darkness Steiner tried to regain his sense of direction. They had already been marching for four hours, and it must be long past midnight. This area was strange to him. They had not followed the highway leading westward, but a country road tending more in a northwesterly direction. The road rose and fell endlessly over hilly country that reminded him of the area around Krimskaya. Everything seemed black, monotonous, limitless and terribly abandoned. Under their nailed boots fine sand squeaked, and in spite of the darkness they could see the kicked-up dust that hung like a translucent veil above their heads and made breathing difficult. Up ahead in the ranks of the First Company a song was started. But it soon faded out wearily in the dull tramp of boots. Occasionally a man stood out of the line of march with his back to the road. They passed by him as though he were a tree. Weariness crawled from their legs into their brains, making them dead-sleepy.

The three behind Steiner had locked arms and were marching with closed eyes. Alternately one of them would open his eyes to see the direction, and would gently press the others toward the middle of the road, so that they would not stumble into the ditch. It was a technique they had developed over thousands of miles. It enabled them to march half-asleep; their legs seemed separate from the rest of the body, independent units which moved automatically.

Steiner walked with drooping head, staring at the shoes of the company commander beside him. März took long strides and whistled under his breath. Once again Steiner found himself thinking about Brandt. The more time that passed since the interview, the more conscience-stricken he felt about it. The devil must have got into me, he thought. He could not understand himself. Several times he had wrestled with the thought of sending a letter of apology. But there was a stubborn defiance in him that forbade such a step. Least of all could he understand the commander's conduct. The longer he thought about that, the more inexplicable it seemed. He would have acceped any punishment as the natural result of his insolence. But this mysterious silence on the commander's part tormented him; it simply did not tally with what he knew of the way superiors acted. Altogether, it was a queer business.

When März spoke to him, he looked up vacantly. "We've made it," the lieutenant said.

"Really?" Steiner asked. Now he became aware that the road before them terminated in a broad highway where stood a line of big trucks. At the same time a loud call came down the column, ordering the company commanders up front. "Bring us good news!" Steiner said. März nodded and hurried off. The men dropped leadenly by the roadside.

"I wonder where we'll drink our next champagne," Schnurrbart remarked.

Kruger grinned. "In Siberia. Where else?"

"How late is it?" Maag sat with legs drawn up, chewing a piece of bread.

Steiner looked at his watch. "Half past three. We marched for five hours."

"Twenty miles," Schnurrbart said, looking at the trucks. The drivers were asleep at the wheels.

After five minutes März returned.

"Where are we headed for?" Steiner asked.

März hooked the map board to his belt. "Guess."

They regarded him curiously. "Italy?" Steiner said hopefully.

März shook his head.

"Crimea?" Schnurrbart guessed.

"No," März said. "You'll never get it. We're going back."

"We've been doing that for the past year," Steiner growled. "You don't mean back to dear old Germany?"

"No, back to Novorossiysk," März stated.

They stared blankly at him. Steiner rubbed his eyes. "Somebody's crazy." Suddenly he grinned. "Then we can go on with our chess match."

"We'll have to play against the Russians," März said. "Tonight they landed at five points on the water front. Two hours after we moved out. Do you notice anything?"

Steiner gaped. "Treason!"

"You could call it that," März replied equably. "But it sounds better if you say: intelligence. In that respect we have still something to learn from the Russians. Last week a radio station of theirs was discovered right in the heart of the city. Probably there were others."

"Incredible," Schnurrbart whispered.

März smiled mirthlessly. "We'll have to get used to the idea. All right, into the trucks."

Cursing, the men got up and scattered among the vehicles. Minutes later the trucks started up. Schnurrbart sat beside Steiner, holding his tommy gun in his hands. "*Scheisse!*" he grumbled. Steiner nodded.

They sat in silence until they reached the outer suburbs of the city. The trucks had covered the distance of the five-hour march in barely an hour. It was already light. Above the city hovered huge clouds of smoke; dull detonations vibrated over the roofs. As the men jumped down from the trucks they noticed that the street was full of splintered glass, scraps of wood and fragmented stone. "You'd think there was a war going on here," Kruger said, gazing with disgust at the black shell holes.

Steiner looked toward the one-story buildings which seemed to be cowering in terror behind the garden fences. Then he recalled there was something he'd wanted to ask about. He put his question to März, who was supervising the unloading of the vehicles: "Where had we been headed for?"

"The Isthmus of Perekop," März replied.

"And what were we supposed to do there?"

"Defend the Crimea."

Steiner nodded. "Then I guess there's no harm in my having sent my letter."

"What letter?" März asked in surprise.

"My last will and testament," Steiner said, and returned to his men. He felt somehow relieved.

They waited until the last of the soldiers had clambered out of the vehicles, then watched the trucks drive off as though the devil were behind them.

Kruger picked at his nose and watched them go thoughtfully. "If I ever come into this world again . . ." he began, but Steiner interrupted him.

"You'll be a truck driver, I know. But I imagine you'll know better than to come into the world again."

From somewhere sounded violent rifle skirmishing. Schnurrbart raised his head to listen. "That's on the water front," he commented. "Must be going hot and heavy down there."

"If it weren't, they wouldn't have sent for us," Maag growled.

Kern sighed. His unshaven face twitched as though pricked by nettles. He wished he could crawl into one of the houses and wait until the show was over. Glumly he watched the head of the First Company start forward. The men formed squad columns, leaving a large interval between each two. They had exchanged their alpine caps for steel helmets and were walking crouched, with heads tilted.

"I wonder whether this area is exposed to observation," Maag remarked uneasily.

Kruger said indifferently, "I doubt it, or we'd have smelled powder by now."

"Just give it time." Schnurrbart hitched up his belt. "I don't like this quiet."

"You call this quiet!" Kruger grinned and nodded toward the water front where a series of heavy explosions rumbled one after the other. The cool breeze from the sea carried the smell of burned powder to the street. Steiner saw März place himself at the head of the first platoon and raise his fist into the air. The company started forward. They passed down several streets swathed in dense smoke and partly converted into rubble heaps.

"Mortars," Schnurrbart commented, glancing distrustfully up at the cloudless sky, which was gradually coloring with the promise of a fine day.

After a quarter hour's march they had come so close to the center of the city that the noise of battle seemed to be raging beyond the next street corner. They could easily distinguish machine-gun fire from hand grenades. Isolated shells passed high above the roofs and exploded with thunderous crashes. Up front there was a pause. Steiner observed the men scattering among the houses while März hurried on, ducking low.

"What's going on?" Schnurrbart asked.

Steiner shrugged. "Don't know. Probably a briefing at battalion. Let's get off the street."

He sat down on a doorstep, lighted a cigarette and looked at the houses across the street. The top stories were already catching the light of the rising sun. A curtain swayed in and out of an empty window frame. The sight was somehow homelike, and Steiner felt his heart grow heavy. Damn it all, he thought, absently puffing on his cigarette. Behind him he heard the voices of Kern and Kruger, who sat in the vestibule of the house, talking loudly. They stopped as the even noise of rifle and machine-gun fire was drowned out by a long dull thunder that reverberated menacingly over the streets, plucking at the nerves.

"Artillery salvo," Schnurrbart muttered.

They had all jumped up and cowered in the doorway. The detonations followed in quick succession somewhere along the water front.

"They'll blow our asses off," Kern whispered, white-lipped. They were all pale, unshaven, tired-faced. Their steel helmets hung low over their eyes.

"You know what we're going to have?" Kruger asked. He laughed savagely. "The same shit like in Kharkov, I tell you. Fighting from house to house and room to room. When we throw them out on one side they'll come in again on the other, and when we're in the cellar they'll be in the pantry. I can do without it." He stared darkly out at the street.

März was coming toward them swiftly. "It's starting," he said laconically. He turned to Kern. "Bring the other platoon leaders here."

Kern returned shortly with Sergeants Schulz and Stober. Steiner knew the two men only slightly. They had come with the latest batch of replacements, and he had exchanged a few words with them once or twice. They entered the vestibule of the house and looked expectantly at März, who was studying the map in his hand. Now he looked up at them. "We're attacking. The goal is a big machine-tool factory on the water front. The Russians have raised a red flag on the factory tower. We're to take it down. Express order from the battalion commander. Special assignment for you, Steiner."

"That's crazy," Stober murmured.

März ignored the remark. "The First and Third companies are advancing toward the water front to our left and right. The attack is set for eight o'clock."

"How far is it to the factory?" Steiner asked.

"About five hundred and fifty yards. We'll be there soon."

"And the main resistance line?" Schulz asked.

März scraped his chin. "Things seem to be confused. In places the Russians are already deep into the city, and at other places they haven't got beyond the water front."

"I don't get it," Stober muttered. "What are we doing on the water front if they're already inside the city?" The man had an angular face with deep hollows in his cheeks and eyes that seemed made of glass.

März spread the map out on the floor and the men looked over his shoulders. "Here's the water front. When we get there, we'll advance along the shore and take the Russians on the flank. They seem to be bent on establishing contact with their units on the other side." März pointed to a spot on the map. "Here is Novorossiysk and here is our southern flank. The front line begins on the other side of the harbor. If the Russians succeed in breaking through, they'll advance along the sea coasts as far as Anapa and seize the ferry landings."

"I see," Stober said. "By landing on the water front he's taking us in the rear. It's like cutting the string on a stretched bow."

"Pretty much," März replied. "If we want to hold the bridgehead we've got to get the Russians out of here. So you know what's at stake."

Schulz straightened up. "That's idiotic," he declared moodily.

"What?"

"That about the factory. How big is the place?"

"I don't know," März replied. "I've never been in that part of town. We'll soon see."

A man came in from the street. "The First Company is leaving, Lieutenant," he reported.

"I know. They have farther to go than we." He folded up the map and thrust it into the map board hanging from his side. He turned to Steiner. "You and your platoon will follow me at the head of the company. In front of us are parts of a navy unit. We will relieve them and then attack at once. Order the men to fall in."

Steiner had a few more words with the two sergeants; Schulz had thrust his hands into his pockets and was glaring furiously after the lieutenant. "Wants to earn the Iron Cross, the dog!" he sneered.

Steiner looked at him reprovingly. He did not like the man. His face appeared extremely brutal. From temple to chin ran a deep scar. The man's brows grew together over the base of his nose, and his broad mouth was embedded in ugly folds.

"Mind your own business," Steiner said sharply and followed the lieutenant.

The men streamed out of the houses and stood waiting in a long row on the right side of the street. Steiner glanced rapidly around to assure himself that Schnurrbart and the others were close by him.

März raised his hand. "Keep a good distance between you," he ordered. "I don't want any casualties before the show starts. March!"

As they moved down the street, keeping close to the row of houses, the artillery fire above their heads increased. The din of battle in front of them went on without pause. The district they were now in must once have been the business center of the city. On both sides of the street gaped the empty frames of huge show windows; the insides of shops were strewn with plaster and broken glass. In many places the pavement on the street had been torn open by shells. As Steiner, following März, went around a heap of rubble, there was an explosion behind them that threw them to the ground and showered large and small pieces of stone onto the street. When the hail stopped, März stood up and dusted his clothes. "That's the start," he said calmly. "Increase distances."

Steiner passed on the order and the men stirred from their frozen positions. März was displaying an astonishing coldbloodedness. Steiner had to smile—the lieutenant was walking as though he were out for a Sunday stroll in a peaceful garrison town. März, happening to turn his head at the moment, caught the grin and stood still.

"What is so amusing?" he demanded.

"You," Steiner replied, wiping the grin from his face. März opened his mouth. Steiner, hearing the shell a fraction of a second before him, pulled him to the ground as he dived. The street vanished under a cloud of smoke. Again a wild hail of stones hurtled against the walls of the buildings. Glowing splinters of iron darted with a horrible hissing noise into the wooden frames of the shop windows. The men lay flat on the ground, pressing their faces into their arms. The next shell exploded a long way ahead of them.

März got up. "I asked you a question," he said to Steiner, who was rubbing an aching elbow.

Steiner looked at him blankly. "Maybe you were going to ask me something."

März thought a moment. Then he nodded. "Right. I wanted to ask you what amuses you so about me."

Steiner glanced back and noticed Schnurrbart's confounded

expression; he was right behind them listening to every word. He turned to März again. "Are you fishing for compliments?"

"Never mind—you can keep it to yourself." März strode on again.

They made a detour around the fresh shell hole. When they reached an intersection they saw that the street dropped steeply to the water front, and that it seemed to be blocked off at the end by a board fence. Coming closer they could see a cross street which ran along the fence and in a wide curve around the harbor.

"We're here," März said. "Send the men into the houses. I'll go to the battalion command post."

"Where is it?" Steiner asked.

"Around the corner here somewhere. I'll be right back." As März trotted off around the corner, Steiner turned and signaled to the men to take cover.

"What's up?" Schnurrbart wanted to know.

"You're to wait here," Steiner ordered. "Get out of sight." He lighted a cigarette and walked slowly forward toward the intersection.

The water-front street was built up only on one side. On the other side was the six-foot high fence. As Steiner turned the corner someone called out to him, "Watch your step, fellow."

He looked up and saw a man glaring indignantly down at him from a window. "What's eating you?" Steiner asked.

The man recognized his rank, and his face showed embarrassment. "You must be careful here, sir. It's all under enemy observation."

Steiner looked around. Close to the window was a door into the building. He went through it. On the steps of the front hallway stood three men in dark-blue uniforms, their faces bearing the marks of fear. "What unit?" Steiner asked curtly.

"Navy," one of them replied. "Are you the relief?"

When Steiner nodded, the faces of all three brightened. "Thank God!" the second man sighed. They reached for their carbines, which were leaning against the wall.

Steiner climbed the four steps to them and asked, "Where are you going?"

The men grinned. "Back," the first of them answered. "We've had all we can take."

"Not any more than we have," Steiner replied with animosity.

"You have no idea," the man said. "You should have been here last night when it started."

Steiner scrutinized him with contempt. "You crawled into the cellar anyhow; if you hadn't the Russians wouldn't have been able to land. And now we've got to clean up your mess."

They glowered at him, and the first speaker said, "We're not infantry."

"That's obvious." Steiner's dislike was mounting steadily. "What's been going on here?"

"Just about everything," the man replied. "There's that factory over there, where at least a regiment of Russians have squatted. If they attack, we're finished."

"Boys probably would be," Steiner growled. "Can the factory be seen from here?"

"Sure. You must have seen the tower already."

Steiner went back down the steps to the doorway. "Careful!" one of the men warned him. Steiner shrugged contemptuously. He saw the tower at once. At the very top of it was a pole from which hung a red cloth that fluttered in the wind. He stared up at it for a few seconds.

The sailors had come up behind him, and one of them said, "That does it. They know how to slap your face!"

"We're supposed to take it down," Steiner murmured. He smiled grimly at their looks of wonder. "Wouldn't you like to help us do it?"

They shook their heads in horror, and his grin broadened. "I'll see how it looks from up above," he said and went back into the house.

Upstairs a door led into an apartment. From the window he could see the entire terrain. The factory consisted of a block of connected eight-story buildings in the shape of a triangle open toward the water front. The tower was on the south wing. The longer Steiner looked, the more hopeless the impending attack appeared to him. From the fence there were some five hundred feet of factory yard completely without cover, offering every opportunity to the defenders and none to the attacker.

He leaned out of the window to glance at the southern end of the factory and jerked back abruptly. Over his head there was an ugly hiss and then a thud as though a board were struck against a stone. A cloud of dust whirled down toward him. Simultaneously a Russian machine gun began hammering away. Steiner stepped quickly away from the window, cursing under his breath. Those boys over there were alert as watchdogs. But he had had time to notice that the chances for an attack from the south were somewhat better, since there the fence approached to within a hundred feet of the building. He moved cautiously to one side of the window again and looked down at the street. To his surprise he saw several men

of the Second Company running across the pavement and
scattering along the fence. He recognized März among them.
Quickly he left the room and ran down the steps.

The sailors had disappeared. On the street he saw März
again, leaning against the fence and watching the company
cross the street in small groups. He saw Steiner and raised his
hand. "Where have you been?" he called impatiently.

Steiner crossed over to him and gestured back over his
shoulder with his thumb. "Sight-seeing."

"You'll take the right wing," März directed briskly. "We'll
start in a moment. We have artillery support."

"Ten rounds," Steiner growled, slipping the tommy gun
from his shoulder.

"I beg your pardon?" März asked in astonishment.

"Ten rounds," Steiner repeated. "It won't be enough to
disturb the Russians at their second breakfast."

"You take too black a view." März reached into his pocket,
took out a pack of cigarettes and offered it to Steiner.

"The only color for it," Steiner muttered morosely, holding
the burning match under the company commander's cigarette.
As he tossed it away, he caught sight of several men kneeling
and using their bayonets to pry the slats of the fence from the
lower bar. He took a step forward. The rest of the company
was engaged in similar work. "What's the idea?" he said to
März.

"What idea?"

"That," Steiner said impatiently, gesturing at the men.

"Look for yourself," März replied. "Do you imagine we're
going to climb over the fence?"

Steiner stared at him incredulously. "Does that mean we
attack from this point?"

"Of course," März said.

They stood in silence. From the direction of the factory a
Russian MG chattered now and then. Further to the south
a violent skirmish seemed to be going on. Heavy artillery
detonations boomed in unbroken succession. Before the mountains loomed dark clouds of smoke that stretched higher
and higher, dirtying the cloudless sky. Steiner looked at the
houses across the street. Their white stucco showed ugly
wounds; they glistened starkly in the cold morning sunlight. An uncomfortable sensation crawled down his spine.
"It's insane," he said softly. "I hope you realize what our
chances are."

"I do." März nodded indifferently. Steiner looked at the
men. They were working eagerly, as though the fence were

the last obstacle between them and a storehouse full of provisions. He laughed aloud. März looked up at him in astonishment. "What's the matter with you?"

"Nothing. I just thought of something funny."

"Of yourself, by any chance?"

"For once, no. I thought of a stupid rat desperately looking for a way into a trap."

"That certainly is funny," März replied. His face was deadly serious.

As Steiner started to turn away, the lieutenant gripped his shoulder. "Don't forget the flag. The commander wants it."

"He can use it to be wrapped in at his funeral," Steiner snapped. He went over to his men, who were sitting on the ground about sixty yards away.

"How does it look?" Schnurrbart held his cold pipe clenched between his teeth. His face looked sunken and weary. Steiner sat down beside him without replying. He leaned back against the fence and stared across the street.

"Are we supposed to attack here?" Kern asked fearfully. Steiner nodded.

Kruger propped himself up on his right elbow. "We won't get across," he stated. "This time we'll all be butchered."

"Maybe with a little luck . . ." This was Maag, and it was evident from his voice that he did not believe his own words.

Faber said nothing. The machine gun tucked between his legs, he stared absently at the ground.

Suddenly they all jerked at once. Above their heads, so close that they imagined they could feel the wind of their passage, a series of heavy shells swished by to explode behind them in the yard.

"It's starting," Steiner murmured.

On their stomachs, they pushed the slats somewhat to one side and watched the barrage. The next round drummed against the factory, and they saw the walls burst apart. The building vanished behind a yellow-black cloud of smoke that slowly mounted upward.

Crap, Steiner thought. The building was solid; there was no reason to think that a dozen holes in the walls would seriously weaken the enemy's resistance. His glance fell on a small black beetle that crawled under the fence and disappeared into a tiny hole. He swallowed. We're much too big, he thought. As he stared at the ground, aware that he was envying a beetle, he suddenly thought of Anne, and his throat contracted so that he had difficulty breathing.

The hellish concert above his head continued. Insanely loud, the shells howled above the roofs, cleaving the air and crashing into the factory. *Hooeeee-vumn, hooeeee-vumn*. It went on and on.

He turned his head and saw beside him Kern's sallow face. Kern lay on the ground, lips twitching, steel helmet pressed against the fence. Faber was squatting, the machine gun clutched in his hands, his eyes shut. Kruger and Schnurrbart were peering through the cracks in the fence at the factory yard, the skin over their cheekbones so taut it seemed on the point of ripping. On his other side was Maag, the freckles on the white skin of his face like drops of blood in snow.

There was an abrupt silence. Somewhere a piercing cry rang out. Steiner saw the men jump up, reach for the slats of the fence and tug at them. The big nails in the wood squealed as though several dozen doors were moving on rusty hinges, and the boards thumped to the ground. Then the yard lay before them. Smooth, flooded with sunlight. A slaughtering yard, Steiner thought, and began to run. Two hundred steps to the factory. Two hundred ridiculous steps to the gray basalt walls behind which the Russians lay. He felt his heart pounding against his ribs, sweat streaming down his face. He panted. Two hundred steps, twenty seconds. Since Anne plunged over the cliff two thousand years had passed, or was it more? Twenty seconds; it was ridiculous.

He heard his breath whistling, saw the scurrying shadows of the men to his left and right, felt biting dust in his eyes and stumbled and ran and gasped. They had covered half the distance when machine-gun fire blazed in their faces. They had taken a hundred steps, and they fell to the ground as though they had stumbled over a wire. Within ten seconds the company lay like a writhing, many-limbed animal in the factory yard; somewhere a man began to scream as though he had three voices. An instant later a second man began to scream, and another, then many. They lay screaming on the ground, and over them and into them pelted the bullets from half a dozen Russian machine guns.

Then came the artillery fire. The yard was transformed into a forest of darting fountains of smoke, as though the earth had broken open in a hundred places, and the screams of wounded and dying men were drowned out by the earsplitting explosions. Two paces away from Kern, Steiner stared at the one-time innkeeper, whose right arm stuck up into the air like a post, fingers curiously outspread. Two paces farther on Maag had his freckled face pressed against the ground as though he had discovered a shaft leading through the earth, as though he saw the blue sky above the Azores on the other side. Steiner lay between the two dead men and felt clods of earth raining down on his back, felt the hot breath of steel fragments hissing by, and in his head was nothing but a roaring which made him scarcely hear the infernal din in the factory yard. In the cemetery, he thought, closing his eyes.

He heard a voice calling his name, but did not stir. He stayed still, his thoughts flying and swooping in great circles, and he heard another voice saying: "And none of you will go without his reward. . . ." But it sounded unreal and remote. It must have been in a barracks yard, he thought. A voice ringing out across a barracks yard in which stood eight hundred men in new uniforms and shining boots. How far away was that? Six million steps and more, and across the factory yard it was only two hundred.

He raised his head and looked toward the road. A hundred paces from the fence, he thought; only half the distance. And between the detonations of the shells he saw several dozen men running, and throwing themselves to the ground, picking themselves up and racing on, until they vanished from sight. Suddenly he realized that it had been Schnurrbart's voice calling his name. At that he pushed himself up. He pushed himself away from the ground, and for a moment stood upright. As he turned around he saw März. The lieutenant came stumbling across the yard, eyes wild, mouth open, arms dangling slackly at his sides. Steiner heard him shouting, but he could not understand a word. When a shell struck near März, he tipped over as though his legs had been knocked from under him. Steiner ran toward him, looking neither to right nor to left. For a second he stared down at him, then slung the man over his shoulder and stumbled blindly through the fire. He ran like a machine, utterly without sensation, eyes closed, thinking: You will all receive your reward. All of you. He tripped over bodies, slid heavily into shell holes that opened before him, panted through dark clouds of smoke, until suddenly he saw the fence before him. The weight of the lieutenant seemed to increase tenfold. As Steiner ran across the street, his knees threatened to give in. Several men in a doorway were shouting at him; he saw a familiar face as Schnurrbart came running toward him. And then the tons of weight fell from his shoulder and he plunged into the vestibule of a house, where he lay groaning and half unconscious. You will all receive your reward, he thought again, and closed his eyes. There was a great stillness within him. . . .

Toward evening Kiesel entered the commander's room. He found the lieutenant colonel studying some papers which he quickly laid aside. His face expressed uneasiness and concern as he asked, "Well?"

"He was lucky," Kiesel replied, sitting down. "I found him at the clearing station. He had already been operated on and was out of ether when I came. By now he is probably . . ." Kiesel glanced at his wrist watch. "At this moment he must be on his way to the ferry. In a few days he'll be in a hospital back home."

"I'm glad for him and for you," Brandt said heartily. "What do you think your sister will say to that?"

Kiesel stared reflectively at the floor. "She will thank his lucky star," he replied. "His lucky star and Steiner."

The commander's head jerked up. "Steiner? What about Steiner?"

"If it were not for Steiner, he would have lain there and bled to death. Steiner carried him back. März told me about it himself."

"Can you guess what I am thinking?" Brandt asked softly. "I am thinking of what would have happened to März if I had accepted your recommendation and transferred Steiner. I can't help thinking of that now."

"I have already thought of it," Kiesel said.

Brandt looked down at him. "Do you remember what you said about Providence?"

Kiesel nodded silently. For a while Brandt stood motionless, looking over his head into a corner of the room. Then he returned to his chair and sat with head bowed.

Through the tall windows the ruins of the city towered into a fiery sky. The light of the setting sun flooded in through the window panes, casting bars of brightness on the intricate pattern of the rug. Kiesel watched as the sunlight neared the wall, flowing over the white-painted wood of the baseboard and almost imperceptibly crawling up the wallpaper. On an antique chest stood a plaster bust of Lenin staring popeyed at the leggy china closet on the opposite wall, in which a delicate Biedermeier tea service was arrayed. Rendezvous of the centuries, Kiesel thought, feeling an odd sense of grief.

The commander picked up a sheet of paper and raised his head. "Captain Morlock was here."

Kiesel raised his eyebrows expectantly. Captain Morlock was chief operations officer of Division. He seldom came down to the regiment; when he did, it was always on something of special importance. Controlling his curiosity, Kiesel waited. He watched Brandt consult the sheet of paper again. Finally he thrust it into a drawer which he carefully locked. "Top secret, for commanders only," he said tersely.

Kiesel's bright, intelligent eyes regarded him steadily. Then he said, "We're evacuating." It was not a question but a statement.

"How do you know?" Brandt asked.

"A guess. It's been in the air a long time."

Brandt nodded wearily. "The day is still secret."

"And why are we attacking?" Kiesel asked.

"Camouflage tactics. As long as we keep on attacking, the Russians won't expect us to evacuate the bridgehead. It has to be done, senseless as it seems."

"When do you think we'll go?"

"Today, tomorrow, the day after." Brandt shrugged. "We're waiting for the cue. The evacuation has been prepared down to the last detail. What bothers the big brass is the unexpected invasion of the Russians in Novorossiysk. They think it important for that to be cleaned up first."

"We're too weak," Kiesel said.

Brandt, who had been pacing the room, paused in front of an engraving in a gilded frame on the wall. He studied the print for a moment. Then he turned toward Kiesel again. "Morlock holds the same opinion. But we dare not leave anything untried. There's too much at stake. According to information reaching Division, the Russians have been concentrating their strength for months. It's going to be a race with time, and everything depends on whether we can carry out the step-by-step evacuation as planned. Novorossiysk is the first monkey wrench in the machinery." He went to the table and leaned over the map. "Vogel has reached the water front. Körner is still fighting around the center. Stransky is stuck in front of the factory, while his First and Third companies are brawling wtih the Russians somewhere and sending alarming radio messages. My picture of it is beginning to be balled up."

Kiesel stood up and looked over his shoulder at the map. "What is Stransky going to do?"

"I've ordered him to occupy the factory after dark. Triebig will lead the Second Company's attack. Let's hope they have more success than they did this morning. As long as the Russians hold the factory, they'll be able to keep their little bridgehead here. There seem to be four or five gunboats in the harbor."

"Hopeless," Kiesel murmured.

"Körner worries me most," Brandt remarked, rubbing his chin. "He hasn't advanced a yard and on both sides has exposed flanks which . . ." He was interrupted by the urgent shrilling of the telephone. "That may be Körner now," he said eagerly, answering. Then he frowned and looked up. "It's from Vogel. What . . ." He listened intently. Kiesel saw his features stiffen. He laid back the receiver and spoke dully: "Vogel is dead."

"Dead?" Kiesel changed color.

"They caught the battalion staff," Brandt said. "Suddenly broke in from the back of the house. Nobody knows where they came from." He leaned forward, probing Kiesel's pale face. "What are we going to do when we lose the war?"

The question was such a bolt from the blue that Kiesel started. He shrugged wearily. "Start life all over again," he said softly.

A dark frown passed over the commander's face. "You may, but not I. I'm too old to start life over again." His big head drooped. "It's no longer worth it."

"There are ways." Kiesel spoke without conviction.

"Certainly." Brandt nodded absently. "Certainly there are ways. Being a salesman, for example. Going from house to house and door to door. Can you imagine it?"

Kiesel did not reply. Several painful minutes passed, until Brandt laughed harshly. His whole body stiffened. "Perhaps we are thinking further ahead than is really necessary. There are other solutions. A hero's grave, for example, or Siberia, or running away across the lines to join General Paulus' National Committee. What do you think about that?"

Kiesel saw the rage and anguish in his face, and something of the commander's hopelessness affected him. "I would prefer the first," he answered.

"That surprises me," Brandt replied loudly. "I would have thought the last."

Kiesel felt that he was looking for a quarrel, and shook his head. "You misunderstand me. That would be an escape into self-deception, and in the long run you can't go on deceiving yourself."

"What about your ideology?" Brandt asked scornfully.

Kiesel looked down at his cigarette and remained silent. When the commander drummed his fingers impatiently on the table, he raised his head. His voice was cold. "I'll put it this way: in principle I can't enjoy a full dinner when others sitting beside me are hungry, especially when they wear the same uniform and have sworn the same oath as I have."

"I'm glad to hear that," Brandt said. His face relaxed. "There is no excuse for the Committee," he said harshly. "Germans call on Germans to desert although they know perfectly well what is awaiting them on the other side. Filthy scoundrels." He began to knead the skin above his cheekbones.

"I've never thought about that before," he went on. "But for several weeks now it's been weighing on me. I really don't any longer see what I'd do with myself if I should take off this uniform today."

"You're still a fine figure of a man," Kiesel said cautiously.

Brandt laughed contemptuously. "You mean I might marry again? Are you mad? I was forty when my wife died. Twelve years have passed since then, and I've become an inveterate bachelor. Don't bring that up." He lighted a cigarette and tossed the match to the floor, where it went on flaming, burning a tiny hole in the rug. They watched it without moving.

Their eyes met, and Brandt laughed bitterly. He pointed to the ugly black spot in the vivid design of the rug and said, "If I were a married man, I wouldn't do that sort of thing. But I'm too old to adjust to domesticity. Too old and full of idiosyncrasies."

"You would have to find the right woman," Kiesel replied.

"That happens only once. You know that as well as I. Why haven't you ever married?"

It was a challenge that struck Kiesel to the quick. He bristled as he said, "Don't you know?"

"Yes, I do know. There's more talk about you than you have any notion of. The division is full of gossip about it. If what they say is true, you were studying for the ministry until you got mixed up with some girl who later threw you over. Is that so?"

"They are well informed," Kiesel replied coldly.

"You should expect that," Brandt said. "You may think me tactless for saying it to you so bluntly. But I'm not one to talk around the bush. When I talk with somebody I want him to know where he stands. You've escaped into the uniform just as I did, and now that we are probably on the point of losing our uniforms, we're right back where we once were. I tell you frankly, I don't look forward to it."

Kiesel regarded him expressionlessly. "You can shoot yourself," he said brutally.

He saw the commander's eyes widen for a moment, but his voice was perfectly tranquil. "The thought is not new. Perhaps I shall some day take it up."

There was something in his face which Kiesel had never see before, which aroused his concern. "You mean that?"

"What do you think?"

"That's no solution," Kiesel said harshly.

Brandt shrugged. "It's no better or worse than the others. It's just—shall I say, more final."

"At first sight," Kiesel said.

Brandt waved that aside. "At last sight, which is what makes the idea appealing." He leaned across the table. "Listen to me carefully, Kiesel," he said in a controlled voice. "You have your philosophy and I have mine. I may envy you for your illusions, but I cannot take them seriously."

The patch of sunlight on the rug had meanwhile traveled to the ceiling where it clung in a corner, shrinking and fading. Kiesel sat rigidly in his chair. His eyes under half-shut lids were fiercely alert. "What do you mean by illusions?"

Brandt sighed. "For heaven's sake, don't start splitting hairs with me. I had illusions, too, Kiesel, but they possessed form and substance. I had my eye on one thing and another, until finally I picked the uniform. That was the greatest folly of my life, not that you could have told me so at the time. It was not that I had no other opportunities. There was a family business—you understand—but it wasn't enough for me. I had ambition, wanted to make a career. Well, did I succeed or not?" He laughed stridently. "Didn't make it to general, as I had hoped, but, still, regimental commander. There hasn't been time to go any further." He fell silent, rose quickly and went to the window where he stood with averted face, gazing out over the roofs.

"You can regard it as an episode," Kiesel said quietly.

Brandt shook his head emphatically. "That sort of thing is not an episode. It's what I have to show for my life. The top step, where I intended to rest, and I have spent fifty-two years reaching it." He turned around, propping his arms on the window sill. His face seemed shattered, but he was smiling. "Fifty-two years. I don't know anybody who started at the beginning again at the age of fifty-two. Not when all bridges were burned behind him."

"There are examples . . ." Kiesel began.

The commander cut him off. "Don't give me any of that. Public welfare case or monk or something. I'm not the type. I'm sick of it all, damn sick of it." At that moment the telephone rang. He went to the table and picked up the receiver. His body stiffened. "Herr General!"

The four of them sat around the table in silence. Schnurrbart was holding a worn letter case in his hands, leafing aimlessly through a number of papers. The only window in the room was shielded by a shelter-half so that no light would fall into the street. The flickering candle cast leaping shadows on the walls of the room. Now and then a machine gun chattered.

Schnurrbart lifted his head. "What'll we do with this stuff?"

"You can give it to Fetscher," Steiner replied. He sat with feet on the table, smoking. Now he held out his hand. "Let me see." As Schnurrbart handed the letter case to him, a picture fell out.

Kruger leaned forward with interest. "What is it?"

"A girl." Steiner held the picture up to the candle and studied the merry face with tight curls framing a clear forehead and crinkles of laughter around the mouth.

"Nice," Kruger murmured. "I wonder what she'll do when she gets the news."

"What's there for her to do?" Schnurrbart replied grumpily. "She'll buy herself a nice-looking black dress, and by two weeks she'll have forgotten him."

Faber shook his head reproachfully. "That's no way to talk. You don't know how they feel about it."

Steiner had turned the picture over. He read the words written in a rather childish handwriting on the back. "For my dear Kurt. Monika." Curious that his name was Kurt, Steiner thought. "Did any of you know his first name was Kurt?" he asked.

"Who?" Kruger asked.

"Maag, of course. I don't think I ever heard his first name."

"Neither did I," Schnurrbart said. "Was it?"

"Says so here," Steiner said. He replaced the picture in the letter case and turned to Faber. "Have you Kern's things?"

"No. They've already taken him away. He must be over at First Company. When I went, Maag was the only one lying there."

"Rotten business!" Schnurrbart shuddered. "You know what surprises me?" They looked up questioningly at him. "That they gave the job to the first platoon instead of us."

Steiner frowned. "That *is* funny. I'll bet there's something behind it."

"I've got that feeling too," Kruger said. "It's a suicide job, picking up the wounded and dead. And the Ivans kicking up the dust with their MG's in the yard."

"At any rate the attack has been called off," Schnurrbart said.

"What's that?" Kruger paused in his vigorous scratching of his head.

"It's obvious," Schnurrbart said. "If we were going to attack again, we wouldn't have to fetch the dead because we could do that a lot better once we were in the factory."

The reasoning seemed cogent. "Let's hope you're right," Kruger said. "I wouldn't like to run across there again. I thought we were all done for when the shooting started."

The memory of that wild flight through the artillery fire marked dark shadows upon his face, and the faces of the others darkened also. "It was sheer madness," Schnurrbart growled bitterly. "It serves them right, the damned heartless slave drivers. Why didn't they try it from the other side?"

"Higher strategy," Steiner said. He was about to stand up when the door opened and Triebig appeared. They stared at him without rising.

He addressed Steiner. "How many men do you have left?"

Steiner gave him a look of disgust. "I haven't counted them yet," he grunted.

"Then do so at once. You will attack in fifteen minutes. With a shock troop and from the south. When you are inside the factory, fire a green flare. That will be the signal for me to follow with the rest of the company. Order of the battalion commander."

There was a silence in the room. Triebig saw the masklike faces of the men and shrugged slightly. "Order of the battalion commander." he repeated in a somewhat softer voice. After a moment's hesitation he added, "Before I forget: you must bring down that flag. The commander wants it."

"To wipe his ass with?" Schnurrbart asked loudly.

Triebig whirled around. "Are you out of your mind? Stand up when I talk to you."

Steiner, at the lieutenant's last words, had put his feet up on the table again. He lighted a cigarette and let it droop from the corner of his mouth as he spoke. "You don't have to play the big shot here. Besides which, I'd advise you not to get on Schnurrbart's nerves. Since that last wound in his head he's got into the habit of firing at anything stupid enough to cross his path. Don't forget that he'll be in the factory before you."

"What has that to do with it?" Triebig asked sharply.

Steiner wagged his head pityingly and glanced at Schnurrbart, who was glaring narrow-eyed at the lieutenant. "Simple enough," Steiner explained. "If we get to the factory before you, you'll get there after us, and it just might happen that a stray bullet would meet you in the darkness." He watched calmly as Triebig's face turned pale. With his tongue he shifted the cigarette from the right to the left corner of his mouth.

Triebig stared at him. This was the first time Steiner had taken this tone to him in the presence of subordinates. To preserve a last remnant of authority, he would have to do something effective. But his fear of Steiner was even greater than his agitation. "I'll inform the commander of that statement, you can depend on it." His voice was shaking and he felt as though he might burst into sobs at any moment.

Steiner stared him down. "I don't know what good you think that will do you," he said. "Do you imagine you'll find anyone here to confirm your charges?" He turned to Kruger. "What were we talking about?"

The East Prussian grinned. "About the shock troop action."

"There, you see," Steiner said, turning to Triebig again. "You're an officer, aren't you? What do you need a big brother for?" His voice was full of contempt.

Triebig started to speak several times. Then he stared into the faces of the men as though imprinting them on his mind. "Very well," he whispered, and left the room.

After the door had closed behind him, there was a silence for several minutes. At last Faber spoke up. "If I hadn't been here, I wouldn't have believed it. There's going to be a big fuss, I imagine."

Steiner shook his head contemptuously. "There won't be a big fuss or a little one, but something else entirely, and very soon." He stood up and turned to Kruger. "How many of us are left?"

"About twenty."

"That's enough. Get ready."

As he went out of the room, the men reached for their gear. Kruger cursed. "What a damned swindle! How are a few poor bastards like us to occupy that whole factory? It's madness, I tell you." He had slung his assault pack on his back and now stood with his clenched fists leaning on the table. "Are you catching on?" he asked. They looked at him blankly, and he laughed furiously. "First Dietz, then Anselm and the doctor, then Hollerbach and Pasternack, and today Kern and Maag. You know what I think?" He looked at each of them in turn. "I don't think a single one of us is going to come out of this bridgehead alive. That's what I think."

Schnurrbart nodded. "I've known that for a long time. That's nothing new."

"So it isn't," Kruger whispered. He stood motionless for a few seconds. His glance fell on a crystal vase that stood on the table beside the candle. Suddenly he picked it up and hurled it with all his might to the floor. It shattered into a thousand pieces. He picked up a chair and hurled it at the sideboard filled with glasses and dishes. Fragments shot in all directions.

As he started to pick up the table, Schnurrbart jumped at him and held his arms. "Stop that!" he roared angrily. "I don't see what good this does, you damned crazy idiot." He pounded him hard on the chest. The blow brought Kruger to his senses abruptly. He dropped like a log into his chair.

When he looked up, he met Faber's eyes; the woodsman had been sitting motionless at the table all the while, face expressionless. Now he spoke. "You can't fight against it. You can see it coming, but you can't do anything about it, and that is good."

"That is good," Kruger aped him, raging. "What's good about our being butchered, what?"

"It's good any way it comes," Faber murmured. He said no more.

Kruger stared at his wooden face, biting his lip. Like a gravedigger, he thought, the man looks like a gravedigger. He bowed his head.

They sat in silence until Steiner returned. He merely glanced at the wreckage in the room, did not waste a word on it and beckoned the men to follow him.

The others were waiting in front of the house. They stood close together, wearing steel helmets and assault packs, and they talked in whispers. In a low voice Steiner gave them instructions. Before they started, Steiner tied ten stick grenades into a bundle. The platoon moved forward. The men kept close to the fence and followed the street around the factory yard. It was about eleven o'clock. Above the roofs hung a narrow crescent moon; the huge mass of factory buildings towered black and threateningly toward the stars. Further to the south artillery explosions rumbled steadily. Now and then tracer shells hissed past the gleaming white limestone slopes of the mountains lighted to the very tops by the glare of tremendous conflagrations. The line of houses past which the men were marching looked like an abstract stage set, the vacant windows gaping blackly out of the whitewashed walls.

Schnurrbart stayed beside Steiner. He was so fearfully tired and indifferent that even the impending assault could not wring any emotion out of him. He held his right hand over his gas mask so that it would not knock against his mess tin and said, "You'd think Triebig would have turned up again."

"What do you want with him?" Steiner replied crossly. "I'm happy not to see that bastard."

"Sure, so am I. But we ought to have discussed the details with him. He doesn't know where we'll be waiting for him."

Steiner snorted. "Do you know?" he asked testily. "He'll see where the flare comes from."

Schnurrbart glanced speculatively across the street. It turned sharply to the west at this point; they ought to be at the assault point in a moment. The fence on this side had been shattered by many shells, and they could see the factory building ominously close at hand beyond the crazily dangling pickets. Luckily it was so dark in the street that movement behind the fence could scarcely be detected. After another fifty yards Steiner stopped and waited until the men had closed ranks.

Kruger pressed through the group to him and whispered, "What now?"

"The place is right," Steiner answered. He turned to the men and explained his plan. "I don't know what it's like inside, but I imagine there'll be one long room. Perhaps with machinery in it. Once we've got ourselves established in the first floor, we'll fire the flare and wait for the others." He spoke to Schnurrbart. "You stay here with the boys. I'll try to get under the window and throw this thing in." He indicated the bundle of hand grenades which he carried in his right hand. "When it goes off, come over, and then in we go. Clear?"

"Clear enough," Schnurrbart said unwillingly. "But wouldn't it be better for us to go all together?"

"Nonsense. If they discover us, we're all through. Besides . . ." He dropped abruptly to the ground. From one of the lower windows a flare rose, hissed over their heads and smashed into the wall of a house. It dropped down and burned out on the ground. The men lay motionless, pressed against the fence. When all was dark again, Steiner turned his head and brought his mouth close to Schnurrbart's ear. "Did you notice which window?"

"I can see without glasses," Schnurrbart muttered. "Must be an MG there."

"Must be," Steiner agreed. He rose to his knees. The men shifted restlessly. Anxiously they eyed the silent factory front.

"Scheisse," Kruger muttered.

Steiner slung the tommy gun around his neck, grasped the bundle of grenades and cautiously crawled through the damaged fence. He continued to inch along on all fours. Halfway to the building he reached a deep shell hole. He dropped carefully into it and waited for the next flare. His shirt was sticking damply to his back, and he had to clench his teeth. Never before had he felt such intense fear. When he laid his hand on his arms, his whole body shook. Damn this hero's death, he thought, closing his eyes.

XIV

AFTER the hot exchange of words with Steiner, Triebig made his way straight to the battalion commander. Quivering with fury, he spilled out his story. "It's an impossible relationship," he concluded angrily, forgetting his customary servile manner.

Stransky sat at his desk, face indifferent. When Triebig finished, he shrugged disdainfully. "You know as well as I why the fellow takes such liberties. Legally there isn't much I can do about him. Legally, Lieutenant Triebig." He smiled maliciously. "But there are other ways. Happily there are other ways. Sit down." He looked thoughtfully up at the ceiling.

During the pause in the conversation Triebig examined the furnishings of the room. After the unsuccessful attack of that morning Stransky had looked around very carefully for a suitable command post and had finally decided on a third-floor flat facing the courtyard of a group of houses. "The higher the better," he had decided. "We don't know how the business will turn out, and if the Russians undertake a counterattack it's better to have them under us than over us."

The pause was prolonged. Finally Stransky seemed to come to a decision. His voice sounded vexed. "I would rather you had avoided that clash with Steiner." As Triebig opened his mouth to defend his conduct, Stransky raised his hand soothingly. "Never mind. What's done is done. I don't like it, but it can't be changed now. You will have to be all the more cautious." He glanced at his watch. "We don't have much more time. Steiner will start in five minutes, and you must follow him at once with the rest of the company. Whether or not he gets into the factory is his business. But you must make it yours to see that he never leaves it again. If you succeed, you'll be first lieutenant in a few days, as sure as my name is Stransky."

Triebig stared at him. "Do you mean that?"

Stransky smiled. "When I make such a statement, you have no reason to doubt it. Incidentally, I may as well tell you that I have already taken steps to have myself transferred back to France. I expect the order to come through any day now. Perhaps—" his smile deepened—"perhaps I can also do something for you in that connection. Or would you have any objection to continuing on as my adjutant in some French city?"

The news took Triebig so much by surprise that for a moment he merely gasped. All the humiliations he had suffered from Stransky were erased. The prospect of transfer made him slightly giddy. "You don't know how grateful I would be to you for that," he stammered at last.

Stransky nodded patronizingly. "You will have the opportunity to prove your gratitude—promptly." His voice changed; it rang like steel. "Get that creature Steiner off my neck and I guarantee that you will survive this war. He must not come back, not even if you have to kill him with your own hands. I want to know that he's dead, dead, dead."

Triebig involuntarily shrank from the savage expression on his superior's face. "I'll do everything possible," he said hastily.

But Stransky shook his head violently. "You must do more than everything possible. You must stop at nothing, and the more daring you are the higher I will value your achievement. Only manage it cleverly, so nothing is apparent. Bear in mind that I cannot cover you if the story should come out."

Triebig hesitated. The more he thought about it, the more frightened he became. But Stransky gave him little time for weighing the matter. He stood up quickly and placed a hand on his lieutenant's shoulder. "You have no cause to be concerned," he said quietly. "I'll make the business easier for you, as far as is in my power. Once you are in the factory with him, there will be a hundred opportunities; it will be up to you to seize one of them." His voice became persuasive. "In any case, it is the lesser evil. I know from reliable sources that the men in the bridgehead have been written off. There is no longer any intention of evacuating. Within two weeks at most the Crimea will be a sack with a closed neck. The Russians are close to Perekop now, and everyone south of Perekop will suffer the same fate as the Sixth Army. Do you want to be here then?"

"How do you know all that?" Triebig stammered through bloodless lips.

"I know. A relative of mine is in the Army High Command. Before that day comes I shall be on my way to France. France . . ." He shook Triebig by the shoulder. "Do you know what that means? It means life, Triebig, in Biarritz or Arcachon or Mont de Marsan or Paris. Think of it, man. Paris, Notre Dame, Champs Elysées, Montmartre . . . What the devil is there to consider?"

Triebig stared up at the man's flushed face, which seemed irradiated by an almost hysterical rapture, and swallowed hard.

He felt his scruples being swept away, and when Stransky went on to describe the fate that probably awaited Triebig if he remained here in the bridgehead, the lieutenant clapped his hands over his ears and jumped to his feet.

"No, no!" he exclaimed.

Stransky studied him with satisfaction. "You have the choice," he declared. "You can either go to the dogs somewhere in Siberia or guzzle champagne in France. Which do you prefer?"

"Steiner will not come back," Triebig said softly. "I am counting on your word—that you will take me with you to France. But may I know one thing?"

"What is that?"

Their eyes were locked as Triebig asked, "Why is it so important to you? If you are leaving here in a few days, it shouldn't matter to you what happens to Steiner."

Stransky stepped over to the window to stare down into the dark courtyard. "What happens to Steiner," he said at last, "is more important to me than whether we win or lose the war. But you will not understand that. It's my personal affair, Triebig. Go now. Otherwise you'll be too late. And don't neglect to keep me informed constantly by radio."

He waited until the door closed. Then he picked up the telephone and called the communications platoon leader. There were no new messages either by radio or telephone from the other companies. Biting his lip, he laid down the receiver. It's sickening, he thought.

Ever since Triebig had returned from the regimental command post that fatal evening, Stransky had had the feeling that he was sitting on a volcano. The regimental commander's threat had been so definite that in the past weeks he had not dared to do anything against Stiener. Consciousness of his impotence had given him some terrible moments. He could do nothing but wait for the proper time, but that time seemed to have come at last. Six feet underground—that was where Steiner belonged. Once this account was settled he could leave the East behind, even without the Iron Cross. At bottom it was Steiner's fault that he was not already wearing one.

So absorbed was he in his painful thoughts that it took several buzzes from the field telephone before he started up and absently reached for the receiver. But as soon as he recognized Kiesel's voice he became keenly alert. He listened attentively to the adjutant's words, and his face paled. What was the fellow saying? Call off all attacks immediately, set up defenses along whatever line had been reached and await further orders. And then: "Has Triebig started yet?"

"No," Stransky stammered. "That is . . ." He paused and thought feverishly.

Kiesel's voice rang coldly in his ears. "Beg pardon?"

"I'll check," Stransky said hastily. "One moment, please."

He dropped the receiver to the table, rushed out of the room to the hallway and into a room facing the street. As he leaned out of the window he saw a number of men standing together, barely recognizable in the darkness. He heard Triebig's muted voice issuing orders. Stransky opened his mouth to call. Then he compressed his lips and watched stony-faced as the company started moving, marched across the street and seconds later disappeared from sight. He brushed the back of his hand over his forehead and felt the moisture. He hurried back into his room and took up the telephone.

"The attack has already begun," he said in a controlled voice. "I can't stop it now." He heard Kiesel exchanging hasty words with someone.

Then the hated voice was in his ear again: "Are they advancing?"

"I have no information yet. As soon as I know details, I'll inform you."

"The commander wishes you to. What do your other companies report?"

"For the past half hour I've had no news from them," Stransky replied. "Couriers are on the way. The last reports said that the Third Company was close to the water front, while the First has scarcely advanced at all; it's fighting practically in the assembly area."

"Very well, Captain Stransky. Make sure that the companies are informed at once. It's of prime importance that they establish contact on their right and left. If it should turn out that the factory cannot be taken, withdraw your Second Company to the street and inform us."

As Stransky laid down the receiver, he thought he heard the sudden blaze of guns. He stepped quickly to the window. He had not been mistaken. The attack on the factory had begun.

Some three minutes might have passed when Steiner heard the soft pop produced by the firing of a flare. Without opening his eyes, he waited the necessary period. Then, with the yard in darkness again, he crept cautiously out of the shell hole. Now that the decisive moment was only a few seconds away, his excitement had abruptly vanished. As he crawled foot by foot toward the black factory wall, his senses were keyed to a pitch of alertness. His eyes were fixed on the dark window opening behind which he guessed the Russian machine gun was posted.

He had come within ten paces of the building when a piercing cry rang out so unexpectedly that he froze. There followed a succession of hasty words, and before Steiner could recover from his initial start of terror, the factory yard was bathed in the merciless light of a flare which hung like a great arc lamp above him. Simultaneously a machine gun began to chatter. The fearful sound of steel-jacketed bullets hissing by, gashing the dry, sandy soil around him, speeding past his head with an ugly whine, revived all his reflexes. Before the traversing fire from the invisible machine gunner could touch him, he bounded the last few yards, slammed heavily into the stone blocks of the factory wall and with all the strength of despair hurled the concentrated charge of ten hand grenades through the yawning void of the narrow window above his head. Then he dropped full length on the ground, pulled the strap of the tommy gun over his head and waited. The MG fire swept wildly across the factory yard; it must be coming from one of the windows farther to the west. Above his head he heard several loud shouts. In his excitement he bit his lips till they bled. He was beginning to fear he had not pulled the fuse cord of the charge properly when, inside the building, there was a crash as though the roof had fallen in.

Before the last rumble of the blast had ceased, Steiner swung himself up on the window sill, jumped off into space, though he could not estimate how high the window was, and landed safely beside a huge machine. The ends of the long hall were lost in darkness. The room seemed to be occupied by a large number of machines of the most varied types, and by several dozen small lathes installed along the windows. The MG fire had stopped, but from the further end of the hall he could hear the hasty tramp of nailed boots along the stone blocks of the floor. The sound mounted to a wild drumming as Steiner emptied the magazine of his tommy gun in that direction.

As he reloaded he heard loud shouts from the yard. From the window he saw them coming, running shoulder to shoulder, rifles held high, Schnurrbart and Kruger leading. Seconds later they poured in through the windows, stumbled over the lathes in the darkness, knocked one another against the machines and shouted, until Steiner's sharp voice restored order. He issued commands precisely and swiftly. While the last of the men were still coming in, he led a rush to the far end of the long hall. A door led to a narrow corridor on the long side of the room, and a few minutes later the entire first floor of the south wing was in their possession. They had encountered no serious resistance.

"You'll get the Knight's Cross for this," Schnurrbart said. He stood beside Steiner in the doorway, scanning their immediate neighborhood. "Crazy place, this." He pointed to the long corridor which ran parallel to the machinery room. "I wonder where that leads."

"Must go to the yard," Steiner replied. "The tower must be up at the front end. Perhaps a stairway leads up." He glanced speculatively at the dozen windows in the left side of the corridor and started cautiously toward one of them. But as soon as he moved a few steps away from the door, a Russian MG let loose. The bullets rattled through the windows. The men dropped to their knees and crawled hastily back through the door into the main hall. The others had meanwhile distributed themselves along the windows.

"No use," Schnurrbart growled, glumly rubbing his hairy chin. "At any rate they can't get in again."

"And we can't get out," Steiner said. "Let's fire that flare."

They sent up the signal and before the light faded made a thorough inspection of the huge room. There were two doors, one on either end, each leading out into the corridor. Although they examined every nook and corner and even looked under the machinery, they found no trace of any Russians. They did find an elevator in the right hand corner of the hall. Behind an iron double door, both halves of which stood wide open, yawned a dark shaft. When Steiner flashed his light down into it, he could see a massive platform hanging in iron guide rails on both sides. It was operated by strong steel cables. His attention was immediately attracted to a row of steel rungs attached at intervals of a foot or so to the front face of the shaft and extending both up and down until they were lost in darkness. They were covered by a thick layer of dust. Upward he could not see to the top of the shaft.

There was no time to study the elevator shaft more closely, for the rest of the company arrived then. In an unfriendly voice the lieutenant inquired about the state of affairs.

"We have to occupy the windows and investigate the corridor," Steiner declared. "How strong are we?"

"About fifty men." Triebig stood with his back to a window, looking uneasily up and down the hall.

"Not many," Steiner said. "I would suggest that we secure the hall with half our men and use the other half to investigate the corridor leads. Perhaps we'll run into a stairway leading to the upper floors."

"That's silly," one of the men objected. Steiner recognized Sergeant Schulz.

"Have you any better ideas?" Steiner asked coldly.

"I'm for our sticking together," Schulz replied. "We won't get far with twenty-five men. In fact, we couldn't occupy this factory if we had a lifetime."

"We must keep our retreat open," Steiner declared. "It's sure we can't hold this building permanently with fifty men. Once the Russians find out how weak we are, they'll make things hot for us."

Schulz growled something under his breath, but when Triebig agreed to Steiner's suggestion he said no more. Angrily he sat down on a machine and let his legs dangle.

Steiner turned to Triebig. "I would suggest that you post an MG outside by the fence. If the Russians should get there before us, our way across the yard will be cut off."

Triebig rejected the suggestion. "We have only three MG's. I can't spare one of them. Besides, I don't think it will occur to the Russians to do that. They need their men to occupy the other floors."

"Whatever you think. I've warned you." Steiner looked around for Schnurrbart, standing near by with Kruger and Faber and paying close attention to the discussion. "Get your men together," he ordered them. "We'll look the situation over now."

"What about the elevator?" Schnurrbart asked.

"That comes later. First we'll try the stairs. If that doesn't work, we can always break our bones on the iron ladder."

"Nice prospect," Kruger grumbled. He looked around the room. All the windows had been occupied by sentries meanwhile, and the rest of the company stood around Triebig, who was talking rapidly with Sergeant Schulz.

"Well, let's try it," Schnurrbart said. He and Kruger assembled their groups, and Steiner went to the door on the right. All was still in the corridor. Through the window he could see into the back yard. Several trucks parked there were undoubtedly usable; they must have belonged to the factory. He turned to the right. Here he could not use his flashlight, since its glow would be seen from the yard. Groping his way forward in the darkness, he kept close to the left-hand wall. He went about thirty feet before the hall ended at a closed door. By feel Steiner decided that it opened outward.

"Watch out," Schnurrbart warned him. Close behind Steiner, he watched anxiously as Steiner reached for the latch. The rest of the men stood pressed against the wall, holding their weapons ready to fire.

The unnatural stillness throughout the entire factory made Steiner nervous. Instead of proceeding cautiously, he kicked out violently at the door, knocking it wide open; at the same time he threw himself to one side.

The consequences were breath-taking and frightful. Through the pitch-black doorway half a dozen Russian tommy guns barked. The cone of fire whipped down the corridor, whirling the men away from the wall as if the rough stone paving blocks of the door had suddenly been transformed into glare ice. The men toward the front were protected by the dead angle, but those further back were helplessly exposed. The animal screams of men who had been hit sounded down the corridor.

Steiner huddled against the wall. Although he had half reckoned with such a possibility, for a few seconds he was paralyzed by fright. Then he feverishly pulled a hand grenade out of his belt, unscrewed the safety cap and pulled out the button. He waited a full three seconds before he tossed the grenade through the door. From the corner of his eye he saw Schnurrbart also throwing a grenade. The detonations rumbled so violently in the narrow corridor that Steiner clapped his hands to his ears, deafened for a moment. Paying no attention to what was going on behind his back, he leaped into the doorway and began blazing away blindly into the darkness. The Russian guns had stopped firing. He thought he heard hasty cries. From somewhere sounded a dull thud as if a heavy door had been slammed shut. Then silence.

When he switched on his flashlight, he saw several steps leading down into a continuation of the corridor at a slightly lower level. In front of him lay the twisted bodies of two Russians. Raising the beam of his flashlight, he saw that the corridor made a right-angle turn and apparently continued on toward the yard. For a second he stood undecided. Then several loud explosions made him whirl around. He bumped against Kruger, who shouted, "They're throwing hand grenades through the windows."

Schnurrbart also came up behind him and urged him to hurry.

Steiner grasped the latch and drew the door closed behind him. "Back to the big room," he said.

From the yard the Russian MG began firing again, raking the row of windows. Further ahead two or three hand grenades exploded. Several men were working feverishly to get the wounded out of the corridor. In the main hall Triebig stood excitedly at one of the windows, barking out a succession of meaningless orders. He caught sight of Steiner and swooped down on him. "What the devil have you done?" he shouted wildly. "Half your platoon is knocked out; did you know that?"

"If you'd been leading them, not one of those men would have come back," Steiner snapped. "Am I the platoon commander or you?" To Schnurrbart he said. "Where is Faber?"

"At the front door with his MG. What'll we do?"

The men were still busy with the wounded, who were being laid on the floor between two big machines. There were eight or ten stretched out there.

"Shall we try the elevator?" Schnurrbart asked.

"We can't get into the yard," Steiner said. "There's no other way although it's insane. If they're up above, they can knock us off as we climb."

"The whole attack on this coffin is insane anyway." Kruger laughed savagely. "And that genius has already sent off a big-mouthed radio message. Factory taken and so on."

"Who?" Steiner asked quickly.

"Triebig. We have a radio section with us, you know. They're up there in the corner, communicating with Battalion."

"I didn't know that," Steiner said.

Triebig was bickering with Sergeant Schulz. "You need not tell me what to do and what not to do," he was saying. "We have orders to take the factory, and that's all there is to it." He caught sight of Steiner.

"What do you think?" Schulz asked Steiner violently. "Do you think we can ever take this building?"

"Sure, with several tons of dynamite and a hundred Stukas, why not?" Steiner addressed Triebig. "We're going to try it up the elevator now. Four of us at first. If we reach the top, I'll signal."

"And if you don't reach the top?" Triebig asked.

"Then you can order us a state funeral. But don't rejoice too soon."

At the elevator shaft Schnurrbart and Kruger were waiting for him, staring up the opening.

"Who's going?" Kruger asked.

"We three and Faber. Get him." Steiner slung the tommy gun around his neck and collected hand grenades from the other men. Then he felt for the rungs.

All the men not posted as sentries thronged around the shaft and watched breathlessly as he slowly started climbing. Someone called after him, "The lieutenant says you're not to forget the flag."

"The lieutenant can kiss my ass," Steiner retorted. He paused and looked down. Seeing Schnurrbart swing himself into the shaft, he reached for the next rung. He felt as if he could not tell up from down. It was so dark that he shut his eyes and depended wholly on his sense of touch. But as yet he felt no fear.

Surprised and instantly on his guard, Stransky greeted Kiesel coldly. It was unusual, to say the least, for the regimental adjutant to call on him at his command post.

"Do sit down." He gestured toward a chair. "To what do I owe the honor?"

"I have orders for you," Kiesel said curtly. "May I see your map?" Stransky spread the tactical map out on the table. Kiesel took a pencil from his pocket and began to explain. "You will withdraw this morning at four o'clock to this line." He traced the line with his pencil. "About five miles northeast of here, at the western exit of the big tunnel. Do you see?"

Stransky leaned over the map and nodded.

"To your right is the Third, to your left the Second Battalion," Kiesel continued. "As soon as you have occupied this position, the lieutenant colonel will expect you at Regiment. Inform your companies. What is your Second Company doing?"

Stransky picked up a sheet of paper from the table. "The last bulletin came in ten minutes ago. See for yourself." He handed the message form to Kiesel.

" 'Factory building occupied without losses,' " Kiesel read aloud. " 'Mopping up has begun. Triebig.' " He nodded approvingly and laid down the paper. "They are not to take any more needless risks. Send a radio directive to that effect. We must conserve our forces. What is the situation with your other companies?"

"Somewhat more stabilized. Only they can't really make contact. The gaps between the companies are too large to close with available manpower. At night practically impossible."

"The eternal evil. Huge sectors and no men to occupy them. If we had one battalion more it would be . . ." He broke off as the telephone rang.

Stransky lifted the receiver. After the first few words his face creased into lines of vast astonishment. He laid down the receiver. "It was the artillery observer who has been watching the factory through his night glasses," he said distractedly. "He has just seen the flag pulled down from the factory tower. I wouldn't have thought it possible."

"What?" Kiesel asked quickly.

Stransky realized that he had made a mistake. He gave an

embarrassed laugh. "The whole thing," he answered evasively. "I wouldn't have thought Triebig would succeed in getting as far as the top of the tower."

Kiesel studied him closely. "What makes you think it is Triebig?"

"Lieutenant Triebig is in command of the company," Stransky replied aloofly.

"Indeed? Had you given orders for the flag to be taken down?"

"Would that be so odd? The flag was undoubtedly a control point for the Russian artillery. I had no idea we were going to pull out and thought it essential for the flag to come down."

"But you assumed it was impossible?"

"As troop commander one gives the right orders irrespective of their feasibility. If aggressive action always depended on its probable outcome, we would never attack at all."

"You're partly right," Kiesel said. "But there is a difference between operations undertaken for strategic significance and those undertaken merely for prestige. Did you by any chance order Sergeant Steiner to fetch that flag?"

The bluntness of the question caught Stransky off balance. "What makes you think that?" he parried.

Kiesel's voice was hard as he answered. "A guess. Captain Stransky, I will tell you something. There are two persons in this world who mean a great deal to me, and Sergeant Steiner saved the life of one of them."

"I don't know what you refer to," Stransky said. "Are you speaking of your brother-in-law?"

"Yes, my brother-in-law, Lieutenant März. You know that he was wounded. Steiner carried him back. It surprises me that you have not yet heard about it."

"Lieutenant Triebig didn't mention it." Stransky shrugged. It took him a moment to adjust to the new situation. When he spoke, his tone was reserved and he chose his words carefully. "Sergeant Steiner is to my knowledge a platoon leader in Second Company. What orders he receives come from Lieutenant Triebig."

"That may be," Kiesel said frostily. "But in case it really was Sergeant Steiner who brought down that flag, I hope the assignment was not given to him with a certain intention." He stood up.

"Will you express yourself somewhat more clearly?" Stransky asked.

Kiesel shook his head. "If my interpretation is correct, I spoke clearly enough. I might, however, add a general suggestion."

"Directed toward whom?"

"Answer that yourself," Kiesel said contemptuously. "My point is that it is risky to play Providence. Many a nasty wish has boomeranged."

Stransky rose slowly to his feet, his face betraying the intensity of his effort to control himself. "That sounds like a threat."

"I never bother to threaten," Kiesel retorted. "Justice does not require advance notice." On the way out he turned briefly. "You will be informed of the position of the new regimental command post."

He let the door slam behind him. Back at the command post he seized the first opportunity to talk with the commander. He urged the immediate transfer of Steiner with such forcefulness that Brandt could not conceal his astonishment.

"I don't know why you are so agitated," he said patiently. "Frankly, I no longer care to meddle with the business. I've given Steiner a chance and I've given Stransky a chance. Let them now settle with each other. What made you go to Stransky, anyway? I needed you."

The commander picked up the telephone, called Captain Körner and talked briefly with him. Then he turned to Kiesel again. "It looks as though we have switched parts," he said harshly. "At least in our relationship to Steiner. I don't want to tell you what to do, but I assure you, it isn't worth it. Believe me, it isn't worth it. Steiner has already come to the point that it has taken me fifty-two years to reach. You'll have no more success with him than I have had, and you'll be kicked in the teeth, besides."

He was silent, his eyes fixed emptily at some spot far beyond Kiesel. Then his sagging shoulders straightened. "Take four or five men, drive to our new command post and get the quarters ready. We will follow in two hours. Send the car back to me." When Kiesel did not respond immediately, Brandt snapped, "Did you hear me?" Kiesel nodded, but did not move. "What are you waiting for?" Brandt asked, frowning.

Somewhere in the vicinity several heavy shells exploded, and Kiesel waited until the din had faded before he spoke. "Permit me one question," he said.

"Yes?"

"What point has Steiner reached?"

Brandt studied him, his own expression noncommittal. Then he picked up his belt which lay on the table with pistol holster attached. "This," he said tersely, slapping the leather holster. "Just this. Is there anything else you want to know?"

"Thank you." Kiesel left the room, his face gray.

Steiner had counted one hundred of the iron rungs when his hand, groping for the next failed to find it. Carefully he felt the wall on his left until he encountered a depression which must be a doorway. He called down in a whisper to Schnurrbart, whose panting breaths were growing louder beneath him, and waited until he felt Schnurrbart's hand touch his boot. He told Schnurrbart to switch on his flashlight. By the bright beam he was able to orient himself. About six feet above his head was the roof of the shaft, to which the heavy elevator mechanism was attached. On his left, an easy step away, he saw the footwide base of the iron door. The door resisted the pressure of his hand. It was undoubtedly bolted from outside, and for a few seconds Steiner was in a quandary.

"What's the matter?" Schnurrbart whispered. He stood with his right arm hooked around a rung, still holding the flashlight. Steiner glanced down. Kruger and Faber were immediately below, and he ordered them to climb down twenty rungs and wait there. Then he took two stick grenades from his belt and unscrewed the safety caps.

"We'll have to blow it open. Buckle yourselves to the rungs with your belts."

"The stuff will fall on our heads," Schnurrbart objected.

"Nonsense. You're safe if you press close to the ladder. The door will blow open outward. Get down."

Grumbling, Schnurrbart climbed downward. He was sweating and the air in the shaft was stale. When he thought of the yawning depths below him, he had to close his eyes to repress a feeling of giddiness. A warning cry from below indicated that he had reached the others.

"What's up?" Kruger wanted to know.

"He wants to blow the door open," Schnurrbart growled, flashing the light up.

Kruger cursed. "He's plain mad."

"That's what I said." Schnurrbart put the flashlight in his mouth for a moment, unbuckled his belt and drew it around a rung. The others followed his example. When Steiner called down to ask whether they were ready, Schnurrbart answered crossly, "We're as ready as we'll ever be. You'll finish us off with your wild ideas."

Quickly Steiner came racing down the ladder to press himself against the rungs just above their heads. The explosion will be heard throughout the building, Schnurrbart had time to think. Then there was a booming crash as though the shaft were collapsing. Above their heads scraps of iron hurled against the walls, and the air blast threatened to wrench their cramped fingers from the rungs. They could already see Steiner scrambling up and before they could detach their belts from the rungs he had disappeared into the wall of the shaft.

Seconds later they stood panting and excited beside him, staring into a broad corridor with large windows through which the reflected light of the burning city shone. On their left were doors, probably leading to offices. Steiner quickly tried these and found them locked. Kruger was examining the door of the shaft. The force of the explosion had torn the bolting device right out of the concrete blocks and blown the door outward. The trick had worked, and they quickly regained their confidence.

Only Kruger was still worried. "What do you figure to do now?" he asked Steiner.

Steiner looked thoughtfully out of a window at a fantastic vision. All along the water front and in the center of the city burning houses stood like gigantic torches against a star-studded sky. The artillery fire had quieted. But through the smashed windowpanes rifle fire could be heard distinctly, rising and falling in intensity and seeming to come from all parts of the city.

Steiner turned around. "We'd better call the others. Until they get here, we can't do anything."

They went back to the shaft and Schnurrbart moved his flashlight in circles. Kruger felt as if he were stooping over a bottomless well. The signal was immediately answered from below. The dancing light from the pitchy darkness seemed to come from another world. "They've seen it," he breathed. "We're lucky bastards."

They waited in suspense. A few seconds passed. Then a dull thud reached their ears, at first inexplicable. There followed so piercing and frightful a cry that they reeled back from the opening. They had heard many kinds of screams. They knew how a man roared when the glowing hot iron of a shell splinter struck into his flesh, when a bullet tore away his intestines or shattered his genitals. But the sound that came up from below was not one of these. There was nothing human about that scream. It filled the entire shaft and did not stop until it was cut off by the chatter of a Russian tommy gun. Abruptly and terribly there was utter silence.

"What was that?" Schnurrbart whispered. None of the others answered.

Steiner took several steps back and went to a window. He peered down into the courtyard. Finally he turned to the men.

"We'll have to find the stairs. We won't get back down that shaft."

He ran with catlike steps down the corridor, the men following. They passed a number of closed doors and at last came up against a wall. On their right a staircase led down.

Behind an open door on the left a few steps were visible; probably these went up to the tower. Steiner stood hesitant. Then he told himself that the five minutes more or less would not matter.

Without a word of explanation he scaled the narrow winding staircase. Schnurrbart followed. They tried to move quietly, but their footsteps echoed with dreadful loudness on the stone steps, which went on and on, winding upward through impenetrable darkness. Finally Steiner stopped and called out a whispered order for the men to wait until he came back. Then he went cautiously on.

Suddenly he heard an indistinct murmur from further up. He dropped to his knees and crawled, careful not to make a sound. The murmuring became louder and more distinct. He could make out individual words. Gray light trickled into the narrow tube of the stairwell, and after one more turning he saw above him a door which was closed except for a narrow crack. He raised himself to his knees, slipped the tommy gun from his neck and listened. For a moment he wondered whether he ought to forget the flag. No, he would not give up now that he was so close. With infinite care he pushed against the crack in the door.

The room was rectangular, quite bare, with windows running around three sides. The glass in most of them was intact. On the right side stood four men in Russian uniforms looking down at the burning city. They were talking unconcernedly in loud voices. Two of them were evidently officers; they wore caps and raincoats under which their high boots were visible. Now that his eyes had grown accustomed to the dim light, Steiner could make out two small boxes on the floor—obviously radio apparatus. Advance artillery observation post. The thought flashed through his mind that they must have heard the explosion that blew open the doors. Why had they not acted? Then all his keyed-up tension gave way abruptly to a sense of relief that made him feel almost gay.

With a kind of eager curiosity he raised his tommy gun. For the fraction of a second he felt inhibited; those backs turned unsuspectingly to him somehow troubled him, and he could not refrain from uttering a hissing noise. He saw the masklike planes of their faces as they turned, had time to observe the drawing-in movements of their necks and their arms, and then he pressed the trigger. The lifeless steel in his hands changed into a roaring, jerking creature that sent the bodies of the Russians spinning as though an invisible lash had struck them. Steiner wondered at how silently they died. Like animals, he thought, and lowered his gun. He felt sick. As he kicked the door in, a frantic trampling sound on the staircase behind him, and Schnurrbart's voice called out. A second later they came swiftly around the next winding of the stairs, weapons held high.

Steiner assured them that everything was in order, and Kruger let loose a string of relieved curses. "Always the same," he griped as he mounted the last few steps. "The bastard was just trying to scare us again. I'll bet there wasn't . . ."

As they entered the room they saw the dead Russians. Steiner stood with his back against the row of windows, his eyes fixed on a narrow iron door in the rear wall, apparently the opening to the peak of the tower.

The men stepped closer to the bodies and looked down at them, shaking their heads. "A radio section," Schnurrbart said. He looked over at Steiner, who was changing the empty magazine of his gun. "Nice work. Didn't they see you?"

"It was too dark for me to introduce myself," Steiner replied. He strode over to the iron door and tried it. It was unlocked. "We'll get that flag now," he said. "Schnurrbart can come with me. You two wait until we're back; you have to stay to keep our retreat open."

"What do you want the stinking old flag for?" Kruger remonstrated. "If the Russians catch on to what's happening up here, we'll never get back down."

Schnurrbart sided with Kruger, urging that they find the quickest way down again.

But Steiner would not listen. "It isn't the flag that matters; it's something else entirely. If you feel things are getting too hot for you, you can run for it. I'm not keeping you." He turned to the door.

"Damned mule," Schnurrbart grumbled, following him.

They found themselves again on the worn steps of a winding staircase even narrower than the other. The stairs rose steeply into a pitchy dark room. Steiner sent the beam of his flashlight hastily around it. The room was windowless and circular, the floor coated with dust. In the center was an iron ladder with wide flat rungs which led to a rectangular opening in the ceiling. At the top of the ladder Steiner encountered a wooden trap door which yielded to the pressure of his hands. He raised it, and a moment later they stood on the roof of the tower with the stars above them. The roof was flat, ringed by a knee-high wall. In one corner, fastened to the wall by iron clamps, the creaking flagpole pointed toward the sky. The flag fluttered clumsily like a big, dark shadow in the fresh breeze that blew from the sea and cooled their hot faces.

Quiet had settled over the city. All was still and dark. Only here and there fires still smoldered, casting a glow into the gloomy gorges of the streets and now and then raining sparks on the roofs. From the elevation of the tower the fires seemed altogether harmless, and the red window openings looked like lanterns. The mountains reached toward the stars, and the Milky Way blazed in a bright arc from horizon to horizon.

"I wonder which one is ours," Schnurrbart said.

"Which what?" Steiner asked.

Schnurrbart waved his hand at the sky. "Which star, I mean. My mother always used to say each of us had one." He was silent, then he asked, "By the way, have you still a grudge against me?"

"What about?"

"Oh, I thought maybe about that business at the bridge, back in the woods."

"I don't know what you're talking about," Steiner said.

"You're just saying that," Schnurrbart muttered skeptically.

"We're not children any more," Steiner said curtly. "A lot of water has passed under the bridge since then. I've forgotten about it. I've forgotten a great deal."

"That's good," Schnurrbart whispered. Obeying a sudden inspiration he added, "Anne too?"

A few seconds passed before Steiner answered, "No. Not her. Never."

Schnurrbart averted his eyes. "What she must have meant to you!"

"That's enough!" Steiner said. With both hands he pulled down the flag. The rusty rollers screeched, and he had to tug hard at the cloth before he could separate it from the wire. They folded it carefully. Then Steiner strapped it to his assault pack and returned to the trap door.

In the lower room Kruger and Faber waited impatiently for them. Quietly they descended the winding staircase and reached the corridor below.

Steiner peered toward the elevator shaft at the other end of the corridor. Not a sound reached their ears. Slowly they went down the stairs to the next floor. Here, too, they paused for a few seconds, listening hard for suspicious sounds in the darkness. Steiner was about to continue when Schnurrbart suddenly held him back. Muffled, but distinctly audible, the din of violent shooting reverberated in the stairwell.

"That must be from the yard," Steiner breathed. "They're attacking the company."

Schnurrbart relaxed his tight grip on Sterner's arm. "What do we do?"

"We must get down. If Triebig runs for it, we'll be stuck in this trap. Let's go."

Disregarding caution, they pelted down the stairs. Suddenly a sharp outcry dropped like a stone at their feet. On the landing below stood a Russian looking up at them. Without thinking Steiner raised his tommy gun. The staircase resounded with the cracking of the shots. The Russian fell.

The four of them leaped over the body, and simultaneously the whole corridor came to life. Doors flew open, men shouted, boots thundered over the paving blocks; a random salvo spattered over their heads. Ducking, they raced on down the stairs, tearing around the banisters. Behind them the racket grew more terrifying from floor to floor.

They reached the end of the staircase. It was blocked by a door that must lead out into the yard, and Steiner desperately tugged at the latch. Behind them footsteps boomed like an avalanche. The searing beams of flashlights ate into the darkness and scraps of words in Russian shrieked in their ears. Panting for breath, they stood still, their eyes frantically searching for a way out.

Kruger saw the other door first. A corner alongside the stairs, a big wooden box, and beside it a narrow door—unlocked. Beyond it more steps into a black tunnel. As they plunged on, total darkness wrapped them like a blanket. Steiner switched on his flashlight. To left and right ran a long, narrow underground corridor. A few iron pipes were attached to the low ceiling, and there were doors on both sides. And in the background impenetrable darkness.

But there was no time to consider—the Russians had reached the entrance to the cellar. Steiner turned to the right. They raced down the narrow tube, only the cones of light from their flashlights severing the darkness. Behind them several shattering explosions boomed. Hand grenades, Steiner thought. He ducked even lower. Any moment now the Russians would be down here with their tommy guns. The corridor seemed to go on forever. No branches, nothing but doors, doors, doors. Every one of those doors concealed a rattrap, and Steiner knew it. Once they were caught in one of those holes, the Russians would have no trouble smoking them out. It was hopeless. He halted so suddenly that the others bumped into him.

"What?" Schnurrbart panted.

"Shut up," Steiner whispered. "Put out your lights and keep going."

"What about you?"

"I'll follow you; go on, damn it." As the men ran on, he flung himself flat on the ground and began to fire blindly into the darkness.

Schnurrbart wanted to stop again. But Kruger's fist caught him hard in the back. "Go on, go on!" They continued running until, in the darkness, they slammed up against a wall.

Their hearts jumped. The corridor turned at a right angle here and led toward a patch of light against which the shadowy outlines of several men could be seen. They stood motionless in an open doorway, and they wore steel helmets. German steel helmets.

Schnurrbart uttered a cry of disbelief and rushed toward the men, shouting, "Sergeant Steiner here, don't shoot! It's us —Sergeant Steiner!" He stormed out of the darkness toward the light. With every step he took his jubilation grew; he could think of nothing but: Saved, we're saved! Already he thought he could distinguish Triebig, standing in the midst of the men, raising his hand. Schnurrbart overlooked the motion. He saw only the familiar uniforms, and he thought of the captured flag. Steiner was the luckiest bastard born and with him a fellow could pull the stars from the sky. By God, the luckiest bastard born! Joyously he threw up his arms. The stars, he thought, the stars from the sky.

Then something fell at his feet and he staggered. He managed to remain on his feet, and he tried to regain his balance. *"Verdammt,"* he stammered, throwing his head back, uncomprehending. With abrupt horror he felt something striking his body. It was as though his chest, his abdomen, were being torn open; fiery pain darted up to the roots of his hair. They're crazy, he thought, sinking to his knees. The rumbling stopped and he saw innumerable shimmering points plummeting toward him. The stars, he thought again.

Then he suddenly heard his mother speaking to him; he knew instantly it was her voice. As he tilted forward from the waist, he smiled distortedly. The stars gathered together, formed big, glowing-hot disks that became a face. He recognized Erika. Or was it his mother still? It's all one, he had time to think. Then a black wall shot through his brain.

XV

CORPORAL NONNENMACHER was leader of the radio section in the signals platoon at Regiment. He was a stocky, powerful man with a ruddy face and good-natured blue eyes that regarded the world with quizzical intelligence. Sitting in his headquarters on the second floor of the regimental command post, he boredly twisted the dial of the radio set. In the back of the room the men of his section were snoring. Nonnenmacher listened to them for a while. Then he fooled with the dial again. Nothing special seemed to be happening to either the First Battalion or the others, and Nonnenmacher yawned mightily. He glanced at his watch. Another hour and a half, he thought. How slowly the time passed!

As he idly continued to turn the dial, listening to the unchanging drone of the ether waves, he wondered what their new quarters would be like. Undoubtedly not so comfortable as these, he thought gloomily, and sighed. Russia was bearable only when you were established in a big city. Novorossiysk had had some conveniences they were going to miss. He stared into the quiet flame of the lantern and sighed again. It was a dreary business, these eternal retreats. When he thought of the imminent winter, the stark snow-covered hills whipped with icy wind, when he remembered the two thousand miles that lay between him and his home in Karlsruhe, an unnamable sadness and hopelessness came over him.

A sudden noise in his ears interrupted his broodings. Automatically he adjusted the headset and leaned forward, intent. As his fingers glided skillfully over the knobs beneath the dial, a voice shouted so loudly out of the earphones that he pulled back in alarm. He regulated the volume and reached hastily for paper and pencil. According to the list of call numbers, it was the Second Company which was sending the message. The contents of the dispatch were dramatic enough.

When the voice stopped and a few moments later a second voice repeated the words, Nonnenmacher uttered an exclamation that startled the snoring men from their bunks. Sleep-dazed, they reeled toward him. "What's going on?" one of them asked.

"Read that," Nonnenmacher said, handing him the slip of paper.

"'Cannot hold the factory any longer,'" the man read aloud. "Sergeant Steiner killed. Request orders.'" The man let the paper flutter out of his fingers. "That would happen just before we're withdrawing," he said. "What are you going to do?"

Nonnenmacher shrugged. "It isn't really any of our business. They'll report it directly to Regiment. I suppose we might inform the commander. Then if he wants he can . . ." Nonnenmacher abruptly broke off.

The voice he had heard before was sounding in the earphones again, a breathless, distraught voice, and Nonnenmacher's pencil skipped across the pad. Then he wrenched the headset away from his ears.

"The Russians are attacking," he told the anxious group around him. "They're signing off now, but asking First Battalion to stay on their frequency. Get the other set and keep check on the other battalions. I want to hear how this thing turns out."

While the men brought another set from the back of the room and hooked it up, Nonnenmacher again listened. Minute after minute passed without any further messages from Second Company. He grew increasingly anxious and wondered again whether it might not be best to inform the commander. But the report must already have been telephoned in from the First Battalion. More than fifteen minutes had passed when a loud whistling tone sounded in his ears.

"They're switching to CW," he said to the men.

Again Nonnenmacher picked up his pencil and waited. The call signal came: *dah, dit, dit . . . dit, dit . . . dah, dah.* Reception was feebler than before; he increased the gain.

"They must be asleep," one of the man said impatiently. Nonnenmacher turned to him. "Were you listening in?"

The man nodded. "It's loud enough. QSA three, I say. David, Ida, Mike—that's the Second. But Battalion doesn't answer. Have they changed frequency?"

Nonnenmacher shook his head. "They're coming in on the same frequency. I wonder what the hell is the matter with Battalion."

Several more minutes passed, during which the call signal came in regularly at shorter and shorter intervals. Finally Nonnenmacher's patience gave out. "I'm going to answer," he said. "Maybe First Battalion's transmitter is on the blink." He placed his thumb and forefinger on the bug, switched the transmitter to CW and gave a continuous tone. Then his fingers flew.

The men watched him with admiration. Nonnenmacher

was undeniably the fastest operator in the regiment; you had to be damned good to copy him.

The answer came. First the call signal and confirmation, then a succession of staccato whistling tones. Nonnenmacher nodded with satisfaction. "They've got us. We're to wait; they're sending AS."

Two or three minutes passed in silence. Then the call signal came again, and the men heard the familiar and exciting signal that preceded every urgent message.

"KR." Nonnenmacher leaned over his pad, frowning with concentration. For a while nothing but the Morse signals could be heard. Then Nonnenmacher sat back. "I can't figure out what's going on here," he said helplessly. "Take a look at this." He turned back to the transmitter, and the men studied the message with equal puzzlement.

"Take it to the commander," Nonnenmacher ordered. "Immediately."

One of the men hurried out and raced downstairs to the commander's room. Lieutenant Colonel Brandt was busy stowing his personal belongings into a large canvas bag. "What is it?" he asked harshly.

The man clicked his heels. His voice rang like a trumpet as he said, "Radio message from Second Company to Regiment."

Brandt turned around to face him. "Well?"

"Second Company surrounded in factory cellar, underneath tower. Lieutenant Triebig dead." The man hesitated. Then he added, "Signed by Sergeant Steiner."

With three long strides Brandt reached the man and snatched the sheet of paper from his hand. "Any more messages?"

"Yes, sir." The man spilled out an explanation: they had picked up the first message and had finally answered when Battalion remained silent.

Brandt heard the story out before he asked, "Have you the text of the first message?"

"Corporal Nonnenmacher has it."

"Bring it here at once," Brandt ordered. "And inform Second Company that we will come to get them out. Hurry up." He waited until the door closed behind the man. As he went to the telephone, there was a dangerous light in his eyes. "Get me Lieutenant Stroh," he barked.

When the prearranged light signal flashed at the top of the elevator shaft, Sergeant Schulz turned his head. "They've made it," he said to Triebig behind him. He signaled into the shaft with his own flashlight and asked, "How many men do you want to send up there?"

The lieutenant nervously fingered the strap of his tommy gun. "Ten will be enough," he ventured. "The rest will stay with me. You too, Sergeant."

"Yes, sir!" Schulz addressed the men standing nearest him: "Up with you, and make it snappy." One after the other they entered the shaft and began to climb. "Speed it up," Schulz called impatiently. He took a step forward, and craned into the shaft.

The fourth man had just swung onto the ladder when a strange noise came from above. There followed a scream that sent the other men reeling back from the doorway. Seconds later a body plummeted past and struck with a dull thud at the bottom of the shaft. Schulz started to shout to the men on the ladder, but as he opened his mouth a Russian tommy gun began roaring up above and the other three plunged also, slamming with a hideous sound upon the iron platform of the elevator. A hissing rain of sparks from hand grenades danced past the doorway; four or five shattering explosions reverberated in the shaft. Then there was a deadly silence.

Schulz looked at Triebig. "We can write them off," he said hoarsely. "Them and the others up there, too. If we don't instantly . . ."

He broke off, for Triebig had abruptly sped off down the long aisle between the machines. Schulz chased after him. He caught up with him in front of the lathe on which the radiomen had placed their apparatus.

Triebig was loudly telling them: "Report to Battalion that we cannot hold the factory another five minutes; we must pull out at once and . . ." He hesitated. "Report that Sergeant Steiner has been killed. Are you connected?"

"They're on permanent reception," one of the men replied. He was wearing a throat microphone.

Triebig nodded, gratified. "Send that right away," he ordered. "I'll wait until you receive an answer."

As the radiomen bent over their apparatus, Schulz stepped up to Triebig's side. "Isn't it premature to report Steiner killed?"

Triebig shrugged impatiently. "It's a dead certainty the Russians have got him. Lord knows what went on up there."

Dubious, but not minded to dispute the matter, Schulz remained silent. He watched with interest as one of the two radiomen spoke into the microphone. Unthinkingly he put his hand into his pocket to take out a crushed cigarette. Halfway through the movement he froze. Through the window sprayed a fiery rain. A deafening rattle of gunfire followed. Schulz dropped to the ground. Beside him Triebig was shouting something. But he could not grasp the words. Innumerable arting, bluish flames were dancing in the big room. They're shooting explosive bullets, Schulz thought. He forced himself to crawl to the windows, where the men huddled on the floor were yelling something. The din grew louder. Screams of pain came from the wounded. From the direction of the corridor hand grenades burst, and as Schulz looked toward the door he saw the sentry there run back into the hall.

He turned and crawled back to Triebig. "They're attacking from both sides!" he shouted in Triebig's ear. "We've got to get out of here. We're trapped."

Triebig jumped to his feet and ran down the aisle to the other end of the hall. He stopped in front of the elevator shaft and waited for Schulz to catch up. Several other men joined them there. Triebig leaned over the shaft. "One man go down there," he ordered, his voice trembling. "Perhaps there's a cellar door below. Go on, Sergeant."

Schulz hesitated, but hand grenades were already flying in through the windows of the hall. He fished with his foot for the rung of the ladder below the door. For a few seconds he remained suspended, peering upward. Above him all remained still. Squinting, he descended the ladder until his foot encountered something soft. As he tried to feel along the wall, his hands met nothing and he felt a draft of cool air in his face. He kicked aside a body lying in his way, and made sure that the opening actually led into a room. Then he scrambled rapidly back up the rungs. The shaft stretched above him, a column of blackness. When he reached the main floor, the full violence of the battle struck his ears.

Triebig gripped his shoulder. "How is it?"

In breathless haste he reported, and the men groaned with relief. "Everyone get down there," Triebig's voice faltered. "Is the radio section here?" One of the radiomen replied, and Triebig turned to Schulz. "Call the men away from the windows. They're all to come down to the cellar."

"What about the wounded?" Schulz asked. Triebig was already swinging down the ladder. Schulz bit his lip. A dirty deal, he thought. Then he shrugged. He raced across the room, now saturated with dust and smoke and in an insane roar.

At one of the windows he found two men kneeling behind an MG, heads low, firing into the yard. He slammed the first man on the back and shouted, "Into the shaft, into the shaft and down to the cellar!" He rushed on, to the next window and the next.

But then he recoiled. In the forepart of the hall great shadows were pouring through the windows, jumping over the lathes and scattering with phantom movements in all directions. For a second Schulz stood frozen. They're here, he thought, the Russians are here!

He whirled and sped blindly back between the machines, stumbled over a body, felt two hands clutching at his coat, heard a gruesome, despairing bellow and with a jerk pulled free. The wounded, he thought. There was no time to take any other path. They lay side by side, filling the narrow aisle between the machines. His boots dug deep into the soft carpet of their writhing bodies. He tripped over outstretched arms until his foot caught somewhere; he plunged full length on his face, and several fists held him fast. He saw a face in front of his, a mouth stammering something. Gasping for air, he raised his tommy gun and struck out blindly with it. He got to his feet again, was pushed from behind and thrown forward.

"Kill him," a voice roared, and many others took up the cry: "Kill him, kill him!"

He defended himself like a wild beast, and finally pulled the trigger and fired until his magazine was empty. The shouts died away into groans and whimpers and helpless sobbing; the hands fell away from his torn uniform. He took three huge leaps, reached firm pavement, dashed with aching lungs toward the shaft.

Behind him a single voice continued to shout, and each word struck him like a blow, "Coward, bastard, traitor!" He dropped the tommy gun and pressed his hands to his ears as he ran on. When he got to the shaft he was shaking so violently he could scarcely stay on his feet.

A knot of men were struggling in front of the door, pushing one another back from the shaft, behaving like madmen. For a moment he halted and stared with bloodshot eyes at the scene. Then he crashed with all his weight against the living wall that blocked his way and carried it down with him into the shaft. He fell about fifteen feet, landed on a clump of intertwined bodies, instantly rolled away from them, leaped to his feet and pelted on. The shouting behind him became muted. Down a narrow corridor toward a glimmer of light he rushed. At a door on the right he heard a harsh voice, and a few seconds later came face to face with Triebig.

When he recognized Schulz, Triebig slowly lowered his

raised tommy gun. There were about fifteen men in the room. Some held flashlights. Schulz closed his eyes against the glare. Then he remembered the Russians and shouted, "Keep going. They're coming; the Russians are coming, Lieutenant!"

Triebig shouted orders, and the men stormed toward the back of the room where Schulz now noticed, another door opened out. As he followed he realized that other members of the company would be coming. He stood still.

"What are you waiting for?" Triebig screamed impatiently.

Schulz silently pointed to the opposite entrance. Two more men came running toward them. One of them shouted, "Hold it there." He collided with Triebig, who violently pushed him back.

"What are you yelling for?" Triebig asked loudly. "What's the matter?"

The man recognized the lieutenant and snapped to attention. "More of the men are coming, sir," he panted, jerking his thumb back over his shoulder.

"Have you seen Russians?" Triebig asked.

"Und wie!" the man burst out. "They must be in the shaft by now and . . ."

"Why didn't you say that right away?" Triebig cursed and sprang to the door. "In with you!" he shouted. "Come on, we can't lose another second." He shoved the men violently inside. The door of solid sheet steel had two big bolts that could be shut from inside.

As Triebig slammed and locked the door behind him, fists thudded against the steel and several voices roared, "Open up, open up!"

"For God's sake, open that door," Schulz stammered.

The men on the other side were now kicking it with their nailed boots.

Triebig did not move. Schulz tried to force past him, but Triebig placed both hands on his chest and pushed him away. "Keep your hands off, you damned idiot!" he screamed.

"But you can't . . ." Schulz whispered.

"Shut up!" Triebig commanded. "I know what I'm doing. Better they than the whole lot of us." He stepped away from the door and ran after the others. Schulz followed. The corridor turned at a right angle and terminated, about a dozen paces farther on, in a large room that was piled to the ceiling with boxes. They flashed their lights over every corner of the room and discovered a second door.

"We have to keep our rear open," Schulz panted. "If we set up an MG at the corner there, nobody can get through the door and we can take our time about looking around."

Triebig agreed. He ordered the radiomen to set up their apparatus. Meanwhile Schulz had the men drag four of the heavy boxes, filled with machine parts, to the right angle, where they were stacked on top of one another. "No bullet will go through that, I tell you," he said with satisfaction. "You're as safe behind those boxes as in a tank."

The MG crew took up positions behind the improvised barricade. Not a sound could be heard. Presumably the locked-out men had run back into the corridor—God knew where it led to. Perhaps they had run straight into the hands of the Russians. Schulz felt an enormous uneasiness. Triebig had left them to their fate. Bad enough about that business with the wounded . . .

Shame and horror welled up within him as he remembered. Suddenly it also occurred to him that he no longer had a gun. He cursed himself for having failed to pick up one in the shaft. But who in such a situation would be likely to think that far ahead? He felt naked. He'd ask around among the men; perhaps one of them would be carrying an extra gun. He turned toward the storeroom, where the men had sat down on the crates and were smoking. What part of the factory were they under now? Beneath the tower probably.

Triebig was standing beside the radiomen, impatiently watching as they set up the long rod antenna. "I hope we'll have some kind of reception here," one of them remarked. "Not a window anywhere in this damned cellar—I don't know."

"Do you need a window?" Triebig asked anxiously.

The man nodded. "You do with these sets. They're not much good except in open terrain. We'll see." He turned the dial. "Not a whisper," he complained. "I'd better try CW right away." He reached for the bug.

Schulz went around among the men until he found one who had a pistol in addition to his carbine. "I'll give it back to you later," he assured the man, examining the weapon.

The soldier waved his hand generously. "What for? You don't seriously think we'll ever get out of this tomb, do you?"

Schulz shrugged. He went over to Triebig who still stood beside the radiomen, shifting his weight tensely from one leg to the other. "That's just a waste of time," he said. "I'd suggest we first see where the corridor over there goes. We have to know what we're up against."

Triebig nodded, but did not stir. When the men looked questioningly at him, some of them with their mouths twisted in an expression of scorn, he pulled himself together. "Take a few men with you," he said to Schulz. "If you discover anything special, send a man back to me."

The sergeant shook his head firmly. "It will be better if you come along," he declared in a loud voice. "It may prove necessary to make a decision that I couldn't take on myself as long as there's a company commander around." There was undisguised mutiny in his voice.

The men had all stood up; as he looked at their hostile faces, Triebig realized how serious his mistake was. He dared not risk angering them any further. Perhaps his life would depend on every one of them in the course of the next hour. Suppressing his rage, he said, "If you are afraid, Sergeant, I'll go with you."

"It isn't a question of being afraid," Schulz said bitingly. "The men here can tell you exactly who is afraid and who isn't." He looked around, saw agreement on all faces. He grinned spitefully. "We have eyes in our heads, Lieutenant, good eyes: we know what's been going on here."

Triebig felt that he was losing control of his temper in spite of his resolve. Without a word he went out through the door. Ten yards down, the corridor suddenly turned again. Triebig paused, checked the direction by his compass and turned to Schulz. "Leave one man here," he ordered curtly. "We may have to come back quickly."

Schulz nodded. "I don't understand why the building has no cellar windows," he said. "If we could find a window we could try getting out."

"If there are any they'll be barred," Triebig said. "Right now we must know where the corridor goes." They walked on until they reaced a door that led into a chamber in which there was a large array of machinery, boilers and enormous pipes that disappeared into the high ceiling.

"Heating plant," Schulz declared with the air of an engineer. He flashed his light around. Toward the rear they came on a pile of coke reaching to the ceiling. An opening in the wall proved to be the entrance to the coal cellar.

"Now it's getting romantic," Schulz muttered.

Triebig watched him climb over the coke and disappear through the opening. "Be careful," he called out and was about to follow.

A sudden noise stopped him. Several men ran across the cellar and stopped in front of a door he had not noticed earlier. The noise grew louder. Now he heard the chatter of a tommy gun. He jumped off the pile of coke and ran after the men. They were gathered in front of a dark corridor.

Before he could order them to switch off their flashlights, a voice rang out in front of them. Triebig staggered back as from a blow, "Sergeant Steiner here, don't shoot! It's us—Sergeant Steiner!" Incredulous and aghast, he saw a man running toward them out of the darkness, arms upraised, while behind him the roar of the tommy gun continued with undiminished insistence.

Triebig's thoughts were in a turmoil. As yet he could see only the outlines of the approaching man's body—Steiner, whose death he had already reported to Battalion! Steiner, who had climbed to the factory tower and was now appearing in the cellar like a ghost; Steiner, whom he hated more than anyone he had ever before encountered in his life; Steiner, who stood between him and the future that Stranksy had promised: Biarritz, Arcachon, Mont de Mersan, Paris, Montmartre. . . .

Triebig forgot where he was. He forgot the men of his company who stood on both sides of him, staring breathless and incredulous into the corridor. And he forgot himself. He raised the tommy gun and pulled the trigger. The man had approached within ten paces. Triebig saw him stumble, sink to his knees and tumble forward on his face. Then hands dragged his arms down, he heard voices shouting, and a blow in the body took his breath away. Someone roared, "One of our men!"

Triebig did not answer. With a strange feeling in his chest he watched men run toward the soldier on the ground; he swallowed. This was the first human being he had ever shot. The first. A wild sensation of triumph rose within him, staggering him with terrible force and distorting his face to a grinning mask.

Behind him Triebig suddenly heard Schulz, and at the same time he became aware that the hammering of the Russian tommy gun had stopped.

The sergeant pressed close to him. "What happened?"

Triebig shrugged and remained silent. Vacantly he watched three more figures appear out of the darkness of the corridor and move toward the man he had shot. He saw them bend over the body, and suddenly his heart began to pound so hard that he clutched at his chest with both hands.

Schulz, eying him from the side, now pushed past him and went over to the others. "What happened?" he demanded. Then he noticed Steiner kneeling beside the man on the ground. He had unbuttoned the other's shirt and was looking down at him, lips compressed.

Steiner raised his head and asked Kruger, "How did this happen?" He spoke in so low a voice that it was barely possible to understand him.

"I don't know," Kruger said dully. "When we turned the corner, he went on running toward the light. I wanted to run after him, but Faber held me back. And then . . ." He hunched his shoulders and stood helplessly among the men.

"And then?" Steiner demanded.

Kruger did not reply. Faber spoke for him. "And then someone fired. We dropped to the floor until the firing stopped." He shook his head. "I don't get it," he said. "They couldn't help seeing it was us."

Steiner nodded. He suddenly saw with great clarity what must have happened.

For a long while he looked down into Schnurrbart's face, which was gradually crumbling to shapelessness like ruined masonry. Then he slowly straightened up. "Who fired?" he asked, and he was certain of the answer.

The men remained silent, but their glances had a single direction.

Steiner raised his flashlight. The beam struck a bloodless face, picked out a pair of nervous eyes. Every sound in the cellar ceased abruptly.

"Take a couple of men," Steiner said to Kruger. "You must hold the corner; the Russians will be along in a moment."

Then he stalked toward the lieutenant. The men followed him as if they had slivers of glass in their shoes. "Why did you shoot?" Steiner asked. He stood in front of Triebig, fixing those evasive, flickering eyes.

Triebig made no reply. When Steiner repeated the question, he blinked to escape the probing of the flashlight. "Shut up!" he barked.

Steiner could feel the skin of his face tighten. Grief knotted his throat like a noose; he panted for breath. "You swine!" At that moment at the corner of the corridor several tommy guns began to roar. Shooting boomed like cannon fire in the confined space.

The men came to life. They tried to get past Steiner, toward the rear, but he blocked their way. "Stay here!" he shouted. He aimed his gun at them, and they pressed themselves against the wall in terror.

He saw Triebig on the point of running. A leap brought him to the lieutenant's side, and he held him fast. Triebig dropped his gun and struck out at Steiner with his fists. Taken by surprise, Steiner staggered back. His flashlight hampered him, and he thrust it into his pocket. In the darkness the men ran past him, although he again shouted to them. Triebig flailed at him like a madman, gasping and swinging blindly.

There was no more time. Steiner raised the barrel of his

gun in both hands and struck brutally, one, two, three times. When he pulled the flashlight out of his pocket, he saw Triebig lying on the floor. There was a gash from his right eye to his chin, and blood was pouring into his mouth. Steiner gripped the officer's tunic and pulled him to his feet. "Come on!" he said.

He pushed him along toward the corner just as Kruger and the others retreated toward them.

"They're coming," Kruger shouted. He stopped and looked at the screaming lieutenant, from whose shattered nose blood was spurting. "What's the idea?" he asked in horror.

Steiner shoved him aside and simultaneously gave the lieutenant a violent push forward. Kruger tried to catch his arm. With a movement almost playful in its agility Steiner ducked and thrust the barrel of the tommy gun into his stomach with so much force that Kruger lost his balance and fell.

As he straightened up, face working with pain, he saw Steiner driving the lieutenant on toward the Russians.

"He's gone mad," one of the men cried; he had come from the corner and was watching, too shocked to do anything.

They shouted at Steiner, but he paid no attention. He was pushing Triebig ahead of him like a ball. He kicked Triebig alternately in the legs, in the buttocks, in the back, repeating over and over, "Keep going, keep going." Rifle fire was clattering into the walls, tearing down the plaster. Ricochets whistled around their ears. They were within ten feet of the corner when there was a crashing explosion in front of them.

Steiner had time to see Triebig reach both hands into the air, reel and plunge heavily to the floor. He paused long enough to fix the sight in his mind. Then he turned and dashed back. The flashlight fell from his hands and shattered. Without pausing he ran on until in the darkness he stumbled over a body and plunged full length. He cursed. Then it occurred to him that this must be Schnurrbart. With one mighty effort he heaved the lifeless body onto his shoulder and ran on, gasping for breath, to where the others were waiting tensely for him at the furnace room.

"Which way?" Kruger asked.

Schulz pointed to the door opposite.

Kruger turned to Steiner. "Let me have him," he said, and took the dead body on his own broad back.

In the next room the men who had remained behind received them excitedly. Schulz waved his hand impatiently. "Not so much talk. We have to block this side with boxes too. The Russians are coming."

In feverish haste they began to barricade the second corridor also. The room seemed ideal for withstanding a siege. From both sides the Russians would have to run down a long corridor completely without cover; they would be stopped easily by the heavy machine guns and could be held off far enough so that their hand grenades would do no damage.

As Steiner ran from one corner to another he was irritated by the men whispering to one another and throwing meaningful glances at him. Kruger and Faber sat on a box, their faces chalky, watching him. Behind them lay Schnurrbart. They're scared stiff, Steiner thought contemptuously. The bastards are all scared stiff. He noticed the radiomen in a corner.

As he approached, one of the two men raised his head. "We have communication with Regiment now," he said.

"What about Battalion?" Steiner asked.

The man shrugged. "They don't answer. God knows what's wrong there."

"I can tell you what." Schulz joined the group. "They've written us off, the swine. As far as they're concerned we're through. Dead and gone." He looked up at the dirty-gray arched ceiling that curved above them like the lid of a coffin.

"Shut up," Steiner said with disgust; and to the radiomen: "How did you get here?"

As one of the men explained, Steiner stood with closed eyes, trying to reconstruct the diagram of the cellar. Finally he nodded. "We've run around the sides of a square and come out under the tower again. If they don't fight through to get us out, we'll have to try it ourselves. Get in touch with them," he ordered sharply.

The radiomen slipped on their earphones.

After receiving the alarming radio message from Triebig, Stransky sat at his desk blankly. The news of Steiner's death brought him none of the inner rejoicing he had anticipated, and he wondered why. The feeling suddenly swept him that a vast cloud of danger was gathering around his head. If they are wiped out by the Russians, he thought, things will be bad here. For a moment he thought of removing the First or the Third Company from its position and ordering it to the defense of his command post. But Brandt would have to approve such a step.

At last he lifted the telephone and spoke with the signals platoon leader. "Get all your available men and take up position in front of my command post," he ordered. "If anything should happen, send a courier up to me."

For a moment there was a dead silence at the other end

of the line. Then Hüser exclaimed in dismay, "I need at least four men for the switchboard and radio communication, sir."

Stransky bit his lip impatiently. "One man is enough for communication," he said imperatively. "The Russians may be on top of us at any moment. You will need every man down in the street below the command post. Once the danger is past, I'll inform you and you can have your men again and resume communications. How many are you?"

"Only six at the moment," Hüser replied, his uneasiness plain.

Stransky frowned. "How is that? Your platoon is fifteen men strong."

"The others are out taking down the telephone lines to First and Third," Hüser explained.

"Then take the couriers also, and hurry up about it, man." He replaced the receiver and lighted a cigarette. But after the first few puffs he dropped it to the floor in disgust and ground it out with his boot. The silence in the room intensified his nervousness. He turned his thoughts to his transfer back to France. If what his cousin had written was accurate, the transfer ought to come through any day now. His cousin could be relied on, he thought, grinning.

Now and then he glanced impatiently at his watch. The battalion was due to start its withdrawal in one hour. The companies, except for Second, had been informed and would evacuate their positions according to plan. Lieutenant Moninger had sent a message that he was in communication with Third and that all was peaceful on both sectors. Peaceful? Stransky smiled grimly. Nothing reassuring about this peacefulness—it plucked at the nerves and was harder to bear than all the racket of yesterday.

Unable to banish his gloomy thoughts, he went over to the window and looked down into the dark back yard. "There is no peace," he murmured to himself. "One is a hunted animal." His thoughts returned again and again to his Second Company. It was really time now to order it to withdraw. Perhaps it will be better after all, he told himself, if I send a courier over there. Was Triebig still alive? He was not eager for Triebig to come back, but he could not put off issuing his order much longer.

Glancing at his watch again, he saw that nearly an hour had passed since his conversation with Hüser. It was twenty minutes to four. He reached for the telephone but it occurred to him that the house was deserted except for the communications platoon out front. He started for the door. Suddenly he recalled the radio message from Triebig. Because he had deliberately failed to report it to Regiment, he returned to the table and carefully burned the message slip over the candle.

As he turned toward the door again, it flew open and Stransky found himself confronted by Kiesel. The adjutant's face bore an expression of outrage and harshness such as Stransky had never before seen in him. Without a word Kiesel strode past him, sat down at the desk, reached into his pocket and accusingly laid a sheet of paper on the desk. The silence became unbearable; it stood like a wall between the two officers.

At last Stransky pulled himself together and managed a dim smile. "You, Herr Kiesel?"

"As you see, Herr Stransky. I have something to say to you." He waited until Stransky had taken a seat. "The commander has sent me. What is the situation of your Second Company?"

Stransky moistened his dry lips with his tongue and tried to keep his voice on a casual, even note. "The last radio message came from Triebig. But you know how Triebig is." He assumed a sardonic air that dissolved at once under Kiesel's icy gaze. "I didn't take his assertions too seriously," he added vaguely.

Kiesel still did not speak, and Stransky's discomfort mounted. He passed his hand nervously over his temple. "What makes you ask?"

"The last radio message came from Sergeant Steiner," Kiesel replied, picking up the paper he had laid on the desk. "He says that Triebig has been killed and the company is surrounded in the cellar of the factory. Didn't you know that?" His eyes probed Stransky's ashen face.

Stransky's lips moved without making a sound. At last he whispered incredulously, "Impossible."

Kiesel regarded him impassively. "You didn't know that?" he asked in mock surprise. "But you have radio communication with the company, Herr Stransky." He spoke now with naked scorn.

Stransky fought to restore some order to his thoughts. To gain time he lighted a cigarette. But his fingers were trembling so hard that he feared Kiesel would notice, and he laid the cigarette on the edge of the desk. "I don't understand it."

There was a knock on the door and a tall, broad-shouldered man in lieutenant's uniform entered. He paused at the threshold and snapped his hand to his cap.

"You're a little earlier than I expected," Kiesel said, rising. "Do you know Lieutenant Gollhofer?" he asked Stransky. When Stransky shook his head, he continued, "He has been commanding the engineer's platoon for the past eight days.

Lieutenant Colonel Brandt has ordered him to go to the relief of Second Company. I have no more time to spend talking with you. You are to take the rest of the battalion as planned to the new position. The commander will expect you in his command post at nine o'clock."

He had spoken very rapidly. Now he pulled the lieutenant out with him into the hall. Side by side they ran down the steps to the street. Several dozen men were huddled close to the wall of the building, talking in whispers. "You know what to do?" Kiesel asked.

Gollhofer nodded.

They looked beyond the fence at the shadowy outlines of the factory. Kiesel bit his lip. Then he shook hands with the lieutenant. "I hope you are successful. The business must not take too long, or you'll lose contact with us. Good luck."

He watched as the men disappeared into the shadow of the fence. Then he hurried on to the next intersection, where his car was waiting. "Back," Kiesel snapped, swinging into the seat beside the driver. He ordered him to drive fast.

So the commander's hunch had been right. From the battalion communications platoon leader in front of Stransky's command post, Kiesel had learned that the radio station had been left untended and communication with the Second Company broken off on Stransky's orders. That will cost him his head, Kiesel thought grimly as the car drew up in front of the regimental command post.

"Wait till I come back," Kiesel ordered the man at the wheel. He bounded up the steps.

The candles in the hallway were still burning, but almost all the doors stood wide open, and his footsteps echoed loudly through the deserted building. The commander sprang to his feet, irritable and impatient, as Kiesel entered the room. "You can tell me about it as we ride," he said quickly. "I must get to the new headquarters. Since the communications men have left I've been up in the air here. Where is the car?" Without waiting for a reply he snatched up his baggage and hurried out.

On the way down to the car he told Kiesel that the rest of the staff had left half an hour ago. "I put them all on trucks," Brandt said. "It will be light in an hour. The time for the withdrawal was set much too late. I don't understand the general."

"Neither do I," Kiesel agreed. "The battalions will reach the new line in broad daylight."

Sighing, Brandt settled on the seat. "Get started, man," he barked at the driver. He turned to Kiesel, who had sat down beside him. "It's exactly four now. I hope there was no last-minute hitch with the withdrawal."

"Let's hope not," Kiesel answered.

Brandt watched indifferently as the car barely missed a fallen telegraph pole. "You can turn on your headlights now," he called to the man at the wheel. Unhappily, he eyed the graying sky. Then to Kiesel: "Now let me have it."

Silently Brandt listened while the car gathered speed, left the last houses of the city behind and reached the highway. When Kiesel finished, there was a long silence. Finally Brandt shook his head. "He must have gone stark raving mad," he said. "In the language of military law there's only one word for that: sabotage. And the rope is the penalty for sabotage. Stransky knows that as well as I. I'd like to know what he could have been thinking of. He must have reckoned on the possibility of this foul business being discovered."

"Certainly," Kiesel said. He looked back. The silhouette of the city was beginning to emerge gradually from the darkness, black against the gray of the sky. "Of course he must have reckoned on the possibility," Kiesel repeated absently. Suddenly he turned to face Brandt. "I feel like a deserter."

"So do I," said Brandt, "but we have done all in our power. H hour couldn't be postponed on account of a single company. The bridgehead has begun to move and will go on moving until the last man has reached the Crimea. A moment of historic significance." He smiled bitterly. "We are making history once more."

Still holding its smile, his face suddenly convulsed. "Drive faster, damn it all!" he shouted at the driver. Frightened, the soldier hunched his shoulders as though he had received a blow and pressed the accelerator to the floor. "But we are like the sorcerer's apprentice," Brant continued in an easy conversational tone. "We have forgotten the magic word for stopping the flood. Or do you perhaps know it?"

"Capitulation," Kiesel said.

Brandt dismissed that with a wave of his hand. "The time for that has passed. What would we get out of it now?"

Kiesel shrugged.

"There you are," Brandt said. "Incidentally, I want to have everything on this business with Stransky in writing. Don't forget any of the details, including those radio messages. I'll need them as evidence."

"Are you intending to start so soon, tomorrow, on . . . ?" Kiesel asked hesitantly.

Something in Kiesel's voice alienated Brandt. His own tone

became more reserved. "As soon as I know how the affair in the factory turns out," he replied crisply.

Kiesel bowed his head. For all his outrage at what Stransky had done, he suddenly felt uneasy at the thought of bringing the man before a court-martial. But did Stransky deserve anything better? He pursued this thought until the commander's voice, louder and somewhat sharper now, made him conscious again of the upholstery and the sway of the speeding automobile. "You are unstable," Brandt said challengingly. "You are unstable and should never have been permitted to wear a uniform. A person like you ought to be careful about entering a sphere where justice is not meted out by the hand of God. In military life there's no time to wait for that kind of justice. But you cannot change your spots any more than I can. If I find fault with you for anything, it's for not perceiving sooner the nature of the individual you work for. If you have perceived it, you should by now have accepted it. *J'y suis et j'y reste.* Since I have been commander of this regiment I have sent several men up before a court-martial, not because it amused me, but because I happen to be commander. In Stransky's case, too, I shall do what is my duty. That's all there is to it." He pressed further back into his corner and fell into a profound silence.

In the beam of the headlights several houses flew past, the shadowy outlines of a railroad yard, tall poles, tracks. The road spiraled up a steep slope that seemed to go on forever. Brandt asked, "How far to go yet?"

"Ten minutes," Kiesel replied after consulting the illuminated dial of his wrist watch. They seemed to have reached the top of the climb now. The road ran on almost in a straightaway along the barren ridge of a series of hills. A few miles farther on, it turned toward the north and dropped precipitately into a narrow valley in whose lap stood a small cluster of buildings. "We're there," Kiesel said, pointing to the houses.

The driver steered the car around a last curve and braked sharply in front of a longish building. The door of the building was flung open and a man came running toward the car. Kiesel recognized him as Lieutenant Mohr, the regimental communications officer. "What's new?" Brandt asked as he stepped out of the car.

"The general has already called you three times," Mohr hastened to report.

"I'm not a magician," Brandt grumbled. "Did he want anything special?"

"I don't think so, sir. He asked how things were going. I

told him that the withdrawal had all gone according to plan so far, and the battalions were on the way to their new positions."

"And Gollhofer?" Brandt asked with apparent casualness. Kiesel waited tensely.

Mohr gave his news: "Gollhofer's already on his way, with the Second Company. Radio message from him just ten minutes ago."

"What's that you say, man!" Brandt exclaimed loudly, snatching the sheet of paper with the report from his hand. There was already enough daylight for him to read the hastily scribbled notation. He read it through twice. Then he turned to Kiesel. "Hey, what do you say to that?" he exploded, and suddenly burst into cheerful laughter.

He crumpled the paper in his clenched fist and thrust it into his pocket. "You're a damned gloomy raven," he said to Kiesel. "I hope you'll admit it." Disregarding Kiesel's blank expression, he asked Mohr, "Where do I hang my hat?"

Mohr gestured toward the door. "Here, sir. There's someone waiting to see you already."

"Who?" Brandt asked.

"A Captain Killius," Mohr replied. "He's come direct from the High Command and says he's to replace a battalion commander; the name of the man he replaces is in a letter which he wants to hand to you personally."

Brandt exchanged a brief glance with Kiesel. Then he followed the lieutenant. As he entered the room which was now his new headquarters, a stocky figure rose from a chair. "Captain Killius," the man said, clicking his heels. "I . . ."

But Brandt cut him off with a brusque gesture. "I've heard," he said curtly. "You have orders for me?"

Plainly depressed by this frosty reception, the captain laid a sealed envelope on the table. "I have, sir," he said stiffly.

While the commander tore open the letter, Kiesel watched his face; it had suddenly lost all expression and looked like a whitewashed wall. For a while Brandt stood staring over the head of the officer. Then he quietly asked Kiesel, "Didn't you once mention Captain Stransky's good connections?"

Kiesel nodded. "There is a Major General Stransky, attached to Army High Command, South. He is, I believe, a cousin of Captain Stransky."

"I see," Brandt said slowly. Grimacing, he tossed the letter on the table. "You can guess what that is, can't you?" he said, indicating the letter as if it were some offensive filth.

"His transfer, of course," Kiesel replied calmly.

"Exactly," Brandt said grimly. "Herr Stransky is to report

to the staff of a battalion in Paris within a week. I believe it is the very assignment he held before he came out here to us."

There was a brief silence in the room. Lieutenant Mohr made bold to murmur, "Miracles still happen."

"You may be right about that," Brandt growled. "But the miracle is going to be a bit different from the kind Herr Stransky expects." He turned to Killius, who had been attending to the conversation in a total fog. "I'm happy to welcome you among us," he said cordially, shaking the new man's hand. "Things are rather hectic at the moment and I must ask you to bear with us. Let me introduce you to everybody. Oh yes, you already know Lieutenant Mohr."

Kiesel was obliged to smile at his superior's sudden shifts of mood.

The telephone shrilled. "That will be the general," Mohr said.

When Brandt hung up, after a brief conversation, his expression had become very grave. "We're staying here only till tonight," he said to the officers. "A courier is on the way with important orders. Let's get to work, gentlemen."

XVI

IN THE cellar nothing had changed. The men perched idly on the boxes, smoking and talking in muted tones. Their spirits were at low ebb, their faces sallow under the steel helmets. Steiner, too, sat on a box, head drooping, eyes empty.

Kruger muttered a curse. He dropped his cigarette to the floor and ground it out. "We have to do something," he said loudly. "This business of sitting around frazzles my nerves. Just look at the cheesy faces on all these guys."

He had spoken to Faber, who hunched his shoulders indifferently. "What do you want to do?" he asked quietly. "We just have to wait until they come for us."

"Until they come!" Kruger laughed wildly. "By the time they come they'll have to scrape us off the walls." He strode over to the radiomen's corner. "Nothing new yet?" he asked.

One of the men shook his head. "They signaled QRX-thirty," he said. "They're moving to new positions and we're to wait thirty minutes. There are still ten minutes to go."

"They've run out on us," Kruger said. "That's what they've done. They've given us up, the bastards, that's all."

His loud voice disturbed the trance of the other men. "What's happened?" Schulz exclaimed.

"Don't ask such dumb questions," Kruger replied violently. "How much longer are we going to sit around on our asses? Any of you think they're going to dig us out? You can wait till you're blue in the face, I tell you."

He had only put their own fears into words. Schulz nodded emphatically. "I think so too," he declared hoarsely. "We're wasting precious time. As it is I don't understand why the Russians haven't come yet."

"You may not, but I do." Kruger snorted. "They'd be idiots to run head on up against our machine guns. They know they can have us cheaper. All they have to do is wait till we've got nothing to eat and we'll crawl right up to them wagging our tails."

"Right." Schulz looked toward Steiner.

"Let him alone," said Kruger, guessing Schulz's thoughts. "Let him alone, I tell you." He lowered his voice. "You don't understand." He stretched and said in a loud voice. "Left or right?"

Schulz grasped his meaning at once. He swung around and indicated the door on the right. "There, I'd say. Maybe we can get back up through the elevator shaft."

Although most of the others looked skeptical, Kruger took up the plan. "We'll block the door with boxes," he declared. "That way we have our rear protected and don't have to leave anyone here."

Schulz nodded. Glad to throw off the leaden weight of inactivity, the men set to work. The machine gunners were pulled back and the door locked, and they piled a dozen of the heavy crates in front of it. Another dozen were stacked behind the first row, so that the entire doorway from floor to ceiling was shielded by their immovable mass.

"That ought to do it." Kruger studied their work with satisfaction. He went slowly over to Steiner and announced, "We're going to try to break out."

"All right," Steiner said without raising his head.

Kruger squinted down at him, his face drawn. Something seemed to be impeding his tongue so that he could hardly talk. "Maybe we can get up through the elevator shaft," he managed to say. Turning his head, he observed that the men were all standing impatiently behind him. "Once we're in the hall," he said in a somewhat louder voice, "we're as good as in the clear."

Steiner stood up heavily. "Take Schnurrbart along," he

said. A shudder passed through Kruger as he looked into Steiner's eyes. He turned to two of the men and ordered them to carry Schnurrbart's body. Then he followed Steiner toward the barricade at the other end of the corridor. They moved the boxes aside to make a small opening through which they could crawl, and cautiously went on toward the next door.

Schulz suddenly recalled the men whom Triebig had locked out. In a whisper he told Kruger about it. "An insane, cowardly trick, but I couldn't do anything."

"He's paid his bill," Kruger said. They watched Steiner move the bolt back.

"Lights out!" Schulz whispered.

Instantly all the men switched off their flashlights. Up ahead the darkness was impenetrable. A faint creaking indicated that Steiner had opened the door. At the same time they felt a fresh stream of air against their faces; it was like something from another world. In the intensity of his excitement Kruger bit his lips until they bled. There's no chance, he thought. If we . . . He recoiled in fright as someone touched his chest.

Then he heard Steiner's voice right in front of him: "Leave your lights out. Where is Schulz?"

"Here," the sergeant breathed.

"Come along," Steiner whispered, and Schulz felt a hand taking his arm. They tiptoed down the corridor, feeling their way along the walls, until they reached a door.

Schulz whispered, "That's a cellar room. The door we want is on the other side, and then the corridor runs left to the elevator."

"Let's go." Steiner's voice was low and steady.

The nails of their boots scraped on the stone floor. At last they came up against a wall. After some searching they found the door. "Get the others," Steiner said. He turned to the left.

A few yards farther on he stumbled on a body that lay across his path. He stepped over it. The current of fresh air was even stronger here. Steiner straightened up somewhat from his hunched position. The last few yards he walked erect until his foot encountered something hard. It was a step. His hands groped over the two halves of an open double door, and he reasoned that this must be the elevator shaft. For a moment he hesitated. But since he could not hear a sound anywhere, he took the risk and switched on his flashlight. The bright beam revealed the crumpled bodies of about a dozen men piled one on top of the other, their faces horrible to behold, blocking the entrance.

There was a noise behind him. Steiner turned and saw the rest of the men. "What is it?" Schulz whispered. Then he caught sight of the bodies and his mouth twisted in sick horror. "Upstairs there will be worse sights," he said.

Kruger joined them. "How do you figure it out?" he asked. Since Steiner gave no reply, Schulz asked, "What?"

"That the Russians haven't let out a peep," Kruger answered impatiently. "Good Lord, they must be hiding somewhere."

Schulz shifted uneasily. "It's funny," he remarked. "And whatever happened to the others?"

"What others?"

"The ones Triebig locked out."

"*Scheisse*," Kruger whispered. He pressed his fist against his right knee which was beginning to quiver like a gearshift. His reason rebelled against the unreality of the situation. He felt the sweat starting on his forehead.

The men remained motionless and silent. Steiner switched off his flashlight, clambered over the dead bodies and groped for the ladder. Slowly he pulled himself up, rung by rung. He reached the first floor. On his left he saw the rectangle of the doorway shimmering dimly, and for a few seconds he hung on the ladder, peering incredulously. Then he carefully moved his leg sideways until his foot found support, and swung over into the opening. Before him lay the machinery hall, dark, silent and lifeless. Through the high windows dull light trickled down on the machines which filled the room like petrified primordial monsters. For no reason he had a feeling amounting to certainty that there were no longer any Russians in the room. Carelessly he walked forward several yards and looked around. Then he returned to the shaft and called to the men.

Kruger appeared first. He thrust his powerful frame through the doorway and stopped in amazement. Behind him came Schulz, and the others followed one by one, pushing one another ahead impatiently, and equally incredulous as they saw the empty hall. "Can you believe it!" one of them said.

"They must be waiting for us outside," Schulz said hoarsely. "It's a trick, that's all."

"Sure," another man whispered. "They can't have run away."

"Don't wear your brains out thinking," Kruger snapped morosely. He turned to Steiner. "Now what?"

Steiner looked around. "Where were the wounded placed?"

"Over there." Schulz pointed to a spot between two machines.

Steiner walked toward the area until his foot encountered

something soft. He switched on the flashlight and stood rooted to the spot.

Behind him a suppressed moan arose. Kruger whispered, "My God!" The men lay scattered over the floor like lumps of raw meat, naked, their uniforms stripped off, abdomens slit open, faces smashed in, bodies bestially mutilated. The floor was red from pools of coagulated blood that had run even underneath the machines.

Steiner switched off his flashlight. "Where is Schnurrbart?" he asked.

"We have him," Kruger replied hollowly.

"Wait," Steiner ordered. He went over to a window. They watched as he swung up on the sill, paused a moment and then jumped into the yard.

"He's crazy," Schulz stammered.

They ran to the window and peered out into the gray twilight of dawn. Steiner was running erect across the yard. They heard his gas mask knocking against his mess tin. Then his figure vanished against the dark wall of the fence.

"He's made it," Kruger breathed. When a green light flashed along the fence, Kruger climbed onto the window sill. "First the two men with the canvas," he ordered. He waited until the men had lifted Schnurrbart's body down.

Then they ran across the yard. They felt as if bells ought to be ringing somewhere as they ran, holding their faces up in the fresh morning air.

Schulz, a short distance ahead, had come within a few yards of the fence when he stopped abruptly. He thought he had heard voices behind the fence.

Kruger caught up with him and panted, "Go on, go on."

At that moment they saw several of the slats of the fence being pushed aside. Steiner appeared in the gap and called impatiently to them. When they reached him they were stunned to see an officer standing beside him, addressing him with many shakes of the head; behind the two stood several dozen men in German uniforms.

"I'm seeing things," Kruger muttered. He turned to Schulz and Faber beside him. "I think I'm losing my mind."

"I've lost mine," Schulz said.

The outlines of the factory were now rising more and more distinctly out of the dissolving darkness. The building presented a black bulk against the paling sky. The officer was shaking his head again and saying, "The case reminds me of something that happened just about a year ago. Maybe the Russians caught on that we were evacuating. In any case I can't understand their fighting it out in the factory when they've already dug in right in the heart of the city. They would have finished you fellows off today anyway."

He thrust his steel helmet back from his forehead. "You've had unbelievable luck," he declared happily. "We were supposed to dig you out and were just going to cross the yard when your sergeant came out the window. I'm glad we didn't fire wildly." He caught sight of the two men with the canvas and asked, "Wounded?"

"No, dead," Schulz replied.

"What are you dragging him along for?" the lieutenant asked in surprise. "Do you expect to carry him six miles?"

"Six miles?" Kruger exclaimed.

The lieutenant nodded and looked at his watch. "It's five to four," he said urgently. "We must hurry. We're evacuating the city at four." He laughed at their astonished expressions. "That's the way it is. If I hadn't got on the track of you right off, or if the Russians had put up a hard fight, I would have had to leave you stuck there in the cellar. God knows what would have become of you. Let's get going." The lieutenant hitched up his belt. "Leave the dead man here. We can't carry him along."

"Who says so?" Steiner asked, his voice taut to the point of breaking.

Gollhofer raised his eyebrows. "I do. Have you a different opinion on the matter?"

"Yes," Steiner retorted. He turned to the men. "Who'll help me?"

"Me," Kruger said. Faber stepped up beside him. The other men held back.

"One more," Steiner said loudly. No one stirred. Steiner gripped two ends of the canvas. "Three can do it."

"Hold on a moment," Schulz said. Without feeling any eagerness for this task, he suddenly felt that he had something to make up for. He took his place beside the other three.

Gollhofer glared at them and considered simply ordering them to let the dead man lie. But something about Steiner's face restrained him. Raising his hand, he placed himself at the head of the column. As they marched with long strides down the street they kept looking back through the battered fence at the factory, which seemed to be watching them through the empty sockets of its windows. At last they crossed the street near the former battalion command post and left the factory behind them. They marched up a dark canyon between towering walls of buildings.

Gollhofer had meanwhile instructed the radio operators to

contact Regiment. "Report that we're on our way. That will give them something to chew on," he added humorously. The consciousness of having carried out a difficult mission so easily filled him with elation.

Suddenly he thought of the men carrying the dead soldier, and his gleeful mood gave way to guilt. He waited until they had gone two blocks further. Then he ordered the company to halt. He walked back to the rear where Steiner and the other three had taken advantage of the halt to lay their burden on the ground. They stood beside it, panting.

"I'll have you relieved," Gollhofer declared so loudly that the rest of the men could not help hearing. "I hope there will be volunteers." He looked the men over, waiting. "As you like," he said after a brief pause. His voice took on a tone of command. "Line up four abreast."

The men obeyed sullenly, while Gollhofer spoke to Steiner. "Take five or ten men and march a hundred yards ahead of the company as advance guard. I'll give you a man who knows the way." Then he went to the head of the line and ordered the first row of four to carry the dead man. "After five minutes you'll pass him to the next, and so on to the end of the line. Then start over at the beginning again."

As Steiner selected his men, Kruger whispered to Faber, "I couldn't have held out much longer." He rubbed his aching arms. "Never knew he was so heavy," he added sadly. He turned to Schulz. "That was damned decent of you. Did you know Schnurrbart?"

Schulz nodded. "*Und wie!* Who didn't know him? Hell, don't mention it. I couldn't leave you to do it all."

They covered a long distance in silence until they reached a street that sloped somewhat uphill. "Do you know this district?" Schulz asked.

Kruger looked around speculatively. "Seems familiar to me. Weren't we here yesterday morning?"

"Sure. Over there, in the next house or the one after, März told us about the attack on the factory."

"Right," Kruger said. His big face started to work; he swallowed, wiped his face with his shirt sleeve and fought vainly against the grief that clawed at his heart. He knew it, he thought. Schnurrbart knew he wouldn't come out of it. The mist of moisture over his eyes grew more and more opaque; he forced his eyes wide open so that he could see where he was going. Their street ran now between a lane of trees into the brightening gray of daylight.

Suddenly he felt that he must have a few words with

Steiner. He caught up with him and asked, "Where are we going?" He had to repeat his question twice before Steiner reacted.

"Doesn't matter," Steiner said.

"Right," Kruger said. "Nothing matters now."

Beyond the trees were one-story houses, small gray cubes each ringed by its green-painted garden fence. "Here's where we got out of the truck," Kruger said.

Steiner did not answer. "Yesterday morning," Kruger said.

Steiner remained silent. But abruptly they all stood still and looked back. In the west a number of low detonations sounded, and a few seconds later a steady rumble thundered up from the city. "They're starting again," Kruger said.

Schulz grinned. "A waste of ammunition." His shoulders twitched with soundless laughter and he held his sharp face toward the sky.

"They should have realized we've cleared out," Kruger commented.

"Guess they haven't," Schulz said. "Why do you think we left so late? That's strategy. The Russians are used to us leaving around midnight when we retreat. By four o'clock in the morning they figured we wouldn't be going."

His reasoning sounded convincing. "Lucky we're not there," someone said. "We really would have been in for something."

The rest of the company had drawn closer, and Gollhofer came running. "What are you loitering for?" he said impatiently. "Let's beat it out of here or we'll get ourselves a dose of the Russian matins." He grinned. "They're going to be in for a surprise when they attack."

They continued on at a smarter pace, and a few minutes later left the suburbs of the city behind. Steiner looked back once more. It was not yet light enough to distinguish more than the gray cones of the mountains suspended in the sky like clouds. The skyline of the city, embedded in the ambiguous dusk of morning, was already almost visible. The sight produced no emotions in him. It was as if all his feeling were frozen and lifeless. But his mind circled incessantly and with great concentration around a single point. He had to settle the account; there was no help for it. Stransky was the man. Triebig had been only his tool. The tool had been eliminated. The hardest task was still ahead. What happened to Steiner himself did not particularly matter, so long as he gave Stransky what was coming to him.

Steiner considered how to do it. Shoot him? That was the simplest way. Where? That question he could not answer until he was back with the battalion.

Gollhofer ran up, calling his name. "For you, Steiner," he said loudly, holding out a scrap of paper. "Radio message from Regiment," he went on respectfully. "You're to go directly to Regiment."

As Steiner indicated neither curiosity nor any other sign of interest, the lieutenant disappointedly thrust the paper into his pocket. "This probably means you're due for the Ritterkreuz," he said with forced gaiety.

Steiner shrugged. The summons troubled him, although he told himself that it could not possibly have any connection with Triebig's death. His expression of sourness deepened.

Gollhofer studied him in wonderment. "What's the matter with you, fellow?" he asked impatiently. "You deserve a decoration. Even if you already have a dozen of them plastered on your chest."

As Steiner remained stubbornly silent, the lieutenant laughed crossly. "You're a queer fish," he said. Offended, he stood still, waiting for the company to catch up with him. Then, as a thought occurred to him, he called out, "You can stay with us; we're going straight to the regimental command post also."

Steiner nodded without turning his head. Faber was marching at his side, and it suddenly struck him that he had not exchanged a word with Faber for hours. The kind of man who never says anything but who's always there when you need him, he thought.

The summons from Regiment continued to prey on his mind. If only he knew what lay behind it. Finally he gave up trying to figure it out. By now it had grown light enough to see the land on both sides of the highway. The vineyards had a melancholy air. The leaves on the harvested vines were already aglow with the colors of autumn, as though they had been dipped into the hot embers of a fire, and as Steiner raised his head he saw the purple veil on the horizon slowly lifting, drawing after it the blue-black shadows of a chain of hills. It looked as if the highway ended in an unearthly radiance shed like a lamp by the earth herself. With an oddly cramped feeling in his chest Steiner watched the sunrise. He saw the faces of the men washed with a pale yellow glow as though they were the souls of the dead marching on the great highroad to heaven. The impression lasted until a blaze flashed across the horizon and the rim of the sun became visible beyond the hills. With silent might it thrust higher, showering light over the last shades of the night. Day had come.

A quarter of an hour later Lieutenant Gollhofer ordered the company to halt. "Your men must continue on from here," he directed Steiner. "They'll do best to stick to the railroad embankment until they reach the tunnel. As far as I know the battalion is somewhere over there."

"Where are we going?" Steiner asked.

Gollhofer indicated a dirt road that branched off the highway on the left and disappeared among the vineyards. "We're taking a short cut. The highway leads to the command post also, but it takes a detour and winds around the hills. We'll be there in an hour if the map is right." While he was speaking he happened to notice Steiner's pack. "What's that you have there?"

At first Steiner did not know what he meant. Then he recalled the captured flag which was still strapped to his assault pack. He had forgotten all about it. "A memento," he said tersely, and turned to Kruger. "Take him to Fetscher," he said hoarsely. "Tell him to make the grave level. Tell him that. So level that nobody will ever spot it as a grave. Clear?" Kruger nodded. "I hope one of you will be able to be present," Steiner went on. "Faber or you. Try."

"Yes," Kruger said.

Steiner hesitated. Then he went over to the men carrying Schnurrbart's body. They had laid him down on the road. Only his nailed mountaineering boots could be seen, protruding from the canvas as though they were things in themselves. Kruger stood beside Steiner, his lips so tightly compressed that they looked like a white streak across his face.

Stiffly, clumsily, Steiner reached over his shoulder and fingered a strap until the red flag fell to the ground. He rolled it up and placed it on the canvas under the dusty boots. "Tell them to cover him with that," he said. They stood side by side, looking down at the dead man.

Gollhofer had quietly come up and was watching the scene, a curious expression around his mouth. "A friend of yours?" he asked.

Steiner turned, crossed the highway and started up the track between the vineyards.

There was a startled silence until Kruger spoke. "He was his brother," he said.

Thin-lipped, Gollhofer watched as they picked up the body and marched off toward the railroad embankment. None of them looked back. When the last man had disappeared beyond the embankment, Gollhofer whirled around and said harshly, "Engineers platoon, march!"

Their way led across a treeless plateau extending westward as far as the eye could see. Suddenly Steiner, who was walking some five hundred yards ahead of them, disappeared as though swallowed up by the earth. Only then did they realize how sharply the land dropped. The valley appeared at their feet so suddenly that they stood stock still. From above, the dip in the land was so extreme as to form what was practically a ravine. Cleft and uneven, the steep slope was almost barren, with only an occasional bush clinging to the rock. A few hundred yards to their right they saw roofs; the highway wound down beyond in four huge spirals. They scrambled down the rough incline. Steiner was waiting for them near the first house. Unhappily Gollhofer observed the dirty-gray walls of the houses and the boarded-up windows. A regular den for bandits, he thought.

A man ran toward them. "The lieutenant colonel wants to speak to you at once, sir," he said to Gollhofer.

The lieutenant nodded. As he pounded the dust from his uniform, he asked where the quarters for the engineers platoon were to be.

The man pointed to a barnlike building. "There, sir." Seeing chagrin on Gollhofer's face, he laughed. "Not as comfortable as Novorossiysk. But it doesn't matter; we'll be moving on again tonight."

"Oh!" Gollhofer exclaimed. His face brightened. "Where to?"

"I don't know. But it's sure that we're pulling out of the bridgehead."

"That's what counts," Gollhofer said. "Where's the commander?"

"In the long building there. I'll take you to him now." The man turned to Steiner. "You're to come too, Sergeant."

In the commander's building they had to wait several minutes in the dirty vestibule until the man came back. "You may come in now, sir," he said to Gollhofer.

"What about me?" Steiner asked.

"Captain Kiesel says you are to wait a little while," the man replied. He wore the chevrons of a staff corporal and had a weary, bored expression.

"If you need me, I'll be in front of the house," Steiner said indifferently.

He went out again. Here in the ravine the shadows had not yet lifted. Only the upper half of the western slope was tinted with a pink which was slowly seeping into the gorge. The houses of this village formed two rows with a lane between. Their chimneys were half crumbled and their slate roofs full of holes. Back of the eastern row of houses the slope was deeply eroded. The ugly ruts led to the dried bed of a stream which was undoubtedly a torrent during the rainy season.

Several vehicles stood on the highway. One of them bore the divisional standard. At the wheel sat a driver, dozing. Steiner slowly wandered about among the houses. Perhaps it was on account of the early hour—it was shortly after six—that so few men were about. At the end of the row of houses a sentry watched in boredom as three men of the signals platoon laid a cable.

Steiner turned and walked toward the other end of the settlement. The gorge led straight for about fifty yards, then bent sharply eastward. The highway, too, following the bed of the stream, disappeared beyond that corner. The last of the buildings stood somewhat at a distance from the others and seemed uninhabited. Glancing in through the glassless windows Steiner saw bundles of straw lying on the bare floor. Behind the house a deep channel wound its way up the western slope of the ravine. In three places the highway cut across this channel. Accustomed to thorough analysis of the most trivial aspects of his surroundings, Steiner traced its course up to the rim of the ravine.

For a few minutes he stood gazing vacantly upward. Then he started back. As he approached the command post he saw the staff corporal standing on the steps, looking around. The man caught sight of him. "The captain is waiting for you."

As he entered the room, Kiesel strode toward him holding out his hand. "I'm very glad you're here!" he said with a cordiality that took Steiner aback. "Make yourself comfortable. You've really been through something. The commander is occupied at the moment, therefore I'm delegated to listen to your story. We may as well get right to it. Smoke?"

Wondering about the captain's intentions, Steiner nodded and accepted a cigarette.

"First of all I'd like to discharge an obligation," Kiesel went on. "I wouldn't have delayed so long except that you've been, shall we say, inaccessible, for quite a while. You saved my brother-in-law's life, and I want to thank you for it. I regret being able to do so only in words, but you've never cared to accept favors from anyone, Steiner, and I hope you understand my feelings."

Steiner shrugged uncomfortably. But his relief was so great that he was able to smile. "He happened to be in my way, so I picked him up, that's all."

A touch of Steiner's sudden geniality passed over into Kiesel's grave face. He nodded as though he had expected some such answer. "We'll drop the subject for the present. Would you mind outlining the events inside the factory from the beginning?"

"If you like." Steiner gave him a summary account. Kiesel scribbled brief notes on a sheet of paper.

At the mention of Triebig's death, the captain interrupted. "A hand grenade, you say?"

"Hand grenade," Steiner assented, scanning Kiesel's face vainly for traces of suspicion. "The lieutenant was standing no more than two feet in front of me when he toppled over."

"Dead?"

"I hope so," Steiner said coldly. "For his sake," he added as Kiesel raised his eyebrows. "If he was not killed the Russians will have butchered him as they did the wounded men whom the lieutenant abandoned to their fate."

Kiesel blanched. "How did that happen?" he asked quickly.

As Steiner went on with his story, the captain's face set in harder and harder lines. Finally he stood up with an awkward movement. "I know you're tired, but we may still need you. Captain Stransky has been ordered to see the commander at nine o'clock. It is possible that in connection with their meeting the commander will have a few more questions for you. Why don't you take a nap until then? Tell the sentry where we can find you. Incidentally . . ." He hesitated, and an edge of curiosity crept into his voice. "What did you do with the flag?"

"Threw it away," Steiner replied curtly. "It was a nuisance to carry."

"Really?" Kiesel's voice expressed doubt. But he asked no more questions and accompanied Steiner to the door, stressing again that he must hold himself in readiness to be called at nine o'clock. "That gives you two and a half hours," he said. "Time to get a bit of rest." He nodded good-by and opened the door.

As Steiner stepped out on the street he wondered whether it had been a mistake to expurgate his story. Originally he had not intended to conceal the manner in which Schnurrbart had been killed. Yet when he came to that part of his report something had compelled him to pass over the matter, although it was highly unlikely that Brandt or Kiesel would infer the connection between the lieutenant's apparent error and his subsequent death. Perhaps the reason had been simply that talking about Schnurrbart at all was still too painful.

But this problem was insignificant in comparison to the vital information that Kiesel had unwittingly given him. As he crossed the street a plan began to form in his mind. With every step it grew clearer. Suddenly a key detail occurred to him. He turned and went back along the street until he met the sentry. "If they look for me," he told the soldier, "I'll be taking a nap in the last house over there. Tell your relief, remember."

The man clicked his heels and said, "Yes, sir."

Steiner headed straight for the house, pleased to note that the sentry was watching him with curiosity.

The house consisted of three small rooms so filthy that Steiner grimaced with disgust. The largest of them had apparently been used off and on as a latrine and stank fearfully. The second room was in somewhat better shape. It was in the center of the house and had a window on the rear. Steiner decided to stay there. With the butt of his tommy gun he hammered the bolt of the door shut and then went to the window. A few yards away the land sloped up toward the highway. He found himself looking directly into the erosion gully. It was six feet deep on the average and from ten to twelve feet wide. Undoubtedly there were more like it in the vicinity, but this, a few steps from the window, was the one for him. The only danger points were the places where the highway crossed it. But it would take a considerable coincidence, Steiner told himself, for anyone to observe him at those points.

Having thought the matter out thus far, he slipped his pack off, laid it on the floor and sat down on it. He was filled with a violent impatience. Waiting seemed intolerable. Nevertheless, he forced himself to sit still for a while.

Finally he swung himself out the window and began to climb the slope. He stayed in the gully, keeping his head low. The ground, soaked by the rain, was slippery and hard going. Panting, he worked his way up to the first winding of the road. There he paused to catch his breath. The roofs of the houses were already a considerable distance below him; he could see the rents in the slates. From above the gorge looked romantically wild. The road crossed the gully on a stone embankment about ten feet high.

Steiner climbed over the stones, scurried across the dusty highway and ducked down again into the continuation of the gully. He had hung the tommy gun across his back in order to leave his hands free. After he had crossed the two other highway embankments he slung it over his shoulder once more, ready to hand, and climbed the rest of the way up the slope. The houses had vanished from his field of vision, but he could survey the ravine for more than a mile. He took a short breather and then followed the road.

Since he could see a considerable distance in both directions, he was safe from unwanted encounters. The land was undulating here, rising somewhat to his left to form a low ridge which would provide good cover if necessary. He had to avail himself of this cover sooner than he had expected. Turning around for a moment, he saw a cloud of dust rapidly approaching. He sprang up the slope, threw himself flat on the ground and watched the approaching vehicle. As it came closer he recognized the divisional car. The driver wore goggles which made his face almost unrecognizable. In the back sat two officers who seemed engaged in an excited discussion. Before he could recognize their rank the car disappeared again behind the billowing dust.

He lay where he was for a few minutes, considering. The regimental command post was still too near. He decided to go on another half mile. As he got up, he wondered about the direction the divisional car had taken. If it kept going at that pace for another half hour, he thought, it would run smack into the Russians. Instead of returning to the road, he continued swiftly on along the top of the ridge, carefully watching the ground to his left. It fell off gently on the other side, then rose again after a few hundred yards to form another ridge. The ground was sandy and slowed him down. After ten minutes he stopped and looked around. The place seemed ideal for his purpose. Here the land dropped off more steeply from the crown of the ridge and he would have to go only a few steps to be completely invisible from the highway.

He unbuckled his belt, took his spade out of its leather case and with the sharp edge marked a large rectangle in the sand. Then he set to work. The ground under the layer of sand was hard and forced him to take many rests. But he made good progress. Now and then he ran to the brow of the hill and gazed westward where the road crawled under the veiled horizon and vanished. Then he resumed his work. Sweat poured down his face and his shirt stuck wetly to his back. After a while he took off his tunic and rolled up his shirt sleeves. He worked until he stood chest-deep in the ground. Then he stopped. Contentedly he looked at the pit; he remembered that a few weeks ago he had done a similar job for Stransky. Its purpose now was different.

As he climbed out of the hole there were grim lines around his mouth. He got into his tunic, buckled his belt and picked up his tommy gun. Then he lay down flat on top of the ridge and waited. It was fifteen minutes after eight.

After dismissing Steiner, Captain Kiesel went into Brandt's office. The commander was sitting with two officers discussing the details of the evacuation of the regiment to the Crimea. As Kiesel entered everyone looked toward him. "All done?" Brandt asked.

Kiesel nodded and sat down. "It's fortunate that Herr Morlock is here," Brandt said, rubbing his sharp chin with the back of his hand. His eyelids fluttered rapidly. "We'll discuss the case afterward," he continued. He turned to Captain Killius, who sat grave-faced beside him. "You know all about it now, so there's no need for you to be here for the conference at ten o'clock. You can set out for the battalion at once and relieve Herr Stransky. Is my car here?" he asked Kiesel.

"You gave it to Lieutenant Stroh," Kiesel reminded him.

"Damn it, so I did," Brandt snapped. "Sorry, Captain Killius, I'm afraid you'll have to walk it. If you keep up a good pace, you'll be there in less than an hour. It's a quarter to seven now. In case Herr Stransky hasn't left yet, you can explain the route to him."

Killius stood up quickly. "I need to stretch my legs anyhow," he said.

Captain Morlock, operations officer of the division, had been listening with interest to the brief exchange. As Killius was about to bid good-by to the commander, he raised his hand. "One moment, please. I believe I can give you a ride, Captain Killius." He bent over the map in front of him. "Yes, you see, here is your road. I drove this same way with the general a few weeks ago. About a mile and a half west of here your road branches off from the highway and runs north until it intersects with the highway again beyond the ravine. For me it will be the smallest detour, while it will save you a good forty minutes."

"I don't want to put you to any trouble," Killius protested.

"Nothing of the sort, Captain Killius. Besides, it will give us a chance to swap some more news." He turned to Brandt with a smile. "Captain Killius and I come from the same town. We discovered it yesterday when we first met at divisional headquarters."

"Then by all means make the most of your chance to talk," Brandt said. "Who knows when you may have another? Perhaps in the Urals," he concluded bitterly.

For the fraction of a second the captain's face changed as a landscape does when the shadow of a cloud passes over it. Then his smile returned, reinforced, and he said, "I do not think our leadership is continuing to entertain such far-reaching goals. We would be content with Baku, sir."

The undertone of reprimand in his words was barely perceptible, but Kiesel detected it. The dark-haired, thin-faced divisional operations officer was well known and feared for his strait-laced ideology. In their occasional meetings Kiesel had strictly avoided anything like a political discussion. Brandt, too, had always been on his guard with the man and had never so much as touched on subjects outside the line of duty.

But now the devil seemed to have entered Brandt. His bass voice rumbled dangerously. "Don't misconstrue what I said, Herr Morlock; I don't like having my words twisted. For the past year our goals have been determined not by us but by the Russians. You know that as well as I." He snorted. "You at Division should be able to see that more clearly than I can."

"Undoubtedly," Morlock said coolly. The shadow had returned to his face. As he spoke he looked at his hands which he had placed palms down on the desk. "Undoubtedly," he repeated. Uneasily Kiesel noted the tightening lines around his mouth. "Precisely because we can see the whole situation more clearly," Morlock went on somewhat more loudly, "we beg to differ with you, sir. I believe the general would be very much surprised to hear your views. Rightly surprised, if I may add my personal opinion."

Brandt looked back at him with an amused twinkle in his gray eyes. "I'll tell you something," he said, glancing at Killius who had sat down again and was taking in the talk with obvious discomfort. "I don't know where the blinkers are made that so many people wear over their eyes. So long as they don't blind me, I don't mind them. But only so long." His tone had suddenly become chilly.

Now he stood up. The leather of his boots squeaked loudly as he went to the window and stood there with averted face, looking out.

With feelings of mingled admiration and nervousness Kiesel looked at Brandt's broad back, and then at the frozen face of the operations officer, who was sitting rigid and unstirring, again studying his hands.

Morlock looked up when Brandt abruptly crossed the room in three big strides, pulled the leather strap of binoculars from the nail in the wall, returned to the window and held the glasses to his eyes. He said nothing, and none of the other men ventured to ask a question.

Killius, leaning across the table to Kiesel, whispered, "Planes?"

"We'd hear them," Kiesel said, shrugging.

Brandt was leaning forward eagerly now, pressing the binoculars to his eyes. His peculiar behavior was highly disturbing.

At last Kiesel could not refrain from asking, "Anything unusual?"

Brandt did not reply. He remained at the window for a moment more and slowly lowered the binoculars. When he turned around there was an expression of deep wonderment on his face. But he did not explain. Instead he said to Killius in a tone of forced calm, "There was one more thing I wanted to say to you. I would appreciate your not mentioning Herr Stransky's transfer to him. I should like to surprise him. I'll send for his baggage."

"Of course," Killius said, rising.

"Didn't you also want to talk with me about Herr Stransky?" Morlock asked.

Brandt looked at him for a moment out of half-shut eyes. He shook his head. "There's time for that later. I must talk with him first." He turned to Kiesel. "You accompany the gentlemen to the car," he said, and shook hands vigorously with Killius. He took leave of Morlock with a curt nod. When the door had closed behind them he went to the window and watched the car start up the winding highway, wrapped in a cloud of dust.

Kiesel returned immediately. The manner in which he took his seat expressed so much concern and incomprehension that Brandt drew up his mouth in a scornful smile. He stood with folded arms, looking at the captain with an air of challenge. At last, in the face of Kiesel's persistent silence, he said, "Well?" The ironic undertone could not be missed.

Kiesel's lined face flashed a variety of expressions. When he spoke, it was with an almost pedantic carefulness. "You pose riddles," he said quietly. "Would you be surprised if some day I should ask you to replace me?"

Brandt's face reflected in rapid succession indignation, disdain and finally vexation. Only in the depths of his eyes was there a trace of the superior expression on his face a moment before. "I don't think I would be surprised," he retorted coolly. "You know perfectly well that I would not let you go. Not because you are indispensable—you aren't, any more than I am—but because I might land a creature like Morlock for adjutant. You get on my nerves at times, but I've grown accustomed to that, and I have the right to ask the same of you—that you get used to me."

Kiesel tilted his head to one side. "It was only a theoretical question," he said serenely. "If I couldn't stand you as my superior officer, I would have one consolation: that my problem will soon be over. Another conversation like the one you've just had with Herr Morlock and there's likely to be a violent solution to the problem."

"I see." Brandt smiled. "Are you afraid?" he asked slyly.

"A person is only afraid for himself," Kiesel replied, shrugging. "After all, it's not my neck you were risking with your loose talk."

Brandt frowned. "Is that all you have to say?"

"No." Kiesel shook his head. "I want to apologize to you," he added gravely.

Brandt went over to his desk and looked absently down at the papers strewn over it. "We can talk about that later," he said. "What did you learn from Steiner?"

"A fascinating story!" Kiesel said and retold it. The commander listened to him in silence, his face expressionless. "A certain imprecision about the report," Kiesel said. "I have the feeling that Steiner concealed one or two details. It might be a good idea to question another participant."

"What for?" Brandt asked.

Kiesel shrugged. "I suspect that Steiner is still trying to save Stransky."

"I doubt that," Brandt said forcefully. Kiesel looked up at him, startled by the emphasis in his voice. Brandt smiled oddly. "Where is Steiner at the moment?" he asked.

"In the house next door, I suppose. I suggested that he sleep for a couple of hours, until we would need him."

"Does he know Stransky is coming here?"

"I don't know," Kiesel said, considering. Then he nodded. "Yes, I remember—I mentioned it."

"You mentioned it!" Brandt repeated. He suddenly broke out into hysterical laughter that shook his whole big body. "You're priceless," he said, gasping for breath. Then he became serious so abruptly that Kiesel could scarcely follow the alterations of mood. He sprang to his feet again and went to the window once more. For a few moments he stook looking up the slope of the ravine.

When he turned around, there was a grim sparkle in his eyes. "I told you this morning that you were unstable, Kiesel," he said. "But you are not only unstable, you are naïve. Do you know whom I observed with my binoculars awhile ago?" His face suddenly looked alien and brutal to Kiesel. "I saw Steiner. Steiner, who you think is next door taking a couple of hours of well-deserved rest. What a fool you are, Kiesel!"

He chuckled and folded his arms across his chest. "Steiner is a product of our times," he said, and Kiesel thought he detected a trace of satisfaction in the commander's voice. "Do you recall what I said to you about justice? Of course you do. And I should like to add that a man like Steiner makes no bones about correcting Providence when the powers above bungle things. What is more, he'd be a thrice-damned fool if he let a good chance slip by because he trusted in heavenly justice. The justice of heaven is a dream of the weak, Kiesel, and it's about time you absorbed that idea."

He became silent and began to pace the room. When Kiesel rose without a word and started toward the door, Brandt blocked his way. "Where are you going?"

Kiesel did not reply, but his pale face answered enough for Brandt.

"You have more imagination than I thought," Brandt said coldly. "But I cannot do without you for the next hour. The march routes for the battalions have to be settled and I'll need your help."

"I'll be back in ten minutes." Kiesel's voice sounded muffled, tense, and resolute.

Brandt shook his head mockingly. "You will stay here," he declared firmly. "Do you understand me?"

Again Kiesel did not reply.

Brandt returned to his desk and bent over the maps. "Come here," he said sharply. Kiesel continued to stand immobile at the door. The commander's tone changed. "In case you are not yet aware of it, I have given you an order."

"I know," Kiesel said. His voice thickened with rage, he added, "You are making me guilty as an accomplice."

Brandt straightened up. "I am on the point of leading my regiment into a cul de sac from which it has not the slightest chance of escaping. To what sort of guilt are you referring?"

"That is still no excuse for this other thing," Kiesel said stubbornly.

"You are evading my question," Brandt retorted. "But as matters stand, I have no time for philosophical debate when there are these important decisions to make. Now will you kindly drop the question and attend to business?" He sat down at the desk. "Let's start with Killius' company," he said crisply.

XVII

IT WAS twenty minutes to nine when a dark spot crawled up over the horizon of the road and slowly drew nearer. Twenty minutes to nine; this must be Stransky, Steiner thought. He laid the tommy gun ready to hand on the ground beside him and peered with narrowed eyes along the gray ribbon of road that wound so forlornly across the undulating landscape. The highway seemed utterly out of place in the context of the scenery; the telegraph poles looked like big posts stuck into the ground for no reason at all.

The dark spot in the distance increased in size. Steiner regretted having no binoculars with him. He continued to lie flat. In spite of the early morning hour he felt the warmth of the sand through his uniform. Tiredness trickled from his brain to his toes. He figured it out—fifty hours since he had last slept. As long as that! he thought in astonishment; again he turned his attention to the dark spot, which had meanwhile come much closer. Still he could distinguish nothing more than a formless something that moved with agonizing slowness down the highway. Often it seemed to stand completely still for minutes at a time. Gradually, however, Steiner made out the figure of a man striding forward at a vigorous pace.

At last he was convinced that the man was Stransky. With a relieved sigh he tucked the tommy gun under his arm and crawled back a little way so that he could no longer be seen from the road. Now that the decision was nearing, silently and steadily, he could feel the sweat that ran, salty-tasting, into the corners of his mouth. His throat seemed choked. His hands twitched restlessly. He inched back a little more, then instantly worked forward again and remained lying still as a stone. Stransky had by now come within some two hundred yards of him. With every step the man took Steiner's face changed like a sand bar under the wind. At last it froze into a mask in which only the eyes remained alive, burning. The oiled steel of the gun lay cool and firm in his hands. As he pushed back the safety, he did so with so utter a lack of feeling that he was not even conscious of the movement.

Suddenly he shot up as though snapped by a spring. For a few seconds he disregarded all caution. Stransky was not

alone. To one side of him there appeared the figure of a
man who must have been marching along behind the commander all the while. Steiner stared at this man as though he
had fallen from the sky. He had thought of some such possibility but only fleetingly. What should he do? If he shot
Stransky, the captain's companion would have to share his
fate. Otherwise, the man would run straight to Regiment
with his tale. There was no way out. As Steiner watched the
two of them he became aware, with grim contempt for himself, of how much value he had placed on a perfect alibi, how
careful he was being to cover his tracks. A few hours ago
he would have maintained that he didn't care. He had thought
he was finished with himself, with everything. That had been
a mistake.

With a gesture of finality he braced the butt of the tommy
gun against his armpit. The two men swiftly approached,
Stransky walking with that peculiar, rather rocking gait of
his, his right hand resting lightly on his hip, while his companion trotted along apathetically behind him. He was a
stranger to Steiner. Probably he had come with the last batch
of replacements, Steiner thought; perhaps he was the captain's
orderly. He could distinctly see Stransky's face now. It wore
an expression of gloom, and the manner in which he stared
at the ground also suggested that his thoughts were none too
happy.

By now they had come within fifty paces, and Steiner
knew it was time to act. Still he held back. Something in the
bearing of the man tramping behind Stransky troubled him,
made him unsure of himself. It was a man like any other,
with a face like all the faces which had permanently peopled
his surroundings for so many months—haggard, weary and
utterly indifferent. The man's arms hung loosely, his body
seemed to be following the movements of his legs with reluctance. A dusty, unpressed uniform without insignia, a
visored cap under which a few strands of hair protruded, and
a carbine slung diagonally across his back. At every step
tiny puffs of dust whirled up from the ground, and his boots
looked as if he had been wading through chalk.

Steiner stared at him. Were there really two men marching
along the highway? Wasn't there just one? He was marching
on a road without end, a road that ran on over the horizon
as though there were no horizon, a straight, dusty-gray, merciless road. A weary, apathetic, hopeless man. And looking at
his face Steiner told himself that the man would never reach
the end of the road, for the road now had no end. The longer
he stared at that face, the more familiar it seemed to him.

Suddenly he thought that it was Dietz. He opened his mouth to scream, but his voice did not obey him. Then, numbed, he thought he recognized Dorn. Again it was not Dorn but Hollerbach, Hollerbach who . . .

He groaned and stirred. Part of his conscious mind noted the movement with which he rose up beside the road. Then reality leaped at him once more. Stransky was there in front of him. Stransky, who had seen him now and was standing petrified. They confronted each other, motionless as the telegraph poles behind them, no more than ten paces separating them.

As Steiner raised the barrel of his gun, the two walking held their breath. Steiner's face was frightful to behold. Stransky saw only his face, like a white disk, and the meaning of this meeting burst on him. He made no attempt to reach for the pistol which hung, ludicrously small, at his belt. Nor did he think of his companion who stood beside him, open-mouthed, stunned. Stransky simply started to run. His right hand dropped away from his hip, and he ran down the road, bending low so that only his back could be seen, his feet drumming a rapid tattoo on the gravel. Steiner followed him with his eyes. He watched him without moving, turning his head just enough to keep Stransky in view. Stransky's companion started forward and ran after the commander, the dust spurting up under his boots.

Steiner slowly let the barrel of the tommy gun slide toward the ground. They won't make it, he thought. He watched as their figures became smaller and smaller. They were still running, desperate and tireless as hunted game, and Steiner muttered, "It is useless," without awareness of what his words meant.

He suddenly felt unutterably tired and sat down. The idiots, he thought, shaking his head. He had the feeling that he had missed the greatest opportunity in his life. But he did not feel unhappy about it and wondered why.

After a while he set out along the road to rejoin his company.

Stransky did not stop until his feet began to stumble and fiery needles were pricking his brain. Gasping for air, he looked back. About fifty yards behind him his orderly was running through the dust like a lame horse, his head jogging from side to side with every step. There was no longer any sign of Steiner. Endless, dusty, deserted, the highway ran due west, and for a moment Stransky was inclined to think that he had been the victim of hallucination. But he rejected the idea at once. Although his nerves had been subjected to great strains of late, he knew he was not so far gone. Steiner's face and the Russian tommy gun in his hands, the whole horrible encounter, were still so vivid in his mind that there was no pretending it had been an illusion. His whole body was trembling, and he pressed his hands against his chest to still the irregular thudding of his heart. Still half mad with terror and shock, he looked at his orderly, who had slowed his pace and was shambling along unwillingly. The man's haggard face had an expression of outrage, and deep within those colorless eyes Stransky thought he detected astonishment mingled with contempt. In a flash Stransky became aware of how frightfully foolish his behavior had been. What must the man be thinking of him?

He turned swiftly so that he would no longer be exposed to that scornful gaze. Without a word of explanation, he continued on his way. The longer he thought about the encounter, going over the wretched role he had played, the more depressed he became. I'm disgraced, he thought, disgraced forever. Rage flickered up in him and quickly faded as he realized soberly that what had happened could not be undone. He had run away from Steiner like a whipped dog; he had no proof at all that Steiner had intended to kill him. He could feel his ego crumbling piece by piece, as though it were the bark of a dead tree.

He walked the rest of the way without paying the least attention to his surroundings. Not until the road dipped into the ravine did he recall the painful interview he was facing. But even this thought failed to produce any emotion in him. All through the morning he had pondered it so steadily that now, with the clash immediately before him, he was capable only of apathy. He was simply at the end of his rope.

When he reached the regimental command post, he instructed the orderly to wait outside. For a few seconds he stood in front of a door through which the commander's booming voice could be heard. He knocked. The conversation stopped and someone said loudly, "Come in."

Stransky opened the door. Directly opposite him he saw Kiesel, who jumped up from his chair by the desk so suddenly that Stransky flinched. The commander remained in his seat. He was looking up, and his face was printed with a mixture of surprise and disappointment that Stransky found utterly perplexing. The odd look persisted as Brandt opened his mouth and exclaimed, "You!"

Stransky struggled for composure. This fantastic reception aroused again that thumping of his heart which he felt down to his finger tips. He closed the door behind him and blinked alternately at the faces of the two officers. The difference in their expressions only increased his bewilderment. As the commander's face grew steadily angrier, Kiesel's seemed to lighten—still further baffling Stransky who had been expecting a particularly frosty reception from the adjutant.

It was Kiesel, too, who broke the already embarrassing silence. With a mysterious twinkle in his clear eyes he said to the commander, "You made an appointment with Herr Stransky for nine o'clock!"

Brandt slowly turned his head. With mounting uneasiness Stransky witnessed the exchange of glances between the commander and his adjutant. He had to lean against the wall to suppress the sudden weakness in his legs.

The movement did not escape Brandt. "You are punctual," he said, and pointed to a chair. "Sit down." As Stransky obeyed, Brandt, with set features, studied a large map on the table before him. Finally he raised his head. "Get me Killius," he said to Kiesel.

A few minutes of tormenting silence passed until Kiesel handed the telephone across the table. "He's on the line, now."

Brandt nodded. Both elbows on the table, he asked a few questions; Stransky was disturbed to hear his name mentioned several times. "Very well, Captain Killius," Brandt said at last and laid down the telephone.

"You missed Captain Killius," he explained to Stransky. "Captain Killius reached your former battalion without meeting you. Didn't you go by the highway?"

Former battalion, Stransky thought; he said, Former battalion. His voice hoarse with agitation, he replied, "Only part of the way. We took a short cut for the first mile or so."

"Who is we?" Brandt asked quickly.

Stransky moistened his dry lips. "I have my orderly with me," he said with an effort. "He's waiting outside."

"I see." Brandt studied him with slitted eyes. Suddenly he turned to Kiesel. "Bring the man in."

Stransky shifted about in his chair. There was no need for my saying that, he thought. The idiot will tell the whole story and . . . The idea took his breath away. My God! he thought.

But Kiesel was already back. Sheepishly, cap in hand, Stransky's orderly followed him into the room. He clicked his heels resoundingly lifted his eyes timidly to the commander's face.

Brandt waited until Kiesel had taken a seat. Then he asked the orderly, "Anything happen on your way here?"

The man threw an embarrassed look at Stransky. Unaware that Brandt was watching him, Stransky blinked his eyes furiously at the orderly. At the sound of the commander's incisive voice he turned around in panic.

"If you can't keep your eyes still," Brandt said, "I'll have you stand in a corner." He turned to the soldier again. "Speak up, man, and don't you dare lie to me or hold back. Is that clear?"

"Jawohl!" the man said, terrified. Kiesel, catching the expression of shame and embarrassment on Stransky's face, once again felt admiration for the commander's sure instinct.

"Well, what happened?" Brandt asked.

The man dropped his eyes. "All of a sudden he was standing in the road," he mumbled awkwardly.

"Who?" Brandt snapped.

"The sergeant. He stood there with a Russian tommy gun in his hand, and the captain ran away."

"Ran away?" Brandt repeated incredulously, leaning across the desk.

The man nodded. "He just ran," he said helplessly. "And then I ran too, I don't know . . ."

He glanced nervously at Stransky. Kiesel bit his lip. He suddenly saw the scene and found it hard to keep a straight face. Even Brandt's glowering features were twitching as he asked, "And why did you run away?"

Again the man threw a perplexed glance at Stransky, who sat motionless, head lowered. "I don't know," the man faltered. "The sergeant was holding his gun in such a queer way."

"Did he fire?" Brandt said quickly.

The man shook his head. "He was one of our soldiers," he said in shocked surprise. "How could he have fired at us?"

"Right." Brandt got up, went to the window and stood there for more than five minutes, face averted from the three in the room. Finally he turned. "Go back to your battalion," he said to the orderly. He waited until the door had closed. Then he went to his desk, picked up a letter and stood for a few seconds looking down at it.

Kiesel watched him breathlessly. He could not have said why, but he had the feeling that he was witnessing a magnificent scene. He was not mistaken. With an inimitable gesture that expressed contempt, superiority and pity all at the same time, Brandt tossed the letter across the desk so adroitly that it fluttered into Stransky's lap. Stransky reached for it with both hands.

Before he could begin to read it, the commander's icy voice

lashed him to his feet. "Examine it outside," Brandt said. "I don't want to see any more of you. Run, you little shit!"

Stransky stared open-mouthed at that stony face. When he did not stir, Brandt said to Kiesel, "Open the door for him."

Kiesel obeyed. At that moment he wanted to embrace Brandt like a brother.

"Go," Kiesel said. He avoided looking at Stransky's face as the man lurched past him to the door. Then he went to Brandt's side and watched with him as Stransky stepped out onto the street and stood still to read the letter. His face remained expressionless. Finally he thrust the sheet of paper almost carelessly into his pocket and moved off down the street, shoulders drooping, growing smaller and smaller until he disappeared from sight around a turn in the ravine.

"What I cannot understand," Brandt said hoarsely, "is why this creature is the one to escape. Stransky, of all people!"

Shaking his head, he returned to his desk and dropped heavily into a chair.

Kiesel remained at the window, his intelligent eyes fixed on the commander. "Why do you say that?"

"Why?" Brandt laughed bitterly. "You know as well as I what awaits us. Hundreds of times we've escaped; hundreds of times we've been caught in the trap and each time found a way out somehow. But this time . . ." He paused. "This time there is no way out," he finished glumly.

Although Kiesel knew how right he was, he tried to find something encouraging to say. "It isn't as bad as all that. Things may still turn out."

"Don't fool yourself," Brandt said surlily. "When they pick on us as the last division for the Crimea, the meaning is another Stalingrad. Even if we should succeed in reaching Sevastopol, we won't find so much as a rowboat to take us off. No, this time our number is up, Kiesel, and perhaps it's just as well. I really think it is just as well."

Kiesel felt a sudden sinking sensation. He looked out the window at the hovels that made up this village and clenched his teeth. Brandt's remarks were certainly not the product of exaggerated pessimism. Rather, they represented the logical conclusion to be drawn from what Morlock had said. The Russians were already established west of Melitopol and were pushing toward Perekop with strong armored forces. If the intention actually was to evacuate the Crimea by water—and that would follow from Morlock's talk about delaying tactics—then it was plain as day that the available shipping space could accommodate only a fraction of the troops stationed in the Crimea. Sooner or later the majority of those troops would suffer the same fate as the Sixth Army at Stalingrad.

During the past several years Kiesel had repeatedly considered where the division would run its last lap. He had thought of many possibilities. But that it would be in the Crimea was something he had never imagined. As he looked out over the ravine, up to the barren rims of the slope, beyond which the blue of the sky glowed like a chalice in eternity, his eyes misted slightly and he felt a dull pressure in his breast. Between clenched teeth he exhaled against the window with a hissing sound.

"What's the trouble?" the commander asked. When Kiesel did not reply, the commander's mouth twisted in a weary smile. "Don't worry about it," he said quietly. "We could scarcely expect anything else, and we have done our duty. You and I and all of us. But we undertook to do too much, and that is our misfortune."

He lighted a cigarette. Casually he added, "Incidentally, whatever happens in the Crimea need not cause you any personal concern. You will not be affected."

"What do you mean by that?"

The tired, superior smile flitted once more across Brandt's stern face. "By that I mean I shall send you on leave before the end is reached."

Kiesel thought he had not heard right. Behind his back he dug his fingers into the wood of the window frame. Never, he thought. "You aren't serious," he said.

"Not serious?" Brandt repeated. He spoke with unfamiliar mildness. "I am always more serious than you're inclined to think, Kiesel. I shall send you on leave before the noose is drawn and knotted, and I see no way for you to block me. . . ."

"Do you think so?" Kiesel whispered.

Brandt nodded quietly. "Your chances of fighting a furlough are practically nil. Should you attempt to provide me with a show of heroism, you'll have a bitter disappointment. I am not a bit impressed by shows of heroism." He leaned forward, smiling. "You see, Kiesel," he said serenely, "you have misunderstood me so often in the past that one more misunderstanding wouldn't matter much. But since I am going to part with you, I want you to know why. You know the story of Noah." His smile broadened. "Noah built the ark and saved himself and his family from the flood. He became the bridge between the old and the new humanity, and he took elements of both into the new world: the good and the evil. I am trying to do the same. I have given evil a chance in the special case of Stransky, and I shall give the good a chance also, and no power in this world will prevent me."

Kiesel still scarcely dared to breathe. After a long pause he said, "You overlook one factor."

"Which is that?"

"Noah saved himself in the ark."

"Noah was not a regimental commander," Brandt retorted. "Any more questions?" Kiesel shook his head silently. "Then we can go back to our work. We still have a great deal to do before the flood. Now let's see, Körner's battalion will . . ."

"One more thing, please," Kiesel said.

Brandt looked up in surprise. "What might that be?" he asked curtly.

"You've forgotten Steiner."

"I haven't forgotten him. Steiner is a case all to himself. How late is it?"

Kiesel looked at his watch and gasped. "Five to ten," he said. "The battalion commanders will be here any moment now."

"Tell the sentry to show them the way," Brandt ordered. "They can wait in the next room till I call them. And one thing more. Telephone Killius and ask whether Steiner has reached the Second Company. Hurry."

He bent over his work again and did not look up until Kiesel returned to the room. Something about Kiesel's expression boded ill. "What's the matter?" Brandt asked.

Kiesel hung back in the doorway. His voice thick, he reported, "Captain Körner has already arrived."

"And?"

Kiesel pulled himself together. "Captain Killius informs me that one of his noncoms, Senior Sergeant Steiner, was wounded by a Russian shell just ten minutes ago. He is already being taken back to the clearing station."

"I see," Brandt said. He kept his eyes on the desk before him as he continued. "There you are—Steiner is a special case. I am glad I did not have to exceed my authority. Keep Captain Körner company for a while. When the rest of the officers are here, let me know. I'll finish this up alone. Go on now."

He waited until Kiesel had left the room. Then he walked to the window. Hands clasped behind his back, he held his face up to the sunlight which slanted down over the ravine. Star and flower, he thought. It was ten o'clock in the morning, and the hill opposite was bare as a board. The words went through his head in endless iteration: star and flower, star and flower. There was no color in his face.

In the distance muted detonations rumbled out of the sky, to be swallowed up in the October stillness. But Brandt did not really hear them. There was a greater stillness in him than the quiet which covered the horizons like a hood of glass. He felt unencumbered and content, like a man who has ordered his life and marked out his road. There was no longer anything to do but wait.

Behind him the door opened and he heard Kiesel saying, "The commanders are here." For a while the officers stood stiffly erect, looking at one another.

Then Brandt walked slowly to his desk and tucked the assortment of papers under his arm. "Well, gentlemen, here we are again," he said.

XVIII

THE battalion had occupied its last position in the bridgehead. Second Company was posted at the exit of the tunnel, its front facing west, and all the men except for the sentries had lain down to catch up on their sleep. Sergeant Schultz was in command of what remained of the company. He sat at the tunnel exit with Kruger and Faber. Their monosyllabic conversation had faded out entirely a few minutes before, and they were watching dully as Kruger, with ferocious care, inspected the miserable remnants of his socks.

Suddenly he cursed and drove his fist through a huge hole where, a few hundred miles back, there had been a heel. "Look at that thing!"

"Put your stinking socks away," Schulz said in disgust. "What can we do about it? Go see the paymaster."

"Paymaster?" Kruger snorted. "Maybe you can tell me where there's a paymaster on the whole eastern front? I tell you, either I'm going to get a new pair of socks or they can stick these up their arses, the damned war profiteers."

"I have only one pair myself," Faber said, shrugging. "You should have asked Fetscher."

"Fetscher!" Kruger waved his hand grumpily. "Did you see what a face he made when he saw Schnurrbart? Pretty near started to bawl. Though we had more reason to than him."

"Where did you bury him?" Schulz asked. He gazed out into the sunny October day.

Kruger's face hardened. "There were a few trees around,"

he said tersely. "About two miles from the supply dump. Well . . ."

Schulz scratched in the dirt with his fingers. "That was decent of Moninger, giving you the cart. You wouldn't have been able to carry him the two miles."

Kruger nodded. After reaching the battalion he had gone to the commander of the First Company and borrowed a horse-drawn, two-wheeled weapons wagon on which they had moved Schnurrbart. Since Stransky had appointed Schulz temporary commander of Second Company until Steiner's return, Kruger and Faber had had no trouble leaving the company for two hours. They had come back a few minutes ago and so far had not said a word about their brief expedition.

Schulz asked no more questions. He began talking about the new battalion commander. The two listened to him in high astonishment.

"It's funny, changing commanders so sudden," Kruger said suspiciously. "Have you had a squint at the new one?"

"Not yet," Schulz replied. "He telephoned and said he would be coming up here this morning to look over the position. Stransky has just up and vanished. I wish I knew where."

"Who cares?" Kruger grunted. He had already lost interest in the conversation and was gloomily studying his dirty bare foot.

Schulz lighted a cigarette. "I wonder where the Russians are." He looked up ahead where a heavy machine gun was emplaced. The sentry stood motionless gazing across the railroad embankment toward the west, where there were no signs of life.

"They'll be along soon enough," Kruger said. "I'd be more interested to know what's happened to Steiner. It's almost ten o'clock."

"Me too," Schulz said. He lowered his voice. "I hope there's no stink about Triebig. If any of those fellows starts shooting his mouth off, there's going to be trouble."

"What's that?" Kruger said sharply. His apathy dropped away all at once. When Schulz shrugged and made no reply, Kruger leaned toward him. His voice sounded so menacing that Schulz edged away from him. "Triebig had a Russian hand grenade blow up in his mug and that's all there was to it. If anybody says any different, I'll personally bash his skull in. Let's get that clear."

"Don't shout about it," Schulz said uncomfortably, looking around with a scared expression.

But Kruger was not so easily subdued. His face flushed a deep red. "I'll shout all I please, and if anybody has something against it he'd better come and see me with his steel helmet buckled on so he can pick up his bones later, the swine."

He seemed on the point of continuing in the same tone. Faber laid a hand soothingly on his shoulder. "Why work yourself up?" he said quietly. "No one is shooting off his mouth, and if anyone does, we're still here. Till then we can hold our fire."

Kruger slowly calmed down. He once more gave himself to the observation of his dirty foot, and thought that he simply had to get a chance to wash soon. Since this idea necessarily was connected with a bathtub, his reflections landed him back home in Königsberg. He sighed.

"What's the matter?" Schulz asked.

Kruger shrugged. "I was thinking about something," he said evasively. He turned to Faber. "Why are you so quiet?"

"I'm not one for talking," the woodsman said.

Kruger nodded. "That's true." It had never really struck him before, but now he realized how little Faber spoke. "That has its points. I once knew a girl who was just as quiet as you."

"She would be the wife for me," Schulz put in. "Why didn't you marry her?"

Kruger did not answer, and the other two did not press the matter. Schulz puffed away at his cigarette. Farther back in the tunnel several men were vying with one another to snore the loudest. The sentry at the machine gun stood with head drooping, half-asleep on his feet.

"*Scheisse*," Schulz said. The other two looked inquiringly at him. He raised his shoulders and explained. "Everything." A thought occurred to him. "Is it true that your father was a Russian?" he asked.

"You mean me?" Kruger asked.

Schulz nodded. "Yes, you. Some one told me that awhile back—I don't remember who."

Kruger drew on his boot. His face had darkened and his voice rumbled dangerously. "Does Kruger sound Russian? If you want to know, he had Russian citizenship, that's all. Besides which, he died five years ago."

"Oh," Schulz said. There was an embarrassed silence. Kruger busied himself with the laces of his boot.

"What about your mother?" Faber asked.

"She's been dead a long time," Kruger said, standing up.

He walked off, shoulders stooping. "*Scheisse*," Schulz said again. He tossed his cigarette butt between the rails and yawned. For a few minutes he sat moping; then he picked up his tommy gun and yawned again. "I'm going to catch a few winks," he said glumly to Faber. "When the new Iron Cross hound comes by, wake me." He walked a short distance back into the tunnel, where the others were sleeping, lay down beside the rails, shoved his pack under his head and closed his eyes.

Faber watched him. Farther back the darkness was like viscous ink, while up ahead, no more than ten yards in front of him, the sunlight flooded into the tunnel entrance with such a glare that Faber had to squint to see at all. He sat still for a while. Then he decided on a short walk to see what the terrain looked like. He went past the machine gunner out into the open. The ridge through which the tunnel passed rose almost vertically above him, its muddy slope quite barren. Halfway up this slope several men were standing waist-deep in a foxhole, looking down at him.

"What are the Russians doing?" Faber called up to them.

One of the men laughed. "Not a sign of them. I'll bet my ass they're still sitting in Novorossiysk guzzling champagne. Where you going? Reconnaissance?"

"Too dangerous," Faber said. He was about to add a word or two, but was interrupted.

From higher up came a loud call, and a man said, "Someone's coming."

"A Russian?" Faber asked. From his position he could not see any great distance.

The man above shook his head. "I doubt it; must be one of our men."

Faber peered westward over the railroad embankment. The tracks glistened in the sunlight and merged in the distance into a single silvery ribbon that ran straight on into the blue sky. "He's coming from the right," the man above said, hitching himself out of the foxhole.

With a sudden feeling of certainty that this was Steiner, Faber asked, "From the highway?"

"Yes."

Faber hesitated a moment longer. Then he said, "I'll go see who it is."

He climbed down the embankment. To reach the highway he had to cross through a wide field of tall grapevines whose thick foliage cut off the view. Careful not to damage any of the vines, he squeezed his big body between wires and posts down to the road. Steiner was trudging toward him, a cigarette drooping from the corner of his mouth. Steiner must surely have seen him, but he did not increase his pace, and his face remained a blank. He covered the rest of the way be-

tween them casually, as though he had been expecting this
meeting. A few feet away he stood still and took the cigarette
from his mouth.

Faber looked back in the direction from which Steiner had
come. "The Russians might have been here by now," he said
reproachfully.

"I'd have seen them," Steiner returned. "I came back the
same way because I didn't know where you were."

"Didn't you find out at Regiment?" Faber asked.

"I forgot to ask. Besides, I didn't report that I was leaving.
Have they asked for me yet?"

Troubled, Faber studied Steiner's face. It was somehow
changed, although he could not have said what was different
about it. "Not yet," he answered slowly. "How did you get
through the front line?"

"I have no idea," Steiner replied indifferently. "What does
front line mean here, anyway? Where's Kruger?"

"He's back there."

"I've got to talk with him right away," Steiner said. "I have
to disappear. Take me to him."

"You have to what?" Faber exclaimed.

"Don't waste time talking," Steiner said impatiently. "I
have to skip out, but fast. Has there been any fuss about me
yet?" Seeing the blank expression on Faber's face, he added,
"I mean on account of Triebig."

"I don't understand you," Faber said. "Why should there
be any fuss?"

"Sometimes you get on my nerves," Steiner snapped angrily. "For Christ's sake, take me to Kruger."

"All right," Faber said. They turned off the road and made
a path through the vines until they reached the railroad embankment. "There's where we're stationed," Faber said, pointing to the tunnel.

Steiner nodded. They still had about a hundred feet to go.
They walked swiftly along the tracks, stepping from tie to tie.

Steiner just had time to hear the shell coming before an
inconceivable force tossed him into the air. In a cloud of
black smoke, he flew to the side and crashed to the ground
like a plank. He uttered one brief shriek. Then he lay motionless. Several men dashed out of the tunnel, lifted him and
carried him back.

When he opened his eyes, he saw Kruger's face above him.
"So there you are," he whispered.

"Yes," Kruger said. He gulped. "I was beginning to think
you'd had it."

What's the matter with him, Steiner thought. "Why are you bawling?" he asked.

"I'm not bawling," Kruger said, turning his head away.

"You are," Steiner said. "Where did I get it?" There were several other faces bending over him. These bothered him. "Go away," he said to them. Then he remembered that Kruger had not answered his question. He attempted to grin. "Is my ass gone?"

"Not your ass," Kruger said.

Steiner tried moving his arms but could not. Because he felt no pain he became impatient and struggled to sit up. But Kruger held him fast. "Don't make a fuss," he said roughly. "They'll come for you in a minute."

"The gravediggers?" Steiner asked. He felt something moist run out of his mouth. He knew it was blood and thought: in the lung. Suddenly he felt the pain. It was everywhere, in his back, in his chest, in his legs, in his brain—everywhere. He groaned and closed his eyes. What rotten luck, he thought.

"Don't be silly," Kruger said. "The medics from the clearing station are coming for you."

Steiner grinned. "Comes to the same thing."

"I wanted to go with you," Kruger said dolefully. "But Schulz won't let me go. I'm the last noncom here." They were silent for a while. Then Kruger looked at his watch. "Where the devil are they?" he murmured restively. "It's more than twenty minutes already."

"Since when?"

"Since you were hit. Took you ten minutes to come to and I was beginning to think you'd had it."

The words sounded familiar to Steiner; when had he heard them before? But suddenly a noise reached his ears that drew his attention. It was like a man screaming with his head wrapped in a thick blanket.

"What's that?" he asked.

"Faber," Kruger answered softly.

"What's the matter with Faber?" Kruger did not answer. Steiner stared at his twitching face. "What's the matter with Faber?" he demanded again.

"I think they're coming," Kruger said. From the depths of the tunnel footsteps thumped over the ties, and a voice called, "Where are the wounded?"

"Here," Kruger called back. "His eyes," he said to Steiner.

"What about his eyes?"

"Gone," Kruger said.

"Gone?"

"Both of them gone."

Steiner let his head drop back. All he could see was the massive vault of the tunnel roof. He felt himself being lifted up and laid on a stretcher. Then Kruger's face reappeared above him, and Steiner said, "Don't bawl."

"I'm not bawling," Kruger said while the tears rushed from his eyes.

"You're the last noncom," Steiner said. "You mustn't bawl." Kruger nodded.

"Are you ready?" a voice asked.

Steiner turned his head and said, "Shut your damned trap. You can take my tommy gun," he said to Kruger. "I won't need it any longer."

Kruger nodded. The men with the stretcher started forward, and Kruger walked alongside for a few paces. "When you come back," he said, "you can bring me another bottle of perfume." In this part of the tunnel there was light enough for him to see Steiner's face, and suddenly he stood still and shouted, "You're bawling too!"

But Steiner no longer answered. He had turned his head to the side and was thinking, Old fellow, good fellow. With closed eyes he felt the darkness gather around him. Darkness and coolness. He was shivering. He tried to draw his legs up closer to his body, and again felt the blood in his mouth. Damn, he thought. The blood trickled over his lips, and when he coughed a pain shot through his body that made him groan aloud.

"We'll be there soon," a voice above him said soothingly. "Clench your teeth."

"All right," Steiner whispered.

When he opened his eyes he saw how dark it was. Like a grave, he thought. Suddenly a terrible fear rose in him, and he began to tremble. He had the feeling that it would always remain just as dark, as dark as it was for Faber who had lost both eyes. My God, he thought, it would be Faber; did it have to be Faber? The conception of Faber blind was so incredible that for seconds he forgot his own pain and stared, forcing his eyes as wide open as possible, at the place where the vault of the ceiling must be. The vault, and above it the blue sky. But for Faber there was no longer a sky; for Faber there were no stars and no trees, no green trees. Steiner felt a sob tugging at his throat. He opened his mouth and groaned. My God, he thought, My God. For a while he lay with closed eyes, listening to the nasty pounding in his chest and in his back. He felt the blanket under him growing wet.

And it seemed to him that as the blood flowed out his body

grew lighter. He felt like a feather sailing through the air toward a light. Toward a light? He opened his eyes and saw that it was getting lighter. At first there was only a gray gleam that crept across his face and slowly became transformed into a sparkling crystal that grew bigger and bigger, until at last its brightness was such that his eyes ached from looking at it. But he fixed his eyes on it and moved his lips and whispered, "Anne."

Then he saw her face distinctly, her mouth, her eyes, looking at him, and he saw her smiling, and he smiled back and said, "I'm coming, I'm coming, Anne."

So they carried him out of the tunnel into the light of day.

ABOUT THE AUTHOR

WILLI HEINRICH is a German novelist whose specialty is the look, smell and sound of military defeat. He came by his competence honestly and bitterly as an infantry officer in a fearfully mauled German division that bit deep into Russia and withdrew its remnants in broken retreat. He was born in Heidelberg and received his education in German grade and trade schools. He is also the author of *Crack of Doom*. His hobbies are chess and fast cars. He lives in Karlsruhe.

"HITLER'S WAR"

From the German point of view and secret Nazi documents never before revealed to the public, here is the whole gigantic drama of the most crucial days of World War II. Bantam now presents the books that individually capture the major personalities and events of the war.

Buy them at your local bookstore or use this handy coupon:

BOOKS BEHIND THE LINES:

The side of war you will never read about in the history books

☐	THE HOUSE ON GARIBALDI STREET Isser Harel	2501	•	$1.95
☐	THE WAR AGAINST THE JEWS Lucy S. Dawidowicz 1933-1945	2504	•	$2.50
☐	THE WALL John Hersey	2569	•	$2.25
☐	THE UPSTAIRS ROOM Johanna Reiss	2858	•	$1.25
☐	THE HIDING PLACE Corrie ten Boom	7903	•	$1.75
☐	THE PAINTED BIRD Jerzy Kosinski	8257	•	$1.75
☐	FAREWELL TO MANZANAR Jeanne Wakatsuki Houston and James D. Houston	8507	•	$1.25
☐	SUMMER OF MY GERMAN SOLDIER Bette Greene	10192	•	$1.50
☐	THE LAST OF THE JUST Andre Schwarz-Bart	10469	•	$1.95
☐	90 MINUTES AT ENTEBBE Dan Stevenson	10482	•	$1.95
☐	HIROSHIMA John Hersey	11077	•	$1.50

Buy them at your local bookstore or use this handy coupon for ordering:

Bantam Book Catalog

Here's your up-to-the-minute listing of every book currently available from Bantam.

This easy-to-use catalog is divided into categories and contains over 1400 titles by your favorite authors.

So don't delay—take advantage of this special opportunity to increase your reading pleasure.

Just send us your name and address and 25¢ (to help defray postage and handling costs).

BANTAM BOOKS, INC.
Dept. FC, 414 East Golf Road, Des Plaines, Ill. 60016

Mr./Mrs./Miss_____
(please print)

Address_____

City_____State_____Zip_____

Do you know someone who enjoys books? Just give us their names and addresses and we'll send them a catalog too!

Mr./Mrs./Miss_____

Address_____

City_____State_____Zip_____

Mr./Mrs./Miss_____

Address_____

City_____State_____Zip_____

FC—6/77